D0335084

select
editions

Reader's
Digest

Reader's Digest

The names, characters and incidents portrayed in the novels in this volume are the work of the authors' imaginations. Any resemblance to actual persons, living or dead, events or localities is entirely coincidental.

The condensations in this volume are published with the consent of the authors and the publishers © 2011 Reader's Digest, Inc.

www.readersdigest.co.uk

Published in the United Kingdom by Vivat Direct Limited (t/a Reader's Digest), 157 Edgware Road, London W2 2HR

For information as to ownership of copyright in the material of this book, and acknowledgments, see last page.

Printed in Germany
ISBN 978 1 78020 018 7

THE READER'S DIGEST ASSOCIATION, INC.

contents

worth dying for
lee child — 9

There is deadly trouble in the wilds of Nebraska . . . and Jack Reacher walks right into it. He should have just kept on going but that's not his style. He wants answers about the hold the Duncan clan has over the terrified county and is determined to get them.

dambuster
robert radcliffe — 157

Tense, thrilling and meticulously researched, Robert Radcliffe's part-fictional account of the Dambuster raid gives an insight into the personal cost of war. A gripping, old-fashioned adventure where love, friendship, heroism and sacrifice abound.

the summer of the bear
bella pollen — 295

The mysterious death of young Jamie Fleming's diplomat father in Germany and an escaped bear on the Hebridean island where the Flemings go to live, become entwined as Jamie tries to make sense of things. Part Cold War thriller, part family drama, this is a haunting tale.

stagestruck
peter lovesey — 443

Bath's Theatre Royal, steeped in tradition and superstition, is the perfect setting for a murder mystery—but the drama is not taking place on the stage. As Detective Superintendent Peter Diamond and his team investigate, the plot thickens.

author in focus

Inspiration for Bella Pollen's *The Summer of the Bear*, came from a real-life, tamed grizzly bear named Hercules, whose owner, a wrestler, took him to an island in the Hebrides to film an advertisement for tissues. But Hercules broke free and went missing for more than three weeks. Bella Pollen was a child at the time, staying on the island with her family, and she searched for Hercules every day. When the bear was finally sighted and netted by helicopter, it was estimated that he had lost more than half his body weight. Yet, despite being close to starvation, Hercules did not hurt a single creature.

in the spotlight

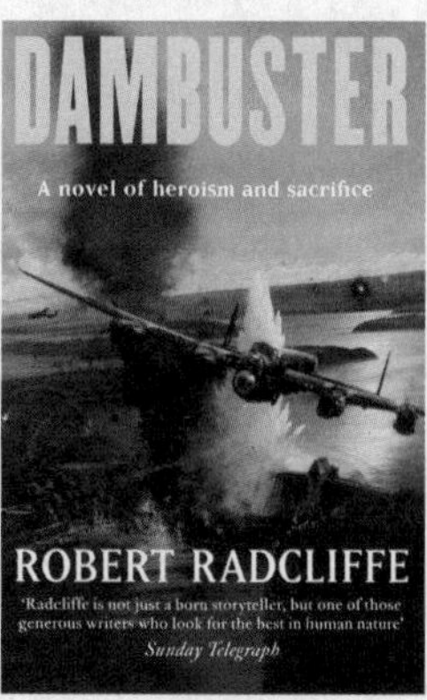

The RAF's 617 Squadron, formed during the Second World War and also called the Dambusters, is probably the best known of all Bomber Command squadrons because of its daring bombing raid on the night of May 16–17, 1943. Nineteen Lancaster bombers targeted the dams of Germany's Ruhr Valley, using the revolutionary 'bouncing bomb' invented by Barnes Wallis. Eight bombers and fifty-six men did not return from the raid, and the dams were soon repaired, but the Dambuster mission undermined enemy morale and was a huge boost for British and Allied troops. *Dambuster*, Robert Radcliffe's wonderful blend of fact and fiction, depicts the courage of the brave crews of 617 Squadron and the sheer audacity of the raid itself.

WORTH DYING FOR

LEE CHILD

For Jack Reacher nothing is routine. Travelling cross-country, he stops to rest at a remote hotel in the wilds of Nebraska and stumbles into the Duncans—a local clan that has terrified the neighbourhood into submission for years. But why? How?

The Duncans want Reacher gone—or better still dead. They've a secret shipment due and don't want any trouble.

But the Duncans have underestimated Jack Reacher—trouble is his middle name.

One

Eldridge Tyler was driving a long straight two-lane road in Nebraska when his cellphone rang. It was late in the afternoon. He was taking his granddaughter home after buying her shoes. His truck was a crew-cab Silverado the colour of a day-old newspaper, and the kid was flat on her back on the rear seat. She was lying with her legs up, staring fascinated at the white sneakers wobbling around in the air two feet above her face. She was eight years old.

Tyler's phone was basic enough to be nothing fancy, but complex enough to have different ringtones against different numbers. Most played the manufacturer's default tune, but four were set to sound an urgent note halfway between a fire-truck siren and a submarine's dive klaxon. That sound was what Tyler heard, in the late afternoon, on the long straight two-lane road in Nebraska, ten miles south of the outlet store and twenty miles north of home. So he fumbled the phone up from the console and said, 'Yes?'

A voice said, 'We might need you and your rifle. Like before. There's a guy sniffing around.'

'How much does he know?'

'Some of it. Not all of it yet.'

'Who is he?'

'Nobody. A stranger. Just a guy. But he got involved. We think he was a military cop. Maybe he didn't lose the cop habit.'

'How long ago was he in the service?'

'Ancient history. He won't be missed. He's a drifter. He blew in like a tumbleweed. Now he needs to blow out again.'

'Description?'

'He's a big guy,' the voice said. 'Six-five at least, probably two-fifty. Last seen wearing a big old brown parka and a wool cap. He moves funny, like he's stiff. Like he's hurting.'

'OK,' Tyler said. 'So where and when?'

'We want you to watch the barn all day tomorrow. We can't let him see the barn. If we don't get him tonight, he's going to figure it out eventually. He's going to head over there and take a look.'

'He's going to walk right into it, just like that?'

'He thinks there are four of us,' the voice said. 'He doesn't know there are five. Shoot him if you see him. Don't miss.'

'Do I ever?' Tyler said. He clicked off the call and put the phone back on the console and drove on, dead winter fields ahead, dead winter fields behind, darkness to his left, the setting sun to his right.

THE BARN had been built long ago, when moderate size and wooden construction had been appropriate for Nebraska agriculture. Its function had since been supplanted by huge metal sheds built in distant locations chosen on the basis of logistical studies. But the place had endured, rotting slowly, leaning and weathering. Around it was an apron of ancient blacktop laced with weeds. The main door was a slider built of great baulks of timber, hung off an iron rail by iron wheels, but the gradual tilt of the building had jammed it in its tracks. The only way in was the judas hole, which was a small conventional door inset in the slider, a little left of its centre.

Eldridge Tyler was staring at that door through the scope on his rifle. He had been in position well before dawn. He was a meticulous man. He had driven his truck off the road, followed tractor ruts through the dark, and had parked in a three-sided shelter designed long ago to keep spring rain off burlap fertiliser sacks. Then he had stepped back to the shelter's entrance and tied a tripwire across it, made of thin cable, set shin-high to a tall man.

Then he had walked back to his truck, and climbed into the load bed, and he had stepped onto the cab's roof, and he had passed his rifle and a canvas tote bag up to a half-loft built like a shelf under the shelter's roof. He had levered himself up after them, and eased a loose louvre out of the ventilation hole in the loft's wall, which would give him a clear view of the barn a hundred and twenty yards north, as soon as there was light in the sky. He had waited for the sun to come up, which it had eventually, pale and wan.

His rifle was chambered for the .338 Magnum and fitted with a 26-inch barrel and had a stock carved from English walnut. It was a seven-thousand-dollar item. The scope was by Leica, with a cross-hairs engraving on the reticle. Tyler had it zoomed through two-thirds of its magnification so that at a hundred and twenty yards it showed a circular slice of life ten feet high and ten feet across.

Tyler worked on the assumption that most people were right-handed, and therefore his target would stand a little left of centre so that his right hand when extended would meet the handle in the middle of the judas hole's narrow panel. A man six feet five inches tall had the centre of his skull about seventy-three inches off the ground, which in terms of the vertical axis put the optimum aiming point about six inches below the top of the judas hole. And a man who weighed 250 pounds would be broad in the shoulders, which would put the centre of his skull maybe a foot and a half left of his right hand, which in terms of the horizontal axis would put the aiming point about six inches beyond the left edge of the door.

Tyler pulled two plastic five-pound packages of long-grain rice from his canvas bag. He stacked them under the rifle's forestock and tamped the fine walnut down into them. He snuggled behind the butt, put his eye back to the scope and laid the cross hairs on the top-left corner of the door. He eased them six inches down, and six inches left. He laid his finger gently against the trigger. Outside, the sun continued to climb. The air was damp and heavy, the kind of air that cradles a bullet and holds it straight and true.

Tyler waited. He knew he might have to wait all day, and he was prepared to. He was a patient man. He imagined the big man in the brown coat stepping into the scope's field of view.

A hundred and twenty yards. A single high-velocity round.

The end of the road.

JACK REACHER was the big man in the brown coat, and for him that particular road had started four miles away, in the middle of an evening, with a ringing telephone in a motel lounge at a crossroads, where a driver who had given him a ride had let him out. The land all around was dark and flat and empty. The motel was the only living thing in sight. It looked like it had been built forty or fifty years earlier in a burst of commercial enthusiasm. Perhaps great possibilities had been anticipated for that location. But the great possibilities had never materialised. One of the four crossroads lots held the abandoned shell of a gas station. Another had a poured foundation, with nothing ever built on it. One was completely empty.

But the motel had endured. It looked like the drawings Reacher had seen as a kid in comic books, of space colonies set up on the moon. The main building was round, with a domed roof. Beyond it each cabin was a circular domed structure of its own, trailing away from the mothership in a lazy curl, getting smaller as they went to exaggerate the perspective. The siding was painted silver. The paths were made of grey gravel boxed in with timbers that were painted silver. The pole the motel sign was set on was disguised with painted plywood to look like a rocket resting on a tripod of slim fins. The motel's name was the Apollo Inn.

Inside, the main building was mostly an open space. There was a curved reception counter and a hundred feet opposite there was a curved bar. The place was a lounge, with red velvet chairs set round cocktail tables. The interior of the domed roof was a cyclorama washed by red neon.

The place was deserted, apart from one guy at the bar and one guy behind it. Reacher waited at the reception counter and the guy behind the bar hustled over and seemed surprised when Reacher asked him for a room. But he stepped to it smartly and coughed up a key in exchange for thirty dollars in cash. He was maybe fifty-five or sixty with a full head of hair dyed a lively russet colour. He put Reacher's thirty bucks in a drawer. Probably made ends meet by pulling quintuple duty as manager, desk clerk, barman, handyman and maid. He set off back towards the bar.

'Got coffee over there?' Reacher asked him.

The guy turned and said, 'Sure,' with a smile. Reacher followed him through the neon wash and propped himself on a stool three spaces away from the other customer. He was a man of about forty. His hands were curled round a glass full of ice and amber liquid. He was staring down at it with an unfocused gaze. Probably not his first glass of the evening. He looked pretty far gone.

The guy with the dyed hair poured coffee into a china mug and slid it across the bar. 'Cream?' he asked. 'Sugar?'

'Neither,' Reacher said.

'Passing through?'

'Aiming to turn east as soon as I can.'

'How far east?'

'All the way east,' Reacher said. 'Virginia.'

The guy with the hair nodded. 'Then you'll need to go south first. Until you hit the Interstate. Where did you start out today?'

'North of here,' Reacher said.

'Driving?'

'Hitching rides.'

The guy with the hair said nothing more. Bartenders like to stay cheerful, and there was no cheerful direction for the conversation to go. Hitching a ride on a back road in the dead of winter in the ninth least densely populated state of America's fifty was not going to be easy, and the guy was too polite to say so. Reacher picked up the mug and tried to hold it steady. The result was not good. Every tendon, ligament and muscle from his fingertips to his rib cage burned and quivered and the microscopic motion in his hand set up small ripples in the coffee. He concentrated and brought the mug to his lips, aiming for smoothness, achieving lurching movement. The drunk guy watched him for a moment, then looked away. He took a sip from his glass. Nobody spoke. The drunk guy finished up and got a refill. Reacher's arm started to feel a little better. Coffee, good for what ails you.

Then the phone rang.

The guy with the hair picked up and said, 'This is the Apollo Inn,' just as brightly and enthusiastically as if it was the motel's first-ever call on opening night. Then he listened for a spell, pressed the mouthpiece to his chest and said, 'Doctor, it's for you.'

The drunk guy said, 'Who is it?'

'It's Mrs Duncan. Her nose is bleeding. Won't stop.'

The drunk guy said, 'Tell her you haven't seen me.'

The guy with the hair relayed the lie and hung up. The drunk guy slumped and his face dropped almost level with the rim of his glass.

'You're a doctor?' Reacher asked him.

'What do you care?'

'Mrs Duncan's your patient and you're blowing her off?'

'Are you the ethics board? It's a nosebleed.'

'That won't stop. Could be serious.'

'She's thirty-three years old and healthy. No history of hypertension or blood disorders. She's not a drug user. No reason to get alarmed.' The guy picked up his glass. A gulp, a swallow.

Reacher asked, 'Is she married?'

'Marriage causes nosebleeds now?'

'Sometimes,' Reacher said. 'I was a military cop. Sometimes we would get to the married quarters. Women who get hit a lot take a lot of aspirin, because of the pain. But aspirin thins the blood, so the next time they get hit, they don't stop bleeding.'

The drunk guy said nothing.

The barman looked away.

Reacher said, 'What? This happens a lot? You're afraid of getting in the middle of a domestic dispute?'

No one spoke.

'Whatever,' Reacher said. 'You'd be no good anyway. You're not even fit to drive to where she is. You should call someone.'

The drunk guy said, 'There isn't anyone. There's an emergency room sixty miles away. But they're not going to send an ambulance sixty miles for a nosebleed. Sure, I'd have a problem driving. But I'd be OK when I got there. I'm a good doctor.'

'Then I'd hate to see a bad one,' Reacher said.

'I know what's wrong with you, for instance. Physically, I mean. Mentally, I can't comment.'

'Don't push it, pal.'

'It's a nosebleed,' the doctor said again.

'How would you treat it?' Reacher asked.

'A little local anaesthetic. Pack the nasal cavities with gauze. The pressure would stop the bleeding, aspirin or no aspirin.'

Reacher nodded. He said, 'So let's go, doctor. I'll drive.'

THE DOCTOR WAS UNSTEADY on his feet. But he got out to the lot OK and then the cold air hit him and he got some temporary focus. Enough to find his car keys, anyway. He patted one pocket after another and eventually came out with a big bunch on a worn leather fob that had *Duncan Transportation* printed on it in flaking gold.

'Same Duncan?' Reacher asked.

The guy said, 'There's only one Duncan family in this county.'

'You treat all of them?'

'Only the daughter-in-law. The son goes to Denver. The father and uncles treat themselves with roots and berries, for all I know.'

The car was a Subaru wagon. It was the only vehicle in the lot. Reacher found the remote on the fob and clicked it open. The doctor made a big show of heading for the driver's door and then ruefully changing direction. Reacher got in and started the engine.

'Head south,' the doctor said.

Reacher put his hands on the wheel the same way a person might manoeuvre two baseball gloves on the end of two long sticks. He clamped his fingers and held on tight, to relieve the pressure on his shoulders. He eased out of the lot and turned south. It was fully dark. Nothing to see, but he knew the land was flat all around.

'What grows here?' he asked, just to keep the doctor awake.

'Corn, of course,' the guy said. 'Corn and more corn.'

'You local?'

'From Idaho originally.'

'So what brought you to Nebraska?'

'My wife,' the guy said. 'Born and raised right here.'

They were quiet for a moment, and then Reacher asked, 'What's wrong with me?'

The doctor said, 'What?'

'You claimed you knew what's wrong with me. So let's hear it.'

'I know what you did,' the guy said. 'I don't know how. You damaged every muscle, tendon and ligament associated with moving your arms, from your little fingers to the anchor on your twelfth rib. You've got pain and discomfort and your fine motor control is screwed up because every system is barking.'

'Prognosis?'

'You'll heal in a few days. You could try aspirin.'

They passed three large homes, set close together a hundred yards off the two-lane road at the end of a long driveway. They were hemmed in together by a post-and-rail fence. They were old places, once fine, now a little neglected. The doctor turned his head and took a long hard look at them, and then he faced the front again.

'How did you hurt your arms?' he asked.

'You're the doctor,' Reacher said. 'You tell me.'

'I've seen the same symptoms before. I volunteered in Florida after a hurricane. People who get caught in a hundred-mile-an-hour wind get bowled along the street, or they catch onto a fence and try to haul themselves to safety. Like dragging their own body weight against the resistance of a gale. Unbelievable stress. But your injuries are only a few days old. You said you came from the north. No hurricanes north of here. And it's the wrong season for hurricanes. So I don't know how you hurt yourself.'

Reacher said nothing.

The doctor said, 'Left at the next crossroads.'

They got to the Duncan house five minutes later. It had exterior lighting, including a pair of spots angled up at a white mailbox. The mailbox had *Duncan* written on it. The house itself looked like a restored farmhouse. There was a long straight driveway leading to a big garage. It had three sets of doors. One set was open.

Reacher stopped the car level with a path that led to the front door. They got out of the car. The doctor took a leather bag from the back of the car. At the door Reacher pushed a brass button. Inside he heard the sound of an electric bell, and then the sound of slow feet on floorboards. The door opened and a face looked out.

It was framed by black hair and had pale skin and frightened eyes and a red-soaked handkerchief pressed tight at the apex of a triangular red gush that had flooded downwards past the mouth and neck to the silk blouse below. The woman took the handkerchief away from her nose. She had split lips and blood-rimmed teeth. Her nose was still leaking. 'You came,' she said.

The doctor focused hard. 'We should take a look at that.'

'You've been drinking,' the woman said. Then she looked at Reacher and asked, 'Who are you?'

'I drove,' Reacher said. 'He'll be OK. I wouldn't let him do brain surgery, but he can stop the bleeding.'

The woman thought about it for a moment and then she nodded and put the handkerchief back to her face and opened the door wide.

They used the kitchen. The doctor was drunk as a skunk, but the procedure was simple and he retained enough muscle memory to get himself through it. Reacher soaked cloths in warm water, passed them across and the doctor cleaned the woman's face, jammed her nostrils with gauze and used butterfly closures on her cut lips. The anaesthetic took the pain away and she settled into a calm and dreamy state. It was hard to say exactly what she looked like. Her nose had been busted before. That was clear. Apart from that she had good skin and fine bone structure and pretty eyes. She was slim, well dressed and solidly prosperous. As was the house itself. The floors were wide planks, lustrous with a hundred years of wax. There was a lot of millwork and fine detail. Reacher checked out the living room —there was a wedding photograph in a silver frame. It showed a younger version of the woman with a tall reedy man in a grey morning suit. He had dark hair, a long nose and he looked smug. Not an athlete or a manual worker. Not a farmer, either. A businessman, probably.

Reacher headed back to the kitchen and found the doctor washing his hands in the sink. He asked the woman, 'You OK now?'

She said, 'Not too bad,' slow and nasal and indistinct.

'Your husband's not here?'

'He decided to go out for dinner. With his friends.'

'What's his name?'

'His name is Seth.'

'And what's your name?'

'My name is Eleanor.'

'You been taking aspirin, Eleanor?'

'Yes.'

'Because Seth does this a lot?'

She paused a long, long time. 'I tripped. On the edge of the rug.'

'More than once, all in a few days? The same rug?'

'Yes.'

'I'd change that rug, if I were you.'

THEY WAITED in the kitchen while she went upstairs to change. They heard her call down that she was OK and on her way to bed. So they left. The doctor staggered to the car and dumped himself in the passenger seat. Reacher started up and reversed down the driveway to the road. He took off, back the way they had come.

'Thank God Seth Duncan wasn't there,' the doctor said.

'I saw his picture. He doesn't look like much to me. I can see a country doctor being worried about getting in the middle of a domestic dispute where the guy drinks beer and has a couple of pit bull terriers in the yard. But apparently Seth Duncan doesn't.'

The doctor said nothing.

Reacher said, 'But you're still scared of him. So his power comes from somewhere else. Financial or political, maybe. Was it him?'

'Yes.'

'You know that for sure?'

'Yes.'

'And he's done it before?'

'Yes. A lot. Sometimes it's her ribs.'

'Has she told the cops?'

'We don't have cops. We depend on the county, sixty miles away. Anyway, she's not going to press charges. They never do.'

'Where does a guy like Duncan go to eat with his friends?'

The doctor didn't answer, and Reacher didn't ask again.

'Are we heading back to the lounge?' the doctor asked.

'No, I'm taking you home.'

'Thanks. But it's a long walk back to the motel.'

'Your problem, not mine,' Reacher said. 'I'm keeping the car. You can hike over and pick it up in the morning.'

FIVE MILES SOUTH of the motel the doctor stared again at the three old houses standing alone at the end of their driveway, and then he directed Reacher left and right and left along the boundaries of dark empty fields to a new ranch house set on a couple of flat acres.

'Got your key?' Reacher asked him.

'My wife will let me in.'

'You hope,' Reacher said. 'Good night.'

He watched the doctor stumble down the driveway and then he threaded back to the main north–south two-lane. He thought, Where would a guy like Seth Duncan go for dinner with his friends?

A steakhouse, was Reacher's conclusion. A rural area, farm country, a bunch of prosperous types ordering a pitcher of domestic beer, getting sirloins cooked rare, smirking about the coastal pussies who worried about cholesterol. Nebraska counties were huge and thinly populated, which could put thirty miles between restaurants. But the night was dark and steakhouses always had lit signs.

Reacher pulled over, killed his headlights, climbed out of the Subaru, grabbed a roof rail, stepped up on the hood and eased himself up on the roof. He turned a full 360 and peered into the darkness. Saw the blue glow of the motel off to the north, and then a distant pink halo maybe ten miles south and west. So Reacher drove south and then west. The glow in the air grew brighter as he homed in on it. Red neon. Could be anything.

It was a steakhouse. It was a long low place with candles in the windows. It had a bright sign along its ridgeline, a bird's nest of glass tubing and metal supports spelling out *Steakhouse* in red light. It was ringed with parked cars and pick-up trucks and SUVs.

Reacher parked the Subaru near the road. He climbed out and stood for a moment, rolling his shoulders, trying to get his upper body comfortable. He had never taken aspirin and wasn't about to start. He was going to rely on time and will power. No other option.

He walked to the steakhouse door. Inside was an unattended maître d' lectern. To the right was a small dining room with two couples finishing up their meals. To the left, the exact same thing. Ahead, a short corridor with a larger room at the end of it.

Reacher stepped past the lectern and checked the larger room. Directly inside the arch was a table for two. It had one guy at it, wearing a red Cornhuskers football jacket. The University of Nebraska. In the main body of the room was a table occupied by seven men, three facing three plus the guy from the wedding photo at the head. He was a little older than the picture, but the same guy. No question. The table held the wreckage of a big meal.

Reacher stepped into the room. As he moved, the guy alone at the table for two stood up and sidestepped into Reacher's path. He placed his hand on Reacher's chest. He was a big man. Nearly as tall as Reacher himself, a whole lot younger, maybe a little heavier.

Reacher said, 'What's your name, fat boy?'

The guy said, 'My name? Brett.'

Reacher said, 'So here's the thing, Brett. Either you take your hand off my chest, or I'll take it off your wrist.'

The guy dropped his hand. 'Are you here to see Mr Duncan?'

'What do you care?'

'I work for Mr Duncan.'

'What are you, security? A bodyguard? What the hell is he?'

'He's a private citizen. I'm one of his assistants, that's all. Sir, you need to leave. Let's get you back to your car.'

'You want to walk me out to the lot?'

'Sir, I'm just doing my job.'

The seven men at the big table were all hunched forward on their elbows, conspiratorial, six of them listening to a story Duncan was telling, laughing on cue, having a hell of a time.

Reacher said, 'Are you sure about this?'

The young man said, 'I'd appreciate it.'

Reacher shrugged. 'OK, let's go.' He turned and threaded his way out to the cold night air. He squeezed between two trucks and headed towards the Subaru. The big guy followed him. Reacher stopped ten feet short of the car. The big guy stopped too.

Reacher said, 'Can I give you some advice? You just swapped a good tactical situation for a much worse one. Inside, there were witnesses and telephones, but out here there's nothing. I could take my time kicking your ass and there's no one to help you.'

'Nobody's ass needs to get kicked tonight.'

'I agree. But I still need to see Duncan.'

'Sir, get real. You won't be seeing anything. Only one of us is going back in there tonight, and it won't be you.'

'You enjoy working for a guy like that?'

'I have no complaints. Sir, you need to move along.'

Reacher put his hands in his pockets, to immobilise his arms, to protect them from further damage. He said, 'Last chance. You can still walk away. You don't need to get hurt for scum like that.'

'I have a job to do.'

Reacher nodded, and said 'Listen, kid' very quietly, and the big guy leaned in fractionally to hear the next part of the sentence, and Reacher kicked him hard in the groin, and then he stepped back while the guy jack-knifed ninety degrees and retched and spluttered. Then Reacher kicked him again on the side of the head, and the guy went down like he was trying to screw himself into the ground.

Reacher headed for the steakhouse door again.

The party was still in full swing in the back room. All seven men were enjoying themselves. Six of them were half listening to the seventh boasting about something and getting ready to one-up him with the next anecdote. Reacher strolled in and stepped behind Duncan's chair. He put his hands on Duncan's shoulders. The room went silent. Reacher leaned on his hands until Duncan's chair was balanced uneasily, up on two legs. Then he let go and the chair thumped forward. Duncan scrambled out of it and turned round, fear and anger in his face, plus an attempt to play it cool for his pals. He looked round and couldn't find his guy, which took out some of the cool and the anger and left all of the fear.

Reacher said, 'I have a message for you from the National Association of Marriage Counsellors.'

'Is there such a thing?'

'Probably. It's more of a question. And the question is, how do *you* like it?'

Reacher hit him, a straight right to the nose, a big vicious blow, his knuckles driving through cartilage and bone and crushing it all flat. Duncan went over backwards and landed on the table. Plates broke and glasses tipped over and fell to the floor.

Reacher walked away, back out to the lot.

THE KEY the red-headed guy had given him was marked with a six, so Reacher parked next to the sixth cabin, went inside and found a circular space except for a straight section boxed off for a bathroom and a closet. The bed was against the wall, on a platform that had been custom built to fit the curve. There was a tub-shaped armchair and an old-fashioned telephone next to the bed. The bathroom was small but adequate.

He undressed and took a shower. He ran the water as hot as he could stand and let it play over his neck, his shoulders, his arms, his ribs. The good news was that his knuckles didn't hurt at all.

SETH DUNCAN'S DOCTOR was more than two hundred miles away in Denver. The nearest ER was an hour away. And no one in his right mind would go near the local quack. So Seth had a friend drive him to his uncle Jasper Duncan's place. He lived five miles south of the motel, in the northernmost of the three old houses that stood at the end of their long shared driveway. The house was a warren, filled with all kinds of things saved against the day they might be useful. Uncle Jasper himself was more than sixty years old, a reservoir of folk wisdom and backwoods knowledge.

Jasper sat Seth in a kitchen chair and looked at the injury. He went away and came back with a syringe and some local anaesthetic. It was a veterinary product, designed for hogs, but it worked. When the site was numb, Jasper used a strong thumb and forefinger to set the bone and then got an old aluminium facial splint. He shaped it to fit and taped it over his nephew's nose. He stopped up the nostrils with gauze and used warm water to sponge away the blood.

Then he got on the phone and called his neighbours.

Next to him lived his brother Jonas Duncan. Next to Jonas lived their brother Jacob Duncan, who was Seth's father. Five minutes later all four men were sitting round Jasper's kitchen table.

Jacob said, 'First things first, son. Who was the guy?'

Seth said, 'I never saw him before.'

Jonas said, 'No, first things first, where was your boy Brett?'

'The guy jumped him in the parking lot. Brett was escorting him out. The guy kicked him in the head. Just left him lying there.'

'Is he OK?'

'He's got a concussion. He's useless. I want him replaced.'

'Plenty more where he came from,' Jonas said.

Jasper asked, 'So who was this guy?'

'He was a big man in a brown coat. With a watch cap on his head. That's all I remember. He just came in and hit me.'

'Why would he?'

'I don't know. But Brett said he was driving the doctor's car.'

'And you're sure it wasn't the doctor who hit you?'

'I told you, I never saw the guy before. I know the doctor. And the damn doctor wouldn't hit me, anyway. He wouldn't dare.'

Jacob said, 'What aren't you telling us, son?'

Seth looked left, looked right. He said, 'OK, I had a dispute with Eleanor tonight. Before I went out. I had to slap her. I might have made her nose bleed.'

The kitchen went quiet for a moment. Jonas said, 'So let's try to piece it together. Your wife called the doctor.'

'She's been told not to do that.'

'But maybe she did anyway. And maybe the doctor wasn't home. Maybe he was in the motel lounge, like he usually is, halfway through a bottle of Jim Beam. Maybe Eleanor reached him there.'

'He's been told to stay away from her.'

'But maybe he didn't obey. And perhaps he was too drunk to drive. So perhaps he asked someone else to drive him.'

'Nobody would dare do that.'

'Nobody who lives here, I agree. But a stranger in the motel lounge might do it. And maybe the stranger didn't like what he saw at your house, and he came to find you.'

Jacob asked, 'What exactly did he say to you?'

'Some bull about marriage counselling.'

Jonas nodded and said, 'There you go. That's how it played out. We've got a passer-by full of moral outrage. A guest in the motel.'

Seth said, 'I want him hurt bad.'

His father said, 'He will be, son. Who have we got?'

Jasper said, 'Not Brett, I guess.'

Jonas said, 'Plenty more where he came from.'

Jacob said, 'Send two of them.'

Two

Reacher dressed after his shower, coat and all. He turned the lights off, sat in the tub armchair and waited. He didn't expect Seth to call the cops. That would require a story, and a story would unravel straight to a confession about beating his wife. No smug guy would head down that route. But a smug guy who had lost a bodyguard might have access to a replacement or two. Reacher knew it wouldn't be hard to track him down. The Apollo Inn was probably the only public accommodation in two hundred square miles. And if the doctor's drinking habits were well known, it wouldn't be difficult to puzzle out the phone call, the treatment, the intervention.

So Reacher sat in the dark, kept his ears open for tyres on gravel.

MORE THAN FOUR HUNDRED and fifty miles north of where Reacher was sitting, the United States finished and Canada began. The world's longest land border followed the 49th Parallel, over mountains and roads and rivers and streams, its western portion running perfectly straight for nearly nineteen hundred miles, from Washington State to Minnesota, most of it unmarked. Between Washington State and Minnesota there were fifty-four official crossings, seventeen manned around the clock, thirty-six manned through daylight hours only, and one unstaffed but equipped with telephones connected to customs offices. Elsewhere the line was randomly patrolled by a classified number of agents, and more isolated spots had cameras and motion sensors buried in the earth.

In Montana, east of the Rockies, the land spent a hundred miles flattening from jagged peaks to gentle plains, most of it thickly forested, interrupted only by sparkling streams and freshwater lakes and needle-strewn paths. One of those paths connected to a dirt fire road, which ran south and in turn connected to a wandering gravel road, which many miles later ended at an inconspicuous left-hand turn off a minor two-lane north of a small town called Hogg Parish.

A grey panel van made that left-hand turn. It rolled along the gravel. Then it turned on to the fire road, a narrow slice of night sky visible overhead. It crawled onwards, many miles, and then the fire road petered out and the sandy track began. The truck slowed and locked into the tyre ruts it had made on its previous trips. It drove for more than an hour and then came to a stop, two miles south of the border. No one was certain where the motion sensors had been buried, but most assumed that a mile either side of the line was the practical limit. Another mile had been added as a safety margin.

The truck backed up, turned and stopped astride the sandy track, facing south. It shut down and its lights went off. It waited.

REACHER WAITED in his tub armchair, tracing the next day's route in his head. South to the Interstate, and then east. He had hitchhiked most of the Interstate before. There were on-ramps, rest areas and a vast travelling population, some of it commercial, some of it private, a fair proportion of it lonely and ready for company. The problem would come before the Interstate, on the middle-of-nowhere trek to it. Since climbing out of the car that had dumped him at the crossroads he had heard no traffic. In fact he had heard nothing at all, no wind, and no night sounds, and he had been listening hard, for tyres on gravel. Then he heard something.

Not tyres on gravel. Footsteps on gravel.

A light, hesitant tread, approaching. Reacher watched the window and saw a shape flit across it. Small, slight, head ducked down into the collar of a coat. A woman.

There was a knock at the door, soft and tentative. A small nervous hand. A decoy, possibly. Not beyond the wit of man to send someone on ahead, all innocent and unthreatening, to get the door open and lull the target into a sense of false security.

Reacher crossed the floor and headed to the bathroom. He eased the window up, clipped out the screen and rested it in the tub. Then he climbed out, stepping down to the gravel. He went round the cabin and came up on the woman from behind. She was alone.

No cars on the road, nobody in the lot, nobody flattened either side of his door. Just the woman, standing there on her own. She was maybe forty, small, dark and worried. She knocked again.

Reacher said, 'I'm here.'

She gasped and spun round and put her hand on her chest. He said, 'I'm sorry if I startled you. Who are you?'

'I'm sorry,' she said. 'I'm the doctor's wife.'

'I'm pleased to meet you,' Reacher said.

'Can we go inside?'

Reacher found the key in his pocket and unlocked the door from the outside. The doctor's wife stepped in and he followed her. He crossed the room and closed the bathroom door against the night air coming in through the open window. He turned back to find her standing. He indicated the armchair and said, 'Please.'

She sat down. Didn't unbutton her coat. She was still nervous. She said, 'I walked all the way over here.'

'To pick up the car? You should have let your husband do that, in the morning. That's what I arranged with him.'

'Morning's too late. You have to get going. You're not safe here. My husband said you're heading to the Interstate. I'll drive you.'

'It's the middle of the night. And it's got to be a hundred miles.'

'A hundred and twenty. My husband told me what happened. You interfered with the Duncans. You *saw.* They'll punish him for sure, and we think they'll come after you too.'

'Punish him how?'

'Oh, I don't know. Last time they wouldn't let him come here to the lounge for a month. It's his favourite place.'

'How could they stop him coming here?'

'They told Mr Vincent not to serve him. The owner.'

'Why would the owner do what the Duncans tell him?'

'The Duncans run a trucking business. All of Mr Vincent's supplies come through them. He signed a contract. So if Mr Vincent doesn't play ball, a couple of deliveries will be late, a couple lost. He knows that. He'll go out of business.'

Reacher asked, 'What will they do to me?'

'They hire football players right out of college. The ones who were good enough to get scholarships, but not good enough to go to the NFL. They'll connect the dots and figure out where you are. They'll pay you a visit. Maybe they're already on their way.'

'How many football players have they got?'

'Nine,' the woman said. 'You're in big trouble.'

'I already met one of them. He's currently indisposed. He got between me and Seth Duncan.'

'What did you do to Seth Duncan?'

'I broke his nose.'

'Oh, my God. Why?'

'Why not? What will happen to Mrs Duncan?'

'She will be punished too. For calling my husband. She's been told not to do that. Just like he's been told not to go treat her.'

'He's a doctor. He doesn't get a choice. They take an oath.'

'What's your name?'

'Jack Reacher. What will they do to Mrs Duncan?'

The woman said, 'Probably nothing much. They might stop her taking so much aspirin. So she doesn't bleed so bad next time. And they'll probably ground her for a month. Nothing too serious.'

'Except this time she inadvertently got her husband's nose broken. He might take that out on her, if he can't take it out on me.'

The doctor's wife said nothing. But it sounded like she was agreeing. The room went quiet. Then Reacher heard tyres on gravel.

He checked the window. There were four tyres in total, big off-road things, on a Ford pick-up truck. The truck had a jacked suspension and lights on a roof bar and a winch on the front. There were two large shapes inside. The truck nosed down the row of cabins and stopped behind the parked Subaru. The headlights stayed on. The engine idled. The doors opened. Two guys climbed out.

They both looked like Brett, only bigger. Late twenties, easily six-six or six-seven, probably close to three hundred pounds each. They had cropped hair and small eyes and fleshy faces. They were wearing red Cornhuskers football jackets.

The doctor's wife joined Reacher at the window.

The two guys stepped to the load bed and unlatched a tool locker. One took out a hammer, the other took out a wrench a foot and a half long.

They attacked the Subaru in a violent frenzy. They smashed the windshield, the side windows, the back window, the headlights, the taillights. They hammered dents into the hood, into the doors, into the roof.

'My husband's punishment,' the doctor's wife whispered.

The two guys stopped as suddenly as they had started. They stood there, one each side of the wrecked wagon, and they breathed hard.

Reacher took off his coat and dumped it on the bed.

The two guys formed up shoulder to shoulder and headed for the cabin's door. Reacher opened it up and stepped out to meet them.

The two guys stopped ten feet away and stood, side by side, weapons in their outside hands, flushed and sweating in the chill.

Reacher said, 'Pop quiz, guys. You spent four years in college learning how to play a game. I spent thirteen years in the army learning how to kill people. So how scared am I?'

No answer.

'And you were so bad at it you couldn't even get drafted. I was so good at it I got all kinds of medals. So how scared are you?'

'Not very,' said the guy with the wrench.

Wrong answer. But understandable. These guys had been the elite for most of twenty years, the greatest thing their neighbourhood had ever seen, then their town, then their county, maybe their state. They had been popular, they had been feted. And they probably hadn't lost a fight since they were eight years old.

Except they had never had a fight. Not in the sense meant by people paid to fight or die. Pushing and shoving at the schoolyard gate was as far from fighting as two fat guys tossing lame spirals in the park were from the Superbowl. These guys were amateurs, accustomed to getting by on bulk and reputation alone.

Case in point: bad choice of weapons. Best are shooting weapons, second best are stabbing weapons, third best are slashing weapons. Blunt instruments are way down the list. They slow hand speed. And: if you have to use them, the backhand is the only way to go, so that you accelerate and strike in the same sudden fluid motion. But these guys were shoulder to shoulder with their weapons in their outer hands, which promised forehand swings, which meant that the hammer or the wrench would have to be swung backwards first, then stopped, then brought forward again. The first part of the move would be a clear telegraph. All the warning in the world.

The guy with the wrench said, 'We've got a message for you. Actually it's more of a question.'

'Any difficult words? You need more time?' Reacher stepped forward and a little to his right. He put himself directly in front of the two guys, equidistant, seven feet away. The guy with the wrench was on his left, the guy with the hammer was on his right.

The guy with the wrench moved first. He dumped his weight on his right foot and started a backswing with the heavy tool, designed to snap forward through a horizontal arc, aiming to break Reacher's left arm. But Reacher had his weight on his left foot, and before the wrench started moving forward the heel of Reacher's right boot met the big guy's knee and drove through it, smashing the kneecap, rupturing tendons, dislocating the joint, making it fold forward the way no knee is designed to go. The guy began to drop and before the first howl was starting in his throat Reacher was stepping past him.

The guy with the hammer had a split-second choice to make. He could spin on the forehand, but that would give him almost a full circle to move through, because Reacher was now almost behind him. Or the guy could flail on the backhand, a Hail Mary blind swing into the void behind him, hoping for a lucky contact.

He chose to flail behind him.

Reacher watched the arm moving, the wrist flicking back, the elbow turning inside out, and he planted his feet and jerked from the waist and drove the heel of his hand into the guy's elbow, that huge force jabbing one way, the weight of the swinging hammer pulling the other, the elbow joint cracking, the hammer falling, the guy crumpling, trying to force his body to a place where his elbow stayed bent the right way around, which left him unsteady and unbalanced and face to face with Reacher, who then head butted him in the face. The guy sagged forward and went down.

Enough, a person might say, if he lived in the civilised world of movies, television and fair play. But Reacher didn't live there. He lived in a world where you don't start fights but you sure as hell finish them, and you don't lose them either, and the best way to lose them was to assume they were over when they weren't. He stepped back to the guy who had held the wrench. He was down and rolling around. Reacher put him to sleep with a kick to the forehead. Then he picked up the wrench and broke the guy's wrist with it, *one*, and then the other wrist, *two*, and turned back and did the same to the other guy who had held the hammer, *three*, *four*. The two men were somebody's weapons and no soldier left an enemy's abandoned ordnance on the field in working order.

THE DOCTOR'S WIFE was watching from the cabin door, terror in her face. 'I wish you hadn't done that. Nothing good can come of it.'

Reacher asked, 'What is going on here? Who are these people?'

'I told you. Football players.'

'Not them. The Duncans. The people who sent them.'

'They're a family. That's all. Seth, and his father, and two uncles. They used to farm. Now they run a trucking business.'

'Where do they live? The three old guys?'

'Just south of here. Three houses all alone. One each.'

'I saw them. Your husband was staring at them.'

'He was probably crossing his fingers for luck.'

'Why? Who are they?'

'They're a hornets' nest, that's what. And you just poked it with a stick and now you're going to leave.'

'What was I supposed to do? Let them hit me with shop tools?'

'That's what we do. We take our punishments and keep our heads down. It's not a big deal.'

'What the hell are you talking about?'

'Throw a frog in hot water and he'll jump right out. Put him in cold water and heat him up slowly, he'll let himself boil to death without noticing.'

'And that's you? Give me the details.'

'No,' she said. 'You won't hear anything bad about the Duncans from me. I've known them all my life. They're a fine family. There's nothing wrong with them. Nothing at all.'

THE DOCTOR'S WIFE set off walking home. Reacher offered her a ride in the pick-up, but she wouldn't hear of it. He watched her until she was swallowed by the dark. Then he turned back to the two guys outside his door. They were going to be hard to move. No way could he lift an unconscious human weighing three hundred pounds.

He opened the pick-up's door and climbed into the cab. He backed up until the tailgate was in line with where the two guys lay. He got out, stepped round the hood and looked at the electric winch bolted to the frame at the front. It had a motor connected to a drum wrapped with thin steel cable. The cable had a snap hook on the end. There was a release ratchet and a winding button.

He hit the ratchet and unwound the cable. He flipped it up over the hood, over the roof of the cab, over the load bed, and down to where the guys were lying behind the truck. He dropped the tailgate flat and fastened the hook onto the first guy's belt. He walked back to the front of the truck, found the winding button and pressed.

The motor started, the drum turned and the slack pulled out of the cable. Then the cable went tight and burred a groove into the front edge of the hood. The drum slowed, but it kept on turning. Reacher walked back and saw the first guy getting dragged by his belt towards the load bed. The guy dragged all the way to the tailgate. Then the cable came up vertically, shrieked against the sheet metal and the guy started up into the air, his back arched, his head, legs and arms hanging down. Reacher pulled and pushed and got him up over the angle and into the load bed. Reacher stepped to the front and stopped the winch. He came back, leaned into the load bed and released the hook, then he did the same things for the second guy.

Reacher drove five miles south, slowed and stopped before the shared driveway that ran towards the three houses huddled together. There was no landscaping. Just gravel and weeds and three parked cars, and then a heavy post-and-rail fence, and then empty fields.

Reacher pulled thirty feet ahead and then backed up into the driveway. Gravel crunched under his tyres. A noisy approach. He risked fifty yards, about halfway. He stopped, slid out and unlatched the tailgate. He climbed into the load bed, grabbed the first guy by the belt and the collar and hauled and half dragged him to the edge and then put his boot against the guy's hip and shoved him over. The guy fell three feet and thumped on his side.

Reacher went back for the second guy and rolled him out of the truck right on top of his buddy. Then he latched the tailgate again, vaulted over the side, got behind the wheel and took off fast.

THE FOUR DUNCANS were still round the table in Jasper's kitchen. On their minds was an emerging delay on the Canadian border. Jacob said, 'We're getting pressure from our friend to the south.'

Jonas said, 'We can't control what we can't control. Tell him he'll get his shipment.'

'When?'

'Whenever.'

'But this time he's agitated. He wants action. And here's the thing. He called me, and it was like jumping into the conversation halfway through. He was frustrated. But also a little surly, like we weren't taking him seriously. Like he had made prior communications that had gone unheeded.'

'He's losing his mind.'

'Unless one of us took a couple of his calls already.'

Jonas said, 'Well, I didn't.'

'Me either,' Jasper said.

'You sure? Because there's no other explanation. This is a guy we can't afford to mess with. This is a deeply unpleasant person.'

Jacob's brothers shrugged. Two men in their sixties, gnarled, battered, built like fire hydrants. Jonas said, 'Don't look at me.'

'Me either,' Jasper said again.

Only Seth hadn't spoken. Not a word. Jacob's son.

His father asked, 'What aren't you telling us, boy?'

Seth looked down at the table. Then he looked up, the splint huge on his face. 'It wasn't me who broke Eleanor's nose tonight.'

Jasper took a bottle of Knob Creek whiskey from his kitchen cabinet. He put four chipped glasses on the table and poured four generous measures. He sat again and each man took an initial sip.

Jacob said, 'From the beginning, son.'

Seth said, 'I'm dealing with it. He's my customer.'

Jacob shook his head. 'He was your contact, but we're a family. We do everything together. There's no such thing as a side deal.'

'We were leaving money on the table.'

'You don't need to go over ancient history. You found a guy willing to pay more for the same merchandise, and we surely appreciate that. But reward brings risks. So what happened?'

'We're a week late.'

'We aren't. We don't specify dates.'

Seth said nothing.

Jacob said, 'What? You guaranteed a date?'

Seth nodded.

Jacob said, 'We never specify dates. We can't afford to. There are a hundred factors outside of our control. The weather, for one.'

'I used a worst-case analysis.'

'There's always something worse than the worst, son. Count on it. So what happened?'

'Two guys showed up. At my house. Two days ago. His people.'

'Where was Brett?'

'I had to tell him I was expecting them. They said they were delivering a message from their boss. An expression of displeasure. I apologised. They said that wasn't good enough. They said they had been told to leave marks. I said they couldn't. I said I have to be out and about. I have a business to run. So they hit Eleanor instead.'

'Just like that?'

'They asked first. They made me agree. They made her agree, too. They made me hold her. They took turns. I told her sorry afterwards. She said, what's the difference? Them or you?'

'And then what?'

'I asked for another week. They gave me forty-eight hours.'

'So they came back again? Tonight?'

'Yes. They did it all over again.'

'So who was the guy in the restaurant? One of them?'

'No, he wasn't one of them. I told you, I never saw him before.'

Jonas said, 'He was a passer-by. Like we figured.'

Jacob said, 'Well, at least *he's* out of our hair.'

Then they heard faint sounds outside. Tyres on gravel. A vehicle, on their driveway. It seemed to stop halfway. There was a thump, and then a pause, and another sound. Then the vehicle drove away.

Jonas was first out the door. From fifty yards he could see strange humped shapes in the moonlight. From twenty he saw what they were. From five he saw what condition they were in. He said, 'Not out of our hair. Not exactly. Not yet.'

Jacob said, 'Who the hell *is* this guy?'

REACHER PARKED the pick-up truck next to the wrecked Subaru and found the motel owner waiting at his door. Mr Vincent.

The guy said, 'I can't let you stay here.'

Reacher said, 'I paid thirty dollars.'

'I'll refund it, of course.'

'They already know I'm here. Where else could I be?'

'It was OK before they told me not to let you stay here. Ignorance of the law is no offence. But I can't defy them now. Not after they informed me.'

'When did they inform you?'

'Two minutes ago. By phone.'

'You always do what they tell you?'

'I'd lose everything I've worked for. I'm sorry about this.'

'You going to offer to drive me down to the Interstate now?'

'I can't do that either. We're not supposed to help you in any way at all. They're putting the word out.'

'Well, I seem to have inherited a truck. I can drive myself.'

'Don't,' Vincent said. 'They'll report it stolen. The county police will stop you. You won't get halfway there.'

'They *want* me to stay here?'

'They do now. You started a war. They want to finish it.'

Reacher looked around. The blue glow of the neon reached as far as the dead Subaru, and then it faded away. Overhead was a moon.

Reacher said, 'You still got coffee in the pot?'

Vincent said, 'I can't serve you. They might be watching.'

'Let's make a deal,' Reacher said. 'I'll move on, to spare you the embarrassment. In return I want a cup of coffee and some answers.'

THE LOUNGE WAS DARK, except for a lone work light behind the bar. A harsh fluorescent tube. Vincent filled the machine with water and spooned ground coffee into a paper filter the size of a hat. He set it going.

Reacher said, 'Start at the beginning.'

Vincent said, 'They're an old family. The first one I knew was old man Duncan. He was a farmer, from a long line of farmers. They grew corn and beans and built up a big acreage. The old man had three sons, Jacob, Jasper and Jonas. The boys hated farming. But they kept the place going until the old man died. So as not to break his heart. Then they sold up. They went into the trucking business. They split up their place and sold it off to their neighbours. Land prices were high back then, but the boys sweetened the deals. They gave discounts, if their neighbours signed up to use Duncan Transportation to haul away their harvests. Which made sense. Everyone was getting what they wanted. Everyone was happy.'

'Until?'

'Things went sour slowly. There was a dispute with a neighbour twenty-five years ago. It was an acrimonious situation. That summer the Duncans wouldn't haul the guy's crop away. It rotted on the ground. The guy didn't get paid that year.'

'He couldn't find someone else to haul it?'

'By then the Duncans had the county all sewn up. Not worth it for some other outfit to come all the way here just for one load.'

'The guy couldn't haul it himself?'

'They had all sold their trucks. No need for them, as far as they could see. And the football players were on the scene by then.'

'Total control,' Reacher said.

Vincent nodded. 'You can work all year, but you need your harvest trucked away, or it's the same thing as sitting on your butt and growing nothing. Farmers live season to season. They can't afford to lose a crop. The Duncans found the perfect pinch-point. When they realised what they had, they started enjoying it.'

'How?'

'Nothing real bad. People pay a little over the odds, and they mind their manners. That's about all, really.'

'You too, right?'

Vincent nodded again. 'This place needed some fixing, ten years ago. The Duncans loaned me the money, interest free, if I signed up with them for my deliveries.'

'And you're still paying.'

'We're all still paying. But no one thing is really that bad.'

'Like a frog in warm water,' Reacher said. 'That's how the doctor's wife described it.'

'That's how we all describe it.' Vincent filled a mug with coffee. He passed it across the bar.

Reacher tried the coffee. It was excellent. He said, 'Aren't there laws? Monopolies, or restraint of trade or something?'

Vincent said, 'Going to a lawyer is the same thing as going bankrupt. A lawsuit takes what? Two, three years? Two or three years without your crop getting hauled is suicide.'

Reacher said, 'Wrecking the doctor's car wasn't a small thing.'

'I agree. It was worse than usual. We're all unsettled by that.'

'All?'

'We all talk to each other. There's a phone tree. We share information.'

'And what are people saying?'

'That maybe the doctor deserved it. He was way out of line.'

'For treating his patient?' Reacher asked.

'She wasn't sick. It was an intervention.'

'I think you're all sick. How hard would it be to do something? One guy on his own, I agree, that's difficult. But if everyone banded together and called another trucker, they'd come, wouldn't they?'

'I don't think another trucker would take the business. They carve things up. They don't poach, in a place like this.'

'Whatever,' Reacher said. 'You can sort it out for yourselves. Or not. It's up to you. I'm on my way to Virginia.'

'What are you going to do?' Vincent asked.

Reacher said, 'That depends on the Duncans. Plan A is to hitch a ride out of here. But if they want a war, then plan B is to win it. I'll keep on dumping football players on their driveway until they've got none left. Then I'll walk on up and pay them a visit. Their choice.'

'Stick to plan A. Just go. That's my advice.'

'Show me some traffic and I might.'

'I need your room key. I'm sorry.'

Reacher dug it out of his pocket and placed it on the bar.

There was no more conversation. Reacher finished his coffee and walked back to the truck. He drove out of the motel lot. If in doubt, turn left, was his motto. So he headed south, rolling slow, lights off, looking for a direction to follow.

The road was a straight ribbon, with dark empty fields to the right and to the left. Then three miles out Reacher saw two old wooden buildings to the west, one large, one small, standing in a field.

Reacher slowed and turned into a pair of deep tractor tyre ruts. The pick-up lurched and bounced. The two old buildings got nearer. One was a barn. The other was a smaller structure. They were about a hundred and twenty yards apart and were fringed with dormant vegetation, where errant seeds had blown against their sides, and then fallen and taken root. In the winter the vegetation was dry and tangled sticks. In the summer it might be a riot of colourful vines.

He looked at the barn first. It was built of timbers that looked as hard as iron, but it was rotting and leaning. The door was a slider big enough to admit some serious farm machinery. But the tilt of the building had jammed it in its tracks. There was a judas hole in the slider, a small door. It was locked. There were no windows.

Reacher got back in the truck, headed for the smaller shed. It was three-sided, open at the end that faced away from the barn. It was about twice as long and a little wider than the truck. Perfect.

Reacher drove in, and stopped with the hood of the truck under a mezzanine half-loft built like a shelf under the peak of the roof. He shut the engine down, climbed out and walked back the way he had come. He turned and checked. The truck was completely hidden.

He thought, Time for bed.

He walked in the tractor ruts, made it back to the road and turned north. Up ahead there was no blue glow. The motel's lights had been turned off for the night. He came up on the crossroads from the south and stopped. No parked cars. No watchers. No ambush.

Reacher came up on the motel from the rear, at the end of the curl of cabins. All was quiet. He stayed off the gravel and minced along the silver timbers to his bathroom window. It was still open. The screen was still in the bathtub. He sat on the sill and ducked his head and slid inside. He closed the window against the cold. His towels were where he had left them after his shower. Vincent hadn't made up the room. Reacher guessed that was tomorrow's task.

Reacher stepped into the main room. He kept the lights off and the drapes open. He slid into bed, fully dressed, boots and all. Not the first time he had slept that way. Sometimes it paid to be ready. He got as comfortable as he could, and a minute later he was asleep.

HE WOKE UP five hours later and found out he had been wrong. Vincent was not pulling quintuple duty. Only quadruple. He employed a maid. Reacher was woken by her feet on the gravel. He saw her through the window. She was heading for his door. There was mist and cold grey light outside, not long after dawn.

The housekeeper used a pass key, pushed the door open and stepped into what she thought was a vacant room. Her eyes passed over Reacher's shape on the bed and moved on and it was a whole second before they came back again. She showed no big surprise. She looked like a capable woman, about sixty years old, white, blunt and square, with blonde hair fading to yellow and grey.

'Mr Vincent believed this room to be empty,' she said.

'That was the plan,' Reacher said. 'Better for him that way. What you don't know can't hurt you.'

'You're the fellow the Duncans told him to turn out,' she said.

'I'll move on today. I don't want to cause him any trouble.'

'How do you plan to move on?'

'I'll hitch a ride. I'll set up south of the crossroads.'

'Will the first car you see stop?'

'It might.'

'The first car you see won't stop. Because almost certainly the first car you see will be a local resident. That person will phone the Duncans and tell them where you are. We've had our instructions. The second car you see will be full of the Duncans' people. You're in trouble. The land is flat and it's winter. There's nowhere to hide.'

Reacher asked, 'You going to rat me out?'

'Rat who out? This is an empty room.'

Reacher asked, 'What's to the east of here?'

'Nothing worth a lick to you,' the woman said. 'The road goes to gravel after a mile, and doesn't really take you anywhere.'

'West?'

'Same thing.'

'Why have a crossroads that doesn't lead anywhere?'

'About fifty years ago there was supposed to be a commercial strip here. Some farms were sold for the land, but that's about all that happened. Even the gas station went out of business.'

'This motel is still here.'

'By the skin of its teeth. Most of what Mr Vincent earns comes from feeding whiskey to the doctor.'

'Vincent's paying you.'

She nodded. 'He helps where he can. I'm a farmer. I work the winters here, because I need the money. To pay the Duncans.'

'Haulage fees?'

'Mine are higher than most.'

'Why?'

'Ancient history. I can't talk about it.'

Reacher got off the bed. He headed for the bathroom and rinsed his face with cold water and brushed his teeth.

Behind him the woman stripped the bed with fast, practised movements. She said, 'You're heading for Virginia.'

Reacher said, 'You know my Social Security number too?'

'The doctor told his wife you were a military cop. So what are you now?'

'Hungry.'

'There's a diner an hour or so south. In town.'

The housekeeper stepped out to the path and took fresh linens from a cart. Reacher asked her, 'What does Vincent pay you?'

'Minimum wage,' she said. 'That's all he can afford.'

'I could pay you more than that to cook me breakfast.'

'Risky. Do you tip well?'

'If the coffee's good.'

'I use my mother's percolator. Her coffee was the best.'

'So we're in business.'

'I don't know,' the woman said.

'They're not going to be conducting house-to-house searches. They expect to find me out in the open.'

'And when they don't?'

'Nothing for you to worry about. I'll be long gone.'

The woman stood for a minute, unsure. Then she said, 'OK.'

REACHER STOOD in the middle of the room and the housekeeper finished up. Then she went to get her truck. It was a battered old pick-up. She looped round the wrecked Subaru and parked with the passenger door next to the cabin door. She checked front and rear. Reacher could see she wanted to forget the whole thing and take off without him. But she didn't. She leaned across the cab, opened the door and flapped her hand. *Hurry up*.

Reacher stepped out of the cabin and into the truck. The woman said, 'If we see anyone, you have to duck down and hide, OK?'

Reacher agreed, although it would be hard to do. The dash was tight against his knees. 'Got a bag? I could put it on my head.'

'This isn't funny.'

She turned left out of the lot, drove through the crossroads, and headed south. In the daylight the land looked flat and featureless. After five minutes Reacher saw the sagging barn and the shed with the captured pick-up in it to the west. Three minutes later they passed the Duncans' houses. The woman's hands went tight on the wheel. Reacher saw she had crossed her fingers.

He said, 'They're only people. They don't have magic powers.'

'They're evil,' the woman said.

THEY WERE IN Jonas Duncan's kitchen, eating breakfast, biding their time. Jacob had a pronouncement to make. His brothers knew the signs. Many times Jacob had sat quiet and contemplative, and then he had delivered a nugget of wisdom that had cut to the heart of the matter. So they waited for it, Jonas and Jasper enjoying their meal, Seth struggling a little because chewing had become painful for him.

Jacob put down his fork. 'We have to ask ourselves if it might be worth trading a little self-respect for a useful outcome. We have a provocation and a threat. The provocation comes from the stranger in the motel throwing his weight around in matters that don't concern him. The threat comes from our friend to the south getting impatient. The first thing must be punished, and the second thing shouldn't have happened. But it has, so we have to deal with it. No doubt Seth did what he thought was best for all of us. Let's think about the stranger first.'

Seth said, 'I want him hurt bad.'

'We all do, son. And we tried. Didn't work out so well.'

'What, now we're afraid of him?'

'We are, a little bit. We lost three guys.'

'You want to let him walk?'

'No, I want to tell our friend to the south that the stranger is the reason for the delay. Then we point out to our friend that he's already got two of his boys up here, and if he wants a giddy-up in the shipment process, then maybe those two boys could be turned against the stranger. That's a win all round. First, those two boys are off Seth's back, and second, the stranger gets hurt or killed, and third, some of the sting goes out of our friend's recent attitude, because he comes to see that the delay isn't really our fault.'

Silence for a moment.

Then Jasper said, 'I like it.'

Jacob said, 'The downside is we'll be admitting to our friend to the south that there are problems we can't solve by ourselves.'

'No shame in that,' Jonas said. 'This is a complicated business.'

'But suppose the delay doesn't go away?' Jasper asked. 'Suppose the stranger gets nailed today and we still can't deliver for a week? Then our friend to the south knows we were lying to him.'

'I don't think the stranger will get nailed in one day,' Jacob said. 'He seems to be a capable person. It could take a few days, by which time our truck could be on its way. Even if it isn't, we could say that we thought it prudent to keep the merchandise out of the country until the matter was resolved. Our friend might believe that. Or he might not. But it's the best we can do. Are we in or out?'

'We should offer assistance,' Jasper said. 'And information. We should require compliance from the population.'

Jacob said, 'Naturally. So are we in or out?'

No one spoke for a long moment. Then Jasper said, 'I'm in.'

'Me too,' Jonas said.

Jacob nodded. 'That's a majority, then. Which I'm mighty relieved to have, because I took the liberty of calling our friend to the south two hours ago. Our boys and his are already on the hunt.'

Three

Reacher was half expecting something nailed together from sod and rotten boards, like a Dust Bowl photograph, but the woman drove him down a long gravel track to a neat two-storey dwelling standing alone in the corner of a spread that might have covered a thousand acres. The woman parked behind the house, next to a line of old tumbledown barns and sheds. Reacher could hear chickens in a coop, and he could smell pigs in a sty. The woman said, 'I don't mean to be rude, but how much are you planning to pay me?'

Reacher smiled. 'Deciding how much to feed me? My breakfast average west of the Mississippi is about fifteen bucks with tip.'

The woman looked surprised. 'That's a lot of money.'

'Not all profit,' Reacher said. 'I'm hungry, don't forget.'

She led him through a door to a back hallway. The place was old and outdated in every way, but cleaned and well maintained for a hundred years. The kitchen was immaculate. The stove was cold.

'You didn't eat yet?' Reacher asked.

'I don't eat,' the woman said. 'Not breakfast, at least.'

'I'm buying,' he said. 'Thirty bucks. Let's both have some fun.'

'I don't want charity.'

'It isn't charity. I'm returning a favour, that's all. You stuck your neck out bringing me here. Take it or leave it.'

She said, 'I'll take it.'

He said, 'What's your name? Most times when I have breakfast with a lady, I know her name at least.'

'My name is Dorothy.'

'I'm pleased to meet you, Dorothy. You married?'

'I was. Now I'm not.'

'You know my name?'

'Your name is Jack Reacher. We've all been informed.'

'I told the doctor's wife.'

'And she told the Duncans. Don't blame her for it. It's automatic. She's trying to pay down her debt, like all of us.'

'What does she owe them?'

'She sided with me, twenty-five years ago.'

ROBERTO CASSANO and Angelo Mancini were driving north in a rented Chevrolet Impala. They were based in a Courtyard Marriott, which was the only hotel in the county seat, which was nothing more than a grid of streets set in the middle of what felt like nothing at all.

They were from Vegas, which meant they were really from somewhere else. New York, in Cassano's case, and Philadelphia, in Mancini's. They had paid their dues in their home towns, and then they had moved up to the big show out in the Nevada desert. Tourists are told that what happens in Vegas stays in Vegas, but that wasn't true for Cassano and Mancini. They were travelling men, tasked to roam around and deal with the first faint pre-echoes of trouble long before it rolled in and hit their boss where he lived.

Hence the trip to the agricultural wastelands. There was a snafu in the supply chain, and it was a day or two away from getting embarrassing. Their boss had promised certain things to certain people, and it would do him no good if he couldn't deliver. So Cassano and Mancini had been on the scene for seventy-two hours, and they had smacked some beanpole yokel's wife around, to make their point. Then some related yokel had called with a claim that the snafu was caused by a stranger poking his nose in where it didn't belong. Probably just an excuse. But Cassano and Mancini were only sixty miles away, so their boss had sent them to help, because if the yokel's statement was a lie, then it indicated vulnerability, and minor assistance rendered now would leverage a better deal later.

They came up the crappy two-lane, rolled through the crossroads, pulled in at the motel and saw a damaged Subaru near one of the cabins. They parked in the lot and got out. Cassano was medium height, dark, muscled. Mancini was pretty much the same. They both wore good shoes, dark suits and wool overcoats. They went inside, to find the motel owner. They found him behind the bar. Some kind of sad-sack loser with dyed red hair.

Cassano said, 'We represent the Duncan family,' which he had been promised would produce results. And it did. The guy almost came to attention and saluted.

Cassano said, 'You sheltered a guy here last night.'

The guy with the hair said, 'No, sir, I did not. I tossed him out.'

Cassano said, 'If he didn't sleep here, where did he sleep? You got no local competition. And he didn't sleep out under a hedge. For one thing, there don't seem to be any hedges in Nebraska. For another, he'd have frozen his ass off.'

'I don't know where he went. He wouldn't tell me.'

'Any kindly souls here, who would take a stranger in?'

'Not if the Duncans told them not to.'

'Then he must have stayed here. You checked his room?'

'He returned the key before he left.'

'More than one way into a room. Did you check it?'

'The housekeeper already made it up.'

'Where is she?'

'She finished. She left. She went home.'

Mancini said, 'Tell us where she lives.'

DOROTHY'S IDEA of a fifteen-dollar breakfast turned out to be a regular feast. Coffee first, while the rest of it was cooking, which was oatmeal, bacon, eggs and toast, served on thick china plates.

'Fabulous,' Reacher said. 'Thank you very much.'

'You're welcome. Thank you for mine.'

'It isn't right. People not eating because of the Duncans.'

'People do all kinds of things because of the Duncans.'

'I know what I'd do.'

She smiled. 'We all talked like that, once upon a time, long ago. But they kept us poor and tired, and then we got old.'

'What do the young people do here?'

'The adventurous ones leave. The others stay closer to home, in Lincoln or Omaha. Some boys join the State Police.'

He asked, 'What happened twenty-five years ago?'

'I can't talk about it. I was wrong anyway.'

'About what? Were you the neighbour with the dispute?'

She wouldn't answer. She said, 'People say you beat up three Cornhuskers yesterday.'

'Not all at once,' he said.

'You want more coffee?'

'Sure,' he said, and she recharged the percolator and set it going again. He asked, 'How many farms contracted with the Duncans?'

'All of us. This whole corner of the county. Forty farms.'

'That's a lot of corn.'

'And soya beans and alfalfa. We rotate the crops.'

'Did you buy part of the old Duncan place?'

'A hundred acres. It squared off a corner. It made sense.'

'How long ago was that?'

'It must be thirty years ago.'

'So things were good for the first five years?'

'I'm not going to tell you what happened.'

'I had three football players sent after me. I'd like to know why.'

She poured the coffee. 'Twenty-five years ago Seth Duncan was eight years old. This corner of the county was like a little community. We were spread out, but everybody knew everybody else. Children would play together at one house, then another. But no one liked going to Seth's place. Girls especially.'

'Why didn't they like it?'

'No one spelled it out. My daughter was eight at the time. She didn't want to play there. She made that clear.'

'What was going on?'

'I told you, no one said.'

'But you knew. Maybe you couldn't prove it, but you knew.'

She said, 'Today they would call it inappropriate touching.'

'On Seth's part?'

She nodded. 'And his father's and both his uncles'. My daughter never went there again.'

'Did you talk to people?'

'Not at first,' she said. 'Then it all came out in a rush. Everyone was talking to everyone else. Nobody's girl wanted to go there.'

'Did anyone talk to Seth's mother?'

'Seth didn't have a mother. Jacob never married. He was never seen with a woman. No woman was ever seen with any of them. Their own mother had passed on years before. It was just old man Duncan and the three of them. Then the three of them on their own. Then suddenly Jacob was bringing a little boy to kindergarten.'

'Didn't anyone ask where the kid came from?'

'People talked a little, but they didn't ask. Too polite.'

'So what happened next? You all stopped your kids from going there to play, and that's what caused the trouble?'

'That's how it started. There were whispers. The Duncans were alone in their compound. They were shunned. They resented it.'

'So they retaliated?'

'Not at first. Not until after a little girl went missing.'

CASSANO AND MANCINI got back in their Impala. They had scribbled down directions given by the motel guy, who was anxious to be accurate, in order to avoid a worse beating than he was getting.

'Left out of the lot,' Mancini read out loud.

Cassano turned left out of the lot.

DOROTHY SAID, 'Seth got bullied in school. I guess eight-year-old boys felt they had permission to go after him, because of the whispers at home. None of the girls would even talk to him. All except one girl. Her parents had raised her to be compassionate. She wouldn't go to his house, but she still talked to him. Then one day she disappeared.'

Reacher said, 'And?'

'It's a horrible thing, when that happens. First, everyone is worried but can't bring themselves to believe the worst. You know, a couple of hours, you think she's playing, maybe out picking flowers, she's lost track of the time. Then you think the girl has got lost, and everyone starts driving around, looking for her. Then it goes dark, and you call the cops.'

Reacher asked, 'What did the cops do?'

'Everything they could. They did a fine job. They went house to house, they used flashlights, they used loudhailers to tell everyone to search their barns and outbuildings, they drove around all night, then at first light they called in the State Police and the State Police called in the National Guard and they got a helicopter.'

'Nothing?'

'Nothing. Then I told them about the Duncans.'

'You did?' Reacher asked.

'Someone had to. As soon as I spoke up, others joined in. The State Police took the Duncans to a barracks over near Lincoln and questioned them for days. They searched their houses. They got help from the FBI. All kinds of laboratory people were there.'

'Did they find anything?'

'Every test was negative. They said the child hadn't been there. The little girl was never seen again. The case was never solved. The Duncans asked me to apologise, for naming names, but I wouldn't. My husband, neither. Some folks were on our side, like the doctor's wife. But most weren't. They saw which way the wind was blowing. The Duncans punished us. We didn't get our crop hauled that year. We lost it all. My husband killed himself.'

'I'm sorry,' Reacher said. 'Was the girl yours?'

'Yes,' the woman said. 'It was my daughter. She was eight years old. She'll always be eight years old.'

She started to cry, and then her phone started to ring.

Dorothy snatched it up, said hello and then she listened, to what sounded like a fast slurred message, and then she clicked off.

'That was Mr Vincent,' she said. 'Over at the motel. Two men were there. They're coming here. Right now.'

'Who?' Reacher asked.

'We don't know. Men we've never seen before.' She opened the kitchen door and glanced down a hallway towards the front of the house. Reacher heard the distant hiss of tyres on blacktop, and then the crunch of wheels on gravel, as a car bumped onto the track.

Dorothy said, 'Get out of here. They can't know you're here.'

'We don't know who they are.'

'They're Duncan people. Who else would they be? I can't let them find you here. It's more than my life is worth.'

'I can't get out of here. They're already on the track.'

'Hide out back. Please. I'm begging you.' She stepped out to the hallway, ready to meet them at the front door. 'They might search. If they find you, tell them you snuck in the yard. Over the fields. Tell them I didn't know.' Then she closed the door on him and was gone.

REACHER CHECKED THE VIEW across the yard at the back. Maybe sixty feet to the parked pick-up, maybe sixty more to the line of barns and sheds. He eased the door open. He turned back and checked the door to the front hallway. It was closed, but he could hear the car crunching to a stop. He turned again to leave. His gaze passed over the kitchen table.

Not good. The table held the remains of two breakfasts.

Two oatmeal bowls, two plates smeared with egg, two plates full of toast crumbs, two spoons, two knives, two forks, two mugs.

He put his toast plate on his egg plate, his oatmeal bowl on his toast plate, his coffee mug in his oatmeal bowl, and he put his knife, fork and spoon in his pocket. He picked up the teetering stack of china and carried it with him, out the door. He held the stack one-handed, pulled the door shut after him and set off across the yard. The ground was beaten dirt. It was reasonably quiet underfoot. But the shakes in his arm were rattling the mug in the bowl. It sounded as loud as a fire alarm. He passed the pick-up. Headed to a wooden barn. It was in poor condition with hinged twin doors. The hinges were shot and the doors were warped. He hooked a heel behind one of them, forced his butt into the gap and scraped his way inside.

It was dark. No light in there, except blinding sparkles from chinks between the boards. He put the stack of china down.

He peered through a crack in the leaning doors. He heard nothing. And he saw nothing, for ten long minutes. Then a guy stepped out the back door, into the yard, and another came out behind him.

They walked ten paces and stood there like they owned the place. They were both on the short side of six feet, both heavy in the chest and shoulders, both dark. Regular little tough guys. They checked the pick-up. Then they moved on, towards the line of barns and sheds. Directly towards Reacher.

Reacher rolled his shoulders and tried to work some feeling into his arms. He made a fist with his right hand, and then his left.

The two guys walked closer still. They sniffed the air.

They stopped.

Shiny shoes, wool coats. City boys. They didn't want to be wading through pig poop and chicken feathers. They looked at each other and then the one on the right turned back to the house and called out, 'Hey, old lady, get out here right now.'

Dorothy stepped out the door. She walked towards the two guys, slow and hesitant. The two guys walked back towards her, just as slow. They met near the pick-up truck. The guy on the right caught Dorothy by the upper arm with one hand and used the other to take a pistol from under his coat. He laid its muzzle against Dorothy's temple. His thumb and three fingers were wrapped round the grip. The fourth finger was on the trigger.

He called out, 'Reacher? You hiding somewhere? I'm going to count to three. Then you come on out. If you don't, I'm going to shoot the old cow. I've got a gun to her head. Tell him, grandma.'

Dorothy said, 'There's no one here.'

The yard went quiet. Three people, all alone in a thousand acres.

Reacher stood still, right where he was, on his own in the dark.

He saw Dorothy close her eyes.

The guy with the gun said, 'One.'

Reacher stood still.

The guy said, 'Two.'

Reacher stood still.

The guy said, 'Three.'

There was a long second's pause. Reacher stood still and watched through the crack. The guy who had been counting stuffed the gun back under his coat. He let go of the woman's arm. She staggered away. The two guys looked at each other. They shrugged, headed round the side of the house and disappeared. A minute later Reacher heard doors slam, an engine start, and a car drive away.

Reacher stayed right where he was. He wasn't dumb. Easiest thing in the world for one of the guys to be hiding behind the corner of the house, while his buddy drove away like a big loud decoy.

Dorothy stood in the yard with one hand on her truck, steadying herself. Reacher guessed she was about thirty seconds away from shouting that he could come out now. Then he saw twenty-five years of caution get the better of her. She walked the same path the two guys had taken. Then she came back, round the other side of the house. She called, 'They're gone.'

He picked up the stack of plates and shouldered his way out between the barn's warped doors. She took the plates from him.

He said, 'You OK?'

She said, 'I was a little worried there for a minute.'

'The safety catch was on. The guy never moved his thumb. I was watching. It was a bluff.'

'Suppose it hadn't been a bluff? Would you have come out?'

'Probably,' Reacher said.

'You did good with these plates. I remembered them and thought I was a goner for sure. Those guys looked like they wouldn't miss much.'

'What else did they look like?'

'Rough. Menacing. They said they were here representing the Duncans. Representing them, not working for them. That's something new. The Duncans never used outsiders before.'

'Where will they go next? The doctor's, maybe?'

'They might. The Duncans know you had contact. I should get back to the motel. I think they hurt Mr Vincent. He didn't sound too good on the phone.'

'There's an old barn and an old shed south of the motel. Off the road, to the west. All alone in a field. Whose are they?'

'They're nobody's. They were on one of the farms that got sold for the development that never happened. Fifty years ago.'

'I have a truck in there. I took it from the football players last night. Give me a ride?'

'I'm not driving you past the Duncan place again,' she said.

'So you want me to *walk* past their place?'

'You don't have to. Head west across the fields until you see a cell tower. Turn north there and skirt the Duncan place on the blind side and then you'll see the barns.'

'How far is it?'

'It's a morning's walk. Make sure you turn north, OK? South takes you near Seth Duncan's house, and you really don't want to go there. You know the difference between north and south?'

'I walk south, I get warmer. North, I get colder. I should be able to figure it out. What was your daughter's name?'

'Margaret,' the woman said. 'Her name was Margaret.'

So Reacher walked round the back of the barns and the sheds and struck out across the fields. The sun was nothing more than a bright patch of luminescence in the high grey sky, but it was enough to navigate by. He saw a cellphone tower looming insubstantial in the mist. The ground underfoot was hard and lumpy, all softball-sized clods of frozen earth.

He turned north at the tower. Far ahead, to the right, he could see a smudge on the horizon. The three Duncan houses, he guessed. He couldn't make out any detail. Certainly nothing man-sized. Which meant no one there could make out any man-sized detail either, in reverse. But even so, he tracked left, maintaining his distance.

Dorothy sponged the blood off Mr Vincent's face. He had a split lip and a lump the size of an egg under his eye. He had apologised for being slow with his warning call. He had passed out, he said, and scrambled for the phone as soon as he came round.

Dorothy told him to hush up.

Mancini had the doctor's shirt collar bunched in his left hand and his right hand bunched into a fist. The doctor's wife was sitting on Cassano's lap. She had been ordered to, and she had refused. So Mancini had hit her husband. She had complied. Cassano had his hand on her thigh under the hem of her skirt.

'Talk to me, baby,' Cassano whispered, in her ear. 'Tell me where you told Jack Reacher to hide.'

She was rigid with fear. 'I didn't tell him anything.'

'You were with him twenty minutes. Last night. The weirdo at the motel told us so. So what were you doing? Did you have sex with him?'

'No.'

'You want to have sex with me?'

She didn't answer.

'Shy?' Cassano asked. 'Bashful? Cat got your tongue?'

He moved his hand another inch, upwards. He licked the woman's ear. She ducked away from him. He said, 'Come back, baby.'

She didn't move.

He said, 'Come *back*,' a little louder.

She straightened up. He got the impression she was about to puke. He didn't want that. Not all over his good clothes. But he licked her ear one more time, to show her who was boss. Mancini hit the doctor one more time. Travelling men, getting the job done. But wasting their time in Nebraska. No one knew a thing. The place was as barren as the surface of the moon. This guy Reacher was long gone, probably halfway to Omaha by the time the sun came up, in the stolen truck, completely unnoticed by the county cops, who clearly sat around with their thumbs up their butts, because hadn't they missed every single one of the deliveries roaring through from Canada to Vegas? Yokels. Retards. All of them.

Cassano jerked upright and spilled the doctor's wife off his lap. She sprawled on the floor. Cassano and Mancini left, back to the rented Impala parked outside.

REACHER TRACKED ONWARDS. He was used to walking. All soldiers were. Sometimes there was no alternative to a long fast advance on foot, so soldiers trained for it. He kept on going, enjoying the fresh air and country smells. Then he smelled something else.

Up ahead was a tangle of low bushes. Wild raspberries or wild roses, somehow spared by the ploughs, now bare and dormant but still dense with thorns. There was a thin plume of smoke coming from them. Not a wood fire. Not a cigarette. Marijuana.

Reacher was familiar with the smell. All cops are, even military cops. Grunts get high like anyone else, off duty.

It was a boy. Maybe fifteen years old. Reacher looked down into the chest-high thicket and found him there. He was tall, thin, with long hair, wearing a parka. He was sitting, his back against a large granite rock that jutted up from the ground. The rock was why the ploughs had spared the thicket. Big tractors had given it a wide berth, and nature had taken advantage. Now the boy was taking advantage, hiding from the world.

'Hello,' Reacher said.

'Dude,' the boy said. He sounded mellow. 'You're the man. You're the guy the Duncans are looking for.'

Reacher said, 'Am I?'

The kid nodded. 'You're Jack Reacher. Six-five, two-fifty, brown coat. They want you, man. We had Cornhuskers at the house this morning. We're supposed to keep our eyes peeled. And here you are. You snuck right up on me. I guess your eyes were peeled, not mine. Am I right?' Then he lapsed into a fit of helpless giggles.

Reacher said, 'You got a cellphone?'

'Yes, but I'm not going to rat you out. You're putting it to the Duncans, I'm with you all the way.' He held out his joint. 'Share?'

'No, thanks,' Reacher said.

'Everyone hates them,' the kid said. 'The Duncans, I mean. They've got this whole county by the balls. They killed a kid. Did you know that? A little girl. Eight years old.'

'That was twenty-five years ago. You sure?'

'No question, my friend.'

'The FBI said different.'

'You believe them? The FBI didn't hear what I hear, man.'

'What do you hear?'

'Her ghost, man. Still here, after twenty-five years. Sometimes I sit out here at night and I hear that ghost screaming, man, screaming and wailing and moaning and crying, right here in the dark.'

Four

Our ship has come in. An old phrase from sea-faring days, full of hope. An investor could spend all he had, building a ship, hiring a crew. Then the ship would sail into a years-long void, unimaginable distances, incalculable dangers. There was no communication. Then, maybe, one day the ship would come back, its hull riding low in the waters, loaded with spices from India or silks from China, making a man rich beyond his dreams.

Our ship has come in.

Jacob Duncan used that phrase, at eleven thirty that morning. He was with his brothers, in a small dark room at the back of his house. His son Seth had gone home. Just the three elders were there.

'I got the call from Vancouver,' Jacob said. 'Our man in the port. Our ship has come in. The delay was weather in the Luzon Strait, where the South China Sea meets the Pacific Ocean. But now our goods have arrived. Our truck could be rolling tonight.'

'That's good,' Jasper said.

'Is it? You were worried before, in case the stranger got nailed before the delay went away. You said that would prove us liars.'

'True. But now that problem is gone.'

'Is it?' Jacob asked. 'Suppose the truck gets here before the stranger gets nailed? That would prove us liars, too.'

'So what do we do?'

'We think. That's what we do. And we find that guy.'

IN LAS VEGAS a Lebanese man named Safir took out his phone and dialled a number. The call was answered six blocks away by an Italian man named Rossi. Safir said, 'You're making me angry.'

Rossi said nothing in reply. It was a question of protocol. He was absolutely at the top of his own particular tree, but there were bigger trees in the forest, and Safir's was one of them.

Safir said, 'I favoured you with my business. But now you're embarrassing me.' Which, Rossi thought, was an admission of weakness. It made it clear that however big Safir was, he was worried about someone bigger. A food chain thing. At the bottom were the Duncans, then came Rossi, then Safir, and at the top came someone else. Safir said, 'I expect promises to be kept.'

'So do I,' Rossi said. 'We're both victims here. But I'm doing something about it. I've got boots on the ground up in Nebraska.'

'What's the problem there?'

'They claim a guy is poking around. A passer-by. A stranger.'

'So how is this stranger holding things up?'

'I don't think he is. I think they're lying to me. I think they're just making excuses. They're late, that's all.'

'Unsatisfactory. Who have you got up there?'

'Two of my boys.'

'I'm going to send two of mine.'

'No point,' Rossi said. 'I'm already taking care of it.'

'Not to Nebraska, you idiot,' Safir said. 'I'm going to send two of my boys across town to baby-sit you. To keep the pressure on. I want you to be aware of what happens to people who let me down.'

THE PORT OF METRO VANCOUVER was the largest port in Canada, the largest port in the Pacific Northwest, and the fifth largest port in North America. It occupied 375 miles of coastline, had twenty-eight terminals, and handled three thousand vessel arrivals every year, for an annual cargo throughput of a hundred million tons. Almost all of those tons were packed into intermodal shipping containers.

Intermodal shipping containers were corrugated metal boxes that were a little more than eight feet high and eight feet wide, of varying lengths. The Duncans' shipment came in a twenty-foot-long container. Gross weight was 6,110 pounds, and net weight was 4,850 pounds, which meant that there were 1,260 pounds of cargo inside, in a space designed to handle more than sixty thousand. The box was 98 per cent empty. But each of the pounds in the container was worth more than gold.

It was lifted off a South Korean ship by a gantry crane and placed gently on Canadian soil, and then it was picked up by another crane, which shuttled it to an inspection site where a camera read its *Bureau International des Containers* code, a combination of four letters and seven numbers. They told Port Metro Vancouver's computers who owned the container, where it had come from, what was in it, and that those contents had been pre-cleared by Canadian customs, none of which was true. The code also told the computers where the container was going, and when, which was true, to a limited extent. It was going into the interior of Canada, and it was to be loaded immediately onto a waiting semitruck. So it was shuttled on ahead, through a sniffer designed to detect smuggled nuclear material, a test that it passed easily, and then out to the marshalling yard. At that point the port computers generated an automatic text message to the driver, who swung his truck into position. The container was lowered onto his flat bed and clamped down. Ten minutes after that it was rolling through the port gates.

It headed east on Route 3 in British Columbia, driving parallel to the international border. Route 3 was a mountainous road, with steep grades and tight turns. Not ideal for a large vehicle. Most drivers took Route 1, which looped north out of Vancouver before turning east later. A better road, all things considered. But Route 3 had long stretches of wild scenery and very little traffic. And occasional gravel turnouts, for rest.

One of the gravel turnouts near the Waterton Lakes National Park had an amazing view, forest to the south, the snowy Rockies to the east. The truck driver pulled off and parked there, but not for the view. He parked there because it was a prearranged location, and a white panel van was waiting for him. The Duncans had been in business a long time, because of luck and caution, and one of their cautionary principles was to transfer their cargo between vehicles as soon as possible after import. Shipping containers could be tracked. Better not to risk a delayed alert from a suspicious customs agent. Better to move the goods within hours, into something anonymous and forgettable and untraceable, and white panel vans were the most anonymous and forgettable and untraceable vehicles on earth.

The semitruck parked and the panel van backed up to it. Both drivers stepped into the roadway and checked what was coming. Nothing was coming, so the van driver opened his rear doors, and the truck driver climbed up on his flat bed, cut the plastic security seal, smacked the bolts and levers out of their brackets and opened the container's doors.

One minute later the cargo was transferred. Another minute after that the van was moving east. The semitruck turned around and headed back to Vancouver for his next job.

IN LAS VEGAS the Lebanese man Safir dispatched his two best guys to baby-sit the Italian man Rossi. An unwise decision, as it turned out. Within the hour Safir's phone rang and he found himself talking to an Iranian man named Mahmeini. Mahmeini was Safir's customer, but there was no transactional equality in their relationship. Mahmeini was Safir's customer in the way a king might have been a boot-maker's customer. Much more powerful and likely to be lethally angry if the boots were defective. Or late.

Mahmeini said, 'I should have received my items a week ago.'

Safir couldn't speak. His mouth was dry.

Mahmeini said, 'Those items are allocated, to certain people in certain places. If they're not delivered on time, I take a loss.'

Safir said, 'I believe the shipment is actually on its way now.'

'A week late.'

'I'm suffering too. And I'm trying to do something about it. I made my contact send two of his men up there. And then I sent two of my men over to him, to make sure he concentrates.'

'I'm sending two of mine to you. To make sure *you* concentrate.'

Then the phone went dead, and Safir was left sitting there, awaiting the arrival of two Iranian tough guys in an office that had, just an hour ago, been stripped of the better half of its security.

REACHER MADE IT to the two buildings without encountering the two out-of-towners or the six remaining football players. But he knew that his hunters were still looking for him, checking the roads and the fields.

The pick-up was still hidden in the smaller shelter. Reacher opened the tool locker in the pick-up's load bed. The biggest thing in there was an adjustable steel wrench about a foot long. Not the greatest weapon, but better than nothing. Reacher put it in his coat pocket, rooted around for more and came up with two screwdrivers, one a Phillips cross-head design, and one with a regular blade. He put them in his other pocket, closed the locker and climbed in the cab. He backed out and then he followed the deep tractor ruts east to the road, where he turned north and headed for the motel.

SAFIR'S TWO TOUGH GUYS arrived in Rossi's office carrying guns in shoulder holsters and black nylon bags in their hands. They unpacked the bags. From the first bag came a belt sander. From the second bag came a propane blowtorch and a roll of duct tape.

Tools of the trade. And an unmistakable message, to a guy in Rossi's world. In Rossi's world victims were taped naked to chairs, and belt sanders were fired up and applied to areas like knees or elbows. Then blowtorches were sparked to life for a little extra fun.

Rossi dialled his phone, and Cassano answered, in Nebraska. Rossi said, 'What the hell is happening up there?'

Cassano said, 'We're chasing shadows. Who knows whether this guy has anything to do with anything? Whatever happens to him isn't going to make the shipment show up any faster.'

'Have you ever told a lie?'

'Not to you, boss. But to other people, sure.'

'Then you know how it goes. You arrange things to make sure you don't get caught out. I think that the Duncans are going to hold the shipment until the guy gets caught. To make it look like they were telling the truth all along. So we're going to have to play the game their way. Find this guy fast, will you? This thing can't wait.'

Rossi clicked off the call. One of the Lebanese guys had plugged in the belt sander. He flicked the switch, just a second, and the machine whirred and stopped.

A message.

REACHER DROVE to the motel, parked next to the wrecked Subaru. He used the smaller screwdriver from his pocket to take the plates off the Subaru and put them on the pick-up. He tossed the pick-up's plates into the load bed and headed for the lounge.

Vincent was in there. He had a black eye and a thick lip and a swelling the size of a mouse's back on his cheek.

Reacher said, 'I'm sorry I got you in trouble.'

Vincent asked, 'Did you spend the night here?'

'Do you really want to know?'

'No, I guess I don't.'

'What kind of car were those guys driving?'

'A rental. Something dark blue, maybe? A Chevrolet, I think.'

'Did they say who they were?'

'Just that they were representing the Duncans. That's how they put it. I'm sorry I told them about Dorothy.'

'Don't worry about it. She's had bigger troubles in her life.'

'I know.'

'You think the Duncans killed her kid?' Reacher asked.

'I'd like to. But there was no evidence at all. And it was a very thorough investigation. I doubt if they missed anything.'

Reacher said nothing.

Vincent asked, 'What are you going to do now?'

'A few things. Then I'm out of here. I'm going to Virginia.'

Reacher walked back out to the lot and climbed into the pick-up truck. He fired it up and took off towards the doctor's house.

MAHMEINI'S TWO TOUGH GUYS arrived in Safir's Las Vegas office about an hour after Safir's own two tough guys had left it. Mahmeini's men were small, dark and rumpled. Safir knew they would have guns under their arms and knives in their pockets. It was the knives he was worried about. Guns were fast. Knives were slow.

Safir dialled his phone. Three rings, and one of his guys answered, six blocks away. Safir said, 'Give me a progress report.'

'Rossi's contacts are Nebraska people called Duncan. They're in an uproar over some guy poking around. Rossi thinks the Duncans are going to stall until the guy is down, to save face, because they've been claiming the guy is the cause of the delay. Rossi thinks nothing is going to happen until the guy is captured. He's got boys up there, working on it.'

'Tell Rossi to tell them to work harder. Tell him I've got people in my office too, and if I'm going to get hurt over this, then he's going to get hurt first, and twice as bad.'

REACHER REMEMBERED the way to the doctor's house. In daylight the roads looked different. More open, less secret. More exposed.

But Reacher arrived OK. The plain ranch house, the couple of flat acres. There were no cars in the driveway. No blue Chevrolet. No neighbours, either. On three sides there was nothing except dirt, waiting for ploughing and seeding in the spring. On the fourth side was the road, and then more dirt, all the way to the horizon.

Reacher parked and walked to the door. It had a spy hole. A little glass lens like a fat drop of water. Common in a city. Unusual in a rural area. He rang the bell. Eventually the spy hole darkened, then lightened again and the door swung back. Reacher saw the woman he had met the night before, looking a little surprised but plenty relieved.

'You,' she said.

'Yes, me,' Reacher said. 'Were they here?'

'This morning.'

'What happened?'

The woman stepped back. A mute invitation. Reacher stepped in and walked down the hallway and found out pretty much what had happened when he came face to face with the doctor. The guy was a little damaged, in much the same way that Vincent was, over at the motel. Bruising around the eyes, swellings, blood in the nostrils, splits in the lips.

Reacher asked, 'Do you know who they are?'

The doctor said, 'They're not from round here.'

'What did they want?'

'You, of course.'

Reacher said, 'I'm very sorry for your trouble.' He turned back to the doctor's wife. 'Are you OK?'

She said, 'They didn't hit me.'

'But?'

'I don't want to talk about it. Why are you here?'

'I need medical treatment,' Reacher said. 'I'd like some painkillers. I haven't been able to rest my arms like I hoped.'

'What do you really want?'

'I want to talk,' Reacher said.

They went to the kitchen. The doctor said, 'Would you like some coffee?'

Reacher smiled. 'A cup of coffee is always welcome.'

The doctor got a drip machine going. Then he took Reacher's arm, like doctors do, his fingertips in Reacher's palm, lifting, turning, manipulating. The guy dug the fingers of his other hand deep into Reacher's shoulder joint, poking, feeling, probing.

'I could give you cortisone,' he said. 'It would help ease the discomfort. It's probably nagging at you, making you tired.'

'OK,' Reacher said. 'Go for it.'

'I will,' the doctor said. 'In exchange for some information. How did you hurt yourself?'

'Why do you want to know?'

'Call it professional interest.'

Reacher said, 'It was like you figured. I was in a hurricane.'

The doctor said, 'I don't believe you.'

'Not a natural weather event. I was in an underground chamber. It caught fire. There was a stair shaft and two ventilation shafts. I was lucky. The flames went up the ventilation shafts. I was on the stairs. So I wasn't burned. But air to feed the fire was coming down the stair shaft just as hard as the flames were going back up the ventilation shafts. So it was like climbing through a hurricane. I couldn't keep my feet. I had to haul myself up by the arms.'

'How far?'

'Two hundred and eighty steps.'

'Wow. That would do it. Recent event, yes?'

'Feels like yesterday,' Reacher said. 'Now go get the needle.'

IT WAS A LONG NEEDLE. The stainless-steel syringe looked big enough for a horse. The doctor made Reacher take his shirt off. He eased the sharp point deep into the joint. Reacher felt it pushing through tendons and muscles and felt the fluid flood the joint. Felt the joint loosen and relax immediately, like healing insanely accelerated. Then the doctor did the other shoulder. Same result.

'Wonderful,' Reacher said.

The doctor asked, 'What did you want to talk about?'

'A time long ago,' Reacher said. 'When your wife was a kid.'

Reacher dressed again and all three of them took mugs of coffee to the living room, which was a rectangular space with furniture arranged in an L-shape along two walls, and a huge flatscreen television on a third wall. Set into the fourth wall was a picture window that gave a great view of a thousand acres of absolutely nothing. No hills, no trees, no streams. But no trucks or patrols, either. Reacher took an armchair where he could see the door and the view at the same time. The doctor and his wife sat on a sofa.

Reacher asked her, 'How old were you when Dorothy Coe's little girl went missing?'

She said, 'I was fourteen.'

'Do you remember when Seth Duncan first showed up?'

'I was ten or eleven. There was some talk. No one knew anything. People assumed he was a relative. Maybe orphaned.'

'What happened when Dorothy's little girl went missing?'

'It was awful. A thing like that, it puts a scare in you, but it's supposed to have a happy ending. Though it didn't.'

'Dorothy thought the Duncans did it. She said you stood by her. Why?'

'Why not?'

Reacher said, 'You were fourteen. She was thirty? Thirty-five? So it wasn't about solidarity between two women or two mothers or two neighbours. It was because you knew something, wasn't it?'

The doctor's wife said, 'I was the Duncans' baby sitter that year. But they didn't really need one. They rarely went out. Or actually they went out a lot, but then they came right back. Then they would be real slow about driving me home. It was like they were paying me to be there with all four of them, not just with Seth.'

'How often did you work for them?'

'About six times.'

'Anything bad happen?'

She looked straight at him. 'No.'

'Was there any inappropriate behaviour at all?'

'Not really.'

'So what made you stand by Dorothy when the kid went missing?'

'Just a feeling. I didn't really understand anything. But I knew I felt uncomfortable.'

'Did you know why?'

'It dawned on me they were disappointed I wasn't younger. They made me feel I was too old for them. It was creepy.'

'And you told the cops about how you felt?'

'Sure. We told them everything. But nothing was ever proved.'

'Did you think the investigation was OK?'

'I saw dogs and guys in FBI jackets. It was like a television show. So yes, I thought it was OK. But they never found her bike.'

The doctor's wife said that Margaret had ridden away from the house on a pink bicycle bigger than she was. Neither she nor the bike was ever seen again.

'I kept expecting them to find the bike. On the side of a road. In the tall grass. Like a clue. But it didn't happen. Everything was a dead end.'

'So what was your bottom line on the Duncans?' Reacher asked. 'Guilty or not guilty?'

'Not guilty. Facts are facts, aren't they?'

'Yet you still stood by Dorothy.'

'It was horrible for her. The Duncans were very self-righteous. And people were starting to wake up to the power they had. It was like the thought police. First Dorothy was meant to apologise, which she wouldn't, and then she was supposed just to shut up and carry on like nothing had ever happened. She couldn't even grieve, because that would have been like accusing the Duncans all over again. The whole county was uneasy about it. It was like Dorothy was supposed to take one for the team. Like one of those old legends where she had to sacrifice her child to the monster for the good of the village.'

There was no more talk. Reacher carried the empty coffee cups out to the kitchen. The doctor joined him. 'So what are you going to do now?'

Reacher said, 'I'm going to Virginia. With two stops along the way. I'm going to drop in on the county cops. Sixty miles south of here. I want to see their paperwork.'

'Will they still have it?'

Reacher nodded. 'They'll have a pretty big file. And they won't have junked it yet. Because technically it's still an open case.'

'Will they let you see them? Just like that?'

'I was a cop of sorts myself, thirteen years. I can usually talk my way past filing clerks. If it looks OK and I don't see any holes, I'll keep on running. If it's not, I might come back to fill in the holes.'

'Showing up in a stolen truck won't help your cause.'

'It's got your plates on it now. They won't know.'

'My plates?'

'Don't worry, I'll swap them back again. If the paperwork's OK, then I'll leave the truck near the police station with the proper plates on it, and sooner or later someone will figure out whose it is, and word will get back to the Duncans, and they'll know I'm gone for good, and they'll leave you people alone again.'

'That would be nice. What's your second stop?'

'The cops are the second stop. First stop is closer to home. We're going to drop in on Seth's wife. To make sure she's healing right.'

The doctor was dead set against the idea. He looked away and paced the kitchen. Eventually he said, 'But Seth might be there.'

Reacher said, 'I hope he is. We can check he's healing right, too. And if he is, I can hit him again.'

'He'll have Cornhuskers with him.'

'They're all out in the fields, looking for me.'

'I don't know about this. You're a crazy man.'

'I prefer to think of myself as conscientious.'

REACHER AND THE DOCTOR climbed into the pick-up truck, headed back to the county two-lane. Reacher threaded through the turns until Seth's house appeared on his right. The long driveway, the garage, the three sets of doors. This time two of them were standing open. Two cars were visible inside. One was a small red sports car, maybe a Mazda, very feminine, and the other was a big black Cadillac sedan, very masculine.

The doctor parked and they got out. Reacher knocked on the door and they heard feet on the boards inside. A light tread. Eleanor.

She opened up. Her lips had scabbed over, dark and thick, and her nose was swollen. 'You,' she said.

'I brought the doctor,' Reacher said. 'To check on you.'

Eleanor glanced at the doctor's face. 'He looks as bad as I do. Was that Seth? Or a Cornhusker? Either way, I apologise.'

'None of the above,' Reacher said. 'It seems we have a couple of tough guys in town.'

Eleanor didn't answer that. She just invited them in. Reacher asked, 'Is Seth home?'

'No, thank goodness,' Eleanor said.

'His Cadillac is here,' the doctor said.

'His father picked him up.'

Eleanor led the way to the kitchen, sat down and tilted her face to the light. The doctor took a look. He asked questions about pain, headaches and teeth. She gave the kinds of answers Reacher had heard from many people in her situation. She said yes, her nose and mouth still hurt, yes, she had a slight headache, and no, her teeth didn't feel entirely OK. But her diction was clear and she had no memory loss, so the doctor was satisfied. He said she would be OK.

'And how is Seth?' Reacher asked.

'Very angry at you,' Eleanor said.

'What goes around comes around.'

She didn't answer. She just looked at Reacher for a long second, then she looked away, an expression of complete uncertainty on her face, its extent limited only by the immobility caused by the stiff scabs on her lips and the frozen ache in her nose. She was hurting bad, Reacher thought. She had taken two blows, probably the first to her nose and the second aimed at her mouth. The first had been hard enough to do damage without breaking the bone, and the second had been hard enough to draw blood without smashing her teeth. Two blows, carefully aimed, carefully delivered.

Reacher said, 'It wasn't Seth, was it?'

She said, 'No, it wasn't.'

'So who was it?'

'I'll quote your earlier conclusion. *It seems we have a couple of tough guys in town.*'

'They were here?'

'Twice.'

'Why?'

'I don't know.'

'Who are they?'

'I don't know.'

'They've been saying they represent the Duncans.'

'Well, they don't. The Duncans don't need to hire people to beat me. They're perfectly capable of doing that themselves.'

'How many times has Seth hit you?'

'A thousand, maybe.'

'Why do you stay?'

'I don't know. Where else would I go?'

'Anywhere else. So what happened?'

'Four days ago two Italian men showed up here. Seth took them into his den. After twenty minutes they all trooped out. Seth was looking sheepish. One of the men said their instructions were to hurt Seth, but Seth had bargained it down to hurting me. Seth held me in front of him and they took turns hitting me. Then yesterday they came back and did it again. Then Seth went out for a steak.'

'I'm sorry,' Reacher said. 'Any ideas about what they wanted?'

'Maybe they were here on behalf of investors,' she said. 'Gas is expensive now. And it's winter, which must hurt Duncan Transportation's cash flow. There's nothing to haul. I see on the news that ordinary banks are difficult now, for small businesses. So maybe they had to find a loan through unconventional sources.'

'Very unconventional. But if this is all about some financial issue with Duncan Transportation, why are those guys looking for me?'

'Are they looking for you?'

'Yes,' the doctor said. 'They were at my house. They hit me and threatened to do worse to my wife. All they ever asked was where Reacher was. Mr Vincent at the motel was also visited. And Dorothy.'

'That's awful,' Eleanor said. 'But I can't explain it. I know nothing about Seth's business.'

Reacher asked, 'Do you know anything about Seth himself? Like who he is, and where he came from.'

'Do you guys want a drink?'

'No, thank you,' Reacher said. 'Tell me where Seth came from.'

'That old question? He's adopted, like a lot of people.'

'Where from?'

'He doesn't know, and I don't think his father knows either. It was some kind of charity network. There was anonymity involved.'

'Doesn't Seth remember anything? People say he was ready for kindergarten when he got here.'

'He won't talk about it.'

'What about the missing girl?'

'I'm not blind to Seth's faults, or his family's, but I understand they were cleared after an investigation by a federal agency.'

'You weren't here at the time?'

'No, I grew up in Illinois. Seth was twenty-two when I met him. I was trying to be a journalist, working at a paper out of Lincoln. I was doing a story about corn prices. Seth was the new CEO of Duncan Transportation. I interviewed him for the story. Then we had a cocktail. At first, I was bowled over. Later, not so much.'

'Are you going to be OK?' Reacher asked.

'Are you? With two tough guys looking for you?'

'I'm leaving. Heading to Virginia. You want to ride along?'

Eleanor Duncan said, 'No.'

'Then I can't help you.'

'You helped me already. You broke his nose. I was so happy.'

Reacher said, 'You should come with me. You should get the hell out. It's crazy to stay, talking like that. Feeling like that.'

'I'll outlast him. That's my mission, to outlast them all.'

Reacher looked around the kitchen at the stuff she would inherit if she succeeded in outlasting them all. There was a lot of high-quality stuff, some of it German, some of it American. Including a Cadillac key in a glass bowl. 'Is that Seth's key?' Reacher asked.

Eleanor said, 'Yes, it is.'

'I'm going to steal his car.'

Five

Reacher said, 'I've got an hour's drive ahead of me. I could use something more comfortable than a truck. The doctor should keep it. He might need it for his job.'

Eleanor said, 'You won't get away with it. You'll be driving a stolen car straight through where the county police are based.'

'They won't know it's stolen. Not if Seth doesn't tell them.'

'But he will.'

'Tell him if he does, I'll come back here and break his arms.' Reacher took the Cadillac key from the bowl, gave the pick-up key to the doctor, and headed for the door.

SETH DUNCAN was at his father's kitchen table, opposite the old man himself, with his uncle Jonas on one side and his uncle Jasper on the other. The four men were still and subdued, because Cassano and Mancini were there. Cassano had made a point of smoothing his shirt into the waistband of his trousers and Mancini had opened his coat and pressed the heels of his hands into the small of his back. Both men's gestures had been designed to show off their semiautomatic pistols in their shoulder holsters. The Duncans had seen the weapons and got the point.

Cassano said, 'Tell me again. Explain it to me. Convince me. How is this stranger disrupting the shipment?'

Jacob said, 'Do I tell your boss how to run his business? I stay out of it.'

'And Mr Rossi stays out of yours. Until he gets inconvenienced.'

'He's welcome to find an alternative source.'

'I'm sure he will. But right now there's a live contract.'

'We'll deliver as soon as this stranger is out of our hair.'

Cassano shook his head in frustration. He stepped out the back door and walked across gravel to where he couldn't be overheard. He dialled his cell and got Rossi. He said, 'They're sticking to their story. We're not getting the shipment until they get the stranger.'

Rossi said, 'How much pressure have you applied?'

'To the Duncans? How much do you want us to apply?'

There was a long pause. Rossi said, 'The problem is, they sell great stuff. I can't burn them. Because I'm going to need them again. So play their game. Find the damn stranger.'

SETH DUNCAN'S CADILLAC was new enough to have all the bells and whistles, but old enough to be a straight-up turnpike cruiser. Reacher liked it a lot. It was long and wide and smooth and silent. It had black paint and black leather and black glass. And a warm-toned radio and a three-quarters-full tank of gas.

Reacher had eased it out of the garage and drove to the two-lane. He had turned left and wafted down the road. Ten miles south there was an old boarded-up roadhouse. After that there was nothing, all the way to the horizon.

THE DOCTOR STARED at the pick-up. He didn't want to drive it. The manner of its misappropriation had been a major humiliation for the Duncans. Therefore to be involved with the truck would be an outrageous provocation. He would be punished, severely.

But he was a doctor. And he had patients. He had responsibilities. To Vincent at the motel. To Dorothy the housekeeper. Both were shaken up. And his wife was eight miles away, scared and alone.

He looked at the key in his hand. He could park behind Dorothy's house and keep the truck out of sight. He could park on the wrong side of the motel office and achieve the same result. Then he could dump the truck to the north and hike across the fields to home.

Total exposure, two miles on minor tracks, and four on the two-lane road. That was all.

He climbed in the cab, started the engine.

ROSSI CLICKED OFF the call with Cassano and thought hard for five minutes, and then he dialled Safir, six blocks away. He asked, 'You've always been satisfied with the merchandise, right?'

Safir said, 'I'm not satisfied now.'

'I understand. But I need this shipment and you need this shipment. So I want to ask you to put our differences aside and make common cause. Just for a day or two. My contacts in Nebraska have a bug up their ass.'

'I know all about that. My men gave me a full report.'

'I want you to send them up there to help,' Rossi said. 'There's no point in having them in my office. I'm thinking your guys could go help my guys and between us we could solve this problem.'

SAFIR CLICKED OFF the call with Rossi and thought hard for ten minutes, and then he dialled his customer Mahmeini, eight blocks across town. He asked, 'Have you ever seen better merchandise?'

Mahmeini said, 'Get to the point.'

'There's a speed bump. It's crazy, but it's there. We all have a common goal. We all want that shipment. And we're not going to get it until the speed bump disappears. So I'm asking you to put our differences aside and make common cause, just for a day or two.'

'How?'

'I want you to take your guys and send them up to Nebraska. I'm sending my guys. We could work together and solve this problem.'

Mahmeini went quiet. Truth was, he was a link in a chain, too, the same as Safir and Rossi, except that he was the penultimate link, the second to last, and therefore he was under the greatest strain. Because right next to him at the top were Saudis, unbelievably rich and beyond vicious. He said, 'Ten per cent discount.'

Safir said, 'Of course.'

THE DOCTOR MADE IT to Dorothy's farmhouse unobserved. He checked on her. She was frightened, but doing OK.

He headed back out to see Vincent at the motel. He found Vincent in the lounge. He had a black eye, a split lip and a swelling on his cheek.

The doctor asked, 'You need anything? Want painkillers?'

Vincent said, 'I want this to be over. That's what I want. I want that guy to finish what he started.'

'He's on his way to Virginia. He said he's going to check in with the county cops along the way. He said he'll come back if there's something wrong with the case file from twenty-five years ago.'

'But what can he find now, that they didn't find then? Saying all that means he's never coming back. He's leaving us in the lurch.'

The room went quiet. 'You want a drink?' Vincent asked.

'Are you allowed to serve me?'

'It's a little late to be worried about that. You want one?'

'No,' the doctor said. 'I better not.' Then he paused and said, 'Well, maybe just one, for the road.'

SAFIR CALLED ROSSI BACK. 'I want a twenty per cent discount. In exchange for sending my boys up there.'

'Fifteen per cent. Because you'll be helping yourself too.'

'Twenty,' Safir said. 'Because I'm talking about sending more boys than just mine. I've got guys baby-sitting me too. I got my customer to agree to send his guys as well.'

Rossi paused. 'That's good. We'll have six men up there. We can take care of this thing real fast. The nearest civilisation is sixty miles south. The only accommodation is a Courtyard Marriott. My guys are based there. I'll book a few more rooms. Then everyone can meet up as soon as possible.'

REACHER KEPT THE CADILLAC ROLLING at a steady sixty, covering a mile a minute. Fifty minutes from where he started he blew past a bar with dirty windows. A mile later a water tower and a Texaco sign loomed up out of the afternoon gloom. Civilisation. But not much of it.

Eight hundred yards out there was a Chamber of Commerce billboard that listed five ways a traveller could spend his money. If he wanted to eat, there were two restaurants. One was a diner, and one wasn't. If he wanted to sleep, the only choice was a Marriott.

Reacher slowed. In his experience most places reserved the main drag for profit-and-loss businesses. Municipal enterprises like cops and county offices would be a block or two over. He passed the first building on the left, a diner. There was a police cruiser parked outside. Next up was a gas station. Then came a hardware store, a liquor store, a bank, a grocery, a pharmacy.

Reacher drove all the way through town. At the end of it was a crossroads. He U-turned and came back again on the main drag. There were three side streets on the right, and three on the left. He made the first right and saw the Marriott hotel ahead. It was four in the afternoon, which was awkward. The old files would be in the police station or a county storeroom, and either way the filing clerks would be quitting at five. He had one hour. Access might take thirty minutes to arrange, and there was probably plenty of paper, which would take more than the other thirty to read. He was going to have to wait for the morning. Or, maybe not.

The hotel was just two storeys, H-shaped, a lobby flanked by two wings of bedrooms. There was a parking lot at the front with spaces for about twenty cars, only two of them occupied. Same again at the rear of the building. Twenty spaces, only two of them occupied.

He made a left and came back north again, parallel to the main drag, three blocks over. He saw the second restaurant. It was a rib shack. He turned left again just beyond it and came back to the main street and pulled in at the diner. The cop car was still there.

Reacher walked in. The cops were in a booth. One of them was about Reacher's age, and one of them was younger. They had grey uniforms, with badges and nameplates. The older cop was called Hoag. Reacher pantomimed a big double take. 'You're Hoag? I don't believe it.'

The cop said, 'Excuse me?'

'I remember you from Desert Storm, the Gulf, in 1991?'

The cop said, 'I'm sorry, my friend, but you'll have to help me out here. There's been a lot of water over the dam since 1991.'

Reacher offered his hand. He said, 'Reacher, 110th MP.'

The cop shook. 'I'm not sure I was in contact with you guys.'

'I could have sworn. Saudi, maybe? Just before?'

'I was in Germany just before.'

'I don't think it was Germany. But I remember the name. And the face. Did you have a brother in the Gulf? Or a cousin?'

'A cousin, sure.'

'Looks just like you?'

'Back then, I guess. A little.'

'There you go. Nice guy and a fine soldier, as I recall.'

'He came home with a Bronze Star.'

'I knew it. VII Corps, right?'

'Second Armored Cavalry.'

'Third Squadron?'

'That's the one.'

'I knew it,' Reacher said again. An old process, exploited by fortune tellers everywhere. Steer a guy through a series of yes-no, right-wrong questions, and in no time an illusion of intimacy built itself up. Most people who wore name tags every day forgot they had them on. And a lot of heartland cops were ex-military. Even if they weren't, most of them had big families. Lots of brothers and cousins. At least one of them would have been in the army. And Desert Storm had been the main engagement for that generation, and VII Corps had been its largest component, and a Bronze Star winner from the Second Armored Cavalry was almost certainly from the Third Squadron, which had been the tip of the spear.

Reacher asked, 'So what's your cousin doing now?'

'Tony? He's back in Lincoln, working for the railroad.'

'Be sure to remember me to him, OK? Jack Reacher, 110th MP.'

'So what are you doing now? He's bound to ask.'

'Oh, the same old, same old. I was an investigator, and I'm still an investigator. But private now. My own man, not Uncle Sam's.'

'Here in Nebraska?'

'Just temporarily,' Reacher said. Then he paused. 'You know what? Maybe you could help me out. If you don't mind me asking.'

'What do you need?'

Reacher said, 'I knew this guy, name of McNally. Another Second Armored guy. Turns out he has a friend of a friend who has an aunt in this county. Her daughter disappeared twenty-five years ago. Eight years old, never seen again. The woman never got over it. Your department handled it, with the FBI as the icing on the cake. McNally's friend of a friend thinks the FBI screwed up. So McNally hired me to review the paperwork.'

'Twenty-five years ago?' Hoag said. 'That means it's an open case. Cold, but open. The paperwork should still exist.'

'That's exactly what McNally was hoping.'

'And he's looking to screw the FBI? Not us?'

'The story is you guys did a fine job.'

'And what did the FBI do wrong?'

'They didn't find the kid.'

'OK,' Hoag said. 'I'll put the word out at the station house. Someone will get you in, first thing tomorrow morning.'

'Any chance of doing something tonight? If I could get this done by midnight, it would cut McNally's bill by one day. He doesn't have much money. You know how it is. One veteran to another.'

Hoag checked his watch. Twenty minutes past four. He said, 'All that old stuff is in the basement under the county clerk's office. You can't be in there after five o'clock.'

'Any way of getting it out?'

'Oh, man, that's asking a lot. I could get my ass kicked real bad.'

'I just want to read it. Where's the harm in that? In and out in one night, who's going to know? I'll help out with the grunt work.'

'Where are you staying?'

'The Marriott,' Reacher said. 'Where else?'

There was a long pause. Hoag said, 'OK, we'll get this done. But it's better that you're not there. So go wait for us. We'll deliver.'

So Reacher drove to the Marriott and put the Cadillac behind the building, where it couldn't be seen from the front. Then he went to the lobby desk and bought a night in a ground-floor room. Forty minutes later Hoag and his partner showed up in a van loaded with eleven cardboard cartons of files. Five minutes after that, the cartons were in Reacher's room.

AND FIVE MINUTES AFTER THAT, sixty miles to the north, the doctor left the motel. He had talked with Vincent, but mostly he had drunk three triples of Jim Beam. It was getting dark. He climbed into the pick-up truck and started the motor and backed out from his place of concealment. He crossed the lot and turned right on the two-lane.

The six remaining Cornhuskers had split up and were operating solo. Two were parked north on the two-lane, two were parked south, one was out cruising the lanes to the southeast, and the sixth was out cruising the lanes to the southwest.

The doctor ran into the two to the north.

Almost literally. His plan was to dump the truck as soon as he found some neutral no-man's-land and then walk home. He was looking around as he drove, the bourbon making him slow and numb. His gaze came back to the traffic lane and he saw he was about one second away from colliding head-on with a truck parked half on the shoulder, facing the wrong way, with its lights off. Eyes to brain to hands, everything buffered by the bourbon fog, a split second of delay, a wrench of the wheel, and suddenly he was heading diagonally for another truck parked on the other shoulder, thirty yards farther on. He stamped on the brake and came to a stop.

The second truck pulled out and blocked the road ahead of him.

The first truck pulled out and blocked the road behind him.

IN LAS VEGAS Mahmeini dialled his phone. His main guy answered, eight blocks away, in Safir's office. Mahmeini said, 'Change of plan. You two are going to Nebraska, right now. Use the company plane. First, find this stranger and take him out. Second, get close to the Duncans. Build up some trust. Then take out Safir's guys, and Rossi's, so that we're bypassing two links in the chain. In future we can deal direct. Much more profit that way.'

His guy said, 'OK.'

THE DOCTOR SAT STILL behind the wheel, shaking with shock and fear. The Cornhuskers climbed out of their vehicles. They walked towards the doctor's truck. The first guy opened the passenger door, and the second guy opened the driver's door. The guy at the driver's door hauled the doctor out and hit him in the gut. The doctor fell to his knees and puked bourbon on the road.

The guy at the passenger door walked back to his vehicle and parked it where it had been before. Then he put the doctor's truck behind it. He rejoined his buddy and between them they wrestled the doctor up into the cab of the first guy's truck. Then they drove away, with the doctor jammed between them, shaking and shivering.

IN LAS VEGAS Safir called his guy in Rossi's office. Safir said, 'I'm sending you two to Nebraska. I'll fax details to the airport. Rossi's guys will meet you at the hotel. Mahmeini is sending guys too. The six of you will work together until the stranger is down. Meanwhile, build a relationship with the Duncans. Then take Rossi's guys out. That way we're one step closer to the motherload. We can double our margin. Take Mahmeini's guys out too. I think I can get next to his customer. We could quadruple our margin.'

His guy said, 'OK, boss.'

THE CORNHUSKERS drove south five miles, and then they turned in to the Duncans' driveway. They took it slow all the way up to the houses. They parked, got out and hauled their prize out after them. They marched him to Jacob's door and knocked. Jacob opened up and one of the Cornhuskers shoved the doctor inside, and said, 'We found this guy using the truck we lost. He put his own plates on it.'

Jacob dragged the doctor into the hallway towards the kitchen at the back. Jacob turned to the Cornhuskers. 'Good work, boys. Now go find Reacher. If the doctor knows where he is, he's sure to tell us, and we'll let you know. But in the meantime, keep looking.'

CASSANO AND MANCINI were still in Jacob's kitchen. They saw the doctor stumble in from the hallway, drunk and terrified. Then Cassano's phone rang. He stepped out the back door, hit the button and Rossi said, 'You're getting reinforcements. Two of Safir's guys, two of Mahmeini's.'

'That should shorten the process,' Cassano said.

'Initially,' Rossi said. 'But then it's going to get difficult. I'll bet they're coming with instructions to cut us out of the chain. So watch your step. You're going to have four guys gunning for you.'

'Rules of engagement?'

'Put Safir's guys down. That way we remove the link above us. We can sell direct to Mahmeini. And put Mahmeini's guys down too, if you have to, for self-defence. Leave now. Pull back to the hotel. You'll meet the others there soon. Make contact and make a plan. Be careful.'

'OK, boss,' Cassano said. And two minutes later he and Mancini were back in their rented blue Impala, heading south.

THE WHITE VAN was still on Route 3, still in Canada, but it had left British Columbia behind and had entered Alberta a few hours ago. It was making steady progress, heading east, completely unnoticed.

Saskatchewan was up ahead. The white van had just skipped a right turn on Route 4, which led south to the border, where the modest Canadian blacktop ribbon changed to US Interstate 15, which ran all the way to Las Vegas and then Los Angeles. It was an obvious artery, with two big prizes at the end of it, and so it was assumed to be monitored very carefully. Which was why the van did not exit there but laboured east on the minor thoroughfare. He made a right turn just shy of a small town called Medicine Hat and headed south on a lonely road that led down towards Pakowki Lake.

It was already fully dark up there. The road was bad, pitted with potholes. It twisted and wandered. It was hard going, and not entirely safe because at that stage a broken axle would ruin everything. So the driver turned left, on a rough grassy track he had used before, and bumped and bounced two hundred yards to a picnic spot provided for summer visitors. In winter it was deserted. He parked under a towering pine and shut down for the night.

THE DUNCANS made the doctor stand upright at the head of the table. Jacob and Seth on one side, Jasper and Jonas on the other. Jacob asked, 'Was it an act of deliberate rebellion?'

The doctor said, 'I don't know what you're talking about.'

'We want to know why you put your licence plates on our truck. Were you retaliating for our having disabled your own vehicle?'

'I don't know,' the doctor said.

'Or did someone else change the plates?' Jacob asked.

'I don't know who changed them.'

'Where did you find the truck?'

'At the motel next to my car. With my plates on it.'

'To drive with phoney plates is a criminal offence, isn't it? Should medical practitioners indulge in criminal behaviour?'

'I guess not. I'm sorry.'

'Don't apologise. We're not a state board. But you might lose your job. You treated my daughter-in-law. After being told not to.'

'I'm a doctor. I had to.'

'The Hippocratic oath? Doesn't it say, first, do no harm?'

'I didn't do any harm.'

'Look at my son's face,' Jacob said. 'You did that. You caused it to be done. You did harm.'

'That wasn't me.'

'So who was it?'

'I don't know.'

'I think you do. The word is out. Surely you've heard it? We know you people talk about us all the time. On the phone tree.'

'It was Reacher.'

'Finally,' Jacob said. 'We get to the point. You were his co-conspirator. You asked him to drive you to my son's house.'

'I didn't. He made me go.'

'Whatever,' Jacob said. 'There's no use crying over spilt milk. But we have a question for you. Where is Reacher now?'

REACHER WAS IN his ground-floor room at the Courtyard Marriott. He had started a quick-and-dirty overview of the police records.

The notes were comprehensive. It had been a high-profile case with many sensitivities, and there had been three other agencies on the job: the State Police, the National Guard and the FBI. The county PD had recorded every move. In some ways the files were slices of history. They were typewritten. The paper was brown and brittle.

Dorothy had called the local cops at eight p.m. on an early summer Sunday. Her last name was Coe. Her only child Margaret had last been seen more than six hours previously. She had been wearing a green dress and had ridden away on a pink bicycle.

The desk sergeant had called the captain and the captain had called a detective, Miles Carson. Carson had sent squad cars north and the hunt had begun. There had been an hour of twilight and then darkness had fallen. The next twelve hours had unfolded pretty much the way Dorothy had described, the house to house canvass, the flashlight searches, the loudhailer appeals to check every outbuilding, the all-night motor patrols, the State Police contribution, the National Guard's loan of a helicopter.

Reacher thought that the loudhailer appeals for folks to search their own property was curious, because what was a guilty party going to do? Turn himself in? Although in Carson's defence, foul play was not yet suspected. The first Carson had heard about local suspicions had come the next morning, when Dorothy had spilled the beans about the Duncans. That interview had lasted an hour and filled nine pages of notes. Then Carson had got on it. But from the start, the Duncans had looked innocent.

They even had an alibi. Five years earlier they had sold the family farm, retaining only a T-shaped acre that encompassed their driveway and their three houses, and they had never marked off their new boundaries. Eventually they decided to put up a post-and-rail fence. They hired four teenagers to do the work. The four had been there dawn to dusk that Sunday, measuring, sawing, digging deep holes for the posts. The three Duncans and the eight-year-old Seth had been with them all day, supervising. The four boys confirmed that the Duncans had never left the property, and no one had stopped by, least of all a little girl on a pink bicycle.

Even so, Carson had hauled the Duncans in. The State Police had to be involved, because of jurisdiction issues, so the Duncans were taken to a State barracks near Lincoln. The three adults were grilled for days. But the Duncans admitted nothing. They allowed their property to be searched. Carson's people did the job thoroughly and found nothing. Carson called the FBI, who sent a team equipped with the latest 1980s technology. The FBI found nothing. The Duncans were released and the case went cold.

Overview completed, Reacher was ready to start in on the details.

THE DOCTOR DIDN'T ANSWER. He just stood there, bruised, sore, shaking. Jacob repeated the question, 'Where is Reacher now?'

The doctor said, 'I would like to sit down.'

'Have you been drinking?'

'A little. I was drinking at home. Then I walked to the motel. I needed some medical equipment from my car.'

'So you were already drunk when you stole our truck?'

'Yes. I wouldn't have done it if I was sober.'

'Where is Reacher now?'

'I don't know.'

'Would you like a drink?'

The doctor said, 'Yes, I would like a drink.'

Jacob took a bottle of Wild Turkey from the cabinet. From another cabinet he took a glass. He carried both back to the table. He placed a chair behind the doctor. He said, 'Sit down, please. And help yourself.'

The doctor sat down, poured himself a generous measure and drank it all. He poured a second glass. Jacob asked, 'Where is Reacher now?'

The doctor said, 'I don't know.'

'I think you do. And it's time to make your choice. You can sit here with us and drink my fine bourbon and pass the time of day in pleasant conversation. Or we could have Seth break your nose.'

'Reacher's gone,' the doctor said. 'He left this afternoon.'

'How?' Jacob asked.

'He got a ride. He was at the motel. I think he changed the plates because he was going to use your truck. But some stranger came along in a white car and he hitched a ride, which was better.'

'Did Reacher say where he was going?'

The doctor drank his second glass. 'He's going to Virginia. But first he's going to the county police. Tomorrow morning, I suppose. He'll look at the file from twenty-five years ago. If it's OK, he's going to Virginia. If it's not, he's coming back here.'

CASSANO AND MANCINI pulled their rented Impala round the back of the Marriott and slotted it next to a black Cadillac. They got out. They figured they had time for dinner before their reinforcements arrived. The diner or the rib shack? They pondered for a second and decided on the diner.

THE DUNCANS let the doctor finish a third glass of Wild Turkey, then they sent him on his way and told him to walk home.

They regrouped in Jacob's kitchen. Jasper asked, 'Should we call the county and stop them showing Reacher the files?'

'I don't see how we could do that,' Jacob said. 'It would draw attention.'

Jonas asked, 'Should we call Eldridge Tyler? Strictly as a backup, if Reacher is coming back?'

'I don't think he's coming back,' Jacob said. 'But ultimately I guess it depends on what he finds.'

Six

Reacher found a detailed statement from the girl's father. Cops weren't dumb. Fathers were automatic suspects when little girls disappeared. Margaret's father was Arthur Coe, a Vietnam veteran. He had refused an offer to classify his farm work as an essential occupation. He had served, and he had come back. He had been fixing machinery in an outbuilding when Margaret had ridden away, and he had still been fixing it four hours later, when his wife came to tell him that the kid was still out. He had dropped everything and started the search. His statement was full of the feelings Dorothy had described, the hope against hope, the belief that the kid was maybe picking flowers, that she had lost track of time. Even after twenty-five years the typewritten words reeked of shock and pain.

Arthur Coe was an innocent man, Reacher thought.

He moved on, to a thin envelope marked *Margaret Coe Biography.* Reacher eased the gummed flap open. There were sheets of paper inside, plus a photograph. Reacher was surprised.

Margaret Coe was Asian.

Vietnamese, possibly, or Thai or Cambodian. Dorothy wasn't. Arthur probably hadn't been, either. Therefore Margaret was adopted. The photo showed a smiling little Asian girl, trust and merriment in her eyes.

And at that point Reacher took a break. He called the desk and asked for room service. The guy told him there was no room service. He mentioned the two restaurants named on the billboard Reacher had already seen.

Reacher headed to the lobby. Two guests were checking in. Both Middle Eastern men. Iranian, possibly. They were small and rumpled. One of them glanced at Reacher and Reacher nodded politely. He decided to go to the rib shack for dinner.

THE DOCTOR MADE IT HOME inside an hour. His wife was waiting. She was worried. After he got through the whole story, she said, 'So it's a gamble. Will Reacher come back before Seth gets home and finds out that you sat there and watched his car get stolen?'

The doctor said, 'Will Reacher come back at all?'

'I think he will. Because the Duncans took that kid.'

The doctor said, 'Maybe Seth won't go home. Maybe he'll spend the night at his father's place.'

'That's possible. People say that he often does. But we shouldn't assume so.'

She started checking the window locks, checking the door locks. She said, 'We should wedge the doors with furniture.'

'Those guys weigh three hundred pounds. You saw what they did to my car. Even if you're right about the Duncans, there's no guarantee Reacher will find proof. There probably isn't any proof.'

'We have to hope.'

REACHER ORDERED baby back ribs and a cup of coffee. The place was dim and dirty. But the ribs turned out to be good. The coleslaw was crisp. The coffee was hot. And the bill was tiny.

Reacher paid and walked back to the hotel.

Two guys were in the lot, hauling bags out of the trunk of a red Ford Taurus. More guests. The guys were Arabs of some kind. Syrians or Lebanese. The two guys looked at Reacher as he passed. He nodded politely. A minute later he was back in his room, with faded paper in his hands.

THE FOUR DUNCANS ate lamb and potatoes in Jonas's kitchen. Afterwards Jasper said, 'We still have six boys capable of walking and talking. We need to decide how to deploy them tonight.'

Jacob said, 'Reacher won't come back tonight.'

'Can we guarantee that?'

'We can't really guarantee anything at all, except that the sun will rise in the east and set in the west.'

'Therefore it's better to err on the side of caution.'

'OK. Put one to the south and tell the other five to get some rest.'

CASSANO AND MANCINI got back from the diner and went to Cassano's room. Cassano called the desk and asked if any pairs of guests had checked in. He was told two pairs had just arrived, one after the other. Cassano asked to be connected with their rooms.

The Iranians arrived first. Mahmeini's men. They were not physically impressive. Only one of them spoke. No names were exchanged.

The Lebanese arrived five minutes later. Safir's men. They were big, and they looked tough. Again, only one of them spoke, and he gave no names. Cassano let the room go quiet.

He said, 'Sixty miles north of here there's forty farms. There's a guy running around causing trouble. Our supplier is taking it personally. Business is on hold until the guy goes down. We'll all move up there and take care of the problem tomorrow morning.'

'Have you seen the guy?' Mahmeini's man asked.

'Not yet.'

'Got a name?'

'Reacher.'

'Got a description?'

'Big guy, blue eyes, white, six-five, two-fifty, brown coat.'

Mahmeini's man said, 'That's worthless. This is farm country. They all look like that. I mean, we just saw a guy exactly like that.'

Safir's guy said, 'He's right. We saw one too. We're going to need a much better description.'

Cassano said, 'We don't have one. But it will be easier when we get there. He stands out, apparently. And there's no cover up there.'

Mahmeini's man said, 'So where is he hiding out?'

'We don't know. But I'm sure we'll find him.'

'And then what?'

'We put him down.'

THE PHYSICAL SEARCH of the area was described in four files, from the county PD, the State Police, the National Guard's helicopter unit and the FBI. The helicopter report was useless. Margaret had been wearing a green dress, which didn't help in corn country in early summer. Nothing significant had been seen from the air. No flash of pink or chrome from the bike, no flattened stalks in the fields.

Both the county PD and the State Police had covered the forty farms at ground level. First had come the loudhailer appeals in the dark, and the next day every house had been visited and every occupant had been asked to verify that they hadn't seen the kid and that they had searched their outbuildings. There was near-universal cooperation.

Nothing was found.

The Duncan compound showed up in three files. First the county PD had gone in, then the State Police, and finally the FBI. The searches had been intense. The lumber for the half-built fence had been taken apart and examined. Gravel had been raked up, and lines of men had walked slow and bent over, staring at the ground. The search moved indoors. Stuff had been taken apart, and voids in walls had been opened up, and floors had been lifted.

Nothing was found.

The FBI contribution was a full-on forensics sweep, 1980s style. Hairs and fibres had been collected, every flat surface had been fingerprinted. Technicians had been in and out for twelve hours.

Nothing was found.

Reacher could hear it in his head right then, the same way they must have heard it years ago: the sound of a case going cold.

It was ten p.m. Reacher's job was done. He packed up all eleven cartons. From the bedside table, he dialled, asked for Hoag.

When the guy came on, Reacher said, 'I'm done. You guys did a fine job. So I'm moving out.'

'OK, leave the stuff right there. We'll swing by and pick it up.'

'I owe you,' Reacher said.

'Forget it,' Hoag said. 'Be all you can be, and all that.'

Reacher hung up, grabbed his coat and headed for the door. He had to walk all the way forward to the lobby before getting outside and looping back to where his car was parked. The stairs came down from the second floor just before the lobby. As Reacher got to them, a guy stepped off the last stair and fell in alongside him, heading the same way. He was one of the Iranian guys Reacher had seen checking in. He glanced across. Reacher nodded politely. The guy nodded back. They walked together. The guy had car keys swinging from his finger. A red tag. Avis. Reacher held the door. The guy stepped out. Reacher followed. The guy looked at him again.

Reacher stepped left. The Iranian stayed with him. Reacher glanced ahead, saw two cars parked there. Seth's Cadillac and a dark blue Chevrolet. Prime rental material. Avis probably had thousands of them.

A dark blue Chevrolet. Reacher stopped.

The other guy stopped.

NOBODY KNOWS how long it takes for thoughts to form. People talk about electrical impulses racing through nerves at a fraction of the speed of light, but that's mail delivery. The letter is written in the brain, sparked to life by two compounds arcing across synapses. The brain floods the body with lots of subtle adjustments at once, because thoughts don't happen one at a time. They come in starbursts and explosions, jostling, fighting for supremacy.

Reacher saw the dark blue Chevrolet and instantly linked it through Vincent's testimony back at the motel to the two men he had seen from Dorothy's barn, while simultaneously critiquing the connection, in that Chevrolets were common cars and dark blue was a common colour, while simultaneously recalling the two matched Iranians and the two matched Arabs he had seen, and asking himself whether the rendezvous of two separate pairs of strange men in winter in a Nebraska hotel could be a coincidence, and, if it wasn't, whether it might imply the presence of a third pair of men, which might be the two tough guys from Dorothy's farm, while simultaneously watching the man in front of him dropping his car key, and putting his hand in his coat pocket, while simultaneously realising that the guys he had seen on Dorothy's farm had not been staying at Vincent's motel, and that there was nowhere else to stay except there, sixty miles south at the Marriott, which meant that the Chevrolet was likely theirs, which meant that the Iranian was likely connected with them, while simultaneously recalling years of experience that told him men like this Iranian went for their pockets in dark parking lots for one of four reasons, to pull out a cellphone to call for help, to pull out a wallet or a passport to prove their innocence or their authority, to pull out a knife or to pull out a gun.

Better safe than sorry. Reacher reacted.

He twisted from the waist and started a low sidearm punch aimed at the centre of the Iranian's chest. Chemical reaction in his brain, instantaneous transmission of the impulse, total elapsed time a fraction of a second, total time to target another fraction of a second, which was good to know because the guy's hand was all the way in his pocket by that point, his elbow jerking up and back, trying to free whatever it was. But Reacher's fist was homing in and the guy's eyes were panicked and his arm was jerking harder and then came his knuckles above the hem of his pocket, all bunched because his fingers were clamping around something big and black.

Then Reacher's blow landed.

Two hundred and fifty pounds of moving mass, a huge impact, the guy's breastbone driving backwards into his chest cavity, the compression driving the air from his lungs, his head snapping forward, his arms, legs and torso going down like a rag doll, the clatter of something black skittering away on the ground, Reacher tracking it in the corner of his eye, not a wallet, not a phone, not a knife, but a Glock 17 semiautomatic pistol. It ended up eight feet away from the guy, out of his reach, partly because of the distance and partly because the guy was down and wasn't moving at all.

In fact he was looking like he might never move again.

Something Reacher had heard about, but never actually seen.

His army medic friends had called it *commotio cordis*, for low-energy trauma to the chest wall. Low energy in the sense that the damage wasn't done by a car wreck or a shotgun blast, but by a line drive in a football collision or a punch in a fight. Gruesome research on laboratory animals proved it was all about luck and timing. Electrocardiograms showed waveforms associated with the beating of the heart, one of which was called the T-wave, and that if the blow landed when the T-wave was between fifteen and thirty milliseconds short of its peak, then lethal cardiac dysrhythmia could occur, stopping the heart like a regular heart attack. And in a high-stress environment like a confrontation in a parking lot, a guy's heart was pounding away harder than normal and was bringing those T-wave peaks around faster than usual, thereby increasing the odds that the luck and the timing would be bad, not good.

The Iranian lay completely still. Not breathing. No signs of life.

The first-aid remedies taught by the army medics were artificial respiration and external chest compressions, but Reacher's rule of thumb was never to revive a guy who had just pulled a gun on him. So he let nature take its course. The Iranian died. Reacher found the car key and picked up the Glock. The key was marked with the Chevrolet bolt logo, but it wasn't for the blue car. Reacher stabbed the unlock button and nothing happened. The Glock was fully loaded. Reacher put it in his pocket.

He walked to the front lot and tried again with the key. A yellow Chevy Malibu flashed its turn signals and unlocked all four of its doors. It was new and plain and clean. An obvious rental. He got in and started it. The tank was close to full. Reacher drove to the back and stopped with the dead guy between the wall and the car. He popped the trunk. It was not a big trunk, but then, the Iranian was not a big guy.

Reacher went through the Iranian's pockets. He found a phone, a switchblade, a wallet and a handkerchief. He stripped the battery out of the phone and put the phone back in the dead guy's pocket. Reacher put the knife in his pocket. The wallet held four hundred bucks, plus a Nevada driver's licence made out to a guy named Asghar Arad Sepehr at a Las Vegas address. Reacher put the wallet back in the guy's pocket. He hoisted him up to fold him into the Malibu's trunk. Then he got a better idea.

He carried the guy to the Cadillac and laid him on the ground. Reacher found the key, opened the trunk, picked the guy up again and put him inside. A big trunk. Plenty of space. He closed the lid, locked up and walked to the Malibu. It was yellow, but fairly anonymous. Probably less conspicuous than the Cadillac, despite the colour. And less likely to be reported stolen. Out-of-state guys with guns and knives in their pockets generally kept a lot quieter than outraged local citizens.

He got in the Malibu, nosed out of the lot and paused. To the left was I-80, sixty miles south, a straight shot east to Virginia. To the right were the Duncans, Eleanor, the doctor and his wife and Dorothy, sixty miles north.

Decision time.

Left or right? South or north?

He flicked the headlights on, turned right and headed back north.

THE MALIBU WORKED OK. As it cruised, Reacher was thinking about the dead Iranian, and the odds against hitting a T-wave window. It had been an unlucky punch. But most likely Reacher would have had to put the Iranian down anyway, probably within just a few more heartbeats. Once a gun was pulled, there were few options. But still, it had been a first. And a last, probably, at least for a spell. Because Reacher was pretty sure the next guy he met would be a football player. He figured the Duncans knew he had gone out of town, possibly for a day, possibly for ever. They would have got hold of the doctor and squeezed that news out of him. And they were realistic but cautious people. They would have stood down five of their boys for the night, and left one lone sentry to the south. And that sentry would have to be dealt with. But not via *commotio cordis*. Reacher wasn't about to aim a punch at a Cornhusker's centre mass. He would break his hand.

He kept the Malibu humming along, and then he started looking for the bar he had seen on the shoulder. There was mist in the air and the Malibu's headlights made crisp little tunnels. Then they were answered by a glow in the air. A halo, far ahead on the left. Neon, in Kelly green, and red, and blue. Beer signs.

Reacher parked. He got out, headed for the door. There was noise inside, the low hubbub and hoo-hah of a half-empty late-evening bar. Reacher threaded sideways between tables and caught the barman's eye. He asked him if he could use a pay phone.

The guy pointed. 'Back corridor.'

'Thanks,' Reacher said.

He worked his way down the line of stools, and he found an opening that led to the restrooms. There was a pay phone on the wall opposite the ladies' room. He dialled information and asked for Seth Duncan, but the number was unlisted. So he asked for the town doctor's number. Once he had the number, Reacher hung up and redialled.

TEN MILES SOUTH, Mahmeini's man was dialling too, calling home. He got Mahmeini, and said, 'We have a problem. Asghar has run out on us. I sent him down to the car to get me a bottle of water. He didn't come back, so I checked. The car is gone, and he's gone too.'

'Call him.'

'I tried ten times. His phone is off.'

'I don't believe it,' Mahmeini said. 'I want you to find him.'

'I have no idea where to look. I don't have a car. And I can't ask the others for help. That would be an admission of weakness.'

'Find him,' Mahmeini said. 'That's an order.'

REACHER LISTENED to the sonorous ringtone. When the doctor answered, Reacher said, 'I need Eleanor Duncan's phone number.'

The doctor said, 'Reacher? Where are you?'

'Still out of town.'

'I didn't tell the Duncans about the Cadillac.'

'Good man. Has Seth gone home yet?'

'He was still with his father when I left.'

'You OK?'

'Not too bad. I was in the truck. The Cornhuskers got me.'

'And?'

'Nothing much. Just words, really.'

Reacher pictured him, standing in his kitchen, quaking, shaking, watching the windows. 'I need Eleanor's number.'

'She's not listed.'

'I know that.'

'She's not on the phone tree. Seth might answer.'

'But she's your patient.'

'I can't. There are confidentiality issues.'

'We're making an omelette here. We have to break some eggs.'

The doctor sighed, and then he recited a number.

'Thanks,' Reacher said. He redialled and listened to more ringtone.

Eleanor picked up. 'Hello?' she said.

Reacher asked, 'Is Seth there?'

'Reacher? Where are you?'

'Doesn't matter where I am. Where's Seth?'

'He's at his father's. I don't expect him home tonight.'

'That's good. I want you to do something for me. In one hour and ten minutes, I want you to take a drive. In your little sports car.'

Eleanor said, 'A drive? Where?'

'South on the two-lane. Just drive. Eleven miles. As fast as you want. Then turn round and go home again. Will you do it?'

'I can't. Seth took my car key. I'm grounded.'

Reacher said, 'He's not carrying it in his pocket. Not if he keeps his own key in a bowl in the kitchen. Do you know where it is?'

'Yes. It's on his desk.'

'On or in?'

'On. Just sitting there. Like a test for me. He says obedience without temptation is meaningless.'

'Why the hell are you still there? Just take the keys, will you?'

There was a long pause. Then Eleanor said, 'OK, I'll do it. I'll drive south eleven miles on the two-lane and come back again. An hour and ten minutes from now.'

'No,' Reacher said. 'An hour and six minutes from now. We've just been talking for four minutes.'

He hung up, pushed out the door and walked to his car.

ELEANOR CHECKED HER WATCH. She had forty-five minutes to go. She stepped into her husband's den. There was a glass bowl on the desk. It had paperclips in it. And her car keys. For her Mazda Miata.

She took the keys. She thought she knew what Reacher had in mind. So she opened the coat closet and took out a white silk headscarf and tied it over her hair. She checked the mirror. Just like an old-fashioned movie star. Or an old-fashioned movie star after a knockout round with an old-fashioned heavyweight champion.

She walked to the garage, She got in her car, unlatched the clips above the windshield and dropped the top. She started up, backed out and waited, the motor running, her heart beating hard.

REACHER CRUISED ONWARDS for three more minutes, watching the right shoulder. The abandoned roadhouse loomed up at him. He slowed, pulled off the road and went into the lot. He drove a full circuit. The rectangular building was long, low and plain, except for two square bump-outs added at the back, one at each end, the first for restrooms, probably, and the second for a kitchen. Between the bump-outs was an empty U-shaped space, enclosed on three sides, open only to the dark fields to the east. Perfect, for later.

Reacher came around to the south gable wall and parked thirty feet from it, out of sight from the north, facing the road at a slight diagonal angle, like a cop on speed-trap duty. He killed the lights and kept the motor running, watching the darkness in the north.

Reacher waited twenty minutes, and then he saw light. Very faint, maybe five or six miles away, trembling a little, bouncing. A moving bubble of light. A car coming towards him, pretty fast.

Eleanor Duncan, presumably, right on time.

Two minutes later the hemispherical glow was bigger, still bouncing, but now it had a strange asynchronous pulse inside it, the bouncing going two ways at once. There were two cars on the road, not one.

Reacher smiled. The sentry. The football player, posted to the south. He knew his five buddies had been sent home to bed because nothing was going to happen. He knew he was facing a long night of boredom. So what's a guy going to do, when Eleanor Duncan blasts past him in her sports car? He's going to follow her, and he's going to dream of a promotion to the inner circle, and he's going to imagine a scene when he pulls Seth aside tomorrow morning, and whispers, *Yes, sir, I followed her all the way and I can show you exactly where she went.*

Two more minutes, and the travelling bubble of light was two miles closer, now flatter and more elongated. Two cars, with little distance between them. Predator and prey. The football player was maybe a quarter of a mile back, following the Mazda's taillights.

Reacher locked the Malibu in first gear, put his left foot hard on the brake and his right foot on the gas until the transmission was straining against the brake and the car was ready to launch. He kept one hand on the wheel and the other on the headlight switch.

Then the Mazda flashed past, its top down, a woman in a headscarf at the wheel. Then it was gone. Reacher flicked his headlights on, took his foot off the brake, stamped on the gas, shot forward, braked hard and stopped sideways across the road. He wrenched open the door and spilled out. Two hundred yards to his right a big SUV was starting a panic stop. Huge tyres howled and the truck went into a four-wheel slide. The rear end fishtailed violently a full ninety degrees. The truck snapped round and came to rest parallel with the Malibu, less than ten feet away.

Reacher pulled the Iranian's Glock from his pocket, stormed the driver's door, wrenched it open and pointed the gun. He screamed GET OUT OF THE CAR GET OUT OF THE CAR as loud as he could, and the guy behind the wheel tumbled out, then Reacher was forcing him face down into the blacktop, the Glock's muzzle in the back of the guy's neck, screaming STAY DOWN STAY DOWN, while watching over his shoulder for more lights.

There were no more lights. No one else was coming. No backup. The guy hadn't called it in. He was planning a solo enterprise.

The scene went quiet. Nothing to hear, except the Malibu's patient idle. Nothing to see, except four high beams stabbing the high shoulder. The Cornhusker lay still. Hard not to, with 250 pounds on his back, and a gun to his head, and television images of SWAT arrests in his mind. The guy was big. Six-six, two-ninety. He had on a red football jacket and baggy jeans.

Reacher said, 'Tell me your name.'

The guy's chin and his lips and his nose were all jammed hard down on the blacktop. He said, 'John,' like a gasp, like a grunt.

Reacher turned the guy's head, jammed the Glock in his ear, saw the whites of his eyes. 'Do you know who I am?'

The guy on the ground said, 'I do now.'

'Whoever you think you are, I'm tougher and more ruthless than you. You know what I did to your buddies?'

'Yes.'

'But, John, I'm prepared to work with you, to save your life. But if you step half an inch out of line, I'll kill you. We clear on that?'

'Yes.'

'Are you thinking about some stupid move? You planning to wait until my attention wanders?'

'No.'

'Good answer, John. Because my attention never wanders. So stand up.' Reacher got up out of his crouch, aiming the gun two-handed, tracking the guy's head. The guy got to his feet. Reacher said, 'See the yellow car? Stand next to the driver's door.'

The guy said, 'OK.' Reacher tracked him round the hood. The driver's door was open. Reacher had left it that way. Reacher aimed the gun across the roof of the car and opened the passenger door.

Reacher said, 'Now get in.'

The guy slid into the seat. Reacher aimed the gun inside the car at the guy's hips and thighs. He said, 'Don't touch the wheel. Don't touch the pedals. Don't put your seat belt on. Now close your door.'

The guy closed his door.

Reacher said, 'Just remember, the Malibu is an OK mid-range product, but it doesn't accelerate like a bullet. This gun has nine-millimeter Parabellums that come out of the barrel at nine hundred miles an hour. Think a four-cylinder motor can outrun that?'

'No.'

Reacher looked up across the roof of the car, and he saw light in the mist to the south. A high hemispherical glow, trembling a little, bouncing. A car, coming north towards him, pretty fast.

The oncoming car was about two miles away. Doing about sixty, Reacher figured. Two minutes. He said, 'Sit tight, John.'

The guy sat still behind the Malibu's wheel. Reacher watched across the roof of the car. The bubble of light was just one car. The glow resolved itself to twin sources spaced feet apart, mounted low on a small low car, a Mazda Miata, red in colour, slowing now.

Then Eleanor Duncan killed her lights, manoeuvred round the Malibu's trunk, and came to a stop. She asked, 'Did I do it right?'

Reacher said, 'You did it perfectly. The scarf was a great touch.'

She was quiet for a second. Then she said, 'Need anything else?'

'No, thanks,' Reacher said. 'Go on home now.'

Eleanor put her lights back on and drove away. After she was gone, Reacher slid into the Malibu's passenger seat and closed his door. He held the Glock right-handed across his body. He said, 'You're going to park this car round the back of the roadhouse. If the speedo gets above five miles an hour, I'll shoot you. We clear?'

'Yes.'

'OK, so let's do it.'

The guy put the car in gear, turned the wheel and bumped down onto the lot, turning behind the building. Reacher said, 'Pull ahead, then back in, between the two bump-outs, like parallel parking.'

The guy lined up and backed into the shallow U-shaped bay. Reacher said, 'All the way, now. I want the back bumper hard against the wood and I want your side of the car hard against the building. Can you do that?'

The guy did pretty well. He left about an inch between the car and the building.

'Now shut it down,' Reacher said. 'Leave the key.'

The guy killed the lights and turned off the motor. He said, 'I can't get out. I can't open my door.'

Reacher said, 'Crawl out after me.' He opened his door, slid out, stood and aimed the gun. The guy came out after him, hands and knees, huge and awkward, feet first, butt high in the air.

'Close the door and step away from the car.'

The guy closed the door and stepped away. The car was invisible from the road.

Reacher said, 'OK, turn round and walk back to your truck.' Reacher kept ten feet behind the guy all the way back to the two-lane. 'Now get in the truck the same way you got out of the car.'

The guy opened the passenger door. He climbed into the passenger seat, lifted his feet one at a time into the driver's foot well, and then he jacked himself over the console between the seats. Reacher climbed into the passenger seat and closed the door. He swapped the gun into his left hand and put his seat belt on. Then he swapped the gun back to his right and said, 'I've got my seat belt on, but you're not going to put yours on in case you're getting ideas about driving into a telephone pole. Where do you live?'

'At the Duncan Transportation depot.'

'Where is that?'

'About thirty miles, give or take, north and then west.'

'OK, John,' Reacher said. 'Take me there.'

Seven

Mahmeini's man was in his room at the Courtyard Marriott. He was on the phone with Mahmeini. The conversation had not started well. Mahmeini had been reluctant to accept that Asghar had lit out.

'I checked all over town,' Mahmeini's man said. 'Which didn't take long. The sidewalks roll up when it gets dark. There's nowhere to hide. Asghar isn't here.'

'Did you try his phone again?'

'Over and over.'

There was a long pause. Mahmeini said, 'OK, let's move on. This business is important. So you'll have to manage on your own.'

'But I don't have a car.'

'Get a ride from Safir's boys.'

'I thought of that. But the dynamic would be weird. I wouldn't be in charge. I would be a passenger. And how would I explain why I let Asghar take off somewhere and leave me high and dry?'

'So rent another car. Tell them you told Asghar to go on ahead.'

'Boss, this isn't Vegas. The nearest Hertz is back at the airport.'

Mahmeini asked, 'Did the others see the first car you were in?'

'No. I'm sure they didn't. We all arrived at different times.'

Mahmeini said, 'OK. You're right about the dynamic. We need to be visibly in charge. So here's what to do. Find a suitable car. Steal one, if you have to. Then call the others, in their rooms. Tell them you're leaving for the north immediately. Give them five minutes, or you're going without them. They'll be in disarray, packing up and running down to the parking lot. You'll be waiting in your new car. But they won't know it's new. And they won't even notice that Asghar isn't with you. Not in the dark. Then drive fast. Be the first one up there. When the others get there, tell them you turned Asghar loose, on foot, behind the lines. That will worry them. They'll be looking over their shoulders all the time.'

MAHMEINI'S MAN walked out of the hotel with his bag, looking for a car to steal. First, he needed a vehicle with a degree of prestige. He couldn't be seen in a rusted pick-up. That would not be appropriate for a Mahmeini operative, especially one tasked to impress the Duncans. Second, he needed a car that wasn't new. Late-model cars had too much security built in. Lone men in the dark needed something easier.

He walked round the H-shaped hotel and saw three pick-up trucks, a blue Chevrolet Impala, a red Ford Taurus and a black Cadillac. The pick-ups were out of the question. The Impala and the Taurus were too new, and they were obviously rentals, because they had barcode stickers in the rear side windows, which meant they almost certainly belonged to Safir's guys and Rossi's guys.

Which left the Cadillac. Right age, right style. Local plates, neat, discreet. Black glass. Practically perfect. He put his bag on the ground next to it, dropped flat and shuffled on his back until his head was under the engine. He had a tiny Maglite on his key chain. He lit it up and went hunting. Cars of that generation had a module bolted to the frame to detect a frontal impact. An accelerometer, with a two-stage function. Worst case, it would trigger the air bags. Short of that, it would unlock the doors, so that first responders could drag drivers to safety. A gift to car thieves everywhere.

He found the module. It was square and small, with wires coming out of it. He took out his knife, used the handle and banged hard. The Cadillac's electronic brain thought it had just suffered a minor frontal impact, not serious enough for the air bags, but serious enough to consider the first responders. There were four thumps from above, and the doors unlocked.

Mahmeini's man scrambled out. A minute later his bag was on the back seat and he was in the driver's seat. He used the tip of his blade to force the steering lock, and then he pulled off the column shroud, stripped the wires he needed with the knife and touched them together. The engine started. He pulled out his phone, called Safir's guys, then Rossi's, telling them that plans had changed, that he and Asghar were leaving for the north immediately. They had five minutes to get in gear, or they would be left behind.

THE SUV WAS A GMC YUKON, metallic gold. It had beige leather inside. It was a nice truck. Reacher said, 'Got a cellphone, John?'

The guy paused a fatal beat and said, 'No.'

'Of course you've got a cellphone. You were on sentry duty.'

The guy didn't answer that. They were on the two-lane road, north of the motel, well out in featureless farm country.

Reacher said, 'Give me your cellphone, John.' The guy took one hand off the wheel and dug in his trouser pocket. He came out with a phone. He went to hand it over, but he lost his grip on it and dropped it in the passenger foot well. 'Shoot,' he said. 'I'm sorry.'

Reacher smiled. 'Good try, John. Now I bend over to pick it up, and you cave the back of my skull in with your right fist. I wasn't born yesterday. So I guess we'll leave it right where it is.'

'I had to try.'

'Is that an apology? You promised me.'

'You're going to break my legs and dump me on the side of the road.'

'That's a little pessimistic. Why would I break both of them?'

'It's not a joke. Those guys you hurt will never work again.'

'They'll never work for the Duncans again. But there are other things to do in life. Better things.'

The guy said nothing. Just drove.

Reacher asked, 'Who are those Italian guys in the overcoats?'

'I don't know.'

'What do they want?'

'I don't know.'

'Where are they now?'

'I don't know.'

THEY WERE IN the blue Impala, already ten miles north of the Marriott, Cassano at the wheel, Mancini beside him. Cassano was working hard to stay behind Safir's boys in their red Ford, and both drivers were working hard to keep Mahmeini's guys in sight. The black Cadillac was really hustling. It was doing more than eighty miles an hour.

Mancini was staring at it. He asked, 'Is it a rental?'

Cassano was thinking hard. He said, 'I don't think it's a rental.'

'So what is it? Those guys have their own cars standing by in every state just in case? How is that possible?'

'I don't know,' Cassano said.

'They fly in on the casino plane, and there's a car for them. How many states are there? Fifty? That's fifty cars standing by.'

'Not even Mahmeini can be active in all fifty states.'

'OK,' Mancini said. 'You're right. It has to be a rental.'

'It's not a rental,' Cassano said. 'It's not a current model. That's an old-guy car. That's your neighbour's granddad's Cadillac.'

'So what is it?'

'It doesn't matter what it is. You're not looking at the big picture. That car was already at the hotel. We parked next to it. Late afternoon, when we got back. Those guys were there before us. You know what that means? They were on their way before Mahmeini was even asked to send them. Something weird is going on here.'

THE GOLD GMC YUKON turned left off the north–south two-lane and headed west on another two-lane. After ten miles and fifteen minutes, Reacher saw a group of dim lights, off to the right. The truck turned, and headed north on a private approach road, leading towards what looked like a half-built industrial facility. There was a concrete rectangle the size of a football field, enclosed on all four sides by a razor-wire fence. The space was empty, apart from two grey panel vans in a marked-off bay big enough to handle three.

The approach road was scalloped out at one point to allow access in and out through a pair of gates. Then it ran towards a long, low one-storey building. It was an office block, built to serve the factory it once stood next to. The factory was a defence plant, almost certainly. Give a government a choice of where to build in wartime, and it will seek the safe centre of a land mass, away from coastal shelling and potential invasion sites. Nebraska and other heartland states had been full of such places.

John said, 'This is it. We live in the office building.'

The building had a long line of windows. A concrete path led from the building to an empty rectangle made of paving stones, the size of two tennis courts. Managerial parking, presumably, back in the day. There were no lights on inside the building.

'And your buddies are in there now?' Reacher asked.

'Yes. Five of them.'

'Plus you, that's six legs to break. Let's go do it.'

Reacher made John get out of the truck the same way he had before. He asked, 'Where are the harvest trucks?'

'They're in Ohio. Back at the factory, for refurbishment.'

'What are the two grey vans for?'

'This and that. Service and repairs, tyres, things like that.'

'Are there supposed to be three?'

'One is out,' John said. 'It's been gone a few days.'

'Doing what?'

'I don't know.'

Reacher asked, 'When do the big trucks get back?'

The guy said, 'Spring.'

'What's this place like in the early summer?'

'Pretty busy. The first alfalfa crop gets harvested early.'

John closed the passenger door and took a step. Then he stopped dead, because Reacher had stopped dead. Reacher was staring at the managerial parking lot. Nothing in it. Reacher asked, 'Where do you and your buddies normally park your cars, John?'

'Right at the front there, by the doors.'

'So where are they?'

The young man's mouth came open a little. He said, 'I guess they're out. They must have got a call.'

'From you?' Reacher asked. 'When you saw Mrs Duncan?'

'No, I swear. I didn't call. You can check my phone.'

'So who called them?'

'Mr Duncan, I guess. Mr Jacob, I mean.'

'He called them but he didn't call you?'

'No, he didn't call me. I swear. Check my phone.'

'So what's going on, John?'

'I don't know.'

'Best guess?'

'The doctor. Or his wife. They're always seen as the weakest link. Because of the drinking. Maybe the Duncans think they have information about where you are and what you're doing.'

'OK, John,' Reacher said. 'You stay here and go to bed.'

'You're not going to hurt me?'

'You already hurt yourself. You showed no fight at all against a smaller, older man. You're a coward. You know that now. That's as good to me as a dislocated elbow.'

'Easy for you to say. You've got a gun.'

Reacher put the Glock in his pocket. He stood with his arms out, hands empty. He said, 'Now I don't. So bring it on, fat boy.'

The guy didn't move.

'Last chance,' Reacher said. 'Step up and be a hero.'

The guy walked away, head down towards the dark building. Reacher looped round the rear of the Yukon, to the driver's door. He got in, started up and turned and drove away.

Twenty miles was a long distance, through the rural darkness. He saw no other vehicles the whole way back to the ranch house with the featureless yard. There were lights on in the house. But there were no pick-ups or SUVs in the driveway. The front door was closed. Reacher parked in the driveway and walked to the door. He rang the bell. The spy hole darkened and lightened and locks and chains rattled and the doctor opened up. His wife was behind him, with the phone to her ear.

The doctor said, 'You came back.'

Reacher said, 'Yes, I did. The Cornhuskers are out and about.'

'We know. We just heard. We're on the phone tree right now.'

'They didn't come here?'

'Not yet.'

Reacher said, 'Can I come in?'

'Of course.' The doctor stepped back and Reacher stepped in. The doctor closed the door and turned two keys and put the chain back on. He asked, 'Did you see the police files?'

Reacher said, 'Yes. They're inconclusive.' He moved on into the kitchen. The doctor followed Reacher.

'Want coffee?' he asked.

Reacher said, 'Sure. Lots of it.'

The doctor filled the machine. Reacher took off his coat and hung it on the back of a chair.

The doctor asked, 'What do you mean, inconclusive?'

Reacher said, 'I mean I could make up a story about how the Duncans did it, but there's really no proof either way.'

'Can you find proof? Is that why you came back?'

'I came back because those two Italian guys who were after me seem to have joined up with a regular United Nations of other guys. Not a peace-keeping force, either. I want to know why.'

'You messed with the Duncans, and they won't tolerate that. Their people can't handle you, so they've called in reinforcements.'

'Doesn't make sense,' Reacher said. 'Those Italians were here before me. So there's some other reason.'

'How many of them are coming?' the doctor asked.

From the hallway his wife said, 'Five of them.' She had just got off the phone. She stepped into the kitchen and said, 'They're already here. That was the message on the phone tree. The Italians are back in their blue Chevy, plus two guys in a red Ford, and one guy in a black car that everyone swears is Seth's Cadillac.'

Reacher poured himself a cup of coffee and thought for a long moment and said, 'I left Seth Duncan's Cadillac at the Marriott.'

The doctor's wife asked, 'So how did you get back here?'

'I took a Chevy Malibu from one of the bad guys.'

'That thing on the driveway?'

'No, that's a GMC Yukon I took from a football player.'

'So what happened with the Cadillac?'

'I left a guy stranded. I stole his car, and then I guess he stole mine.

Probably not deliberate tit for tat. Probably just coincidental, because there wasn't an infinite choice down there.'

'Did you see the guys?'

'I didn't see the Italians. But I saw the other four.'

'That makes six, not five. Where's the other one?'

'I promise you something,' Reacher said. 'The guy who took the Cadillac put his bag on the back seat, not in the trunk.'

'How do you know?'

'Because that's where the sixth guy is. I put him there. I think whatever else they're doing, they're coming here to get me first. The way I see it, they assembled tonight in the Marriott, the Italians gave the others a vague description because they haven't actually laid eyes on me yet, and then I bumped into one of the others, in the lobby, and he was looking at me, like he was asking himself, Is that the guy? We got out to the lot, he put his hand in his pocket and I hit him. You heard of *commotio cordis*?'

'Chest wall trauma,' the doctor said. 'Causes fatal cardiac dysrhythmia.'

'Ever seen it?'

'No.'

'Neither had I. But I'm here to tell you, it works real good.'

'What was in his pocket?'

'A knife and a gun and an ID from Vegas.'

'Vegas?' the doctor said. 'Do the Duncans have gambling debts?'

'Possible. No question the Duncans have been living beyond their means. They've been getting extra income from somewhere. Seth lives like a king and they pay nine football players just to be here. They couldn't do all that on the back of a seasonal enterprise.'

The doctor's wife said, 'We should worry about that later. Right now the Cornhuskers are on the loose, and we don't know where or why. That's what's important. Dorothy might be coming over.'

'Here?' Reacher asked. 'Now?'

The doctor said, 'That's what happens sometimes. It's like a sisterhood. Whoever feels the most vulnerable clusters together.'

They took cups of coffee and waited in the dining room, which had a view of the road. The road was dark. They sat quietly, on hard upright chairs, with the lights off to preserve their view out the window, then the doctor said, 'Tell us about the files.'

'I saw a photograph,' Reacher said. 'Dorothy's kid was Asian.'

'Vietnamese,' the doctor's wife said. 'Artie Coe did a tour over there. Something about it affected him, I guess. When the boat people thing started, they stepped up and adopted.'

'Did the Duncans go to Vietnam?'

'I don't think so. They were in an essential occupation.'

'So was Arthur. Who was chairman of the local draft board?'

'Their father. Old man Duncan.'

'So the boys didn't keep farming to please him. They kept on to keep out of the war. They're cowards, apart from anything else.'

The doctor said, 'Tell us about the investigation.'

'The lead detective was a guy called Carson. It started out as a missing persons issue, and then it slowly changed to a potential homicide. And Carson didn't really revisit the early phase in light of the later phase. The first night, he had people checking their own outbuildings. But later he never searched those outbuildings independently. At some point Carson should have treated everyone as a potential suspect. But he didn't. He focused on the Duncans only. And they came out clean.'

The doctor's wife said, 'I still think it was the Duncans.'

'Three different agencies disagree with you,' Reacher said. 'It's clear that the Duncans never left their compound, and that the kid never showed up there. There are witnesses to both facts. And the science came up negative. But the Duncans could have had an accomplice. A fifth man. He could have taken the kid somewhere.'

'Who would the fifth man have been?'

'A friend, maybe. Did you ever see one, when you baby-sat?'

'I saw a few people, I guess. Where would he have taken her?'

'Anywhere, theoretically. And that was another mistake. Carson never looked anywhere, apart from the Duncans' compound. But there was one place Carson should have checked. And he didn't.'

'Which was where?'

But Reacher didn't get time to answer, because right then the window blazed bright and the room filled with moving lights and shadows. Headlight beams. A car, coming in fast from the east.

IT WAS DOROTHY COE, in her old pick-up. She stopped short of the house. She had seen the Yukon in the driveway. A Cornhusker's car. The doctor's wife undid the locks and chain, opened the front door, and waved. Reacher joined her. He pointed to the Yukon. *My truck.* Dorothy moved on again and turned in. She shut down, got out and walked to the door.

They all stepped back inside and the doctor closed up, locks and chain, and they went back to the dining room. Dorothy took off her coat. They sat and watched the window. It was almost one o'clock in the morning. Reacher asked Dorothy, 'The Cornhuskers didn't go to your place?'

She said, 'No. But Mr Vincent saw one, passing the motel. About twenty minutes ago. He was watching out the window.'

Reacher said, 'That was me. I came that way in the truck I took. There are only five of them left now.'

'OK, but I would expect one of us to have seen at least one of them, roaming around. But no one has. Which means they aren't spread out. They're bunched up. They're hunting in a pack.'

THE MOTEL WAS CLOSED for the night, but Vincent was in the lounge watching out the window. He had seen the gold Yukon go by. It belonged to a very unpleasant person called John. A bully.

Vincent had called in the Yukon sighting and then he had gone back to the window.

Twenty minutes later, he saw the five men everyone was talking about. Their convoy pulled into his lot. The blue Chevrolet, the red Ford, Seth's black Cadillac. A small rumpled man slid out of the driver's seat. Then the two men who had roughed him up climbed out of the Chevrolet. Then two more got out of the Ford, tall, heavy, dark-skinned.

The five men were talking. Vincent couldn't hear what they were saying through the closed window, but he continued to watch them.

MAHMEINI'S MAN was saying, 'I let my partner out a mile back. He's going to work behind the lines.'

Cassano said, 'You should have kept him around. We need a plan.'

'For this? We don't need a plan. It's just flushing a guy out. How hard can it be? With luck we'll get it done by morning. Then we'll spend the day leaning on the Duncans. We need that delivery.'

'So where do we start?' Cassano asked.

'You tell me. You've spent time here.'

'The doctor. He's the weakest link.'

'OK, go talk to him. I'll go somewhere else. If you know that he's the weakest link, then so does Reacher. Dollars to doughnuts, he ain't there. So you go waste your time, and I'll go do some work.'

The rumpled man slid back into Seth's Cadillac and the big black car turned left on the two-lane and took off south.

The other four men watched until the Cadillac's taillights were lost to sight, and then they turned back and started talking again, each one of them with his right hand in his right-hand coat pocket.

Cassano said, 'He doesn't have a partner. There's nobody working behind the lines. What lines, anyway? It's all bull.'

Safir's main man said, 'Of course he has a partner. We all saw him, right there in your room.'

'He's gone. He took the car they rented. That guy is on his own now. He stole that Cadillac from the lot. We saw it there earlier.'

No reply.

Cassano said, 'Unless you had a hand in it. We're all grown-ups here. We know how the world works. Mahmeini told his guys to take the rest of us out, and Safir told you guys to take the rest of us out, and Rossi sure as hell told us to take the rest of you out. Mahmeini, Safir and Rossi all want the whole pie. We know that.'

'We didn't do anything. We figured you did. We were talking about it on the way here. It was obvious that Cadillac isn't a rental.'

'We didn't do anything to the guy. We were going to wait for later.'

'Us too. So what happened?' Safir's man asked.

'He ran out. Maybe chicken. Or short on discipline,' Cassano said. 'We have a vote here, don't you think? The four of us? We could take out Mahmeini's other boy, and leave each other alone. That way Rossi and Safir end up with fifty per cent more pie each. They could live with that. And we sure as hell could.'

Safir's guys glanced at each other. Not a difficult decision.

VINCENT WAS STILL WATCHING. He saw quiet conversation, some major tension, then some easing, the body language relaxing, some tentative smiles. Then all four men took their hands out of their pockets and shook.

The two dark-skinned men climbed into their red Ford. They closed their doors and got set to go and then the Italian who had done all the talking turned back and tapped on the driver's glass.

The window came down. The Italian had a gun in his hand.

The Italian leaned in and there were two bright flashes, all six windows lighting up, and two loud explosions. Then the Italian stepped away and Vincent saw the two dark-skinned men slumped in their seats, their heads lolling down on their chests.

The other Italian opened the Ford's trunk and found two nylon suitcases. He unzipped one of the bags and rooted around and came up with a shirt on a wire hanger. He tore it off the hanger, crushed the hanger flat, opened the Ford's filler neck, used the hanger to poke the shirt down into the tube, with a sleeve trailing out. He lit the trailing cuff with a match. Then he walked away, got in the blue Chevrolet's passenger seat and the other Italian drove him away.

Vincent fell to the floor and vomited. Then he ran for the phone.

THE ROAD OUTSIDE the dining room window stayed dark. The doctor and his wife and Dorothy sat quiet, waiting it out.

Reacher was waiting it out, too. He knew that Dorothy wanted to ask what he had found in the county archive. But she was taking her time getting around to it, and that was OK with him.

After fifteen minutes, she asked, 'Did you see the files?'

'Yes, I did.'

'Did you see her photograph?'

'She was very beautiful.'

'Wasn't she?' Dorothy said. 'I still miss her. She would be thirty-three now. I don't know what she might have become, if she would have been a mother, or a career girl, maybe a lawyer or a scientist.'

'Where was she going that day?'

'She loved flowers. I think she was going searching for some.'

'I was a cop of sorts for a long time. So may I ask you a question? Do you really want to know what happened to her?'

'Can't be worse than what I imagine.'

'I'm afraid it can. Sometimes it's better not to know.'

She said, 'My neighbour's son hears her ghost screaming.'

'I met him. He smokes a lot of weed. I don't believe in ghosts.'

'Neither do I, really. I mean, look at me.'

Reacher did. A woman worn down by work. Greying, solid, capable. She said, 'Yes, I really want to know what happened to her.'

Two minutes later the phone rang. The doctor's wife ran out to the hallway to answer. She said hello, and then just listened. The phone tree again. The others heard the distorted crackle of a loud panicked voice from the earpiece. Some kind of surprising news.

The doctor's wife came back in. She said, 'Mr Vincent just saw the Italians shoot the men from the red car. They're dead. Then they set the car on fire. Right outside his window. In the motel lot.'

Reacher said, 'Well, that changes things. I thought maybe we had six guys working for the same organisation, with some kind of a two-way relationship, them and the Duncans. But they're three pairs. Three separate organisations, plus the Duncans make four. Which makes it a food chain. The Duncans owe somebody something, and that somebody owes somebody else, and so on. They're all here to safeguard their investment. And as long as they're all here, they're trying to cut each other out.'

'So we're caught in the middle of a gang war?'

'Look on the bright side. Six guys showed up this afternoon, and now there are only three of them left. Fifty per cent attrition.'

The doctor said, 'We should call the police.'

His wife said, 'No, the police are sixty miles away. And the Cornhuskers are right here, right now. That's what we need to worry about tonight. We need to know what they're doing.'

Reacher asked, 'How do they normally communicate?'

'Cellphone.'

'I've got one,' Reacher said. 'In the truck I took. Maybe we could listen in. Then we'd know for sure what they're doing.'

The doctor undid the locks and they all crowded out to the driveway. Reacher opened the Yukon's passenger door, rooted around in the foot well and came out with the phone, slim and black. He said, 'They'll use conference calls, right? This thing will ring and all five of them will be on?'

'Check the settings for an access number,' the doctor said.

'You check,' Reacher said. 'I'm not familiar with cellphones.'

He handed the phone to the doctor. Then he looked to his left and saw light in the mist to the east. A high hemispherical glow, trembling, bouncing.

A car, coming west towards them, pretty fast.

Reacher recognised it at two hundred feet out. Eleanor Duncan.

A hundred feet out the Mazda slowed. Its top was up this time.

Twenty feet out, it swung wide and started to turn.

Ten feet out, Reacher remembered three things.

First, Eleanor was not on the phone tree. Second, his gun was in his coat. Third, his coat was in the kitchen.

The Mazda jammed to a stop right behind Dorothy's pick-up. The door opened and Seth Duncan stepped out holding a shotgun.

Eight

Seth had an aluminium splint on his face. He was wearing dark trousers and a dark sweater with a parka over it. The shotgun in his hands was an old Remington 870 pump. Probably a twelve-gauge.

Seth's finger was on the trigger. He was aiming it from the hip at Reacher, which meant he was aiming it at Dorothy and the doctor and his wife, too, because buckshot spreads a little, and all four of them were clustered together, ten feet from the front door. Seth started to move up the driveway. He raised the Remington's stock to his shoulder. He stopped thirty feet away. 'All of you sit down. Right where you are. On the ground.'

Nobody moved.

Reacher watched and thought. He said, 'It's too cold to sit down outside. Let's go inside.'

'I want you outside.'

'Then let them go get their coats. You're wearing a coat. If it's warm enough not to need one, then you're a pussy. If it's cold enough to bundle up, then you're making innocent people suffer.'

Seth thought about it. He said, 'OK, one at a time. Mrs Coe goes first. Get your coat. Nothing else. Don't touch the phone.'

Dorothy went inside. She came back wearing her coat.

Duncan said, 'Sit down, Mrs Coe.'

Dorothy tugged her coat down and sat.

Reacher said, 'Now the doctor's wife.'

Duncan said, 'Don't tell me what to do.'

'I'm just saying. Ladies first, right?'

'OK, the doctor's wife. Go. Same rules. Just the coat.'

The doctor's wife peeled out of the cluster. A minute later she was back, wearing her coat, and a hat, and gloves. She sat down next to Dorothy.

Reacher said, 'Now the doctor.'

'OK, go,' Duncan said.

The doctor was gone a minute. He came back in a blue parka.

Reacher said, 'Now me.'

Duncan said, 'No, not you. I don't trust you. Sit down.'

Reacher didn't move. Then he glanced to his right and saw lights in the mist, and he knew that his chance had gone.

THE CORNHUSKERS came on fast, five of them in five vehicles, three pick-up trucks and two SUVs. They jammed to a stop on the road, five doors flung open, and five guys in red jackets spilled out. They swarmed in, coming in wide of the Remington's potential trajectory.

Duncan said, 'Take the three others inside, and keep them there.'

Rough hands grabbed at the doctor, his wife and Dorothy, hauling them to their feet, hustling them across the gravel, pushing them through the door. Eight people went in, and a minute later four of the football players came out to where Reacher was standing.

Duncan said, 'Hold him.'

Reacher was spending no time on regret or recrimination. People who wasted time and energy cursing recent errors were certain losers. Not that Reacher saw an easy path to certain victory. Not right then. Right then he saw nothing ahead but a world of hurt.

The four guys stepped up close. The Remington stayed trained on its target. Two guys came in from wide positions, never getting between Reacher and the gun. They stepped alongside him, grabbed an arm each, hooking their ankles in front of his ankles, holding him immobile. A third guy came behind him and wrapped massive arms round his chest. The fourth stood ten feet from Duncan.

Reacher didn't struggle. No point. Each man holding him was taller than him by inches and outweighed him by fifty pounds. He could move his feet a little, and he could move his head a little, but that was all. And all he could do with his head was duck his chin to his chest, or jerk it back a few inches. He was stuck, and he knew it.

Seth walked forward and handed off the gun to the fourth guy. He stopped face to face with Reacher. He was quivering from fury or excitement. He said, 'I have a message for you, pal.'

Reacher said, 'What's the message?'

'It's more of a question. The question is, how do *you* like it?'

Reacher had been fighting since he was five years old, and he had never had his nose broken. Plenty of people had tried, over the years, but none had succeeded. It was a fact Reacher was proud of.

The blow came in exactly as he expected it to, a straight right, hard and heavy. Reacher kept his head up, his eyes open, watching down his nose, timing it, then jerking forward from the neck, smashing a perfect head butt into Duncan's knuckles, a high-impact collision between the thick ridge in Reacher's brow and the delicate bones in Duncan's hand. No contest. Reacher had a skull like concrete, Duncan screamed, snatched his hand away and cradled it against his chest, stunned and whimpering.

Duncan glowered from either side of his splint, hurting and angry and humiliated. He jerked his head, looking first at Reacher, then at his fourth guy, who was standing there, holding the gun. *Get him.*

The fourth guy stepped up. Reacher was pretty sure he wasn't going to shoot. No one fires a shotgun at a group of four people, three of whom are his friends. Reacher was pretty sure it was going to be worse than shooting. The guy reversed the gun. Right hand on the barrel, left hand on the stock.

The guy behind Reacher wrapped his left arm round Reacher's throat, and he clamped his right palm tight on Reacher's forehead.

The fourth guy raised the gun horizontal, butt first, two-handed, cocked it over his right shoulder, then he took a step, aimed carefully and jabbed the butt at the centre of Reacher's face and:

CRACK

BLACK

JACOB DUNCAN convened a middle-of-the-night meeting with his brothers. His mood was celebratory. 'I just got off the phone,' he said. 'You'll be pleased to hear my boy has redeemed himself. He captured Reacher.'

Jonas asked, 'How?'

Jacob said, 'I drove Seth home, as you know, but I let him out at the end of his road, because he wanted to walk a spell in the night air. He got within a hundred yards of his house, and he was nearly run over by a car. *His* car. His own Cadillac, going like a bat out of hell. Naturally he hurried home. His wife was induced to reveal all the details. It turns out Reacher stole the Cadillac in the afternoon. The doctor was with him. Misguided, of course, but it seems the poor fellow has formed an alliance with Mr Reacher. So Seth took his old Remington pump and set off in Eleanor's car and sure enough, Reacher was indeed at the doctor's house, large as life.'

'Where is he now?'

'In a safe place.'

'Is he alive?'

'So far. But how long he stays alive is what we need to discuss. Seth wants to finesse the whole thing, right down to the wire and, frankly, I'm tempted to let him try.'

Jasper asked, 'What does Seth want to do?'

'He wants to wait until our shipment is about an hour away, whereupon he wants to unveil Reacher to Mr Rossi's boys, whereupon he wants to fake a phone call and have the truck arrive within the next sixty minutes, as if what we've been saying all along about the delay was indeed true.'

'Too risky,' Jonas said. 'Reacher is a dangerous man. We shouldn't keep him around a minute longer than we have to.'

'He's in a safe place. Plus, if we do it Seth's way, we'll be seen to have solved our own problems, without any outside assistance.'

'Even so. It's still risky.'

'There are other factors,' Jacob said. 'We've never known what happens to our shipments once they're in Mr Rossi's hands. We've supposed they pass down a chain of sale and resale, to an ultimate destination. Now that chain is visible. As of tonight, three participants have representation here. It's clear they have agreed to work together to break up the logjam. Once that's done, it's equally clear they will be under instructions to eliminate one another, so that the last man standing triples his profit.'

Jonas said, 'That's not relevant to us.'

'Except that Mr Rossi's boys are jumping the gun. Our stooges on the phone tree tell me that two men are already dead. So my idea is to give Mr Rossi's boys enough time to shorten the chain a little more, so that Mr Rossi will be the last man standing, whereupon he and we can have a talk about splitting the extra profit equally.'

A long silence. Then Jonas said, 'The doctor lied to us. He told us Reacher hitched a ride in a white sedan.'

Jacob said, 'I'm told he's being a model of cooperation now. He says Reacher left Seth's Cadillac sixty miles south of here, and that it was restolen by an operative further up the chain. He was the one who nearly ran Seth over. The doctor also says Reacher saw the police files.'

Jonas said, 'And?'

'Inconclusive, the doctor says.'

'Conclusive enough to come back.'

'The doctor says he came back because of the men in the cars. But the doctor also claims Reacher asked Mrs Coe if she really wants to be told what happened to her daughter.'

'Reacher can't possibly know. Not yet.'

'I agree. But he might be beginning to pull on threads.'

'Then we have to kill him now. We have to.'

'It's just one more day. He's locked up. Escape is impossible.'

Then Jonas asked, 'Anything else?'

'Eleanor helped Reacher get past the sentry,' Jacob said. 'She and Reacher conspired to decoy the boy away from his post. We'll have to fire him. And Seth has broken his hand. It appears Reacher has a very hard head. That's all the news I have. We need to make a decision about the matter at hand. I vote to let my boy keep Reacher concealed until our truck is close by. It's a minor increase in risk. One more day is all.'

Jasper said, 'I'm in.'

And Jonas said, 'OK,' a little reluctantly.

REACHER WOKE UP in a concrete room full of bright light. He was on his back on the floor, at the foot of a flight of steep stairs. He had been carried down, he figured, not thrown. Because his limbs were intact. He could see, hear and move. His face hurt like hell.

The lights were regular household bulbs, six or eight of them, randomly placed. The concrete was smooth and pale grey. The angles where the walls met each other and the floor were chamfered and radiused, just slightly. Like a swimming pool, ready for tiling.

Was he in a half-finished swimming pool? Unlikely. Unless it had a temporary roof. The roof was boards laid over heavy joists.

He felt confused. He had no idea what time it was. The clock in his head had stopped. His nose was jammed with blood and swellings. He could feel blood on his lips and his chin. It was thick and almost dry. A nosebleed. Maybe thirty minutes old.

There were other things in the concrete room. Pipes. Green metal boxes. Some wires, some in steel conduit, some loose. There were no windows. Just the walls. And the stairs, with a closed door at the top. He was underground.

Huge waves of pain were boring into his head. Bad pain. It was insane. In the past he had been wounded with shrapnel, shot in the chest and cut with knives. This was worse. Much worse.

Something was wrong. He had seen busted noses before. No fun, but nobody made a fuss about them. People got up, winced, walked it off.

He raised his hand to his face. Slowly. He knew it would be like shooting himself in the head. But he had to know. He touched his nose. He gasped. The ridge of bone on the front of his nose was broken off. It had been driven around under the tight web of skin and cartilage to the side. It was pinned there, like a mountaintop sliced off and reattached to a lower slope. It hurt like hell.

He knew what he had to do. He had to reset the break. He knew the pain would lessen, and he would end up with a normal-looking nose. Almost. But he would pass out again. No question about that. Touching the injury with a gentle fingertip had nearly taken his head off. Fixing it would be like machine-gunning himself.

He closed his eyes. He raised his hand. He grasped the knob of bone. Atom bombs went off in his head. He pushed and pulled.

No result. The cartilage was clamping too hard, holding the thing in place. In completely the wrong place. He tried again. No result.

He knew what he had to do. Steady pressure was not working. He had to smack the knob of bone back into place with his hand.

He rehearsed the move. He needed to hit low down on the angle of cheek and nose, with the side of his hand, like a karate chop. He needed to drive the peak back up the mountainside. It would settle OK. Once it arrived, the skin and cartilage would keep it in place.

He dragged himself across the concrete, and he sat up against a wall, half reclining, his neck bent. He got as stable as he could, so that he wouldn't fall. No point in cracking his skull as well.

Show time, he thought. *On three.* One. Two.

CRACK

BLACK

MAHMEINI'S MAN had driven around for twenty minutes, then he had come to a house with *Duncan* written on a mailbox. The house was a decent place, expensively restored. Their HQ, he had assumed. But no. All it contained was a woman who claimed she knew nothing. She said there were four Duncans, a father, a son and two uncles. She was married to the son. They were all elsewhere. She gave directions to a cluster of three houses.

As he set off in that direction, driving fast, almost running down some idiot pedestrian who loomed up at him out of the dark, from the two-lane he had seen a gasoline fire blazing to the north. He had hustled towards the fire and found it was in the motel lot. It was a car. Or, it had been a car. Judging by the shape it had been the Ford that Safir's boys had been driving. They were still inside it.

Rossi's boys had killed them, obviously. Which meant they had killed Asghar too, almost certainly, hours ago. Rossi's plan was clear. He already had a firm connection with the Duncans, at the bottom end of the chain. Now he intended to leapfrog Safir and Mahmeini and sell to the Saudis direct. Rossi had had his boys start early. They had lain in wait for Asghar, taken him down and disposed of his car, all within thirty minutes. Asghar was tough and wary, not easy to beat. A good friend, too, now crying out for vengeance. Mahmeini's man could sense his presence strongly, like he was still close by. All of which made him change his plan. The stranger could wait. His primary targets were now Rossi's boys.

CASSANO AND MANCINI were parked four miles north, with their lights off. Cassano was on the phone with Rossi.

Cassano asked, 'You and Seth Duncan made this deal, right?'

Rossi said, 'He was my initial contact, back in the day. It turned into a family affair pretty soon after that.'

'But as far as you know it's still your deal?'

'Of course it's still my deal,' Rossi said. 'Why are you asking?'

'Seth Duncan lent his car to Mahmeini's guy. There was an old Cadillac at the Marriott when we got there this afternoon. Later we saw Mahmeini's guy using it. At first we thought he stole it, but the locals here say it's Seth Duncan's personal ride. Therefore Seth must have provided him with it. He's probably hanging out with the Duncans right now. We're getting screwed here, boss.'

'Can't be happening.'

'Boss, your contact lent his car to your rival. They're in bed together. How else do you want to interpret it?'

Rossi said, 'OK, I guess nothing is impossible. Go ahead and deal with

Mahmeini's boys. Do that first. Then move in on the three old guys and Seth Duncan. Tell them if they step out of line again we'll take over the whole thing, all the way up to Vancouver.'

REACHER WOKE UP for the second time and knew instantly it was two in the morning. The clock in his head had started up again. And he was in the basement of a house, not an unfinished swimming pool. The concrete was smooth and strong because Nebraska was tornado country, and either zoning laws or construction standards or insurance requirements had demanded an adequate shelter. Which made it the basement of the doctor's house, almost certainly, partly because not enough time had elapsed for a move to another location, and partly because the doctor's house was the only house Reacher had seen that was new enough. In the old days people just built things themselves and hoped for the best.

Therefore the pipes were for water and the sewer and heating. The green metal boxes were the furnace and the water heater. There was an electrical panel, full of circuit breakers. The stairs came down and the door at the top would open outwards into the hallway.

Reacher sat up. His neck was a little sore, which he took to be a good sign. It meant the pain from his nose was relegated to background noise. He raised his hand and checked. His nose was still tender, and there were open cuts on it, and pillowy swellings, but the chip of bone was back in the right place. More or less.

He got to his feet. There was nothing stored in the basement. No crowded shelves, no piles of dusty boxes, no pegboards full of tools. Reacher figured all that stuff was in the garage. There was nothing in the basement, except the house's mechanical systems. Reacher crept up the stairs, put his ear to the door. He heard voices, low and indistinct, first one and then another. A man and a woman. Seth Duncan, he thought, asking questions, and Dorothy or the doctor's wife answering them.

Reacher tried the door handle, slowly and carefully. It turned, but it was locked, as expected. The door was stout, set tight in a wall that felt very solid. He let go of the handle, crept back downstairs.

He had a number of options. He could turn off the hot water, but that would be a slow-motion provocation. Equally he could turn off the heat, which would be more serious, given the season, but response time would still be slow, and he would be victimising the innocent as well as the guilty. He could kill all the lights, at the electrical panel, but there was at least one shotgun upstairs, and maybe flashlights too. He was on the wrong side of a locked door, unarmed, attacking from the low ground. Not good. Not good at all.

Nine

Seth Duncan had his right hand on the doctor's dining table, with a frozen bag of peas laid over it. The cold was numbing the pain, but not very effectively. He needed another shot of his uncle Jasper's pig anaesthetic, and he was about to go get one, but first he had wanted to talk to the doctor, his wife and Dorothy. He led them one by one through a series of questions about the events of the night.

Duncan was alone on one side of the table, and the doctor and his wife and Dorothy were opposite him, lined up on three upright chairs. He had a Cornhusker standing in the dining-room doorway, holding the Remington pump, and he had another in the hall, leaning on the basement door. The other three were out in their cars, driving around in the dark, pretending to hunt for Reacher. The illusion had to be maintained for Rossi's boys—Reacher's capture was scheduled for much later in the day.

While Duncan was talking to Dorothy, out in the hallway, three inches from the Cornhusker's hip, the basement door handle turned a quarter-circle, and paused a beat, and turned back. No one noticed.

Finally, Duncan got up. 'You three stay here. My boys will look after you. Don't attempt to leave the house, and don't attempt to use the phone. Don't even answer it. The phone tree is off limits tonight. Punishment for non-compliance will be swift and severe.'

Then Duncan put his parka on, awkwardly. He headed for the front door. The people in the house heard the Mazda drive away.

MAHMEINI'S MAN drove the Cadillac south on the two-lane five miles, and then he turned the lights off and slowed to a walk. He saw the three old houses on his right. There were four vehicles parked out front, three of them old pick-up trucks and the red Mazda Miata he had seen at the restored Duncan farmhouse. The daughter-in-law's car. Maybe she had reported the encounter with the strange Iranian man, and she had been told to come in for safety's sake. None of the cars was a new blue Chevrolet. But the Chevrolet would come. Mahmeini's man was sure of that.

Mahmeini's man rolled past the end of the Duncans' driveway, U-turned and parked a hundred yards south on the opposite shoulder, his lights off, the car nestled in a slight natural dip, about as invisible as it was possible to get.

Mahmeini's man waited. The mist in the air that was helping to hide him was fogging his rear window. An approaching car with its lights off might be difficult to see. He groped for the rear defogger button. It was hard to find. With the lights off outside, the dash was unlit inside. And there were a lot of buttons. He found one and pressed it. The radio came on. He tried another button. The trunk lid clunked and popped and raised itself up, slowly and smoothly, all the way open, completely vertical. Blocking his view.

He was going to have to get out and close it.

CASSANO AND MANCINI had been in the area three days, and they figured their one advantage over Mahmeini's crew was their local knowledge. They knew the lie of the land, literally. They knew it was flat and empty, no ditches, no hedges, the ground frozen and hard. So even though their car was a street sedan, they could drive it cross-country, pretty much like sailing a small boat on a calm sea. And they had seen the Duncan compound up close. They could loop around behind it in the car, lights off, invisible in the dark, then they could climb the post-and-rail fence, and storm the place from the rear. Surprise was everything. There might be eyeballs to the front, but in the back there would be nothing except the Duncans and Mahmeini's guys sitting around, probably toasting each other with bourbon and sniggering about their newly streamlined commercial arrangements.

Cassano came south on the two-lane and switched off his lights at the motel. The Ford was still burning in the lot. Four miles south of the motel and one mile north of the Duncan place he slowed, turned the wheel, and struck out across the open land. The car lurched. He had to steer round a bramble thicket. But after that it was easy. They could see a pool of faint yellow light ahead. The southernmost house. Jacob Duncan's place.

Cassano let the Chevrolet coast towards the compound. A hundred yards out he brought it to a stop. Cassano and Mancini climbed out. They drew their Colts and walked forward, shoulder to shoulder.

MAHMEINI'S MAN climbed out of the Cadillac. There was a light in the trunk throwing a pale yellow glow into the mist.

He took a step past the rear passenger door and raised his left hand, palm flat on the metal maybe a foot from the edge of the lid, so that the force of his push would act on both hinges equally, so that the lid would go down smooth and easy.

He leaned into the motion, and his change of position hunched his shoulders a little, which brought his head forward a little, which changed his eye line a little, which meant he looked into the lit interior.

Asghar Arad Sepehr stared back at him.

Mahmeini's man stood absolutely still, his hand on the cold metal, his mouth open, not really breathing. He forced himself to look away. Then he looked back. He wasn't hallucinating. He started breathing again. Then his heart started thumping. He started to shake and shiver.

Mahmeini's man raised his head and his arms and howled silently at the moon, his eyes screwed tight shut, his mouth wide open in a desperate snarl, all alone in the vast empty darkness.

Then he started thinking. His friend had been killed sixty miles away, by an unknown person, and then locked in the trunk of a car that could have absolutely nothing to do with either Rossi's boys, or Safir's. Then his own rental had been taken away, so that he had been forced to steal the very same car, the only possible choice in an entire town, like a puppet being manipulated from afar by a grinning intelligence much greater than his own.

It was incomprehensible. But, facts were facts. He steeled himself to investigate further. He began an examination of Asghar. He had no broken bones, no bruises, no cuts. All around him were the usual things a person might expect to find in a trunk. There was an empty grocery bag with a week-old receipt inside, some browned leaves and some crumbs of dirt as if items had been hauled home from a plant nursery. Clearly the car belonged to someone who used it in a fairly normal manner.

So, whose car was it? Mahmeini's man stepped away to the front passenger door, opened it, leaned in, and opened the glove box. Inside it he found a registration document, and an insurance document. He held them close to the light inside the glove box.

The car was Seth Duncan's.

Which was logical, in a sudden, awful way. Because everything had been miscalculated, right from the start. There was no giant stranger on the rampage. No one had seen him and no one could describe him, because he didn't exist. The delivery delay was bull. It had been staged, from beginning to end. The purpose had been to lure everyone to Nebraska to be killed. The Duncans were severing the chain, intending to remake it with nobody between themselves at the bottom and the Saudis at the top, with a massive increase in profit. They were not the clueless rural hicks everyone thought they were. They had foreseen Mahmeini as their strongest opponent, and they had crippled his response from the word go by taking Asghar down, before the bell had even sounded. They had probably also burned Safir's guys to death in the motel lot. Rossi's boys hadn't done that. Rossi's boys were probably already dead themselves.

Mahmeini's man felt completely alone. He *was* completely alone. He had no friends, no allies, no familiarity with the terrain. And no idea what to do next, except to fight back, to seek revenge.

He closed the trunk lid on Asghar reverently. Then he walked back to the passenger door, and picked up his Glock on the seat. He closed the door, crossed the road, and walked parallel with the Duncans' fenced driveway, his gun in his hand.

THE DOCTOR, his wife and Dorothy were sitting quietly in the dining room, but the football player with the shotgun had moved from the door and gone into the living room, where he was sprawled on the sofa, watching NFL highlights on the doctor's big television. His partner had moved off the basement door and was leaning on the hallway wall, watching the screen from a distance. The phone had rung three times, but no one had answered. Apart from that all was peaceful.

Then all the power in the house went out.

The TV picture died abruptly and the sound faded away, and the hum of the heating system disappeared. Silence clamped down.

The football player in the hallway pushed off the wall and stood still. His partner in the living room swivelled his feet to the floor and sat up straight. He said, 'What happened?'

The other guy said, 'I don't know.'

'Doctor?'

The doctor got up from behind the dining table and fumbled his way to the door. 'The power went out. Could be the whole area.'

The guy in the hallway asked, 'Where are the circuit breakers?'

The doctor said, 'In the basement.'

'Terrific. Reacher's awake. And he's playing games.' The guy crept through the dark to the basement door. He identified the door by touch and pounded on it. He called, 'Turn it back on, jerk.'

No response. Pitch black throughout the house.

'Turn the power back on, Reacher.'

No response.

The guy from the living room found his way out to the hallway. 'Maybe he isn't awake. Maybe it's a real outage.'

His partner asked, 'Got a flashlight, doctor?'

The doctor said, 'In the garage.'

'Go get it.'

The doctor shuffled down the hall, fingers brushing the wall, colliding with the first guy, sensing the second guy's hulking presence and avoiding it, making it to the kitchen. He trailed his fingers along the counters, passing the stove. He found the garage door, opened it and stepped into the space beyond. He found the workbench, reached up and traced his fingers over the items clipped above it. A hammer, good for hitting. Screwdrivers, good for stabbing. He found the flashlight, pulled it from its clip, thumbed the switch and a bright yellow beam jumped out. He turned and found the football player from the living room next to him.

He took the flashlight and turned away, using the beam to paint his way back into the house. The doctor followed. The football player said, 'Go back in the dining room,' and shone the beam ahead, showing the doctor the way. The doctor went back to the table and the football player said, 'All of you stay right where you are,' and he closed the door.

His partner said, 'So what now?'

The guy with the flashlight said, 'We need to know if Reacher is awake.' He stepped back down the hallway to the basement door. He pounded on it with his hand. He called, 'Reacher, turn the power back on, or something bad is going to happen up here.'

No response. Silence.

The guy with the flashlight said to his partner, 'Go get the doctor's wife.' He aimed the beam at the dining room door and his partner went in and came back out holding the doctor's wife by the elbow. The guy with the flashlight said, 'Scream.'

She said, 'What?'

'Scream, or I'll make you.'

She paused, and then she screamed, long and loud. She stopped and the guy with the flashlight called, 'You hear that, Reacher?'

No response. Silence.

The guy with the flashlight jerked the beam towards the dining room and his partner led the doctor's wife back down the hallway and pushed her inside and closed the door on her. He said, 'So?'

The guy with the flashlight said, 'We wait for daylight.'

'That's four hours away.'

'You got a better idea?'

'I'm not going down there. Not with him.'

'Me either. We can wait him out. It ain't rocket science.'

They followed the dancing beam back to the living room and sat side by side on the sofa with the old Remington propped between them. They clicked off the flashlight, to save the battery.

MAHMEINI'S MAN walked parallel with the driveway for a hundred yards and then came up against a fence that ran across his path. It was made of five-inch rails, easy enough to climb. He got over it without difficulty. The southernmost house was in front of him. The centre house was the only one that was dark. The southernmost and the northernmost houses had faint light in them, as if only back rooms were in use. He hesitated. Left or right?

CASSANO AND MANCINI came on the compound from the rear, out of the dark and dormant field, and they stopped on the far side of the fence opposite the centre house, which was Jonas's. It was closed up and dark, but both its neighbours had light in their kitchen windows, spilling out across the weedy backyard gravel. The gravel would be noisy. Their best play would be to stay on the wrong side of the fence, and then head directly for their chosen point of entry. That would reduce the sound of their approach to a minimum. But which point of entry? Jasper's place or Jacob's?

ALL FOUR DUNCANS were in Jasper's basement, hunting for veterinary anaesthetic. The last of the hog dope had been used on Seth's nose, and his busted hand was going to need something stronger anyway. Jasper figured he had something designed for horses. He planned to flood Seth's wrist joint with it.

Jonas asked, 'Is this it?' He was holding up a round brown glass bottle. Its label was stained and covered in Latin words. Jasper squinted across the dim space and said, 'Good man. You found it.'

Then they heard footsteps on the floor above their heads.

Jacob was first up the stairs. When he got to the kitchen he found a small dark man, pointing a gun at Jacob's chest. Jacob stood still.

Behind him his son and his brothers crowded into the kitchen. The man moved the muzzle of his gun, left and right, back and forth. The four Duncans lined up, shoulder to shoulder.

Jacob asked, 'Who are you?'

The man said, 'You killed my friend.'

'I didn't.'

'One of you Duncans did. Which one of you is Seth?'

Seth paused a beat and then raised his good hand.

The little man said, 'You killed my friend and you put his body in the trunk of your Cadillac.'

Jacob said, 'No, Reacher stole that car this afternoon.'

'Reacher doesn't exist.'

'He does. He broke my son's nose. And his hand. Reacher was at the Marriott today. We know that. He left the Cadillac there.'

'Where is he now?'

'We're not sure. Close by, we think. Who are you?'

'I represent Mahmeini.'

'We don't know who that is.'

'He buys your merchandise from Safir.'

'We don't know anyone of that name either. We sell to a Mr Rossi in Las Vegas, and after that we have no further interest.'

'You're trying to cut everyone out.'

'We're not. We're trying to get our shipment home, that's all. But we can't bring it in until Reacher is down.'

'Why not?'

'You know why not. This kind of business can't be done in public. You should be helping us, not pointing guns at us.'

The little man kept the gun level. 'Safir's men are dead too.'

'Reacher,' Jacob said. 'He's on the loose.'

'What about Rossi's boys?'

'We haven't seen them recently.'

The little man was quiet for a long moment. Then he said, 'OK. Things change. From now on you will sell direct to Mahmeini.'

Jacob said, 'Our arrangement is with Mr Rossi.'

The little man said, 'Not any more.'

CASSANO AND MANCINI opted to try Jasper Duncan's place first. They walked north parallel with the fence to a spot opposite Jasper's kitchen window. They climbed the fence, flattened themselves against the wall and peered inside. Not what they expected.

There was only one Iranian, not two. There was no happy conversation. No bourbon toasts. Instead, Mahmeini's man was standing there with a gun in his hand, and all four Duncans were cowering away from him. Jacob Duncan's urgent voice was faintly audible.

He was saying, 'We have been in business a long time, sir, and our arrangement is with Mr Rossi. Perhaps he can sell direct to you, now that Mr Safir seems to be out of the picture.'

The little man said, 'Mahmeini won't take half a pie when the whole thing is on the table.'

'But it isn't on the table. I repeat, we deal with Mr Rossi only.'

'Do you really?' the little man asked. He tracked the gun slowly back and forth along the line of men. Finally the gun came to rest aimed at Jonas. The little man's finger whitened on the trigger.

Then simultaneously the window and the little man's head exploded, and the room filled with powdered glass, smoke and the massive barking roar of a .45 gunshot, and the little man fell to the floor, and first Mancini and then Cassano stepped in from the yard.

AFTER LESS THAN AN HOUR the two football players were bored with sitting in the dark. And not just bored, but exasperated. They were the big dogs, and being denied heat, light and NFL highlights was insulting.

One said, 'We have a flashlight and a shotgun, damn it.'

The other said, 'It's a big basement. He could be anywhere.'

'Maybe he's still unconscious, and we're sitting here like idiots.'

'He has to be awake by now.'

'What if he is? He's one guy, and we have a gun and a flashlight. We could tape the flashlight to the gun barrel. Go down, single file, like they do in the movies. We'd see him before he sees us.'

'We're not supposed to kill him. Seth wants to do that himself.'

'We could aim low. Wound him in the legs.'

'Or make him surrender. With the shotgun and all. We could tape him up, with the tape we use for the flashlight.'

'We don't have any tape.'

'Let's look in the garage.'

They went to the garage, and on the workbench was a fat roll of duct tape. They carried it back with them and tied the flashlight against the shotgun barrel. The flashlight fitted pretty well, ahead of the forestock, and underslung because of the front sight above the muzzle. The plastic lens was about an inch in front of the gun.

One asked, 'Well?'

The other said, 'Let's do it.'

He propped the gun across his knees and held the flashlight in place. The first guy juggled the roll of tape, making tearing noises, winding it round and round, until the assembly was mummified. The other guy swung the gun left and right, up and down. The flashlight stayed in place, its beam moving with the muzzle.

'OK,' he said. 'We're good to go. The light is like a laser sight.'

They followed the light out to the hallway and stopped near the basement door. The guy with the gun said, 'You open it and step back and then get behind me. I'll go down slowly and I'll move the light around as much as I can. Tell me if you see him.'

'OK,' the first guy said. He put his hand on the knob. 'On three. Your count.'

The guy with the gun said, 'One.'

Then, 'Two.'

The first guy said, 'Wait. He could be right behind the door. Just waiting to jump out at us before we're ready.'

'That would mean he's been waiting there a whole hour. I could fire through the door.'

'The door has a steel core.'

The guy with the gun asked, 'So what do we do?'

'I'll open up fast, and you fire one round immediately, right where his feet would be. Don't wait and see. Just pull the trigger.'

'OK. I'm ready.' The guy with the gun braced himself, the stock to his shoulder, one eye closed, his finger tight on the trigger.

'On three. Your count.'

'One.'

'Two.'

'Three.'

The first guy flung the door open and the second guy fired, with a long tongue of flame and a huge roaring twelve-gauge boom.

REACHER HAD DECIDED to cut all the circuits at once, because of human nature. He was pretty sure that the football players would turn out to be less than perfect sentries. Reacher figured that those in the house above him would stay on the ball for about fifteen minutes, and then they would get lazy. Maybe they would turn on the TV and get comfortable. So he gave them half an hour to settle in, and then he cut the power, to be sure of killing whatever form of entertainment they had chosen.

Whereupon human nature would take over again. The Cornhuskers were used to getting their own way. Being denied television or warmth for these guys was like a poke in the chest on a sidewalk outside a bar. It would eat away at them. Ultimately they would respond, first with anger, and then threats, and then intervention, which would be inexpert and badly thought out.

Reacher hit the circuit breakers, found the stairs in the dark, crept up to the top step and listened. He didn't hear much, except bouts of hammering an inch from his ear, and then the scream from the doctor's wife, which he discounted, because it was clearly staged.

He waited in the dark. All went quiet for the best part of an hour. Then he sensed movement on the other side of the door. He imagined that one guy would hold the gun, the other would hold the flashlight and they would shuffle down behind the gun. He figured their primary intention would be to capture him because Seth would want him alive for later entertainment. So if they were going to shoot, they would aim low. If they were smart, they would shoot immediately. They would have to realise that his best move would be to be waiting at the top of the stairs, for the sake of surprise.

He felt the doorknob move, and then there was a pause. He put his back flat on the wall, on the hinge side of the door, and he put one foot on the opposite wall, at waist height, and he clamped himself tight, and then he lifted his other foot into place, and he walked himself upwards, palms and soles, until his head was bent against the ceiling and his butt was jammed four feet off the ground.

He waited.

Then the door flung open and he got a glimpse of a flashlight taped to a shotgun barrel, and then the shotgun fired, at point-blank range and a downward angle, right under his bent knees, and the stairwell was full of deafening noise and flame and smoke and wood splinters from the stairs and shards of plastic from where the muzzle blast blew the flashlight apart. Then the muzzle flash died and the house went dark again and Reacher vaulted out of his position, his right foot landing on the top stair, his left foot on the second, using the bright fragment of visual memory his eyes had retained, leaning down to where he knew the shotgun must be, grabbing it two-handed from the guy holding it, back-handing it hard into where the guy's face must be, achieving two results in one, making the guy disappear backwards and recycling the shotgun's pump action, and then shouldering the swinging door away and feeling it crash against the second guy, and bursting out of the stairwell and firing into the floor, not seeking to hit anyone but needing the light from the muzzle flash, seeing one guy down on his left and the other up on his right, launching himself at that new target, bringing him down, kicking his fallen form, then kicking the first guy in the dark, until he was sure no more was required.

Then he stopped and listened. He heard panicked breathing from the dining room. He called, 'Doctor? This is Reacher. No one got shot. Everything is under control. But I need the power back on.'

He heard movement in the dining room. A chair scraping back, a hand touching a wall. Then the door opened and the doctor came out. Reacher asked him, 'Do you have another flashlight?'

The doctor said, 'No.'

'OK, go switch on the circuit breakers for me. Take care on the stairs. They might be a little busted up.'

He heard the doctor feel his way along the wall, heard his feet on the stairs, slow cautious steps, the creak of splintered boards underfoot, and then the confident click of a heel on solid concrete.

Ten seconds later the lights came back on, and the television picture jumped back to life. Reacher looked down at the two guys on the floor. He found the roll of duct tape on the sofa. Five minutes later both guys were trussed up and bound together back to back.

Job done, Reacher thought.

Job done, Jacob Duncan thought. Seth's Cadillac had been retrieved from the road, and both dead Iranians had been hauled to the door and left in the yard for later disposal. Then the kitchen wall and the floor had been wiped clean, and the broken glass had been swept up, and the busted window had been patched with tape and wax paper, and Seth's hand had been taken care of, and now all six men were sitting round the table, the four Duncans plus Cassano and Mancini. The Knob Creek had been brought out, and toasts had been drunk, to each other, to success and to future partnership.

Jacob had drunk with considerable satisfaction. He had glimpsed Cassano at the window, had seen the aimed .45, and had loudly proclaimed his undying loyalty to Rossi, all the while waiting for Cassano to shoot, which he had. Quick thinking, courage under pressure, and a perfect result.

Cassano and Mancini's minds had been changed by the dead man in the Cadillac's trunk. Now they both accepted that Reacher was a genuine threat. How else could they react? The dead man had no marks on him. So what had Reacher done to him? Frightened him to death? Cassano apologised to Jacob for not taking him seriously about Reacher and vowed that he and Mancini would find him.

Jacob sat back in his chair, relaxed. Reacher was locked safely underground. Cassano and Mancini would waste long and fruitless hours and then in good time Reacher would be revealed, and Rossi would take a small hit and the playing field would tilt, just a little.

Doubled profits stretched ahead in perpetuity. And the shipment was on its way, which was the most wonderful thing of all, because as always a portion of it would be retained for the family's use.

The doctor's wife told Reacher to sit down in a chair. He did, and she examined him. She said she had trained as a nurse. 'Your nose looks terrible. My husband should look at it. It needs to be set.'

'I already did that.'

'No, seriously.'

'Believe me, it's as set as it's ever going to get. But you could clean the cuts, if you like.'

Dorothy helped her. They started with warm water, to sponge the crusted blood off his face. Then they got to work with cotton balls and a thin astringent liquid. The open edges stung like crazy. It was not a fun five minutes. But finally the job was done.

The doctor's wife asked, 'Do you have a headache?'

'A little bit,' Reacher said.

'Do you know what day it is?'

'Yes.'

'I should bandage your face.'

'No need,' Reacher said. 'Just lend me a pair of scissors.'

She found scissors and he found the roll of duct tape. He cut an eight-inch length and laid it glue-side up on the table. Then he cut a two-inch length and trimmed it into a triangle. He stuck the triangle glue-side to glue-side in the centre of the eight-inch length, and then he picked it up and smoothed it across his face, hard and tight, a silver slash that ran from one cheekbone to the other, right under his eyes. He said, 'This is the finest field dressing in the world.'

'It's not sterile, and it can't be very comfortable.'

'But I can see past it. That's the main thing.'

Dorothy said, 'It looks like war paint.'

'That's another point in its favour.'

The doctor came in and asked, 'What happens next?'

Ten

They went back to the dining room and sat in the dark, so they could watch the road. There were three more Cornhuskers out there somewhere, and it was possible they would come in and out on rotation, swapping duties, like shift work. Reacher hoped they would show up. He kept the duct tape and the Remington close by.

The doctor said, 'We haven't heard any news.'

Reacher nodded. 'Because you weren't allowed to use the phone. But it rang, and so you think something new has happened.'

'Three things may have happened. Because it rang three times. Maybe the three men left in the gang war are all dead now.'

'They can't all be dead. The winner must still be alive, at least.'

'OK, then maybe it's two dead. Maybe the man in the Cadillac got the Italians.'

Reacher shook his head. 'More likely the other way around. The man in the Cadillac will get picked off easily. Because he's alone, and because he's new up here. This terrain takes some getting used to. The Italians have been here longer than him.'

'So what kind of gangs are these?' the doctor's wife asked.

'The usual kind that makes big money out of something illegal. It's not gambling debts. It's something physical. With weight, and dimensions. It has to be. That's what the Duncans do. They run a transportation company. They're trucking something in.'

'Drugs?'

'You don't need to truck drugs south to Vegas. You can get them direct from Mexico. But certainly it's something valuable, which is why they're in such an uproar. And it's late now, possibly, which is why there are so many boots on the ground here. They're anxious. They want to see it arrive. Either the Duncans are late for some other reason and they're using me as an excuse, or this is something a stranger can't be allowed to see. Have you ever been told to stay away from anywhere for periods of time?'

'Not really.'

'Have you seen weird stuff arrive? Any unexplained vehicles?'

'We see Duncan trucks all the time. Not so much in the winter.'

'I heard the harvest trucks are all in Ohio.'

'They are. Nothing more than vans here now.'

Reacher nodded. 'One of which was missing from the depot. So what kind of a thing is valuable and fits in a van?'

THE ROAD OUTSIDE the dining-room window stayed dark.

The doctor said, 'I don't like just sitting here.'

'So don't,' Reacher said. 'Go to bed. Take a nap.'

'What are you going to do?'

'Nothing. I'm waiting for daylight.'

'You're going out?'

'Eventually. Places to go, things to see.'

'One of us should stay awake. To keep an eye on things.'

'I'll do that,' Reacher said. 'You guys go get some rest.'

They didn't need more persuading. The doctor and his wife headed off together. Dorothy followed, presumably to a spare room. Doors opened and closed, water ran and toilets flushed, then the house went quiet. The heating system whirred and the taped-up football players grunted and snored on the hallway floor, but apart from that Reacher heard nothing at all. He sat upright on the hard chair and kept his eyes open and stared out into the dark.

No one came. Then pale streaks of dawn started showing in the sky, and a knee-high mist rose up off the dirt. A new day. But not a good one, Reacher thought. It was going to be a day full of pain, for those who deserved it, and for those who didn't.

FIVE HUNDRED MILES NORTH, up in Canada, the first of the morning light touched the white van at the end of the rough grassy track. The driver woke in his seat, and blinked, and stretched. He had seen and heard nothing all night long. No animals, no people. He had been warm, because he had a sleeping-bag filled with down, but he had been uncomfortable, because panel vans had small cabs, and he had spent the night folded into a seat that didn't recline very far.

He climbed out and ate and drank from his meagre supplies. The sky was brightening. It was his favourite time for a run to the border. Light enough to see, too early for company. He had just twenty miles to go, most of them on an unmapped forest track, to a point a little less than four thousand yards north of the line. The transfer zone, he called it. The end of the road for him, but not for his cargo.

He climbed back in the cab and started the engine. Then he turned the wheel and moved slowly down the rough grassy track.

The road petered out after Pakowki Lake. The blacktop surface finished in a forest clearing with no apparent exit. But the van lined up between two pines, drove over stunted underbrush and found itself on a rutted, neglected track. Ahead of it was nothing but trees, and then the Montana town of Hogg Parish. But the van stopped halfway there, two miles short of the border, exactly symmetrical with its opposite number in America, which was already in place and waiting, for the last leg of the journey.

REACHER HEARD a toilet flushing, a tap running, a door opening and closing. Then the doctor came past the dining room, stiff with sleep. He skirted the football players and headed for the kitchen. A minute later Reacher heard the gulp and hiss of the coffee machine.

The doctor came in with two mugs of coffee. He put one mug in front of Reacher and sat in a chair on the opposite side of the table.

He said, 'Good morning. How's your nose?'

Reacher said, 'Terrific.'

'There's something you never told me. You said twenty-five years ago the detective neglected to search somewhere because of ignorance or confusion. Is that where you're going this morning?'

Reacher took a sip of coffee. 'Yes, it is.'

'Where is this place?'

'Dorothy told me that fifty years ago two farms were sold for a development that never happened. The outbuildings from one of them are still there. Way out in a field. A barn, and a smaller shed.'

The doctor nodded. 'I know where they are.'

'People plough right up to them.'

'I know,' the doctor said. 'I guess they shouldn't, but why let good land go to waste? The subdivisions were never built. So it's something for nothing, and God knows these people need it.'

'When Detective Carson came up here twenty-five years ago, what did he see in the early summer? He saw acres of waist-high corn, he saw houses dotted around here and there, and he saw outbuildings dotted around here and there. He stopped at every house, and every occupant said they'd searched their outbuildings. That old barn and shed fell between the cracks. Because Carson's question was, Did you search *your* outbuildings? Everyone said yes, probably truthfully. Carson saw the old barn and shed and assumed they belonged to someone, and that they had been looked at. But they didn't belong to anyone, and they hadn't been looked at.'

'You think that was the scene of the crime?'

'I think Carson should've asked about it twenty-five years ago.'

'There won't be anything there. Those buildings are ruins now. They've been sitting empty for fifty years, just mouldering away.'

'Then why have they got wheel ruts all the way to the door? I hid a truck in the shed my first night. No problem getting there. I've seen worse roads in New York City. Quite well-established ruts.'

The doctor asked, 'So you think someone scooped the kid up and drove her to that barn?'

'I'm not sure,' Reacher said. 'They were harvesting alfalfa at the time, and there would have been plenty of trucks on the road.' He looked out the window at clumps of frozen weeds. The lawn was dry and brittle with cold. He said, 'You're not much of a gardener.'

'No talent,' the doctor said. 'No time.'

'Does anyone garden?'

'Not really. People are too tired. And farmers hardly ever garden. They grow stuff to sell, not to look at. Why do you want to know?'

'I'm asking myself, if I was a little girl, and I loved flowers, where would I go to see some? No point coming to a house like this. Or any house, probably. Or anywhere at all because every inch of ground is ploughed for cash crops. I can think of just three possibilities. I saw two big rocks in the fields, with brambles around them. Nice wild flowers in the early summer, probably, but in the early summer they would be completely inaccessible, because you'd have to wade a mile through growing corn just to get to them. But there was one other place I saw the same kind of brambles. Around the base of that old barn. Wind-blown seeds, I guess.'

'You think she rode there on her own?'

'I think it's possible. Maybe she knew the one place she was sure to see flowers. And maybe someone knew she knew.'

The doctor said, 'Maybe she went in the barn with her bicycle. She might have injured herself on something in there. Or got stuck. The door is jammed now. Maybe it was baulky then. She could have got trapped. No one would have heard her shouting.'

'Maybe,' Reacher said.

The doctor went quiet.

Reacher said, 'Now there's something you're not telling me.'

'In probably half an hour the other Cornhuskers will come here. Their buddies are here, so this is their temporary base. They'll make my wife cook breakfast for them. They enjoy feudal stuff like that.'

'I'll be ready,' Reacher said. 'Can you watch the road? I'll be back in ten.' Reacher picked up the Remington and found his way to the garage. There was a workbench, well organised, with a vice, and a pegboard above, loaded with tools logically arrayed.

Reacher unloaded the Remington, five shells from the magazine and one from the breech. He clamped the gun upside-down in the vice. He found an electric jigsaw and fitted a woodcutting blade. He plugged it in, fired it up, put the blade on the walnut and sawed off the shoulder stock. He found a rasp and cleaned the whole thing up.

He swapped the jigsaw blade for a metal cutter, then laid it against the barrel an inch in front of the forestock. The saw screeched and the last foot of the barrel fell on the floor. He found a metal file and cleaned the burrs of steel off the new muzzle. He released the vice, lifted the gun out and reloaded it. A sawn-off with a pistol grip, not much longer than his forearm.

He found the coat closet on his way back through the house and got his parka. The Glock, the switchblade, the two screwdrivers and the wrench were still in the pockets. He used the knife to slit the lining inside the left-hand pocket, so the sawn-off would go all the way in. He put the coat on. Then he went back to the dining room.

THE CORNHUSKERS came in separately, the first exactly thirty minutes after the doctor had spoken, in a black pick-up. He pushed in through the door like he owned the place, and Reacher laid him out with a blow to the back of the head. The guy toppled forward. Reacher dragged him onwards across the shiny wood, and he taped him up, quick and dirty, not a permanent job, but enough for the moment. The thump of the guy falling and Reacher's grunting woke the doctor's wife and Dorothy. They came out of their rooms wearing bathrobes. The doctor's wife looked at the new guy on the floor and said, 'I guess they're coming in for breakfast.'

Reacher said, 'But today they're not getting any.'

The doctor's wife said, 'You want us to stay out of the way?'

'Might be safer. You don't want a guy falling on you.'

'Another one coming,' the doctor called from the dining room.

The second guy went down exactly the same as the first. There was no room to drag him forward. Reacher taped him up right there.

The last to arrive was the guy who had broken Reacher's nose.

And he didn't come alone.

A white SUV parked on the road, and the guy who had broken Reacher's nose climbed out of the driver's seat. Then the passenger door opened and the kid called John got out. The kid Reacher had left at the depot. *Go to bed*, Reacher had said. But the kid hadn't gone to bed. He had hung out until he'd heard that things were safe, and then he had come out to claim his share of the fun.

Reacher opened the door and stepped out to meet them head on. He drew his sawn-off across his body and aimed it at the guy who had hit him. But he looked at John. 'You let me down,' he said.

Both guys came to a dead stop and stared at him more urgently than he thought was warranted, until he remembered the duct tape on his face.

Like war paint. He looked at the guy who had hit him. 'It was nothing that couldn't be fixed. But I'm not certain you'll be able to say the same. Take out your car keys and toss them to me.'

The guy said, 'What?'

'I'm bored with John's Yukon. I'm using your truck today.'

The guy dipped into his pocket and got his keys. He tossed them to Reacher, who made no attempt to catch them. They landed on the gravel. Reacher said, 'John, lie face down on the ground.'

John didn't move. Reacher fired into the ground at his feet. John howled and danced. Not hit, but stung in the shins by gravel fragments kicked up by the blast. Reacher pumped the gun, a solid *crunch-crunch*, probably the most intimidating sound in the world.

John got down on the ground and lowered himself face down. Reacher called over his shoulder, 'Doctor? Bring me the duct tape.'

The doctor came out with the tape. He gave the roll to Reacher and went back inside. Reacher tossed the tape to the guy who had hit him. 'Make it so your buddy can't move his arms or legs.'

The guy got to work. He wrapped John's wrists with a tight three-layer figure of eight, and then he did the same to his ankles.

Reacher shrugged out of his coat and let it fall. Then he laid the sawn-off down. He looked at the guy who had hit him and said, 'Fair fight. You against me. Bare knuckles. No rules.'

The guy looked blank for a second, and then smiled, as if an unbelievable circumstance had unveiled itself right in front of him.

Reacher smiled too, just a little. The guy had no idea. No idea at all. He was six-seven and three hundred pounds, but he was nothing more than a prize ox, big and dumb, going up against a gutter rat.

The guy bobbed and weaved, up on his toes, jiggling around, wasting energy. Reacher stood still, watching the guy's eyes and his hands and his feet. And soon enough a left jab came in, powered by the arm only, with no real contribution from the legs or the upper body. Reacher watched the big pink knuckles getting closer, and then he moved his own left hand, fast, and he slapped at the inside of the guy's wrist, hard enough to deflect it away from his face and send it buzzing harmlessly over his moving shoulder.

His shoulder was moving because he was already driving hard off his back foot, twisting at the waist, hurling his right elbow, aiming to hit him on the outer edge of his left eye socket. The blow landed with 250 pounds of moving mass behind it. The guy staggered back. His legs folded from under him and he went down on his back.

But the guy didn't quit. He started scrabbling around on his back, like a turtle, trying to get up again. Reacher kicked him in the face, and the crunch of the guy's shattering nose was clearly audible.

Game over. Reacher taped the guy up where he lay. Then he stepped back into the hallway and did a better job on the two who had come in first. He slid them round on the shiny parquet and taped them together, back to back, like the two from last night.

Then a phone rang, muted and distant.

It was Dorothy's cell. She came out of her room with it in her hand. She said, 'That was Mr Vincent at the motel. He wants me to work this morning. He has guests.'

Reacher asked, 'Who are they?'

'He didn't say.'

Reacher thought for a moment. He told the doctor to keep a medical eye on the six captured football players, then he went back outside, put his coat on and put the sawn-off in his pocket. He found the car keys on the stones, and then he headed to the white SUV.

ELDRIDGE TYLER MOVED, just a little, to keep himself comfortable. He was into his second hour of daylight. He was a patient man. His eye was still on the scope. It was still trained on the barn door. The rifle's forestock was still secure on the bags of rice. The air was wet and thick, but the sun was bright and the view was good.

But the big man in the brown coat hadn't come.

And perhaps he never would, if the Duncans had been successful during the night. But Tyler was cautious by nature. He always took his tasks seriously. Maybe the Duncans hadn't been successful during the night. In which case the big man would show up soon.

THE WHITE SUV turned out to be a Chevy Tahoe. It drove just the same as the GMC Yukon, big and sloppy and inexact. Reacher went back to the two-lane, turned right and headed south.

He slowed and then parked on the shoulder, two hundred yards short of the motel. He got out of the truck and walked quietly on the blacktop. First, he saw the burned-out Ford in the main lot. Then he saw the doctor's damaged Subaru, outside room six. Then he saw the dark blue Chevrolet parked outside room seven or eight.

Reacher came in off the road and walked to the lounge door. He saw Vincent behind the reception desk hanging up the phone. He stared at Reacher's duct-tape bandage. 'What happened to you?'

'Just a scratch,' Reacher said. 'Who was on the phone?'

'It was the phone tree. Three Cornhusker vehicles were tooling around aimlessly all night. All four Duncans are in Jacob's house.'

'You have guests here,' Reacher said.

'The Italians,' Vincent said. 'They woke me up. They were very bad tempered. I put them in seven and eight. I don't think I'm going to get paid. They asked if I had seen you.'

'When did they get here?'

'About five this morning.'

Reacher nodded. A wild goose chase all night long, no success, eventual fatigue. 'OK,' he said. 'Call them. One minute from now. Talk in a whisper. Tell them I'm in your lot, looking at the wreck.'

Reacher stepped back out to the lot and walked on the silver baulks of timber, behind rooms seven and eight, and came out near room nine. He stood in a narrow gap, the circular bulk of room eight in front of him, room seven one building along. He took out the dead Iranian's Glock. He heard the room phones ring, behind closed doors. He pictured men rolling over on beds, struggling awake, finding the phones on the night stands, answering them, listening to Vincent's urgent whispered messages.

He knew what was going to happen. Whoever opened up first would wait in the doorway, half in and half out, gun drawn, craning his neck, watching for his partner to emerge. Then there would be gestures, sign language and a cautious joint approach.

Room eight opened up first. Reacher saw a hand on the jamb, then a pistol pointing almost vertical, then the back of a head.

Reacher heard room seven's door open. He sensed tapped chests assigning roles, raised arms indicating directions, spread fingers indicating timings. The obvious move would be for the guy from room eight to leapfrog ahead and circle the lounge on the blind side, hitting the lot from the north, while the guy from room seven waited a beat then crept up from the south.

They went for it. Reacher heard the farther guy step out and wait, and the nearer guy step out and walk. Eight paces, Reacher thought, before the latter passed the former. He counted in his head. On six he stepped out, on seven he raised the Glock, and on eight he screamed FREEZE and both men froze, guns held low near their thighs, tired, just woken up, and disoriented. Reacher screamed DROP YOUR WEAPONS and both men complied instantly.

Reacher looked at them from behind. They were both in trousers, shirts and shoes. No jackets, no coats. Reacher said, 'Turn around.'

They turned round. The one on the left said, 'You.'

Reacher said, 'Finally we meet. Turn out your trouser pockets.'

They obeyed. Quarters and dimes and pennies rained down, and cell-phones hit the gravel. Plus a car key, with a bulbous black head.

Reacher picked up one of their guns. He ejected the magazine and it fell to the ground and he saw it was full. He picked up the other gun. Its magazine was one short. 'Who?' he asked.

The guy on the left said, 'The other Iranian. You got one, we got the other. We're on the same side here.'

'I don't think so,' Reacher said. He moved towards the small pile of pocket junk and picked up the car key. He pressed the button set in the head and the Chevy's doors unlocked. 'Get in the back seat.'

The guy on the left asked, 'Do you know who we are? We work for a guy named Rossi, in Las Vegas. He's got money. There's a deal going down here. We could cut you in. Make you rich.'

'I'm already rich. I've got everything I need. Get in the back of your car. We're going for a drive.'

The two men didn't dare believe their luck. Them in the back, a solo driver in the front. Reacher tracked them with the Glock, all the way to the car. After they got in, Reacher opened the driver's door. He put his knee on the seat and leaned inside.

The guy who had spoken before asked, 'So where are we going?'

'Not far. I'm going to park next to the Ford you burned. Then I'm going to set this car on fire.'

The two men didn't understand. The one who had spoken before said, 'You're going to drive with us in the back? Like, loose?'

'You can put your seat belts on if you like. But it's hardly worth it. It's not far. And I'm a careful driver. I won't have an accident.'

The guy said, 'But ...' and then nothing more.

'I know,' Reacher said. 'I'll have my back turned. You could jump me. But you won't.'

'Why not?'

'Because you'll be dead,' Reacher said, and he shot the first guy, in the forehead, and then the second, a brisk double tap, *bang bang*. The rear window shattered, and the two guys settled peacefully, like afterthoughts, like old people falling asleep but with open eyes.

Reacher checked room seven and found a wallet. There was a Nevada driver's licence in it, made out to Roberto Cassano. There were four credit cards and ninety dollars in cash. Reacher took sixty, got in the Impala, drove forty yards and parked against the shell of the Ford. He gave sixty bucks to Vincent in the lounge, two rooms, one night, then he borrowed rags and matches, and as soon as the fuse was set in the Chevy's filler neck he hustled back to the Tahoe. The first major flames were showing as he drove by, and he saw the fuel tank go up in his mirror, about four hundred yards later.

Reacher drove south on the two-lane road and coasted to a stop a thousand yards beyond the barn. It stood on the dirt a mile away to the west, close to its smaller companion, crisp in the light.

He ignored the tractor ruts and walked straight across the dirt.

DOROTHY COE used the guest bathroom and showered fast, ready for work at the motel. She stopped in the kitchen to drink coffee and eat toast with the doctor and his wife, and then she changed her mind about her destination. She asked, 'Where did Reacher go?'

'He's working on a theory.'

Dorothy asked, 'Where did he go?'

The doctor said, 'The old barn.'

Dorothy said, 'Then that's where I'm going too.'

ELDRIDGE TYLER heard the truck stop. Just the whisper of faraway tyres on coarse blacktop, barely audible in the rural silence. It was a mile away, he thought. It was not one of the Duncans with a message. They would come all the way, or call on the phone. It was not the shipment, either. The shipment was still hours away.

He rolled on his side and looked back at the tripwire. Should someone come, he would snatch back the rifle, roll on his hip, sit up, swivel round and fire point blank. No problem. He faced the front again and put his eye on the scope and his finger on the trigger.

TEN MINUTES LATER Reacher was halfway to the barn. It was on his right. The small shelter was on his left. The brambles at their bases were dry sticks in the winter, possibly a riot of colour in the summer.

He stopped fifty yards out. His theory was either all the way right or all the way wrong. The eight-year-old Margaret Coe had come for the flowers, but she hadn't got trapped by accident. The bike proved the proposition. A child impulsive enough to drop a bike on a path might have dashed inside a derelict structure and injured herself. But a child earnest and serious enough to wheel her bike in with her would have taken care and not got hurt at all. If there had been an accident, the bike would have been found outside. The bike had not been found, therefore there had been no accident.

And: she had gone to the barn voluntarily, but she had not gone inside the barn voluntarily. Why would a child looking for flowers have gone inside a barn? Barns held no secrets for farm children. A kid interested in colours and nature and freshness would have felt no attraction for a dark and gloomy space full of decaying smells. The slider was jammed now, and it might have been jammed then. Could an eight-year-old have lifted a bike through the judas hole? No, someone had done it for her. A fifth man.

Because the theory didn't work without the existence of a fifth man. The Duncans were alibied, but Margaret Coe had disappeared even so. Therefore someone else had been there. He would be bound to the Duncans, by a terrible shared secret. His loyalty and service were guaranteed. In an emergency, he would help out.

All the way right, or all the way wrong.

Reacher looked at the barn, and the smaller shelter.

If the theory was right, the fifth man would be there.

Best move would be for him to be inside the barn, sitting six feet from the door, a shotgun across his knees, waiting for his target to step through in a bar of bright light. Second-best move would put the guy in the smaller shelter a hundred and twenty yards away, prone with a rifle on the mezzanine half-loft. In either case, the smaller shelter should be checked first.

Reacher headed quietly for the smaller shelter. Chances were good the fifth man had served. He might not be a specialist sniper, but he might know the basics, foremost among which was that when a guy lay down and aimed forward, he got increasingly paranoid about what was happening behind him. Therefore, he might have set up a physical early-warning system.

Reacher walked quietly towards the entrance, drew the shotgun, and inched forward. And saw a tripwire, a thin cable tied shin-high across the open end of the structure, filmy with the part-dried remains of the morning dew, which meant it had been in place before dawn, which meant the fifth man was a cautious and fully invested person. And it meant he had been contacted the day before, by the Duncans, which confirmed that the barn was important. Reacher smiled. All the way right.

He walked an exaggerated curve, working on the assumption that most people were right-handed, so he wanted to be on the guy's left before he announced himself, because that would give the guy's rifle a longer and more awkward traverse before it came to bear on his target. He saw a truck inside the shelter, parked under the mezzanine floor. He approached within six inches of the wire and stood still, letting his eyes adjust. The inside of the shelter was dark. Above the truck was the loft, and there was a humped shape up there, butt, legs, back and elbows, backlit by daylight coming in through the ventilation louvres. The fifth man, prone with a rifle.

Reacher stepped over the tripwire carefully, and eased into the shadows. He inched along the left-hand tyre track. He made it to the back of the truck. He could see the man's feet, but nothing more. He needed a better angle. He needed to be up in the truck's load bed, which meant that a silent approach was no longer an option. The sheet metal would clang and the suspension would creak.

ELDRIDGE TYLER heard nothing until a sudden cacophony erupted eight feet below. There was some heavy metal implement beating on the side of his truck, then footsteps were thumping into the load bed, a loud voice was screaming STAY STILL STAY STILL, then a shotgun fired into the roof above his back with a pulverising blast. The voice said, 'Take your hands off your gun, or I'll shoot you.'

Tyler took his right forefinger off the trigger and eased his left hand from under the barrel. He turned. He saw a big guy holding himself awkwardly, like he was hurting. He was exactly as advertised, except for a length of duct tape on his face. He was holding a shotgun.

REACHER SAW A MAN between sixty and seventy years old, with thin grey hair and a weather-beaten face. Beyond him and beneath him was an expensive hunting rifle, resting on stacked bags of rice.

Reacher asked, 'What's your name?' The guy didn't answer.

Reacher said, 'Come down from there. Leave your rifle.'

The guy didn't move. Reacher saw him running through the same basic calculation any busted man makes: *How much do they know?*

Reacher said, 'I know most of it. I just need the last few details. Twenty-five years ago a little girl came here to see flowers. Probably she came every Sunday. One particular Sunday you were here too. I want to know how fast the Duncans picked up on the pattern. Three weeks? Two?'

The guy's head stayed where it was, but his hands crept back towards the gun. Reacher said, 'I'll shoot you if that muzzle starts turning towards me.'

The guy stopped moving, but he didn't bring his hands back.

Reacher said, 'I'm going to assume they noticed her the first Sunday, they watched for her the second Sunday, they had you in place for the third go-round. I want to know when the Duncans called you and when they called those boys to build the fence.' No response.

Reacher said, 'You need to talk to me. It's your only way of staying alive.'

The guy closed his eyes. His hands started creeping again. He didn't want to stay alive. He was going to commit suicide, not with the rifle, but by moving the rifle. Reacher knew the signs. Suicide by cop, it was called. Common, after arrests for certain crimes.

Reacher said, 'It had to come to an end some time, right?'

The guy nodded. The rifle kept on moving.

Reacher said, 'Open your eyes. I want you to see it coming.'

The guy opened his eyes. Reacher shot him with the sawn-off. He died more or less instantly, which was a privilege Reacher figured had not been offered to young Margaret Coe.

REACHER STEPPED on the roof of the cab and climbed onto the half-loft shelf. He took the dead man's rifle and climbed down. It was a fancy toy, custom built around a Winchester bolt action, a .338 Magnum in the breech and five more in the magazine.

He carried the rifle to the mouth of the shelter and stepped over the trip-wire. Then he headed for the barn. The judas hole was secured with a lock normally seen on a suburban front door. Reacher aimed the rifle, fired twice, at where he thought the screws holding the lock in place might be. The door sagged open half an inch before catching on splinters. He put his fingers in the crack, pulled. The door came free and he stepped inside the barn.

Eleven

Reacher stepped out of the barn again eleven minutes later, and saw Dorothy's truck driving up the track. Dorothy was at the wheel, the doctor was in the passenger seat, the doctor's wife between them. Reacher stood still, completely numb, blinking, the captured rifle in one hand. Dorothy slowed, stopped and waited thirty feet away, as if she already knew.

A long minute later the truck doors opened and the doctor and his wife climbed out. Then Dorothy got out. Reacher walked to meet her. She was quiet for a moment, then she asked, 'Is she in there?'

Reacher said, 'Yes.'

'Are you sure?'

'Her bike is in there.'

'Still? After all these years? It must be all rusted.'

'A little. It's dry in there.'

Dorothy went quiet. 'Can you tell what happened to her?'

Reacher said, 'No,' which was technically true. He was no pathologist. But he had been a cop for a long time. He could guess.

She said, 'I should go look.'

He said, 'Don't.'

'I have to.'

'Not really.'

'You can't stop me.'

'I know. I'm asking you, that's all. Please don't look.'

'I don't have to listen to you.'

'Then listen to Margaret. Pretend she grew up. She wouldn't have been a lawyer or a scientist. She loved flowers. She loved colours and forms. She would have been a painter or a poet. An artist. In love with life, and full of concern for you. She'd look at you and smile and she'd say, "Come on, mom, do what the man says." She'd say, "Mom, trust me on this."'

'But I have to see. It's just her bones.'

'It's not just her bones.'

'What else can be left?'

'No,' Reacher said. 'I mean, it's not just *her* bones.'

UP ON THE 49TH PARALLEL, the white van had parked for the final time in a forest clearing a little more than two miles north of the border. The driver had got out, taken a long coil of rope from the passenger foot well, walked to the rear doors and opened them. The women and the girls had come out with no hesitation at all, because passage to America was what they wanted, what they had paid for.

There were sixteen of them, all from rural Thailand, six women and ten female children, average weight close to eighty pounds each, for a total payload of 1,260 pounds. The women were slim and attractive, and the girls were all eight years old or younger. They all stood and blinked in the morning light and shuffled their feet a little, stiff and weary but excited and full of wonderment.

The driver couldn't speak Thai and they couldn't understand English, so he started the same dumb show he had performed many times before. First he patted the air to get their attention. Then he raised a finger to his lips, so that they all understood they had to be silent. He pointed at the ground and then cupped a hand behind his ear. *There are sensors.* The women nodded. He pointed to himself, and then to all of them, and then pointed south. He used both hands, palms down, stepping on the air gently. *Now we all have to walk softly and keep very quiet.* The women nodded again.

The driver uncoiled his rope, measured off six feet from the end and wrapped that round the first woman's hand. He measured another six feet and wrapped the rope round the first girl's hand, and then the next, and then the second woman, and so on, until he had all sixteen joined together. The driver picked up the free end of the rope. Then he led them quietly south between bushes and trees.

THEY WALKED ON CAREFULLY, patiently enduring the third of the four parts of their adventure. First had come the shipping container, and then had come the white van. Now came the hike, and then there would be another van. Everything had been explained beforehand in a shipping office above a store in a town near their home. There were many such offices, and many such operations, but the one they had used was considered the best. The price was high, but the facilities were excellent. The shipping container was equipped with lamps inside with bulbs that simulated daylight, wired to automobile batteries. There were mattresses and blankets. There was food, water and chemical toilets. There were ventilation slots disguised as rust holes. There were washing facilities.

And the best thing was that there was no bias against families with girl children. Some organisations smuggled adults only, because adults could work immediately, and some allowed children, but older boys only, because they could work too, but this organisation welcomed young girls. The only downside was that the sexes had to travel separately for the sake of decorum, so fathers were separated from mothers, and brothers from sisters, and then on this particular occasion they were told at the last minute that the ship the men and the boys were due to sail on was delayed, so the women and the girls had been obliged to go on ahead. Which would be OK, they were told, because they would be well looked after in America, for as long as it took for the second ship to arrive.

They had been warned that the four-mile hike would be the hardest part of the trip, but it wasn't. It felt good to be out in the air, moving around. It was cold, but they had warm clothes to wear. The best part was when their guide stopped and traced an imaginary line on the ground and mouthed, 'America.' They passed the line one after the other and smiled happily, on American soil at last.

THE DUNCAN DRIVER in the grey van on the Montana side of the border saw them coming a hundred yards away. His Canadian counterpart was leading the procession, holding the rope. The Duncan driver opened his rear doors, ready to receive them. The Canadian handed over the free end of the rope, and then he turned and walked back into the forest. Before each of his passengers climbed aboard, the Duncan driver looked at their faces, smiled and shook their hands, in a way his passengers took to be a formal welcome to their new country. In fact the Duncan driver was trying to guess which kid the Duncans would choose to keep. The women would go straight to the Vegas escort agencies, and nine girls would end up somewhere further on down the line, but one of them would stay in the county. Buy ten and sell nine, was the Duncan way.

DOROTHY STOOD BEHIND her truck's open door for ten minutes. Reacher stood in front of her, hoping he was blocking her view of the barn, happy to stand there for as long as it took, ten hours or ten days or ten years, anything to stop her going inside. Eventually she asked, 'How many are in there?'

Reacher said, 'About sixty.'

'Oh my God.'

'They got a taste for it,' Reacher said. 'An addiction. There are no ghosts. What the stoner kid heard from time to time was real.'

'Who were they all?'

'Asian girls, I think.'

'Where were they all from?'

'Illegal immigrant families, probably, smuggled in, for the sex trade. That's what the Duncans were doing.'

'Were they all young?'

'About eight years old. There are photographs. In silver frames.'

There was a long, long pause. Dorothy went quiet again and watched the horizon. Then she asked, 'What should we do now?'

Reacher said, 'I'm going over to the Duncan houses. They're all in there thinking everything is fine. It's time they found out it isn't.'

Dorothy said, 'I want to come with you.'

Reacher said, 'Not a good idea. Could be dangerous.'

'I hope it is. Some things are worth dying for.'

The doctor's wife said, 'We're coming too. Both of us. Let's go.'

Dorothy got behind the wheel of her truck again and the doctor and his wife slid in beside her. Reacher rode in the load bed, with the captured rifle, back to where he had left the white Tahoe. Reacher got in and drove it and the other three followed behind. They went south on the two-lane and stopped half a mile shy of the Duncan compound. Reacher unscrewed the Leica scope from the rifle and used it like a miniature telescope. All three houses were clearly visible. There were five parked vehicles. Three old pick-up trucks, plus Seth's black Cadillac and Eleanor's red Mazda.

Reacher climbed out of the Tahoe and walked back to meet the others. He took the sawn-off from his pocket and handed it to Dorothy. He said, 'You all head back and get car keys from the football players. Then bring me two more vehicles. Choose the ones with the most gas in the tank. Get back here as fast as you can.'

Dorothy took off north. Reacher waited in the Tahoe.

THREE ISOLATED HOUSES. Wintertime. Flat land all around. Nowhere to hide. Standard infantry doctrine would be to call in an artillery strike or a bombing run. The guerilla approach would be to split up and attack with grenades from four sides simultaneously. But Reacher had no forces, no grenades or air support. He was on his own, with a middle-aged alcoholic man and two middle-aged women, one of whom was in shock. They had a rifle with two rounds in it, a Glock pistol with sixteen rounds, a sawn-off shotgun with three rounds, a switchblade, two screwdrivers, an adjustable wrench and a book of matches. Not exactly overwhelming force.

But time was on their side. They had all day. And the terrain was on their side. And the Duncans' fence was on their side. The fence, built a quarter of a century before, was still strong and sturdy.

Reacher put the Leica to his eye again. Nothing was happening in the compound. It was still and quiet. Reacher waited.

Fifteen minutes later, he checked the Tahoe's mirror and saw a convoy heading for him. First was Dorothy's truck, then came John's gold Yukon with the doctor at the wheel. Last was the doctor's wife, driving the black pick-up the first Cornhusker of the morning had arrived in. They parked nose to tail behind the Tahoe.

Reacher climbed out, the other three gathered around and he told them what to do. He told Dorothy to keep the sawn-off, he gave the Leica scope to the doctor's wife, and he took her scarf and her cellphone in exchange. As soon as they understood their roles, they got into Dorothy's truck and headed south. Reacher was left alone on the shoulder of the two-lane, with the Tahoe and Yukon and the pick-up, with the keys for all of them in his pocket.

The black pick-up was the longest of the three vehicles, so Reacher decided to use it second. The Tahoe had the most gas in it, so Reacher decided to use it first. Which left the Yukon to use third.

Reacher walked back and forth along the line and started all three vehicles. Then he leapfrogged them forward, moving them closer to the mouth of the Duncan driveway, a hundred yards at a time, getting them in the right order. He got the black pick-up within fifty yards, he left the gold Yukon right behind it, and then he drove the white Tahoe into the mouth of the driveway and eased it to a stop.

He slid out of the seat, crouched down and clamped the jaws of his adjustable wrench across the gas pedal, so that the stem of the wrench stuck up above horizontal, then he turned the knob tight. He hustled round the tailgate, opened the fuel-filler door, took off the gas cap, poked the end of the borrowed scarf down the filler neck with the longer screwdriver and lit the free end of the scarf. He hustled back to the driver's door, leaned in and put the truck in gear. The engine's idle speed rolled it forward. He kept pace, put his finger on the button and powered the driver's seat forward. The cushion moved slowly, past the point where a person of average height would want it, on towards where a short person would want it, and then the cushion touched the end of the wrench, and the truck sped up a little. Reacher kept his finger where it was, the seat kept moving, the truck kept accelerating, Reacher ran alongside, and then the seat arrived at its limit and Reacher let the truck go on without him. The ruts in the driveway were holding it straight. The scarf in the filler neck was burning pretty well.

Reacher jogged back to the road, to the black pick-up. He got in and parallel-parked it across the mouth of the driveway, between the fences. The Tahoe was already halfway to its target, trailing a bright plume of flame. Reacher pulled the black pick-up's keys and jogged back to the Yukon on the road. He took the rifle off the seat, leaned on the blind side of the Yukon's hood and watched.

The Tahoe was well ablaze. It rolled on through its final twenty yards, and it hit the front of the centre house and stopped dead. There was no major crash. The wood on the house splintered, the front wall bowed inwards a little, and glass fell out of a ground-floor window, and that was all. But that was enough.

The flames at the rear of the truck licked out under the sills and crept towards the front of the Tahoe. Then the fuel line must have ruptured because there was a wide fan of flame, a fierce lateral spray that beat against the front of the house and rose up all around the Tahoe's hood, licking the house, lighting it. Air sucked in and out of the broken window and the flames started licking at its frame.

Reacher dialled his borrowed cell. 'The centre house is alight.'

Dorothy answered, from her position half a mile west, out in the fields. She said, 'That's Jonas's house. We can see the smoke.'

'Anyone moving?'

'Not yet.' Then she said, 'Wait. Jonas is coming out his back door. Turning left. He's going to head round to the front.'

'OK,' Reacher said. 'Stay on the line.'

He laid the phone on the Yukon's hood and picked up the rifle. It had a front iron sight at the muzzle. Reacher raised it to his eye and aimed at the gap between the centre house and the southernmost house. He saw a figure enter the gap from the rear. A short, wide man, maybe sixty years old. Round red face, thinning grey hair. The guy hustled stiffly between the two homes and stopped dead. He stared at the burning Tahoe and started towards it. Then he stopped and stared at the pick-up parked across the far end of the driveway.

Reacher laid the front sight on the guy's centre mass and pulled the trigger. The .338 hit Jonas between his lower lip and his chin. He went down vertically and sprawled in a grotesque tangle of limbs, and then he died.

Reacher picked up the cellphone and said, 'Jonas is down.'

Dorothy said, 'We heard the shot.'

'Any activity?'

'Not yet.'

Reacher kept the phone against his ear. Jonas's house was burning nicely. The front wall was on fire, and there were flames inside, curling flat and angry against the ceilings.

Dorothy said, 'Jasper is out. He's running, heading for Jacob's.'

Reacher saw him, flitting across the narrow gap between Jonas's house and Jacob's, a short wide man similar to his brother. On the phone Dorothy said, 'He's gone inside. We see him in Jacob's kitchen. Through the window. Jacob and Seth are in there too.'

The fire in Jonas's house was burning out of control. Glass punched out of the house's windows ahead of flames that followed horizontally before boiling upwards. The roof was alight. The left-hand gable tilted inwards and the right-hand gable fell outwards, across the gap to Jasper's house. Sparks showered all around and thermals caught them and sent them shooting a hundred feet in the air. Jonas's right-hand wall collapsed into the gap and piled against Jasper's left-hand wall, and vivid new flames leaped up. Then Jonas's left-hand wall folded in half, the top part falling inwards into the fire and the bottom part angling outwards, propping itself against Jacob's house. Huge flames licked upwards and outwards and sideways.

Reacher said, 'I think we're three for three.'

Dorothy said, 'Jasper is out again. He's heading for his truck.'

Reacher saw Jasper run for the line of cars and slide into a white pick-up, start it up and back it out. It turned and aimed for the driveway towards the parked black truck. It stopped behind it, and Jasper scrambled out. He stood still, momentarily unsure. Reacher put the phone on the Yukon's hood. Distance, forty yards. Which was really no distance at all. Reacher shot him through the head. Reacher picked up the phone and said, 'Jasper is down.'

Then he dropped the empty gun on the road behind him and climbed inside the Yukon. Lack of replacement ammunition meant that phase one was over, and that phase two was about to begin.

Reacher drove the Yukon beyond the mouth of the driveway, and then he turned right, onto the open dirt. He drove a wide circle until he was level with the compound and then he stopped, the engine idling, his foot on the brake. To the left he could see Dorothy's truck in the fields.

He put the phone to his ear. 'I'm end-on now. What do you see?'

Dorothy said, 'Jonas's house is about gone. All that's left is the chimney. Jasper's house is on its way. Jacob's is burning pretty fierce. Has to be getting hot in there.'

'Stand by, then. It won't be long now.'

It was less than a minute. Dorothy said, 'They're out,' and Reacher saw Jacob and Seth spill round the back corner of the house. They ran ducked down, zigzagging, afraid of the rifle they thought was still out there. They made it to one of the remaining pick-up trucks and Reacher saw them open the doors from a crouch, climb in and hunker down. Behind them the north end of Jacob's house swelled and came down, slowly and gracefully, with burning timbers tumbling, reaching almost to the boundary fence, and then the south end of the house fell backwards and collapsed into the fire.

Reacher saw Jacob at the wheel, shorter and broader than Seth in the passenger seat. The truck backed up ten yards, almost into the fire, and then it drove forward and hit the fence, butting against it, trying to break through. The pick-up's front bumper bent out of shape, the hood crumpled a little. The fence shuddered, but it held.

Jacob tried again. He backed up, much less than ten yards this time because the fire was spreading behind him, and then he shot forward once more, but the fence held.

Jacob changed his tactics. He manoeuvred the nose of the truck halfway between two posts. Then he came in slow, in a low gear, pushing the grille into the rails, easing down on the gas, pushing hard, hoping that sustained pressure would achieve what a sharp blow had not. It didn't. The rails bent, and bowed, but they held.

'Here they come,' Reacher said.

Behind them the last vestigial support under the blazing structure gave way and the burning pile settled slowly into a lower and wider shape. Big curled flames danced free. Heat distorted the air and gouts of fire hurled themselves a hundred feet up. Jacob and Seth shrank back, shielded their faces with their arms and ducked away. They climbed the fence. They dropped into the field. They ran.

JACOB AND SETH ran thirty yards, a straight line away from the fire and then they stopped. They saw the Yukon as if for the first time, and they stared at it in confusion, because it was one of theirs. Then they saw Dorothy's truck off in another direction and they understood. They looked at each other one last time, and they ran again, in different directions.

Reacher raised his phone. He said, 'If I'm nine o'clock on a dial and you're twelve, then Jacob is heading for ten and Seth is heading for seven. Seth is mine. Jacob is yours.'

Dorothy said, 'Understood.'

Reacher took his foot off the brake and followed a lazy curve, heading north and then east. Ahead of him Seth was stumbling through the dirt, heading for the road. Reacher saw something in his hand. He heard Dorothy's voice on the phone, 'Jacob has a gun.'

Reacher asked, 'What kind?'

'A handgun. We think it's a regular six-shooter.'

'OK, back off, but keep him in sight. Let him get tired.'

'Understood.'

Reacher laid the phone down and followed Seth, staying thirty yards back. The guy was really hustling. Reacher had no scope, but he was prepared to bet the thing in Seth's hand was a revolver too.

Reacher accelerated and pushed on to within twenty yards. Seth was racing hard, knees pumping, arms pumping. The thing in his hand was definitely a gun. The two-lane road was forty yards away.

Then Seth stopped running, whirled round and aimed his revolver two-handed. His chest was heaving, his limbs were trembling and despite the two-handed grip the muzzle was jerking. Reacher slowed and stood thirty yards off. He felt safe enough. The chances of a panting man hitting the truck with a handgun at ninety feet were slight.

Seth fired three times with a jerky trigger action and no lateral control at all. Reacher didn't even blink. He just watched the muzzle flashes and tried to identify the gun, but he couldn't. Too far away. He assumed it was a six-shooter and that there were three rounds left in it. The phone squawked. He picked it up and Dorothy asked, 'Are you OK? We heard shots fired.'

'I'm good,' Reacher said. 'Are you OK?'

'We're good.'

'Where's Jacob?'

'Still heading south and west. He's slowing down.'

'Stay on him,' Reacher said. He put the phone back on the seat.

Seth rested, bending forward from the waist, forcing air into his lungs. He straightened and aimed the gun again, this time with better control. Reacher turned the wheel, stamped on the gas and took off to his right, and then he feinted to come back on his original line but wrenched the wheel the other way. Seth fired into empty space and then aimed and fired again. A round smacked into the top of the Yukon's windshield, on the passenger side, six feet from Reacher's head. One round left, Reacher thought.

But there were no rounds left. Reacher saw Seth thrashing at the trigger and he saw the gun's wheel turning and turning to no effect. Eventually Seth gave up and hurled the empty gun away. Then he turned and ran again, and the rest of it was easy.

Reacher stamped on the gas, accelerated and lined up carefully and hit Seth from behind doing close to forty miles an hour. The Yukon was a big truck with a high blunt nose, about as subtle as a sledgehammer. It caught Seth flat on his back, and Reacher felt the impact.

Reacher slowed, steered a wide circle and came back to check if any further attention was required. But it wasn't. Reacher had seen plenty of dead people, and Seth was more dead than most of them.

Reacher took the phone off the passenger seat and said, 'Seth is down,' and then he drove away fast, south and west across the field.

Jacob Duncan had got about two hundred yards from his house. That was all. Reacher saw him up ahead with nothing but open space all around. He saw Dorothy's truck a hundred yards farther on. It was holding a wide curve, like a vigilant sheepdog.

On the phone Dorothy said, 'I'm worried about the gun.'

'OK,' Reacher said. 'Pull over and wait for me.'

He clicked off the call, crossed Jacob's path a hundred yards back and headed for Dorothy. When he arrived she got out of her truck and headed for his passenger door. He dropped the window with the switch on his side and said, 'No, you drive. I'll ride shotgun.'

He got out, stepped round and they met at the front of the Yukon's hood.

Dorothy's face was set with determination. She got in the driver's seat, motored it forward and checked the mirror, like it was a normal morning and she was heading out to the store. Reacher climbed in beside her and freed the Glock from his pocket.

She said, 'Tell me about the photographs. In their silver frames. I need to know there's no doubt they implicate the Duncans. Like evidence.'

'There's no doubt,' Reacher said. 'No doubt at all.'

Dorothy nodded and the truck took off. She said, 'The doctor says we should burn down the barn. But I'm not sure I want to do that.'

'Your call, I think.'

'What would you do?'

Reacher said, 'I would nail the judas hole shut and I would leave it alone, never go there again. Let the flowers grow right over it.'

They got within fifty yards of Jacob. He was still running, but he was stumbling and staggering, a short wide man limited by bad lungs and the aches and pains that come with age. He had a revolver, the same dull stainless and stubby barrel as Seth's, and likely to be just as ineffective.

Dorothy asked, 'How do I do this?'

Reacher said, 'Pass him on the left. Let's see if he fights.'

He didn't. Reacher buzzed his window down and hung the Glock out and Dorothy swooped fast and close to Jacob's left and he didn't turn and fire. He just flinched away and stumbled onwards. Reacher said, 'Now come around in a big wide circle and aim right for him from behind.'

'OK,' Dorothy said. She continued the long leftward curve, winding it tighter and tighter until she came back to her original line. Then she hit the gas and the truck leaped forward. Jacob glanced back in horror and darted left. Dorothy flinched right, and she hit Jacob a heavy glancing blow in the back with the left headlight, sending the gun flying, hurling him to the ground.

'Get back quick,' Reacher said.

But Jacob wasn't getting up. He was on his back, one leg pounding away like a dog dreaming, one arm scrabbling uselessly in the dirt, his eyes open and staring, up and down, left and right.

Dorothy drove back and stopped ten yards away. 'What now?'

Reacher said, 'I think you broke his back. He'll die slowly.'

'How long?'

'An hour, maybe two.'

'I don't know.'

Reacher gave her the Glock. 'Or go shoot him in the head. It would be a mercy, not that he deserves it.'

'Will you do it?'

'Gladly, but you should. You've wanted to for twenty-five years.'

She nodded. She stared down at the Glock. She opened the door. And climbed down. 'For Margaret. And for Artie, my husband.'

She went, slowly, with reluctance, and then she crossed the open ground, small neat strides on the dirt, ten of them, twelve, turning a short distance into a long journey. Jacob watched her approach. She stepped up close and pointed the gun straight down, holding it a little away from herself, separating herself from it, and then she said some words Reacher didn't hear, and then she pulled the trigger.

THE DOCTOR AND HIS WIFE were waiting in Dorothy's truck, back on the two-lane road. Reacher and Dorothy parked ahead of them and they all got out. The Duncan compound was reduced to three chimneys and a wide spread of ashy grey timbers. The sun was as high as it was going to get, and the rest of the sky was blue.

Reacher said, 'You've got a lot of work to do. Get everyone on it. Get backhoes, bucket loaders and dig some big holes. Then gather the trash and bury it. But save some space. Their van will arrive at some point. The driver is just as guilty as the rest of them.'

'You're leaving now?' Dorothy asked.

Reacher nodded. 'I'm going to Virginia,' he said.

'What about the football players at my house?'

'Turn them loose and tell them to get out of town. They'll be happy to. There's nothing left for them here.'

DOROTHY DROVE REACHER the first part of the way. They climbed back in the Yukon together and checked the gas gauge. There was enough for maybe sixty miles. They agreed she would take him thirty miles south, and then she would drive the same thirty miles back, and then after that filling the tank would be John's problem.

They drove the first ten miles in silence. Then they passed the abandoned roadhouse and Dorothy asked, 'What's in Virginia?'

'A woman. Someone I talked to on the phone. I wanted to meet her. Although now I'm not so sure. Not yet, looking like this.'

'What's the matter with the way you look?'

'My nose,' Reacher said. He touched the tape. He said, 'It's going to be a couple of weeks before it's presentable.'

'Well, I think you should go. I think if this woman objects to the way you look, then she isn't worth meeting.'

THEY STOPPED on the road halfway between the Apollo Inn and the bar where Reacher had used the phone. Reacher opened his door and Dorothy asked him, 'Will you be OK here?'

'I'll be OK wherever I am. Will you be OK back there?'

'No,' she said. 'But I'll be better than I was.'

She sat behind the wheel, a sixty-year-old woman, worn down by hardship, fading slowly to grey, but better than she had been before. Reacher climbed out and closed his door. She looked at him once and then she turned across the width of the road and drove back north. Reacher jammed his hands in his pockets against the cold, and got set to wait for a ride.

He waited a long, long time. Then he sat down on the shoulder. He was tired. He pulled his hood up over his hat and lay down on the dirt. He crossed his ankles and went to sleep.

It was getting dark when he woke. He sat up, and then he stood. No traffic. But he was a patient man. He was good at waiting.

He waited ten more minutes, and saw a vehicle on the horizon. It had its lights on. He stuck his thumb out. The vehicle was bigger than a car. He could tell by the way the headlights were spaced. It was tall and narrow. It was a panel van, the same kind of panel van as the two grey panel vans he had seen at the Duncan depot.

It slowed and came to a stop right next to him. The driver leaned over, opened the passenger door and a light came on inside.

The driver was Eleanor Duncan. She said, 'Hello.'

Reacher didn't answer. He was looking at the truck. It was travel-stained. It had salt and dirt on it. It had been on a long journey.

He said, 'This was the shipment? This is the truck they used.'

Eleanor Duncan nodded.

He asked, 'Who was in it?'

'Six young women and ten young girls. From Thailand.'

'Were they OK?'

'They were fine. Not surprisingly. It seems that a lot of trouble had been taken to make sure they arrived in marketable condition.'

'Where are they?'

'They're still in the back of this truck.'

'What?'

'We didn't know what to do. They were lured here under false pretences. They were separated from their families. We decided we have to get them home again, so I'm driving them to Denver.'

'What's in Denver?'

'There are Thai restaurants.'

'That's your solution? Thai restaurants?'

'We can't go to the police. These women are illegal. They'll be detained for months, in a government jail. We thought they should be with people who speak their own language. Some restaurant workers were smuggled in themselves. We thought perhaps they could use the same organisations, but in reverse, to get out again.'

'Whose idea was this?'

'Everybody's. We discussed it all day, and then we voted.'

Reacher said nothing. There was a long pause. The van idled, the sky darkened, the air grew colder.

Then Eleanor said, 'You want a ride to the highway?'

Reacher nodded and climbed in. They didn't talk for twenty miles. Then Reacher said, 'You knew, didn't you?'

Eleanor said, 'No.' Then she said, 'Yes.'

'You knew where Seth came from.'

'I told you I didn't. Just before you stole his car.'

'And I didn't believe you. Up to that point you had answered all my questions with no hesitation at all. Then I asked you about Seth, and you stalled. You offered us a drink.'

'Do you know where Seth came from?'

'I figured it out eventually.'

She said, 'So tell me your version.'

Reacher said, 'The Duncans liked little girls. People like that form communities. Back before the Internet they did it by mail, clandestine face-to-face meetings and photo swaps. There were alliances between interest groups. My guess is a group that liked little boys was feeling the heat. They went to ground. They fostered the evidence with their pals. It was supposed to be temporary, until the heat went away, but no one came back for Seth.

The guy was probably beaten to death in jail. So the Duncans were stuck. But they were OK with it. Maybe they thought it was cute, to get a son without the involvement of a woman. So Jacob adopted him.'

Eleanor nodded. 'Seth told me Jacob had rescued him out of an abusive situation. I believed him. Then over the years I sensed the Duncans were doing something bad, but what turned out to be the truth was the last thing on my mental list. Because I felt they were so opposed to that kind of thing, that rescuing Seth had proved it. I thought they were shipping drugs or guns.'

'What changed?'

'Things I heard. It became clear they were shipping people. Even then I thought it was regular illegals, like restaurant workers. But I was getting more suspicious. There was too much money. And too much excitement. Even then I didn't believe it. I thought Seth would find that kind of thing repulsive, because he had suffered it himself. I didn't want to think it could cut the other way. But I guess it did. I'm so ashamed. I'm not going back.'

'So what are you going to do?'

'I'll give this truck to whoever helps the people in it. Then I'm going somewhere else. I'll hitchhike, like you, and start over.'

'Take care on the road. It can be dangerous.'

'I know. But I don't care. I feel like I deserve whatever I get.'

'Don't be too hard on yourself. At least you called the cops.'

'But they never came. How do you know I called the cops?'

'Because they came,' Reacher said. 'That's the one thing no one ever asked me. Everyone knew I was hitchhiking, but no one ever wondered why I had been let out at a crossroads that didn't lead anywhere. Why would a driver stop there?'

'So who was he?'

'A State Police cop, in an unmarked car. He picked me up way to the north and told me he would have to drop me off in the middle of nowhere, because all he was doing was heading down and back. He pulled over, let me out, then turned round and took off.'

'Why would he?'

Reacher said, 'After I got here, I wondered if they'd had a call, and they knew they weren't going to do anything about it, but they needed to be able to prove they'd showed up. Later on I wondered if it was you who'd called.'

'It was me. Four days ago. I told them everything I was thinking. Why didn't the guy even get out of his car?'

'I bet you mentioned Seth beat you,' Reacher said.

'Well, yes, I did. Because he did.'

'Therefore they ignored everything else you said, putting it down to a wronged wife making stuff up to get her husband in trouble. The cops weren't going to tackle the domestic issue. Not against the Duncans. Because of local knowledge. Dorothy told me some neighbourhood kids join the State Police. The message was the same in that corner of that county, you can't mess with the Duncans.'

'I don't believe it.'

'You tried,' Reacher said. 'You tried to do the right thing.'

They drove on and blew past the Chamber of Commerce billboard, past the diner, past the gas station with its Texaco sign, past the hardware store, the liquor store, the bank, the grocery and the pharmacy, and onwards into territory Reacher hadn't seen before. The van's engine muttered low, and Reacher heard sounds from the load space behind him, people talking occasionally, even laughing.

Then an hour and sixty miles later, Reacher saw bright vapour lights at the highway cloverleaf, and big green signs pointing west and east. Eleanor slowed and stopped and Reacher got out and waved her away. She used the first ramp, west towards Denver and Salt Lake City, and he walked under the bridge and set up on the eastbound ramp, one foot on the shoulder, one in the traffic lane, and he stuck out his thumb and smiled and tried to look friendly.

lee **child**

For many people redundancy is a truly frightening prospect, but for some it can be a catalyst for change and take them down a completely different path. This is exactly what happened to Lee Child.

Born Jim Grant in 1954 in Coventry, he started out studying law but switched to a more compelling interest in drama. That move led to a successful eighteen-year career in television at Granada studios in Manchester, where he worked in production on a number of prestigious series such as *Brideshead Revisited*, *Prime Suspect*, *The Jewel in the Crown*, and *Cracker*. 'It was a great job—I loved it,' Child says. 'Absolutely loved it. And if I hadn't been fired, I would still be doing it and still loving it. But I was fired.'

Suddenly, without a job at the age of forty, and with a wife and young daughter to support, he took an enormous risk. 'What I wanted was to stay in the world of entertainment,' Lee Child says. 'I mean, that's all I've ever wanted to do. It's all I've ever been good at. And I thought, Well, I know the audience, I know how they think. Let's try writing a book.' But Jim Grant, now with the pen name Lee Child, also knew that the odds were stacked against him. 'I remember, when I lost my job, my dad said, "What are you gonna do?" And I said, "I'm gonna write a book." And he said, "I'll lay ya ten thousand to one it won't work." And I guess that's pretty accurate—ten thousand to one—probably those were about the right odds.'

Undaunted by the uncertainty, Lee Child sat down at his kitchen table with nothing but a legal pad and a pencil, coffee and cigarettes to hand, and began to write. It took him five months to finish *Killing Floor*, which is set in the United States and introduces the character who would secure Lee Child's place as one of today's greatest mystery writers: a 6 foot 5 inch tall, 250-pound, ex-US Army military cop named Jack Reacher. A hard guy with a tough-sounding name that, ironically, Child came up with while grocery shopping with his wife Jane. 'I was out of work, so we went to the supermarket. And every time that I've ever been in a supermarket, I walk in, and a little old lady comes up to me and says, "You're a nice tall gentleman. Would you reach me that can?" So my wife said, "You know what? If this writing gig doesn't work out, you could be a reacher in a supermarket." And I thought, Good name!'

Lee Child has now written fifteen books starring Jack Reacher, all of which have gone straight into the best-seller lists, selling more than forty million copies in seventy-five countries and translated into more than forty languages. 'It's a funny feeling,' the author says. 'You don't want to come right out and say, "Yeah, you know, I'm thrilled about it." But I am. It's really a great thing to know that all around the world, right this second, somebody is reading one of those books.'

But there was a moment when his legions of fans thought they might have read the last Reacher adventure. At the end of *61 Hours*, the novel before *Worth Dying For*, Lee Child left his readers on a cliffhanger, with Jack Reacher trapped in an underground bunker, his fate unclear. 'How could he not survive? I've got bills to pay,' quips Child.

One question he gets asked more than any other is how an Englishman, who drives a Jaguar and supports Aston Villa, can write something as distinctly American as the Jack Reacher crime series? 'I really can't help it. I live in America. I travel a lot. I see stuff everywhere. And it makes an impression . . . There are five hundred 24/7 cable channels, a million websites, a million magazines, and everyone has a story, everyone knows a guy who knows a guy. Americans are friendly and unguarded and talkative. Plus—and here's the thing—every crazy thing happens here.'

Like Dirty Harry and Phillip Marlowe, Reacher is the latest incarnation of the noble loner . . . strong silent types who drift into trouble, righting wrongs along the way. 'We walk around and, whoever we are, we're somewhat nervous, somewhat intimidated,' Lee Child says. 'Wouldn't it be great just to know for sure, for absolute certain, that you've got nothing to be afraid of? Reacher's one hundred per cent confident. He walks into those situations—three bad guys, six bad guys, whatever—he knows they're gonna lose, you know? It's simply a question of, are they gonna be limping for a week, or are they gonna be in a wheelchair the rest of their lives?'

In the hands of this master craftsman, Jack Reacher has become that rare literary creation—a character so well drawn he's inspired a cult following that call themselves, 'Reacher Creatures' and competitions have taken place worldwide to find Reacher look-alikes. With a fan base like this, it's little surprise that Hollywood has come calling, optioning all the Jack Reacher books, amid much speculation surrounding who the actor will be who could fill Jack Reacher's shoes.

In his New York City apartment, Lee Child is already hard at work on Reacher's next adventure . . . coffee and cigarettes still close to hand. After fifteen books has his style and approach to writing changed? 'I still don't write a plot outline,' he says. 'I try to feel the same excitement that I hope the reader will: never knowing what's coming on the next page.'

AJ

Dambuster

Robert Radcliffe

RAF Scampton, Lincolnshire, May 1943.

Wing Commander Guy Gibson and the brave men of the newly formed 617 Squadron have been set a most audacious objective, using Barnes Wallis's innovative bouncing bomb.

As they train and fine-tune their plans around the clock, the critics are many, the believers few . . .

Tense, thrilling and meticulously researched, this re-telling of the legendary Dambuster story blends fact and fiction, breathing new life into the airborne action, as well as creating a new and gripping human drama.

CHAPTER 1

Sometimes, Quentin Credo mused, it wasn't murderous rivers of machine-gun bullets that destroyed a bomber and its crew, or exploding antiaircraft shells fired from below, or collisions with other bombers in the darkness, or even being hit by bombs dropped from aircraft above. Sometimes it had nothing to do with bullets and bombs at all. Sometimes it was just bad luck. He leafed through the file in front of him, picturing as he did so exactly how it must have been for Flying Officer Peter Lightfoot and his crew . . .

'NAVIGATOR TO PILOT.'

'Go ahead, Navigator.'

'Our estimated position is sixty miles northeast of Lyon. We should probably start the climb to twenty thousand feet.'

'Understood, Navigator, thanks.' Probably? Peter glanced up from the blind-flying panel to the windscreen. Probably was not a word his navigator used routinely. But then little about this mission was going routinely. He peered through the windscreen. Beyond it lay an impenetrable black fog, the same fog that had enveloped them within minutes of leaving Nottinghamshire. In the three hours since, he and his crew had seen nothing—no ground, no moon, no stars, nothing. And nothing, disconcertingly, of the fifty other bombers growling through the turbulent night sky around them. All they'd seen was cloud and darkness. And now a layer of rime-ice was building up on the wings; one more cause for concern. One among several. He turned his gaze back to the artificial horizon, only to find another: the Lancaster was flying left wing low again. He hauled it level, reaching once more for the aileron trim wheel, yet, despite patient adjustment, the bomber doggedly refused to fly on an even keel. He gave up trimming and resigned himself to flying an out-of-kilter aeroplane. Unaided. Beside him the automatic pilot panel glowed uselessly, an 'Unserviceable' label hanging from it like a taunt. No autopilot meant hand-flying the thirty-ton aeroplane all the way to Turin and back. Eight hours or more without a break, all of it on instruments, and one wing drooping. He reached for the intercom switch. 'Pilot to Navigator, just how estimated is that position, Jamie?'

'Very,' replied his navigator. 'I got a reasonable Gee fix about an hour ago, but Chalkie thinks the set's on the blink. There's no chance of a star-sight in all this clag, so it's strictly dead reckoning. We should probably start that climb to twenty thousand, don't you think?'

Yes, we should, Peter acknowledged privately. But up there lurked some very unpleasant weather indeed, the Met officer had cautioned: embedded cumulonimbus with the possibility of severe turbulence, icing and associated thunderstorm activity, and Peter was in no hurry to fly into it. On the other hand, the Met officer had added cheerily, the weather on the other side would be much better. So that was all right then. As though as a foretaste, the creaking Lancaster lurched suddenly, bucking in turbulence like a bus hitting a pothole, and Peter was jerked hard up against his straps as he wrestled for control. Comments followed:

'Ouch, that was a big one.'

'Now I've spilt my soup, damn it!'

'Did you feel the wings flexing? God, this aeroplane's a wreck.'

'Are you sure we haven't been recalled?'

'Navigator to Pilot, ah, about that climb—'

'It's all right, Jamie,' Peter cut in. 'Any minute now.'

He steadied the bomber. Jamie sounded anxious, he thought, but then Jamie always sounded anxious. His navigator sat in a tiny cubicle behind the Lancaster's flight deck, a curtain drawn round him so he could use his map light without disturbing the pilot's night vision. In all the missions they'd flown together Peter had never known Jamie voluntarily open his curtain, no matter how bloody the action, how intense the antiaircraft fire, or how violent the escape manoeuvres Peter subjected the aeroplane to. Yet the twenty-two-year-old clerk from Croydon never allowed his fear to affect his navigation, which at times bordered on the miraculous. So if Jamie thought it was probably time to climb to 20,000 feet, then it probably was.

Because despite the horrible weather up there, and Chalkie at the radio missing two command broadcasts because of static, and the ice building up on the wings, and the starboard outer engine running hotter and hotter—despite all the snags and niggles, to complete the mission they *had* to make the climb to 20,000 feet. To get over the Alps.

Turin, the Alps, they'd done it once before, but beneath clear skies and in good weather, when in the moonlight the mountains were magnificent to behold. Attempting it in February, at night, in zero visibility, though, was little short of lunacy. Peter was amazed the mission hadn't been aborted due to bad weather, but there was little choice other than to press on, prepare to unload their bombs on the Fiat aero-engine works. The only positive note amid all the negatives was an uncanny absence of the enemy. Not a peep, all the way down through France; no night fighters, no searchlights, no flak, nothing. All sitting by the fire warming their feet, Peter supposed, and who could blame them?

He reached for the throttle levers. Time to start that climb. As he did so his flight engineer, MacDowell, sitting on his fold-down seat beside him, turned and looked at Peter, eyes questioning. Though they sat inches apart, normal conversation was impossible above the mind-numbing thunder of four Rolls-Royce Merlin engines. They could use the intercom, which meant fiddling with the switches in their masks, but after many missions together Peter had learned to read MacDowell's expression. Currently it spoke of resigned exasperation. Peter held up four fingers, then a wavering thumbs-up, which meant: How is the number-four engine behaving? MacDowell gestured at the engine's temperature gauge, which had now almost reached the red line, then rolled his eyes and shrugged, which meant: Your guess is as good as mine, this aeroplane is a piece of junk.

'Navigator to Pilot. I really think we ought to be starting that climb.'

'Yes, you're right, Navigator, we're just about to. Hello, Pilot to Crew, we're going to make the climb now, be sure your oxygen is fully on, and you might want to strap in tight, it's likely to get rough up there.'

'Oh joy.'

'Is that ice I see on the wings?'

'Are you sure we haven't been recalled?'

'Pilot to Radio. Anything, Chalkie?'

'Not a thing, Pilot. But the static's awful.'

'Right, well, we'd better get it over with. Everyone check in, please.'

One by one they checked in: flight engineer, navigator, radio operator, mid-upper gunner, rear gunner, everyone but the bomb aimer. Then:

'Bomb Aimer to Pilot.'

'Yes, hello, Bomb Aimer, what is it?'

'That awful smell down here in the nose. The one I told you about? Well, it's a dead rat. I just found it under my seat. What should I do with it?'

'Tie your hanky on it for a parachute then chuck it out over the target!'

'The Eyeties will think it's a spy in disguise and shoot it!'

'Eat it more like, knowing Italians.'

'Rat-a-touille.'

Peter reached for the four throttle levers once more. This time he eased the throttles forward, the thunder of labouring engines turned to a roar and the Lancaster began the long climb to 20,000 feet.

'Rear gun to Pilot.'

'Hello, Rear, what is it?'

'Nothing. Just making sure you received my check-in message.'

HERB GUTTENBERG had a fixation about intercom messages being received and acknowledged. Peter had become aware of this soon after he and his new crew began flying together. 'The rear gunner,' he murmured to MacDowell one day. 'Guttenberg. Why do you think he keeps asking for intercom checks?'

'Perhaps he's a wee bit deaf or something,' MacDowell suggested.

'I'll have a word with the upper gunner, Bimson, they seem to be mates.'

They had first formed as a crew of seven six months before, in the summer of 1942, while training to operate Lancasters at a Heavy Conversion Unit in Yorkshire. All seven men were sergeants, proudly equal under the eyes of God, and not an officer among them. And all had, against intractable odds and at some personal cost, already survived one tour of thirty operations. Apart from MacDowell, who was oldest by a decade and thus had always been nicknamed 'Uncle', none was over twenty-four. Comprising an English pilot, navigator and radio operator, two Canadian gunners, a bomb aimer from New Zealand and a Scots flight engineer, the seven men were highly experienced, highly attuned to the job, and, unsurprisingly, given all they'd endured, not a little highly strung.

Herb Guttenberg no more so than any other. He and Billy Bimson were indeed best friends, MacDowell reported, following Peter's query about intercom checks. The pair had joined the Royal Canadian Air Force together straight from school, trained together as gunners, but parted when they had transferred to Bomber Command in England. Bimson joined 50 Squadron and Guttenberg joined 102 Squadron as a rear gunner in Whitleys. One autumn morning in 1941, Bimson related, Herb's Whitley returned from a long mission over enemy territory to find England blanketed by fog. Tired, anxious and low on fuel, the pilot flew in hopeless circles trying to locate his position and find a way down. Eventually he set the controls on autopilot and gave the order to bale out. But Herb never heard the order, for his intercom hadn't been working properly all night. So while the rest of the crew floated to safety, he flew on alone, idly watching the fog-bound earth drifting by below. Twenty minutes later, the Whitley crash-landed itself into a field outside Kettering. Herb clung on grimly as the machine careered across the field before slewing to an undignified halt.

'Bit of a rough landing, Pilot,' he scolded over his dead intercom, then clambered from the wreckage to find himself alone. Only luck had saved the rear gunner's life and everyone knew it.

So Herb made frequent intercom checks, and that was fine with Peter, because after forty or fifty missions everyone had foibles. Even Uncle MacDowell, who was utterly unflappable, even he had foibles, wearing a clean uniform for every operation, and shining his shoes. And during the run-in to the target, when the aircraft flew straight and level for endless minutes, Chalkie White, who could strip down and rebuild a radio blindfold, his foible was to hold a photo of his wife Vicky inches from his face and stare into her eyes. All that mattered was being good at your job, and Peter's crew quickly became superb at it.

THE MISSION had been recalled. From Turin. They just didn't know it, for along with many other defects in the replacement aeroplane they were flying, the long-range radio was faulty. It worked, but not to full power, which together with the extreme distance and poor atmospheric conditions meant that Chalkie had not received all the half-hourly command broadcasts, the last two of which had signalled cancellation of the mission.

Buffeted by increasingly fierce turbulence, Peter fought to keep the bomber upright and climbing. Twelve thousand feet, thirteen, with each passing milestone the machine felt heavier and more lethargic in his hands. Glancing outboard he saw ice was now accumulating rapidly on the wings and round the engine air intakes, while a look up through the Lancaster's huge 'greenhouse' canopy showed no hoped-for clearing of the sky above, only the churning black, now lit occasionally by flickers of lightning. Then a storm of hailstones began hitting the windscreen like flung gravel, deafening even above the roar of the engines. Peter urged the bomber upwards, while the others hung on to their seat-straps, then twenty-year-old Billy Bimson, perched in his vantage point in the upper turret, let out a shout.

'Jesus, look at the propellers! They're on fire!'

Faces peered out in alarm. Sure enough, arcs of eerie blue light shimmered round the propellers, glowing like fiery blue haloes. Billy Bimson saw them, Kiwi Garvey in the nose could see them, MacDowell saw them too and turned to Peter in incomprehension.

Herb in the tail couldn't see them. 'What did Billy say?' he called uneasily. 'Did he say fire?'

'It's all right!' Garvey called. 'It's that St Elmer's thing. Static electricity, from the thunderclouds. Nothing to worry about.'

'Well it looks like fire to me.'

'It's St *Elmo*, Kiwi,' Chalkie corrected. 'Not *Elmer*. They used to see it on the masts of sailing ships when . . .'

Just then, and with an earsplitting crash, a lightning bolt exploded against the fuselage, instantly filling the interior with acrid smoke and dancing blue sparks that leapt round the airframe like sprites. Fuses blew, circuit breakers popped, gyros toppled; in a stroke the aircraft was blinded and crippled. On the flight deck the panel-lights failed, plunging the instruments into darkness. Out on the wings the port outer engine, maimed by the lightning, faltered, belched smoke and sparks, and with a tortured whine began to seize on its mountings.

Peter stamped right rudder as the Lancaster yawed towards the doomed engine, the whole airframe shuddering from its death throes. 'I can't hold her, Uncle!' he shouted.

MacDowell snatched up a torch, playing its beam over the instruments. 'It's blown a bearing! We'll have to kill it now before it tears the wing off.' Peter nodded, grimacing with effort as MacDowell swiftly shut off fuel to the engine, pulled back its throttle and mixture levers and pushed the propeller feather button.

In moments the dreadful juddering eased. A few seconds more and Peter had retrimmed the rudders and regained control of the stricken bomber.

MacDowell held the torch on the blind-flying panel. 'OK?' he shouted.

'I . . . I think so.' Peter scanned the panel through the haze of smoke, retrimming as he went. Under normal conditions he knew a fully loaded Lancaster should fly acceptably on only three engines. It might even be persuaded to climb a little. Under normal conditions. Which these weren't. 'She feels heavy, but all right, I think. Though half the instruments are out, so God knows. What about the others? Try the intercom.'

The smell of smoke in the cockpit was strong. Both men feared fire back in the fuselage. Still gingerly testing the controls, Peter waited for the reassuring clicks of his crew checking in, but though MacDowell's mouth was working, no voices filled his ears. MacDowell shook his head. 'Nothing!' Then Kiwi's face appeared in the nose-tunnel by their feet, tapping his ear and shaking his head. MacDowell gestured the bomb aimer up and gave him the torch. 'I'll go aft!' he shouted, unbuckling his harness.

Ten minutes went by. With lightning still flickering all around, and Kiwi at his side holding the torch, Peter flew the aeroplane and took stock. It was a grim audit. Apart from the dead engine and blown instrument lights, his gyrocompass repeater was dead, as was his direction indicator, which left only the small standby magnetic compass to give heading information. But the standby compass wandered in useless circles, confounded by the magnetic interference of the storm. So he had no means of telling direction.

And there was more. The altimeter was working, as was the air-speed indicator, but little rate of climb showed and the air speed was inexorably falling, despite full power to the remaining three engines. And every few seconds a loud report rang through the aeroplane, as though someone was throwing rocks at them. Ice forming on the propellers was flying off in chunks to strike the fuselage. He risked another look out at the wings, where thick accretions of clear ice now covered the leading edges. He could feel the weight of it overloading the bomber, and the shape of it degrading its lift. Much more and the Lancaster would simply fall from the sky. He lowered the nose to preserve speed. Now the bomber was barely holding level.

'Flight Engineer to Pilot.' A Scots voice broke over the headphones.

'Yes, Uncle, Pilot here! What's happening? Is everyone all right?'

'Everyone's fine. I'm with Chalkie. Couple of small electrical fires are out, smoke's dispersing and we've managed to get battery power to the intercom. Hydraulics are out, burst manifold somewhere. Chalkie's working on the direction finder and trying to get some lighting back, Jamie's navigating by torch, everything else—radios, Gee set, nav equipment, bomb panel—is pretty well smoked.'

Bomb panel. The 14,000 pounds of high explosives nestling in the huge bomb bay. Without power to the panel, he'd be unable to release them.

'Pilot to Navigator.'

'Navigator here.'

'Jamie, I've got no DF and no standby compass, so I'm probably going round in circles.'

'So I see. Can you hold present heading for a minute or two? There's a spare compass in the emergency bag. I'll get Billy to bring it up.'

'Thanks I, ah, stand by a moment . . .' The wheel had begun to shake in Peter's hands. Suddenly the stall warning shrieked. At once he pushed forward, but too late. There came a falling sensation, like a big dipper at the funfair, a mushing feeling in the wheel, then a wing began to drop sideways. He kicked full rudder to hold it, seconds of agonised waiting followed, then with a lurch the nose fell, the shaking stopped and the Lancaster was diving, losing height, but recovering speed and control. It had stalled, nearly fallen into a full-blown spin, lost 500 feet in seconds, and, Peter knew, might never have recovered. He held the nose down now to gain more speed, before carefully raising it back to horizontal. His eyes checked the panel, Kiwi white-faced beside him with the torch. The bomber was flying again, but only just. Something was happening to the engines. They sounded strained, and their note was changing.

'Navigator to Pilot. Is everything all right up there, Peter?'

'Yes. No. The ice. We stalled, and the engines don't sound . . . Can you get Uncle up here?'

'Will do. What height are we at?'

'Thirteen and a half thousand and we're starting to lose it. And we're also losing power, get MacDowell up here!'

But MacDowell was already there, torch beam searching the dials.

'What's happening?' he said, plugging in his intercom.

'I . . . I don't know. It's the engines. The throttles are wide but they're losing power.'

MacDowell shone the beam over the wings. 'Christ! It's the air intakes. Look, they're all iced up. The engines are starved of air!'

Thirty seconds later, the Lancaster's remaining three engines, their air intakes completely blocked by ice, spluttered one by one to silence.

It was to be their final mission. Ever. Yet of B-Baker's crew, only Peter knew. He had found out that morning. Squadron Leader Walker had called him in for a chat, then begun scattering bombshells like confetti. Barely was Peter through the door before the first one exploded.

'Come in, Peter, and do sit down.' Walker beamed. 'Or, should I say, *Flying Officer* Lightfoot!'

Peter was astonished. And shocked. Commissioned as an officer? After so long in the ranks. *Flying Officer*. His crew would have to call him 'Sir'.

'You'll make a splendid officer, I'm sure,' Walker went on. 'And, by Jove, you've earned it. You've also earned this . . .' He handed Peter a memo. 'It's the Distinguished Flying Cross. Harris himself has approved it, look: "*In over fifty missions with Bomber Command, F/Sgt Lightfoot has demonstrated unflinching determination and dependability. This award could not be better deserved.*" What do you say to that, Peter?'

Peter still didn't know what to say. And before he could think of anything, the squadron leader dropped his third bombshell.

'Splendid. Now then, here's the thing. 61 Squadron is being detached to Aldergrove in Northern Ireland for a spell with Coastal Command. But I'm finishing your tour after tonight. You and your crew have done enough.'

'But . . . but, sir, we've still got two or three missions to . . .'

'I'm aware of that, Peter, but a second tour's a movable feast, as well you know. Twenty missions plus or minus a couple, what's the difference? You've done nearly sixty in all, and Group agrees that's more than enough. What's the matter? I should think you'd be delighted.'

'Well, yes, sir, I am, of course . . .'

'That's the spirit. So tonight is your last op out of Syerston, your last op of the war, and, you'll be happy to hear, an easy one to finish with . . .'

And he'd gone on to explain about Turin, and the need to go back there, to bottle up enemy forces as a diversion to Allied landings in North Africa, to demoralise the Italians who seemed ready to throw in the towel, and to knock out the Fiat factory, which was a key strategic target. But Peter wasn't listening, he was in shock. It was over, he kept thinking, everything he'd worked for, trained for and fought for. This was the moment he'd yearned for, and yet somehow dreaded, for more than three years. He didn't know whether to laugh or cry.

Walker was still talking and, impossibly, still dropping bombshells. 'There'll be about fifty aircraft taking part, from 1 and 5 Groups, plus a

Pathfinder flight to mark the target. The weather looks a bit iffy, but nothing you can't handle. Should be a breeze. Oh, but there is one more thing . . .'

Peter could barely take it in. 'There is?'

'You can't use your usual aeroplane, Q-Queenie. A supercharger needs changing apparently, so you'll have to take B-Baker. Bit of a hack, but it should get you there all right.'

B-Baker? Peter was aghast. B-Baker. The squadron spare. It was a joke, a total wreck. Crews avoided it like the plague. Peter wanted to protest, but Walker was already on his feet, pumping his hand and ushering him outside to the adjutant's office, where the final bombshell awaited.

'Sergeant Lightfoot?' the adjutant said. 'I've your mail here.' Peter took the two letters and stepped outside into the freezing February morning. I'll keep it as a surprise, he decided. About this being our last op. I won't tell the others until we get safely back. Then he'd opened his letters. One, he read with sinking heart, contained his orders to go on leave after the mission, then report to 19 OTU in Lossiemouth, Scotland, where he was to become a flying instructor. The other, impossibly, after six years of silence, was a letter from the girl who had got him into all this: Tess Derby.

STRANGELY, PETER FELT no panic when the Lancaster's remaining engines failed. Choices were gone, he realised. Now it was just a matter of procedure, and time. Quickly and calmly he lowered the nose and retrimmed, until the Lancaster was gliding down the freezing air at a steady 130 mph, a descent rate of 900 feet per minute. Settled in the glide, Peter glanced at MacDowell, then flicked on his intercom.

'Pilot to Crew. Sorry, everyone, she's had it. Bale out and let's be quick about it. We'll go out through the nose-hatch, it's safer. Kiwi, you go and open it, everyone else check in.'

One by one they checked in, then began squeezing onto the flight deck and down the narrow access-way to the bomb-aimer's position.

Chalkie White stopped. 'What about you two sods?'

'Uncle goes after everyone else,' Peter replied. 'Then I secure the wheel and follow.'

He met MacDowell's glance. Both knew that without an autopilot the chances of Peter making it out were slim. Chalkie waited his turn to enter the tunnel, feet braced against the sloping deck. Behind him, Jamie Johnson hovered near his navigator's cubicle, stuffing pencils and maps into his pockets as he clipped on his parachute. A moment later a blast of freezing air signalled that Kiwi had successfully jettisoned the nose-hatch.

Kiwi grimaced. 'Told you I should've joined the Navy!' he said. 'Right then, boys, here goes nothing!' He unplugged his intercom and lowered his legs into the slipstream until he was sitting in the narrow hatchway.

Just then they heard it. A cough, far out on the starboard wing, followed by a loud report, like a gunshot. Bimson and Guttenberg looked at each other. 'What was that?'

'Hold on!' Peter's voice rang over the intercom. 'Hold on, for Christ's sake, I think we're getting one back!' An engine. One of the engines was firing. They could hear it, banging and spluttering like a backfiring lorry. All except Kiwi Garvey, who was half out of the hatch.

Up on the flight deck, MacDowell was juggling throttle and mixture levers to the starboard outer engine. 'Come on, you big bastard,' he muttered furiously. 'You can do it, come ON!'

Chalkie looked on. 'What the hell's happening?'

'Lower altitude.' Peter stared at the engine's rev counter. 'Ice must be melting a bit.'

Still MacDowell nursed the controls, cursing and coaxing, while the giant bomber slipped steadily downwards. Then, with a sudden tattoo of explosive backfiring, the Merlin roared to life. 'Got you!'

Peter felt the exhilarating surge through the controls as the engine powered up, but at the same instant knew it wasn't enough. 'Well done, Uncle!' he encouraged. 'Try the port inner. If we can get another going we've a chance.' MacDowell quickly throttled the number four to full power, while Jamie Johnson dived back into his cubicle. In the nose, Bimson and Guttenberg struggled to drag Garvey back aboard.

'Come back! Uncle's got an engine running!'

In a short while Uncle had a second engine running, the port inner, but that was all, for the port outer was wrecked and the starboard inner refused to unfeather. Using maximum throttle on both good engines, Peter was gradually able to reduce the rate of descent until he had it stabilised at 8,000 feet. A few minutes later, with everyone still in the forward part of the aeroplane, intercoms were plugged in and an impromptu conference convened.

'This is Navigator. I can't be sure, but the fact we're still here suggests we've cleared the highest peaks. Or we got lucky and transited through the Col Madeleine or something.'

'Well, boys, I'm for staying,' Kiwi said firmly. 'I've been out there and I can tell you it ain't hospitable.'

'A mighty long walk to anywhere too,' Uncle added.

'Too right. I vote we stick with the crate and try to make it home.'

'Yeah, but the crate's a total wreck.'

'Herb's right,' Peter interjected. 'We're flying in a ruined machine on only two engines, one of them badly overheated. If either loses power again we've had it. But if we can stay airborne for fifteen minutes or so, we'll be clear of the mountains and over Italy. It'll be safe to jump then.'

'I'm with Herb on this,' Billy Bimson said. 'I think we should jump.'

'So jump then, you crazy Canadian, I'm staying.'

'Well, would you look at that,' MacDowell's Glaswegian tones broke in. He was staring upwards through the greenhouse roof. 'Up there lads, aye, look.' Seven heads peered skywards. And saw stars, sparkling against the firmament like jewels on velvet. Just for a few seconds, then they were gone. Somehow the sighting changed everything.

'The cloud's breaking,' MacDowell went on quietly. 'I think it's a good sign. I think we should all return to our positions and do what we can to get this aeroplane home.'

So they did. They held their original southerly course, stayed away from Turin, cleared the mountains past Vinadio, then turned southwest. With dawn soon to break, all agreed that turning north to fly home through occupied France—an unescorted British bomber flying low and slow in broad daylight—was to invite certain disaster, so Jamie plotted a westerly route to the Bay of Biscay, then a curving sweep out over the Atlantic, before turning northeast for Cornwall. It was as ambitious a plan as it was long, but all agreed it was the safest option, and set eagerly to the task.

By the time they coasted out over the Atlantic near Arcachon, daylight was flooding the flight deck. Peter and MacDowell exchanged hopeful glances. The land was behind them, together with its threat of detection. Below them now lay a different foe: the cobalt-blue waters of the ocean. Fuel was going to be tight, but their luck had held thus far, so maybe, their eyes said wordlessly, just maybe . . .

IT WAS NOT to be. They were working on a means of jettisoning the bombs. Fuel was getting critical, and no one wanted to make an emergency landing with bombs still aboard. But with no hydraulics and no electrical power, opening the bomb-bay doors and safely releasing the bombs was problematic. A back-up compressed-air system was available to blow open the doors, but no one knew whether enough compressed air would remain to close the doors again and lower the wheels for landing. In the end the fuel situation won the day and they elected to try the doors. Uncle pressurised the system; down in the nose Kiwi removed the safety pin and pressed the lever. With a resounding hiss the doors blew down, and seconds later Peter felt the Lancaster surge upwards as the bombs fell to the ocean.

Without warning, the starboard outer engine then blew up. It had been running hot all night, since the Alps, and finally it had failed. Just as the bomb doors were hissing shut, they all heard a bang on the wing, gouts of black smoke and sparks flew, slicks of boiling oil poured forth, and the engine wound swiftly down to silence.

Little was said, for little needed saying. With just one engine remaining the Lancaster was finished and everyone knew it. Once again, Peter found himself lowering the nose and trimming for descent, while around the aircraft everyone else prepared, resignedly and without fuss. Parachutes were discarded, spare clothing donned, Mae West life vests inflated. Water bottles, uneaten sandwiches, soup flasks, chocolate bars, were gathered in a bag together with first-aid kit, torches, a flare gun and cartridges. Chalkie White used the last of the battery power to send out an SOS, before screwing down the Morse key in permanent transmit.

'What about the pigeons?' Billy Bimson asked at one point. In the event of forced landing or ditching at sea, two homing pigeons were carried in a canister on every British bomber on every mission. Opinions varied as to the correct procedure to use them.

'Hang on to them until after we ditch, do you think?'

'I heard you were supposed to chuck one out before ditching and one after. You know . . . in case of a problem during the ditching.'

'Chuck one out at a hundred miles per hour and it'll be blown to bits.'

While Billy held the birds, Jamie wrote details on slips of paper that he then rolled into tiny cylinders attached to each pigeon's leg. Then Billy replaced both birds in the canister.

'We've about a minute, everyone,' Peter called. 'Everyone take up crash positions aft the main spar. Get the dinghy released as soon as possible after we ditch. Good luck, see you in the water.'

Alone now in the cockpit, he made ready. The sky was completely free of cloud and bright shards of sunlight ricocheted off the sea, which raced by below like burnished steel. He banked a little to line up parallel to the waves, then at sixty feet he throttled the remaining engine back to idle, noting how breathtakingly near the sea looked at that height. The left wing was hanging slightly low, he noted, so he lifted it level one final time. Then he settled the Lancaster onto the water.

It was worse than expected, and it was better. The bomber hit, skipped once like a stone on a pond, then hit again, this time for good. The nose dug deep, everyone was hurled forward, the tail rose almost to vertical, then slowly sank back level. In the cockpit Peter watched in awe as the view outside turned green, then darker green, while a solid shaft of freezing ocean jetted up at him from the open nose-hatch. She's diving for the bottom, he thought. In seconds the water was swirling waist-deep round him. Gasping in the sudden cold he freed his straps, clambered onto his seat and began hammering at the Perspex escape hatch in the roof. At first it wouldn't budge, sealed by the weight of water pressing on it, then suddenly he saw sunlight as the bomber resurfaced, the catches freed, the hatch sprang clear and he was hauling himself up into daylight.

The others were already out, swimming gamely for the life raft, which had popped automatically from its housing in the wing. The Lancaster was sitting level but settling fast. Peter ran back along the fuselage roof to join them, as one by one they flopped into the dinghy, gasping like landed fish. A moment of panic ensued, when Billy remembered the pigeons and swam back to retrieve the canister. Then another panic as the Lancaster began to sink and Kiwi had difficulty severing it from the dinghy. Finally Uncle took an axe to the cord, they quickly paddled clear, and then watched in silence as B-Baker slipped quietly beneath the waves and vanished.

'Bugger me, it's gone.' Kiwi shivered.

Their enemy now was the cold. And the clock. The North Atlantic in midwinter, in a tiny open boat, was no place to linger. Their Type 'J' inflatable life raft was little bigger than a tractor tyre and offered no protection from the elements. Though the sky was clear and the sea slight, waves constantly slopped aboard, requiring them to bail frequently and ensuring that their legs were permanently soaked. In no time they were stiff with cold. They had food and water enough, but long before they ran out of either, exposure would sap the life from them. Probably within two days.

For a long while nothing was said. Apart from the effects of shock and cold, all were drained and exhausted. Then, late morning, Uncle broke up a bar of chocolate, poured the remainder of Chalkie's soup into a mug and passed them round. 'All right, lads, let's see you tuck in.'

'No, thanks, Uncle,' Herb said. 'Couldn't keep it down.'

'I'm no joking, laddie. If you don't eat, you'll die.'

'Uncle's right,' Chalkie added. 'Try a little, Herb. My Vicky made it.'

'Oh, well, OK . . .' Herb sipped soup, then passed the mug on.

'Say, Kiwi, it looks like you got your wish to join the Navy.'

'Ha bloody ha.'

'Chalkie, do you think anyone heard your SOS?'

'God knows. If they did the air-sea rescue boys will be on their way.'

'Well, I bloody hope so, because it's bloody cold.' Kiwi shuddered.

'The pigeons.' Jamie Johnson straightened from reverie. 'The homing pigeons. We should release them.'

The canister was duly retrieved and the birds withdrawn. Having checked that his notes were still attached, Jamie held the first pigeon aloft, then to a cheer from the others tossed it skywards. The operation was repeated, with increased vigour, but this time the bird merely flew round in a circle then landed back on the dinghy.

'Stupid bird!' Chalkie cursed, swatting it feebly.

'We could always eat it,' Billy mused. 'If things got desperate.'

'In case you hadn't noticed, you daft Canuck, things *are* desperate.'

'Kiwi, I told you before about using that word, now take it back.'

'Take it back? I'd like to see you make me.' A half-hearted kicking match followed, enough to slop more water into the dinghy.

'Right, you two can just stop that,' Uncle ordered.

'Oh, yes?' Kiwi countered. 'Says who?'

'Me,' Peter said quietly. 'I order you to stop.'

'What?'

'They've made me an F/O.'

The men looked at each other in bafflement.

'Blimey. Flying Officer la-di-da Lightfoot. Who'd have thought it?'

'There's something else. This was our last op. Group's finishing our tour early. Squadron's being detached to Aldergrove, they want the aircraft to train new crews. They say we've done enough.'

'They got that bloody right.'

'Jesus! I don't believe it. We're done. Finished.'

Further silence followed as they digested this, then slowly, and rather solemnly, the seven men leaned across and shook hands with one another.

'Well done, Jamie, old mate.'

'Congratulations to you too, Chalkie.'

'Drink-up tonight eh, boys?'

'Well done, Herb, well done, Billy. No hard feelings, eh?'

'Thanks, Kiwi. And thanks, Uncle. For everything.'

'You're welcome. Well done, everyone.'

The morning dragged on. Around noon cloud began to amass from the west, bringing a bitter wind that cut through their wet clothing and splashed more water into the dinghy. With their discomfort complete, and now dangerously chilled and fatigued, they began to bail less, talk less, and care less. Knee-deep in the freezing water, one by one they lapsed into torpor.

Peter, too. He found himself thinking of Tess, the girl he hadn't seen or spoken to in six years, yet whose memory remained for ever fresh. Why now, he wondered, after all this time, had she decided to get in touch? Her letter, still carefully tucked in his breast pocket, said so much, yet so frustratingly little. *I'm all right*, it said, at the end. *Really I am*.

Someone was nudging him.

'Peter! Come on, wake up!'

Reluctantly he opened salt-stung eyes to find that dusk had fallen. White-topped waves hissed menacingly about them. The others lolled against each other like drunken puppets. Uncle was talking in his ear.

'Peter, lad. We've got to keep everyone awake and moving. If we can do that and make it through the night, we've a chance of getting picked up. But if we nod off, we're dead. Peter, are you listening?'

Peter felt a harder nudge. 'Yes! I'm listening. But what do you want me to do?'

'It's time to take charge, son. You're an officer now. Come on, think!'

'Yes.' He sat up. 'Right. Ah . . . Jamie.'

No reply, only the ceaseless slap of sea against Neoprene.

'Jamie, wake up.' Still nothing. 'Pilot to Navigator!'

'What the hell is it?' Johnson's head rose reluctantly from his chest.

'Where are we?'

'What? Bay of Biscay, of course, where d'you think?'

'No, but I mean, where exactly?'

Jamie struggled upright. 'Well, best estimate, Western Approaches, I'd say. Cornish coast is about a hundred and fifty miles northeast. Why?'

Others, Peter saw, were also beginning to stir. 'Listen,' he went on. 'The wind's southwesterly, right? So it's blowing us in the right direction, at maybe a couple of knots. And the Gulf Stream's also flowing northeast at two or three knots, right?'

'So . . .?'

'So we row it! And sail it! We rig a little sail using a paddle for a mast, take turns rowing, we should easily be able to add three knots to our speed. Don't you see? Fifteen, twenty hours or so and we've cracked it.'

'Hold on,' Chalkie croaked. 'Are you telling us that if we start paddling, by opening-time tomorrow night we could be downing pints in Blighty?'

'Yes, exactly! We could!'

They couldn't, and he knew it, not in a million years. But it didn't matter. They believed him and were prepared to give it a try. And the effort of it sustained them through the freezing hours of darkness until the coming dawn brought renewed hope, and they could safely collapse, spent, back into stupor. There they lay, throughout that second day, until less than an hour before sunset a Coastal Command Sunderland flying boat out of Plymouth picked them up and flew them back to land.

And that night they were downing pints in a pub in Blighty.

. . . And the irony was, Credo jotted, before closing the file, the irony was that it was Tess Derby's husband who saved them.

CHAPTER 2

The call had come at eleven in the evening, by which time Squadron Leader Walker, the forty-year-old officer commanding 61 Squadron, had been without sleep for forty-eight hours. Apart from snatched cat naps at his desk, he rarely slept on operations nights, preferring to busy himself through the long hours of waiting with the mountains of paperwork squadron COs were burdened with.

B-Baker had been the only Lancaster he'd dispatched to Turin not to return out of a combined force of fifty. A cruel irony, he felt, because although he couldn't tell Peter and his crew, he'd known all along the operation would be abandoned due to weather. Which was why he'd rostered them in the first place—so they would have an easy final mission. But his gesture had backfired, they had vanished and, as always, Walker felt personally responsible.

So he'd stayed up to wait, drinking cocoa, toiling through his papers, and endlessly rehearsing scenarios he knew so well. Options began sprouting on his blotter like branches on a tree. B-Baker had enough fuel for nine hours' flying, so might simply be crawling home in slow time, with an engine out, perhaps. But as an icy dawn broke, he was forced to accept that Peter's crew could no longer be airborne. More branches sprouted. They could have diverted to another base, because of fuel shortage perhaps, in which case they would soon be telephoning him.

But when nine o'clock passed without word, Walker knew the situation was much worse. Only four viable options now grew on his tree. The first—that they were down on friendly ground but unable to contact him—was the most optimistic, yet least probable. The other three branches acknowledged they were in hostile territory: down but all safe, down with dead or injured, or down and all dead.

Then followed the long middle watches of the day. It was a Sunday, so Walker attended chapel where, hunched in his pew, he prayed for the safety of Peter, Uncle and the others. Afterwards he telephoned his wife, who was on a visit to her parents in Gloucestershire.

'How was your night?' she asked lightly, knowing there'd been an op on.

'One astray,' he confided sadly.

Halfway through their conversation a tap came on the door and his adjutant appeared bearing a slip of paper. Walker read it and hurriedly ended the call. A Morse message had been picked up by Portishead Radio on 600 metres, the standard distress frequency. The message had been faint, but the operator thought he heard 'QR', which were 61 Squadron's code letters. Chalkie White's final transmission from B-Baker.

Five minutes later Walker was through to Portishead.

'Operator wasn't sure what he heard, sir. Then there was lots of routine traffic to sort through so it was a while before I got to it.'

'Corporal . . .' Walker struggled for calm. 'This is very important. Please tell me everything you can about this message.'

'The slip just says an unconfirmed SOS was picked up via Dorchester receiving station at oh-seven-forty-eight, strength one and broken, possibly with code letters QR or YR attached. Then transmission stopped.'

'Was there a bearing, a range, anything?'

'No, sir. Although it would have been green sector.'

'What's green sector?'

'West, sir. Roughly. From Dorchester.'

'Over the sea, you mean?'

'Oh, yes, sir. Over the sea, definitely.'

They were down. Ditched in the ocean. Walker hung up then telephoned 5 Group headquarters, who channelled his news to 19 Group, Coastal Command, in Plymouth. Within an hour, two Lockheed Hudsons and a Shorts Sunderland were fanning out across the Western Approaches in search. But by now the afternoon's winter light was waning, so after two hours they were recalled with instructions to resume at daybreak.

Walker spent another sleepless night tossing and turning on a campbed in his office, and at six the next morning Coastal Command telephoned to say the search aircraft were aloft and concentrating their hunt in an area southwest of the Devon coast. With each hour, hopes of a happy outcome for Peter and his crew dwindled. Twice during the morning he broke off from his duties to telephone his opposite number at Coastal Command. 'Nothing yet, old chum,' the man told him. 'But don't give up.'

Then at noon the breakthrough finally came in an extraordinary telephone call.

'Squadron Leader Walker?' a cultured voice enquired. 'Flight Lieutenant Quentin Credo here, sir. SIO, 57 Squadron.'

'Oh, yes?' Walker frowned. 57 Squadron, another Lancaster unit over at Scampton, in Lincolnshire. 'How can I help you, Lieutenant?'

'Well, I'm rather hoping I can help *you*, sir. I've got one of your pigeons, you see.'

Credo had gone on to explain that Scampton's pigeon loft, run by a certain Sergeant Murray, was the regional centre for the rearing of 5 Group's homing pigeons.

'. . . In short, a rather bedraggled bird landed back here this morning with note attached. Murray brought it straight to me, and I think it could be one of yours. May I ask, sir, are you missing any aircraft?'

'Yes, for Christ's sake! What does the note say?'

'"Lancaster QR-B-Baker ditching 0800 Feb 25 position 48°19′ north, 6°44′ west."'

Within minutes Walker had telephoned the coordinates to Coastal

Command. A nail-biting two hours followed, then shortly before dusk Walker received the call he'd been praying for. B-Baker's crew had been found and picked up. Frozen, exhausted, but alive.

Some hours later, just as Walker was preparing to leave his office, he received one last call. It was Peter Lightfoot, he was in a pub in Plymouth, and he was drunk. 'Jus' wanted check in, sir. Let you know we're ol' right.'

'Splendid news, Peter. Can't tell you how relieved we all are.'

'Yessir. All done . . .'

An odd pause followed. 'So, Peter . . . Got any plans for your leave?'

'Well, thought I'd pop up 'n' say a few thank-yous and goodbyes . . .'

'Good idea. There's an SIO called Credo over at Scampton you should thank. And a pigeon fancier name of Murray.'

'Scampton, sir? A what?'

'Never mind. All will become clear.'

'Oh. Right, sir . . .' Another awkward silence.

'Everything OK, Peter?'

'Yessir. Only . . .'

'Yes?'

'Well . . .' Suddenly the dam broke. 'I don't want to come off ops, sir! I mean, I don't know what I'll do . . . I mean, I only know ops flying.'

'Peter, what are you saying?'

'That I'll make a terrible instructor, sir, Let me stay on ops!'

'I can't, Peter, you've done your bit. You will make a fine instructor.'

'No, sir, please, I just want to keep flying. There's nothing else for me.'

Nothing else? Walker rubbed tiredly at his temples. What on earth did that mean? Then he made a reasoned guess.

'Peter.' He sighed. 'Does this have anything to do with a girl?'

Dear Peter,

I hope this letter finds you well. And after six years, doesn't come too much as a shock! Why am I writing it? Because I found myself thinking about you, that's all. Truthfully I suppose I never stopped. I learned through a contact that you were in the RAF, and on bombers too, which is a coincidence as I'm married to an RAF man on a bomber base. The contact kindly found where you were stationed, so I decided to write. I hope you don't mind.

How has your life gone since our childhood back in Bexley? I miss our friendship greatly and feel particularly bad about how it ended. After the business at home it was decided I should begin a new life elsewhere and not contact you. I came up here to Lincoln and moved in with my father's sister, who was good to take me in after what happened. Since then I have had no contact with my mother, although my father writes occasionally. I tried to continue my school studies here but it didn't work out, so I left school and got a job in the local library. Then in '38 I met Brendan and we decided to get married. He was ten years older, and is a sergeant mechanic in charge of grounds maintenance. We've been married four years now.

I won't pretend it's easy, Peter, because it isn't. My life hasn't turned out as I'd hoped. (Remember our great plans?) I didn't go to university and will never have a career. But you reap what you sow, as they say, and I'm all right, really I am.

And what about you? How has your life turned out? Have you found someone to share it with? I'd love to hear your news, should you ever feel like sharing it. If not then I understand.

Take care of yourself, I know well the risks you bomber crews face.

With sincere best wishes,

Tess

According to Credo's file, the 'business' Theresa Derby referred to in her letter happened in 1936. She and Peter were sixteen, childhood friends and neighbours in the London suburb of Bexley where they lived—the Derbys in modern detached splendour, the Lightfoots across the road in terraced modesty. Though the children were close and the adults cordial, the two families led very different lives. Tess's father managed a bank in the City, while Peter's was a clerk at a factory. Mrs Derby held coffee mornings for good causes, Mrs Lightfoot cleaned Mrs Derby's house. The Derbys were strict Roman Catholics, the Lightfoots lapsed C of E. The Derbys expected their daughter to go to university and marry well, while the Lightfoots expected Peter to get a job to help pay the rent.

As young children these differences were invisible. At five they attended primary school together. On their first day, seated side by side at the same table, Peter expressed admiration at Tess's leather pencil-case, while Tess marvelled at Peter's dark eyes and dexterity with Plasticine. In no time the friends were inseparable.

At eleven they moved on to secondary school, where Peter, compact, strong, dark, performed best in classroom tasks involving practical problems. Tess, taller, fair, willowy, outshone all with her logical mind, quick grasp and immaculate homework. They remained close, and mutually supportive, she cheering his goal-scoring from the touchline, he rapturously applauding her Titania on the school stage. One Christmas, out carol-singing, Tess leaned across and stole a kiss during 'Silent Night'. Peter felt his heart falter at the touch of her lips, and knew he was hers for ever.

But it couldn't last. With the onset of puberty and shifting world events, trouble brewed on the horizon like a storm. For the first time an awareness of their differing status arose between them. Peter began to resent that his father was perpetually cashless, that his mother cleaned for the Derbys. At the same time, arousal smouldered within him, he felt tense and giddy when Tess drew near, and his nights were troubled by guilt and lust. Tess too felt unfamiliar stirrings at his touch, and sometimes ached physically for embrace, yet at the same time she couldn't understand his moods, sensing they were her fault somehow but not knowing why.

Tess's approaching departure to an expensive finishing college only served to heighten the tension between them. Then, one sultry afternoon in July of 1936, everything came to a head. Tess and Peter were sixteen, the school term had just ended, both families were preparing to depart for their summer holidays—the Derbys to Scotland, the Lightfoots to Margate. Bored with packing, Tess and Peter escaped to the greenhouse at the bottom of her garden. Behind it, hidden from view, lay one of their many hideaways, a huge mound of leaves and grass-mowings from the lawn.

They stretched out on the pungent softness of the leaf-pile, Tess reading, while he watched clouds wander through the sky.

'I'm signing up for the RAF,' he murmured. 'Soon as war comes.'

Tess turned a page. 'Father says war won't come. Chamberlain will make sure.'

'It's coming, no doubt about it. And I aim to be ready.' Peter reached into his pocket. 'I got you this,' he said, producing something in tissue paper. 'For when you go away.'

Tess unwrapped a tiny silver medallion. 'A St Christopher. Peter, it's beautiful!'

'It's to keep you safe. On your journey. Wherever you go.'

He helped her put it on and, as he did so, one strap of her summer dress slipped from her shoulder. He reached out to replace the strap, but suddenly found himself on top of her, pinning her arms above her head. Twin spots of pink coloured her cheeks.

'Kiss me, Peter,' she whispered. 'Really kiss me, and hold me tight.' Her breathing was heavy, her lips full. The medallion pulsed at her throat.

He hesitated. 'Tess, I love you.' Then his mouth was on hers and their hands were writhing like snakes across their bodies. Her breast was round and firm beneath his palm, her fingers found the buttons of his fly, her back arched as his hand pressed between her thighs, they kissed again, more urgently. Then her hand was holding him, pulling him towards her. 'Come on!' He thrust desperately, felt the enclosing warmth, and exploded.

Then Mrs Derby appeared behind the greenhouse and let out a scream.

The act was as unpremeditated as it was predictable, but the repercussions would change their lives for ever. Nothing was said in the immediate aftermath. The next day the Derbys left for Scotland and the Lightfoots for Margate. Upon his return Peter searched the mail for news but found none. And though three weeks later Mr Derby came home with his son, Tess and Mrs Derby remained absent—visiting relatives, Mr Derby explained stiffly.

Peter waited again, anxiously haunting the hallway of his house for word—a letter, a postcard, even a secret telephone call. But his wait was in vain and soon the days were turning into weeks.

The holidays ended and Peter returned to school, alone and bereft, trying to ignore the whispers of school friends.

Then, one evening in October, a taxi appeared outside the Derby house. Suitcases were disgorged onto the pavement, but only Mrs Derby appeared among them. And that night an envelope was dropped through the Lightfoots' door. Inside it were two notes. One, addressed to Peter's mother, explained that Theresa was continuing her education at a boarding school in Cheshire, and since both Derby children were now effectively gone, Mrs Lightfoot's domestic services were no longer required. The second note was from Tess and addressed to Peter:

Dear Peter,

I'm going to be studying away for the foreseeable future therefore it would be best if we were not to see each other again, nor you to attempt to contact me. I wish you well for the future.

Yours sincerely,

T. Derby

The hand was hers, but not the words, Peter sensed instantly. Why, he wondered, was this happening to them? Was their offence so shameful? His studies suffered, he avoided his friends, his relationship with his parents, who since Mrs Lightfoot's dismissal, had banned all mention of the Derbys, grew strained. Only one thing mattered, that Tess still loved him, and would find a way to come back. But at Christmas she did not come back, nor make any contact, and he was forced to accept that she had rejected him.

It was like being imprisoned, then forgotten. Two years went by without a single word. In 1938 he turned eighteen and left school, accepting the first job he was offered—a filing clerk at an insurance office. He hated the work but kept his head down and his eyes on the newspapers, channelling his frustration into the approaching cataclysm. The day after Chamberlain broke the news to the nation, Peter packed a bag, headed for the nearest RAF recruiting office, and went to war.

AND BECAME A WARRIOR, and a man, focused, dependable, flying and fighting for three years straight, until the day he ditched B-Baker into the ocean, thus concluding a remarkable fifty-eight operational flights against the enemy. But with that he was through, no longer wanted, rejected in effect, once again, by that which he held most dear. Trapped by his inability to act. Like the years of waiting for Tess. The forgotten bird in its cage.

Two days after being plucked from the sea, Peter and his crew returned to Syerston to say their farewells. By now they'd had their fill of riotous celebration, so their final parting was a muted affair. A glass of sherry with Squadron Leader Walker, a few backslaps in the mess, and it was over. All were due two weeks' leave. Peter and Uncle MacDowell decided to go straight to RAF Scampton in Lincolnshire.

The purpose of this visit, as far as Uncle was aware, was to thank two key people involved in their rescue—Scampton's intelligence officer, Flight Lieutenant Credo, and the pigeon-loft man, Murray. After all, as Squadron Leader Walker reminded them over the sherry, had it not been for the quick thinking of these two, the chances of B-Baker's crew being found were minuscule. Uncle wholeheartedly agreed, but had another reason for going to Lincoln. He had nothing better to do. A widower with no children, he had lost his wife in an air raid a year previously, which was why he'd signed up early for a second tour. So, unaware that Peter's motives were equally ambiguous, he asked to tag along.

They arrived at Scampton mid-afternoon and reported to the station commander, a Group Captain called Whitworth, who received them warmly and sent them along to Credo's office. There they introduced themselves, said their piece, and tried not to look shocked at the appallingly burned face and gloved claw of the intelligence officer.

'Tea, gentlemen?' Credo enquired, rising to his feet. Then he quickly dismissed his injuries, as he always did, because aircrew fretted about these things. 'Excuse the appearance, Wellington hit by flak over Heligoland last year. Bloody careless. I got scorched putting out the fire. Milk and sugar?'

Politely they sat listening to the cups rattling like castanets as he fumbled to serve them one-handed. As as he poured, he chatted, his voice soft and refined, at odds somehow with his shattered visage and clumsy manner. 'Have you met Murray yet?' he asked, glancing at Peter, who shook his head. 'He'll be along in a minute. Quite a character. Charming wife too.'

While they waited they drank their tea, and at his bidding recounted the story of B-Baker's last flight. 'You did well.' Credo commented when they finished. 'Kept your heads, did everything right, and in the end it paid off.'

'It didn't feel like it at the time.'

'Believe me, less experienced crews would have panicked. And paid the price for it.' He picked up a pen and began jotting notes, awkwardly. His uniform bore the maroon and blue ribbon of the DSO, the Distinguished Service Order, awarded for individual acts of outstanding bravery. It wasn't hard to guess what. Beneath fair hair, the flesh of his forehead, mouth and cheeks—the exposed parts round a flying helmet—were cruelly burned, red-raw, blistered and mottled with ugly yellow grafts like leather patches. His nose was a purple stump, his mouth an angled gash, grotesque like a clown's. Only his piercing blue eyes seemed untouched. He looked up, catching their stares. 'Wore my goggles,' he said quietly. 'Useful tip.'

'Did your crew make it?' Uncle asked.

'Two did, four didn't.'

'Tough.'

'Indeed.' He sat back, surveying the pair. MacDowell was tall, with ginger hair and bristly moustache, Lightfoot shorter, dark and watchful, earnest and edgy. 'Anyway, gents, enough of me. I hear you're all done and dusted and heading off to teach others how to do everything right now.'

Peter cleared his throat. 'Yes, sir. Although I wanted to ask about that.'

'Really? Fire away.'

'Yes, well, I heard that some aircrew manage to get signed up for a third tour of operations.'

Uncle stiffened beside him. Across the desk Credo blinked.

'Did you now? And where would you hear a thing like that?'

But before Peter could reply, a loud knock came on the door and Murray burst in. 'Is this them?' he roared.

'It is.'

'God's sakes, they don't look like much! And after all the bloody trouble I went to!'

'Quite. Ah, Flying Officer Lightfoot, Sergeant MacDowell, may I introduce Sergeant Murray.'

'The Irish pigeon fancier.' Uncle grinned, pumping Murray's hand.

'That I am! And you're a Scotchman, but nobody's perfect!'

He was big: big-shouldered, big-chested, with a big red face, wavy hair and forearms like hams. He turned to Peter, nearly a foot shorter. 'And this little fellow's English, God help him, but never mind!' And before Peter knew it he was swept into a bear hug that drove the breath from his body. 'Lightfoot, you say? Bless me, are you a Red Indian or something!'

Formalities over, Sergeant Murray took them on a tour of the airfield, which was much like Syerston only bigger and more modern, followed by a hair-raising drive in a van to a far corner of the field to inspect the pigeon loft, housed above a barn filled with agricultural machinery. 'My private empire!' he explained, conjuring whisky from a cupboard. Then he led them up a ladder to the loft, a large caged-in area next to a scruffy office. Here he showed them the pigeons, cooing tenderly at them as he explained how they were reared and trained. Then he reached in and lifted one out, and Peter and Uncle looked in awe at the bird that had saved their lives.

'Incredible,' Uncle murmured, 'that this wee pigeon could fly so far. And so fast.'

'It's what God made him for,' Murray replied. 'Luckily for you.'

RAF SCAMPTON came under the jurisdiction of 5 Group, Bomber Command, and was currently home to just one unit, 57 Squadron, although it was big enough to house two. 5 Group itself consisted of ten Lancaster squadrons, located at eight airfields in the Lincolnshire area, with a headquarters in Grantham. That was just one of the six Groups comprising Bomber Command.

While Peter and Uncle were admiring pigeons at Scampton, Bomber Command's leader, fifty-year-old Air Chief Marshal Arthur Harris, a pugnacious, no-nonsense bulldog of a man, was sitting in a darkened room in Teddington, Middlesex, watching a middle-aged scientist with white hair fiddle with a film projector. And rapidly losing patience.

'For God's sake, man!' he scowled. 'I have to be at the Ministry by six!'

'Any moment now,' the scientist replied nervously. A few seconds later it clattered to life and on the screen appeared a grainy black and white image of a beach with seascape beyond.

'Where are we this time?' Harris demanded.

'Chesil Beach, sir. The Wellington appears in a moment.'

A twin-engined Wellington bomber appeared on the screen, flying low over the sea. Hanging beneath it, clearly visible, were two spheres, each about two feet in diameter. As the bomber drew level with the camera, one of the spheres detached itself and fell to the sea, whereupon it began bouncing gamely over the waves, like a football kicked across a pitch.

'So it bounces, Wallis, we know all this!' Harris growled. 'And I've read your blasted paper. But it's too small for the dams, you said so yourself.'

'Yes, but I can make the full-size one now.'

'Which won't fit under a Lancaster, because the diameter's too big!'

'Not since I changed the shape. It's not spheroid any more, you see. It's an *oblate* spheroid now. A flattened sphere, more like a barrel.'

'Which means?'

'That the diameter's reduced because it's longer. So now it will fit under a Lanc.'

'And does it work?'

The man gestured at the screen. 'You've just seen it working. At least the scaled-down version.'

'Really? That was a barrel, not a ball?'

The man smiled modestly. 'Come next door, sir, to the tank. It won't take a minute.'

Harris followed him along a corridor and through swing doors to a vast, low-ceilinged shed. Dominating the shed was a shallow tank, twenty feet wide and barely three deep, but stretching over 600 feet long. 'National Physical Laboratory let me use it a while longer,' he said. 'Jolly decent of them. Here, sir, this way. We'll watch at the receiving end.'

They set off along the tank's length, eventually arriving at a scaffolding supporting a curved barrier in the water. Like a dam. Several white-coated assistants hovered nearby, two young women among them.

'Ready everyone? Good-oh. Right you are, ladies, in you pop.'

To Harris's surprise, the women mounted stepladders on either side of the tank, before climbing as modestly as possible into narrow metal cylinders sitting in the water.

'They're glass-sided,' the scientist explained. 'So that we can film what happens underwater. Bit of a tight fit though, what with the cameras and everything. Hence the young ladies.'

'Fascinating.' Harris glanced at his watch. 'Will this take long?'

'Less than three seconds.' The scientist picked up a microphone and peered towards the far end of the tank. 'Very well, Walter,' he shouted. 'On my count. Three, two, one, shoot!'

Harris heard a distant crack, like a rifle shot, then a series of hissing sounds as something approached rapidly up the tank. Like kissing, he thought, *kiss, kiss, kiss*, the noise went. Then he glimpsed the projectile itself, bouncing towards them at enormous speed before it slammed into the wall with a resonant thud, bouncing off it to splash a foot or so back.

'Watch!' the scientist said, leaning over the tank.

Harris watched. The projectile, metallic, and about the size of a cricket ball, sank from sight, still spinning, but as it did so it drifted back into the wall until, with a barely audible clunk, it made contact and stopped.

'Good grief,' Harris said, genuinely surprised. 'Does it do that every time?'

'Usually. As long as the water's reasonably flat.'

The two men adjourned outside, where a staff car awaited Harris.

'What range and speed are we talking about? For the real thing?' he asked.

'It would need to be dropped four hundred yards from the dam, at about two hundred and twenty miles per hour.'

'Height?'

'One hundred and fifty feet.'

'I don't know, Wallis,' he said, shaking his head. 'Deep down I still think it's all poppycock.'

'It's not, sir. It's proven science. You've just witnessed it.'

'Hmm. And you really think you can develop a full-sized version, from scratch, get it built, and tested, and working reliably, all in three months?'

'Yes. Given the resources. And the commitment.'

'Well, we'll have to see.' They shook hands. 'I'll speak to Portal again,' Harris said. 'But I make no promises. It's the diversion of resources I can't stomach. That and putting men's lives at risk for something so utterly crackpot. No offence, that is.'

'No offence taken, sir. Thank you for coming.'

'You're welcome. Ultimately it's not my decision, thank God. But, for what it's worth, I still bet my shirt it'll never work!'

SEVERAL WHISKIES LATER, and with a wintry moon rising over the airfield, Peter and Uncle reboarded Murray's van for a second hair-raising drive, out through the airfield gates, down into Lincoln, and a succession of rowdy, smoke-filled pubs. Everywhere they went, the reception was warm and the hospitality generous. And everyone in the city knew Murray, it seemed, and wanted to buy him drinks. Peter struggled to keep up.

Murray was from County Louth in Northern Ireland. Born within sight of Dundalk racetrack where his father was groundsman, the young Brendan was raised on a seasonal diet of horseracing, hare-coursing, bare-knuckle boxing, hurling and, of course, pigeon-racing. By sixteen he was six foot four, and knew most of what there was to know about sports, and gambling, and how to look after turf. In his twenties he crossed to England, where he worked as a navvy until joining the RAF. His timing was propitious, for with hostilities looming the RAF was embarked on a huge airfield expansion programme. Murray's ground-management skills were quickly recognised, and he was soon overseeing maintenance at a succession of airfields, before settling at Scampton.

'What t'at means, Uncle,' he explained, 'is that I supervise the subcontractors who take care of the grounds. Make sure they do a proper job.'

'Important work at a base like Scampton,' Uncle agreed groggily. 'Eh, Brendan'—he prodded Murray's arm—'I was wondering about that wee pigeon. The one that saved us. Might you no' consider selling him?'

'Selling him? To you? What for?'

Uncle leaned closer. 'So's I can have him stuffed for my mantelpiece.'

Murray looked appalled, then saw Uncle's face, and in a moment the two older men were doubling over with guffaws. Peter, smiling politely, looked away, and suddenly saw Tess coming through the door.

She was wearing a belted overcoat and blue beret. She was older, the innocence had gone, but not the beauty. The shock of seeing her was like a physical jolt. Peter's heart lurched and his body went rigid. Tess's eyes widened and looked startled when she saw him, yet also relieved somehow, as though a die had been cast.

'There she is at last!' Murray bellowed. 'Tess! Over here, girl! Come and meet two lovely lads from Syerston.'

For nearly an hour she stood at the bar sipping her drink and pretended she didn't know Peter. She'd been sure that her letter would bring him to her, and she knew now that her feelings for him were undimmed, but she wasn't yet ready to confront all that this implied. So she stood close beside Brendan, smiling as best she could, and she stole sidelong looks at Peter, who was dark and guarded and even more handsome as a man than as a youth. Then, just as they were preparing to leave, Brendan said he had to relieve himself, and Uncle said he had to go too, so they went together, leaving her alone with Peter, who hesitated only a second before coming to the point.

'Why didn't you try to contact me?' he pleaded. 'At the beginning?'

'I did try,' she replied. 'But they said they'd have you arrested if I did. For rape.'

'*What?* But why, for God's sake?'

She licked her lips. 'Because of the baby.'

CHAPTER 3

Some days later, Quentin Credo closed the door of his Scampton rooms, turned the key, dropped his messages onto a side-table and headed for the drinks cabinet. After extracting Scotch, he wedged the bottle under his armpit, pulled the cork with his good hand, slopped liquor into a glass, and drank.

He slumped into an armchair, waiting for the alcohol to begin its work. Pain was coming at him in waves, beginning at its source among the ravaged tissue of his right hand, gathering momentum up his arm and shoulder. It had been building all afternoon, ever since the pethidine wore off.

As the whisky slowly blunted the pain to its customary throb, his blurred gaze fell on his messages. Tess Murray had telephoned again, he saw, the Irish pigeon-fancier's wife. Telephoned as she had telephoned most days in the fortnight since her pilot friend had reappeared. He'd phoned today, too, the messages said. Twice. Quentin was impressed by their persistence, and their commitment, but what they wanted was as preposterous as it was impossible. They wanted him to get Lightfoot's orders magically changed, so he could transfer to 57 Squadron, there at Scampton, and fly a third tour of operations. Something far beyond Quentin's authority.

Briefly scanning his other messages, he hauled himself to his feet. He wanted to excuse himself further pain, but that would be weak. So he crossed the floor to the basin near his bed, filled it with scalding water, and poured in a measure of salt crystals. Then he rolled up the right sleeve of his shirt and plucked carefully at the black leather glove covering his hand until it came off, revealing the claw-like fingers and raw flesh between, where tissue had been cut away that afternoon at the hospital. With a gasp he plunged the hand in. Dizziness and nausea assailed him, as for ten excruciating minutes he stood at the basin flexing his fingers and letting the salty water begin its work. Finally, therapy over, he lifted the hand from the basin and moved unsteadily to his bed, wiping a single rogue tear from the scarred skin of his cheek. He lay down, opened a stoppered bottle, and dribbled clear liquid onto the surgical mask beside it. Then, checking the elastic attaching the mask to his bed was secure, he pulled it over his mouth and sucked at the astringent vapour until he fell into sublime unconsciousness.

HE'D BEEN ON a routine checkup to the pigsty, the fond if unflattering nickname for the Queen Victoria Hospital in East Grinstead. Nestling amid wooded grounds, the hospital was home to a unique military institution, one which under the leadership of its charismatic director, Dr Archie McIndoe, had evolved into the most advanced burns unit in the country. Its patients originated almost exclusively from the RAF, where fire was an ever-present danger, and their treatment was cutting-edge, experimental even, which is why they referred to themselves as guinea pigs, and the hospital as the sty. But always with respect, for the Queen Victoria was a place of compassion, and hope, and courage beyond measure.

'Well now, Credo,' McIndoe had begun at the checkup that afternoon. 'How are we getting on?'

'Not too bad, sir,' Quentin replied, self-consciously turning his head for McIndoe to examine.

'Not bad? Looks pretty bloody brilliant, I'd say!'

'Yes, sir. Only, the hand . . .'

'We'll get to the hand in a minute. Now, I'd say we're about ready to build you a new nose, yes? You know the WTP drill, of course.'

'Yes, sir, but—'

'Good-oh. So, the waltzing tube pedicle. First step is to separate a ten-inch-long strip of skin tissue along the top of your shoulder, turning it under to form a tube, yet keeping it attached at both ends, so it looks like a suitcase handle. Then, when we're sure it's healthy and growing, usually three weeks or so, we detach one end of the tube from your shoulder and sew it onto your face, right here where your nose was. You can go home, carry on as normal, etcetera, while the pedicle takes.'

'With a tube of skin joining my face to my shoulder.'

'Don't be facetious, Credo, it's worth the inconvenience. The next step will be to cut the shoulder end free, but leave it untrimmed. You'll look like a proboscis monkey for a while, but then the final step is to trim the proboscis back into a proper nose shape, including septum and nostrils. Leave it for a couple of months until the swelling goes down, and Bob's your uncle! Bloody marvellous—here, look at these photos . . .'

Quentin took the photos, although he didn't need them. He knew all about the waltzing tube pedicle, so named for the way it waltzed from your shoulder to your nose, or your eyelid, or your lip. He'd seen countless during the four indescribable months he'd spent as an inpatient at the sty. McIndoe was a maverick, often discarding established techniques in favour of the unconventional.

But the results were often remarkable, Quentin conceded, glancing through the photographs. Indeed one man's finished nose looked no worse than an average rugby player's. But the process was complex, and painful, and above all lengthy, and it was this protractedness that concerned him most.

McIndoe was waiting. 'What do you say, old chap, shall we book you in?'

'Well . . .' Quentin began cautiously, McIndoe was famously intolerant of procrastination. 'It certainly sounds marvellous, sir, as you say. But I'm to be re-evaluated for operational flying soon, sir. And much as I'd like a new nose, it's the hand I really need . . .'

'For God's sake!' McIndoe fumed. 'You pilots, haven't you had enough?' The surgeon eyed him witheringly, then began at last to examine Quentin's talon-like fingers. 'Hmm. Seen better. Still bathing them in hot saline?'

'Absolutely, sir. But there's still very little movement. And unless I can get them working . . .'

'No chance of flying, yes, I know. All right, listen, Quentin, I suppose I could try cutting away some of the tissue between the fingers, so they're less webbed. That might free up movement a bit.'

'Thank you, sir, I'd greatly appreciate it.'

'We can do it now.'

Quentin swallowed. 'Now?'

'Yes, now, under pethidine, if you're up to it. It'll hurt like hell, but you'll be home in time for supper.'

Quentin felt a familiar lassitude, as his body's pain-defence mechanism prepared for the coming onslaught. As it had done so often over the months.

'Yes, sir,' he found himself saying, as if in a trance. 'Now would be fine.'

At nine that evening, Scampton's station commander, Group Captain John 'Charles' Whitworth, a short, energetic, habitually worried-looking man of thirty, arrived by car at the former Victorian mansion in Grantham that was serving as 5 Group headquarters, and was shown to a panelled study. A few minutes later, a hawk-faced man wearing the uniform of air vice-marshal entered.

'Charles.' He gripped Whitworth's hand. 'Good of you to come at such short notice. Please sit, let me pour you a brandy and soda.'

Glasses filled, the Honourable Ralph Cochrane, aristocratic and impressively effective commander of 5 Group, got straight down to business.

'Everything we're about to discuss, Charles, it goes without saying, is absolutely top secret, understood?'

'Of course, sir.'

'Good. Ever heard of a boffin called Barnes Wallis?'

Whitworth nodded. 'The Vickers chap? Co-designed the Wellington?'

'That's him. Looks like a country parson and talks utter gobbledegook, persistent as hell, too, but a sound enough fellow and a mind like a razor.'

'Yes, sir.'

'So. As you know, for some time Portal has been focusing bombing efforts on German heavy industry, particularly the Ruhr Valley, where all the major foundries, power stations and factories are.'

'Yes, sir.' Air Chief Marshal Portal was head of the RAF, reporting directly to Churchill.

'Well, to cut a long story short, Wallis has been working on ways to inflict serious damage on targets in the Ruhr, and he's come up with something Portal believes might do the trick.'

'Really? What's that, sir?'

'I can't tell you. But Portal's very gung ho about it. Harris is less keen, in fact he says it's dangerous twaddle. But he's under pressure from Portal. So much so that he's ordered 5 Group to take it on.'

'That's excellent news, sir. But, ah, take what on?'

'I can't tell you that either. I can only tell you he showed me some film footage yesterday, and it's, well, astonishing. But more to the point, it's going to require a dedicated squadron, some heavily modified Lancasters and a lot of training to pull it off. Now, how are things at Scampton?'

He's giving it to me! Whitworth realised with a thrill. Whatever it is, he's giving it to me. 'They're absolutely fine, sir. Quieter obviously, since 49 Squadron moved out. 57 Squadron is due to follow when . . .'

'How's the grass?'

'Firm, sir, no problems. We've an excellent chief groundsman.'

'Good, make sure it stays that way. These modified Lancs will be heavy. What about security? Who's your SIO?'

'A young chap called Credo, sir. A flight lieutenant from 57 Squadron.'

'Is he sound?'

'Well, yes, sir. I believe so. Although he's only acting SIO, strictly speaking. He's a pilot normally, off flying ops following a bad fire in a Wimpy. But very bright, went to Oxford, trained as a barrister, all that sort of thing. And keen as mustard to get back in the fray.'

'I see. Well, he'll have to do, at least until RAF Intelligence can draft in bigger guns. But be sure he stays on his toes, Charles, secrecy is absolutely paramount. Secrecy and speed, that is. Because Harris wants to form a new squadron especially for this one job. That's why we picked Scampton, because you've got the space to house them.'

'A whole new squadron? Seven hundred men? It'll take months.'

'We don't have months. They've got to be flying in a fortnight.'

'Jesus.'

'Indeed. So they're going to need a lot of support, Charles, and practical assistance. That's where you come in. Think you can do it?'

'Well, yes, of course. Who's going to command this new squadron?'

'Harris wants the CO of 106 Squadron. Some chap called Gibson.'

MID-MORNING NEXT DAY, a knock came on Quentin's office door.

'Young lady to see you, sir.' The adjutant winked. 'A Mrs Murray. Works part-time in the NAAFI, her husband is stationed here, she says it's urgent.'

'Thank you, Corporal. Would you ask her to wait a few minutes, please?'

Quentin withdrew a file from a drawer, opened and read it. He'd been expecting this visit. And not just since Tess Murray and Peter Lightfoot began badgering him for a transfer to Scampton.

He'd first met Tess the previous October. He'd just started his job as intelligence officer, following release from the pigsty. Returning to Scampton, he'd been turned down for flying because of his injuries. 'Get that hand working,' his CO had suggested. 'In the meantime, perhaps you can take on the vacant intelligence job, on a temporary basis.' A week later, and with his feet barely under the desk, Tess had come to see him. She'd sat there, chewing her lip, looking embarrassed and avoiding his eye, a reaction he was learning to live with, but it turned out her discomfiture wasn't because of him. 'I need to get in touch with someone,' she'd explained, in an educated but hesitant voice. 'A man I used to know a long time ago. I believe he's in the RAF, possibly as a pilot.' Then she'd looked straight at him and held his gaze, and in that instant he recognised something in her. Something they recognised in one another. This woman, so young yet so knowing, had experienced great pain and terrible loss. Like him. So he'd dispensed with questions, latched onto that one word 'need', and found himself offering to help. In days he'd tracked down Peter Lightfoot over at Syerston, and duly passed on his address. Without ever questioning why.

Which was far from brilliant work, coming from an intelligence officer. But now she was back, and this time he would be more vigilant.

'Mrs Murray,' he began, when she was seated. 'Hello again. I trust you are well.'

'I'm fine, thank you. Um, have you received my messages?'

'Yes, I have, and I apologise for not returning them. However, it's clear to me that your reasons for wanting this transfer are personal and not operational, and so I don't see how I can help you.'

'Are you married, Lieutenant Credo?'

That threw him. A sudden glimpse of Helen, and the scent of her blonde hair as it caressed his face. Then she was gone. 'I don't see what . . .'

'Are you?'

'I . . . well . . . I was engaged once, but not any more.'

Still she held his gaze. 'I'm sorry. Things rarely turn out as we imagine.'

'Indeed.'

'It's not what you think, you see. Peter and me.'

'And what do I think?'

'That we're having some sort of affair, or something.'

'Then . . . What?'

'He beats me,' she murmured. 'My husband beats me. One day he'll probably kill me. Only Peter knows this, and only Peter can help. Now are you satisfied?'

And there it was. Confirmation. Murray, the genial Irish giant, was not the man he seemed—as Quentin had already begun to suspect. In October, a week after Tess had asked him to find Lightfoot, Quentin had dropped by the Murrays' quarters to pass her the details, which he'd sealed in an envelope. But as he'd leaned towards the door to knock, he'd heard a man's raised voice inside, followed by placatory entreaties from a woman. He'd retreated guiltily to his office. Next day he found her in the NAAFI and gave her the envelope. She thanked him, clutching it to her with relief. But there was no hiding the purple bruising on her neck.

Then followed Lightfoot's arrival at Scampton, and their plea for his transfer there. It was all starting to fit together. Yet there was more.

'Well, that is . . . appalling,' Quentin blustered. 'But if it's a matter of marital problems, you should talk to the welfare people.'

She wasn't listening. 'It began shortly before the station moved here from Feltwell. He became secretive and moody, and drank more. Then one night he came in late, I asked where he'd been and he flew into a rage and put his hands round my neck. I didn't know what to do, so I came to you, the station intelligence officer, and asked for help to find the one person I could turn to. Now you're sending him away.'

Quentin sighed. 'It's not me sending him away, Mrs Murray, it's his job. The orders come from Bomber Command. I can give you an address . . .'

But she had given up. Determined still, yet resigned to inevitable defeat.

'I had a daughter, you see,' she went on, more calmly. 'We did. Peter and I. A baby daughter. Long before I was married to Brendan. She was taken from me. Peter never knew about her until now. She's nearly six, and we want to try to look for her. But if Brendan found out . . .'

'I see. I'm sorry. I don't know what to say. I wish I could help. Really. But operational orders . . . Well, they're practically set in stone.'

'So I gather.' She rose to leave.

'Although, perhaps, your daughter'—he found himself saying—'I could make a few enquiries. See what your options are, that sort of thing.'

'I wouldn't want to cause any more trouble.'

'You wouldn't.'

'Then, thank you.'

PETER TIGHTENED the drawstring of his duffle bag and hoisted it to his shoulder, checking round his bedroom one final time. A child's room still, he realised, surveying the *Flight* magazine posters and model aeroplanes.

He closed the door and clumped downstairs, dumping his bag in the hall. He entered the kitchen, nose twitching at another souvenir of youth—fried Spam and overcooked cabbage.

'Tea's ready, love,' his mother said. 'Goodness, don't you look smart.'

'Thanks, Mum.'

His father lowered his newspaper. 'What time's your train?'

'Eleven thirty. It's the sleeper.'

'Do you get a compartment?'

'I've no idea. I doubt it.'

'Bloody well ought to. Seeing as you're an off—'

The telephone rang and Peter escaped to the hall. 'Hello?'

'It's me.'

'Tess! Thank God. I was worried I'd miss you. I'm catching the night train to Glasgow. I'm so worried, you're all alone there . . . with everything.'

'Don't be. I'm fine.'

Peter leaned his forehead to the wall. It was three weeks since he'd been reunited with Tess, three weeks of elation and despair, as he learned of her life over six lost years, of the awfulness of her situation with Brendan, and of the revelation of their daughter. And now, so soon after they had found each other, they were being forced apart.

'It's only for a while, Peter,' she said, reading his thoughts. 'Six months, a year maybe . . .'

'I love you, Tess. It's wrong, but I can't help it. I love you and always have.'

'It's not wrong. I love you too. Keep in close touch, Peter. Write to me. Write here, care of the NAAFI, it's safer. And let me know a number where I can reach you.'

'Yes, yes, I will, of course.'

Silence yawned, there seemed so much to say, then nothing at all, so they murmured unhappy goodbyes and hung up. Peter stared at the receiver, listening to its forlorn hum, then with a bitter curse slammed it down.

'Who was that, love?' his mother said as he returned to the kitchen.

He couldn't tell them, couldn't say anything. 'No one. Wrong number.'

His parents exchanged glances. 'Come and have your tea then, before . . . Where are you going?'

He strode down the hall, hurt and frustration seething within him. It was their fault, those people across the road. Six years he'd lost her, six long years of sadness and yearning and not knowing why. And now he was going to lose her again, it was more than he could bear. He threw open the door, marched down the path and across the darkened street. Everything was exactly as he remembered: the tiled step, the brass letterbox, the bell pull.

Except Mr Derby, who looked older and smaller.

'Good heavens. It's young Lightfoot, isn't it?' he said. 'Flying Officer Lightfoot, I see. And is that a DFC?' Interest flickered, then quickly waned as his guard came up. 'Well, now, and what can we do for you?'

'Can I come in?'

'Ah . . . We're just about to listen to the news . . . Africa . . .'

'It won't take a minute.' He pushed past him into the front room, Mr Derby trailing in his wake. The room was even grander than he recalled: chintz upholstery, gilt mirror, mahogany bookcase, a grand piano bearing framed photographs of the Derbys' son, David, in uniform, David in cricket whites, David in top hat and tails. Not one of Tess.

'Mrs Derby?'

She glanced up from her needlework, looked momentarily startled, then quickly composed herself. 'Oh.' She plucked at a thread. 'It's you.'

'Yes, it is. I'm sorry to disturb you, but have you spoken to Tess lately?'

'Theresa lives in Lancashire. She's married now. We don't hear from her.'

'It's Lincolnshire, as well you know, and that's not what I asked.'

'What business is it of yours if I've spoken to her?'

'She's my friend, that's what. She needs help, from you, from her family.'

'If she needs help, she'll ask. Anyway, she has family. She has a husband.'

'Who treats her badly.'

'That is her business. She chose him, we weren't consulted, nor were we invited to the wedding. We've never even met him. Now, if there's nothing else . . .' She set aside her needles and began to rise.

'Why didn't you tell me about the baby?'

'What did you say?'

'My daughter. I had a right to know.'

'You? A right?' Long-pent-up anger flared. 'You're damn lucky you weren't arrested for rape!'

'Um . . . Emily . . . surely there's no need . . .'

'Keep out of this, Bernard! This . . . this monster ruined our daughter, and brought shame on us. Now he has the gall to come here telling us what to do!'

'No, I'm not telling you, I'm begging you.' Peter snatched a photograph from the piano. 'Look, where is she? Your other child? She still exists, you know, and she needs you. Contact her, Mrs Derby, offer her help. Please.'

A hand touched his arm. 'Leave it, Peter, you're only making it worse.'

Tears were pricking his eyes. 'Please, Mrs Derby, say you still love her.'

'For God's sake, Bernard, get him OUT!'

With a resounding crash Peter threw the photograph to the floor. The Derbys gaped in horror. Peter glared at them, then turned for the door.

'For religious people, you know, you're completely bloody heartless.'

AT SCAMPTON, organised chaos. It had begun two days earlier with the arrival of the mystery squadron's vanguard—a contingent of ground mechanics shipped in from 97 Squadron. Soon the numbers were swelling fast, with every hour bringing more. Loaders, armourers, engineers, fuellers, drivers, meteorologists, mappers, plotters, cooks, clerks, typists, orderlies, the entire human fabric of an operational bomber squadron descending on Scampton.

In the admin building, Station Commander Whitworth and his team struggled to keep up—assigning accommodation, allocating transport, organising catering, and the laborious task of processing the new squadron's personnel. As security officer, this last fell to Quentin, whose desk was soon bowing beneath mounds of lists, documents and files. Every single man and woman on the manifest had to be cleared by him.

Then came the aircrew and with them the first hint that X Squadron, as it was presently dubbed, was to be no ordinary outfit.

'Look at all the gongs!' an orderly murmured, reading over Quentin's shoulder. 'DFC and Bar, DFC and DSO, DFM, DSO and Bar. Look, this bloke's got two DFCs *and* he's a ruddy squadron leader! What do you think it means, sir?'

'Haven't a clue,' Quentin replied innocently. But he knew tongues were already wagging about X Squadron.

Early on the fourth day, he was at his desk, wading through the latest batch of files, when a round-faced officer burst through the door.

'Where's Whitworth! I need . . . Christ, what the hell happened to you?'

'Oh, er, bit of trouble, sir. Last year. Wellington. Fuel fire thing . . .'

'Bloody Wimpys, high time they sorted that fuel system out. What outfit?'

'57 Squadron.'

'I heard about you!' The man grinned. 'Credo, isn't it? Bloody fine job.'

It had been a simple gardening mission—mine-laying in Heligoland Bight—when 57 Squadron was still at Feltwell in Norfolk and operating the twin-engined Wellingtons. Newly promoted to flight lieutenant, Credo had been detailed to take a new crew on a gardening mission, flying as supervisor, an extra pair of hands as needed. But, inexplicably, a flak ship was lying in wait for them, and a couple of deadly salvos riddled the Wellington with white-hot shrapnel, setting the starboard engine ablaze. Only Credo's bravery and quick-thinking prevented the whole blazing aircraft from exploding.

'Thank you, sir,' Credo replied, 'although . . .'

Whitworth entered. 'Ah, Guy, there you are. Quentin, have you met Wing Commander Gibson? He's X Squadron's CO.'

'Good to meet you, Credo.' Gibson held out a hand, then quickly offered the other. Just twenty-four, short and portly, he had a youthful face and dark wavy hair. 'Intelligence, you say? Well, we've got rumours coming out of our ears. In fact we must put a stop to them before they get out of hand.'

'Yes, sir, I've been giving it thought. Some sort of cover story perhaps . . .'

'Good idea, let me know.' He turned to Whitworth. 'Sir, I came to see you about the crews. I'm still several pilots short.'

'Perhaps we can help,' Whitworth said. 'Quentin, you have the files?'

They gathered round Quentin's desk and began poring over names. Gibson, it seemed to him, as well as being lively and enthusiastic, appeared tightly wound, impatient with detail. But some jumpiness was understandable, he conceded, for Gibson had just completed his third tour with Bomber Command. A staggering total of 172 missions.

'So, I've got Hopgood, Shannon and Burpee from my old unit, 106 Squadron,' he said after a few minutes. 'Then from 97 Squadron I've got Munro, Maltby and McCarthy, who are all good chaps. Who's on the list here from 57 Squadron?'

'Rice and Astell, sir,' Quentin offered. 'Both pilots I can vouch for.'

'Good. Anyone else from 57?'

'Young has come forward. He'd make a fine addition.'

'Dinghy Young, yes, I know him. Good. Who else?'

'We've a couple from 50 Squadron, two from 49, one each from 207 and 467, and one from 61—'

'Only one? What's the matter with them?'

'Not sure, sir. Barlow, his name is. Australian, I believe.'

'So how many's that in all?'

Whitworth totted names. 'Sixteen, plus a handful of probables.'

'Sixteen? I need twenty-one and a couple of spares.'

'I'm sure more will come forward in due course, Guy.'

'That's not good enough. I need them now!'

To Quentin's surprise, a fist hit the table. Gibson was not just impatient, but volatile. Whitworth was his superior, although Gibson seemed oblivious. But Whitworth was unconcerned as he went on studying the lists.

'What about you, Credo?' Gibson suggested suddenly. 'You're a good egg. Are you checked out on the Lanc?'

'Me? I, well, ah, I'd like nothing better . . .'

'Quentin's off ops'—Whitworth patted his shoulder—'until this hand of his gets fixed. Look, Guy, why don't you give us a couple of hours to ring round? I'm sure we can come up with more names.'

'All right.' Gibson looked dazed. 'All right, yes, sir, thank you. I've got to see the engineers anyway. Anything you can do, greatly appreciated . . .'

'Talk about a firebrand,' Whitworth breathed, when Gibson had gone. 'But that's why Harris picked him. He gets things done, no matter whose toes he treads on. And he is under monumental pressure. Fancy trying to put a whole squadron together in a week. Madness, I say. Now, Quentin, what about this pilot shortfall. Any ideas? 5 Group chaps, of course.'

Quentin fingered his files. 'One name, sir. Possibly.'

'AH, TESS, LOVE, there you are.' Murray closed his notebook and rose from the table. 'Been down in town, have you?'

'Just to the library. And a little shopping.'

She had neither books nor goods, but if he noticed he gave no sign. In fact she had spent the afternoon at Lincoln Town Hall, seeking advice about how to trace her daughter from the Citizens Aid Bureaux, a new service set up like mobile clinics, in schools, church halls, even pubs, offering free advice to civilians.

'You look all fagged out, girl, let me fix you a cuppa.'

'I should get on with your tea. There's brisket left over.'

'Nonsense, I'll grab something later. You just sit yourself down now.'

'Are you going out?'

'Chief groundsman's work is never done, you know. Especially with this new mob arriving. They want to get flying right away, apparently, so it's all hands to the pumps. Thank God the weather's been dry, I say.'

She allowed him to steer her to a chair, then watched as he busied himself with teapot and milk. His wire-bound notebook lay on the table. It contained his lists of jobs to be done, and notes about grass-seed and tractor-oil and pigeon-feed. And details of the bets he took from men on the station, which he thought she didn't know about. Along with the little black-market fiddles. His war diary, he called it, and carried it everywhere.

'Have you heard the latest crack,' he said, 'about their new CO?'

'No. What about him?'

'Utterly priceless.' He pocketed his notebook. 'The t'ing is, half the new boys don't have full uniforms, right, it all being such a rush and everything. So one of our busybody MPs starts writing them up for being improperly dressed, puts seventy-five of them on a charge. Then he takes the list to their CO, this fellow Gibson, who goes raving spare, rips up the list and throws the beggar out. Then he phones Stores and orders them to issue new uniforms for every man jack. "Can't be done," Stores says, "because we don't have 'em." "It will be done," says Gibson. Next morning, every single man's in proper uniform. Incredible, no?'

'Phyllis at the NAAFI says they're getting special Lancs too.'

'Phyllis talks too much. And where would she hear a t'ing like that?'

'Her husband's working in Hangar 2. One of the fitters.'

'Then he should know better. Careless talk costs lives. Even between husband and wife.'

He handed her a cup of tea then stood behind her, his big hands resting on her shoulders. 'I mean, I wouldn't go telling anyone your secrets, would I? And you wouldn't go telling anyone mine, would you, girl?'

'Secrets?' She felt his fingers on her neck. 'No, Bren, of course not.'

'That's right.' But he stayed behind her, his fingers stroking and squeezing her neck. Tess felt terror rising in her throat. Seconds passed and then at last the fingers left her. 'Good girl.' He kissed her head and left the room.

She stayed at the table, listening to the metallic thud of his footfall receding across the yard. Then she lowered her head into her hands.

'WHY ARE WE GOING back to the station, Uncle?' Peter asked, following MacDowell down Argyle Street. 'It's hours until my train goes. Isn't it?'

'You'll see. Now, get a move on, we're wasting valuable drinking time.'

'Indeed we are.' Although he'd had enough. Hours ago. Glasgow was wonderful, he decided, but they'd been walking all day and drinking all day, and now he was exhausted. Barely had they entered the station when a familiar antipodean whoop echoed through the rafters and Kiwi Garvey's grinning face appeared, followed by Billy Bimson and Herb Guttenberg.

'Good God, it's the three musketeers!' Peter exclaimed, gripping their hands. 'What on earth are you doing here?'

'Come to see you two, of course! Think we'd miss out on a booze-up?'

'You're early, lads.' MacDowell grinned. 'But we forgive you. Right, first stop the station buffet.'

Herb and Billy, it emerged, were kicking their heels in Liverpool, awaiting a troopship back to Canada. 'Weeks, they said it might be,' Billy explained. 'So when we heard from Uncle that you were coming to Glasgow, we thought what the hell, and wangled a two-day pass.'

And also contacted Garvey, Herb added, who was similarly in limbo, pending repatriation to New Zealand and a new life as a gunnery instructor.

'You must be excited, Kiwi,' Peter said. 'To be going home at last.'

'Too right.' Kiwi stared into his glass. 'Can't wait.'

'You could apply for that transfer to the Navy.' Peter couldn't shake the impression his crewmates were subdued.

'I might just do that.'

'What about you, Herb? Home to Canada? I bet you can't wait.'

'No,' Herb agreed. 'I can't. Although . . .'

'Although what?'

The men eyed each other, unable to say the unsayable. So Uncle said it for them. 'They think it doesn't feel right, laddie.'

'Well, it doesn't!' Billy said vehemently. 'We came here to do a job. Now they're sending us home before it's done. It's . . . unfinished business.'

'Unfinished business, that's it!'

Peter nodded. It was exactly as he felt. And, earlier that day, Uncle had voiced similar thoughts. 'There's nothing for me now, laddie,' he'd said sadly. 'With the flying over and Mary gone . . .'

Peter glanced at his friends. 'I have a daughter. I only just found out.'

Incredulous stares were exchanged. 'What?'

'Years ago. With a girl. Someone I grew up with. We lost touch . . .'

'The one you kept muttering about?' Kiwi sat forward. 'In the life raft that night. Bess, isn't it?'

'Tess. Finally we met up again. Now they're sending me to Lossiemouth.'

'Typical.' Silence fell as they considered. 'Bloody war.'

Eventually, Uncle raised his glass. 'Instead of all this carping and moping, I vote we thank our lucky stars. We came through, didn't we? We're all alive, while thousands, never made it. That's a miracle, and we should count our blessings and drink to absent loved ones.'

'Hear hear!'

'Lucky stars!'

'Absent loved ones!'

As their mood lifted and the beer flowed, a full-blown party ensued. Soon Peter was blissfully intoxicated once more, cocooned by his friends, safely anaesthetised from the realities of his predicament, if only for a while.

Then he remembered his train. 'Jesus, what's the time?'

Uncle squinted at his watch. 'Time to go!'

They ran through rain-splashed streets, arriving at the station with scant minutes to spare. Then the Tannoy was announcing Peter's train and Uncle and the others were carrying him, shoulder-high, to his platform.

Where two military policemen waited.

'Oops,' said Billy.

'Well, now,' one MP said dourly. 'And what have we got here?'

'Disorderly airmen, looks like,' said the other. 'Horrible to behold.'

Uncle stepped unsteadily forward. 'Sorry, gents. Just letting off a little steam.'

'Um, my train . . .' Peter mumbled, pointing at the gate.

'Not so fast, *sir*.' The first MP produced a notebook. 'So, which one of you reprobates is Lightfoot?' he said, thumbing the pages of the book.

Peter froze. 'Pardon?'

'Are you deaf as well as English? I said *Light-foot*. Flying Officer Peter Lightfoot.'

'Well, that's me, yes. But my train . . .'

'You won't be needing it. Here, sign this, then clear off, the lot of you.'

Peter signed, the MP handed him an envelope, he sliced it open and started to read, the others crowding round.

'Bugger me.'

'I don't believe it.'

'Wow! Count me in.'

'Yes, but it just says Lightfoot. What does that mean, Peter?'

But Peter was beyond speech. Slowly his knees sank, until he was sitting on the ground, staring in amazed disbelief at the telegram in his hand.

IMMEDIATE TO F/O PJ LIGHTFOOT STOP REPORT RAF SCAMPTON LINCS W/CDR GP GIBSON OC 617 SQUADRON IMMEDIATE STOP SIGNED AVM RA COCHRANE OC 5 GROUP RAF BOMBER COMMAND ENDS.

'Sent by Cochrane himself no less.'

'Who's 617 Squadron? I've never heard of 'em.'

'You have now.'

CHAPTER 4

Quentin straightened from the Elsan toilet, eyes smarting from the disinfectant sloshing about within. Never, he cursed furiously to himself, never in more than 200 flying hours had he been sick in an aeroplane before, no matter how rough the conditions, nor how stomach-turning the action. Until now. His humiliation was complete, or so he believed, glancing guiltily about. Yet he saw no one. The Lancaster was almost surreally empty, thundering through the afternoon air like a ghost ship. A second later, he was doubling over the Elsan once more. And in that moment he knew it wasn't airsickness he was suffering from. It was terror.

The flight had seemed such a good idea. 'I'd like to come on one of your practice sorties,' he'd said to Peter Lightfoot, who owed him a sackful of favours for getting him and his crew assigned to the newly named 617 Squadron. 'See what you chaps get up to all day.' Whitworth liked the idea too. It was a golden opportunity to assess Gibson's training regime, he said.

But what Quentin hadn't told either man was his main reason for going on the flight. Which was to see if his nerves could stand it.

Now he had his answer. He raised his head wearily from the bowl, only to find the rear turret doors had opened beside him.

'You don't look so good, Lieutenant.' Herb Guttenberg held out a bag. 'Barley sugar. I find it helps.'

'Thanks.' Quentin accepted the sweet. 'Do you get sick, Sergeant?'

'Used to. First tour. Not any more.'

Quentin rose unsteadily to his feet. First tour, he pondered. This baby-faced Canadian had flown two full tours. Voluntarily. And was now signed up for this latest madcap venture, without even knowing what it was. Amazing. Quentin waved a grateful parting and set off up the fuselage.

In fact they were all amazing, these 617 crews, he'd decided. On the ground, just disparate gaggles of boozing, bickering, fool-about rascals, but put them together in their aeroplanes and they were magically transformed into something extraordinary. A fantastic seven-faceted machine, precision-engineered with just one function in mind—to wreak havoc on the enemy.

He ducked round the vacant upper turret, continuing forward to the first obstacle in his path: the three-foot step up onto the roof of the Lancaster's thirty-foot bomb bay. Once up, it was forward again, stooping now, until he reached an even greater barrier. This was the main spar, the boxed-in girder supporting the Lancaster's vast wings. The noise and vibration here were indescribable—the whole airframe shuddered from four roaring Merlin engines. Quentin shut his mind to the din and struggled on to the forward fuselage, bending almost double to squeeze through the gap between spar and roof. Halfway through he lost his balance and a hand grabbed him.

'Whoops there, Lieutenant!' Chalkie White leaned over from his wireless station. 'Mind the step.'

Quentin quickly recovered. 'Missed my footing, damn clumsy, thanks . . . So, how's it going up here now?'

Chalkie turned to his console, wedged into the side of the fuselage. 'Still a cockup, if you ask me. We can't talk to Barlow's Lanc except by flashing messages with an Aldis lamp, and we can't send or receive command broadcasts from base because we're too low to receive anything.'

'I see. Well, everything will get fixed in good time, I'm sure of it.'

'I bloody hope so, or this little caper could turn into a right balls-up . . . Whatever it is.'

'Indeed.'

'Such as sinking the *Tirpitz*?'

Quentin smiled. 'I wouldn't know. I'm only an intelligence officer.'

A few paces forward of the radio-operator's station was the navigator's cubicle, which was enclosed by a curtain, even though it was broad daylight. Quentin lifted a corner and saw that the navigator, Johnson, was hunched over what appeared to be an unravelling roll of toilet paper with lines and symbols drawn on it. Navigating at low level was proving almost as problematic as radio communications: with planes covering a mile every fifteen seconds, landmarks and turning-points were flashing by too fast to be identified. So 617's navigators were having to evolve new methods of finding their way, including using hand-drawn paper-roll maps, and the bomb aimer in the nose to act as their eyes. With only varying success.

He lowered the curtain and stepped onto the flight deck itself. Peter and his flight engineer had their backs to him, Peter in the big pilot's seat to the left, MacDowell on the fold-down seat beside him. Both were deeply immersed in the job at hand, and thankfully so, Quentin thought, because the job at hand involved flying the Lancaster at 250 mph, at barely treetop height, over hilly Yorkshire countryside, in close formation with a second Lancaster. While wearing blacked-out goggles. Spellbound by the speed, Quentin edged behind Peter's seat and plugged in his intercom. Instantly his head filled with the calm but insistent tones of Garvey, the New Zealand bomb aimer, lying in his Perspex blister in the nose.

'River coming in left to right. Copse of trees three o'clock. Village with church two miles eleven o'clock. Hill with ruin coming up beyond it. Line of pylons below peak. That's the next turning-point, right, Navigator?'

'Yes, it is. OK, Pilot, turn left heading two-two-oh degrees, Derwent reservoir should then be straight ahead, eight miles, caution Margery Hill to left, which rises to eight hundred—'

'Pylons! Jesus, pull up, Pilot, pull up *now*!'

Reflexively Peter hauled back on the controls, MacDowell rammed the throttles wide, and Quentin stared in breathless awe as the Lancaster soared skywards, engines screaming. Seconds ticked, the aeroplane strained, clouds beckoned, then came Guttenberg's voice from the tail. 'Pylons cleared!'

Immediately Peter bore downwards once more, eyes fixed to the windscreen. 'Sorry, everyone, that was a bit close.'

'You're telling me!'

'Well spotted those pylons, Billy.'

'Couldn't miss the durn things. Even with these God-awful goggles.'

'Aye, they'll need to come up with something better for night-vision training.'

'And keeping the nose gunner's feet out of the bomb-aimer's ears!'

'Sorry, Kiwi, but there's nowhere to put them . . .'

'Hey, where did Barlow go?'

Eyes peered outboard for the second Lancaster. 'I think he veered off, no wait, there he is . . . he's lost his trailing aerial!'

They all watched as Barlow, minus aerial, edged back into formation.

'Say, fellas . . .' Guttenberg commented. 'Would you say this operation is getting a tad dangerous?'

'I think you could safely say that, Herb.'

A pause. 'Whatever it is!'

THEY FLEW BACK to base without further incident, completing a four-hour training sortie that had begun with an eighty-mile leg over the North Sea, followed by a formation cross-country to Derwent reservoir, several low-level runs over the reservoir, and low-level attacks over the bombing range at Wainfleet, before finally flying back to Scampton. On that last leg, to Quentin's surprise, Peter offered him the pilot's seat. And to Quentin's further surprise, when he settled into that seat, and his left hand gripped the control column and his feet found the rudders, he found that all fear and nausea left him, and calmness enveloped him like a blanket. And even if his useless right hand refused to grip the controls, so that Uncle MacDowell had to operate the trim-wheels, the throttles, and pretty much everything, and even though this meant he might never fly again operationally, those few minutes were magically cathartic.

Walking back to dispersal, the crew pronounced the mission a success, despite the technical difficulties.

Guy Gibson pronounced it something else.

'Useless!' he roared. 'Completely bloody useless, the whole lot of you!'

They were assembled in the briefing room to receive their leader's ire. The general thrust of which, Quentin gathered, was that because 617 Squadron had only ten borrowed Lancasters to train with, they had to be nursed, and used wisely. That afternoon all ten had been dispatched on training flights. But two had come back on three engines, two more gave up after getting lost, one returned with engine-intakes stuffed with foliage, Barlow's came back minus an aerial, and one didn't come back at all.

'That was Carter,' Gibson growled. 'He phoned a while ago. From Manchester. His navigator made an error, they ended up flying in circles, then ran low on fuel.' He broke off angrily, pacing.

'Carter said he'd be home in a couple of hours,' he went on. 'I told him to leave his navigator behind, because he was sacked. Carter said if his navigator was sacked, then his whole crew was sacked. I told him to make his choice. So he made it, and they're gone. Off the squadron.'

Shocked murmurs circled the room, airmen glanced around uneasily, yet astonishingly there was more. One crew had failed to fly, Gibson added, for three days because of illness. 617 had no time for illnesses, he said, real or imagined, so they too were off the squadron. Which left just twenty crews to fly the mission.

Whatever it was.

'Can't you tell us anything, Guy?' one of his inner circle, Maltby, asked a few minutes later. Oddly, following news of the sackings, the mood in the room had lifted.

'Sorry, chaps, I can't. But I can tell you that if we get this job right, the result might even shorten the war. But to get it right, we must practise low flying day and night, over land and water, until we can do it blindfold.'

'So it is a ship then!' another stalwart, Hopgood, quipped.

'Maybe, Hoppy.' Gibson grinned, glancing at Quentin. 'You won't get it from me.' Then he became serious again. 'Two things will decide the success or failure of this operation. Training and secrecy. We've already talked about training, but that's only half the battle. If the enemy are ready for us, it'll be a bloody disaster. That's why you must all shut up about the mission. Stop asking, stop speculating, stop the rumourmongering.'

'That's all very well, boss, but how?' someone else asked.

Whitworth had entered the back of the hall, Quentin saw. Together with two men in suits. Somehow he sensed trouble. Sure enough, while Gibson was repeating his tirade about secrecy, Whitworth signalled him outside.

'Quentin, these gentlemen are squadron leaders Arnott and Campbell,' Whitworth introduced stiffly, 'from Intelligence Section, the Air Ministry.' Greetings were murmured, hands shaken. Neither seemed like an airman, Quentin felt, despite their rank. And why no uniforms? he wondered.

'You're the SIO?' Arnott eyed him dubiously.

'That's right, sir. Although, only acting SIO, strictly speaking.'

'Do you know the target for this operation?'

'No, sir. Of course not. Hardly anybody does.'

'Correct. Let's walk.' Leaving Whitworth outside the briefing room, they set off across the field, the two men flanking Quentin. Dusk was falling, the April evening cool. Nobody spoke until they were hundreds of yards into the open.

Campbell lit a cigarette. 'You've done all right, Lieutenant. Up to now.'

'Thank you, sir.'

'It can't have been easy, with that hand, and everything.'

'The hand's not a problem, sir.' Why was he speaking in the past tense? Quentin wondered.

Arnott glanced around again, to be sure they were out of earshot. 'So. Using *Tirpitz* as a cover story. That was your idea?'

'Well, yes, sir, I suppose it was.'

'How did you know it wasn't the real target?'

'I checked the idea with Group Captain Whitworth and Wing Commander Gibson. If *Tirpitz* was the real target, I knew they'd never approve it.'

'A reasonable deduction. So how did you go from there? How did you put it about that the target was the battleship *Tirpitz*?'

'Well, actually, I didn't. People just began to assume it. I merely didn't contradict them.'

'Very ingenious.'

'Thank you, sir. I call it rumour management.'

'How droll. When did it start?'

'Within a few days of the squadron forming. Why, is something wrong?'

They didn't reply, but stepped aside to confer. Quentin waited. The German battleship *Tirpitz*, currently hiding in a Norwegian fjord, had been a thorn in the Allies' side for years. Several attempts had been made to attack it, or flush it into the open, but ringed as it was with mines and massively defended by antiaircraft guns, no one had yet got near it. Most at 617 Squadron, not unreasonably, assumed it to be the target of their mission.

Arnott and Campbell finished conferring. 'Thank you, Lieutenant. You're being relieved of your responsibilities as station intelligence officer.'

'Have I done something wrong?'

'Not at all. It's just that the job is too big for one officer. It's a major operation. You're still on the team. It's just a much larger team now.'

'I see.' Easing him out, in other words. 'But why all the extra security?'

'Because, Lieutenant, 617's mission is too important to fail. Mainly.'

'What's the other reason?'

The men glanced at each other.

'I have a right to know.'

'No, you don't. But since you ask, the Germans are moving *Tirpitz* north to a new base in Altafjord.'

Quentin felt a chill. 'But why? I mean after all this time, why now?'

Then he realised why. The Germans had learned of a plan to attack it.

QUENTIN'S CAR was a 1938 MG TA, a neat sports two-seater, glossy black with red leather trim, spoked wheels and a fold-down roof. Since his injuries, driving it had been difficult, so the car saw little use. Lending it to Peter for the evening therefore, as a thank-you for his ride in the Lancaster, was no inconvenience.

It was Tess and Peter's third meeting since his posting to Scampton. The first two, emotionally charged daytime trysts on a bench in the park, served mainly to reconfirm the strength of feeling between them, which was more profound than either had realised. But by the third assignation, outside the church in Scampton village, they were more organised, and their emotions more controlled. Slightly. As Peter pulled up in the MG, Tess emerged from the shadows and climbed in .

'How long have you got?' he asked.

'I must be home by ten. Come on, let's get away from here.'

They drove out of Scampton, following blacked-out streets until they were clear of Lincoln.

'What did you tell Brendan?' he asked.

'That I'm going to the pictures with Phyllis. I don't know if he believed me, he's terribly suspicious at the moment, about everything.'

'God, I hate this. You're taking so much risk.'

She forced a wan smile. 'It's worth it.'

After five miles they left the main road, following country lanes until they found a village with a quiet-looking pub. Soon they were settled in a corner, drinking half-pints of watery bitter.

'You look tired, Peter. Is everything all right?'

'Yes, I think so. Hard work, plenty of problems, and the CO's never satisfied, always tearing someone off a strip. But that's the job, I suppose.' He sipped beer. 'Oh, I nearly forgot. Credo gave me this.'

He handed her an envelope. She slit it open, withdrew some pages and quickly read. 'It's a list of addresses. Regional offices of the Children's Adoption Agency. He says to write with any information about the baby's name, date and place of birth, parents, and so on. They might be able to trace her . . . assuming she was adopted.' She broke off. 'What does that mean?'

'I don't know. What if she wasn't adopted? I suppose. What if she's still in an orphanage?'

They looked at each other. 'Waiting to be adopted!'

'It's possible, isn't it?'

'Yes! I must get onto the letters first thing. Peter, what if we find her?'

'Yes . . .' He hesitated.

'Peter? What is it?'

'Nothing.' He gazed into his glass. 'Nothing. I was just thinking. About the baby. And Brendan. What he'd do if he found out.'

'Yes.' Tess sighed. 'God knows. He's so unpredictable. Laughing and joking one minute, angry and morose the next. Working all hours too.'

'He's feeling the pressure, like everyone. Is he treating you properly?'

'He gets angry, but mostly at himself. Then he smashes things, crockery and so on. It scares me.'

'Do you think he suspects us?'

'I don't know. The other night he came in, furious about something, shouting about how everything was fine until some gardening job in Feltwell.'

'What gardening job?'

'No idea, a grounds-keeping thing, I suppose. But it wasn't what he said, it was how he said it. White with rage, he was, and staring wildly.'

At the bar, the landlady polished glasses, watching them suspiciously, as if she knew.

'Tess,' Peter said quietly, 'I have to ask. Why did you marry him?'

She took his hand. 'Because he was kind at first. And attentive, and made me laugh for the first time in years. And he seemed to offer security, hope for a future, things I'd long given up on. But it was a mistake, a sham, and I've regretted it ever since. Then the violence started, and it was like . . .'

'What?'

'The final punishment. Only I couldn't take it. I didn't know what to do. Except try to find you.'

He squeezed her hand. 'Thank God you did.'

They talked a while longer, finished their beer then went out to the car and Peter drove home. At the church he switched off the engine and they held on tightly to one another.

'I wish I could get you away from here,' he said at length. 'Right now, that is.'

She patted his hand. 'I'll be careful. Apart from which, it's you we should be worrying about. Do you still have no idea what it's about?'

'The CO has told us to stop asking and concentrate on the training. So we're all agreed, Uncle and the boys and me, that's what we're going to do.'

Tess snuggled closer. 'Good idea. I'll stop asking too.'

Peter checked his watch. 'Nearly ten, Tess.'

'I know. Just five more minutes.'

'Of course.' He hesitated. 'May I ask you something?'

'Anything.'

'It's just, I never knew about the . . . the baby. Having it. And losing it. What actually happened? What was it like?'

LIKE DYING. Over and again. Like a nightmare that never fades but remains ever-fresh in the present, no matter how hard she blots it from memory.

The morning after the 'incident', the Derby family leave for Scotland in tightlipped silence. As the days pass, and still the matter goes unspoken, Tess realises it will remain so, left to rot like last year's leaves. She spends the days mostly alone, exploring rock pools on the beach, or walking the scrubby heather, or lying on her bed. Then one evening her mother comes in. 'Has our friend arrived?' she asks, knitting her fingers. But Tess doesn't understand. 'What friend?' And her mother snaps, 'You know damn well!'

And Tess realises she means her monthly period, which hasn't arrived, and as more days pass and no friend comes, her mother grows angrier, and more tearful, and more religious, going to Mass every day, while her father shakes his head and steals sad looks at her.

At last the holiday ends, but Tess and her mother don't return to Bexley, they go to stay with her mother's relatives in Anglesey, then with others in Prestatyn. But Tess becomes too pregnant for staying with relatives, so they move into a guesthouse overlooking the sea at Southport, where they stay a month. Lonely and desperate, Tess attempts to contact Peter. She creeps downstairs at night to use the guesthouse telephone. But the landlady hears her and comes storming down, saying the telephone is not for public use. Then she summons Tess's mother and tells her they must leave, saying the guesthouse is no place for good-for-nothing girls in trouble. So next morning her mother pays the bill, and pushes Tess into a taxi.

The confinement home, where Catholic girls in trouble go to have their babies, is in a wing of a convent outside Chester. The rooms are freezing, the food foul and the nuns severe. Between chapel and chores they attend scripture classes, or lessons about the error of their ways. Winter comes, then Christmas. She receives one card, from her father, expressing his sadness at her predicament, and the hope she is learning a lesson from it.

Her pains start one night in late March 1937. A midwife comes and tells the nuns to telephone Tess's mother. 'I don't want my mother,' Tess screams, but they telephone anyway. The midwife attaches Tess's legs to metal stands, then forces freezing fingers into her, tells her it's too soon. The woman goes away, and a while later the pains start in earnest. Towards dawn, feverish with exhaustion, she feels a hand touch her brow, opens her eyes and sees her mother. Compassion shows in her, just for a second.

The baby is born, a little girl, who is quickly bundled up and taken away. Tess's only memory of her is hearing her tiny cries receding down the corridor, then she is given a pill and told to sleep. Later her mother rouses her with tea. She looks calm, relieved and in control, for the first time since the incident behind the greenhouse.

'Everything's taken care of,' she says. 'The baby is in good hands, in foster care. Daddy and I have signed the necessary papers, and in time she'll go to an orphanage, then be adopted into a nice family.'

'But can't I see her?' Tess pleads.

'No,' her mother says, 'because that would be wrong. You will leave here and stay with Aunt Rosa in Lincoln, then in a few weeks when you're feeling better, you'll go to your finishing school in London.'

'But what about Peter?' Tess asks.

Her mother's face hardens. 'Never mention his name again. If you do, or if you try to contact him, we'll press charges and he'll go to prison.'

So Tess goes to Lincoln and stays with Aunt Rosa, her father's sister, who is scatty and kind-hearted. And in a few weeks, Tess writes to her parents saying she feels it will be better for everyone if she stays in Lincoln to finish her education. To no one's surprise they agree, and, apart from an annual Christmas card from her father, her parents never contact her again.

CHAPTER 5

At RAF Manston, in Kent, Air Vice-Marshal Cochrane, Charles Whitworth, Guy Gibson and an official called Ashwell from the Air Ministry, were meeting with a subdued-looking Barnes Wallis. Also present at the meeting, somewhat to his surprise, was Quentin Credo.

'Who's he?' demanded Ashwell, straight away.

'My ADC,' Whitworth replied smoothly. 'Flight Lieutenant Credo. He's synchronising the security effort at Scampton.'

'Very well. Let's get on with it. I've a train to catch.'

That morning, following two failed demonstrations of the weapon just off the north Kent coast, Ashwell had called a crisis meeting. He opened proceedings by summarising the day's events—two test drops, two failures—then began to argue the case for cancelling the project. Quentin half followed, hampered partly by his limited knowledge, but also because his head was reeling. Had Whitworth really said ADC? His aide-de-camp? Quentin had assumed his presence at Reculver, the small resort town three miles east of Herne Bay where the tests were carried out, was merely a consolation prize for being sacked. Now, apparently, he was his personal aide. Synchronising the security effort, whatever that meant.

Ashwell was still speaking. '. . . Believe me, Wallis, nobody is more respectful of your skill and ingenuity, but this is the third occasion I've watched this contraption fail. Now it's time to call a halt. After all, the latest date this mission can be carried out is less than four weeks away.'

'Yes,' Wallis admitted quietly. 'Full moon, the middle of May. Water levels at the dams will be at their highest. After that they start going down.'

'Well, there you have it. A splendid idea, but too ambitious, given the timeframe. Maybe next year. Now, I propose to return to London, draft the necessary paperwork cancelling the programme and—'

'No!' Wallis interrupted fervently. 'It just needs more testing. It *will* work, I'm sure of it!'

'So am I.' To everyone's surprise Guy Gibson stepped forward. 'If Mr Wallis says it'll work, that's good enough for me and my crews. After all, we're the ones flying it.'

Everyone knew Gibson's view was pivotal. If he remained supportive then Wallis had a chance. Over the weeks of testing the two men had grown close and, standing there at Wallis's side, Quentin saw a different Gibson from the firebrand scourge of Scampton: more like a doting nephew with a favourite uncle. Earlier that afternoon, when the second bomb failed, disintegrating as it hit the water, onlookers had witnessed the forlorn sight of Wallis peeling off shoes and socks and wading into the freezing water to search for wreckage. Most had turned away in embarrassment, but not Gibson, who had stayed at the water's edge to help.

'Gentlemen,' Ashwell was saying, 'let's be honest. This is not just about the bomb. This whole programme is costing us hugely in other ways—manpower, technical support, production facilities, not to mention cash. Resources that are badly needed elsewhere. And what about all the other snags? The radios don't work, navigation's a problem, the list is endless . . .'

'Nobody said it would be easy,' Wallis murmured.

'We're not asking for easy. We're asking for feasible.'

'It is feasible. I can fix the bomb and the other problems too, I'm sure.'

Ashwell surveyed the room, head shaking. Then picked up his briefcase. 'A week, gentlemen. Get it working by then, or the whole crackpot scheme is cancelled.'

The door slammed behind him. Then Cochrane spoke for the first time.

'Barnes, I'm briefing Harris in the morning. Is it really feasible? Given all the problems, the timing issues, technical hitches and so on?'

'Probably. Oh, I don't know.' Wallis sighed. 'Only if our luck changes.'

Over the next hour Quentin learned all there was to know. The bomb was code-named *Upkeep*, the mission was Operation Chastise. Its aim was to fly the twenty Lancasters of 617 Squadron into the dragon's den, the heavily defended Ruhr Valley area of Germany's industrial heartland, there to attack three key dams using Wallis's bomb. These dams held the millions of tons of water vital to the many foundries, power stations and factories situated along the valley. Smashing the dams would not only unleash a monstrous tidal wave of destruction, but also render any surviving installations useless. Germany's war machine, it was hoped, would grind to a halt.

The devil, as always, was in the detail. Firstly, to have any chance of reaching their objectives, and getting home again, the Lancasters must fly the entire mission at ground level, by moonlight, using special routes planned for stealth and surprise. Secondly, assuming they made it, they must then attack the dams in the exact manner prescribed by Wallis, who believed just one bomb, precisely delivered, was enough to destroy a dam.

Which was just as well, Quentin reflected, for each Lancaster would carry only one bomb, and the manner of delivery was very precise indeed. To begin with, the bomb had to be spun at an alarming 500 revolutions per minute, backwards, using a belt-driven winch in the bomb bay before it could be dropped. The attack had to be made head-on, over the water, at right angles to the dam. The aircraft's wings must be held precisely level, height above the water kept at exactly 150 feet and the air speed fixed at 232 mph. The backwards-spinning bomb must then be released precisely 450 yards from the centre of the dam. Too soon and it would sink short, too late and it would smash against the parapet, or skip harmlessly over. Correctly dropped, however, it should bounce across the lake to the dam wall, whereupon it would explode, causing fatal damage to its structural integrity. The monstrous weight of water behind would do the rest.

Quentin absorbed the information in breathless silence. It was as inspired a plan as it was audacious, the perfect marriage of daring and ingenuity. Although not yet fully formed, he reminded himself. Not proven. Because despite all the proven hydrodynamics, and the weeks of tank tests at Teddington, the full-sized *Upkeep* had yet to bounce. Even once.

The evening wore on, discussion became heated, cooled, reheated again. Finally Wallis tossed aside his pencil.

'There is only one way,' he sighed wearily. 'In the available time, that is.'

'Well, spit it out, man.' Cochrane's patience was wearing thin.

'Get rid of the bomb casing altogether. Drop it in its cylindrical form.'

'Will that work?'

'Yes. But only if we reduce the impact. By dropping it lower. Sixty feet should do it.'

Stunned silence followed. Then Gibson cleared his throat.

'Um, that's less than the wingspan of a Lancaster, you know. Bank the aircraft a little, or sneeze, and you'd hit the water. That would be that.'

'I know, Guy,' Wallis said gently. 'That's why I couldn't ask you to do it.'

'By day it's easy,' Gibson went on, gazing at the table. 'You've lots of cues to judge height. But at night you've none. That's the problem. We need a way of judging height, accurately, at night, over water. If we can solve that, we could do it at sixty feet.'

Cochrane looked round the table. 'Yes, but how?'

NEXT MORNING, Quentin began his new job as Whitworth's ADC. The title was unofficial, he knew, a throwback to an era when an aide-de-camp was a leader's trusted adviser, and at first the job seemed little different to the old one. But, as the morning wore on, strange things began to happen. First a tray of tea and biscuits arrived, brought by a steward from the officer's mess. Then an adjutant dropped by, asking if Quentin needed any typing. Finally, a workman screwed a nameplate to his door—*F/L Q. Credo DSO*.

Then there was Chloe Hickson, a WAAF corporal, fluttering about the corridor like a trapped moth. When he left his office she sprang up and saluted, when he returned she saluted and sat down.

Eventually, bemused, he confronted her. 'Bad form saluting indoors, Corporal. I'm not wearing a cap, so can't return it.'

'Oh. I see. Sorry, sir,' she replied, saluting once more.

'That's quite all right. Except you did it again. Um, who are you exactly?'

'Corporal Hickson, sir. Your driver.'

'My driver!' Suddenly Quentin found himself laughing, for the first time in months. 'A driver, ha! How marvellous, Corporal, you've quite made my day! And have we got a car?'

'Of course, sir. Would you like to see it? It runs, you know.'

'A driver, a car, and it runs! My cup overfloweth.' He glanced up the corridor. Arnott, one of the new intelligence offiers, was approaching. 'Thank you, Corporal, I'd love to, perhaps later?'

He returned to his desk. The unsmiling Arnott followed and locked the door behind him.

'I hear Reculver was another fiasco,' he began, sitting opposite Quentin.

'Not entirely successful, no.'

Arnott shook his head, then withdrew a sheet from his briefcase. 'This is a list of infringements and breaches of security rules, which we'd like you to follow up.'

Quentin glanced through the list: times, dates, misdemeanours, names. At once one jumped out. *Sgt B. Murray*. 'Of course, sir, I'll look into it.'

'Right away, please.'

'Yes, um, have you unearthed anything, may I ask? Anything serious?'

Arnott leaned over. 'Lieutenant, there are no serious security breaches at Scampton. If there were we'd know about them.' He paused. 'One more thing—one of 617's pilots is carrying on with a married woman on the station. Lightfoot, his name is. Put a stop to it.'

After he'd gone Quentin read the list. The 'infringements' were very routine: a security pass mislaid, a harmless comment dropped, an innocent question posed. Almost as if Arnott and Campbell were deliberately distracting him from the real business of security. Yet what of Peter and Tess? he wondered. How had they been discovered? Something was amiss. He pocketed the list, gathered up his driver and descended to the pavement.

Where a decidedly careworn Austin 8 awaited. Which his driver couldn't drive. Quentin took the front passenger seat, clearly unnerving Chloe, who expected him in the back. Then the engine wouldn't start, and she turned it over and over until it flooded. When it did finally explode into life, she was unable to engage gear, one hand stirring the stick while onlookers smirked and the gearbox snarled in protest. Eventually Quentin rammed it into gear with his good hand, whereupon Chloe let the clutch out with a bang and the car promptly stalled.

At that he ordered her out. 'Swap seats, for heaven's sake. You change gears, I'll steer with my left hand and call them out. Got it?'

'Yes, sir.' Chloe was close to tears. 'Sorry, sir.'

'Don't apologise, worse things happen at sea. So I'm told. First gear!'

They set off round the perimeter, erratically to begin with but soon settling to a rhythm, Quentin operating the pedals, Chloe changing gear and occasionally steering as required. First stop was Hangar 2, to caution a fitter heard grumbling about 'all this bleedin' low flying'. Next, to the telephony room where an inconsequential message had gone astray, and so on until Quentin had crossed all but one name off the list.

Then he went in search of Brendan Murray.

Whose offence, he read, had little to do with security, but related to his black-market activities. Apparently he'd short-changed an engineering sergeant over a carton of cigarettes. Quentin, unsure how much Murray knew about Tess and Peter, sensed he must tread carefully.

They found him in the equipment barn, eating lunch with his civilian contractors. 'Well, and what have we here!' Murray grinned, as though expecting him. 'Come on in, sir, and how the devil are you?'

'Well enough, thank you, Sergeant.' Quentin stepped into the gloom. Eight men sat at a table strewn with sandwiches and illicit bottles of beer.

'Gents, this is Flight Lieutenant Credo,' Murray explained. 'A wonderful fellow and first-class hero. Got caught out on a mine-laying trip, flew his burning machine clear of Jerry's deadly clutches, then put the flames out with his own bare hands, thus saving the lives of half of his crew.'

Murmured platitudes and discomfited glances as always, Quentin noted dully. Then a cough came from behind. Chloe, petite, steadfast, strikingly pretty suddenly, was framed in the doorway.

'Hello, and who's this beautiful young thing?'

'Oh, this is my driver, Corporal Hickson.'

'And welcome to you, young lady.' Murray rose, pocketing the black notebook on the table before him. 'Come and have a sandwich with the fellows here, so's Mr Credo and I can talk outside.'

'No, thanks,' Chloe replied lightly. 'I've already eaten.'

'Suit yourself.' They walked into the sunlight where Quentin outlined the complaint against Murray. As he did so Murray seemed to relax, he noted. As though he'd been anticipating worse.

'That bastard is a liar!' he countered immediately. 'And he owes me five guineas for betting.'

'That's as may be, Sergeant, but trading in contraband is illegal.'

'So's the gambling, but everyone does it and where's the harm?'

'The harm, I suppose, is where you draw the line. This is a bomber station at war.'

'And my private dealings have never interfered with that. Ever. But I tell you what. I'll scale them back a bit, if you like. Put the lid on things. Just till this present nonsense is all finished.'

'What present nonsense?' Quentin asked.

'The new squadron. The hush-hush training, the fellows in dark suits.'

'You don't miss much, do you?'

'Best not to, in my experience.'

'Indeed. How did you know what happened on my last mission?'

'Common knowledge. I was at Feltwell that day too. Bad business.'

'Of course. I forgot.'

'Will there be anything else?' Murray smiled warily.

'Not for now. Thank you for your cooperation.'

'A pleasure. My regards to Charlie Whitworth.'

'Yes.' Quentin hesitated. 'And mine to your wife. I trust she's well?'

The eyes darted sideways. 'She's fine, sir. Quite fine.'

They parted at the barn. Back in the car Chloe was incredulous. 'Cheeky so and so!' she exclaimed. 'He doesn't care, sir, does he? About anything!'

'So it would seem. Second gear, please. And have you already eaten?'

'No, but I didn't want to miss anything. Like the question about his wife, sir. What was that about, if I may ask?'

'Nothing. Just a pleasantry, Corporal.'

'Well, he didn't like it. Not one bit.'

'Really? How could you tell?'

'Woman's intuition.'

IN FLIGHT OPS, a breakthrough at last. At three that afternoon, all twenty of 617's pilots were invited to assemble in Number 2 hangar beside one of the Lancs. Gibson then called them onto the flight deck in groups of four. As usual his inner circle went first: Hopgood, Martin, Maltby and Young, replaced ten minutes later by Shannon, Maudslay, Astell and Knight. Peter and the others waited their turn, feigning nonchalance. Gibson's eight favourites always took precedence, then Peter's group of six, then the final back-up group of five. Peter's group, an affable Commonwealth assortment, had been increasingly rostered to fly together, led by Flight Lieutenant 'Big Joe' McCarthy of 97 Squadron, a twenty-four-year-old from Brooklyn, New York, who had enlisted via the Canadian Air Force. Also from 97 Squadron was Les Munro, a farmer from Gisborne, New Zealand. From Saskatchewan, Canada, was Vernon Byers, who at thirty-two was the oldest of 617's pilots. Then came Peter's 61 Squadron cohort, the Australian Norm Barlow, who'd lost his aerial training over Yorkshire. Finally the only other Englishman, Geoff Rice, who was recruited from 57 Squadron.

The development Gibson wanted to show them was night-training equipment. A new system called Two Stage Blue, whereby all the cockpit windows were covered with blue filters, while the pilot's, navigator's and bomb-aimer's goggles were tinted with amber. The result was an uncannily accurate simulation of night, and meant that all training could now be undertaken under real or simulated night conditions. There was more. New wireless equipment had been installed to improve communications, and down in the bomb-aimer's compartment, the padded chest-rest had been lowered, stirrups had been rigged to keep the front gunner's feet clear of the aimer's head, and on his seat lay a curious wooden triangle.

'It's just a sighting aid,' Gibson explained vaguely. 'A chap called Dann knocked it up. Surprisingly simple, yet highly accurate.' He handed it to Peter. An adjustable V-shaped triangle with a peephole at the apex and two nails in either corner, it certainly looked and felt rudimentary. 'You hold it up to your eye,' Gibson went on. 'Then, when the two nails line up with the aiming points on the target, you know you're at the right range, press the bomb-release tit and Bob's your uncle. We start trying them out today.'

'Where?' Big Joe asked innocently.

'Derwent reservoir. The two towers on the dam there. It's as good as anywhere. I also want you to try getting as low as possible to the water. Say sixty feet or so. Your altimeter will be useless at that height so you'll have to judge it by eye. Be careful.'

Owing to the ongoing shortage of aircraft, Peter's formation of three didn't get airborne until evening. In the meantime they were kept at readiness in the ops room, chatting, dozing, or simply sitting in companionable silence. Finally they got airborne, just as full darkness was falling. Broken cloud obscured a waning half-moon, otherwise the sky was clear and visibility good. Peter led a loose formation of three, Geoff Rice to his left, Vernon Byers to his right. The route to Derwent was a prepared one, tried and tested over many sorties. Halfway across Nottinghamshire, Peter became aware of a presence behind him. A moment later a click came over the headphones. 'Navigator here. I'm on the flight deck.'

'Jamie?' Peter queried. 'Everything all right?'

'The navigators had a meeting,' Jamie said. 'We all agreed that staying at our desks on a low-level mission like this is pointless. Far better we navigate from the flight deck'.

'Well, good, it definitely will help, but are you OK with it?'

'Fine. I think.' He laughed nervously.

'Good for you, Jamie lad,' Uncle said.

'Wow, Jamie on the flight deck. Who'd have bet on that?'

'Kiwi would.'

'No, I wouldn't.'

'Rear gunner to Pilot.'

'Yes, hello, Herb, what is it?'

'Nothing. Just an intercom check.'

The three Lancasters reached Derwent without incident and took up a circling pattern a mile to the north. Below them the reservoir lay like a long, narrow shard of black glass nestling amid tree-covered peaks. Studying it closely, Peter signalled the others to wait, then wheeled over for the first run, the Merlins popping and crackling as Uncle throttled back to lose height. The altimeter read 100 feet, the water looked much nearer. He disregarded his instruments, fixed his eyes on the gleaming black, and let the bomber settle lower. Then lower still, until the shadowy landscape was rising up all around as though he was about to land. Beside him Uncle held the throttles, adjusting power to maintain speed; behind him, breath held, Jamie watched the tree-lined banks flash by in a dizzying blur. And, lying down in the nose, Kiwi tried to ignore the hurtling blackness beneath him, picked up his wooden triangle and held it to his eye.

'Can't see a bloody thing,' he reported. 'No, wait, hang on . . .' Far in the distance emerged the faint, dark line of the dam, a square sluice tower at either end. 'OK, there it is, I see it. Come right a bit, Pilot, that's it, right a little more . . . OK, that's good, hold it there.'

The lake curved left, then right again, and Peter eased into a shallow S-turn to line up with the dam. As he did so, the aircraft slid under the shadow of the left-hand bank and he lost all visual reference.

'I . . . I can't see, can't see the height . . .'

'Pull up! Pull up now!' A cry from Guttenberg. Peter wrenched back, Uncle slammed the throttles wide and the Lancaster soared skywards, run aborted. Seconds passed, the engines strained, Peter hauled harder, stamping a foot on the panel for leverage, dark hills filled the windscreen, then at last the starlit sky appeared and the danger slid by beneath.

In a minute, normal order was restored, the power throttled back, and the Lancaster was settled in level flight once more. Then came the analysis.

'All right, lads, well done, good effort,' Uncle encouraged.

'Good effort? It was a bloody disaster!' Kiwi countered. 'The towers weren't in line or anything.'

'This is crazy,' Billy added from the nose turret. 'Like riding a motorcycle blindfold. What the hell happened?'

'Propeller wash,' Herb replied. 'In the water suddenly, trailing behind, you know, like a speedboat. Only four speedboats, one from each prop.'

'Jesus, how low do you have to be for that?'

'Too bloody low, the props could only have been inches off.'

'Pilot to Crew, well spotted there, Herb, that was my fault. I lost vision in the shadows, must have dipped a bit. We'll try again in a minute . . .'

'Maybe I could keep a lookout for height?' Jamie suggested. 'Then, you know, tap on your shoulder or something to signal up or down. That way you could keep your eyes on the view ahead.'

'Good idea, Jamie, we'll give it a try.'

It was midnight by the time they landed back at Scampton. Predictably Gibson was still up and wanting an immediate update. Peter went to his office. He had made three runs, he reported, all with the same result: the new sight worked well, but blind-flying the Lancaster down to sixty feet, in total darkness, was nigh on impossible. Not without risking disaster.

'I know,' Gibson replied, his voice unusually subdued. 'I tried it too and damn near hit. Apparently there's some new kit arriving tomorrow, maybe it'll do the trick. In the meantime, the ADC wants to see you.'

'Now, sir?'

'Yes.' Gibson shuffled papers. 'In his rooms. Right now.'

Peter hurried along the station's darkened paths to the accommodation blocks. Reaching Credo's door, he knocked and it opened at once.

The room was in shadow, lit by a single table lamp. One other person was present, a female, sitting on the edge of a chair.

'Tess!'

'Peter, thank God!' She rose and hugged him with relief.

'What is it? What's happened?'

'It's all right. I'm OK.'

Quentin handed him a drink. 'Here, have this, you're going to need it.'

'For God's sake, tell me!'

'In short, I interviewed Murray this morning. Tonight he attacked Tess.'

'What!'

'It's true.' Tess cupped his face. 'But I'm all right, it's nothing . . .'

Her cheek was bruised, he saw then, and one eyebrow swollen. 'Nothing? Look at you! And what's this scarf? Tess, tell me.'

She touched the scarf she wore at her neck, then pulled it aside to reveal angry red welts.

'Jesus, what has he done?'

'She must get checked by a doctor first thing,' Quentin said. 'There's also bruising. Ribs mostly.'

'My God.' Peter searched her eyes, feeling fury rise inside him. 'I'll kill him. I'll get my service revolver and shoot him dead. Right now.'

'No, Peter, I beg you. Sit down for a moment. There's more.'

She explained how Brendan had come back very late that night, drunk and abusive. 'You shopped me,' he'd shouted. 'You shopped me to that bastard Credo.' But she hadn't understood, hadn't known what he meant. 'No, Brendan, I haven't done anything.' 'Don't lie,' he'd yelled. Suddenly he came at her, grabbing her round the throat with both hands. She'd tried to fight free, but was powerless, unable to breathe, and as unconsciousness beckoned he'd brought his face close to hers and hissed, 'I fixed him, and I'll fix you. And I'll fix your pilot boyfriend you think I don't know about. I'll fix the whole lot of them.' Then he'd flung her to the floor and kicked her in a wild frenzy before, panting breathlessly, he'd stormed off.

In Quentin's rooms, silence. Peter, aghast, struggled to find a voice. 'You must leave him,' he whispered. 'We'll get a room. I'll protect you.'

'I'm sorry, but you can't,' Quentin said. 'Gibson knows about you two. There was some tip-off to the intelligence people, I think. The point is, he says you're to stop seeing each other or you're off the squadron, Peter.'

'Fine. Then I resign.'

'No.' Tess knelt at his side. 'That's not what you want, Peter, and not what we agreed. Remember? We said you'd see this through, then we'll go away together.'

Peter shook his head. 'That was then, this is now.'

'OK, but consider this,' Quentin went on. '617 Squadron is already down to twenty crews. If you pack it in, they'll be down to nineteen. You'll be putting everybody in even greater danger. Is that what you want?'

'I don't care. Tess is more important.'

'You do care. So does Gibson. He says you're one of the best. He said if he didn't regard you so highly he'd have already sacked you.'

'Think of your crew,' Tess coaxed. 'They've put everything into this too.'

'All right.' Peter sighed. 'All right, but Murray then. We'll get him arrested. For common assault.'

Tess and Quentin exchanged glances. 'We could try, yes . . .' Quentin agreed. 'But this is a military base on full alert, remember, so a complaint would be handled by the Provost Marshal's office. And what would we tell them? That a key staff member turned violent when he discovered his wife was seeing another man? They might not be too sympathetic.'

'God.' Peter was shaking his head. 'I don't believe this . . .'

'Please try.' Tess touched his arm. 'Quentin thinks there's more to it than we realise. He thinks it's better to keep Brendan here. Under watch.'

'Yes, but I'm not leaving you alone with him.'

'You don't have to.' Quentin checked his watch. 'There's a taxi waiting at the main gate. I've booked a room at the Royal. Tess can stay there tonight, then tomorrow find a room somewhere quiet. She'll write a note telling Murray she's gone home to her family for a while. He'll never know. In the meantime, you keep your head down and concentrate on the job.'

At Quentin's insistence, Peter left first, returning by a roundabout route to his quarters. Then Quentin followed with Tess. As he helped her into the taxi she said, 'What did Brendan mean? When he said he fixed you?'

Quentin straightened from the window. *Tirpitz*, he'd thought immediately, when Tess told him what Murray had said. He'd tipped off Arnott and Campbell about his *Tirpitz* cover story, and thus got him fired. For helping Tess. Either that, or something so dreadful he could barely bring himself to consider it. 'God knows, Tess.' He sighed. 'God only knows.'

He turned from the taxi and went back to his rooms.

CHAPTER 6

And at that point, Quentin reflected, consulting his file, the stage was effectively set. Tess moved into a guest house in Lincoln, took sick leave from her NAAFI job and dropped out of sight. Peter stayed in contact as best he could, by note and occasional clandestine meeting, although as April turned to May, leaving the station became impracticable. Meanwhile, heavy rain and escalating aircraft movements kept Brendan Murray fully occupied tending Scampton's runways. Quentin kept his file up to date and watched from afar.

As for the dams mission, as is so often the way with grandiose British ventures, just when all seemed hopeless, everything began to go right . . .

'QUENTIN!' WHITWORTH hissed over the intercom a few days later. 'It works!'

Quentin glanced at Chloe, busy at his filing cabinet. 'Beg pardon, sir?'

'The *thing*. It works! Quick, get in here!'

Quentin hurried to Whitworth's office and shut the door behind him.

Whitworth handed him a photograph. 'This was taken at Reculver yesterday. I saw the whole thing. It actually bloody works!'

Quentin studied the photo. It showed exactly the same stretch of coast as before, and a similar gaggle of onlookers, including Ashwell, Gibson, Whitworth and a bare-headed Barnes Wallis. Who was waving his arms triumphantly, like a conductor. At the massive drumlike bomb careering across the sea towards the beach.

'Gracious!' Quentin stared at the picture. 'It's three feet in the air!'

'Yes. Quentin, if only you'd seen it. And you know what that means?'

'The operation is on?'

'Precisely.' Then Whitworth nodded at some more photos on his desk. 'Want to see the target?'

Quentin picked up the photos, a sequence taken from above a vast hook-shaped lake surrounded by fields and woodland. At one end lay the long bowed wall of a dam, topped by two sluice towers.

'That's the Möhne,' Whitworth said. 'Quite a monster, isn't it? A photo-reconnaissance Spitfire took the pictures from thirty thousand feet. Each picture is a week apart, the last one taken yesterday. What do you notice?'

Nothing, was Quentin's initial reaction, apart from differences in light and angle. Then he looked closer. 'The water level. On the dam. It's higher in each picture.'

'Well spotted. It's fed by snow-melt and winter rain. By May the targets reach their fullest, which is when Wallis says they must be attacked.'

Quentin checked the wall calendar. 'And the crews need a full moon to fly the operation . . .'

'Which falls around the middle of this month.'

'Good grief.'

'Precisely. We have very little time indeed.'

Quentin retreated to his office, where he found Chloe waiting with a tray of tea. 'There are two messages for you, sir,' she said. 'A Mrs Barclay, from Staffordshire Council, returned your call of last week. She has some information for you. Shall I phone her back?'

'No, thanks. I'll deal with it later. Anything else?'

'There's a message from the control tower. The first batch of the new Lancs is due any minute.'

Quentin picked up his cap. 'Then I propose we drive out to meet them.'

They took the Austin, he at the wheel, she shifting gears, and sped across the rain-puddled concrete to a far corner of the airfield. There a reception committee of 617 aircrew waited by a control caravan.

One of the pilots ambled up as Quentin disembarked. It was John Hopgood, a twenty-two-year-old Londoner from 106 Squadron.

'Any sign of the new Lancs?' Quentin asked.

'Any time now.' Hopgood scanned the horizon, one hand cupped to his eye. 'I heard what you did, Credo. In that Wimpy. Dinghy Young told me. Bloody brave, it was. We all think so. Just wanted you to know.'

'Thanks. I appreciate it.' Quentin glanced at Chloe, surrounded by fawning airmen. 'How's the night training? Are the new lights working?'

'Yes. Two spotlights, see, mounted on the underside of the Lanc, one aft of the bomb bay, the other under the nose. Both angled so from the cockpit you can see them shining on the water, forward of the starboard wing. The boffins set the angles so the two beams converge at a height of sixty feet. Works like a dream! Tried it myself last night. Navigator stands by the pilot, watching the spots and calling the height, you know, up a bit, down a bit . . . Meanwhile the bomb aimer sings out the range with his Dann sight thing. That leaves the pilot free to concentrate on the flying.'

'That's very good news. What about the radios?'

'Latest plan is to fit VHF, like the fighter boys use, so the Lancs can talk to one another, at least over short distances. We'll use standard W/T to send and receive Morse signals over long distances.'

Quentin cocked his head. From the west rose the drone of distant engines. 'It's beginning to sound as if it's all coming together, Hoppy.'

'And not a moment too soon. All we need now is a weapon . . .'

'Hmm. Can't comment there. But how about some new Lancs to play with? Here they come! What's it called, by the way, this version of the Lanc?'

'It's not called anything. Just the type modification number. Lancaster Type 464 Provisioning.'

The drone rose to a rumble, and then to a roar, as five of the modified Lancasters thundered overhead, settled into a wide left-hand circuit and descended, one by one, to land. A few minutes later, they were taxiing towards the waiting airmen, whose reaction was predictably scornful.

'Jesus! What have they done to the bomb bays?'

'They're all cut away, look, and the bomb doors have gone.'

'And what are those fork things sticking down?'

But there was no hiding their excitement. All those relentless weeks of training and borrowed aircraft, whispered rumours, and jibes from other units, and suddenly the job they'd signed up for was becoming a reality. Quentin watched as the leading Lancaster shut down engines, to be immediately mobbed by airmen swarming round it like excited children.

Over the next few days the remaining aircraft were delivered and assigned to their crews. 617 Squadron's identification letters, 'AJ', were painted in red on the side of each, together with a third call-sign letter. Allocating aircraft was a random matter, thus AJ-A for Apple went to Dinghy Young, AJ-B for Baker went to Bill Astell, Gibson got AJ-G for George, Hopgood AJ-M for Mother, and so on. Peter's crew, to their delight, were allocated AJ-V for Victor, which they immediately rechristened Vicky in honour of Chalkie's wife. Barely had the engineers signed it off and towed it outside, when they were clambering aboard for a test flight.

'Nose turret looks in order,' Billy Bimson reported. 'Clean as a whistle.'

'The new radios are in too,' Chalkie added, seating himself at his station. 'Latest Type 1143 VHFs and thanks very much.'

'New Gee set, too,' Jamie added.

'Same old Elsan,' Herb Guttenberg muttered, pushing past the toilet to the rear turret, sixty feet away from his crewmates in the nose. Unperturbed, he closed his turret doors and squeezed into his seat, sniffing the oil on the four Browning .303 machine guns. Each gun fired twelve bullets a second, four guns meant nearly fifty withering rounds every second, devastating firepower if properly used. Recently 617's gunners had come to a decision. Normally ammunition was loaded with every fourth bullet a tracer round, so gunners could follow their shots. Herb and his cohorts, sensing they'd be flying into the teeth of a storm, planned to shoot with 100 per cent tracer, to create a visually shocking effect, maximise accuracy, and fool the Germans they were firing cannon. Wishful thinking, Herb knew, but disconcerting the enemy, even for a few seconds, might mean the difference between life and death.

Far away in the nose, Kiwi stowed his kit then stretched out to inspect the huge Perspex nose blister. In his pocket was a piece of string, of specially measured length and with a strategically placed knot in its centre. He and other bomb aimers had found that by tying the string to either side of the blister, then holding it to your nose to form a triangle, exactly the same geometric effect could be achieved as with the wooden Dann sight, only simpler and easier to hold steady. In theory, when the sluice towers at Derwent lined up precisely with two grease-pencil marks made on the Perspex, the bomber would be exactly 450 yards from the dam. Kiwi pulled out his pencil and unravelled the string. Tonight he'd try it for real.

Above his head, Billy Bimson checked his two Brownings, his feet securely stirruped out of harm's way.

'You all set up there, Billy boy?' Kiwi asked.

'All set, Kiwi,' Billy replied. 'Just wish we could get on with it.'

They finished strapping in, powered up the master circuits, donned flying helmets and plugged in intercoms. Communication checks completed, they continued down the checklist. Five minutes later V-Vicky went bumping across the grass towards the downwind corner of the airfield.

As soon as the green light flashed on the control caravan, Peter released the brakes and eased up the starboard throttles, turning the bomber into wind. Then he ran each engine up to full power, checking the two-stage blower, the propeller pitch controls and the magnetos. Finally all was ready.

'OK, Uncle, let's go.'

'Flaps thirty.'

'Thirty.'

'Radiators closed.'

'Closed.'

'Throttles locked.'

'Locked.'

'That's it everyone, hold tight, here we go!'

TESS WOKE UP with a jolt. The nightmare once again. Hands clamped at her throat, wringing the breath from her. She sat up, shaking, fingering her neck. Overhead, a rumble of engines receded into the distance. It was these that had woken her, she realised. Lancs. They were training night and day now. She swung her legs to the floor and a crumpled page fell to her feet. She bent and recovered it, smoothed it, then pressed it to her heart. Quentin's note. The one delivered that afternoon. The one she had waited six years for.

He'd found an address for her daughter, in Croxton, Staffordshire, forty miles from where she was born. All the research and the letter-writing had finally borne fruit. At first a tentative confirmation: *Yes, Mrs Murray, a record of your daughter does exist.* Then a follow-up letter: *Yes, Mrs Murray, your daughter was adopted by a family living near Stafford: 'CT T. and Mrs G.', who also have an older son. She is healthy and doing well.* Then a stone wall: *No, Mrs Murray, we cannot give contact details.*

But Quentin had done the rest, helped by a twist of fate. The letter had contained an unintended clue. 'CT' was a military rank—Chief Technician—a senior NCO in the RAF. A couple of phone calls later, and

'CT T. G.' was identified as Chief Technician Thomas Groves, married with two children, of 23 Poplar Lane, Croxton, Staffs.

And there it was, waiting on the hall table when Tess had returned from the library that afternoon. She'd spotted Quentin's ragged handwriting on the envelope and had known somehow that his message was momentous. At the instant of reading it she'd felt herself falling, as though in a dream, and she'd sunk to her bed, turned to her pillow, and sobbed as though her heart would burst. And then finally she'd found sleep.

Now she must go there. Today, right away. She reached for her coat, but as she did so she heard a floorboard creak, right outside her door. She froze, rigid with terror. Then came the knock, softly, almost apologetically.

'Tess, dear. It's me.' A man's voice.

She crept to the door, one hand to her mouth, and opened it. He'd aged, she saw at once, and shrunk, his posture stooped, his face drawn and lined.

'Father?' she said. 'Father, is it really you?'

'I'm so sorry, turning up unannounced like this.' Rheumy eyes took in the room. 'I wasn't sure . . . Is this where you live?'

'No. Well, yes . . .' she blurted. 'For the moment. How did you find me?'

'With some difficulty!' he joked, then burst into coughing. 'Taxi dropped me at Scampton. Terrible palaver. Barbed wire, armed guards . . . They weren't letting me in, that's for sure. They fetched a security officer, dreadfully disfigured, poor fellow . . . He asked me a lot of damn-fool questions, then I managed to convince him I meant you no ill, whereupon he gave me this address. And here I am.' He shrugged.

'Yes. Here you are. After all this time. But why . . . why now?'

'Because it's long overdue. And life's too short.'

They walked up the hill to the cathedral, pausing frequently to rest. He was ill, she realised, breathless and weak. Soon she was slipping an arm round him to give him support. It felt strange, after all the years, embracing her father again, strange but not unnatural.

They arrived in time for choral evensong, where in the vaulted transept they listened to Howell's haunting *Nunc Dimittis*, and watched the evening sunlight pour through the great southern window.

'Exquisite,' her father murmured. 'And I'd forgotten it was so big.'

'You've been here before?'

'Once. On holiday with your mother. Before you were born.'

Tess looked up at the distant ceiling. 'When the weather's misty, which is quite often round here, the bomber crews say the cathedral seems to float in the air like a ship on an ocean, guiding them to safety.'

'I can imagine.' He nodded. 'Peter's in bombers, I believe. He came to see us. He was worried about you. It didn't go well, I'm afraid.'

'He told me. We're . . . well, we're in touch.'

'I'm glad.'

Afterwards he bought her supper in a nearby pub, and as they talked she realised he was there to seek peace and comfort, even reconciliation. David was doing well in Africa, he said. As for her mother, he said she was in good health and left it at that. He ate little and his wine stayed untouched, and, all too soon, clearly exhausted, he asked her to walk him to his hotel.

'It's the cancer, Tess,' he confessed, at the door. 'In my chest and bones.'

'I'm so sorry.'

'No, it's me who should apologise.' He gripped her hands. 'I've an early train in the morning. Don't bother seeing me off.'

'Would you like me to visit you in Bexley?'

'Very much. But only if you feel up to it.'

'And Peter?'

His eyes searched hers. 'What happened, Tess, the way we treated you, was terribly wrong. I pray you can find it in your heart to forgive us.'

'What about Mother?'

'Her faith sustains her. Don't expect too much.'

THE BOMBS ARRIVED, thirty-seven of them, on a convoy of low-loaders shrouded in tarpaulins, and were driven straight to a guarded hangar away from view. With them came specially modified bomb trolleys, a mobile crane and a wheeled gantry for loading. An additional nineteen practice bombs, identical in every detail except concrete-filled, were delivered to Manston for tests at Reculver. At last 617's crews got to see the weapon they'd trained so hard to use—and have a try at using it.

Results were encouraging, although not problem-free. Spinning the bombs up to speed took time and caused the aircraft to vibrate, sometimes alarmingly, which affected handling and performance. Their rotation affected magnetic compasses too, and with accurate navigation vital, these had to be carefully re-swung. As for dropping the bombs, the weeks of training had not been in vain and most practice drops went smoothly, the bombs typically bouncing four or five times over distances of 400 to 600 yards.

Which was good enough. Another week passed, the days grew longer, the weather turned mild and dry. Back at Scampton training continued, but the priority shifted onto procedural matters, communications and navigation. The three groups that emerged in training were now consolidated: a primary flight of nine led by Gibson in G-George, Peter's second flight of six led by Big Joe McCarthy in Q-Queenie, and a back-up flight of five led by Warner Ottley in C-Charlie.

Security on the ground was tighter than ever. Guards patrolled fences and checked passes. Doors were barred, gates locked, barriers erected, while Number 2 hangar was practically a fortress. A virtual communications blackout was imposed, with news filtered, phone calls listened to and paperwork censored. Private correspondence too was opened and read, such that many gave up writing to loved ones until the furore passed.

And every day the water crept a little higher up the dams. Photographs arrived regularly, taken by reconnaissance pilots flying specially adapted high-altitude Spitfires.

'Look at these, Quentin,' Whitworth said one morning. 'Just arrived, hot off the press. I've called Gibson, he's on his way. This is the Eder dam, and this the Sorpe. Or targets Y and Z as we should now be calling them. See the water? It's just feet from the top.'

'Yes, sir, they look fit to burst. How about the Möhne?'

Gibson burst in. 'It's target X, Credo! Target X! Don't ever let me hear you calling it by its name!'

'No, sir. Sorry, sir.'

'Good. Now, let's have a look.' He began studying the photos. Quentin and Whitworth stood back, exchanging glances. Gibson looked a wreck, his black hair dishevelled, his eyes bloodshot. Unless he rested, they both suspected, or flew the mission and got it over with, he would crack.

'We should get on with it,' he muttered, as though reading their thoughts. 'We're ready, we should bloody get on with it!'

'I know, Guy,' Whitworth soothed. 'But it's a political decision now. Churchill's fully briefed, and Portal too. He's in America, seeing Roosevelt, it's all very delicate. But everyone's right behind you.'

'Then they should make the bloody decision.'

'What's that?' Quentin bent to one of the photos.

'What?'

'There. On the Möh . . . I mean, on target X.'

Whitworth peered. 'Quentin, what are you talking about?'

Quentin picked up a magnifying glass and focused it on the dam. 'That.' Then he leaned closer, and his neck prickled. 'Crates. There on the dam. Wooden crates. And they weren't there yesterday.'

CHAPTER 7

Within an hour the RAF's photo-intelligence unit (PIU) at Medmenham in Buckinghamshire telephoned to confirm they too had observed anomalies in the latest dams photos. By lunchtime, Quentin found himself in the boardroom at 5 Group's HQ in Grantham, together with Guy Gibson, Charles Whitworth, Ralph Cochrane and an aide to Arthur Harris, who was waiting at the end of a phone in High Wycombe. Also present were Quentin's intelligence superior, Frank Arnott, and a senior technician from the PIU. Scattered across the table were blow-ups of the Möhne dam photograph.

'So there's no doubt,' Cochrane said, after a long period of inspection.

'None at all, sir,' the technician replied. 'Wooden crates, twelve in all, about ten feet by four. Arrived last night under cover of darkness.'

'Bugger.' Cochrane shook his head. 'The question is, what's in them?'

'That I can't say, sir. It could it be antiaircraft artillery, or more torpedo defences or simply spare parts for the sluice towers.'

'When's the next photo flight?'

'Later this afternoon sir, but there's eight-eighths cloud cover in the Ruhr Valley, so we may not get any more photos for a while.'

'Christ. And Harris needs to know now. As do others . . .'

A lull followed as everyone digested the discovery. Much was at stake with this mission, including reputations, and a disaster was unthinkable. Quentin knew Cochrane's 'others' included Charles Portal, head of the RAF, currently in Washington, and, not least, the Prime Minister.

Cochrane turned to Arnott. 'What do you make of it all?'

'I'm confident the operation has not been compromised, sir. Not from within Scampton, that is. I'm for pressing ahead.'

'Hmm. Credo?'

'Sir.' Quentin began doggedly. His head was aching and he felt hot and feverish; from the moment he'd first spotted the crates, he'd begun to feel ill with foreboding. 'My understanding was always that if there was the slightest chance the Germans were expecting us, then the mission could not go ahead. The risks to the crews would be unacceptable.'

'There's no evidence they are expecting us.' Arnott waved a photo. 'These boxes could contain anything. Lavatory paper, for all we know!'

'But we should consider the possibility the Germans know,' Credo said. 'After all, the *Tirpitz* got moved.'

'And whose fault was that?'

'Gentlemen!' Cochrane held up a hand. 'We're desperately short of time. Ultimately this is an operational decision.' He turned to Gibson at the end of the table. 'Guy, old chap. What's your view?'

Gibson lifted his head from his hands. He seemed to have aged ten years in three months. 'Well, sir, the way I see it, every day that passes increases the risk. So I think we should go, immediately. Or call it off.'

'Very well.' Cochrane pushed back his chair. 'Thank you, gentlemen, please wait here. I'm going to speak to Harris.'

They waited and a steward brought a tray of sandwiches that nobody touched. Finally, nearly an hour after he'd left the room, Cochrane returned.

'Sorry everyone, no easy matter conducting a three-way conference across the Atlantic.' He held up a slip of paper. 'This is from Portal: "*Operation Chastise. Immediate attack of targets X, Y and Z approved. Execute at first suitable opportunity.*"'

It was Friday, May 14, 1943.

QUENTIN RODE in the car back to Scampton with Gibson and Whitworth. At first nobody spoke, each wrapped in thought. Quentin sat in front, nursing a giddy head, and his arm, which throbbed like the devil. He could sense, however, that Gibson was relieved at Cochrane's announcement—as though casting the die had lifted a weight from his shoulders.

'The moon is good for Sunday night,' he murmured after a while. 'I'd like to take off at twenty-one hundred hours, weather permitting.'

Whitworth said, 'Excellent. I'll put the wheels in motion.'

The next day, the Saturday, dawned misty and mild. As the morning wore on, the skies began to clear and temperatures to rise. Unusually, 617's

Lancasters remained on the ground, undergoing maintenance and servicing, as did the aircrews who lounged in the mess or sat soaking up the sun on the grass. At lunchtime the head of 5 Group himself arrived, Air Vice-Marshal Cochrane, to be met by station commander Whitworth and whisked off for meetings. Then, early in the afternoon, a light aircraft landed and the passenger, a worried-looking civilian with white hair, who someone identified as the inventor Barnes Wallis, was also spirited away.

'What the hell's going on?' Kiwi grumbled. Peter's crew were sprawled on the grass. Across the airfield, shimmering in unseasonal heat, a mower spewed grass-clippings high in the air.

'Balloon's going up,' Chalkie replied firmly. 'Can't be any doubt.'

'About time too. This waiting is driving me nuts.'

Peter glanced over at Uncle, who was sitting apart, deeply engrossed in a dog-eared letter.

'All right, Uncle?' he murmured, squatting beside him. The letter, he knew, was the last Uncle had ever received from his wife.

'She . . . Mary wrote it from her sister's,' Uncle whispered hoarsely. 'I said Liverpool could be dangerous, what with the docks getting bombed and that. But Mary said her sister was poorly and needed help for a few days. So off she went.'

'You always said she was strong-spirited,' Peter encouraged.

'Aye, that she was!' Uncle forced a grin, though his eyes were glistening. 'That's why I loved her so. For her spirit.' His gaze returned to the letter. A moment later a single tear fell onto the page.

'Uncle . . .' But the Scotsman could only shake his head. Peter rested a hand on his shoulder and turned his eyes to the distant mower. Brendan Murray could well be manning it, he reflected. And Peter hadn't seen nor spoken to Tess in a week. Not knowing about her situation, her well-being, was torture. Last night, in desperation, he'd asked Credo for help. A message, he'd pleaded, a brief meeting, anything, just for a few minutes. But Credo had been unusually brusque, 'Jesus, Lightfoot! Not now for God's sake!' Everyone, it seemed, was on the ragged edge.

'Look!' A shout came from Billy. 'Here comes Jamie, and in a hurry, too! Maybe he's learned something.'

All gathered round as Jamie pedalled up on a bicycle. 'I've just come from the hangar,' he puffed. 'They're loading bombs. Real ones. On a couple of Lancs. As if making sure they fit.'

Chalkie let out a whistle. 'Well, that's it then, boys. Job's on. Wouldn't you say, Peter?'

'It's certainly starting to look that way.' He glanced at Uncle, who was carefully folding his letter away. Beyond him a battered staff car was making its way slowly round the apron, stopping at each knot of airmen.

A minute later the car pulled up and Quentin leaned from the window.

'Briefing in the ops room at 1800 hours,' he said. 'Pilots, navigators and bomb aimers only.' He turned to Peter. 'Flying Officer Lightfoot, could I speak to you a moment?'

Peter approached the car. Quentin was perspiring, he saw, his face waxy and pale. Beside him sat his driver, Hickson. 'Sir?'

'Lightfoot. About last night . . .'

'Don't worry, sir. I shouldn't have asked, you've done too much already.'

'No, but listen. The southwestern perimeter. By the village road. Tonight at midnight. She'll be there. For God's sake keep it short. Also . . .' He broke off, wiping his brow with his sleeve.

Peter waited. Outside Number 2 hangar, a Type 464 Lancaster was being towed onto the grass, G-George, Gibson's own. 'Sir, are you all right?'

'I'm fine,' Quentin replied. 'Slight fever, that's all. Listen, Peter, this is important. Be careful, do you understand?'

'Of course, sir, no one will know, I'll make sure . . .'

'I'm not talking about tonight.' He nodded towards the Lancaster. 'I'm talking about that. When it comes down to it, just be terribly careful.'

THAT EVENING 617'S sixty pilots, navigators and bomb aimers gathered in the ops room above Number 2 hangar. All had been briefed on important operations before, but the air this time was more highly charged than any could remember. On a raised dais stood three tables bearing boxes draped in cloths. At six on the dot the rear doors opened, everyone stood up, and four men walked up the central aisle to the dais: Gibson, Wallis, Cochrane and Whitworth. Gibson took centre stage, bade everyone sit, seconds of scraping chairs followed, then the room fell to attentive silence.

'You are going to hit the enemy harder than a small force has ever done before,' he began. Short, squat, feet braced, hands on hips, he looked every inch the leader in control. 'Very soon we are going to attack the major dams of western Germany. Smashing them will bring enemy industry to its knees and help shorten the war.' At that he picked up a billiard cue and pulled back a curtain that hid a huge map of Europe. 'Here they are, the Möhne, the Eder and the Sorpe dams. We will attack them in three separate waves flying by different routes, shown here in red. Opposition will be stiff, but if we follow these routes accurately and attack the dams as we practised, then everything will be fine. If, as hoped, all three main dams are successfully breached, we will attack secondary reserve targets of the Lister, Ennepe and Diemel dams. In a moment I'll go into the details, but first I'd like to introduce the inventor of our weapon, Mr Barnes Wallis, who will explain the importance of the dams, and how we are going to smash them.'

Wallis rose shyly to his feet. 'Did you know . . .' he began, 'it takes eight tons of water to make one ton of steel . . .'

The briefing went on. After Wallis finished, Cochrane made a call-to-arms speech of encouragement: '. . . If Bomber Command is a bludgeon to Hitler, you are the rapier-thrust to bring him down,' before handing back to Gibson, who then delivered the mission briefing proper.

'What about getting home?' someone piped up, when he'd finished speaking. A ripple of nervous laughter followed.

'Ah yes, almost forgot!' Gibson grinned. 'Apart from the flight leaders, who will stay to coordinate things, as soon as each aircraft releases its weapon it will make its own way home via the safest route—still at low level. The leaders will follow, then we'll all meet back here for breakfast. And a drink.'

'Or ten!'

'Absolutely. The whole show shouldn't take more than eight hours. Now, come and look at these.' He moved to the three tables and withdrew their cloths. Upon each was a scale model of one of the dams and its environs. 'I want you to memorise these in every detail until they're fixed in your minds, and you can find and recognise them blindfold.'

'Thankfully it isn't the *Tirpitz*,' someone from Peter's wave murmured, as they shuffled forward with the others. 'At least with these we've a chance.' Soon all were crowding round the Sorpe model.

'Doesn't look too bad, does it, boys?' McCarthy said, after an interval.

'No sluice towers to line up on,' Kiwi pointed out. 'We'll have to estimate the range from the banks. Shouldn't be too difficult.'

'No, it's a good straight run-in, not too much high ground around.'

'Not like that Eder one,' Barlow said. 'Nasty tight approach, steep drop to the water, hills everywhere. That's going to be a tough nut.'

'What about defences?' Jamie was still peering at the Sorpe model. 'This town here, Langscheid, any flak emplacements, do you think?'

'That's an unknown,' McCarthy said. 'I guess we'll find out on the night.'

TESS WAITED ANXIOUSLY in the back of Quentin's car, which was parked in a quiet lane close to the perimeter fence. Sitting behind the wheel was Quentin's driver, Chloe Hickson.

'It's terribly kind of you to go to all this trouble,' Tess said. Overhead the full moon, haloed by a summer mist, cast eerie shadows over the scene.

'Not at all. I'm just following Flight Lieutenant Credo's instructions.'

'So you said. Um, is he well?'

'He's resting. He's been a little poorly. Why do you ask?'

'I was hoping to see him, that's all. To thank him. For everything he's done for me. For us.'

'Perhaps you can thank him some other way.'

'Yes.' Tess wondered what she meant, and for a moment thought of Brendan's notebook, but at that moment she detected movement beyond the fence. 'There's Peter!' she whispered. 'Don't bother waiting, I'll walk back.'

She slid from the car and hurried to him. A moment later they were pressed against the fence, fingers entwined, kissing awkwardly.

'Tess, thank God. Are you all right?'

'I'm fine, just missing you.' Behind them she heard the car drive off. 'What about you?'

'I'm fine. Hating being separated like this. Just counting the days.'

'Me too. How's it going?'

'It's on, Tess! Soon, very soon. And the moment it's over I'll come and find you, and we'll get away from here, from Brendan, from everything.'

'I can't wait.' She stretched up and they kissed again.

'What about your news?' Peter went on. 'Have you heard anything? From the adoption people?'

'No. Nothing of interest.' She smiled. No important news, she'd decided earlier, nothing that might trouble him. Only the encouraging, or mundane. 'But guess what? My father came to see me!'

'Good grief! When?'

'Last week. Turned up out of the blue. Thanks to you. He said you visited them and spoke up for me, which impressed him no end. He came to make his peace. I think we've reached an understanding.'

'Well, that's wonderful. And what about your mother?'

'In time, perhaps.'

'Tess, that's fantastic, I'm so relieved for you.' He glanced behind him. In the distance echoed the sound of workshops in full swing. 'I have to go, they've got guards patrolling every fifteen minutes.'

'Wait!' She fumbled at her neck. 'I want you to have this.' She passed the St Christopher through the fence. 'It's to keep you safe on your journey.'

He stared at the medallion, glinting in the moonlight. 'Thank you, Tess.'

'God speed, Peter.' She pressed herself to the wire one final time, and touched her lips to his. 'I'll be there with you, every step of the way.'

They kissed once more, then he turned and vanished into the night.

Chloe meanwhile drove round to the main gate, showed her pass, parked, and hurried up to Quentin's quarters. Where there was no answer. She hesitated, unsure what to do. When she'd seen him in his rooms two hours earlier he'd looked awful: pale, sweating, and almost incoherent with fever. She knocked again, still no answer, then tried the door, which was unlocked, and entered. The room was in darkness save for his reading light, and at first she couldn't see him. But there was an overpowering smell: ethyl alcohol, she recognised, and something else. Something sweet and sickly.

He was on his bed, unconscious with fever. His shirt was plastered to his chest, his gloved right hand hung limply in space, while his left clutched a surgical mask attached by elastic to the bedhead.

'Quentin?' she whispered fearfully. 'Quentin, what's happening to you?'

TEN MINUTES LATER, Whitworth arrived with the station medical officer.

'He's burning up,' the MO said, peeling back Quentin's eyelids.

'An infection of some kind?' Whitworth asked.

'No, sir.' Gently he raised Quentin's right hand. 'It's this. It's gangrene.'

'Christ. What can we do?'

'Hospital. Right away. And pray it isn't too late.'

'I'll take him, sir,' Chloe said immediately. 'Please. It'll be quickest.'

The MO stood back. 'He should go to East Grinstead. McIndoe's place. They've got his records and McIndoe's his best chance. I'll set him up on a drip and send an orderly with him.'

'Quick as you can. I'll phone East Grinstead.' Whitworth gazed down at Quentin. 'The poor boy. I was just trying to help, you know, help him get over it. Not being able to fly. Keep him busy, make him feel useful. He should have been at McIndoe's all along. I just made matters worse.'

'No, you didn't, sir,' Chloe said. 'You really did help him, I saw it. He belongs now, he has a role, everyone respects him. This is not your fault.'

SUNDAY, MAY 16 passed in a blur of activity. Preparing a squadron of Lancasters for a mission was a massive undertaking, requiring the coordinated actions of hundreds: fuellers, armourers, signallers, radio technicians, fitters, parachute packers, planners, cooks, drivers, not to mention the 140 aircrew the twenty aircraft would carry. Preparing 617 Squadron that day required many scores more, for the new radio equiment, the preparation of the navigation routes, the codes, the signals and, not least, the weapon itself.

The hours ticked by. Soon any pretence at practice missions was forgotten. A meal was served for all aircrew, the traditional pre-mission feast of bacon, two eggs and as much tea and toast as anyone wanted. Conversation was stilted, the tension palpable, stewards exchanged glances, everyone knew the boys would be fighting for real that night. Then there were the continual briefings—another sure giveaway. Weather briefings, navigation briefings, bombing briefings and, late in the afternoon, a second full briefing for all aircrew. At last, barely hours before they would take to the air, every crewman learned where they were going, and why. As before, Gibson went through the details of the mission, Barnes Wallis explained the science, Cochrane exhorted them to heroic action.

Then suddenly, as the early evening sun began to go down, a meditative hush fell over Scampton. The work was finished, twenty Lancasters stood at their dispersal points, fuelled, armed and ready to go. Their crews donned flying clothes, collected their harnesses, parachutes and Mae Wests, and wandered out into the evening air to wait, smoking, talking, or just staring out over the wide Lincolnshire countryside in contemplative silence.

At 8.30 p.m. Gibson received the final go-ahead. The weather was clear across Europe, no abnormal activity was reported on the dams, diversionary ops were being dispatched, the way was clear for Operation Chastise to proceed. Dressed coolly in tie and shirtsleeves for the mission, wearing his parachute harness and prized German life vest, he wandered among his men, offering a joke, a word of encouragement, a shake of the hand. Then shortly before nine he casually turned his wrist.

'Well, chaps. My watch says it's time to go.'

CHAPTER 8

It was to be an inauspicious beginning. All crews except those in Wave 3 boarded their aircraft and prepared for flight. Then at 2115 hours Gibson fired a red Very light, signalling engine-start. Fifteen Lancasters cranked sixty Merlins to life, but one, on McCarthy's Q-Queenie, sprang a coolant leak and had to be shut down. In the cockpit of V-Vicky, Peter and Uncle watched anxiously. McCarthy's wave was to take off ten minutes before Gibson's. Big Joe was its leader, his was the honour of leading 617 Squadron into the air. And V-Vicky was second in line.

'You know what, laddie?' Uncle watched as maintenance trucks careered across the field towards Q-Queenie. 'I'd say it's up to us.'

'You're right.' Peter reached for the throttles, released the brakes and began the long taxi to the end of the airfield. Behind, the others formed up in line, leaving Q-Queenie stranded.

Beside the control caravan, and in true Bomber Command tradition, a crowd of well-wishers had gathered to see them off. At a flash of green from the caravan, Peter gunned the throttles, turned the overladen bomber into wind, and set off down the runway. Slowly, laboriously, the aeroplane began its run, the giant bomb bulging incongruously between its wheels. Then the Lancaster's tail rose, and the Merlins began to bite, settling to a brassy snarl as V-Vicky picked up pace. Now the great machine was charging the distant fence like a spreading swan, engines singing, the sunset brilliant on its wings, and the well-wishers breathed with relief as it rose triumphantly into the evening air, tucked away its undercarriage, and turned east for the sea. Operation Chastise was under way.

On board all was quiet as V-Vicky's crew settled to their tasks. Soon they were crossing the coast and heading out across the North Sea. Peter eased the bomber down towards the water. Dusk was falling, the air warm and smooth and, after weeks of training, racing along above the calm sea felt almost effortless. Behind V-Vicky, strung out at one-minute intervals were the four remaining aircraft of Wave 2: Barlow in E-Easy, Munro in W-Willie, Byers in K-King and Rice in H-Harry. Elsewhere, they hoped, Gibson's Wave 1 was getting airborne and heading south.

All went well for about an hour. They stayed low to elude radar and, as darkness gathered, V-Vicky's twin belly-lights were switched on to fix height above the sea. Meanwhile Jamie Johnson dropped regular smoke floats to check for drift, passing small course adjustments to Peter. The minutes ticked, tension rose, then jumped as he called 'enemy coast ahead'. To cross it safely, the Lancasters must pass over the tiny island of Vlieland in the Frisian archipelago, then drop down again for the run across the Waddensee to the mainland.

The margin for error was small—stray a fraction north and they'd cross the next island, Terschelling; south and it was Texel, both aggressively defended. As the five Lancasters raced towards the shore in scattered formation, Vernon Byers's K-King was seen to climb and bank slightly to clear the northern tip of Texel. Moments later flashes of light split the night as a flak battery opened up. K-King was hit at once, flew out of control, and exploded into the Waddensee. It had taken barely seconds, and watching in shock all knew there could be no survivors.

At the same time Les Munro's W-Willie was also hit, sustaining damage to its communication and navigation systems. After a gloomy conference with his crew, Munro turned for home, his radios dead and compasses spinning uselessly.

Meanwhile Geoff Rice cleared Vlieland unscathed and was hastily dropping down to the safety of the Waddensee. But, shaken by Byers's crash, he misjudged the height, rounded out too low and H-Harry struck the waves, tearing off his *Upkeep*, which punched the rear-wheel up through the fuselage and buckled the Lancaster's tail. Fighting for control, Rice just managed to force H-Harry back into the air. But his weapon was gone and he had no choice but to abandon the mission and limp for home. Wave 2 had lost three aircraft in as many minutes.

That left just two, Peter and crew in V-Vicky, and his 61 Squadron cohort Norm Barlow in E-Easy. Without hesitation the pair closed up, flattened out low over the moonlit landscape, and set course for Germany. Fifty minutes later, Kiwi called a caution to Peter on the intercom.

'Pylons ahead, Pilot. Eleven o'clock one mile.'

'Got them, thanks.' Peter eased back on the controls to rise over the cables, but to his right Barlow's aircraft flew steadfastly on. A second later and in a blinding flash, E-Easy ploughed into the wires and dived to the ground in a ball of flame. Peter looked on in stunned disbelief.

What had started out as a wave of six aircraft was now reduced to just one. 'Pilot to Radio,' he called, after an interval of silence. 'Chalkie, you'd better let them know the situation back at base.'

'Will do, Pilot.'

'And tell them we're going on.'

The leading section of Gibson's Wave 1 was also approaching Germany. They too had encountered problems with enemy searchlights and flak. All three aircraft—Gibson's G-George, Martin's P-Popsie and Hopgood's M-Mother—had received hits from ground fire. So bad was the flak in one location that Gibson broke radio silence to transmit a warning back to 5 Group headquarters, who swiftly rebroadcast it to all aircraft. The flak that had struck Hopgood's M-Mother had set an engine alight and immobilised the rear turret, injuring several crew, including the pilot. Anxious seconds passed as the flight engineer shut down the burning engine and Hopgood fought for control. Finally, order of a sort was restored. Hopgood called up his crew. All but the navigator and flight engineer had received injuries, he learned. Hopgood himself was bleeding profusely from a head wound, and from the front turret came only ominous silence.

'What do you want to do, Hoppy?' his radio operator called painfully. His leg was so badly injured it was almost severed.

'Keep going.' Hopgood mopped his bloodied head. 'It's why we're here.'

Ten minutes behind them, Gibson's second section of three—Shannon, Maltby and Young—were halfway across Holland and as yet undetected. And ten minutes behind them the third trio of Maudslay, Astell and Knight was nearing the Dutch coast. Their landfall was accurate and they met no opposition as they thundered in over the dunes and turned east for Germany. Incredibly, they slipped past two night-fighter stations without detection. Navigation now required a course change to intersect the Rhine. Astell in B-Baker was a fraction late on the turn and dropped behind. Searching through the darkness for the telltale blue glow of the Lancasters' exhausts, his became the second aircraft to succumb to high-tension wires. B-Baker smashed into an unseen pylon, broke apart and cartwheeled into the ground. Maudslay and Knight knew nothing of its loss until the massive detonation behind them signalled the explosion of Astell's *Upkeep*.

Twenty-one dead and not a single bomb dropped. Back at 5 Group headquarters at Grantham, Cochrane, Whitworth and Wallis, now joined by Air Marshal Harris himself, were gathering anxiously in the ops room, unaware that out of twenty aircraft dispatched to the Ruhr, only fourteen remained. Of the others, one was unserviceable, two were coming home damaged, and three had crashed.

One, however, miraculously, was getting back in the fray, or at least its crew was. Having abandoned their beloved Q-Queenie as unserviceable, Big Joe McCarthy and his crew had raced across the airfield to the squadron spare, T-Tommy. Shortly afterwards, T-Tommy was taxiing hastily out for take-off. Now it was well on its way, thundering across the Netherlands.

At the same time Gibson's trio was arriving at the Möhne, having picked its way into the Ruhr itself, weaving past the searchlights of Duisburg, Essen and Dortmund, bending north to bypass Hamm's lethal flak, until finally turning south for the run to the lake. Ahead dark hills loomed. As the three aircraft crested them, the lake came into view, huge and silver-grey in the moonlight, together with its vast dam.

The Lancasters began a wide orbit of the scene. As they did so, tracer curled up from emplacements on both sluice towers and in the fields beside the lake. Keeping a wary distance, Gibson sized up the approach. Twelve guns, he estimated, probably 20mm, from four or five emplacements. Briefly his thoughts strayed to the wooden crates of two days earlier. Were the Germans expecting trouble? He'd be first to find out. The initial approach was shielded by a wooded promontory, he saw, but once that was cleared, the sharp right turn and final straight mile to the dam would be in the open, exposed to the full force of the flak. Nearly fifteen long seconds, he estimated, at the speed they'd be travelling.

'Signal from HQ, Skipper,' his radio operator called.

'Go ahead, Radio.'

'Wave 3 is outbound. Wave 2 four aircraft lost or aborted. V-Vicky continuing alone and in your vicinity. T-Tommy following, position unknown.'

'What the hell happened to everyone?'

'They don't say. But B-Baker's gone too from Wave 1. HQ suggests V-Vicky join us to replace him.'

'Understood, stand by a moment.' Gibson broke off, shocked, to gather his thoughts. Wave 2 decimated, leaving only Lightfoot and perhaps McCarthy. Wave 1 intact save for flak damage, injuries aboard M-Mother, and poor Bill Astell in B-Baker who was gone. Wave 3 on the way and hopefully intact. As he looked, he saw three Lancasters cresting the moonlit ridge north of the lake. Shannon, Maltby and Young had arrived, and not a moment too soon. Barely four full hours of darkness remained, and enemy night fighters might appear any second.

'Yes, OK, acknowledge, Radio. Call Lightfoot and get him here.'

'Will do.'

'Hello, all aircraft, Leader here. Prepare to attack in order, I'm going in now. M-Mother, stand by to take over if anything happens to me.'

'Understood, Leader. Good luck.'

With that the attack on the dams finally began.

Gibson throttled back and entered a wide descending turn, down-moon to the eastern end of the lake, four miles or more from the dam. Suddenly he felt very alone, and his Lancaster very small.

All went well. He skimmed the promontory, then came the right turn, and with it the flak, coloured balls of fire looping up and past from the sluice towers and bank. Forcing himself to ignore it, he settled G-George down lower. The spotlights came on, the bomb aimer squinted down his Dann sight, the flight engineer eased up the power.

As the flak grew more intense, Gibson was struck by the mesmerising brilliance of it, scores of brightly glowing shells flashing by from several directions. But inaccurate, he noted, the only advantage of going first—the gunners had no idea what he was doing, or why. Suddenly only seconds remained, snapshot images filled his head: the engineer's white-knuckled hands on the throttles, the navigator urging him lower towards the spotlights, G-George shuddering from machine-gun fire as the nose turret opened up, while the bomb aimer called corrections over the headphones: '. . . left a bit. Straighten up, steady, hold it there, that's good, hold it, that's good . . .'

'Bomb gone!'

G-George bobbed upwards at the bomb's release, then soared over the parapet, Gibson hauling on the controls for height. In the tail the rear gunner began shooting furiously at the sluice towers. 'It's bouncing!' he shouted excitedly. 'The bomb, it's bloody bouncing, look!'

Above the lake five circling crews looked on. G-George had made it unscathed. And its *Upkeep* seemed to drop on target. As they watched, it bounced three times, but then it began to veer, and slow, then stop, finally sinking thirty yards short of the left sluice tower. A few seconds later it detonated, sending out a ghostly shock wave followed by a massive column of white water thrown hundreds of feet in the air.

'Good show, Skipper!' someone called. 'I think you've done it!'

'No. Wait.' Gibson turned in his seat, staring at the scene as G-George climbed away. The entire surface of the lake seemed to be boiling, as though lashed by a squall, with giant waves breaking in sheets over the parapet. Then gradually the tumult subsided, the water settled, and the spray drifted clear. And everyone could see the dam was still there.

At that moment V-Vicky crested the ridge.

A crackle came over the headphones.

'Hello, all aircraft, Leader here, stand by for next attack. Hello, V-Vicky, good to see you, join left circuit and await instructions. Hello, M-Mother, can you hear me?'

'I hear you, Leader.'

'Your turn. Wait for the water to settle, then go. Good luck.'

All waited as Hopgood prepared, breaking from the circuit towards the eastern end of the lake. As they did so, the final two aircraft of Wave 1—Maudslay's Z-Zebra and Knight's N-Nan—arrived on the scene, bringing the total number of planes circling the Möhne to nine. Hopgood began his run. At first it went like Gibson's, the circling descent to the end of the lake, the straight run in to the promontory, followed by the sweeping right turn into the attack. They saw his spotlights come on, saw them converge as he drew lower, saw the flak begin to spew out towards him, but much more accurately than on Gibson's run. They saw, unaccountably, that Hopgood's nose gunner was not firing back, and they saw the flash as the left wing was hit, then the trail of yellow flame as a fuel tank ignited. They saw him resolutely holding height and heading, and the moment of bomb release, which looked straight, but later than Gibson's. They saw M-Mother clear the parapet, trailing flame like a comet and struggling for height. And then they saw the left wing detach and the stricken bomber explode. A moment later they were dazzled by a blinding flash, as his *Upkeep* blew up. It had bounced over the parapet and smashed into a power station in the basin below.

TWO FAILURES, another crew lost. After a shocked pause, the dismal news was tapped out over the W/T for Harris and the others waiting at Grantham. There was no reply, for none was needed. Operation Chastise had so far cost four crews and six aircraft, all without breaching a dam. The Möhne's defences were clearly formidable, and now that the Germans understood the direction and method of attack, they were focused and accurate. John Hopgood was one of Gibson's closest friends, his crew well liked by everybody. Other leaders might have baulked at this point, weighing up mounting losses against a dwindling probability of success.

But Guy Gibson wasn't other leaders. 'Hello, P-Popsie, are you ready?'

'We're ready,' Martin replied.

'It's your turn next. But we've got to do something about the flak, so I'll come in with you to draw their fire. A-Apple, you stand by to take over if anything happens.'

'Understood, Leader.'

All watched in awe as Martin swung his Lancaster towards the head of the lake, with Gibson's G-George following.

'Can't we do anything to help them?' Kiwi said, watching in V-Vicky.

'Yes, we can.' Peter reached for the throttles. 'We'll make a pass downstream of the dam to try to confuse the flak.' He wheeled V-Vicky about, making for the valley beyond the dam. Maudslay, he noted, was following in Z-Zebra. Meanwhile Martin was dropping P-Popsie down towards the water, with Gibson tight on his flank. Above them, the remaining Lancs circled like watchful hawks.

The tactic worked. Beyond the dam, Peter watched as Martin and Gibson cleared the promontory and swung into view. Their spotlights came on, brightly pinpointing their position, and Gibson's navigation lights began flashing to further distract the flak gunners, who flung furious strings of tracer at the two aircraft, which both responded in kind.

At the same moment Peter felt V-Vicky shudder as Herb and Billy both opened up on the sluice towers. Six machine guns firing seventy tracer shells a second, with Maudslay following with more. He glimpsed flashes as bullets struck masonry, saw figures in grey sprinting along the parapet for cover, caught sight of Martin and Gibson charging towards the dam, guns blazing. Then Vicky was past and clear, and he was hauling her round for another pass. But the attack was already over, Martin's bomb bouncing across the lake as he and Gibson climbed to safety. All watched hopefully, yet this bomb, too, lurched towards the bank and erupted in a huge blast of mud and water.

Disbelieving silence followed, then came Martin's exasperated shout: 'The drop was good, what the hell happened?'

'Nothing happened,' Gibson replied. 'It didn't bounce straight that's all. We'll wait for the water to settle then try again. Hello, A-Apple, stand by, you're next.'

AT GRANTHAM the tension was palpable. The ops room was located deep beneath the building, a long windowless cellar with a raised platform down one side, maps of Europe covering the walls, a desk for the radio operator, and the ops blackboard itself, for chalking progress of the raid.

Wallis was close to despair. 'No, no, it's no good!' he moaned, as news of the third failure came over the Tannoy. 'I don't understand, Roy. One bomb should do it.'

Roy Chadwick, co-designer of the Lancaster, did his best to console him. 'Buck up, old boy,' he murmured. 'Plenty of time yet. Plenty of bombs too.' He glanced at Cochrane, whose expression was sombre.

Harris sat stony-faced. 'I knew this was madness,' he kept muttering angrily. 'I bloody knew it.'

Charles Whitworth, unable to stop himself, turned from the ops board. 'Excuse me, sir, but these boys have flown their guts out preparing for this mission. At least let's give them a proper chance to pull it off.'

AND BACK AT the Möhne, they were finally about to. Three bombs gone and the dam seemingly unscratched, but, unknown to them, its flak defences were buckling under the onslaught from the Lancasters' machine guns. Dinghy Young swung A-Apple to the head of the lake for his attack, this time flanked by both Gibson and Martin, while the others made diversionary passes over the dam. As he ran in, the flak was noticeably slacker and, shielded by Gibson and Martin, Young was able to manoeuvre A-Apple into perfect alignment and deliver a bomb accurately to the centre of the dam wall. As Barnes Wallis had predicted, having been delivered correctly, that one bomb did its job.

But not immediately. At first, to everyone's dismay, they saw only the same eerie shockwave, the same exploding waterspout flung into the air, the same waves slopping over the parapet to the basin below, the same ring of white spreading out across the lake. And then everything settled down and the water subsided, the mist drifting clear. And the dam stood defiant and unbowed, like a vast, unmoving battleship.

Yet, unknown to everyone, one fatally damaged below the waterline. Meanwhile, the Lancasters circled, watched and waited, and once again, Gibson didn't hesitate. 'Hello, J-Johnnie,' he called, summoning David Maltby. 'Attack when ready. V-Vicky stand by, you're next.'

Maltby circled, descended, and ran in, covered by Young and Gibson, while the others looked on. Maltby's run looked good at first, but water vapour and drifting smoke from the burning power station below were obscuring the target. And something else was happening—the whole dam seemed to be moving, heaving, crumbling along its crown.

'Christ, it's going!' someone shouted.

'Don't drop!' Gibson yelled. 'Break off, it's going!'

Maltby veered off, but his bomb was already on its way, exploding just as the base of the dam burst outwards, unsheathing a solid shaft of water that spurted out into the valley as though from a giant hose. Seconds later the crown collapsed and a 100-yard breach appeared, releasing the full weight of the reservoir. A giant wave of water arced into the basin below and set off down the valley, smashing all in its path.

For seconds they could only look on in awed silence. Then a chorus of wild cheers and shouting broke over the radio, to be echoed 400 miles away in Grantham, as Gibson's radio operator tapped out the code for success. Before their eyes, a thirty-foot tidal wave thrashed down the valley. The power station, roads, bridges and factories, all were swept before it as though by a giant broom. The destruction was instant and merciless.

Gibson quickly silenced the chatter. Dawn was drawing nearer and, if the enemy hadn't guessed their purpose before, they certainly knew it now. 'Time to get going,' he said, directing Maltby and Martin home. Four unused bombs remained in Wave 1, with much work still to be done. Calling Shannon, Maudslay, Knight and Lightfoot into order, and taking Young with him as reserve leader, Gibson set course for the Eder.

CHAPTER 9

The time was now 0100 hours. Back at Scampton all was tensely quiet, as if the whole station were holding its breath. Everyone knew that 617 was flying for real, braving the enemy's defences to deliver its oddly shaped weapon. Now, it was just a matter of waiting.

Tess arrived at the main gate by bicycle, showed her NAAFI pass, and was admitted on site. Security was still tight, she noted, but somehow the mood had changed, the obsessiveness and the paranoia gone. As though now the mission was under way, the fanatical need for secrecy was over.

She slipped along the darkened pathways to the NCO married quarters. Brendan would be in the barn with his pigeons, she knew. He always stayed near his loft when a squadron flew ops. Because, as he was fond of boasting, it could mean the difference between life and death. His intervention had saved Peter all those weeks ago, she reminded herself, for which, if nothing else, she would be for ever grateful. She mounted the stairs and paused at their door. No light showed beneath, all seemed quiet within. Withdrawing her key, she let herself in.

Immediately his smell hit her—cigarettes, beer, fertiliser, grass clippings. Fearfully she paused, ears straining, but the flat was silent. Turning on a table light, she scanned the room. Discarded newspapers, empty beer bottles, a pile of washing-up at the sink. But nothing unusual or suspicious. She unfolded a holdall and began moving quickly through the room, collecting her post office book from the sideboard, a stack of her letters—one in her father's hand and already opened. Then came the trinkets and her one family photo, of her grandparents, given to her by her aunt Rosa. Swiftly she gathered them into the bag. All she needed now was some clothes.

He was waiting in the bedroom, on the bed, hands propped behind his head, his face in half-shadow from the open doorway.

'There she is,' he said, as though expecting her.

She should have run. She should have dropped the bag and sprinted for the door. But she couldn't move, frozen like a rabbit in headlights.

'What are you doing here?' she gasped. 'I thought you'd be in the barn.'

'With the pigeons? Not tonight, old girl.'

'But why not?' *He shouldn't be here.* It was all she could think.

'Well, you see, your fancy boy and his little friends . . . where they've gone, no one can help them. Not even my darling birds.'

'What do you mean? How do you know where they've gone?'

'Well, now, that's for me to know and you to guess, wouldn't you say?' He sat up, stretching lazily. 'Anyways, I had this little feeling you might pop by tonight. Just to see your old man, eh?'

At that Tess found her feet and began backing through the doorway. But in a flash he was off the bed and shoving her roughly aside. A moment later she heard the key turn in the front door.

'Listen, Brendan,' she began, fighting for calm. 'I'm sorry. I should have got in touch sooner, to explain everything.'

'What's to explain? That you've run out on me and are living in sin with your fancy boy?'

'No. You're wrong. I'm not. But there have been . . . well, developments.'

'Oh, really? Would that be developments about your adulterous doings with your fancy boy, whose wort'less skin I saved? Or maybe developments about bleating to that piteous sod Credo about my private dealings? Or about telling your family about your terrible life with your cruel husband?'

'Brendan, I have never told my family anything about you!' Now she was circling round the dining table, eyes searching in panic for escape, he following, stealthy, watchful, like a cat with a mouse.

'Is that so? Then why does your father write that he's sorry to hear of your troubles?'

'Because he's ill, Brendan. He came to see me. He wants to make up.'

'Very touching. So that's the developments you're talking of?'

'Yes.' She hesitated. 'Yes, that's right.'

'You're a lying whore!'

'No, it's true!'

'What about your bastard child?' He lunged then, grabbing her arm. She yelped, wrenched free and fled to the kitchenette, and its one window. Which was locked.

'Well, and here we are now,' he taunted. She was cornered, with no possible escape. 'Didn't think I knew about that, did you? Your bastard child.'

'No,' she whispered tearfully. 'Brendan, what do you want?'

'Want? Only to be left in peace.'

'All right. I will leave you in peace. We need never see each other again.'

'Ah, yes, but it's not quite as simple as that. What with you and all your blabbing to people. And there's the matter of your fancy boy too, and poor old Credo, and now your bastard daughter.' Sweat glistened on his forehead, his breathing heavy. He took another pace forward. Tess stepped back, hands fumbling behind her as she collided with the sink. Now she had no place left to run. And at that, despite the frantic beating of her heart, she began to think calmly. And to confront the inevitable.

'You . . . you're a spy, aren't you?'

'Is that what you've heard?'

'It's what I think. You pass information to people who pass it to the Germans.'

'Really? And how would I be doing that?'

'Something . . . the notebook. I don't know.'

'No, you don't. You don't know anything. For you're nothing but a deceiving adulteress, with a child out of wedlock and now carrying on with another man behind her husband's back.'

'I am not. I have never been unfaithful to you.'

'So you say. But who will they believe? The respected RAF sergeant, or the lying adulteress covering her deceit with fanciful stories of spies?'

'I . . . Brendan, wait . . .'

He'd taken another step nearer. Now he was so close she could smell his breath and see flecks of spittle on his lips. 'This is a military base, you see, Tess. These are my people, we look after our own. So this business will be handled with discretion, and without fuss, let me assure you.'

'What business? What are you talking about?'

'The military police, Tess. They'll look into the matter and find the respected Sergeant Murray was attacked by his wife, who, as everyone knew, was having an adulterous affair with a pilot. And the poor, provoked Sergeant Murray was only trying to defend his dignity, and his honour, when she accidentally fell down the stairs and got tragically killed.'

'Brendan, for God's sake, I promise . . .'

'No, you don't! You lie!' He lunged at her, full force, arms outstretched for her throat. But as he lunged, her hand came from behind her back, and the kitchen knife she was holding plunged deep into his chest.

THAT WAS HOW it happened, Quentin would later record, Murray's death, in the kitchen of their quarters on the night of the dams raid. Not that Quentin was present, or even compos mentis at the time. He was 150 miles away, in a bed, in a darkened room, in a hospital. He'd been slowly coming round, slipping in and out of consciousness, his fevered mind tormented by dreams of fire and an agonising car-ride through blacked-out streets. Finally he came to his senses. It was night, he realised, he was thirsty and nauseous and his head hurt. As did his right arm, which felt numb and painful within its thick cocoon of bandages.

The room was oppressively warm and airless, despite the open window where a curtain stirred listlessly and beyond which a lone nightingale sang wistfully. He turned his head to listen to it and saw a young woman in WAAF uniform curled on a chair by the window, asleep. Quentin wanted to speak to her, but suddenly found his throat constricting and before he knew it he was weeping inconsolably. Weeping for the crewmen he'd lost in the Wellington and all the countless others who never came home. Weeping for the fair-haired boy of his youth, so smiling and carefree, but now lost and afraid. Weeping for the tragedy of war, weeping for the souls of its victims, and for the heartbroken host left behind.

'Chloe . . .' he sobbed. 'Chloe, please wake up.'

And she woke, and came to him, and gave him water through a straw, and bathed his burning brow, and shushed and calmed him, until at last the crying stopped and he fell quiet.

Later they talked.

'It's gone, hasn't it,' he said. 'The hand.'

'Yes, Quentin. Dr McIndoe says we caught it just in time. You were very poorly. I've notified your parents. They'll be here tomorrow.'

'Thank you, Chloe. You are a remarkable girl.'

'I hardly think so.'

'I do. You work for Arnott and Campbell, don't you?'

'How did you guess?'

Quentin forced a smile. 'Mysteriously promoted to Whitworth's ADC. Given a driver who doesn't drive, but who follows me everywhere, watching my every move. They assigned you to keep an eye on me, didn't they?'

'Something like that. Although I prefer to call it helping with your work. And I do drive, by the way. Rather well, as it happens. The car was Whitworth's idea. He felt you should get out more.'

'He's a good man.'

'Yes. And so are you.'

'Not a traitor, then?'

She patted his hand. 'Not even close.'

He turned his head away. 'So it was all a pretence . . . being friends?'

'Is that what you think?'

'I don't know. I'm afraid . . . I couldn't bear—'

'Quentin. It's all right. Don't upset yourself.'

'Sorry,' he whispered. 'Self-pity. Inexcusable.'

'Perfectly excusable, given what you've been through.'

'Doesn't do any good though.' He sniffed. 'Emotions. I learned that.'

'You think so? Why do you think I'm sitting here with you?'

'Because those are your orders.'

'No, silly!' She laughed. 'It's because I want to.'

They sat together quietly. After a while she reached out, and slipped her hand into his. Then in the distance came the chime of a church clock.

'What time is it?' he asked.

She checked her watch. 'A quarter to two.'

His eyes widened. 'And what day?'

'It's Sunday. Well, Monday now.'

'So, they're up there! They're doing it right now! Peter and the others?'

'Yes, Quentin. They're up there. Doing it right now.'

BIG JOE MCCARTHY was doing it in T-Tommy at the Sorpe. Alone.

'You sure we got the right lake, buddy?' he asked his navigator, as they circled the deserted lake.

'Quite sure. Look there's the town just to the north of it, with the church tower and everything.'

'OK. Right. But it looks damn quiet. No smoke, no fires. Where the hell is everybody?'

The crew looked on in pensive silence. Below them lay a scene of almost surreal tranquillity. The sleepy village nestling in the hills, beside its mist-covered lake, its earthen dam solid and peaceful, like a dozing giant. An unblemished dozing giant. Yet six aircraft had been sent to attack it with enough explosives to demolish a battleship. Where were they?

'They couldn't have bought it, surely.' Someone voiced their thoughts. 'Not all of them. Could they?'

'Christ knows. I vote we get on with it and clear off.'

'Me too. This place gives me the creeps.'

With that Joe banked T-Tommy over for the attack. Only to find the strike plan unworkable. This dam was differently constructed to the Möhne and Eder, straight not curved, comprising a central concrete core supporting sloped earthen sides. To crack the Sorpe, Wave 2 had been briefed to fly in low, lengthways along the dam, and drop their weapons in the middle, without spin. The hope was that the bombs would roll into the water, explode and cause a breach. But as Joe realised, the terrain was much steeper than anticipated, causing problems not only with the approach but also the climb-out, which was up a suicidally steep hill.

Nine times they tried, nine times they failed, struggling without success to get T-Tommy into position. So low was the approach above the rooftops that the church tower flashed by above them; so steep was the climb-out that it felt like scrambling up a cliff. And at each attempt, no matter what Joe tried, the run would end in a 'No drop!' cry from the bomb aimer.

The tenth time, Big Joe cut the power earlier and glided in, levelling out barely thirty feet above the crest, and at a slow 170 mph.

'Go! Now! Do it!' Joe yelled.

'Bomb gone!'

With that, throttles were slammed wide, the Merlins roared and the lumbering machine began its scrambling ascent to safety. As it did so, seven faces peered aft to see the results of their labours.

The bomb had been placed precisely in the centre of the dam. As they watched, it rolled down as planned, then exploded, a phenomenal blast that lit the scene like a flashbulb, churned water to foam and threw a column of earth high in the air. Big Joe and his crew had done precisely what they were supposed to.

But it wasn't enough. And as the smoke cleared and spray settled, they saw it had all been for nothing. The dam was completely intact. Scarcely believing their eyes, they set course for the long flight home.

Meanwhile the five aircraft of Wave 3 were heading into Germany. Theirs was a roving brief, each Lancaster controlled individually from Grantham using Morse code. The first to take off was twenty-year-old Warner Ottley and his crew in C-Charlie. They flew into Holland via Gibson's southern route, pushing on undetected towards Germany and the Ruhr. Nearing the flak-ringed city of Hamm they received a Morse message directing them to the Lister dam, south of the Möhne. Acknowledging the message, they adjusted course accordingly. Three minutes later, a second message changed their target to the Sorpe. Again the course was altered but, possibly confused by the contradiction, C-Charlie strayed too close to Hamm. Twenty miles away and heading for the Ennepe dam, Bill Townsend and his crew saw a distant aeroplane coned by searchlights, followed by streams of tracer, then a monstrous flash as its bomb blew up.

'That's one of ours,' Townsend said without hesitation. He was right. C-Charlie was gone.

And 100 miles back, Canadian Lewis Burpee was threading S-Sugar between the night-fighter stations west of Eindhoven. These bases too were on high alert following repeated fly-pasts of 617 Lancasters that night. Captured in the beam of a single searchlight, Burpee pulled up for safety—

straight into the sights of the flak gunners. S-Sugar received multiple hits, burst into flames and cartwheeled to the ground. Seconds later its *Upkeep* went off, destroying many buildings. A sixth Chastise crew was dead.

AT THE EDER, there were problems for Guy Gibson and the remaining crews of Wave 1, who were running dangerously behind schedule. Late leaving the Möhne, having expended too much time destroying it, they all had problems finding the Eder, which lay amid forested hills and dark valleys interlaced with many lakes and rivers. David Shannon in L-Leather actually squared up to attack a completely different dam before realising his mistake. Eventually Gibson found the correct target and began firing off Very lights to round up the others.

Who arrived on scene to find it unassailable. Time after time they ran in, only to abort because they were wrongly aligned, or too high, or too slow. An increasingly impatient Guy Gibson and his deputy Dinghy Young fussed around overhead, nagging them like nervous sheepdogs.

The problem was the topography. The lake lay among steep-sided hills like a lizard in a burrow, narrow and serpentine, with a sharp twist at its head where the dam stood. To approach it required a two-mile run-in, starting high on the northern shore and at ninety degrees to the dam. From there the bombers had to plunge 1,000 feet to the lake, cross to the southern shore, pop up again over a wooded spit, make a sharp ninety-degree turn to port, then drop down to attack height for the last short dash to the dam. And, after the run, like at the Sorpe, a dangerously steep pull-up was required to avoid a hill. To further complicate matters, early-morning mist now drifted over the scene. The only good news was the absence of flak.

At Maudslay's next failed attempt, Gibson called Shannon back into the fray. 'Hello, L-Leather, Leader here. Look, Dave, we must get on with it. Give it another try and just do the best you can. Z-Zebra, stand by to follow.'

Shannon circled L-Leather into position, the others watching closely as he dived for the water, crossed the lake, turned over the spit and ran in. The bomb fell free, they saw it bounce, then impact the dam, but well to the right of centre. A few seconds later came the familiar flash of the shockwave, followed by the upsurging tower of spray and spreading ring of water.

Shannon was exultant, certain he'd succeeded. Yet no breach appeared. Gibson waited to be sure, then called in Maudslay in Z-Zebra. But almost from the start his run appeared problematic, with Maudslay wrestling the bomber down to the lake, overshooting the turn, and struggling to line up for the drop, which was dangerously late. A blinding flash illuminated the valley as his *Upkeep* exploded against the parapet, just as Z-Zebra was passing over it. All feared he'd blown himself up, flames, smoke and debris obscured everything, anxious seconds passed, then they glimpsed the bomber heading away down the valley, trailing smoke.

'Hello, Z-Zebra.' Gibson called. 'Are you OK?'

Maudslay's reply was eerily faint. 'I . . . I think so, Leader. I don't . . .'

'Z-Zebra, can you hear me?'

But after a ghostly hiss of static, Maudslay's radio was silent.

Two armed aircraft remained. Les Knight went next, the no-nonsense Australian. His run in N-Nan looked better, crossing tidily to the southern shore, up over the spit for the steep turn to port, then quickly back down for the drop. His spotlights lined up, his heading was true and his bomb-release timely, his *Upkeep* making three bounces before impacting the dam and sinking from sight.

Then it went off, the lightning flashed, the lake erupted, the veil of spray drifted. And nothing happened.

Knight looked on in disbelief. 'What do we have to do to crack this bastard?' he lamented over the VHF.

'Good try, N-Nan,' Gibson replied. 'OK, V-Vicky, it's up to you.'

P*ETER HAS BEEN READY all his life. This is what it was for, his modest beginnings in Bexley, the taunts of the moneyed and the secondhand shoes. His childhood with Tess, a friendship, then adolescent love. The desperation of their parting, the lonely years of silence. Then war, the recruiting office, the sixty operations in Wellingtons, Beaufighters, Manchesters and finally 61 Squadron and the mighty Lancaster. All for this. A thirty-second dash across a lake to attack a dam.*

'Pilot to Crew. Call in, please.'

They all call in. Jamie standing behind him, watching the spotlights, one hand ready on his shoulder. Kiwi prone in the nose, his string-sight in one hand, bomb-release in the other. The two gunners, hunched in their turrets. Chalkie at the radios, ready with his Morse key. Uncle at his knobs and dials, tending his quivering charge like a trainer with a thoroughbred.

Peter settles lower in his seat and throttles back. 'Ready, Uncle?'

'Ready.'

'Good. Let's have twenty degrees flap.'

'Twenty degrees.' Uncle reaches for the lever.

A voice breaks suddenly over the radio. 'Say, Peter mate. You might want some flap.' It is Knight, circling overhead in N-Nan.

'I didn't bother with flap,' Shannon adds helpfully.

'Yes, and look at your run!' Young quips.

Uncle glances at Peter. 'You want this?' Peter shakes his head, and with a flick of the switch the radio goes dead. 'That's better. So what's the plan?'

'We do it like Knight. Only steeper down to the water, a faster run to the far side, and tighter turn onto finals. All right?'

'Aye.' Uncle grins. 'But we're not a bloody Stuka y'know!'

'We are now!'

With that he snatches back the throttles, shoves the controls forward and V-Vicky, engines popping, plunges over the edge like a gannet off a cliff. The sky vanishes, the hillside blurs, forest and lake fill the windscreen. Down he dives, slipstream shrieking, altimeter spinning, before hauling back against the protesting airframe, to level off 100 feet from the surface.

'Flaps up, full power!'

The Merlins roar, the bomber surges forward, hurtling over the water towards the southern shore. Ahead dark hills rise steeply. They cross the lake in seconds, then thunder up the bank, and pull up and over into the turn, left wingtip brushing the trees. Peter looks up through the Perspex, waiting, a whirl of black trees, the wildly canting horizon, the aircraft shuddering in his hands as he tightens the turn yet more. Suddenly the angled shadow of the dam swings into view. Quickly he rolls level again, throttles back the power and kicks V-Vicky into a harsh side-slip, the wings banked left, rudders forced right, skidding the aircraft down to the water.

And the last dash to the dam, dead ahead. Seven seconds away.

'Spotlights on!' He levels off, flat-turning to line up. Immediately a squeeze from Jamie—go lower—while beside him Uncle eases up the power.

'Two hundred mph, two-ten, two-twenty . . .'

'Target in sight.' Kiwi from the nose, his string-sight to his eye. 'That's good, but go left, left more, good, steady . . .' Five seconds.

'Two-thirty dead-on!' Uncle at the throttles.

Kiwi: 'Left a touch more, hold it there, yes, steady . . .' Three seconds.

A light squeeze on his shoulder, down a fraction. A pat, hold it there.

'Steady . . . Steady . . . Hold it . . . Bomb gone!'

V-Vicky bucking upwards as though breaking from a leash, Uncle slamming the throttles wide, Peter hauling back for the stars, arms crooked round the controls for leverage, one foot pushing against the dash-panel.

Herb in the tail, watching their bomb. 'It's bouncing! It's bouncing!'

Anxious seconds scaling the hilltop, still straining, then breaking clear at last, levelling off, throttling back and circling to see. Breathless silence on the intercom. Then the flash on the water, the ring of blue lightning, and the whole lake jumping, and blurring, and bursting apart, blasting a tower of white 1,000 feet in the air. Then the misty curtain hanging, and drifting, while rubble and masonry fall back with a splash.

An unruffled report from Uncle.

'We've damaged her, lads,' he says quietly. 'There, look, halfway down.'

A furious circular jet is escaping the dam, like foam past a shaken bottle-top. Then, as they stare, the whole section blows out and solid water spurts from the hole as though from a hose. Seconds more and the crown above begins to collapse, crumbling into the breach, which spreads and widens until a 100-yard gap has opened in the wall.

Releasing the mighty waters behind. They've done it, they realise, breached the Eder! In seconds a tidal wave thirty feet high is storming down the valley, flattening all in its path.

'Jesus Christ!' Chalkie intones. 'Would you look at that.'

'Well done, everyone,' Uncle says. 'Well done, Kiwi, spot-on.'

'Thanks, boys. Nice work yourself, Pilot. And Jamie.'

'I'm real proud of us all,' Billy announces simply.

'Yes.' Peter wipes sweat from his eyes. 'Yes, we all did it.'

'Rear gunner here. Why's it so quiet on the radio?'

Peter and Uncle exchange guilty glances. The radios are still off. Peter reaches for the switch, but Uncle stays his hand. 'In a minute, laddie.' He grins. 'Let's just savour the moment.'

IT WAS THE SECOND and last dam to be breached on Operation Chastise. But not the last attempt. Nor the last casualty.

Five minutes later Wave 1 split up and headed for home, using pre-planned exit routes. Meanwhile the three remaining aircraft of Wave 3 were approaching the area, still armed and still pressing on. Two full hours after Joe McCarthy had left the Sorpe in T-Tommy, Canadian Ken Brown arrived there in F-Freddie, only to encounter the same problems. Despite placing his *Upkeep* near the centre of the dam, the result was disappointing. Signalling the failure to Grantham, he turned for home.

Cyril Anderson in Y-York had a similarly frustrating trip. Arriving in the Hamm area late, flak-chastened, and with an unserviceable rear turret, he, like Ottley, was first directed to one dam, the Diemel, before being diverted to the Sorpe. This too caused confusion on board, and with thick mist below further hampering navigation, Y-York was soon lost. With the clock ticking remorselessly towards dawn, Anderson gave up and turned for home.

Meanwhile, in thickening mist, Bill Townsend and crew in O-Orange were running in to attack the Ennepe. But the bomb failed to reach the required spin rate, so when it was dropped, in line and on target, it bounced just twice before sinking fifty yards short of target, exploding harmlessly. All watched as the ring of white spread out and subsided. Then came the voice of Townsend's navigator.

'Um, Navigator here. I think we attacked the wrong dam. I've a feeling, looking at it now, that it's the Bever, about five miles from the Ennepe.'

'Well, chaps,' Townsend said resignedly, 'the bomb's gone and there's not a thing we can do about it, so, Navigator, let's have a course for home. High time we got out of here.'

Meanwhile elements of Wave 1 were nearing the coast and safety. As Shannon, Gibson and Knight thundered out to sea, exultant cheers rang over their intercoms, together with promises of wild celebrations to come.

Henry Maudslay and his crew would not be joining them. Miraculously, Z-Zebra had survived the explosion of its bomb at the Eder, and its crew had nursed the ailing aircraft back across Germany. But, almost within sight of the Dutch border, they had strayed too close to flak batteries and had been shot down. Chastise had claimed its seventh crew.

The eighth was Young in A-Apple. Having flown a textbook mission to the Möhne, breached it, continued to the Eder, then flown all the way west again, Dinghy Young, so nicknamed for his habit of successfully ditching in the sea, drew near to the coast at Castricum, five miles north of Ijmuiden. There he made one fatal mistake. Seeing the beckoning sea ahead, and exhausted after many hours flying at ground level, he allowed A-Apple to rise a little. A flak battery spotted the Lancaster, catching it with one lucky burst. A-Apple exploded into the sea. This time there were no dinghies.

Which just left V-Vicky. The ninth and final victim of Operation Chastise. Shot down by a night fighter over Borken in Germany.

CHAPTER 10

It is late afternoon. A young woman sits on a park bench in Stafford. Children play on swings nearby. One, a little girl, sits alone on a roundabout, singing to herself, and trailing a hand through the air as it turns. An older woman watches her, reminds her to play carefully, then comes to sit on the bench.

'Looks a bit like rain,' she says, studying the gathering shower clouds.

'I'm sorry?' The younger woman stirs. 'Oh, yes.'

'Come here often, do you?'

'No.'

'Just on a visit, then?'

'A visit. Yes.'

'Relatives?'

The younger woman looks at her, her face crumples and she bows her head. And after a pause, tears start falling onto her lap.

The older woman is concerned. 'Gracious me, dear, what on earth is it? Are you feeling ill?'

'No,' she whispers. 'I'm sorry. It's . . . I lost someone. Someone close.'

'Oh, you poor thing. Here, take this.' She produces a handkerchief and offers it to the younger woman, patting her lightly on the back, like a child.

'Thank you.'

'You keep it, dear. This blooming war, breaks your heart.'

They sit in silence a while. At length the younger woman raises her head.

'All right?' The older woman studies her. 'Feeling a little better now?'

'Yes. Thank you. I'm so sorry.'

'Don't be silly. We all need a good cry sometimes.'

The younger woman nods. 'The little girl on the roundabout. She's yours, then?'

'Peggy, you mean? Yes, she's mine all right.'

Peggy. Peggy Groves. A nice name. 'She's very pretty.'

'Pretty mischievous you mean!' The older woman laughs. 'No, but she's a good girl really. Apple of my eye.'

'I can see.' The young woman hesitates. 'Is she . . . a happy girl?'

'Oh yes, happy as they come. Bright too, spot-on with her reading and that. Bit of a dreamer, sometimes, but there's no harm in that, is there?'

'Dreaming? No, no harm at all.' She begins buttoning her coat.

'You off, then?'

'Yes. I . . . it's time.'

'You sure you're well enough? Do you want us to walk with you?'

'No. Thank you, you've been too kind already. I have to . . . I wonder, is there a police station near here?'

'Police station? Why, have you lost something?'

'Lost? No. Not lost . . .'

'Oh. Well, the police station's off the High Street. Behind the town hall. About ten minutes' walk.'

'Thank you.' She holds out her hand. 'It was nice to meet you. Goodbye.'

The older woman, face quizzical, watches her walk away.

One evening, ten days or so later, I was sitting at home in my parents' house in Chiswick, reading the papers, when I received a telephone call. It was a recall to duty, and not a moment too soon, for what with my mother's doleful looks, and endless sympathy visits from friends and relatives, I was more than ready to escape. And the call, unknown to me, was the precursor to a most extraordinary day.

The caller was Charles Whitworth.

'Quentin, dear boy, how are you?'

'Hello, sir. I'm well, thank you, all things considered. And I must thank you for stepping in when you did. It was a close-run thing.'

'Nonsense, that Hickson girl of yours saved the day. How is she?'

So he knew about Chloe. 'She's well, sir, so I believe.' But I hadn't heard. She had been summoned back the day after the raid.

'Good. Good.' Whitworth sounded distracted.

'Sir.' I lowered my voice. 'No word, I suppose. Survivors . . .'

'No. No word. But it's much too soon, Quentin, you know that.'

'Yes, sir.'

'Now then. Feel up to a little work?'

'Of course. What did you have in mind?'

'Well, the thing is, someone you know is in a hell of a pickle. I can't talk about it over the phone, but if you can get to Lincoln city police station in the morning all will become clear.'

A mechanic arrested on a drunk-and-disorderly charge was my first thought. Hardly urgent, I guessed, but any excuse would do. I glanced at my parents, busy pretending not to listen. 'Yes, sir, that does sound serious. If I catch the early train I could be there mid-morning.'

'Fine. And when you're done there, Quentin, come up to Scampton. And wear your best uniform, there's someone I want you to meet.'

I arrived at Lincoln at ten the next morning. The air was summery and mild, and it felt good to be back. At the police station I gave my name to the desk sergeant. A few minutes later he led me to a back room, guarded unusually by an armed military policeman. 'All yours, Guv.' The sergeant winked. 'And best of luck with it. Bang on the door when you're done.'

It wasn't a hung-over mechanic sitting forlornly at the table, it was Tess Murray. For a second I barely recognised her. She'd changed beyond all recognition, thin and pale, lank hair tied back, her shoulders slumped.

'Tess? Good God, Tess, it's me, Quentin.'

She didn't look up. Just hugged herself, rocking slightly.

'Tess, what on earth happened?'

Still the eyes never left the table. She said. 'He's dead. I killed him.'

I thought she meant Peter. I thought she was blaming herself for getting him into 617 Squadron and Operation Chastise. But why then was she under armed guard?

'Well, now,' I encouraged lamely. 'We don't know that, do we? Officially, he's just missing.'

She shook her head. 'Brendan,' she murmured. 'I killed Brendan.'

'You what?'

'I killed him. And they're going to hang me for it.'

Gradually it all came out. How she'd slipped into their quarters on the night of the raid to recover a few essentials before leaving next morning with Peter. Finding Brendan in the bedroom, the deadly circling round the table, the lunge in the kitchen and the knife. She spoke hesitantly but clearly. She offered no mitigating circumstances, made no claims of self-defence, she simply recounted the facts. And expected full punishment for it, resignedly.

Shocked and incredulous, I realised this was her formal statement so, fumbling notepad and pen from a pocket, I began to take notes. After the killing, it transpired, she'd fled in panic to her lodgings to await Peter's return so that together they might present the true facts to the authorities, in the hope of a sympathetic hearing. But when daylight dawned and no knock came at the door, she began to despair. Finally, around nine, she went to a phone box and got through to her friend Phyllis in the NAAFI. Who was beside herself with anguish. Oh, Tess, she sobbed, so many of those brave boys gone! But what of Peter? Tess asked fearfully. Gone, they're all gone, Phyllis kept repeating.

She'd wandered the streets in shock, then returned to her rooms and lain on her bed without moving. The next morning she'd taken the train to Stafford, found her daughter's address and followed her to the park with her adoptive mother. Having seen her little girl, and satisfied herself that she was safe and well, she'd handed herself in.

Now she was back in Lincoln under arrest for murder. And if she did plead guilty, as she seemed bent on doing, then she might well hang for it. Which was unthinkable, given Murray's record of violence, drinking and other nefarious activities. Everything was recorded in the file I'd passed to Arnott and Campbell. With that dossier, the worst she should expect was a manslaughter conviction, or even a full acquittal based on the *crime passionnel* principle. All that was needed was time to assemble a case.

'Tess, listen to me. You didn't mean to kill Brendan, you acted in self-defence and I know we can prove it. But you must have faith, and hope, and show some determination.'

'For what purpose, Quentin?' she replied then, gazing at me dully. 'I pushed my family away, my daughter has another mother, and I lost the only man I ever loved. Then I killed my husband. I have no friends, no future, absolutely nothing to live for.'

'Of course you do!' I racked my brains. 'What about Peter?'

'Peter's dead. They all are. Everyone says so.'

'But we don't know that. All we know is he's missing. He could be a prisoner, or injured, or even on the run, Tess, trying to get back to you.'

The eyes flickered briefly, with something resembling hope, like embers stirring in a fire. Then died again. 'No. I brought him here. And it killed him. I did it, just like I killed Brendan.'

'All right.' Exasperated, I tried one last tack. 'Maybe you're right. But don't you think you should at least give him a chance to prove you wrong?'

I left my contact details with the desk sergeant, and some money, and a list of basics to get for her, and told him to ring me any time, no matter the reason. Then I caught the bus for the short ride up to Scampton, only to find pandemonium. There were long queues at the gate, armed military police everywhere, sniffer dogs on leads, the works. Fortunately, a gate guard spotted me and waved me forward.

'Welcome back, Lieutenant!' he grinned. 'Glad you could make it.'

'Make what, Corporal? What on earth's going on?'

'Royal visit, sir. Didn't you know? The King and Queen are coming today. To meet the dambusters.'

Dambusters. I'd seen the words in the papers, but this was the first I'd come across it within the RAF itself. 617 Squadron, it seemed, were now officially the dambusters, complete with royal seal of approval. But royalty aside, I had business to attend to, so ignoring the holiday atmosphere, strings of fluttering bunting and cheery greetings from colleagues, I set out for Number 2 hangar, and the offices of Arnott and Campbell.

Only to find everything being packed into boxes and loaded onto a van.

Frank Arnott was there, standing amid the detritus, dressed in full squadron leader's uniform, complete with pilot's wings and medals.

'Ah, Credo, there you are,' he said. 'I trust you're recovered. Wouldn't want to miss the fun, eh?'

'Group Captain Whitworth asked me to attend, sir. Um, are you leaving?'

'We certainly are. Job's done and we've other fish to fry.'

'Really? So, Operation Chastise. All the security work here at Scampton. 617 Squadron. The files are closed?'

'That's right. Closed and on their way back to HQ. One or two loose ends to tidy up, but nothing that need detain us here.'

I wondered which loose ends. 'I see. Only the thing is . . .'

'Yes?'

'Sergeant Murray. The groundsman I wrote to you about.'

'Ah, yes. Nasty business. Stabbed clean through the heart by his wife. Body lay there undiscovered for four days.'

'Yes, sir. Only she didn't murder him. She was acting in self-defence. Murray had a history of violence towards her, and was also mixed up in petty crime, black-marketeering and so on. It's all in the file I sent you.'

'Is it?'

'Yes, sir.' I held my breath. 'As are matters relating to his possible spying.'

'For which you have presented not one shred of evidence.'

'Sir,' I persevered, 'Murray's behaviour was secretive and suspicious, and some of the things he said to his wife suggested the actions of someone engaged in subterfuge.'

'All right, Credo.' Arnott broke off from filing. 'Such as what, precisely?'

'He told his wife, when drunk one night, that everything started going wrong following a gardening job when the squadron was at Feltwell. I believe he meant gardening, as in mine-laying.'

'So.' Arnott nodded. 'That's what this is about. You think he tipped off the Germans about your mine-laying flight?'

'Possibly.'

'Is it not also possible, and perfectly understandable, that you're simply looking for someone to blame? Other than the enemy, that is?'

'Yes, it is. But taking everything as a whole—'

'I've read your file, Credo. It amounts to nothing. You've no proof.'

And I'd argue otherwise, but as far as he was concerned, he'd done his job, the mission was over, and Murray was dead. Arguing with him was pointless. As it was, other matters were pressing.

'That file, sir,' I went on, after a pause. 'It is vital to his wife's defence.'

'I doubt it.'

'The court must have it. It can't be withheld.'

'It most certainly can. That file is top-secret military intelligence. No civilian court in the world can subpoena it. Right now it's on a lorry back to HQ, where it will be stored. For at least fifty years.'

'But the case for Tess Murray's defence rests in that dossier.'

'I'm sorry, Credo, you can't have it and that's final. Anyway, has it not occurred to you she's lying? Our analysis is that she had it all planned out in advance, so she could be with her boyfriend. And if I were you, I'd watch your own back, you're not exactly un-implicated.'

Another file hit the box with a thud. 'What do you mean?'

'For God's sake, man. You got her boyfriend posted here. You helped them find ways to see each other. You paid for a room in a hotel. You even lent them your bloody car for their little love trysts!'

Chloe. As thorough as ever. Bless her. He knew everything. Almost.

'Did you get his notebook?'

That slowed him. 'What notebook?'

'He kept a notebook. Of everything he did. It's all in my report. No doubt you searched his rooms after his body was discovered. Did you find it?'

'I've no idea what you're talking about.'

An awkward pause followed, him sorting files while I stood by and fumed. In the hangar, freshly uniformed ground crew were gathering, smoking and chatting excitedly, while outside a brass band limbered up.

'Where's Corporal Hickson?' I asked.

'Away. On a training course. Look, Credo,' he went on reasonably, 'try to think of the bigger picture. This is a rare chance, amid all the grime and drudgery, to celebrate a success. This whole operation was a massive undertaking involving thousands of individuals, who all worked together and pulled off a great victory. You included. And you can rest assured your contribution hasn't gone unnoticed. So let's just enjoy the party.'

But I wasn't having his platitudes. 'A great victory, sir? We sent twenty Lancasters over there. Only eleven made it back. Nine didn't, nine whole crews, that's sixty-three men lost, and probably dead. I'm afraid "great victory" doesn't do them justice.'

'What's justice got to do with it? If you want justice, Credo, sue the Nazis. They started this war.'

'They were expected, sir. Gibson and the others. They must have been, to sustain losses like that.'

'Christ, you and your bloody conspiracy theories!' He strode to his desk and rifled through a pile of photographs. 'Here, this is the Möhne, taken the day after the raid. Look at it, Credo. Kindly note the hundred-yard gap where the bomb smashed through the dam. And the empty lake behind.' He thrust the photo at me. 'Crushing the enemy, that's what this is about!'

I studied the photograph. 'Yes, sir. Fantastic job. I never said otherwise.'

'Correct. Now look again. What else do you see? Trees, Credo, trees! Your famous wooden crates. Do you know what was in them? Ornamental conifer trees. In pots. To decorate the dam.'

I looked again.

He was right. Trees had appeared, at either end of the dam, and at odd intervals along its length, as though to blend it into the surrounding forest. 'Camouflage.'

'If you like.' He lit a cigarette and wandered to the window.

'But that's my whole point. It could have been flak, or searchlights, or anything. It just happened to be camouflage. And what made the Germans camouflage the dam just before we were due to attack it?'

'Who the hell cares?' he bellowed. 'It's over, Credo, mission accomplished! Nothing else matters!'

'It does to me!'

Which is when I threw the furniture. Well, kicked a wastepaper basket, but then I was convalescing. And it was a metal one, and flew gratifyingly straight and only narrowly missed him. Twenty minutes later, bizarrely, I was standing beside him being introduced to the King. Everyone had assembled outside in the sunshine, while Ralph Cochrane and Charles Whitworth shepherded the royal entourage along, occasionally pausing here and there for a chat. To my consternation, the King stopped in front of me.

'J-jolly bravely done, old ch-chap,' he murmured, in his quiet stammer. 'Did anyone else in your crew get h-hurt?'

'I . . . Ah . . . Well, no . . . You see, sir, I wasn't actually . . .'

Whitworth stepped swiftly forward. 'Flight Lieutenant Credo wasn't flying that night, Your Majesty,' he explained. 'He was my aide-de-camp, sir, during the operation. In charge of synchronising the security effort.'

A derisive snort from Arnott beside me. Nor was Whitworth's use of the past tense lost on me. He *was* my aide-de-camp, he'd said. Clearly I was out of a job again. The King looked baffled, then mustered a smile. 'J-jolly bravely done,' he muttered again, and moved on.

Afterwards came a reception, at which I finally got to speak to aircrew on the raid. But not until the formalities were over. Champagne, sandwiches, and hours of queuing, like guests at a wedding. Followed by endless rounds of speeches from Cochrane, Whitworth, Gibson. Then Barnes Wallis himself stepped up and, in his anxious self-deprecating way, made a rather melancholy speech about sacrifice and loss and the tragic futility of war.

'Poor bloke,' the Australian Les Knight murmured in my ear. 'Been inconsolable since he heard about the casualties. Says he'd never have gone ahead if he'd known.'

Finally the speeches ended and I was able to corner Les and a few other pilots. With their tongues loosened by champagne, hopefully they were ready to unburden themselves to one of their own.

'Rotten luck, Geoff,' I commiserated to Rice, who was a former 57 Squadron colleague. He'd lost his bomb and narrowly escaped disaster pancaking H-Harry into the Waddensee. He'd also received a grilling from Gibson for it and still looked upset two weeks later.

'Thanks, Credo. But I cocked up and everyone knows it.'

'Don't think like that. You did well getting your crew safely home.'

'Too right he did!' Les clapped us both on the shoulder. 'God bless all you 57 Squadron boys.' Rice shot me a sad glance. Both the other crews from our squadron, Dinghy Young's and Bill Astell's, had been lost.

David Maltby sauntered over, glass in hand. It was his bomb, following Young's, that had sealed the Möhne's fate. 'I say, did you hear about Cyril Anderson?' he murmured conspiratorially. Heads leaned forward to listen. Anderson had also been on the receiving end of Gibson's wrath, having abandoned his mission in Y-York because of a faulty rear turret and problems with fog. Now it seemed he was to be sacked. 'Not just for giving up, but for bringing his bomb home, completely against orders.'

'Congratulations on your DSO, Maltby,' I said. 'I hear your bomb pitched up a perfect yorker at the Möhne.'

'More of a googly, actually.' He smiled. 'And the dam was already going when I attacked. Dinghy got it really.'

'Why do you think it took four bombs? Wallis swore one should do it.'

Maltby shrugged. 'The first three weren't on target. The CO's went left and short, Martin's was a complete wide, and poor old Hoppy's went straight over the top.'

Glances were exchanged. One of the unwritten rules of aerial combat is you don't discuss death. Not in direct terms, only in euphemisms: he got the chop, he bought the farm, he didn't make it.

'What happened?' I tried gently.

'M-Mother was riddled in flak, a complete flamer, before he'd gone halfway. Kept right on with the attack and even got his bomb away, but too late and we saw it bounce over the dam. M-Mother flew on down the valley, burning furiously, trying to gain height, then blew apart in the air.'

A pause while we stared at our shoes and upended our glasses, then peered round for the steward. I glimpsed a laughing Joe McCarthy, stalwart of the Sorpe, standing head and shoulders above the throng. And the ever-boyish David Shannon, so sure he'd cracked the Eder, and celebrating his twenty-first birthday that very day. But so many faces I'd grown to know were missing: Barlow, Maudslay, Byers, Burpee, and fifty-nine others. Including Peter, Uncle, Chalkie and the rest.

'V-Vicky bought it on the way home,' Les Knight went on, reading my thoughts. 'I know you were friendly with Lightfoot and his boys. They pulled off the perfect run at the Eder, you know, really. I never saw anyone fly a Lancaster like that. Lightfoot threw that thing around like a Spitfire, finishing with a power-off sideslip with flap, down to the water for the final run-in. Bloody marvellous. The drop was spot-on, too. The bomb punched a hole in the dam like a fist through wet cardboard.'

The afternoon wore on, the champagne flowed, the noise levels grew. At some point the royal party, wisely sensing the onset of disorder, departed for quieter pastures. With them went any pretence at decorum. Ties were loosened, gin and whisky bottles appeared, as did wives, girlfriends and WAAFs rounded up from the women's quarters. A piano arrived, shunted in by cheering airmen, and before long a singsong was under way, together with dancing, games and general tomfoolery. The pilots' way, I reflected, watching them play like overexcited children. Fly hard, party hard and don't think. For tomorrow you fade and die, just like the bubbles of your dreams.

I stayed on the periphery until, with my head spinning somewhat, and feeling oddly forlorn, I left them to it. Outside the air was filled with the scent of dewy grass and rambling roses. I inhaled deeply, gazing out over the verdant airfield and the wide Lincolnshire sky.

'Hello, Quentin. Lovely evening.' Charles Whitworth strolled up, brandy glass and cigar in hand. His tie was loosened, his cap slightly askew.

'Hello, sir. Yes, it's been quite a day.'

'I'll say. How's the Murray woman?'

'In a pickle, sir, as you said.'

'Can you help?'

'I'm not sure. I hope so.'

'Let me know if you need anything.'

'Thank you, sir.'

He puffed on his cigar, surveying his domain. 'Do you know, I've loved being station commander here. Best posting I ever had. They're closing it soon, though. To lay the concrete runways. It won't be the same here afterwards. One of the last of the all-grass bomber stations and that. But then everything changes, doesn't it? Sooner or later, if you get my drift.'

I did. I wasn't a pilot any more, and never would be. I wasn't an SIO, nor was I his aide-de-camp. I wasn't anything, except an embarrassment to the Service. I didn't belong here. It was time to leave, and I felt ready.

'You have absolutely nothing to reproach yourself for, Quentin,' he went on intuitively. 'And much to offer. Common sense for a start, operational experience, good judgment, a compassionate heart. The RAF needs these things. Say the word and I'll have you on 5 Group staff in a trice.'

'It's kind of you, sir, but it's the front line for me, or nothing. I'm ready for a change. A new start.'

'Thought so. And does Corporal Hickson figure in this new start?'

'I, well, gosh, I don't know . . .' I blustered. 'I'd like to hope so . . .'

'Good. She's in London, by the way. Cooped up at RAF Intelligence HQ, and none too happy about it by all accounts. It's in Highgate, a place called Athlone House.' He grinned, then slipped a note in my hand. 'Telephone them, tell them you're my ADC and ask for Signals. That should get you through.'

'I . . . well, I don't know what to say, sir.'

'Don't say anything. Just get on with it. *Carpe diem* and all that. But for God's sake don't tell anyone!' With that, cigar in mouth, he turned and ambled away across the grass.

So I called her. Not ten minutes later.

'Quentin! Thank God. I've been out of my mind. Where are you?'

'Scampton. Lunching with the King. As one does.'

'Bad boy. You're supposed to be on sick leave.'

'I got bored. And things came up. How are you?'

'Missing you. Hating this. It's odd, I used to love this job. But since you and I began working together, you know, on the operation, everything changed. And now I don't feel the same about it.'

'Hmm. Exactly my thoughts. Which is why I'm packing it in. Resigning my commission. Medical discharge or somesuch.'

'Crikey. What will you do?'

'Not sure. Take a break. Get the face fixed. Become a barrister.'

'Goodness. Well, that's absolutely marvellous. How does it feel?'

'It feels good. Would you care to join me?'

A pause. But only a short one. 'As your driver, I suppose?'

'Very funny. As my wife, Chloe. Will you marry me?'

'I'd love to. More than anything. When?'

'Soon as we can arrange it. But, Chloe, I have a request.'

'Yes?'

'I can't tell you now. But I am going to need your help with something.'

We signed off. I stood for a moment, hefting the receiver, scarcely daring to believe it. I was engaged. To the most wonderful girl in the world.

I went back to my rooms, opened the window and poured myself a Scotch. The sounds of merrymaking continued outside and somewhere a gramophone was playing Glenn Miller. I raised my glass to the night, and drank.

Five minutes later, Guy Gibson came barging through the door.

'*Après moi le déluge*,' he spluttered in French.

'I beg your pardon, sir?'

'*Après moi le déluge*. It's our new squadron motto. What do you think?'

'Well, I think it's very good, sir. Most appropriate.'

'Martin thought of it. Ah! I heard you had whisky. Thank God for that!'

'Oh, yes, I do. Would you like one?'

'No, I'd like three! And make them doubles. And have one yourself!'

'Well, yes, all right, sir, if you insist . . .'

'I do. And stop calling me sir.' He winked. 'At least until tomorrow.'

He was drunk and dishevelled, his cheeks flushed. I poured him a glass, he took it and slumped into a chair, eyeing me curiously.

'You lost the hand, I see, Credo. Sorry about that.'

'Can't be helped. Actually, I'm better off without it.'

'Bit tricky for the flying though. But then there's always that Bader chap, flying fighters with no legs, so anything's possible. Although I hear his rudder control's awful.'

They were very alike, I realised, Bader and Gibson. Both hot-tempered, pig-headed taskmasters. Both equally convinced of their own immortality. Both awe-inspiring leaders.

'They're giving me a bloody VC, you know, Quentin.'

'So I heard. Many congratulations. And, may I say, richly deserved.'

'You think so? I was terrified. Absolutely quaking, from start to finish.'

'Of course. You'd be inhuman not to be. But you trained these men, and inspired them, gave them confidence. Then led them to the dams, from the front, and succeeded against all odds. And brought them home again.'

'It was orders, I had no choice.'

'You're wrong, Guy. At the Möhne, after Hoppy bought it. When you went in alongside Martin to draw the flak. That wasn't orders. It was magnificent. And worth a Victoria Cross alone in my view.'

'Maybe.' He downed his glass. 'But we still lost far too many.'

A reflective silence followed. Outside in the corridor airmen were heading noisily for bed. I leaned across and refilled his glass, sensing now might be my only chance. 'May I ask you something?'

He waved his hand. 'Fire away.'

'Do you think they were expecting you? At the Möhne, that is. Did you get the impression the Germans were ready for you, in any way?'

A nail-biting pause while he considered, his eyes focusing unsteadily on mine. Then a knock came on the door.

'Sorry to disturb you, Lieutenant,' an orderly said. 'Telephone call. City police station.'

'Thank you, I'll be right there.'

Gibson was still thinking, still remembering, still staring glassily.

'Guy?'

He began levering himself to his feet. 'God knows, Quentin,' he said finally. 'But I will say this. It certainly bloody felt like it.'

TESS WAS on the telephone. She sounded tired, but more composed.

'Tess. Are you all right? Has something happened?'

'No. Nothing. I'm all right. Thank you for the toiletries and things. And thanks for contacting my family. My father sent a telegram. About arranging representation and that.'

'Good. They had to know, Tess. You can't do this on your own.'

'I suppose not.' She paused. 'About the notebook . . .'

'Yes.'

'I tried.' She sighed at the memory. 'I searched him, afterwards . . . you know. And I did look round our rooms. But I couldn't find it. I'm sorry. I know how important it was to you.'

'No matter. Thanks for trying. It can't have been easy.'

'No.' Another pause. 'Quentin, do you think there's a chance Peter's alive?'

CHAPTER 11

There was.

Peter woke. He was lying on a straw palliasse, in a small room with concrete walls, steel door and tiny barred windows set high in the wall, through which daylight poured, together with the now familiar sounds of boots on gravel and revving auto-engines. The cell was mostly below ground, but by standing on tiptoe he could see out onto a vehicle compound surrounded by high stone walls. Wrought-iron gates opened onto a busy street, from where grey-painted staff cars and motorcycles drove in and out, carrying Germans clad in Luftwaffe uniforms.

He rose from his palliasse and went to the window. Soon would come breakfast, hard black bread and a mug of bitter coffee, then they'd come to get him for the day's first session with Major Kessell on this his fifteenth day in captivity.

He'd first come to his senses on the night of the raid, lying on his back in a clump of bushes. It was cold, and dark, and quiet, and whispering white silk billowed round him like a cloud. He didn't know where he was, nor how he'd got there, he only knew that blood leaked from a handkerchief tied over a gash to his head and that V-Vicky was gone. Of her last moments, and those of her crew, he could remember nothing.

He'd stayed on his back for a while, fighting an unbearable urge to weep. Grief seemed to wash over him like waves onto a deserted beach, yet he didn't know why. Eventually he'd rolled onto his knees and, fighting the pounding in his head, forced himself to his feet. Fumbling with catches, he'd released his parachute and hidden it among the bushes, along with his Mae West. Turning his back on the brighter sky to the east, he'd set out for home.

Three miles into the gathering dawn, he was spotted by a soldier on a bicycle returning from a night on fire watch. The soldier blew loudly on his whistle, unslung his rifle and gestured for Peter to approach with hands held high. Having searched him for weapons and stolen his watch, the soldier then marched him at rifle-point into the nearest village, where he was locked into the back room of a hall and the authorities notified.

The local doctor came and stitched the wound on his head. 'You are fortunate, young man,' the doctor murmured in heavily accented English. 'People don't like being bombed, you know.'

Peter said nothing, just gritted his teeth as the needle pierced him. Then he asked the doctor where he was, and whether any other airmen had been found the previous night.

'There was a crash,' the doctor replied. 'Several kilometres away. Bodies were recovered. That is all I know.' He added that they were in Westphalia, which meant nothing to Peter.

Apart from the doctor, nobody visited. Then, next morning, two plain-clothes policemen collected him in a car and drove him east, deeper into Germany. Word had spread that a downed British airman, an officer at that, was in custody. Furthermore, the officer in question might be a survivor of the extraordinary raid on the Ruhr dams, which had wreaked such havoc and caused a furore in Berlin extending up to the Führer himself. Consequently Section 1L of the Abwehr, the department of Germany's military intelligence responsible for aviation-related matters, was most keen to interview the aforesaid officer. Within twenty-four hours Peter had been collected and driven to the converted mansion in Dortmund that served as the Abwehr's district headquarters. Where the questioning began.

SOMEHOW, MIRACULOUSLY, a handful of those lost on Operation Chastise had survived. But desperately few. Vernon Byers and his crew in K-King were the raid's first victims, downed at 2300 hours by a chance flak round as they coasted in over the Dutch island of Vlieland. Some days later K-King's *Upkeep* exploded, harmlessly, in the Waddensee.

Fifty minutes after K-King's loss, Byers's Wave 2 associate, Norm Barlow, was racing E-Easy low across the Rhineland when it struck high-tension wires and pancaked into a field before exploding. E-Easy's *Upkeep* became detached on impact, and rolled away into trees, but didn't go off. Later, the military arrived and took it away for defusing and examination. Within a fortnight Luftwaffe engineers knew every aspect of Wallis's revolving bomb.

No one survived from Bill Astell's B-Baker, which was the third to be lost at 0015 hours, when Astell collided with a pylon and crashed into a field near Marbeck. Local farm residents watched as a huge drum-shaped object rolled away in flames. Seconds afterwards, the *Upkeep* went off in a monstrous explosion.

Fifteen minutes later the end came for John Hopgood's M-Mother. Having been hit by flak en route, M-Mother lost the final battle on its run-in to the Möhne. Raked by flak as it sped over the water, M-Mother burst into flames and, having narrowly cleared the parapet, was seen heading north, trailing fire. Hopgood knew the aircraft was finished and gave the order to bale out. In the nose, the bomb aimer, Fraser, jettisoned the hatch and parachuted to the ground. The rear gunner, Burcher, also baled out, but landed heavily and badly injured his back. Both men survived.

The Canadian Lewis Burpee and his crew died at 0200. They had taken off in S-Sugar as part of the Wave 3 mobile reserve, but were caught over Holland by flak batteries.

Twenty-year-old Warner Ottley's C-Charlie, another part of Wave 3, was also brought down by flak. Crashing into a field beside a wood, C-Charlie's *Upkeep* went off, demolishing the aircraft. The rear turret was sent flying yet, incredibly, after coming to rest, its occupant, Sergeant Fred Tees, crawled out alive. Shocked and burned, he walked from the scene but into captivity. At around the same time, 0230 hours, Henry Maudslay's Z-Zebra was brought down near the oil town of Emmerich. Having sustained damage and injuries when their *Upkeep* exploded against the parapet at the Eder, Maudslay and his crew had nursed their ailing machine almost to within sight of the Dutch border, when the flak found them.

Then came Dinghy Young, whose brilliantly placed bomb so fatally damaged the Möhne. He'd hedge-hopped all the way to the Dutch coast, where, with the dawn growing at his back, Dinghy had allowed A-Apple to rise into the sky above Vlieland. A chance flak-burst had caught him and the Lancaster had exploded into the sea. Nobody had survived.

Which just left V-Vicky.

Peter finally learned of its fate in Dortmund, that fifteenth day of his captivity.

After his breakfast and a visit to the washroom, he was escorted as usual to the first-floor office of his inquisitor, Major Leopold Kessell. The office was comfortable and well appointed, with shuttered French windows leading onto a balcony. Peter was admitted by an adjutant and shown to his chair before a mahogany desk.

'Good morning, Flying Officer Lightfoot,' Kessell began in his flawless English. 'And it is a fine one, quite warm, no? Now then, you'll be relieved to hear that the injuries to Sergeant Tees are not life-threatening. He has flash-burns, but is receiving excellent hospital treatment. Pilot Officer Burcher's injuries are more serious, I regret, but he is in good hands.' He opened a file labelled: 617 SQUADRON, 5 GROUP, RAF BOMBER COMMAND.

While Kessell studied the latest sheets, Peter said nothing and kept his expression neutral, his by now well-rehearsed response to probing. He also made a point of showing no interest in the file or its contents.

'. . . Some further bodies from other crews have been recovered and buried with appropriate military honours,' Kessell went on, flicking through the sheets, 'though sadly many have yet to be identified, owing to the severe nature of their injuries . . . Oh, but some better news just in, two Canadian sergeants, Bimson and Guttenberg, have turned up alive and well.'

The matter-of-fact delivery, the hypnotic turning of pages, Peter fell for them completely. 'What?' he gasped. 'Where?'

'Bocholt, it seems. A military hospital for NCOs, fifty kilometres from where you were picked up.' Kessell smiled. 'So you do know them, Peter.

This confirms you are from 617 Squadron, and the crashed Lancaster AJ-V was yours.' He went back to his papers. 'But I'm afraid your second pilot, MacDowell, did not survive. He was found at the controls. Nor did the wireless operator and navigator, sadly, ah, what were their names?'

'White. And Johnson,' Peter replied dully. Kessell would find out soon enough. Or perhaps already knew. Chalkie and Jamie. And Uncle. All gone. It was beyond bearing. A fragment of memory came to him: Uncle leaning across him, shouting something and hauling at Vicky's controls while someone, Jamie perhaps, or Chalkie, wiped blood from his eyes with a handkerchief.

'One man is as yet unaccounted for . . .' Kessell was still talking. 'Which would be the bombardier, yes? What was his name, Peter?'

Kiwi. They hadn't got him. Which might mean he was alive. And running for it. 'I'm not telling you another damn thing,' he said angrily.

'Your mission, Peter—what the English newspapers are calling the Dambusters—was an exceptional undertaking, so brave and imaginative. But far too costly, and ultimately of trivial effect. Nearly half those young men were wiped out, you know, a criminal waste of courageous lives.'

Peter leaned over. 'I watched two dams go, Major, and there was nothing trivial about it. And we went there because we wanted to. We were volunteers. All of us. Nobody died in vain.'

'But . . .' Kessell gaped. 'Do you mean, it was you? The second dam?'

He rose from his chair, chuckling in disbelief, strolled to the windows, closed and locked them. As he did so, Peter slipped the Major's letter-opener into his cuff.

'Well, well, well.' Kessell resumed his seat and picked up his pen. 'So, Flying Officer Lightfoot and his crew were at the Möhne and the Eder, where they successfully broke the dam. So this must mean you were part of Wing Commander Gibson's main attack force. Tell me about that, please.'

'No. I refuse. I want to go back to my cell.'

A wince, as of pain. 'That would be so foolish. Because, as I've said before, if you refuse, I must hand you to the Gestapo, whose methods for obtaining information are quite barbaric. I couldn't bear that. So stay, Peter, and help me here. Oh, and may I borrow that letter-opener . . .'

THAT NIGHT, the rest came back to him. For hours he lay on his mattress, staring at the fading square of light at his window and thinking of Uncle and the others. More fragments of memory were surfacing now, wreckage from a sunken ship. Panicked shouts on the intercom, an engine in flames, the smell of cordite and the taste of blood.

VICKY IS DYING, and her crew are injured, Jamie Johnson mortally so, hit in the chest by a cannon shell. Chalkie too is hit, blood pumping from a shattered left arm. In the cockpit Peter can feel himself fainting. Blood pours from a head wound, running in hot gouts into his eyes and mouth. He can't see, his arms are like lead, and unconsciousness beckons. But he can feel the rudders, slack and useless beneath his feet, and sense the intense fire raging on the wing, and knows it's over. 'She's had it, Uncle,' he murmurs feebly. 'She's had it. I'm sorry.'

After the Eder, they'd scurried west for the border. Which is where the night fighter had found them. A Messerschmitt Bf110, fast, twin-engined, carrying four 20mm cannon. Its first burst ripped into the port wing and destroyed an engine; the second poured cannon into the fuselage and cabin. The attack was over in less than a minute. But the damage was done.

Peter's teetering on the edge of oblivion. Strong arms haul him from his seat and wipe blood from his face with a rag. 'Leave it to me, now, laddie,' a comforting voice says. 'Everything's all right. Have you got him, Kiwi?'

'I got him.'

'Good. Time to go now. All of you.'

With that Peter falls into unconsciousness. And it's Uncle that takes over, and gives the order, sitting there, straight-backed in the pilot's seat, resolutely hauling the doomed bomber heavenward.

'Off you go then, lads.'

PETER WOKE in pitch blackness to the wail of an air-raid siren. For a moment he lay, disorientated and confused by the unfamiliar sound. Then he heard the rumble of approaching engines, and leapt from his mattress. Dortmund was under attack. The engine noise grew from a drone to a throb. Peter was sure he heard Merlins, scores of them, Lancasters that meant, or the Mark 2 Halifax. He strained at his window, but could see only the criss-cross beams of the searchlights and flash of distant artillery. Then the bombs fell and he felt the ground quake and heard the rumbling crump of explosions. With each explosion, flickering light lit the courtyard. A fire engine raced past, bell trilling. They'd forgotten him, he realised, left him to die like a bird, forgotten in a cage. Then came a searing flash, a deafening explosion and a shockwave that punched him like a fist in the back. He dropped to his knees and crawled to the door. 'Let me out!' he shouted. 'For God's sake, please let me out!'

THE MORNING AFTER the air raid, instead of being taken to Kessell's office, Peter was escorted outside to the rubble-strewn compound and into the back of a Luftwaffe staff car. Minutes later Kessell himself joined him.

'Good morning, Flying Officer Lightfoot,' he breezed as usual. 'I trust you passed a comfortable night.' He was freshly shaved, crisply dressed, and unshakably cheerful, as if the air raid never happened. But their progress soon slowed as the car threaded its way round debris and craters, and Kessell was forced to take notice. 'Many of the bombs fell in the residential quarter,' he said, peering at a shattered building. 'Thirty dead in all, so I'm told. Which is regrettable, I'm sure you agree.'

Peter was thinking of Uncle, struggling at the controls of V-Vicky. And of how the death of his adored wife, Mary, taken from him by a German air raid, had erased his will to live. Now they were both gone. 'You bombed the people of London,' he replied. 'And Liverpool and Coventry, and the rest. You killed thousands, old and young, women and children. That's what I regret. I regret you ever started this war.'

Kessell seemed oblivious. 'The commercial sector suffered some damage,' he went on. 'As did the industrial quarter. But the canal is quite unharmed, you know, and the docks only superficially damaged. Rest assured, all will be restored to full serviceability in a few days.'

They drove on, out of town. 'Where are we going?' Peter asked uneasily. Apart from the driver, a guard was sitting in front, holding a pistol.

'Be patient, Peter.'

Two hours passed. The landscape became more rugged, the hills angular, the forest primordial. Finally they rounded a bend and arrived at a road-block. Explanations were exchanged, papers passed, Peter's face closely scrutinised, then they were waved through. They continued another half-mile, passed between entrance gates, ascended a twisting driveway, and broke suddenly into the clear.

Spread out before them was the vast expanse of the Eder reservoir. Or what was left of it: a shrivelled river twisting through 3,000 acres of empty lake bed and stretching away to distant tree-lined shores. Sailing boats and ferries lay stranded like beached fish; a pleasure steamer, frozen in mid-motion, cruised the drying mud, while piers and jetties jutted out to nowhere from the shores. Peter stared in awestruck fascination. A mile away on the northern shore, a Gothic castle stood guard, high on its hill overlooking the scene. The starting point, he recognised, for V-Vicky's dive to the water before the final attack.

'So, Peter.' Kessell gestured expansively. 'Behold the fruits of your efforts.'

Minutes later Peter found himself standing on the curved wall of the dam itself, where the scene was one of urgent yet organised activity. Scaffolding had been erected, cranes and hoists swung busily to and fro, while labourers hurried to the barked orders of engineers waving plans. One such engineer, a bespectacled civilian in his fifties, approached them.

'Ah, Herr Doctor,' Kessell greeted him. 'Peter, this is Dr Holzmann, the engineer supervising repairs. Herr Holzmann, may I present Flying Officer Lightfoot? The man who broke your dam.'

A stiff nod from Holzmann, who eyed Peter balefully, as though confronted with the hooligan caught vandalising his car. Behind him a younger assistant looked on curiously.

'Shall we visit the breach, Major?' Holzmann suggested.

They all set off along the parapet, passing beneath the right-hand sluice tower, then on another 100 yards towards the centre of the dam. Which ended abruptly at the edge of a cliff.

Kessell peered into the abyss. 'Look what you have done, Peter.'

Peter looked. The drop was dizzying. Seventy feet straight down to where the river still trickled into the valley beneath. At its base the dam was over 100 feet thick and built of solid reinforced concrete, yet it had been cleaved as though by a giant axe.

'The point of penetration was about ten metres down,' Holzmann explained. He was speaking in English, for his benefit, Peter gathered. 'The explosion caused a small breach, which widened under the pressure of water. The parapet above then collapsed and rolled over the edge.'

'Extraordinary. How bad is the damage?'

'Minor. We shall have the breach repaired in time for the autumn rains.'

'Really? That is remarkable.' Kessell glanced pointedly at Peter. 'And the collateral damage?'

'Insignificant also, Herr Major. Some loss of industrial production, some power shortages and water restrictions. But everything will be restored to normal within three months. Herr Director Speer has visited and promised everything we need. Including forced labour.'

'Casualties?'

'Seventy. Mostly civilians.'

The message being, Peter assumed, as they started back, that the mission had been a waste of time and effort. And lives. He stooped to pick up a fragment of steel rod, snapped in two as though a toothpick.

'The hydrodynamic energy required to do that is phenomenal,' a voice murmured beside him. Peter looked up, and saw Holzmann's young assistant. 'Thirty kilotons of reinforced masonry was blown out by the blast. That required very precise placement of a very specific charge. Your attack was a work of genius, Herr Lieutenant, as was the scientist behind it. I'd very much like to meet him.'

'Come to England. I'm sure it can be arranged.'

'It was my intention to study in London. But the war came.'

'Ah.'

'So much suffering. So much bloodshed. It is regrettable.'

'Indeed.'

The youth glanced cautiously about. 'Do not pay too much attention to Herr Holzmann's pronouncements, Herr Lieutenant.'

'Why?'

'Because, yes, the dam will be repaired, and in the timescale he states. But the damage is greater than he admits. Lateral cracking from one of the other bombs, structural fragilities in the base, it will be years before we can operate at full capacity again. And the collateral damage is also worse. Four power stations destroyed, many factories rendered useless, rail and road bridges swept away, not to mention severe disruption to water supplies. And that's just from the Eder. The damage from the Möhne is even worse.'

Back in the car, Kessell appeared satisfied. 'Now, Peter, I hope you have found this instructive. Your mission failed, you see, failed to starve us of water, failed to deny us power, failed to hinder armament production. So now you will return to Dortmund with your guard, and tomorrow we will continue our discussions.'

'Are you going somewhere, Major?'

'I have meetings to attend in Hamm, so I will drop you at the railway station there. You and your guard will return to Dortmund by train. Please try not to be a nuisance.'

BUT PETER *was* a nuisance. The train crept along at a snail's pace because of flood-damaged tracks. Also caused by him. Soon dusk was falling over the mist-clad countryside. '*Toiletten, bitte*,' Peter hissed to his guard, who ignored him. In the seat opposite a dozing mother sat with her daughter, a young girl of just six or seven, with dark eyes and pigtails, who stared at him in open fascination. '*Toiletten!*' he repeated, grimacing and holding his stomach. But the man only scowled and shook his head. At which the little girl reached over and jabbed the guard with her finger, gabbling at him in bossy tones, a single word of which Peter recognised as '*Diarrhöe*'.

Muttering irritably, the guard led him to the cubicle. '*Fünf Minuten!*' he warned, holding up five fingers.

Which was enough. The toilet floor was of wood and partly rotten. In no time, Peter had levered up the pedestal, a minute or two more and the hole beneath was wide enough to squeeze through. With no further ado, he lowered himself into the gap and dropped to the tracks.

CHAPTER 12

Not that we knew much about it back in Blighty, mused Credo, and as he turned the pages of the file he thought back to those dark days when nothing was known of V-Vicky's survivors . . . For Peter it was to be the beginning of many months on the run. Months during which he would jump trains, ride buses and swim rivers, masquerade as a tramp, a factory worker, even a wounded German soldier. Months during which he would change and grow, acquire new skills, discard old habits, learn stealth and cunning, patience and vigilance, how to forage, to scrimp and to survive, and how to kill with his bare hands, yet never once lose his urge to return home to the woman he loved.

ONE AUTUMN MORNING, many weeks after he'd escaped from the train, Peter woke in a Gascon farmhouse to see snowcapped peaks far to the south. 'The Pyrenees,' his host told him. 'Once across, you are in Spain.'

'How long will that take?' Peter asked.

'You will need to be patient, and learn to live and work with the Maquis,' the farmer replied, referring to the bands of freedom fighters hiding in the region. 'Then, when the time is right, they will guide you to safety.'

So Peter took to the road and became a mountain outlaw.

These things, as I say, we would not learn for months to come. All we knew was he was missing-feared-dead, a status detrimental both to Tess's predicament, which was becoming acute, and her state of mind, which was more and more defeatist. Peter was not just her best friend and ally, he was the key witness in this drama, and without him her defence was weak.

All was looking increasingly desperate, but then, just when we needed it most, providence took a hand, and we had a small but significant breakthrough. It came in the form of a curious letter from Mrs Barclay of Staffordshire Council, with whom I'd liaised during the search for Tess's daughter. She wrote saying the girl's adoptive mother, June Groves, had been to see her. Apparently June had met a distressed young woman at the park in Croxton one day, and something—intuition, empathy—led her to believe that the woman had come purposely to see her and her daughter Peggy. She sensed the young woman might have been Peggy's birth mother.

To cut a long story short, June Groves said she had no objection to Tess visiting again, so that they might all get to know one another a little. A wonderful gesture and exactly the stimulus Tess needed. I came up to Lincoln to break the news, and from her relieved demeanour and much grateful tear-shedding, I could see a will to live had been rekindled.

Meanwhile, events were unfolding in the Credo camp. Firstly, and most importantly, Chloe and I were married one Saturday in July, a gloriously celebratory event despite the privations of rationing. Apart from an excellent turnout from family and friends, Charles Whitworth also attended, together with a few 617 stalwarts, including Les Knight and Geoff Rice.

Chloe was enchanting and radiant in a beautiful satin gown borrowed from a cousin. Standing next to her at the altar, new life seemed to surge through my veins and I felt the happiest I'd ever been. Thank you, I found myself saying to her afterwards, thank you for everything. Her family came from Suffolk, so we honeymooned in a borrowed cottage there, passing an idyllic fortnight lounging on deck chairs by the sea, sailing a day boat on a river, and wandering the local sights.

After the honeymoon, I was due to check into East Grinstead for the facial reconstruction work. But it had to be be put off, yet again, by events outside my control. A date had been set for Tess Murray's arraignment, so it was all hands to the pumps to prepare her case. I spent many days at her barrister's chambers in London, working up the documentation with him.

Crucial to Tess's defence was evidence that Murray was violent towards her, something we knew, but as yet couldn't prove. What we could prove was that he drank, was prone to fighting, and involved in petty crime, racketeering and the rest. Not enough to justify murder, but better than nothing. Essential to everything, however, was the dossier I'd compiled. The one buried in the vaults of RAF Intelligence HQ.

So I got Chloe to 'borrow' it. So I could make a copy. This was the favour I asked over the phone the day I proposed marriage, and would be one of her final acts before resigning from the job—just as well, as the intelligence community takes a dim view of employees snaffling files. Yet all went smoothly, with the file replaced in just a couple of days.

While this file-copying was going on, Tess's lawyer had researched Murray's past and turned up a number of interesting details, including convictions for theft and assault, plus a previous wife whom he'd forgotten to divorce when he fled Ireland leaving a trail of debts in 1936. The girl in question was quickly traced and, crucially, was willing to testify that Murray attacked her, several times, once so severely that she had to go to hospital.

Her testimony combined with Tess's, together with a diminished responsibility plea, should prove sufficient to convince a court his killing was in self-defence, and thus save her from the gallows. But I still had an axe to grind, and one rainy evening that July I arranged to meet Frank Arnott. To grind it.

The last time I'd seen him was six weeks earlier, at Scampton on the day of the King's visit. He hadn't lost any of his charm.

'Ah, Credo!' he called loudly as I entered the busy bar. 'There you are, you frightful beggar. Filthy night, eh? Here, let me get you a drink.' From his collection of empty glasses, I gathered he was ahead of me on that score. So much the better. I let him buy me a beer and suggested we adjourn to a table in the corner.

'What for?' he quipped. 'Going to throw something again?'

I was, in a manner of speaking, although it was a while before he realised it.

Quietly, I explained everything. Gradually he began to follow. As he did so, his mood sobered. 'What the bloody hell . . .' he spluttered, when I produced my copy of the dossier. 'Where did you get that?'

'From my head mostly. I sat down, went through it all in my mind, and reproduced it from memory. That and from the carbon copies I made.'

'Well, you can just unreproduce it. That material is top secret. You absolutely can't have it. Nor can you use it. Not in court, Credo. I've already warned you about that.'

'I don't intend using it in court. I'm selling it to the newspapers.'

Now he was aghast. 'You're what? You wouldn't dare.'

Technically speaking I was still in the RAF, and he my superior officer. But we were both wearing suits, and sitting there on neutral ground with the gloves off, so to speak. 'Wouldn't I? Imagine the headlines: MURDER VICTIM WAS DAMBUSTERS DRUNKARD, or BIGAMY AT 617 SQUADRON, or'—I lowered my voice—'WAS SLAIN PIGEON FANCIER A SPY?'

'It's preposterous! You're an RAF officer. I order you not to . . .'

'I'm out of the Service, Frank. Believe me, I can. And will.'

Stunned silence settled over the table. I sipped my beer, watching him. Time, I decided, for the *coup de grâce*.

'I've got this too.' Furtively I opened my jacket, lifting a notebook from the breast pocket. 'It's his, Frank. The notebook I told you about. The one you couldn't find.'

He eyed it glassily. 'Where did you find that?'

'Under the floorboards, in their quarters. Tess put it there after the killing. It's got everything, Frank. Names, dates, times, messages, the lot.'

Thus, the crux. For us both, really. Was Brendan Murray a spy, as I suspected? Frank and his chums never believed it, nor did they want to. As far as they were concerned, their security operation at Scampton had been watertight. Any suggestion now that it was not could prove highly embarrassing to a lot of people. Heads might roll. Frank's included.

Another pause, followed by a resigned sigh. 'So what do you want?'

'Quash all charges. She's innocent and you know it. You also know how to fix it with your opposite number in the Home Office, who will tell his boss, who will tell the Home Secretary that it's not in the country's interests to proceed with this case. State secrets, defence of the realm, wartime exigencies, call it what you will, there's no hard evidence and the case should be thrown out. If it isn't, 617 Squadron will inevitably become embroiled, and every document in this file will come out, including my suspicions about Murray. And his notebook. My God, Frank, Gibson himself may have to take the stand. You too, probably. Is that what you want?'

'This is blackmail, Credo.'

'No. It's justice.'

'And if we do quash the charges?'

'That's the end of it. I'll destroy the dossier and the notebook. The whole thing goes away. You have my word.'

And that, more or less, was the end of it. In due course the charges were dismissed, citing self-defence and new evidence from Murray's violent past. Tess went home to Bexley to be with her ailing father. Afterwards I kept my promise, took the file and notebook (which I'd bought at Woolworths and filled with scribble) to the bottom of the garden and burned them both to ashes. Arnott, I suspect, did exactly the same with the original file, thus erasing Brendan Murray from the intelligence archive altogether. A while later I sent him a postcard saying our business was concluded, and never heard from him again. Except once.

After that, it was finally off to East Grinstead for the refurbishment work on my face. It was long, tedious and painful. There's no need to go into details, except to say Archie did a WTP for a new nose, and several ops to improve my lips and cheeks. He also tidied up the stump on my arm, the better to accept a prosthesis eventually. All in all I was there nearly two months. Chloe was wonderful—if not for her I'd have certainly gone mad. We booked her into a bed and breakfast nearby, and daily she would appear, smiling and dispensing good cheer like Florence Nightingale. Only prettier.

During my stay I wrote up my notes on Operation Chastise, and caught up with news of 617 Squadron. Overnight, it seemed, 617 had become like the crown jewels, a potent symbol of national unity, too precious ever to be used. As such, sending it back into action was a nonstarter, as was disbanding it. A temporary fudge was agreed, while Bomber Command pondered the dilemma of what to do with it. First everyone was sent on leave, then upon their return a trickle of replacement crews began to arrive, who all required training, so a flying programme of sorts resumed. Low flying, night flying, zooming across reservoirs using the spotlights and Dann sights, the regimen was much as before. But, without a mission, the training seemed pointless. Rumours abounded, as always, about possible attacks on dams in Italy, canals in the Netherlands, or U-boat pens in the Atlantic, but nothing materialised. Except grumbling and frustration.

Weeks passed, training continued, crew numbers rose, replacement aircraft arrived, but still no sign of a return to operations. Boredom set in, and bickering. Worse still, 617 was becoming a joke within 5 Group, whose other squadrons were busier than ever bombing Germany. The one-op wonders, they became known as, to their chagrin. Or the armchair heroes. Or even the bedbusters.

Then, in July, a mission at last. Relief and excitement spread through the squadron, only to turn to dismay when it emerged that the great 617 Squadron was to fly to Italy and drop leaflets urging demoralised Italians to throw in the towel. 'I know how they feel,' Big Joe McCarthy grumbled. 'We're nothing but newspaper boys.'

A few days later, a double hammer-blow. Wing Commander Guy Penrose Gibson, VC, DSO, DFC and Bar to both, was to be grounded. Not only that, but replaced as officer commanding 617 Squadron. 'You've done all anyone could ever ask of a man,' Cochrane told him. 'Now it's time to stop, and take a well-earned rest.' That was the official line. Privately a high-level decision had been taken that Gibson was simply too valuable to risk losing. Winston Churchill was shortly to depart on a flag-waving tour of America, Gibson would go with him, then take an extended period of leave. Gibson was distraught. Flying was his life, he knew nothing else. He'd joined the RAF from school and given it his all. Now, after a staggering 173 operations, it was clipping his wings.

ONE AFTERNOON, I was sitting in the hospital in East Grinstead poring through my notes, when an extraordinary telephone call came through. By then my convalescence was well advanced, and in truth I was itching to get out of the place and on with married life with Chloe. As I walked up the corridor to reception, my new nose seemed to dominate the view ahead, although McIndoe swore it was his best work, and Chloe said I looked like Stewart Granger. At reception I picked up the phone.

'Credo?' a familiar voice enquired. 'Arnott here.'

'Hello, Frank,' I replied cautiously. 'What can I do for you?'

'You can forget we're having this conversation.'

More cloaks and daggers. 'Yes, all right, Frank.' I sighed. 'What is it?'

'Radio intel bods at RAF Chicksands picked up some Sigint. From Belgium.'

Sigint. Signals intelligence. A radio message, in other words. 'I see. What sort of Sigint?'

'A transcript. Of a weekly transmission from a Belgian Resistance operative. Routine stuff, he's just checking in with a news update, weather report, shopping list, that sort of thing. But tagged on the end is an RTV.'

'RTV? For God's sake, Frank, can't you speak English!'

'Request to vouch. Could we vouch, in other words, for someone he was in touch with. Another operative, for instance, or a nosy neighbour, escaped POW or something.'

Hairs were prickling on my neck. 'Vouch for who?'

'A friend of yours. One Flying Officer Lightfoot.'

'My God! Peter? Really?'

'Which means he's alive. And on the run. Or was, when this message was sent. Weeks ago by the look of it. Just thought you'd like to know. For the Murray woman, and so on.'

'Well, yes, Frank, yes, I'm delighted to know. And so will she be. Thank you. Thank you very much.'

'My pleasure. We're not all total bastards, you know. Goodbye, Quentin.'

I wandered back to my room in a daze. Later Chloe dropped in and we marvelled at the news, and its implications. One of which was the excuse I'd been waiting for to discharge myself. 'We'll tell Tess in person,' I decided. 'Bexley's not far from here. We can drive up tomorrow in the MG. It'll be a marvellous surprise for her, don't you think?'

Chloe agreed and we began making arrangements. But, incredibly, more was yet to come. The next afternoon, I packed my bags, said goodbye to Archie and the guinea pigs, and sat waiting, somewhat apprehensively, for Chloe. I had mixed feelings leaving the hospital after so long. It was like an exciting, terrifying blind leap into the unknown.

'Flight Lieutenant Credo?' an antipodean voice asked. I looked up to see a broad youth with wavy hair standing nervously before me. He was in RAF sergeant's uniform, the letter 'B' for bomb aimer on his wings. It took a moment—he'd lost weight, and aged a little—then I got it.

'Garvey! It's Kiwi Garvey! Good heavens, how marvellous to see you!'

'You too, sir. I see you got your new nose.'

'And you made a home run, you clever chap. How did you do it?'

By sea, we learned, as we drove with him up to Bexley. The young New Zealander, who'd been a stevedore before the war, had returned to his roots and stolen home aboard a ship. Or rather, several ships, over several weeks.

As the miles passed in the MG, his story emerged, along with more details about V-Vicky's fate and that of his crewmates.

After baling out of the burning aircraft, Kiwi Garvey had managed to hook up with Bimson and Guttenberg, but they could find no sign of Peter.

'I'm sure he was alive when we got him out,' Kiwi said anxiously.

'He was,' I was able to reassure him. As for Chalkie, Jamie and Uncle, they all feared the worst, having seen no further parachutes emerge from the stricken bomber, which crashed into a field several miles away. Herb had injured an ankle on landing and was unable to walk unaided. Billy and Kiwi helped him as best they could, but the going was slow and agonising, so with daylight growing round them, a short conference was called.

'You go on, Kiwi,' Billy urged. 'I'm staying with Herb, we'll take our chances.' The last Kiwi saw of them, they were sitting by the roadside, waving bravely. Later that day they were taken into captivity.

Meanwhile, Kiwi struck out in a westerly direction until after several days, eighty foot-slogging miles and many close calls, his seaman's instincts brought him to the Dutch port of Rotterdam. The port was heavily secured and crawling with Germans. But by waiting and watching, Kiwi was eventually able to steal into a warehouse overlooking the docks. Three nights later he saw what he was waiting for. A mixed cargo-carrying coaster with Scandinavian markings being loaded by conscript labourers, toiling up and down a gangplank bearing boxes. Timing his moment, he slipped from the shadows, picked up a crate and joined them. No one gave him a second glance, and within minutes he was hidden beneath the canvas cover of the ship's lifeboat. He left that ship at Trondheim in Norway. A second ship came back to the Polish port of Gdansk in the Baltic, where he boarded another bound for the neutral port of Helsingborg in Sweden. There, at the harbourmaster's office, he handed himself in. His final ship, two weeks later, having been checked and cleared, was to Newcastle-upon-Tyne.

'That was a month ago,' he recounted. 'Since then I've been kicking my heels waiting for transfer papers and trying to track everyone down. I went to see Chalkie's wife, and Jamie's Mum and Dad. I hope it helped. Then someone told me you'd left to get married and where to find you. Congratulations on your wedding by the way, sir. You too, Mrs Credo.'

'Why, thank you, Sergeant,' Mrs Credo replied warmly.

CHLOE, KIWI AND I arrived in Bexley in time for tea, finding the address along a tree-lined avenue. On one side of the road the houses were closely packed terraces; on the other, the Derbys' side, stood rather grander detached residences. We parked and walked up their path. The door was opened by Mrs Derby, a small, grey-haired woman with a steely gaze.

'You've come about the Lightfoot boy,' she said. 'I'll get Tess.'

Tess appeared, looking terrified, and suddenly my surprise idea didn't seem so clever. Chloe saved the day. 'It's all right!' she beamed, squeezing Tess's hand. 'It's the best possible news!'

'I must tell the Lightfoots,' Tess fussed, once she'd recovered herself. 'Mother, I must run and tell them right away.'

'Why not ask them over for tea?' her mother replied. A momentous gesture, I was later to appreciate. Relations had clearly thawed between Tess and her mother. There was still an awkwardness between them, but they cooperated and produced tea together, and made us feel welcome, and tended to Mr Derby, who sat in an armchair bundled in blankets.

'Thank you,' he whispered, when I bent to say hello. 'Thank you for what you did for Tess.'

Tess herself took me aside a little later. 'Look,' she whispered, producing a photograph. A little girl, with fair hair and apple cheeks, was sitting on the knee of an older woman. 'Peggy,' she said proudly. 'Peggy with her mother. They sent it to me.'

Then the Lightfoots arrived, in their fifties, unassuming, and managing to look both worried and relieved at the same time. 'Can it really be true?' Mrs Lightfoot asked anxiously.

It can, I assured her, although our optimism must be tempered with caution. 'The message was sent several weeks ago, you see. But the fact that Peter was safely in the hands of the Resistance must be a good sign.'

'Too right!' Kiwi added, waving a biscuit. 'Mark my words, the lad'll come through and no worries.'

Tea went on, the conversation a little stilted at first, but before long polite smiles were breaking out, even the occasional titter. A form of reconciliation was taking place, I realised, as I looked on; a moment of healing and release. Six years of pain, bitterness and enmity coming to an end. Because of a son's survival at war. Which seemed appropriate.

A WEEK OR SO later, Chloe and I drove to Scampton to collect the last of my belongings from my rooms, and to take a last look at the place before finally leaving the Service. Out of respect, and to make it easier getting in, we both wore our RAF uniforms, for what would be the final time.

The place was deserted, just a few skeleton staff in evidence as 617 had moved down the road to Coningsby—no thundering Merlins, no hammering workshops, no whistling or singing or shouted commands. Just the busy chatter of birdsong, and the distant rumble of contractors' vehicles, busy laying swathes of concrete across the virgin turf.

'Shall we take a walk?' Chloe suggested, slipping her hand in mine.

We visited my old office, and Number 2 hangar, and the ops room and the mess, to find them all empty. Then we strolled across the grass to see the work on the runways. A temporary HQ had been set up in the equipment barn by the contractors, with bulldozers, steamrollers and tipper-trucks parked outside. A civilian engineer stood at a table, poring over drawings.

'How's it going?' we asked.

'It's going to plan. Just about.' The man grinned. 'Ground's firm, which helps. Turf's in good condition too. Makes it easier to plane off. Whoever tended it knew his stuff.'

Chloe's eye caught mine, we chatted with him a while longer, then began to move off.

'Don't know anything about the birds do you?' he asked.

'What birds?'

'The pigeons. In the loft above the barn here. Hundreds of 'em. They make a terrible racket sometimes. We feed them on bread and old sandwiches and that. But they seem to have been abandoned.'

We went into the barn and climbed a rickety ladder to the caged-off area above the workshops. The pigeons eyed us warily.

'Poor things,' Chloe said. 'They've been completely forgotten.'

'With Murray gone, I suppose nobody gave them a thought.'

'We must release them, Quentin. Open the shutters so they can fly.'

We duly clambered among the roosts and perches, soiling our nice clean uniforms on dust and feathers until we reached the windows and pushed them wide open. Sunlight flooded the loft suddenly, causing the birds to start and shiver in restless anticipation. But none dared move, so we began stamping and shooing noisily, at which they suddenly took to the air in a great squall of clapping wings and poured out through the windows.

We descended the ladder and went outside. Overhead the pigeons wheeled in joyous celebration.

'Quite a sight!' the engineer said. 'That's the last we'll see of them.'

We peered upwards, watching as they danced and darted like a shoal of fish. Beyond them a light aeroplane was preparing to land.

'I doubt it,' Chloe said. 'They're homing pigeons, you know.'

As we wandered back across the field, arm in arm, the light aeroplane came in to land, taxied up and shut down. A tall, handsome-looking man stepped nimbly down, wearing the uniform of a group captain. Disconcerted somewhat, Chloe and I stepped apart, came untidily to attention and saluted.

'Hello, you two.' The man smiled. 'Sorry to drop in unannounced. But this is Scampton, isn't it?'

'Yes, sir, it is. But I'm afraid nobody's here.'

The man peeled off flying gloves and stared around. 'I know. I just wanted to look at the place, you know, get a feel. I'm Cheshire, by the way.' He reached over and shook hands. 'Leonard Cheshire. I'm the new CO of 617 Squadron. Or will be in a few weeks.'

I'd heard of him. A 4 Group man. Brilliant in the air, by all accounts, a matchless pilot with three full tours under his belt, and great plans to turn bombing into a precision art, yet modest and approachable on the ground. A born leader, and exactly what 617 needed. 'That's very good news, sir. They've been having a difficult time lately. Morale and so on.'

'Yes. We must do something about that.' He leaned across to pluck a pigeon feather from my lapel. 'And you are?'

'Oh, sorry, sir. Quentin Credo. Flight Lieutenant, formerly of 57 Squadron. This is my wife, Corporal Chloe Hickson, er, Credo, that is.'

'Well, I'm delighted to meet you both.' He smiled again. 'Did you say formerly?'

'Yes, sir. Invalided out of ops. Then became SIO here at Scampton, then ADC to Group Captain Whitworth. For the dams raid, and so on.'

'Really? You were here for that? How wonderful. And what are you doing now?'

'Nothing, sir. Leaving the Service, actually. Taking up law.'

'Ah.' Cheshire nodded, and cupped his eyes to the setting sun.

'That seems a pity,' he murmured. 'I'll be needing a good ADC.'

robert **radcliffe**

RD: How did your writing career begin?

RR: My first job in journalism was on *Boat* magazine, a tiny, monthly periodical with an editorial team of three. I loved it, and the great thing was I learned to do everything from reporting to pasting up and photography—the lot. It was great training. Sadly, *Boat* sank and I was made redundant. I then worked for an advertising agency, writing and producing house journals—*Fisons News* and *Industrial Vacuum Cleaners Weekly* spring to mind—for a wide range of companies. I learned how to write good copy on subjects I knew little about and was not necessarily interested in. I also learned the importance of writing to deadline and to length—important skills for an aspiring novelist. I enjoyed the work but I was restless for something bigger so, meanwhile, I was trying to write my own stuff at home.

RD: Was it an easy decision, in 1997, to give up the career and move to France to try full-time writing?

RR: It was a mad decision made at a desperate time. By 1994, I had managed to get one small novel published, *A Ship Called Hope*, and it had sold about ten copies. Meanwhile, I had also started a PR/Design business that was starting to take over my life. I had to decide whether to carry on with it and give up writing, or sell up and try to write a more successful novel. I chose the latter, sold the business and my house, packed up the car and set off for a borrowed cottage in France. It was very rash, very high-risk. But, as I stood on the ferry watching the white cliffs of Dover recede, I literally felt a weight lift from my shoulders. Six months later I had written *The Lazarus Child,* which sold over a million copies and was translated into twenty languages.

RD: In 2002 you switched to writing about the Second World War and published *Under an English Heaven*, about an American bomber crew based in Suffolk. What attracts you to the subject of airmen and their lives? Does the fact that you spent ten years as a commercial pilot play a part?

RR: Yes, it does. I've been fascinated by aeroplanes and aviation since boyhood, and also the whole notion of aerial conflict. I mean, just flying an aeroplane is demanding enough, yet to fly those old aeroplanes and fight for your life in them . . . What must that have been like? That's what I try to give readers a sense of in books like *Under an English Heaven* and *Dambuster*.

RD: What kind of planes did you fly, and where?

RR: I started as a flying instructor at an Ipswich flying club, then qualified as a commercial pilot and worked for air taxi companies in Norwich and Luton. Then I joined Airship Industries—the only company in the world that was at that time flying airships commercially. I worked all over the place, flying airships on sightseeing trips over cities like London, San Francisco and New York, as well as TV cameras over major sporting events, and security and surveillance flights over G8 meetings, Olympic Games and so on. I even flew in a James Bond movie! Currently, I fly a desk, though I do miss the real thing a bit.

RD: You obviously did a great deal of research for *Dambuster*. What aspects of Operation Chastise fascinated you the most?

RR: Yes, I did a lot of research. So much about it fascinates me. I guess at one level it is the perfect marriage of ingenuity and daring—the brilliant scientist coming up with a half-baked idea that the brave men of 617 Squadron subsequently have to turn into reality. Then there's the technical aspect: getting the bomb to work, fixing the height accurately, low-level navigation at night, the little wooden sighting aid to determine range from the dams—all fascinating stuff. Ultimately, too, there's the human drama: the struggle against the odds, the physical demands, the risks, the triumph . . . And of course the characters. Marvellous ingredients for a writer!

RD: Did you visit RAF Scampton in Lincolnshire and, if so, what were your impressions of it?

RR: Yes I did visit. Much of it remains exactly as it was, including Guy Gibson's office, the officers' accommodation and mess, and many of the buildings. It is a slightly spooky place as it is unused by the RAF now and largely deserted. They have an interesting little museum there, though, manned by a very helpful team of volunteers.

RD: Would you like to have flown with Guy Gibson's 617 Squadron?

RR: Maybe, when I was young, headstrong and carefree! But when you consider that of the 133 aircrew involved in the raid only forty-eight survived the war—then, no thanks. It puts the incredible bravery of the men of Bomber Command into perspective. Only now is their valiant sacrifice being properly appreciated and memorialised.

RD: What do you love most about Suffolk, where you now live?

RR: The countryside, the walks, the fresh air, the space, the big skies.

RD: And when you're not writing, how do you most like spending free time?

RR: With my family in Suffolk or at our little house in France. Walking, exploring, sailing a little, sitting on a beach in the sunshine . . .

The Summer of the Bear

Bella Pollen

In the summer of 1979, on a remote Hebridean island, a tamed grizzly bear escapes its keeper.

Meanwhile, the unexpected death of British diplomat Nicky Fleming has left his wife Letty and their three children grief-stricken. As the family relocate from Cold-War riven Germany to the Hebrides, Letty is also haunted by terrible doubts: is it possible her husband may have been a spy? Could it be that his death was no accident, but murder or suicide?

Only eight-year-old Jamie keeps his calm, clinging to the one thing he knows for sure: his father has promised to return, and Nicky Fleming was a man who never broke a promise . . .

Outer Hebrides, Summer, 1979

It was the smell that drove him wild. As though the ocean itself was a tantalising soup made from the freshest ingredients and he couldn't get enough of it. Oh, for a crust of bread big enough to sop up that wonderful bouillabaisse—the head of a mackerel, tails of lithe and saithe. As he swam on, each new flavour presented itself: an underlying broth soaked from the shells of mussels and winkles; a dash of seasoning from the juice of the sea anemone; a sprinkling of plankton for texture. When he jerked his head it was a simple greedy lunge for more. Still, it was enough. The cord snapped and, instantly, the pressure round his neck was relieved. He paused, trod water, understanding coming to him slowly. Freedom.

In front of him lay the horizon, behind him the island bobbed up and down. He spotted a blur of a man, pushing to his feet out of the foaming lines of surf on the beach. His keeper, a wrestler, stood up and raised his arms in salute, and yet still he hesitated, torn. He might be a contented prisoner but a rope was a rope, whoever was tugging on it. So he turned his back on the big man, dived under the salty waters of the Minch and swam on.

TRAFFIC OR NO TRAFFIC, weather good or bad, the journey from London to the island always took three days. For the children to be confined with one another for such a lengthy period of time seemed nothing short of punishment, and Georgie decided she'd rather be strapped to the roof rack along with the suitcases and take her chances with the low-level bridges than feel the evil eye of her younger sister boring into her for one minute longer.

Last night, when her mother had turned on the weather forecast, the weatherman had staked his usual ground in front of a map of the United Kingdom. 'A cool summer's evening, followed by a moderately warm day,' he pronounced, moving a couple of plastic suns onto southern England. He tossed a few more stickers towards Liverpool. By the time he had finished, the entire British Isles had been covered by cheerful yellow suns—except for the exact place in the Outer Hebrides to which they were heading. A solitary grey sticker hovered like a storm warning over their future.

Her mother had been right about leaving early, though. There were hardly any cars on the road. A sudden flash caught Georgie's eye and she turned to see the old Peugeot's reflection in the metal wall of an industrial building. 'Always drive a Peugeot,' she could hear her father saying. 'Africa's favourite car! They've brought affordable transport to millions.' Quite why her father had still felt obliged to sanction Africa's favourite car after they had moved to Bonn, she didn't know. Compared to the brand-new sedans driven by some of his embassy colleagues, the 1967 404 Saloon was something of an embarrassment, with its fin-tailed rear lights and jerry-built roof rack. Her father had adored it, referring to it as a faithful old thing and complaining fondly about its arthritic gearstick as though it were a decrepit great-uncle who had been graciously allowed to live with the family.

Georgie closed her eyes. Packing, sailing, driving, unpacking. Life was something you could gather up and take with you—that was the way it was in the diplomatic service. When she had been nine, her father had been posted back to London. They had sailed out of the Gulf of Guinea, all their belongings lashed and secured in the hold beneath them. When the packing cases had been unloaded in their new quarters, there had not been an inch of floor space left. Now all their worldly goods fitted onto a single roof rack.

'Are you all right, darling?' Her mother was looking over at her.

'Fine.' She faked a smile before turning back to the window.

IT ANNOYED GEORGIE'S SISTER, Alba, that people accused her of hating things indiscriminately. It wasn't true. She had her reasons for feeling the way she did and they were good ones. For example, she despised over-polished furniture, easy-listening music and shiny food, as represented by, say, the glaze on doughnuts or the sweaty sheen of a tomato ring. She loathed any form of sentimentality and strongly believed that doors should be kept either open or shut, but never in-between. In fact, if someone cared to ask her—and God knows, she often wished they would—she could dredge up a bona fide irritation for every letter of the alphabet.

Steadfast, too, was the scorn she felt for her fellow human beings: vegetarians, religious fanatics, English teachers, weathermen . . . But the person she despised the most, the person who was to blame for everything that had happened to their family, was, without a shadow of a doubt, her brother, Jamie. There he was now, sitting across from her on the passenger seat. What a revolting sight.

'Retard,' she whispered.

Jamie was rubbing his legs. Smooth strokes, up and down and—

'Stop doing that!'

'But I'm not touching you.'

'You're annoying me, which is worse.'

'Leave him be, Alba.' Her mother's hand snaked through the divide and connected with Jamie's knee. 'He's just tired.'

Alba scowled. This was it. Exactly it. Excuses were always being made for her brother. In her opinion, if he wasn't babied so much, he'd be obliged to grow up. Jamie was nearly nine years old but still unable to read or write and the only reason he could count to ten was because he'd been born with the visual aid of fingers and thumbs. Jamie was stupid, spoilt and whiny beyond endurance.

'Retard,' she mouthed at him as soon as their mother's attention was reclaimed by the road.

'My legs hurt. Rubbing them makes them feel better.'

'I don't care.' She fashioned her thumb and forefinger into a pincer.

'Ow,' he cringed in anticipation. 'Stop it.'

But Alba had no intention of stopping. And for every pinch successfully delivered, she felt that much better.

'Alba, for goodness' sake!' Now it was Georgie who turned round. 'Just be nice.'

'What's so good about being nice?' she retorted, then, when no one responded, added, 'Dada was nice to everyone and look where it got him.'

'Where?' Jamie asked, immediately alert.

'Alba!' her mother hissed.

'Alba, shhh.' Georgie threw a meaningful glance towards her brother.

How predictable, Alba thought. It was always Jamie everyone worried about, as if he had somehow acquired sole rights to the family's grieving. What about her? Why did no one seem to care how she felt? She was sick of being shushed before she had finished. She was sick of half-truths and unspoken truths and all the lame excuses in between. She didn't believe in God, Father Christmas or the Tooth Fairy and she was damned if she'd believe any of the other lies that parents told their children.

IT WASN'T THAT Jamie Fleming didn't have the vocabulary to fight back—his vocabulary was far more sophisticated than that of most boys his age—but Alba unbalanced him. She turned him into a juggler with too many balls, a pobble with a mass of toes.

'Store your words, then. Keep them in your head,' Nicky Fleming had advised his son. 'Think of them as your secret army and one day you will be able to do battle with your sister.' Jamie liked the analogy, but oh, what an unruly army of words they were. Stationed safely in his head, they kept themselves in an orderly line, but as soon as he gave the command to go, it was as if an internal siren had been triggered. The words stumbled and butted up against each other in their haste to leave and, by the time they left his mouth, they were in too chaotic a state to be of any use.

Then there were the bodily manifestations of his 'condition'. It was as though Jamie's internal wiring had been connected to a faulty electrical socket. Physically his timing was sporadic, his reflexes sluggish. Bats and balls fell regularly through his fingers. But if the sports field was a minor skirmish, the dinner table was a war zone. In Jamie's uncoordinated little digits, knives and forks managed to point themselves any which way except towards his plate.

'You are repellent,' Alba would shout. 'You are useless. You are nugatory!'

'What does "nugatory" mean?' Jamie had taught himself to collect words the way other boys jotted down train numbers and he was always up for a new one, however personally insulting.

'Who cares? Just say it.'

'I am nugatory,' he repeated obediently.

If Jamie sometimes felt home life was hell, it was still a big improvement on school. There, each hour promised its own level of purgatory. He was the worst on the playing field, remedially the worst in class. Jamie Fleming, everyone privately agreed, was just plain dumb. Even Georgie, his chief protector, accepted his lack of intellect as a sad fact and told him it didn't matter.

Only his parents stood fast, taking him to doctor after doctor in the hope that one might hold the key to unlock their child's ability to read and write.

'Of course there's nothing wrong with you,' his father had reiterated after every specialist's appointment. 'It's just that your brain hasn't been properly switched on yet.'

Jamie knew he wasn't stupid. Even as he committed the word 'nugatory' to memory, he could feel his brain growing like one of those miracle car-wash cloths that boasted a capacity of ten times its size when immersed in water. How he longed for his family to understand the scale of his thoughts. They were big and grown-up but, without the ability to articulate them, he was destined to converse only with himself. His war of words frustrated him almost as much as it worried his parents. What if he could never read a book or write a story?

'Don't worry. There's a word for what you are,' his father told him, and whispered it into his ear.

'Is that good?'

'Well, I think so,' his father said, 'but then I happen to be one, too.'

But if Nicky Fleming's polymath abilities were put to use in the everyday world, Jamie's breadth of knowledge became the building blocks of a convoluted fantasy life, peopled by an astonishing number of characters. Alba could call him what she liked. Inside his head he was a storyteller capable of threading together titbits of conversation and snippets from the paper into a sweeping plot of which he was almost always the hero.

In Jamie's world anything was possible. Wolves spoke as men and goblins ruled governments. Waterfalls flowed upwards and inanimate objects made conversation with him whenever they pleased.

There were so many clues that the crossed wires in Jamie Fleming's head would not just spontaneously unravel. Somebody should have noticed but nobody was paying attention. If only they had been. If only his family had understood the strange workings of that clever little mind, they would have watched him so much more carefully.

LETTY FLEMING WAS NOT a confident driver. She sat stiff in her seat, gripping the steering wheel as though scared that it might, in a moment of rebellion, decide to hurl itself out of the window and roll merrily along the motorway. At the thought of the 700-odd miles in front of her, a furrow of concentration cut into her forehead. Surely car journeys had not always been like this, a grim determination to get from A to B? She felt brittle with exhaustion. If only Nicky could be here, if only Nicky could take over everything for her. *If only*. These were the words that governed her every waking moment. If only she had known. If only she had done things differently, but the further back she tried to roll time, the more paths it opened up to her. Painstakingly, she had gone down every one of them looking for a different journey, another road, but in the end they all led to the same place. Fate was fate. Its outcome could not be manipulated.

Bonn, West Germany, 1970s

Information was Nicky Fleming's religion. He respected it, he traded in it, he made his career out of it. He was the missionary who wished to convert all others to his faith and so, as soon as the Fleming girls were old enough to read, he announced that each of them should find an interesting story in the day's paper and discuss it with him. This was an extension of, but by no means a replacement for, his habit of lobbing general-knowledge questions at them when they least expected it.

'What is tax?' he might demand as the children sat down unsuspectingly at the dinner table. 'What does it pay for and is it fair?'

All three children were in agreement: news was a drag. But their father was adamant. There was bound to be one story, however small, that would appeal to them. And thus a daily ritual was born. Every morning, along with the *General-Anzeiger Bonn* and the embassy's digest of all the main national newspapers, a copy of the London *Times* was delivered. Nicky worked his way through the broadsheets over breakfast and, after he was done, *The Times* would be passed to the children in reverse order of age.

In the evening, after Nicky returned from the embassy, he would sit in his favourite chair, a chaise longue with matching footstool that had travelled from country to country with them, and he would invite his three children to sit with him and justify their pick of the day.

Jamie liked animal stories: the sighting of a grey wolf in the Bavarian forest; the discovery of fossilised dinosaur eggs; the story of a Hungarian dancing bear rescued from its persecutors. He was fascinated by pictures of natural disasters and spent long hours planning to save his family from them. He was particularly intrigued by earthquakes and the idea that the world could open up and swallow people, buildings, cities.

'So this earthquake,' Jamie would say after the article had been read to him. 'How did it feel to fall? How long did it take to reach the centre of the earth? Would everyone's houses and cars still be OK when they got there?' And Nicky, having no intention of describing the agony of a man whose bones were being ground to dust, abandoned his passion for facts and turned instead to his imagination. No, people didn't die! Of course they didn't fall for ever! Yes, there was salvation down there: entire cities where buildings had landed intact, precisely into their allotted space. There was a train station too, just like the one in Bonn, complete with a uniformed guard who announced in loud German the arrival times of new citizens. Down in the centre of the earth, Nicky told his son, was a whole new world where people lived and worked and mined the earth's core for untold riches.

Jamie's other favourite topic, as he grew older, was the Cold War. The Cold War—he would roll the words round his mouth, giving them different inflections, sometimes adding a dramatic little chatter of his teeth for effect. Despite his inability to read, he recognised the phrase 'Cold War' when it appeared in a headline and was entirely au fait with all its associated acronyms: CIA, KGB, NATO, MI6, SIS. For Jamie, as for most spy-mad boys, the Cold War conjured up a James Bond world of traitors and dissidents, of intrigue and deceit. He had little idea that the Cold War was the actual world in which he lived; that a hop, skip and one very high jump away from the embassy stood the physical and ideological divide of the Berlin Wall.

Nothing made Alba happier than sensationalism: a gory family murder or a brutal armed robbery. Her chief aim when choosing her story *du jour* was to find something so subversive, so blatantly unsuitable for Jamie's ears that her father would be required to fudge the more sordid details, whereupon Alba would take a sadistic delight in self-righteously correcting him.

Finally, it would be Georgie's turn. There would be a redistribution of limbs on the side of the chaise longue, Nicky would slide his arm round his eldest daughter's waist and say, 'What about you, my George? What caught your attention today?'

But Georgie was shy. The whole business of preference-stating had always made her self-conscious and, besides, she could never dredge up a particular interest in any of the headlines, so she would fidget and say, 'Um, I'm not sure,' all the while turning the pages of the newspaper as slowly as she dared, praying that something would jump out at her. As the minutes ticked by, the room seemed to go very still with the weight of her father's expectation. How she envied Jamie with his headlines, pre-edited and presented as multiple choice. She desperately wanted her father to think of her as intelligent, but all she felt was uninteresting and stupid.

'There must be something,' Nicky would urge, as she stared in mounting desperation at the newsprint. Finally, when she could stand it no longer, Georgie would stab her finger arbitrarily at the nearest headline.

'*President Defiant in Bucharest*,' her father read. 'Why this one, Georgie?' he probed gently. 'What is it about this one you find so intriguing?'

And she would turn her head and blink back the tears while Alba groaned cruelly.

On January 21, 1979, no papers were delivered to the Flemings' house in Bad Godesberg. If they had been, the children would have found only one page of *The Times* to be of collective interest.

THE DAY AFTER Nicky died, the machinery of the Embassy Wives' Club began to turn. The kindness was as overwhelming as it was stifling. The order had come from the top: Letty Fleming was not to be left alone for a minute. A rota was formed, food was cooked, the kettle boiled in shifts. A grieving widow simply could not be made to drink too much tea.

Every afternoon at precisely the same time, Gillian, the Ambassadress, came to the house in person. Letty stared at the woman's ramrod back, at the way her knees were pressed together in perfect symmetry, and wondered whether she herself had overlooked the chapter entitled 'How to Sit Elegantly in a Pencil Skirt' in the guide to embassy etiquette.

The Ambassadress poured the tea and, noting that Letty made no move to pick it up, gently took the younger woman's hand and placed the cup and saucer in it. 'Are you sleeping, Letitia?'

'A little, thank you,' Letty lied.

'And you're eating, I trust?'

Letty nodded. There were only so many times a day she could answer the same questions without screaming.

'And the children?' the Ambassadress asked. 'How is little James?'

Letty turned her head to the wall.

'My dear, you must be strong. The children will take their cue from you. Too much emotion will only upset them.' The Ambassadress produced a handkerchief. 'Show them you can get through this, and they'll find that they can too.'

Letty blew her nose and promised to grieve quietly and considerately.

'There is one more thing,' the Ambassadress announced. 'Naturally, I don't have to explain how these things work. You understand that a replacement for Nicky must be found.'

A film of ice formed round Letty's heart. No, it had not occurred to her. There had been no time to think of England and the blip in its diplomatic relations. The Ambassadress was right—the business of Queen and Country could not shut up shop for untimely deaths. 'Of course,' she murmured.

'There's a good man just arrived back in London,' the Ambassadress continued. 'He's spent the last three years as cultural attaché in Japan. Made quite a success of it. Excellent references. He was hoping to stay in England for a bit, but we believe he'll be willing to rise to the occasion.'

'How long, do you think?' Letty projected herself into the future through sheer need. Nicky had left no will, made no provision for his family. The house, the children's schools, their entire way of life came courtesy of the government. Quite how courteous the government would feel towards them under current circumstances remained to be seen.

'Sir Ian believes we can bring him over by the end of next month.'

Panic rolled through Letty. What was she to do? Where were they to go?

'So.' The Ambassadress placed her teacup carefully back in its saucer. 'You can manage that?' It had not been a question. The Ambassadress patted her arm. 'Good for you, Letitia. Sometimes the thought of positive action is all it takes to make one feel a little better. We will help you with any arrangements you might require.'

As always, the Ambassadress's word was her bond. Within weeks, the Fleming family were out of their residence and on a boat back to England.

Outer Hebrides, Summer 1979

It was futile, his continued battle with the elements. Water was coming at him from all sides—enormous swells tossed and turned him, the cold squeezed his chest. He conceded defeat, blinked his sore eyes and allowed the current to float him towards the island as though he were a piece of driftwood. It was not the friendliest of landing spots: a stone plateau, guarded by sentinels of rock that buffeted him back and forth like the levers of a pinball machine. A wet tumble of seals barked at his approach, unprepared for such an oddity dropping unannounced into their world.

The swell withdrew, then, in one almighty forwards rush, propelled him up and out of the water, dumping him on land. He was not the first creature to have underestimated the power of the northern elements. Over the years, this barren Hebridean isle had been a refuge for all manner of lost souls. Now it was his turn to be blown off course, and it was a late summer slot he was about to share with an equally adrift family of four.

The Highlands, Scotland, Summer 1979

Letty had come to resent borders, those pencil-thin divides where culture, power and religion were destined to grate against each other. She resented the intolerance they represented, the secrets and lies they necessitated and, above all, the amount of Nicky's time they had stolen. The Scottish border, however, was distinguished by only a lay-by, a warped sign for Gretna Green and a van jauntily stencilled with 'The Frying Scotsman', from which Letty bought bacon baps and sugary tea in stout paper cups. The bacon was spitting hot and salty, the inside of the rolls soft and warm. Even before the children had wiped their mouths of the dustings of flour, Letty ordered a second round.

A few miles short of Inverary they stopped at a petrol station for a lunch of sweets and crisps, and not long after that on the verge of the road for Jamie, whose stomach had suffered the consequences.

Letty hovered a respectful distance behind, tissues in her hand.

'It won't come,' he sighed apologetically. 'I want it to, but it won't.'

'Never mind. Does your tummy still hurt?'

'A little,' he fibbed.

He waited until his mother began picking her way back to the car before hastily taking the map from his pocket and concealing it under a large stone. It was the third such map he'd hidden since leaving London. Two had already been safely stowed—one in the petrol station, the other impaled on a fence post somewhere in Cumbria—but this was a long stretch of road without distinguishing landmarks and another clue would surely help his father to follow them.

As Jamie straightened up and wiped his hands on his shorts, the shadow of a passing coach fell over him. To his utter amazement, he saw that its side was painted with an immense picture of a grizzly bear.

'Mum,' he squealed, 'look!'

'Mmm.' Letty had unfolded a scarf from her bag and was busy tying it round her hair.

'Did you see?' He danced an excited little jig. 'The bear!'

'Darling, there are no bears in Scotland.'

'It was on a bus.'

'Was it, darling?' She smiled indulgently. 'I do hope it was off somewhere nice on holiday then.'

'Come on, Jamie.' Georgie wound down the window.

'Did you see it, Georgie?'

Whatever 'it' referred to, Georgie shook her head. She loved her brother, but found him unfathomable. 'I was reading, sorry.'

'Do you think there's going to be a circus?'

'Jamie, why would there be a circus? We're in the middle of nowhere.'

'Get in the Godalmighty car, Jamie,' Alba said. 'Or there will be heavy corporal penalties.'

'Don't swear, Alba,' Letty murmured.

Alba rolled her eyes and withdrew to her outpost in the corner back seat. The whole journey she'd had to listen either to the inane bleatings of her brother or the muffled crackle of the radio. Surely her mother could have fixed it before they left?

'Did you see it, Alba?' Jamie reached the car and yanked open the door.

'Of course. As you know, I'm fascinated by every tiny thing you choose to point out.'

'You are?' Jamie found himself momentarily diverted.

'No, Jamie, I'm not. That was an example of the use of sarcasm. Now, I know how keen you are on spelling things correctly, so allow me to help you out. S. a. r. c. a. s. m.'

'But did you see the bear?' Jamie hid his confusion with perseverance.

'Ah, well, if you mean that large brown animal running along the road wearing a kilt and playing the bagpipes, of course. Why do you ask?'

'Do you think it was my bear?'

'I'm sorry, I wasn't aware you had your own bear.'

'Yes! The one from the *Zirkusplatz*! The one I have the picture of. The one Dada was going to take me to see at the circus the day he—'

'Oh, Jamie, of course,' Letty intervened quickly. 'I know exactly which one you mean. He did look like an awfully nice bear.'

'Then can you drive faster to catch him up?'

'Darling, I can't drive any faster than I'm supposed to.'

Jamie swallowed his disappointment. He stared at the road ahead. Even if his mother drove at over fifty miles an hour, which she never did, they would still not catch up with the bear. He closed his eyes and concentrated on retrieving the image on the side of the coach, the starkness of the brown fur against the glossy white paintwork. The big grizzly had been standing on his hind legs, one colossal paw extended in a wave. Hesitantly, Jamie raised his own hand. 'Hello, bear,' he whispered.

Hello, boy, answered the bear, inside Jamie's head.

Bonn, West Germany, 1970s

There had never been much to do in Bonn at the weekends. They were quiet, boring affairs, and particularly so for a small boy. There was the Haribo sweet factory of course, amiable strolls through the Naturpark and damp walks along the Rhine, but the outing Jamie enjoyed above all others was to the Museum Koenig with his father. As natural history museums go, it was both well curated and surprisingly inspirational—and it had an outrageously large, stuffed grizzly presiding over its foyer. It was an impressive creature, standing over nine feet high on its hind legs.

'The grizzly is one of the largest of all land carnivores,' his father once translated off the plaque on the wall. It was five-year-old Jamie's first visit to a museum, his first grizzly bear, and he shrank behind his father. Each of the bear's claws was the length of his hand and sharp as a machete. Its teeth were so yellow they might have been made of solidified poison, but it was the bear's eyes that scared him the most.

'There's nothing to be scared of, old chap. This one's a nice bear. The fangs and claws are only for show. The truth is, he was once a child's teddy who grew too large to keep in the house and so he left home to seek his fortune. He's in this museum today only because he became very famous and made his mark on the world.'

Jamie crept out from behind his father's back. 'What did he do?'

'Ah, well, let's see . . .' Nicky pretended to consult the museum's leaflet. 'It says here that his achievements are too numerous to be listed, but I quite often sneak down here to have a chat with him when you're at school.'

'He can talk?' Jamie's eyes stretched wide.

'Of course. Bears are highly intelligent and this particular one has been well educated. He speaks fluent German, perfect English, passable French and a smattering of Russian, which he picked up on a state visit.'

'How do I make him talk?'

'Well, you have to be introduced first. Like most people in the service, he's a stickler for protocol.'

'Can you ask him to talk to me?'

'If you like.' Nicky stepped up to the grizzly, cupped a hand towards the bear's musty ear and began whispering.

'What are you telling him?' Jamie demanded.

'That you're a pretty decent fellow and you want to have a quick word.'

Jamie took a tentative step towards the bear.

'Go on,' Nicky encouraged. 'Don't be shy.'

'Hello, bear,' Jamie croaked.

Nicky covered his mouth with his hand and pretended to rub his chin. 'Hello, Jamie,' he growled.

The Highlands, Summer 1979

'This looks like it!' Letty steered the Peugeot down a muddied track. 'We came here once before . . . I expect you were too small to remember,' she added quickly.

The previous evening, in Fort William, Letty had had to scout in ever-widening circles until she'd found a B and B with a vacant family room. Now, the purple heather of Rannoch Moor was behind them, and there, in the distance, was the misty shark fin of Ben Nevis. They had already negotiated the pot-luck timing of the little Ballachulish ferry, and the drive through Glencoe, where she and Nicky had once blown out two tyres simultaneously and ended up walking for hours through those menacing black hills, while Nicky tried to spook her with bloodcurdling stories of the massacre. As if he could. She'd been driving through Glencoe since she was a girl. She'd been in love with the west of Scotland her whole life.

From Glencoe there was the smell of wet bracken and a salty wind to blow them north until, finally, they were in reach of the coast road and the sea, with the promise of the islands to come.

It was hardly the weather for a picnic, but Georgie understood her mother's need to live in the past. And besides, it was a beautiful spot. The track petered out into a circular clearing on the bank of a river. A fish jumped, dragonflies hovered over clumps of desiccated reeds. The scene had all the ingredients of an idyllic summer's day—save for any genuine warmth in the air.

Georgie wandered down the bank, rolled up her trousers and induced Jamie to pitch some twigs into the swirling eddy, but the water was cold so she soon steered him up to where Letty was laying their jackets on the heather and spreading a picnic on top. An emergency dash into Fort William had produced buns, hard-boiled eggs, thick slices of ham with a crumbly yellow edge, and a bag of still-warm sausage rolls. Georgie sat cross-legged on her anorak and squeezed the last of the Primula cheese onto her tongue. Jamie had sequestered the packet of Jaffa Cakes and moved to a rock he had deemed a safe distance from Alba.

Had Alba liked Jaffa Cakes, no distance would have been safe, and Georgie was mildly surprised that her sister hadn't already snatched the biscuits off him, if only for the fun of it, but that was the thing with Alba: just when her level of malice had you thumbing through the Yellow Pages for the nearest child-catcher, she would perform a bewildering volte-face, and was now curled into Letty's body, holding her mother's arm protectively round her.

Georgie relaxed and allowed herself to tune into the near-silence. She decided she liked sitting up on the hill, feeling the prickle of the heather, watching the river twist and flow towards the low grumble of the waterfall. Her eyelids had almost drifted shut when a flash of movement brought her back to the present.

'Mum?' She frowned at the roof of the Peugeot below them.

'Mmm?' Letty rolled sleepily onto her back.

Alba sat up and shielded her eyes with a hand. 'The car,' she said. 'It's moving. It's rolling backwards.'

Jamie was already up and running.

'Jamie, no!' Too late, Letty launched herself down the hill after him, but age had her at a distinct disadvantage. Jamie's eight-year-old bones were as supple as willows, every sinew elastic and forgiving. Uncoordinated he might be, but, compared to his mother, his feet were winged. And now the car was gaining momentum, its front end slowly tilting upwards as its back wheels connected with the bank's incline.

'Don't worry,' Jamie yelled, 'I'll stop it!'

As it dawned on Georgie exactly what her brother was thinking, her heart pulsed with fear. Next to her, Alba was yelling. Something must have penetrated, because Jamie glanced up, as in—what on earth is all the fuss about?

He quickly dismissed his sisters, because, let's face it, weren't they always shouting at him? So much so that sometimes it was all he could do to think for himself? Besides, it felt good to have identified a problem and be dealing with it.

'It's down to you, Jamie.' The Ambassadress had patted his head with her hard, flat hand. 'You must be brave and look after your mother. After all, you're the man of the family now.' Until his father returned, it was the truth. Jamie had no uncles or brothers . . .

The Peugeot was rolling into the river and strapped to its roof was his suitcase, and inside his suitcase were those things that mattered most to him—the flier from the *Zirkus*, the box of IOU promises from his father, his roll of comics—all destined to be lost for ever. No! He would not let that happen. He would hold the car back from the brink! He closed his ears to the screaming and powered on.

The car was almost in the river by the time Jamie caught up with it. Nevertheless, duty was duty. He stretched out his arms, shut his eyes—and in the same instant felt himself blindsided by the full weight of his mother's body. There was a breath of wind on his cheek as the car rolled by. The wheels hit water, the exhaust snapped with a muffled pop. The momentum of the car's backward roll drove it ten feet along the riverbed before it jammed to a stop. The current rose quickly and surrounded the roof rack, until, with a further succession of splashes, the suitcases slid one by one into the river.

On his stomach, his face mashed into the soil, Jamie searched for air while his mother's voice reverberated with anger and fear. 'What were you thinking? How could you be so stupid?' Finally, she pushed herself off his crushed chest and only then, as oxygen sawed up through his deflated lungs, was Jamie able to burst into tears of rage and humiliation.

'I want Dada!' he wailed. 'Where is my Dada?'

THIS MUCH JAMIE KNEW: his father had suffered an accident. He'd gone away for some time, then somehow—Jamie didn't fully comprehend how—his father had got lost.

In the months that had passed since his father's disappearance, he had turned these facts round and round in his head, examining them for a clue, something tangible to hold on to.

That there had been an accident was unfortunate, but not necessarily odd. Accidents were just bad luck and you had to grin and bear them. As for his father having gone away, Jamie didn't like it, but he was used to it. His father travelled all the time. When Jamie had been smaller and noticed the suitcase stationed by the front door, he would burst into tears, wrap himself round his father and beg him not to leave. 'Now, come along, fish-face.' Nicky would gently prise him loose. 'I'll be back before you know it.'

'But where are you going?'

'Ah, well, since you ask, I'm going on a mission.'

'Really,' Jamie breathed. 'A secret mission?'

'Naturally.'

'Is it dangerous?'

'No . . .'

Jamie's face fell.

'Well,' Nicky relented. 'Perhaps just the teeniest bit dangerous.'

'Do the others know?'

'No, and you mustn't tell them, either. It's to remain between us.' He tapped his finger to his nose and winked.

'But you will come back soon, won't you?'

'Of course I will, and when I do, I'll come and find you and maybe'—he picked up his son and swung him round—'if you've been exceptionally good, I'll bring you a present.'

His father never told fibs. He always came back and he always gave Jamie a present. A Russian babushka, a waxed package of stamps, a lead soldier on a charging horse. This time, however, everything had been different—and it had made no sense at all. The last time Jamie had seen his father had been the day before the circus opened. Nicky had been picking at breakfast and scanning the papers when Jamie had asked for help with his homework.

'What's the subject?'

Jamie pushed over his exercise book. Nicky looked at the hieroglyphics of his son's attempt at the English language and sighed. There was already a mound of paperwork on his desk in the embassy that needed deciphering.

'When is it due in?'

'Monday,' Jamie said dolefully.

'Well, that's not so bad, is it? Do what you can on your own and we'll tackle the rest before supper this evening. That way it will all be done before we go to the circus tomorrow.'

As luck would have it, the Circus Krone was being erected on the barren area of an undeveloped piece of land behind the embassy.

'Promise you'll be back in time?'

'Cross my heart, hope to die.' Then, at his son's puzzled frown, Nicky scribbled a few words onto the top of his newspaper and ripped away the corner. 'Here.' He handed it to Jamie. 'Happy now?'

Jamie nodded as he folded the scrap into his pocket. His father did not fib and he did not break promises. 'My work can be hopelessly unpredictable,' he'd explained to his children. 'Things crop up, meetings drag on, so you mustn't ask me to make promises I might have trouble keeping . . . Oh, cheer up.' He'd laughed at their dismal faces. 'It's not so bad. When I do make a promise, I'll honour it. In fact, you can write it down and keep it in a box like an IOU.'

But he hadn't come back in time for homework, or even for bed.

In the morning Jamie had been up early, dressed in clean trousers and his favourite green alligator shirt. He extracted the paper flier from beneath his pillow and smoothed it out onto his bed. The letters *ZIRKUS* were blocked over a picture of a cheerful-looking brown bear wearing a minuscule top hat and riding a unicycle.

Jamie wondered whether to take the flier with him to the circus, then, remembering that he'd torn it off a lamppost when no one was looking, and that, technically, this constituted stealing, he hid it under his pillow again.

The door opened suddenly.

'You're not ready,' Jamie accused his mother.

Letty touched her hand to her chest. Her heart felt as raw as butcher's meat. 'Jamie.' She sat heavily down on the edge of his bed.

'Is Dada ready?' Jamie demanded suspiciously.

Letty took his hand and rubbed the pads of his fingers with her thumb. Jamie decided something was wrong. His mother's voice had sounded reedy, thin—as though she'd left the bulk of it in another room.

'Jamie,' she said for the second time. She gulped at some air and squeezed his hand even harder. 'I have something to tell you.'

Jamie waited for the axe to fall. The circus had been cancelled. Perhaps his father had been detained at the embassy. It had happened before and the apology often came from his mother. But this did not happen when there was a promise. Never when his father had promised.

'Something important, sweetheart. I'm so sorry.'

Jamie tried to crack the code of his mother's expression. She didn't look particularly sorry. If anything she looked scary. Angry almost.

'Daddy's had an accident,' she said.

'Oh!' Jamie pulled his hand away. This was not what he had been expecting. He pictured his father tripping and spraining an ankle. 'Poor Dada,' he said sympathetically. 'Did he cut himself?' he ventured.

'No, Jamie. No, darling.' Letty drew in a breath. Every step of explanation felt like walking across broken glass. 'He . . . well . . . he had a fall.'

Jamie's brow cleared. Falls were painful, no doubt about that, but to a boy who had made a lifelong habit of falling, they were rarely cause for serious concern.

'Does he have to get stitches?' Jamie faltered. A hospital trip meant that the trip to see his unicycling bear would be called off.

The strength went from Letty's arms. The girls had cried themselves to a sleep from which they had yet to wake, but she could not close her own eyes without seeing Nicky on the ground, the pool of blood lacquered round his head. And now here was Jamie, and she was his knock on the door, his war telegram. Jamie was still living in the before, while Letty would for ever exist in the after, and the gap between them was immeasurable. She knew she had no choice but to shatter his world, but into how many pieces was something she did have control over. She must find a way to tiptoe through the land mines of his age, his innocence.

'Find words that won't frighten them.' The Ambassadress had put her arm round Letty's shaking shoulders and gently, firmly pulled her away. They hadn't wanted Letty to go to the embassy. Nicky could not be moved for some time. It was a question of jurisdiction, they said, of government formalities, but Letty couldn't bear for him to lie there on the tarmac, cold, alone. She had taken his coat to lay over him, then knelt beside him, until finally, with the permission of the Ambassador, he had been loaded into an ambulance by the authorities.

Letty summoned every ounce of steel she had remaining. 'Jamie, Daddy's not in hospital . . . Daddy's gone.'

'Oh, I see.' Jamie slumped down on his bed. He didn't see at all, but he matched his mother's solemnity of tone. 'When is he coming back?'

'Darling, Daddy isn't coming back. Try to understand.'

'But when will I see him again?' His voice began to rise plaintively.

'Oh, Jamie.' The fragile shell holding Letty together splintered and broke. 'Not for a long, long time.' She began to cry. 'I'm sorry, Jamie, oh God, I'm so sorry, but Dada's gone now and you have to be brave.' She pulled him to her and held him tight. 'We all have to be so brave.'

Jamie went very quiet. When he was finally released, he looked at his mother's tear-stained face with more than a trace of annoyance.

'Who's going to take me to the circus, then?'

The Minch, Scotland, Summer, 1979

In the perpetual dusk of a summer's night, the ferry at long last shunted its way into Lochbealach harbour. Like some freakish sea monster, it opened its mouth, laid down the metallic tongue of its gangplank and began spewing out the contents of its belly. One hundred or so mildly traumatised sheep were the first off, followed by a windswept line of foot passengers.

It had proved an unexpectedly stormy crossing and the crew had taken several attempts to bring the ferry in. Letty was not overly concerned. The crew of Caledonian MacBrayne were widely admired for their skilful handling of this particular strait and it was their determined 'What won't sink must float' attitude that was responsible for them having once set sail on Christmas Eve in a force ten gale, on the basis that it was every islander's God-given right to be returned home in time for a fine roast lunch. Opening into the Sea of the Hebrides, the Minch was a notoriously angry stretch of water.

On the fourth attempt, the crew's persistence was rewarded. The wind and current momentarily aligned and the ferry surged neatly forwards, eventually butting up against the heavy fenders lining the pier.

Letty stood with the children on the upper deck and listened to the noise of the motors grinding beneath the boat. She tilted her face upwards to catch the rain, which was falling in a light mist against her cheek.

The grisly little Pimlico flat and the handouts from the Diplomatic Wives' Fund were finally behind them. As were the negotiating of Nicky's pension; the sorting out of his affairs; the endless bureaucracy and loneliness of it, all the time wondering if there was a point, a life ahead of them. Now they were home. Everyone has a place where they fit into their skins, a place where they are able to make sense of the world, and the island was hers.

There were no rules, no protocol, no politics or intrigue. There was no Cold War, no Russia, no spectre of power waiting to corrupt. On the island there was only sand and rock and the rain to wash over them.

'Why are you crying?' Georgie asked, alarmed. 'What's wrong?'

'It's only spray, darling.' She kissed Georgie's hand and quickly wiped her cheek. 'Come on, we'd better go.'

The Peugeot had made a miraculous recovery, drying out in the care of Macleod Motors, a dour father-and-son team who had arrived at the river with a tow truck and much chain-smoking and head-shaking. A couple of days later, the children were able to ease themselves gingerly back onto the damp, eggy-smelling seats to complete the journey north.

'Aye,' Macleod Senior commented drily, 'best let the sea air blow through her. It's the interior that's taken the damage. I've stapled the carpet back but that plywood of yours will go rotten soon enough. I can pull it out for you now if you like. Give you more luggage room.'

There followed a silence broken by the clang of metal—a dropped spanner or rolling hubcap—and only then did Letty realise that Macleod was peering at her with an expectant air, handing her the worn leather key ring.

'I'm sure it's fine, thank you.'

Later she would recall a thread of this exchange that had jarred, a whisper in her ear to pay attention, but at the time there had been the ferry to make and the clock was already against them.

Unloading the ferry was almost as laborious a process as docking it and it was a further three-quarters of an hour before Letty was given the nod to start the engine. She drove onto the metal turntable, where, dwarfed by a Mother's Pride truck, the old Peugeot was hoisted up and finally released into the brackish air of the Outer Isles.

THE ISLAND'S SINGLE ROAD was a meandering tarmac track barely wide enough to accommodate the chassis of the average car, let alone a tractor or plough. Every half-mile or so, crescent-shaped passing places had been gouged from the verge as an afterthought, as though the possibility of two-way traffic had been so laughable it had not been worth planning for.

After the dramatic pageantry of Scotland's west coast and the Wagnerian scenery of Skye, there seemed precious little to admire in the island's flat, barren topography. There was instead the squat architecture of the townships—the islanders' were predisposed to building modern bungalows right on the doorstep of their more picturesque crofts—broken rusted cars, dishevelled Highland cattle and never-ending barbed-wire fences that criss-crossed the bog-leaden ground. Pity the few day-trippers, lured to the Outer Isles by some 'Visit Scotland' guide's tepid promise of breezy sands and unique culture. How could they know that the ugliness was superficial—that the whole island was magic?

Georgie breathed in the familiar smell of peat smoke. They had turned at the church and were juddering past the ghostly whitewash of old Euan Macdonald's croft.

'Look, there's Alick now!' Letty exclaimed as a swaying pinprick of light came into view at the end of the road. She slowed the car and wound down the window.

'Ah, Let-ic-ia.' Alick's rubbery face broke into a grin.

For as long as she could remember, Alick Macdonald, her neighbour, friend and protector had met them off the ferry like this, his black serge jacket buttoned over a navy boiler suit, the lantern swinging in his hands.

'Oh, Alick.' She took his hand and squeezed it. 'You're so good to wait for us.' It didn't matter how firmly she told him it was unnecessary, Alick was as stubborn as an ink blot and she knew perfectly well he'd been standing there, cold rain slanting across his face, for the full two hours the ferry had been delayed. He was a short, wiry man, somewhere in his early forties, with piercing eyes under mildly surprised brows and sprigs of tightly coiled hair that looked as if they'd been blown back by the wind for so many years that they'd given up trying to grow in any other direction.

'Shall I help you in with the luggage, Let-ic-ia?'

'We'll unpack the car in the morning, Alick. It's late and I want to get the children to bed.'

'Can we put out the flag for you?' Jamie piped up.

'Aye, first thing. Put her out.' Alick ran a hand through his whorls of hair. 'Put the flag in the stone and I'll be down.'

'Thank you, Alick.' Letty gripped his arm.

'Ah, *mo gràdh*.' His sharp eyes softened. 'Welcome to the country.'

BALLANISH, PERCHED ON the western tip of the island, in Scotland's westernmost archipelago, was neither a pretty nor structurally interesting house but it was a tough one, designed to take no nonsense from the elements. It didn't matter how violently it stormed, how hard the wind blew, the house simply arched its back, closed its eyes and patiently waited out each assault. Every time Letty drove up to find the roof intact and the doors on their hinges, she silently thanked the architect for his lack of creative inspiration.

'Georgie, you take Jamie. Alba, help me with the food. Everything else can wait until morning.'

Alba lugged the cardboard box into the larder. She hated this room with its pinching cold and lingering smell of mutton. Bad things happened to good food in larders. Butter became sullied by traces of Marmite and jam; bricks of Cheddar cracked like heel skin; even the faintest hint of jellifying soup was enough to make her gag.

'No,' she heard her mother say, 'not in there, Alba, put them in the fridge.'

The fridge . . . She stood stock still.

Her mother was standing by the kitchen door, arm raised to the wall. 'Ta-da!' She pressed a switch and the room flooded with light. 'I got some builders in from Skye,' Letty said. 'They made an awful mess, but they got the job done. What do you think?'

'I don't believe it.' In the corner of the kitchen a brand-new Electrolux was humming with power. 'The whole house has electricity?'

Pleased, Letty nodded, but Alba, already regretting her momentary lapse into enthusiasm, frowned. 'Why?'

When, a decade earlier, electricity had finally made it to the Outer Islands. Letty had been one of the few to hold out against it. 'Nostalgia,' Nicky diagnosed. 'Your mother appears to think there's some kind of romance to life in the Dark Ages.' And the Flemings continued to use a push-me-pull-you carpet sweeper and strain their eyes reading with torches under their blankets.

'You've kept the gas lamps,' Alba hedged.

'I couldn't bear to get rid of them. They give off such a pretty light. Besides . . .' Letty hesitated. 'Well, they remind me of your grandpapa.'

Up until then, Victorian glass sconces had provided the only light in the evening. Alba could still picture her grandfather moving from one to the next putting a match to their muslin cones. The burning gas had emitted a comforting buzzing noise as though the whole place was inhabited by a swarm of beautifully house-trained bees.

'Look in the outside room,' Letty ordered.

Connected to the main house by a draughty corridor, the outside room was the dumping ground for all family detritus: fishing reels, amusingly shaped lumps of driftwood, splintered oars, duck decoys and a miscellany of unclaimed clothing so encrusted with sea water that it had achieved the consistency of salted cod. Still, fishy and damp though it was, it smelt, to Alba, of freedom and summer. The new spartan hint of soap in the air unnerved her and then, beneath the virgin glow of overhead lighting, she saw a brand-new chest freezer and state-of-the-art washing machine.

'Well?'

At the touch on her shoulder, Alba recoiled.

Letty stared in bewilderment at Alba's hard little face. The day before leaving London her daughter had locked herself in the bathroom with a pair of needlepoint scissors. Now, as Letty's eyes shifted to the blunt line of her daughter's newly shorn hair, she felt something twist in her heart. When had Alba become so hard, so lacking in compassion, and how had she not noticed it before?

Only Nicky had ever been privy to Alba's more malleable side. In the mornings, his youngest daughter would leap onto his bed and wrap herself round him—tugging at a chest hair or fondly rubbing the wasteland of his bald patch. As he moved from bedroom to bathroom, she would cling to him, forbidding his departure before he had been kissed two or three times and hugged many more. As her limbs were forcibly pruned from him one by one, the wail would rise, 'Oh, no, please, don't go, Dada,' until finally she would collapse in defeat on the floor, weeping. 'When are you coming back? When will I ever see you again?'

'In about half an hour,' Nicky would remind her sternly, whereupon Alba would dissolve into shameless giggles.

'Dada is my love-beetle,' Alba had once explained matter-of-factly to Letty. 'I love you too, of course, but I love Dada a little bit more.'

And Letty had smiled. 'All girls love their father a little bit more. It will probably be like that the rest of your life.'

'It must have cost a fortune,' Alba now said accusingly, of the new freezer.

'But it was worth it, don't you think?'

Alba didn't know what to think. The significance of electricity was not lost on her. In their family's uncharted future, one thing was certain: without light and heat, life became untenable on the island after October, when daylight ended at three in the afternoon. She had always loved summers there, but electricity lent a permanence to their situation that she'd been studiously ignoring. The present was a world she hadn't yet made sense of, let alone the future. She eyeballed her mother, willing her to answer all the suspicions she didn't dare voice. Were they poor? Were they in exile? How long was this for? Was it really conceivable it could be for ever?

ON THE ISLAND, of all the elements, the wind ruled. It blew, gusted and roared a soundtrack to everyday life, like a man with a terrible grievance he couldn't help airing. It was the last thing Georgie listened to before falling asleep and the first thing she heard on waking. On occasion it became so loud she would dream a tidal wave was rolling towards her and she would wake, expecting to find an immense wall of water bearing down on the house. Always, though, there was the same view on the other side of her window: the mist collecting over Loch Aivegarry, the rolling, sandy flats of the machair and the silver line of the sea beyond. The only thing between the house and America was the vast emptiness of the Atlantic.

It was past midnight now, but darkness never truly fell during the summer. Instead, it was as though a rubber had been taken to a charcoal drawing of the sky, smudging the lines between night and day. Georgie loved her room with its brass bed and candy-stripe curtains. Every inch of wall space was covered with watercolours of island birds painted by her father. 'This red, black and white gentleman over your head is an oyster-catcher, my favourite wader,' he had told her. Above the chest of drawers he had hung two studies: the head of a golden plover, complete with scale measurements of its beak, and a painstakingly detailed wing of a mallard.

'Why did you draw only the wing?' Georgie had asked.

'To study the mechanics of it,' Nicky had said. 'I like to know how things work.' And this Georgie knew to be true. Her father devoured specifics and data with the same relish he reserved for smoked oysters on toast.

'You know something, my little George?' he would whisper as he kissed her good night. 'Have you noticed that the call of the corncrake sounds exactly like someone running their fingernail along the teeth of a comb?'

Even as she thought about it, Georgie picked up a faint rasping sound — but it didn't sound much like a corncrake. After a while she realised it was coming through the wall of the next-door room. She brought Jamie into her bed and curled herself round his trembling body. 'What is it, Jamie, why are you crying?'

'I don't know where Dada is.'

'Oh, Jamie.' She tightened her grip on him. 'Dada's in heaven.'

'No, no.' He pulled away, agitated. 'Why do people keep saying that? Dada didn't get to heaven.'

'It's OK, Jamie,' she soothed. 'Of course Dada got to heaven. It's OK now, it was a bad dream, that's all.' She stroked his damp hair and launched into a rationalisation of heaven's geography and how its size made the locating of one individual impossible without maps, until Jamie was sufficiently baffled to drop the subject. She wiped her eyes with the back of her hand. She was always careful not to cry in front of Jamie. Besides, what good were tears? They were hardly adequate for what she was feeling.

'Go to sleep now.' She buried her face in his neck. 'Take a big breath.'

Obediently, he gulped down air and immediately started hiccupping.

'Oh, Jamie,' Georgie said helplessly.

'I can't help it.' He hiccupped again. 'You'll have to scare me.'

'Don't be silly.'

'Tell me a story then. Tell me the Flora Macdonald story. Please, Georgie.' His voice caught pitifully.

'All right.' She sat up, rubbing her eyes with her fist. 'Well, let's see . . . Years and years before Grandpa bought this house, it was owned by a rich islander called Captain Macdonald, and Captain Macdonald'—she settled Jamie in the crook of her arm—'was a pig of a man.'

Jamie sighed in appreciation. It didn't matter how many times he heard it, he loved this story. Captain Macdonald had been a notorious baddie, employing many of the islanders for menial jobs, such as rowing him out to distant islands in order for him to shoot a few duck. He was a snobbish man, too, and when it fell to him to welcome the King to the island for an official visit, he began to harbour dreams of scaling the prestige ladder and sent his only daughter to the annual ball on Skye in the hope of her catching the eye of one of the posh boys attending.

Flora did indeed catch the eye of a boy—a young fisherman on the quay, called Neilly McLellan. The Captain was horrified. Swiftly deciding to marry her off to his factor—the man who collected rent on his properties—he lost no time in arranging the nuptuals. Neilly McLellan was heartbroken and sent word of his intention to rescue Flora from this unhappy fate. The plan was to wait for fine weather then row across the Minch and signal his arrival by shining a light from the mouth of Loch Aivegarry.

Weeks passed while Flora pined, then finally, one moonless night, there it was, the beam of a lantern.

'Without hesitation, Flora wrenched open the window and, as you know,' Georgie said, 'under her window—my window—is the only tree on the whole island and she threw out her sack of belongings and climbed down it.'

'Is it true, though?' Jamie asked. 'Did she really? Alba says nobody could climb down that tree because it's covered in thorns.'

'A few thorns would never stop someone who was in love.'

'Alba says that the tree is too far away from the window and that Flora wouldn't have been able to reach it.'

'Jamie, why do you care about anything Alba says?'

'She doesn't lie about things.'

'Nor do I!' Georgie said, stung.

'You pretend, like Mum.'

'Look.' Georgie sighed. 'How old is Alba?'

'Fourteen.'

'Right. That means she only knows about things that happened in the last fourteen years, OK? This story happened ages ago.' Jamie's slavish adoration of his sister had always riled Georgie.

'Did the story happen more than seventeen-and-three-quarters years ago?'

'Oh, Jamie.' Georgie kissed the top of his head. Her brother's literalness, the unyielding pedantry that so enraged Alba, she found charming. She settled him back. 'Just listen. Flora escapes in the boat with her fisherman and two of his cousins and off they sail to Skye, but unfortunately a gale picks up and they're blown onto the southern shore of Harris. So, there they are, drenched, lost and scared. But they can see a light in the distance and eventually they get to a croft, knock on the door and guess who opens it?'

'Flora's auntie!' Jamie supplied.

'Exactly! Of all the bad luck! Of all the houses on all the islands! Flora's auntie was not best pleased to find such a bedraggled collection of runaways on her doorstep. Even less amusing was the moment she recognised her niece among them. Incensed at their story, she dismissed the boys and kept Flora under lock and key until she could be safely returned to her father. The lovers, however, did not give up. The second time around, the plan worked. Flora and her fisherman escaped to Skye and from there to the mainland, where they eventually boarded a ship bound for Australia.'

'And lived happily ever after,' Jamie finished. 'People in stories always live happily ever after, don't they?'

Georgie's eyes slid to her dressing-table mirror, where a small snapshot was wedged between glass and frame: their parents on honeymoon, leaning against the rail of a ferry, wearing sunglasses and grins. What a happy-ever-after day that had been.

'Go to sleep, Jamie.'

'Yes,' he said, but his eyes remained open long into the night.

Bonn, West Germany, February 1979

Protected from hard facts about his father, Jamie began to hoard scraps of information, but it hadn't been until two weeks after his father's accident that the first significant clue had come his way.

A party was given at the Ambassador's residence. Jamie understood neither what the party was for, nor why he was required to attend. All he knew was that it was boring. Everyone was old and wearing black. There were no other children invited except Georgie and Alba.

A man wearing a black tail-coat handed round plates of cucumber sandwiches. Jamie crammed four into his mouth, trying to satisfy the hollow feeling inside him, which he incorrectly identified as hunger.

He felt a hand drop onto his head and looked up to find Tom Gordunson standing beside him. Jamie liked Tom. He reminded him of a wolf with his shaggy head and crumpled suits. Tom was his father's oldest friend, the best man at his parents' wedding, and he always gave Jamie presents at Christmas even though, technically, he was Georgie's godfather.

'How are you doing, old boy?' Tom asked.

'God supports us in our troublous life,' Jamie intoned.

'Ah, I see you've been talking to the vicar.'

'He said Dada has gone to a better place.' Jamie followed Tom's gaze to where the vicar was chatting, holding a cup of tea poised in the air. 'Has he?'

'Yes, I think he probably has.'

'Better than Bonn?'

Tom smiled faintly. 'Yes, better than Bonn.'

'But then why didn't he take us with him?'

'He couldn't,' Tom said gently. 'It doesn't work like that.'

'But I miss him, and I want him to come home.'

'Of course you do, old chap, of course you do.'

'He was going to take me to the circus,' Jamie said forlornly. 'He promised I could see the bear. He promised to help me with my homework.'

Tom dropped to one knee. 'Listen to me, Jamie.' He laid his hands on Jamie's shoulders. 'Your father will always be with you. Always. Every night when you say your prayers you must believe that he can hear them.'

'How though? Does he have special powers?'

'Yes . . . I suppose in a way he does.'

'Like a spy? Like James Bond?'

'Yes.' Tom smiled again. 'A little like James Bond.'

Jamie sucked in a breath. He knew it! His father had gone on one of his secret missions. Tom Gordunson worked for the Foreign Office. He had one of the most important jobs in the whole of England. If Tom didn't know what he was talking about then no one did.

'I'm going to tell Mummy.'

Jamie tried to wriggle free but Tom held him back. 'Why don't we keep it hush-hush—just between you and me, eh?' He touched a finger to his nose and winked.

And there it was! His father's secret sign.

Tom, an intense, honourable man, couldn't have known that this one simple gesture, coupled with the boy's fierce desire to believe, would harden into an unshakable conviction that his father would be coming back.

Jamie hurried off. If he couldn't tell his mother, he would find Georgie. But he bumped into a woman with a thickly powdered face and a tight grey bun, a long-term intimate of Bonn society whose husband was a political commentator on the radio. Had anyone asked her, she would have crisply informed them that she did not approve of the Ambassador's 'wake' for Nicholas Fleming. A suspected traitor was as good as an actual traitor.

Now, caught unawares by the turncoat's living, breathing offspring in front of her, she instinctively stepped backwards, then rallied with a fatuous question about school. Jamie answered politely. The fur stole round her neck interested him far more than social chitchat. The fox's head nestled on her shoulder while its legs dangled slackly down her back. Just as he stretched out his hand to touch it, he felt the sharpness of Alba's fingers.

'Don't do that, Jamie.' She pinched him.

Jamie started crying and the woman's awkwardness was dispelled. The relief seemed universal as everyone turned to look at the children—the one wailing, the other shushing. For the first time in this whole sorry event, there was a focus for their embarrassment and pity. Poor bereaved children. Poor little fatherless boy.

JAMIE NEVER GOT to tell Georgie and he didn't dare tell Alba. Instead, he carried his secret with him. To school in the mornings, to bed at night. Everywhere he looked for his father, secure in the knowledge that it was only a matter of time.

But then they left Bonn.

'Does everyone know we're going to London?' he asked his mother the night before they sailed. The house looked bare and unfriendly, stripped of their possessions. 'Will Dada know where we are?'

Letty stopped packing and drew him into a hug. 'Of course, darling. Daddy will always know where we are.' And his heart had soared. His father had not lied. Tom Gordunson had not lied. His father was on some kind of mission and, what's more, his mother knew about it.

'Mum,' he whispered. 'It's all right. I know. Daddy's a spy, isn't he?'

It was as if he'd burned her with a poker iron. Letty stiffened and held him at arm's length. 'Why do you say that, Jamie? Who told you that?'

'No one,' Jamie said, frightened. 'I mean, Tom said . . .'

'Tom?' she repeated incredulously. 'Our Tom?' Two red petals of anger bloomed in her cheeks. 'He said that Daddy was a spy?'

'Sort of, I mean, yes.' He had never seen his mother like this. Her mouth twisted, her eyes stormy. 'I'm sorry, Mummy, I was just trying to . . .'

'Don't you ever believe that.' She shook him, her fingers digging into him hard. 'And don't you dare say it, not to me, or anybody. Not ever. Do you understand?'

He had understood and he had felt ashamed. You were not supposed to talk about secret things.

Outer Hebrides, Summer 1979

When his strength returned, the bear pushed himself to his feet and took a look around. Ahead, the sea stretched to the horizon. Behind him a natural archway dead-ended in a crater, flanked on all sides by black rock in whose crevices fulmars were nesting. The cliff was sheer and the only section benign enough to climb—a spine of screed cushioned on either side by moss—offered no foothold within easy reach. Still, the crater was filling up like a kettle under a tap and soon the only way out would be to swim.

He more or less chanced upon the cave, tumbling backwards through the opening. Once again, floored by the elements, he lay still while his eyes adjusted to the dark. The cave was large, with a floor sloping sharply upwards. The incoming tide was boiling past the entrance, but a happy combination of gravity and speed kept the water outside in the channel. He peered out of the opening and spotted a small boat hugging the shoreline. It was travelling slowly, east to west. They were looking for him.

SEVENTEEN YEARS OLD—and she knew nothing. Her entire life, Georgie had been bookish, above-average clever. She thought of the sheer variety of knowledge she had absorbed, the sedimentary rocks studied, the vocabulary memorised and grammar mastered. And for what? She'd been taught everything except the one lesson she really needed—what to do when your father dies. Now, to add to her confusion, her mother had turned turtle and drawn a hard shell over her head and Georgie didn't know how to reach her.

Letty was sitting at the table, a pile of blank white envelopes in front of her. She had always been an inspired letter writer, but whereas letter writing had once been a hobby, now it was an obsession: lawyers, the Home Office, banks, insurance firms, she had written to every person Nicky had ever worked with, looking for answers—a resolution. Yet again, Georgie was overcome with an urge to grab her and tell her about East Berlin—because the knowledge was heavier than she thought possible and she was sick of hauling it around with her, day and night.

'Mum.' She laid a hand on her mother's shoulder.

Startled, Letty turned. 'Darling, sorry, million miles away.'

Georgie searched her mother's face. 'Who are you writing to?'

'Oh, you know . . .' She gave a dismissive little wave, but Georgie knew. She hadn't been writing to anyone. There was no one left to write to. 'Sleep all right, darling?' Letty asked vaguely.

'Fine,' Georgie lied. 'You?'

'Fine,' Letty lied back, then smiled brightly to prove it.

IT WAS QUITE an ordeal kissing Alick's mother. Firstly, it went on for an astonishing amount of time; then there was the odd bristle to contend with; thirdly, the kiss itself was of the wet, full-lipped variety. Nevertheless, it was an unspoken requirement of the Ballanish township that visits to

Alick's parents be made on the first day of the holiday and so the children duly surrendered to Mrs Macdonald's embraces.

She met them at the door of her croft, a warm-hearted woman with ample bosom, wearing a pinafore tied over a tweed skirt. 'And how is the mammy today?' she cried, hugging Letitia and ushering them all into the croft to shake hands with Alick's father, Euan, a neat, self-contained man with ear muffs of white hair and long elegant fingers.

Once inside, the children were positioned on the wooden bench for the ritual of present-receiving. Mrs Macdonald had worked for many years at the knitwear factory and every summer produced a triptych of unusual-coloured jumpers from the seconds pile. This year it was a polo neck in egg yolk for Alba, a slime-green tank top for Jamie, and a dung-coloured V neck for Georgie. The children were compelled to endure the enthusiastic endorsements of their mother. 'Why, they're lovely, Mrs Macdonald, how very generous of you.' And there was nothing else to be said, because it was astonishingly generous of her, but the children fervently wished she would not spend what little money she had on them.

Afterwards, they sat roasting gently in front of the fire while Mrs Macdonald set about making the tea. 'I'm surprised the ferry came in at all,' she said. 'Quite a storm it was, Letitia, and it's been that way all winter, right enough. Many's the croft that lost a roof, and a fishing boat struck the rocks near St Kilda, why, no' more than a for'night ago.'

'Did it sink?' Jamie asked.

'Aye, three men gone and with their bodies not yet recovered.' She transferred the kettle to the hotter of her two griddles.

'Will they wash up on the beach?' Jamie asked.

'You'll no' be wanting to find them if they do, young Jamie, they'll have been tossed around plenty so there's no telling what they'll look like.' She turned to encounter Letty's strained face and corrected herself. 'Though it's more likely God will have taken them before that.'

'Taken them where?' Jamie asked eagerly.

Mrs Macdonald collapsed onto a stool and squeezed her hands together in an effort to milk inspiration out of them. 'They say that sailors and fishermen who drown at sea come back as seagulls, and the sky and the ocean become their kingdom. Ach, you can imagine them swooping down, with the sky always blue and the fish plentiful for the rest of time. There now.' She snatched a scone from the trolley and pressed it into Jamie's hand.

Letty smiled gratefully. She didn't know—how could she possibly—what a child like Jamie could do with such imagery.

The Macdonalds' tea trolley was a three-tiered affair that would not have looked out of place in the finest hotel in Edinburgh. The teapot and crockery were kept on the top, a bowl of carrageen and a plate of sandwiches below and, on the very bottom, a basket of warm scones. Mrs Macdonald's scones were famous on an island already famous for scones, but her tea trolley was approached in strict hierarchical order from above. Tier one presented no problem as the children were not deemed old enough to drink tea; however, enduring the carrageen, a quivering blancmange of a dish made by boiling milk and seaweed together for days, was a feat. And there were other foodie dragons to slay. Mrs Macdonald's sandwiches were grouted with a thick layer of margarine and tinned luncheon meat. How to avoid them was a subject often discussed in the Fleming household and, inevitably, Letty found herself working her way solo through the white triangles, feeling the benevolent eyes of Mrs Macdonald and Euan upon her.

Alick's parents might have five sons, but Letty was their spiritual daughter and they treated her accordingly. In turn, she loved Euan for his gentle manner and thoughtful mind. She was always eager to hear his stories.

While Euan spoke slowly and quietly, Mrs Macdonald more than compensated by delivering a ceaseless stream of news. The news that she was currently preoccupied with was the closure of the seaweed factory.

'It's created terrible unemployment on the island, Letitia. There's only the lobster and the knitwear now. The councillors called a meeting in the school and the whole township came. Back in May it was, but it didn't make a bit of difference.'

Euan sucked his teeth. 'No, indeed it didn't.'

'It's a terrible shame,' Mrs Macdonald said indignantly. 'But it'll no' affect the carrageen, don't you worry.' She emptied a second helping into Alba's bowl. 'I can fetch seaweed from the water myself, but that factory stuff went into all sorts. Soap, postage stamps, even the froth on the top of beer. Why, it was a very useful thing, that seaweed.'

'They started importing it from Tasmania. They said it was cheaper.' Euan shook his head sorrowfully. 'But how can it be? It makes no sense.'

'No sense at all,' Mrs Macdonald echoed.

Jamie sat quietly, preoccupied by the image of the fishermen turning into seagulls. It seemed so odd. Why couldn't they remain as fishermen in their heaven and still be rewarded with plentiful fish from the ocean? And what of the fish? Were they real fish or heaven fish? And what if a particular fisherman had hated fishing? Were heaven's rewards always career-appropriate?

Before Jamie could push these thoughts to any conclusion he found his face being marinated in another of Mrs Macdonald's kisses, then suddenly the door to the croft was opened and Alba was shoving him outside.

Outer Hebrides, Summer 1979

For the first few days the bear stayed put. Time would come when he'd have to search out food and water but in the meanwhile he simply listened to the wind and watched the birds freewheeling in the sky.

One day, as he was sitting there, waiting for the tide to recede, there was a popping noise and a glass bottle bounced over the lip of the entrance. He examined it curiously, rolling it around, and noticed a piece of paper inside. He smashed the bottle and played clumsily with the piece of paper.

It was a map of Europe, drawn in black crayon. A single dot marked the northwest of Germany and from there, tiny red arrows marched across France, forded the channel and made their way to London, where they turned right to Scotland. They advanced up the west coast, across the Minch, and, had he been adept at the art of map-reading, it might have occurred to him that the line of red arrows led almost directly to his cave. Except the map didn't depict a cave. 'X' marked the spot over a house, its name childishly written and misspelt: BALERNICSH, July 1979, *the map was dated. Underneath the date, a message was written in a barely legible scrawl: 'To Dada. If yu ar lukin for uss . . . we ar heer.'*

Bonn, West Germany, January 1979

Letty spared Jamie Nicky's funeral—if that's what the small, awkward, under-attended service in Bonn could be called—and she spared him her tears. She tried to spare all three children the talk. Heaven knows there had been plenty of that.

Appropriately, it had been the press attaché who had found the letter, the morning after the accident, in Nicky Fleming's office, and the smoked end of a cigarette on the embassy's roof. The letter was a draft, clearly an unsatisfactory one, crumpled into a ball and left on the desk. It had been addressed to Letty, but neither its existence nor its contents were disclosed to her for a further six days, by which time it had been examined and re-examined for its implications.

My darling love, it began. *How wrong it feels to be writing this, when all I want to do is take you in my arms and tell you everything. It's ironic, really, given how much of my job is spent talking to strangers, that I have not found a way to reach the one person I love above all others . . .*

And there the letter ended. Below this single paragraph, however, were a number of disjointed phrases, some crossed through, others scrawled at odd angles, and it was these that Letty read over and over again.

Something I've been keeping from you, something that's been preying terribly on my mind
protect you and the children . . . ~~*in doing so I fear*~~
a moment of madness
taken the only way out I thought possible
Forgive me, my love

The letter was a private matter, Letty argued. It proved nothing. But according to Nicky's colleagues, it said everything. An internal investigation was launched into 'the matter of Fleming'.

Over the previous few years, while the Flemings had been stationed there, Bonn had suffered a number of 'irregularities' that, once discovered, had been hard to ignore. The Ambassador and those directly under him were privy to enormous amounts of intelligence. The leaks were small—yet suspicion persisted. Distrust settled over the embassy.

Diplomats, particularly high-ranking ones, did not often jump from the roofs of their own embassies. Fingers were quick to point to Nicky's polymath abilities—that unusual, God-given skill for absorbing information. Oh, yes, everyone agreed, Fleming had been extravagantly well informed. So who knew what he had really been up to, what cards he'd been holding? Suspicion lit its own fire and it was only a matter of time before it burned a trail towards the greatest sin of all: betrayal of Queen and Country.

To Letty, the speed with which Nicky's colleagues lined up to condemn him came as a shock. She had been collected and taken to the embassy, where she was questioned by two men from MI6. The more senior of the two, Porter, did most of the talking. He was a stocky man in his early forties with a damson smudge of tiredness beneath each eye and an expression in them that seemed untroubled by even a flicker of uncertainty about the world. His subordinate, Norrell, was a good deal better looking. He stood, back to the door, while Porter conducted his questioning.

After he had finished, Letty stared at Nicky's letter on the table in front of her. 'My husband's stepmother, Gisela, the woman who raised him, was born in East Germany,' she said eventually.

'Yes, we know,' Porter agreed.

'On her twenty-fifth birthday, she stepped outside her house and tripped over a phosphorus bomb. Her leg was so badly burned that three months later, when the Russians came, she still found it hard to run.'

The MI6 men bowed their heads in dutiful respect as she told them the story. It was 1945 and everybody knew the war was over. Rumours had spread: the English, French and Americans were coming. The Russians were coming. Gisela's family lived in the east and knew that Stalin's army was hungry for vengeance and about to unleash its barbaric fury at the gates of Berlin. Terrified for the women, Gisela's grandfather sent them on ahead with a local farmer, who took them as far as the Elbe and instructed them to swim to a train on the other side. Of the forty-two people who tried to swim the Elbe that day, twelve drowned, including Gisela's mother and sister.

'The Russians slaughtered Gisela's grandfather. They expropriated the house, stole the land and handed it over to a collective,' Letty finished.

'Yes, yes, it's all a matter of record,' the man from MI6 reassured her.

'And yet on the basis of this—' She touched the edge of the letter. 'You're suggesting my husband is a traitor.'

'Tomorrow we would like to speak to your eldest daughter.' Porter checked his notes. 'Georgiana.'

'No.' Letty's jaw felt tight from lack of sleep. 'Absolutely not. What can you possibly want to talk to my daughter about?'

'Berlin,' Porter said. 'Your husband has recently spent considerable time in East Berlin, has he not?'

'He's part of an allied delegation there,' Letty said, unconsciously slipping Nicky back into the present where he belonged. 'He's to and fro all the time.'

'Effectively giving himself a channel of both travel and communication within East Germany.'

'What do you mean?' she said quickly. 'No, it's not like that at all. He's involved with that industrial accident.'

'Schyndell,' Porter supplied.

'Schyndell, yes.'

There had been an explosion at a nuclear power plant in East Germany, releasing into the air unknown quantities of radioactive isotopes, with few resources in place for clean-up. The initial response of the Soviets had been to play it down, but it had grown too big, too complex. The plant was experimental and was being shut down when the accident occurred. A delegation of scientists, safety experts and diplomats had been assembled by the Allies to investigate.

'Four years as First Secretary.' Porter consulted his file. 'A stint in London at the Foreign Office. Back to Bonn, this time as Counsellor. This was your husband's second term in Bonn, correct?' Porter said.

'The Ambassador requested him specifically,' Letty said.

To return had been the last thing she'd wanted, but the personnel department had put pressure on Nicky. *I hope you're not going to be difficult about this* was the exact phrase they'd used. You can say no to them once, Nicky had cautioned, but career-wise, it would not be the most prudent thing. So they'd returned to Bonn and, almost immediately, Schyndell had happened, effectively doubling Nicky's time away from home.

'A little coincidental,' Porter said, when they touched on this. 'A little convenient, don't you think?'

'I don't understand.'

'Was your husband asked to be part of the delegation or did he apply?'

'Nicky speaks fluent Russian and German. He knew he could be of help.'

'Quite,' Porter said. 'And at Schyndell he would have had access to a considerable amount of sensitive information on nuclear technology.'

'As would everyone on the delegation.' Fear made her voice deepen.

'Which is why the question of trust is so significant,' Porter said silkily.

Norrell stepped forwards to the table and pulled out a chair. 'And then, of course, this most recent trip with your daughter was just after your husband heard about Rome,' he said.

'Rome?' she repeated crossly.

'The position of Minister, for which Nicky applied.' Norrell clarified.

She frowned. 'But that hasn't been . . . what's that got to do with anything?' She'd been aware that Nicky was in the running. It was a posting they'd both been anxiously waiting to hear about, but he'd never said anything about it being announced. Was it possible he hadn't told her?

'Mrs Fleming, your husband would not be the first official operating at top level found guilty of corruption of some kind.' Norrell looked at her intently. 'Men turn for all sorts of reasons, ideological, fiscal, sexual. They are turned by inadequacy, by disillusion or jealousy. They betray their country out of greed, revenge, self-loathing, desire. But sometimes,' he said gently, 'all it takes is a little disappointment.'

Ballanish, Outer Hebrides, Summer 1979

When Letty forbade Alick to touch any of the new white goods, she could see from his bemused expression that he was at a loss to understand why. He sat at the kitchen table, a mug of coffee between his oil-stained fingers, while Georgie read, Jamie crayoned and Alba stared moodily out of the window.

'Well, Let-ic-ia, and what if they break down?'

'They're brand new, Alick, and they're under guarantee. If you take them apart, the guarantee won't be valid any more.'

Letty was well aware of delivering a crushing blow to his pride, but she remembered only too well coming home once to find Alick lying on his back on the kitchen floor surrounded by every component part of the Raeburn, ranked by size and cross-referenced according to function.

'Alick, why have you dismantled the oven?' She'd been aghast.

'Ach, just to see if I could,' had been the reply.

Alick was a genius of a mechanic. There was nothing he couldn't fix or build. Had life been fair and designed to reward the brilliant, a man of his capability might have made his career with Ford in Detroit or been snapped up by NASA, but life was particularly inequitable towards a man born in the Outer Hebrides. There was limited scope for his energy and imagination on the islands, so Alick contented himself with whatever Letty needed doing around the house—mowing the lawn, bringing in the peats, tinkering with the Peugeot, which managed to break down almost every other day.

'A guarrrrantee, eh?' Alick rolled his tongue suspiciously round the word as if examining it for contractual flaws. He dropped some tobacco into a cigarette paper and began working the thin tube between his thumb and middle finger. 'Well,' he declared grandly, 'I'd like to see this so-called guarantee take a spanner to the pipes when she blows.'

'Don't be offended, Alick,' Letty teased him. 'It's so good to see you. Tell me how you've been.'

'Aye, not bad,' he grinned, mollified. 'Not bad at all.' He struck a match to his roll-up and leaned forwards. 'What do you think of the beast then?'

'The beast?'

'Have you no' seen it, Let-ic-ia?'

'A beast?' Jamie stopped crayoning. 'Does it have horns?'

'It's a young beast, Jamie, barely two years old.'

'Is it a lion?'

Alick stowed his cigarette end in his breast pocket. 'Why, I've never heard tell of a lion on the island.'

'Is it a dragon, then?'

'Maybe it's an ugly hobgoblin,' Alba grumbled.

'Aye, it's a dragon right enough.' Alick jumped to his feet. 'Come in the garden and I'll show you.'

The garden was a fancy name for an acre of thistle enclosed by a ruined stone wall. From time to time Letty tried to encourage Alick to grow lettuce and vegetables there, but Alick's heart beat for metals, not soil, and only the potatoes ever survived.

Jamie pushed past Alick as he opened the gate, and Alba followed them.

'There she is,' Alick said. 'Over in the far corner.'

Jamie squinted at the tumbledown section of wall. No lion. Instead, a lone cow was breathing steam from its nostrils and stamping a foot.

'Whatever is it doing in here?' Letty frowned. 'Is it trapped?'

'Ach, now you can get your milk here and not walk all the way up to my father's house.'

'Oh, but I don't mind the walk.'

'Indeed, but it's a lot of bother.'

The unpleasant possibility that the cow might be some form of present was only now occurring to Letty. Fetching the metal churn from outside Euan's croft was a morning ritual she enjoyed. 'Oh, Alick, you're not really expecting me to milk this thing, are you?'

'It's no' so hard. I can teach you in a jiffy. You'll get the hang of it soon enough.' He approached the cow with his bucket.

'Be careful, she looks awfully cross.'

As if to confirm this dim view of its mood, the cow punched out an irritated moo as Alick ducked between its legs.

'Does that creature belong to us?' Alba said to her mother.

'I don't think so. I should imagine it's on loan for a bit.'

'I bet Alick stole it.'

'Don't be silly. He hasn't got a dishonest bone in his body.'

'See, it's easy, Letitia!' Alick was now wringing the cow's teats like church bells. 'She's a fine-tempered beast and this milk is as fresh as you'll ever taste, and all for a few moments' milking.'

'She doesn't look fine-tempered at all,' Letty said warily.

On cue, the cow twisted its head and aimed a hefty kick at the bucket.

'You bugger!' Alick roared. He staggered out, his boiler suit covered in milk. The cow bucked.

'Go, devil cow!' Alba roared delightedly.

'Alick, take her away,' Letty implored. 'I can't possibly deal with her.'

'I'll do it,' Alba said suddenly. 'It'll relieve the tedium of my life.'

'Good girl.' Alick was still wiping froth from his trousers. 'If she's to be your beast, then you'd best name her.'

Alba scrutinised the cow with something approaching respect. 'We'll call her Gillian,' she pronounced.

'Oh, I don't think that's a very suitable name,' Letty said faintly.

'Fine.' Alba turned her evil eye on her mother. 'In that case, we'll call her the Ambassadress.'

DONALD JOHN'S BRIGHT BLUE front door opened abruptly, and he appeared in front of the three children, stooping a little under the low frame.

'Donald John!' Jamie hurled himself at the islander.

'Why, Jamie!' Donald John caught him under the armpits and gave his head a vigorous patting. 'And Alba and Georgie too? Well, well. How today? How today?' He grinned and beamed and every version in between, ushering the children into the croft and shouting double commands over his shoulder. 'Come in, come in. Sit down! Sit down.'

'So, how are you, Donald John?' Alba enquired.

'Not so bad, not so bad at all.' He dusted off a bottle of Cherry Coke from his store cupboard and produced a plate of ginger nuts.

Donald John, their nearest neighbour and Alick's first cousin, was the youngest of a confusingly named line-up of brothers: John, John Donald, Donald and Donald John. He had lived alone in the croft his entire adult life but bachelorhood appeared to suit him. Despite his fifty-odd years, he hadn't a wrinkle on his waxy face and boasted an almost god-like smile of pearly whites. His voice was shrill and he tended to deliver everything in a gleeful shout accompanied by a selection of verbal paroxysms, all of which were ruthlessly mimicked by the children as soon as they left the croft.

'So, Donald John, I could hardly believe my ears,' Georgie teased. 'Alick says you've actually been off the island this year.'

'Aye, I went to Inverness to visit my sister-in-law, but that was a good many weeks back now, a good many weeks indeed. The weather was just awful.' He shook his head vigorously. 'Oh, boo boo, it was just terrible.'

'Was it very wet?' Georgie said sympathetically.

'Not wet, Georgie, it was hot! Yes indeed, it was terrible hot.'

'Was it, perhaps, say, a whopping sixty-nine degrees?' Alba said.

'I canna' say it was as high as that, but sixty-five degrees anyways. Oh, what a day,' he reminisced, sucking air into his cheeks and noisily expelling it again. 'I hate the heat. It was awful.'

'Imagine if you had to go to a desert then. It's a hundred and twenty degrees in the Sahara,' Jamie said. 'Don't you want to see a desert, Donald John? Don't you want to go somewhere exciting, like abroad?'

'Abroad?' This warranted an extra strenuous slap of the knee. 'No, no, I've never been to that place,' he admitted gaily, 'and I'm sure I never will.'

The fact was that Donald John had been born on the island and would die on the island and he felt heartily sorry for anyone for whom this was not the case. The very concept of travel was abhorrent to him. Should the children mention a business trip their father had made, Donald John would adopt a terminally mournful expression. 'Paris? Well, well, poor soul, poor soul.'

Jamie loved Donald John's kitchen with its custard-coloured walls and shiny blue Raeburn. He sipped his cherry fizz and looked round at the never-changing objects on the mantelpiece—a school photo of his nieces, a postcard from Glasgow and the plastic clock whose twelve numerals were depicted by small songbirds. When the big hand reached the wren, Donald John knew to put on his cap and go out to tend the cattle. On the hour of the starling he prepared dinner for himself. Visitors seemed to arrive between the thrush and the finch. When not entertaining, Donald John spent his evenings in silence. No television, his radio switched off, just sitting in his chair, absorbing each tick of the clock. If the world slowed around grown-ups, Jamie thought, time crawled around islanders.

'So,' Alba said, 'have you found a wife since we last saw you?'

'No, no.' He dutifully roared with laughter and reassured the girls he was saving himself for them.

'What other news?' Georgie asked. 'Any good gossip?'

'You'll have heard about the beast, I suppose?'

'Oh, yes, we love the beast!' Alba said.

'You've seen it, then?' Donald John sounded surprised.

'Alick took us.'

'Is that so, Georgie. Is that so?'

'Alba thinks it's deranged,' Jamie said.

'It is deranged,' Georgie agreed. 'It tried to kick Alick—and he was only trying to milk it.'

'Was he now!' Donald John began rocking backwards and forwards in amusement. 'Why, you'd have a hard job milking a wild thing like that!'

'Alba's going to try next,' Jamie pressed on. 'Alick is going to teach her.'

To the children's growing puzzlement, Donald John was now wiping tears of laughter from his eyes. 'Well, you'd better not get too close, Alba, no indeed, it'll take your fingers off. Ach, it's to be expected. Why, it's not right to cage a beast up like that!'

'It's hardly caged up,' Georgie said. 'And at least it has all the food it wants. It never stops eating, as far as I can see.'

'Aye, fifteen pounds of meat for its dinner every night!'

'Meat?' Georgie stole a look at Alba, an uncomfortable suspicion forming between them. Teasing was exclusively their department. This was the first time they had received any of their own treatment in return and it made them profoundly uncomfortable. 'What do you mean, "fifteen pounds of meat"?'

'Why, he feeds it steak for dinner and bacon for breakfast. I've heard it said the beast guzzles it down! You'd think it was human the way it carries on.'

'Donald John, have you gone mad?' Alba said. 'Cows don't eat meat. And who's feeding it?'

'Why, the wrestler is feeding him. It's his beast an' all.'

'What are you talking about?' The children stared at him in bewilderment.

'The bear, of course.'

'The bear?' Jamie stopped gargling his Cherry Coke.

The girls looked at each other in stupefied silence. 'We've been talking about a bear all this time?' Alba said. 'What kind of bear?'

'Well now, I'm not sure what species exactly,' Donald John said placidly, 'but a big one right enough.'

'But we were talking about the cow Alick put in our garden. Are you saying there's an actual live bear on this island right now?'

'Aye, he belongs to that wrestler, Andy Robin, and he's quite famous. He even has his own bus.'

Suddenly, the loose wires in Jamie's head began to spark and fizz. He jumped to his feet. 'I've seen him! I saw him on the way up here,' he spluttered. 'He's my bear. A grizzly bear. I told you, remember? On the road.'

'Why would anyone bring a bear up to the island?' Alba said scornfully, elbowing Jamie down into his seat.

'Oh, they say he's a hard-working beast, Alba. I've heard tell he's filming an advertisement—for Kleenex.'

'Does he do tricks?' Jamie asked. 'Can he ride a bicycle?'

'I can't say, but I'm sure you'll be wanting to go and see him, young Jamie.'

Jamie had already disappeared inside his own head. How was it possible? The bear from the museum. The bear on his flier. The bear waiting for him at the *Zirkusplatz* the day of his father's accident. And now here he was on the island. His island. His bear. 'Hello, bear,' Jamie whispered.

Outer Hebrides, Summer 1979

'Can we go now?' Jamie said feverishly. 'Can we?'

'In a minute, darling,' Letty whispered.

'How many minutes?'

'Oh, I don't know. A few, ten, fifteen . . .' Though increasingly aware of her son's need for precision, Letty was often unsure how best to supply it. 'As soon as possible,' she amended, turning back to the islander. 'So, how much do you want for it, Roddy?'

Dolefully she eyed the sideboard through the window. They both knew she would end up buying it, just as she had ended up buying the unspeakably hideous wardrobe that was always going to be too big for the house and the iron bedstead that still languished in the outside room.

'Mum, pleeease?' Jamie said fretfully.

'Jamie, be patient. I'm having a cup of tea with Roddy.'

Jamie watched the old wall-builder as he spooned a fourth sugar into his mug. He was the oddest-looking man Jamie had ever seen. His head resembled something carved out of rock. His wiry eyebrows grew as untrimmed as a hedge of twigs. His ears were like handles of clay and the deep lines etched into his cheek ran clear down to the prominent ridge of his jaw. The most startling aspect of Roddy's appearance, though, was the lump of bone on his back, which had bent his spine into an unyielding curve.

To compensate for this dreadful physical burden, Roddy had been granted a more spiritual gift. He was the seventh son of a seventh son and, as such, had been endowed with that most precious of island characteristics—second sight. By rights, second sight should have opened up the universe to him. It should have been his telescope to far-off lands, where mountains rose out of the sea and waves of sand burned under the desert heat. But, alas, Roddy's gift appeared to have been given to him for a more pedestrian use—the prediction of births, deaths and who would bring home the prize for best cow at the Highland Games.

'I'll take twenty pounds for it,' Roddy said finally.

Twenty pounds! 'I'll take it for ten, Roddy,' she said firmly.

Roddy removed his cap and scratched at the sparse hairs on his head, 'Well, then, ten pounds it is.'

'Good.' Jamie pushed back his chair. 'Can we go now, Mum, please?'

'Where are you away to in such a hurry?'

'Jamie wants to see the bear,' Letty said apologetically.

'Oh, aye? Too late for that, lad. He's gone.'

'Oh no.' Jamie sank unhappily back into his chair. 'Are you positive?'

'Aye, it was last night I had news of it.' Roddy noisily slurped at his cold tea. 'He's escaped, run off . . . Frightened poor Fergus McKenzie to death. I'm surprised you've not heard!' Roddy said with satisfaction. 'Why, the beast's been loose on the island these many few days.'

Bonn, West Germany, 1979

Disappointment. That was the best the investigative powers of MI6 and the British government came up with. Nicky Fleming, disgruntled employee, passed over for promotion, had sought revenge on his country by filtering some as-yet-undiscovered information to an as-yet-undiscovered source. Unable to live with the guilt, he had confessed to his wife in a 'suicide note' and cast himself from the embassy roof. Simple. Tidy. Case closed.

There was one flaw in the in-house trial of Nicky Fleming: that he was guilty was accepted as fact, but of what, no one was sure. No documents had been discovered missing; there was no sign of files having been copied;

evidence of an affair was not forthcoming. Nothing seemed out of place, except, of course, Nicky Fleming himself, dead on the unforgiving ground. The investigation was as thorough as it was useless and, by the end of it, there were still no more answers.

'They can't leave it like this, Tom, they can't.' Letty paced the kitchen. 'You know him better than anyone. You know he wasn't capable.'

'Of course not.' Tom spread his hands in a gesture of helpless sympathy, but in the weeks following Nicky's death, Letty had become expert at picking up on the nuances of people's tones. Tom was the last person from whom she would expect it—nevertheless, it had been there, the faintest hesitation in his answer. She looked at him intently. 'Make them dig deeper, Tom,' she said. 'Make them keep the file open until his name is cleared.'

And there it was again. A flicker.

'Tom?'

'Let it rest, Letty, maybe it's for the best.'

'For the best! Dear God, how can it be for the best when everyone believes Nicky's a traitor?'

Tom was silent.

'You don't believe in him, do you?' Her voice began to rise.

'Letty, you must understand how ruthless the machinery of government can be . . . Nobody's life can stand up to this much scrutiny. I've seen it before. They grind you down until there is nothing left.'

'You don't believe in him,' she said hollowly. 'I can see it in your eyes.'

'Letty.' He gripped her arm.

'No, don't touch me.' She slumped in a chair and covered her face with her hands. 'How could you?' she whispered. 'You, of all people.' Letty lifted her head. 'Protecting your position, Tom?'

'That's not fair.'

'Then what is it? Tell me, goddamnit!'

'All right, Letty, all right.' He sat down heavily. 'Look, about nine months ago, Nicky and I had lunch at the Travellers Club. He told me he'd come into contact with someone. Someone he needed to help.'

'What do you mean? Who, where?'

'East Berlin. I don't know who. He asked only whether he could count on my help.'

'So what did you tell him?'

'That I couldn't possibly evaluate what he was asking out of context but that it was insanity to be involved in anything underhand, particularly in East Berlin. I told him he must talk to the Ambassador, go through the official channels.'

'You turned him down?' she said incredulously.

'Try to understand, Letty. A man in Nicky's position is particularly vulnerable. He would have to assume that anybody with whom he came into contact would likely be an informant or a potential plant. You have no idea the internal soul-searching that goes on in assessing the risk factor of any chance meeting, let alone one in the German Democratic Republic. For Nicky to become entangled with someone in East Berlin would mean going against all his instincts, all his training.'

'So why would you think him capable of such a thing? Why are you convinced it was underhand?'

'Because, had it been above board, there would have been no reason to ask for my help.' Tom stared unseeingly at the table. 'You think I haven't turned it over and over since? Letty . . .'

'You can never truly know someone, can you? You never know who your friends are until you really need them.' She watched Tom flinch. 'Nicky was your recruit.' She was glaring at him now, her eyes brimming with misery. If Nicky was under suspicion then why not Tom, who had been so closely involved in Nicky's career? Tom travelled often to Berlin. If Tom had crossed any lines, then how expedient for blame to be laid at Nicky's door. 'Is there a reason it suits you to distance yourself from him now?' she accused.

Tom pushed back from the table. 'Don't lecture me about loyalty or friendship,' he said bitterly. 'I have been a better friend to Nicky than you will ever understand.'

'No. You betrayed him, you betrayed us both.' She was in the grip of some kind of madness, and it felt so good to vent her own anger.

'You talk about knowing someone. Well, you're right,' Tom flung back at her. 'Nicky loved you with all his heart, but he has never been the man you thought he was.'

'How *dare* you.' She rose and slapped him in one swift movement. 'How dare you try to poison me against him. He was a better man than you'll ever be. I know one thing about my husband—you were his closest friend and he would have taken a bullet for you.'

Her hand was still raised when he caught her wrist. 'It doesn't matter about me, Letty. Hold on to what you believe. That's all that's important.'

Ballanish, Outer Hebrides, Summer 1979

'There's something wrong with my heart,' Jamie announced, skipping along the sandy path behind his sisters. He clutched his chest solemnly. 'Sometimes I feel the wind blowing right through it.'

'Then zip up your jacket, stupid,' Alba said, 'and don't fall behind.'

Jamie skipped faster. In spite of the ache in his chest, he felt cheerier than he had done in weeks. Fate could not have stuck its nose in his business in a more obliging way. Now he could search for the bear and keep a lookout for his father at the same time.

He touched the bottle in his pocket. He'd already launched three maps from different points on the island, not including the one he'd dropped over the side of the ferry. If his luck held, maps in glass bottles would soon be bobbing on the ocean towards every corner of the globe.

'I say we do this methodically.' Georgie squinted towards the sea. 'A different beach each day. It's bound to be in hiding. So we'll have to track it.'

'Like check for footprints or poo?'

'Splendid idea, Jamie.' Alba grabbed her brother and pushed his head towards the acidic splatter of a cowpat. 'Is this bear poo, Holmes? Is it? Is it? Take a sniff and tell us, why don't you?'

'I think this is cow poo,' Jamie offered nervously. He calculated the odds were low that his face might end up actually immersed in the steaming mass, but Alba's unpredictability was unnerving.

At the penultimate moment, she released him with an amiable ear twist. 'Cows are utterly disgusting,' she declared.

'I thought you liked them.' Jamie moved discreetly to Georgie's side and took her hand. 'What about the Ambassadress?'

'The Ambassadress is different. This lot are a bunch of Nazis. Look, why are they standing in a circle? Do you think they have a plan?'

'There's no plan,' Georgie sighed. 'They're cows.'

'I don't like the way they're rounding us up. Get away, you herd of hamburgers. Shoo!'

Jamie giggled. When Alba was in a good mood the sun shone into every dark corner of his world.

'By the way,' she mused, 'it's far more likely the bear will be tracking us rather than the other way round.'

'Why would it track us?'

'We're food, idiot.'

'The bear doesn't eat people. It eats steak.'

'A human can't get a steak on this island, let alone a bear.'

'It could eat fish.'

'It doesn't know how to catch fish. It's a tame bear. It doesn't know how to do anything but wrestle. I'm telling you, when it gets hungry enough, it will track down the smelliest, most putrid thing on the island—you, Jamie—and then bingo, it will leap out from behind a rock.'

'But I want it to leap out from behind a rock. The bear won't eat me.'

'It'll eat you if it gets hungry enough. I'd eat you if I was hungry enough. I'd eat you even if I wasn't hungry—just to get rid of you.'

A bird was skimming low over the reeds. Distracted, Jamie followed it with the binoculars. 'Is that a curlew, Alba?'

'How the holy hell should I know? What's more, I don't care. Birds are pointless.'

'No, they're not.'

'Jamie, you don't think you're pointless but that doesn't mean you aren't.'

'But I need to know for my bird book.'

'Why, so you can mark down that you've seen a curlew? How thrilling. Are you going to shoot the curlew and eat it? Are you going to adopt it or convert it to Christianity? The question you have to ask yourself is—will identifying this bird change your life in any way, and if the answer is no, then I think we can all agree that birdwatching is a pathetic hobby.'

'To you,' Jamie said with uncharacteristic spirit, 'but not to me. Can't you think about me for once?'

'Jamie, *you* think about you the whole time. If I were to think about you as well, it might create a dangerous imbalance in the universe.'

'It couldn't do that. Thinking doesn't weigh anything.'

'Fine, smarty-pants.' Alba snatched the binoculars from him and aimed them at the sky. 'Yup, it's a curlew.' She turned the glasses sideways and machine-gunned the bird. 'And now it's a dead curlew. Oh, dearie me.'

Jamie giggled. 'I love you, Alba.' He moved to hug her but she pushed him away. He looked momentarily defeated, then ran to catch up with Georgie.

'Hey, there's someone on the beach,' he heard his older sister shout.

'What?' Alba ran to the top of the dune. Below them, a man and a woman were hovering over a small child who was troughing into a wet channel of sand with a plastic spade.

'Tourist pig dogs!' Alba narrowed her eyes. 'A pox on them!'

'Should we go and say hello?' Jamie said hopefully.

'No, they might think we're friendly.'

'Aren't we friendly?'

'No, we are not. In fact, I'm going to get rid of them.'

'Alba, wait!' Georgie called, but Alba was already zigzagging down the dunes waving her arms at the small family. The couple looked up.

'I'm sorry'—Alba stopped, panting, in front of them—'but I had to warn you. You mustn't let your child play on this beach.'

The couple stared at her. 'Why on earth not?' asked the mother.

'Jellyfish.' Alba made a gesture designed to take in not only the entire length of beach, but most of the island, too. 'They're poisonous this year.'

'Poisonous!' The couple exchanged a look. 'In Scotland?'

'Yes, I know, that's what we thought, but my beloved little brother Jamie . . .' she hung her head. 'Well, he was stung a few months ago. The jellyfish were only small, normal looking. No one knew . . . no one could have known.' She broke off and began wailing. The couple were taking no chances. Hurriedly, they scooped up the toddler and thrust a tissue at Alba.

'Sweetheart,' the woman said, her own eyes brimming. She glanced desperately up and down the beach. 'Are you all right? Are your parents with you?'

'My mother's at home and my father . . . well, the thing about my father,' Alba continued in a tiny voice, 'is that he's dead too.'

The couple reeled back in unison.

A recently deceased parent had its uses, Alba had discovered. The merest reminder of her father's accident was enough to silence most people and a particularly stricken look that she'd developed had saved her from school detention on numerous occasions. Even the manner of her father's death could be adapted to suit every eventuality. Over the past six months, she'd had him murdered, executed by the Red Army and falling out of a plane. These fabricated stories were, Alba found, easier to believe than the truth.

'How could he have fallen?' she had shouted hysterically that terrible night when Letty had first told her the news. 'People don't just fall.'

Letty had hugged her close, crying herself. 'It was an accident, darling, no one's fault, just a terrible, terrible tragedy.'

As time went on she picked up on an undercurrent, a certain fear and reluctance on the part of her mother to explain. And not only her mother.

'What do you mean, they want to see you at the embassy?' she'd demanded of her sister.

'They just do.'

'There has to be a reason. They're sending a car for you.'

Georgie had shrugged. 'They want to know about Berlin.'

'Berlin?' Alba said indignantly. 'Did something *happen* in Berlin?' It was bad enough she hadn't been allowed to go herself, but the idea that something noteworthy had occurred there was too much to bear and when Alba caught the hesitation in her sister's answer, it sent a sharp signal to her brain—information was being kept from her.

The woman on the beach now clutched Alba to her breast and grasped her husband's arm for comfort. 'Oh, you poor girl. Look, we have a car. Can we take you somewhere? Why don't we drive you home?'

Alba had intended to round off the encounter with a theatrical blow of her nose, but suddenly her real feelings converged with her fake ones and she felt tears welling up. She shook her head and waved them away.

The thing was, some days it was all she thought about: how and why her father had died. One day he had been a man with a job to go to, a family to love and a set of ethics to live by. The next moment, he was gone.

'That was quick.' Georgie was always appalled by, yet at the same time secretly admiring of her younger sister's behaviour. 'Did you tell them there was a grizzly loose on the island?'

'A grizzly?' Alba quickly swiped the tears from her eyes. 'Don't be ridiculous, Georgie, they'd never have believed that.'

East Berlin, East Germany, December 1978

The trip had taken place the month before her father died. It was the first time Nicky Fleming had ever taken any of his children away with him on business and Georgie experienced a degree of smugness at being the chosen one—a smugness that grew after Alba became inconsolable on discovering she was not to be invited. But then Alba did not boast her elder sister's credentials. On August 13, 1961, at the precise moment that armed military units of the GDR sealed East Berlin from the rest of the world and began construction of the wall, Georgiana Gisela Fleming was speeding through the underpass of her mother's womb towards a freshly changed hospital bed in St Thomas' Hospital, London.

Despite the shared birthday, Georgie had initially had little enthusiasm for the subject, and had feigned an interest with the sole purpose of impressing her father. There were almost always references to East Berlin in the *General-Anzeiger Bonn*—snippets for her to latch on to during those agonising newspaper trials on the chaise longue. But, in the end, it had been the Wall itself, with its electric fences and creepy observation towers, that had caught her imagination. She had found herself devouring stories of houses cut in two, of families leaping from the window of one country to the soil of another. Bonn was full of refugees who had fled East Germany—her own grandmother, Gisela, had been one of them. By the time Georgie turned fourteen, the Wall had become for her the very embodiment of danger and romance and she declared herself desperate to see it.

'One day,' her father had said. 'Maybe when you're seventeen and beginning to get some lefty ideas,' he'd joked. 'Perhaps then I'll take you.'

'Promise?' She watched him hesitate, weighing up the commitment.

'Yes, all right. I promise.'

It was the first and only time she thought he might break his word. But she was holding a trump card, in the form of a written IOU posted in her promise box, and eventually she played it.

'A most unusual request,' the head of the delegation declared when Nicky had applied for permission, but a concession was made. Georgie had been ecstatic. East Berlin was West Berlin's evil twin and she was to go there for real. She was to lay flowers on her great-grandfather's grave, spend solo time with her father—and Alba's tears be damned.

THE FIRST THING that struck her about East Berlin was the fine yellow dust hanging in the air and the phosphorous smell that accompanied it.

'Lignite,' her father said as she wrinkled her nose. 'It's why car engines here are so noisy. That little Wartburg, for instance,' he said as a tin can of a taxi heaved alongside them emitting a succession of scatological explosions from its exhaust, 'is definitely running on lignite.'

'Why do they use it, if it smells so bad?'

'Because East Germany is rich in the stuff and they're not allowed to import oil. In fact they're not allowed to import coffee, fruit or anything. That's why we filled up the Peugeot on the other side.'

Her father almost always flew to Berlin, but at the last minute he'd changed his mind. 'A road trip will be more interesting. We'll make it fun.'

As a teenager, Georgie had yet to appreciate the romance of a 'road trip'. Nevertheless, she had loved having her father to herself and on the journey he'd chatted and joked, somehow managing, in the process, to impart a folder full of information. Did she know that one in every six citizens was an informant? That hotels and taxis were uniformly bugged? That there existed a mortuary garage at one of the checkpoints where coffins were searched to confirm the occupants were truly dead?

As they'd approached the border, the atmosphere had changed. Georgie had watched her passport travelling along a conveyor belt towards the processing building and had experienced a strong urge to snatch it back and run. The police manning the border area looked like prototypes for humans before God had breathed heart and compassion into their souls. The whole process had taken for ever.

When finally they'd been reunited with their papers and allowed to continue on their way, her father had grinned at her. 'So, how was it, your first experience of totalitarianism?'

Georgie had shrugged. Just before the trip, a rogue thought had crept into her head. Was the Cold War, this eternal battle where nothing appeared to happen and nobody took up arms, really so awful? But that was before she'd seen the wall. It was the *Grenzmauer*, her father told her, the third wall, a new and improved version consisting of 45,000 sections of reinforced concrete bordering the raked gravel of the 'death strip'—a sheer unscalable monument to fear.

She'd told Norrell and Porter about it, when they'd questioned her.

'You do not tell my daughter about the letter,' Letty had said to the two men beforehand. 'If you so much as put the idea of suicide in her head, I will come after you with everything I've got left—and please don't underestimate what that is.' It had been a bluff, of course. She had nothing left, but for the first time she had glimpsed a modicum of respect in their eyes.

It had not occurred to Letty that Georgie had anything to say to MI6 about her trip to East Germany. It had not occurred to Georgie either, but sitting at the table, facing Norrell and Porter, it was easy to imagine herself back there. In East Berlin she had felt under the same scrutiny—from the fish-eyed stare of the blue-uniformed People's Police, the *Volkspolizei*, or Vopos, for short; from the guards staring down from their watchtowers. Even on the road home, she had been unable to shake the feeling that someone was watching them, listening to them.

Porter had directed the questioning. Who had her father met? Had there been contact with anyone outside the convention? A chance encounter on the street? Georgie had responded with the polite minimum. She told how her father had checked them into the drab, state-owned Interhotel. How the next morning, at the meeting of delegations, she'd been left to read her book in Room IV of some government headquarters. How the Peugeot had broken down and been towed to a garage . . .

'Torsten was the only person my father met up with,' she told Porter.

Torsten was her father's friend on the delegation, a pleasant-looking man, with brown curly hair and an intermittent stutter. The conversation had been as interesting as watching sand trickle through an egg timer. Georgie read one chapter while Torsten and Nicky reminisced about a convention where they had originally met, and a second chapter while they worked their way through the banalities of their respective lives in Stockholm and Bonn. Nicky, noticing his daughter was restless, tapped the cover of her book with his pen. 'You realise we're being watched, don't you?' he whispered.

Georgie looked up.

'Ever since we sat down.'

'Really?' she said doubtfully. She knew her father well enough to suspect she was being set up.

'Trust no one,' he winked. 'They're all watching you.'

'Who?'

'Stasi.'

Instinctively, Georgie hunched behind her book. 'How do you know?'

'That's one there.' Her father tilted his head towards an ordinary-looking individual sitting at a nearby table. 'Another there.'

Georgie peered through to the reception area, where a man standing under an exit sign was attempting to straighten a map. 'They don't look like policemen,' she said uncertainly.

'Stasi are chameleons,' Torsten said. 'They understand how to blend in.'

'So how can you tell?'

'Oh, after a while, you get a nose for them,' he said airily.

'We've been under observation since the moment we arrived in Berlin,' her father said. 'Today, a precise record will have been made of what Torsten is wearing, right down to his rather dubious choice of footwear.'

Torsten smiled the weary smile of a foreigner acknowledging himself to be the butt of an English joke.

Georgie looked at the Swede's muddy-coloured nylon jumper, his khaki knit tie and orange shoes. If he had dressed to blend in, then fashion in East

Germany was more woefully behind the times than she'd thought.

'The fact that we are here in this restaurant will have been logged, along with a record of exactly what we chose to eat. I, for instance, took milk in my coffee. You've been reading Thomas Hardy. All this information will be stored in a file, which, later on, some official will study and analyse.'

'But why do they care?'

'Guess.' Her father's eyes flickered almost imperceptibly towards Torsten and Georgie felt her pulse quicken.

'Really,' she breathed. She turned to him. 'You are?'

Torsten put a finger to his lips and glanced meaningfully at her school notebook, lying on the table.

Georgie snatched up her pen. *Are you a spy?* she scribbled. Then, fully expecting Torsten to laugh at her, she blushed.

'Almost everyone else in East Berlin is one,' he said. 'I, however, am a nuclear physicist.'

Ballanish, Outer Hebrides, Summer 1979

Doubt was a tenacious emotion and Letty found it increasingly hard to judge which memories were real. On good days, she held on to what she believed—that the man she had loved was no liar, never a traitor. On bad days, the weight of her grief simply rolled over her. She had no appetite, barely spoke to the children. Suspicions about Nicky loomed, plausible, unanswerable. *He has never been the man you thought he was*, Tom had told her . . . If Tom was capable of turning his back on his oldest friend, then what might Nicky have been capable of?

'Marry me, and we'll travel the world,' Nicky had said when he'd proposed, and she had seen herself working tirelessly by his side, building dams, administering vaccines. She had fallen for the idea of a love binding them together through passion and adversity, and was ready to bear anything diplomatic life threw at her.

Their first posting, Liberia, for all its overpowering heat, poverty and Third World bureaucracy, had been the place she'd been happiest.

There had been nothing romantic about Bonn's suburban spires and provincial formality. Diplomatic life there was about entertaining at every level and Letty constantly had to watch what she said and work on her formalities. There were endless dinners to attend, back-to-back functions to grace. The dress code frustrated her. Always a brooch to be pinned onto a jacket, shoes to be matched to a dress. Even her hair required taming into diplomatic sobriety. She found the number of engagements exhausting and the adherence to rules a torture.

In the beginning she tried pleading childcare as an excuse.

'I'm afraid it's just not done,' the Ambassadress informed her quietly.

'Heartless old ogress,' she said to Nicky. 'I think the children might actually be dying before she gives me the right to refuse.'

'Go on strike,' Nicky said. 'Everyone else does these days.'

Much as she was taken with the idea, Letty knew there was no place for a conscientious objector in embassy life. As the wife of the First Secretary and then the Counsellor, she had signed up for certain duties. At functions she soon learned she was required to draw the fire of the lesser guests, to laugh at their least amusing anecdotes, to free the Ambassadress for those who had something relevant to say. 'My role is to be the filter through which the uninteresting and the unimportant must not be allowed to pass,' she said to Nicky one evening.

'You're far too clever and beautiful to be allowed near anyone interesting. Gillian feels threatened by you—all the wives do, for that matter.'

'I don't know about that, but I swear to God there isn't anyone less suited to the job,' she said ruefully. 'Conversationally, I have the knack of making a sow's ear out of a silk purse.'

'Rubbish, you charm everyone and, what's more, you know it.'

'No.' She kissed him. 'But as long as I charm you, who cares?' She sighed. 'I miss Liberia.'

'I know you do.' He took her in his arms. 'The problem with Bonn is that its two principal industries are spying and *Gummibär* confectionery. There isn't much in between.'

The rest of the wives were a Stasi of well-turned-out women who operated in a strict hierarchy according to the seniority of their husbands. They kept each other under constant surveillance and were never short of advice, solicited or not. Letty's distaste for gossip prevented her indulging in the fruits of the intelligence grapevine. From time to time there would be 'big' news: a divorce, someone who had cracked under the pressure. So-and-so's wife might be described as 'a bit unsafe'. 'She wasn't one of us,' the whispers went. 'She wasn't . . . diplomatic.' These sorts of utterances were too close to the bone for Letty and so she kept her own counsel.

The problem was that if you weren't inside the circle, you were outside, and so Letty had no way of knowing that the other women had begun to whisper about her, and the softest whisper of all was that Nicky Fleming might never make Ambassador—because of his wife.

Outer Hebrides, Summer 1979

Hunger made the bear leaner and fitter with every passing day. He swam for miles, from one stretch of coast to another, through shoals of shrimp and schools of minnows, their backs tattooed with silver. When he returned to the cave it was not the thought of the big wrestler that soothed him. It was the map. He would stare at the red arrows, at the misspelt words and badly drawn letters. The markings of language that looked so foreign, yet at the same time so achingly familiar.

Eventually, the thought came to him—his time was finite and he was wasting it. What he was looking for was not to be found there. So he left the cave one night, when visibility was grainy and uncertain. Barely a kick and a splash away was a grand curve of a beach overlooked by high dunes that led to a machair, an immense, sanded prairie blanketed in wild flowers. From there, he explored the island, taking each point of the compass in turn. But it was to the west that he kept returning, the west with its seductive loneliness, the iridescent turquoise and emeralds of its bays, and those startling bleached-bone sands. And wherever he went, he searched . . .

THE KETTLE WAS A NICKNAME for a deep ravine in the Scolpaig cliffs, a couple of hundred feet inland from the sea. Some topographical quirk made this enormous gash in the earth invisible from a distance and a person not paying attention to where they were going might easily find himself dropping into the abyss before realising that land and luck had run out.

The sides of the Kettle were sheer, but there was a way down. Bisecting the ravine was a narrow slope, on wet days as lethal as the Cresta Run. The children, of course, were forbidden to attempt it, but Nicky had once made the descent using clumps of tough grass as hand-holds. At the bottom, he had discovered a cave. There was also a tunnel through which, during a storm or spring tide, the sea 'boiled', churning round the walls with such centrifugal force that it shot a frothy spray 100 feet up through the Kettle's 'spout', covering those lying at the top in thick, yellowing foam.

It was dead low tide by the time the children reached Scolpaig and so the Kettle bottom was dry, save for the odd rock pool filled with green slime. Georgie and Jamie lay on their stomachs, a big Ordnance Survey map spread between them.

'You know what they should build here?' Alba rested her chin in her hands and gazed out to sea. 'A high-security prison. It's the perfect place. We're on an island in the middle of the Atlantic with no way off.'

'Except a ferry and a causeway and a plane once a week to Glasgow,' Georgie commented.

'The causeway leads to another island, so that's a dead end, and convicts aren't allowed to catch ferries or planes. Then the Minch is lethal to swimmers. It's like the Bermuda Triangle of the British Isles. There's no escape. We're stuck here for life with no parole and no visiting hours.'

'Perfect place for you, then,' Georgie said. 'Hey, look how clear St Kilda is.'

'Which is St Kilda?' Jamie asked.

'The one shaped like a witch's hat.' Georgie pointed at a shadow of land out to sea. 'Where the cliff game came from.'

Jamie squinted at the horizon. The cliff game was a form of Russian roulette Alba had devised for playing when a gale blew at force eight or higher. They would all stand round the top of the Kettle, backs to the wind, then, on a countdown from three, lean back and allow the wind to support their weight. If it did, they would step a few inches closer to the edge and try again until someone chickened out. The game filled Jamie with equal measures of excitement and dread. To be allowed to join in was an honour, a chance to earn Alba's respect, but he could never help wondering—what of those split seconds between gusts? What would it feel like to fall?

'If a St Kildan man wanted to get married,' Alba said, 'they made him stand on the edge of a cliff on one leg to prove he could support a wife.'

'But what happened if he fell?'

'Bad luck on him,' Alba said, chewing her hair.

'What happened if he didn't fall?'

'Then it was wedding bells and gannet pie for the rest of their lives.'

'But they can't only have eaten gannet pie.'

Alba lined up a row of sheep pellets and flicked them off the edge one by one. 'Of course not. For breakfast they had porridge with boiled puffin in it. For lunch they scrambled a few baby fulmars and they tore the feet off gannets and made jam out of them for tea.'

'That's horrid.' Jamie's brain flashed him an image of the head and shoulders of a puffin staring accusingly at him. 'Why don't we send them food?'

'Nobody lives there any more. They were evacuated. They asked the government to help them leave the island, although they didn't all want to go,' Georgie explained.

'It's pathetic,' Alba said. 'I would have refused to be pushed around.'

'Well, you're the only one of us brave enough to,' Georgie said generously. 'Alba's been to St Kilda, Jamie; don't you remember?'

'And bloody awful it was, too,' Alba said.

The summer of her eleventh birthday, Alisdair, the fisherman, had offered to take her fishing and Alba had been so excited that Letty had agreed.

'So what was it like?' Jamie said now.

Alba shrugged. 'The island is one massive rock. Underneath one of the cliffs there are about a billion gannets nesting. We only stayed a minute because we had to go fishing, although, honestly, I wish we had stayed as the fishing was awful. I was so miserable.'

'You didn't drown?' Jamie said.

'No, village idiot, as you can see, I didn't drown.'

'Did you cry?'

'Yes.'

'Would you cry again?'

'No. I don't cry any more.' Alba shrugged again. 'I can't imagine anything that would make me cry.'

She looked away and Jamie, sensing the abrupt change of mood, leapt to his feet. 'Come on, let's play the cliff game now.'

'It's not windy enough,' Georgie said quickly.

'One go.'

'No.'

'Why?'

'Because we say so,' Alba said. 'Now shut up and sit down.'

But Jamie was already spreading his arms. 'Tell me when.' He took a step backwards. Alba seized his arm and yanked him down to the ground. 'Stoppit. You do as you're told, Jamie Fleming,' she said, gritting her teeth in sudden fury. 'Do you understand? You do as you're bloody well told!'

LETTY FOUND THE CANVAS sorting through a packing crate full of long-forgotten rubbish—old fishing flies, dried-up paint tubes, kites with knotted strings. The painting was at the bottom, wrapped inside a plastic bag. The subject matter, the soaring white statue of Our Lady of the Isles, was set against a backdrop of radar domes—the missile firing-range at Gebraith. The strangely bright colours of the picture bore no relation to the weather on the washed-out, monotone afternoon when she and Nicky had made the trip to the statue years ago. Alba had been small enough to be carried on her father's shoulders and they'd decided to catch the ferry from Oban to Loch Baghasdail, driving up to the north of the island from the toe of the south.

When the white statue had come into view, Nicky had pulled the car into a passing place. 'That's it, isn't it?' he'd asked. 'Our Lady of the Isles. That's where the missile firing-range is.'

'Yes,' she had said shortly.

He'd switched off the engine. 'Let's walk up. I've never seen it close up.'

In the late 1940s, the Ministry of Defence had announced its intention to build an army training base and rocket range at Gebraith. Initially the proposal was greeted with enthusiasm—jobs were scarce on the island—but everything changed once the islanders got wind of the sheer scale of the plans, which required the 'relocating' of every islander in their way.

The most impassioned critic had been the local minister, who had stirred up enough support to commission the building of a twenty-five-foot statue on a hill directly overlooking the intended military site—as a godly act of defiance. The literature on Our Lady of the Isles described it as the 'Protector of the Gael'. Eight months after the statue's completion, the Ministry of Defence revealed a massive scale-down of their plans. Even so, the range they had built was an aberration. Giant twin golf balls perched on the hill, dwarfed by a radio mast. The very sight of it made Letty feel ill.

'First they appropriate St Kilda,' she'd fumed that day, struggling to pull Georgie up the hill behind Nicky and Alba, 'next they go ahead and build this monstrosity. And do you know what they promised the locals? That during the lambing season, "the use of the rocket firing-range will be kept to a minimum", thank you very much. It's so arrogant! I can't stand the way the MoD treats the Highlands and Islands like their playground. They only got away with it because they think the islanders are an easy touch.'

'You can't object to progress just because it doesn't suit your romanticised idea of how this island should be preserved,' Nicky had said mildly. 'If it were up to you, no one up here would ever be allowed to join the twentieth century. People have to live and work and the range provides much-needed jobs.'

Letty had bitten her tongue. It was the very insularity of the island, its lack of ambition and blanket rejection of outsiders that had allowed it to remain a strange, closed world—and she knew that she, too, was an outsider, just as her father had been. The unintended consequence that came with their class and money meant, by definition, that they were themselves destroying the island by being part of it.

'If you think that a missile firing-range is suitable employment for the islanders, then it shows you have no understanding of the kind of people who live here,' she'd said tightly.

'Or maybe you're as guilty of underestimating their intelligence as the MoD,' Nicky had retorted.

'It's no use arguing with you,' she'd said resentfully. 'You won't hear anything negative about your precious government.'

'It's your precious government too, Letty,' he'd reminded her gently. 'Don't forget that. You seem to have an innate distrust of your own country.'

'And you don't? With everything you know about their methods?'

'No,' he'd said quietly. 'I don't. I couldn't very well do my job if I did.'

They had not spoken again until they'd arrived at Ballanish.

'Try to understand,' she'd told him later, 'this island is my sanctuary. It's where I belong, it's where I feel the possibility of hope and faith, and every morning when I look out of the window I fall in love with it all over again.'

Now, Letty stared at the canvas, perplexed at the almost luridly bright blues and purples. Why had Nicky painted it and when? She turned the picture over. It was finished at the back with brown paper stretched across the wooden frame. *CO-60, NI-60, MG-137*. She squinted at what she presumed to be colour-codings that Nicky had written in one corner, and tried to match them to the tubes of old paint in the crate. Then, with a stubborn determination to find an answer to something, anything, she tried to match them to every other tube of paint she could find in the house—but none of the reference numbers came close. She stared at them, waiting for meaning of some kind to come to her, but nothing did. Cobalt, nickel, magenta. Blues, silvers, purples. Sky, sea, heather. They were the colours of the island, that's all.

I paint things to study them, she could hear Nicky saying as she took the canvas to the kitchen table and set it down. *To understand how they work.*

Suddenly—out of nowhere as she was thinking this—the word appeared in her mind. *Schyndell.* The power plant in East Germany.

She sat down abruptly. There was no reason to make a connection, and yet . . . Schyndell. *A little coincidental*, Porter had said. *A little convenient, don't you think?*

She tried to think back. Had Nicky applied to be part of the delegation, or had it been the other way round?

It was when she turned the canvas over again that she heard it—an almost imperceptible noise of paper sliding against paper. Nicky's paintings were crudely framed affairs, with the raw edges of the canvas stapled straight to the wood. She stared at the double thickness of brown backing paper, punctured the corner of it and ripped it away. A white envelope fell out. On the front was a single sentence written in Nicky's tidy script: *Everything and every event is pervaded by the Grace of God.*

She read the line twice, uncomprehendingly, then she turned the bulky envelope over and slit the flap.

Outer Hebrides, Summer 1979

An 800-pound grizzly with the run of a Hebridean island was a rare occurrence, and teatime most days found Donald John's small kitchen bulging with visitors all engaged in the island's most popular pastime: gossip. Weeks had passed since the flight of the bear and the excitement was beginning to die down. Nevertheless, when Jamie walked in, he found Peggy from the shop, Roddy and elderly Mrs Matheson, all deep in speculation about the animal's fate.

'If it isn't wee Jamie,' Mrs Matheson broke off. 'Why, many's the long day since we've seen you!' She grasped Jamie's thin hands in her own complicated, knotted ones, then continued her story as Jamie ran the gauntlet of head pats before squeezing himself next to Roddy on the bench. 'Aye, everyone's after the thousand-pound reward that's being offered,' she said. 'The army have got aerial photographs, helicopters and the whatnot, why, they've even got the coastguards in Skye looking for him.'

'Tse, so much fuss about that beast still.' Donald John produced a bottle of Cherry Coke for Jamie. 'He'll have gone over a cliff long before now.'

'No, he won't,' Jamie said. It made him furious when people said the bear was dead. The bear was huge, one of the largest of all land carnivores, his father had told him. Nothing on the island could threaten it. If all the cows and bulls ganged up and head-butted it together, the bear would still be stronger. As for the idea that he'd fallen off a cliff—bears weren't stupid! They didn't trip over their claws. Bears lived in Russia and in Canada. They were used to cliffs.

He didn't care that Georgie and Alba had given up. He had devised his own system for searching. The Kettle was his headquarters. He wasn't sure why but he was drawn back there again and again, and from the top of the cliffs he could see all the way to the road and up to the heathery tip of Clannach beyond. Way in the distance, he could make out Donald John's croft and even the yellow gate of Ballanish. If the bear went in any direction, he would see it. If his father walked down the road to Ballanish, well, he would see him too . . .

In the last couple of weeks, Jamie's doubts had resurfaced. Despite his father's promise, despite all the prayers and the maps he'd put into bottles and tossed off the rocks, his father had still not returned. Slowly, the dark truth had come to him: no one was looking for his father any more. And now people had given up looking for the bear. He stared balefully round the room. Why was he the only person who believed in anything? Did faith and optimism disappear when you grew up? His father was still lost—just as the bear was still lost—and he, Jamie, would find them both.

'The beast isn't in Skye and he's no' dead either,' Roddy said, rubbing at the bags under his eyes. 'Why, only the other evening, I was listening to the wireless when I heard noises. It was a stormy night, right enough, but I went outside and there in front of me I saw the red eyes of the bear glowing in the dark. Ach, a terrible sight! Why, if I'd only had a pitchfork to hand,' Roddy sighed, 'that reward would have been mine.'

'Maybe you should go out and look for it, Donald John,' Jamie said. 'You could get the reward.'

'Oh, boo boo, it would take a lot to tackle that bear.'

'The wrestler fights it all the time.'

'Aye, the wrestler can put that beast down all right, but he's a hardy man. Why, he's been out on the hills every day in the wind and the rain dressed in nothing more than his wrestling boots and trunks.'

'That's right,' Mrs Matheson said. 'Quite bare-chested. It's a wonder he hasn't taken a terrible chill.' She levered herself slowly to her feet. 'I must away, Donald John.'

'Right you are, then. Bye for now.' He helped her to the door.

'Come on, Donald John,' Jamie said, following. 'Can you and me take the tractor and go now?'

'Ach, let it be. I'm not gallivanting round the island looking for a bear. If he's not dead, he'll be in hiding and I'm quite sure he's very hungry by now.' He shook his head vigorously. 'Why, if that beast turns renegade, it could be the end of us.'

TWO SMALL PHOTOGRAPHS had dropped out of the white envelope hidden behind the painting. Two passport-sized photos—stamps of treason—along with East German ID papers.

Mechanically, Letty now stirred split pea and ham soup in the kitchen. Whose was the blank face that stared out at her, and what did he represent? A trap? A double agent? Had Nicky owed him or needed him?

'Go and put out the flag for Alick,' she heard Alba ordering Jamie, and she identified the edge of claustrophobia in her daughter's voice.

The children were defeated and listless and Letty couldn't blame them. It was nearly three weeks since the bear had run off and everyone was in agreement: the beast was dead. He had drowned in the bogs or been carried out to sea and, despite the offer of £1,000, most people had stopped caring. The children had seen nothing in their searches. And now there was nothing to fill their days except bickering and carping.

Summers had been so easy when they had been small. They'd all potter round the house in the morning, then after lunch there would be an outing—dune jumping, digging for razor clams, a game of boules on the beach with washed-up lobster floats. If the weather was bad, they'd head to the tweed shop, or brave the cliffs of Scolpaig to look for colonies of seals. Afterwards they'd drive home, the smell of damp wool settling around them, while Nicky wiped the rain off his face with one hand and negotiated the serpentine road with the other.

'Do concentrate, Nicky,' she'd say, 'and try not to hit that nice boy on a bicycle. You could drive a tiny bit slower, maybe?'

And Nicky would turn round to the children in the back seat: 'On and on she goes, your mother. Never stops grumbling, it's quite extraordinary. You'd think there was actually something wrong with her life, the way she goes on.' Then he would smile secretly at Letty and take her hand in his.

Letty caught a rogue tear with her sleeve. She had to get through this, she had to, but how, when it was all spinning perpetually round her head? The painting, the missile firing-range, the bleached-out face in the photographs . . . Why hadn't Nicky confided in her? When had they stopped talking? She was certain now that he had done something wrong and the knowledge felt like a rock in her throat.

Tom had rung twice in the last month, each time getting one of the children to fetch her urgently, but she had refused to come to the phone. What was she to say? Fear, suspicion, pride, loyalty, shame . . . She no longer knew what emotion was driving her. The feeling of unreality that accompanied her day and night had grown so strong that she thought it was amazing she still existed at all. Maybe this was why her children no longer responded to her. She had become invisible.

She stole a look at them. Georgie, pale as a piece of silk, her head in a book; Jamie, hunched in his woolly jumper. Alba, prowling the room like a caged tiger. The truth hit Letty like a body blow—this might be her home, but it was not *theirs*. Bonn was their home—Bonn, where their schools were, where their friends lived. The island offered them a summer holiday. Now it was the place where they were forced to live without their father.

She heard the rumble of the tractor. *Thank God for Alick.* Without Alick to take the children off her hands, she would have gone mad. Barely a day passed without one of them hanging their anoraks on the stick fixed into the old stone grinder in the garden. In the past the children had been forbidden to summon Alick this way, for their amusement. 'He is not a genie in a bottle, you know!' Letty had told them. But this year, the anorak wrapped round the stick had been her literal SOS flag. As soon as Alick spotted it, down he raced and whisked the children off on whatever chore he happened to have that day. Cutting peats, lifting potatoes or rescuing a calf stuck in the bog. God knows, she didn't care, as long as he took them away.

Bonn, West Germany, 1978

The afternoon the Ambassadress had paid her a visit in Bad Godesberg, Letty had been preparing a dinner party for eighteen, chewing her finger over possible menus.

At the bell, she'd opened the door to find the wretched woman outside, dazzling in a pastel tweed suit. Nervously, Letty had straightened her shirt. It always seemed as if the presence of the Ambassadress was carefully designed to downgrade her subordinates from ministers' wives to mice. Moreover, her timing was unfortunate. It wasn't so much the cooking of the dinner—the caterers would take care of that—as the infinite tedium of getting ready. The straightening of the hair, the choosing of the outfit . . she pulled herself together, made Gillian coffee and offered her a chair.

The Ambassadress interrogated her about the children's schools, their general health and happiness. Letty waited for the axe to fall, unaware that it had been dropping for some minutes in a controlled fashion towards her neck. 'And you, my dear, how are *you* getting on?' Gillian ventured. As always, the erectness of her back, even the symmetry of her knees, seemed a tribute to order and self-discipline.

'Oh, quite well, thank you,' Letty said, but Gillian was not to be fobbed off so easily.

'The welfare of the wives is one of my main obligations,' she reminded Letty, 'and, of late, I've been concerned. I know how isolating it can be for a woman to be shipped from pillar to post with a young family. Unhappiness is not unknown. Perhaps you should involve yourself more in embassy life? Some of the other wives find it terribly rewarding, you know.'

'You're very kind,' Letty said, 'but I'd really rather devote my time to Nicky and the children.'

'Yes,' Gillian said gently, 'but you see, that's rather the reason I've come to see you.'

Letty felt her insides cramp. 'I'm not sure I quite understand.'

'Letitia, my dear, Nicky is being fast-tracked. He could go far, given the right circumstances—all the way, I suspect. As his wife you have a pivotal back-up role to play. A good diplomatic wife cannot afford to be too needy or distracting.' Gillian paused to remove a speck of fluff from her stockings. 'A good diplomatic wife must sacrifice her own desires and needs in order to allow her husband to get on and do his job.'

'And are you saying that I'm not?'

'My dear, selflessness, self-discipline, are prerequisites of the position. Nicky really must be shielded from the trivia of domestic life.'

'Are you asking me to sacrifice the well-being of my family?' Letty said incredulously.

'Letitia, a post is coming up in Rome and Nicky's name has been put forward. Now, I know that you'll want to do anything in your power to support him,' Gillian said quietly, 'so, I want you to understand that you are equally under consideration. Think about what Nicky wants, think about how he would feel if he were passed over for, well . . . for the wrong reasons.' She stretched out a hand. 'The truth is, Letitia, a diplomatic wife can make or break her husband's career.'

Letty knew now, as she remembered that visit, exactly why she and Nicky had stopped talking. Rome. It was what Nicky had wanted. It was what Gillian had wanted for both of them.

Ballanish, Outer Hebrides, Summer 1979

The first thing Alba stole was a bar of Cadbury's Fruit & Nut. The second was a packet of Fruit Pastilles. One minute she was staring at them stacked on the shelf in the shop, the next they were in her hand and, without a thought to the consequences, propelled up the sleeve of her Fair Isle jumper.

Stealing put Alba in a good mood. And now that the bear was missing, presumed dead, shoplifting was also the only viable option for an afternoon's entertainment. Today, her mother had gone on one of her hateful walks and Georgie and Jamie had gone with Alick to the beach to chop up driftwood. But Alba was fed up with the beach. Had she felt the need to justify her shoplifting, she would have done so on the grounds that she was owed. She was owed for the death of her father and the zombie that passed for her mother. And for the emptiness of her future confined to this damp island with only her rhesus monkey of a brother for company.

Then there was her sister. At the thought of Georgie, she could almost taste the bile in her mouth. The week before, when everybody had been scattered to different parts of the island, Alba had wandered round the house looking for something to destroy. She'd ventured into the kitchen, where Angus Post Office had left a pile of letters stacked on the counter. Alba flicked idly through them before stopping at one addressed to Georgiana Fleming. *University College London*. For a moment, Alba stared numbly at the return address then she switched on the kettle and held the flap of the envelope to the spout.

Afterwards, she had sat at the kitchen table for a long time, Georgie's university offer letter in her hands. Why hadn't Georgie said anything? Why hadn't she warned her? Two B grades and an A, that was all her sister needed to get a place at university. The whole world was about to open up to Georgie, while she, Alba, would be left alone. She had taken the offer letter and envelope to the sitting-room fireplace and, shoving them deep into the pit of ashes, had set them on fire. When and if the actual A-level results came in, she resolved to do the same.

So now, standing in the aisle of the shop, she ran her eyes over the cans of cock-a-leekie soup and Crosse & Blackwell stew. It was her turn to cook supper. The cooking rota had been her idea—a response to the disintegrating quality of family meals. Food in Bonn, while never inspired, had always been comforting, but ever since her mother had surrendered to a colourless version of herself, it was as though all taste and flavour had also vanished from her cooking.

Alba wandered past the refrigerated section, but there was only a pack of oily bacon with a single Scotch egg nestling behind it. The fruit and vegetable rack offered a choice of two battered apples and a pitifully starved onion.

At the till, Peggy was gossiping with Morag. Alba moved along the aisle until the women's voices became no more irritating than the drone of flies. There were logistical problems to theft. Crisp packets were too crackly to store up her jumper. Tubs of ice cream gave her skin-freeze. She settled for two cans of tuna and a wedge of Cheddar cheese, pocketed the cans, then headed for the front counter.

'Can you put this on Mum's account, please, Peggy?' She plonked down a loaf of Mother's Pride bread.

'Is Mammy not with you again today?'

'Evidently not,' Alba said rudely. Peggy was a committed gossip and theft required a fast getaway.

'Strange that I've no' seen her these good few weeks.' Peggy noted down the Mother's Pride in her ledger.

'Well, she doesn't go out much.' Alba shrugged. 'You can imagine . . .'

'Ach, it's no surprise she's taken it hard, poor soul, what with your grandfather passing on only last year and all. And as for your father, well, a man of the highest order, Mr Fleming was. Always a kind word for everyone.'

At the mention of her father, Alba, to her surprise, felt an unwelcome stinging behind her eyes. He'd become a forbidden subject at home. Now, suddenly, she felt his arm round her and the grate of his chin against her cheek . . . While her grandfather's funeral service had been held at the Guards Chapel in Westminster, her father's had been in a small church in Bad Godesberg. Surely there ought to have been some kind of official ceremony? Instead, the service had felt almost furtive. She had been expecting friends and colleagues to stand and speak about character and achievements, but there had been nothing except for that creepy, awkward gathering at the Ambassador's residence. How *dare* the government treat her father so badly and how *dare* her mother have allowed them to?

Unseeingly, Alba printed her name in the shop's ledger.

THE FIRST TIME Georgie saw him was through a window. Most days after lunch she retired to the upstairs bathroom and locked the door. The window faced northeast and through it she could usually run her eyes along a flat, three-mile strip of the island without seeing another soul. One afternoon, however, perching on the low window-sill, she spotted a toothpick of a figure sitting on the wall by the corner of Euan's croft. He looked as if he was waiting. He looked like she felt—as if he'd been waiting for ever.

She watched him with vague curiosity, then went on scanning the roads until she spotted what she was looking for: the red dot of the Post Office van. She held her breath as it approached, then experienced a pinch of disappointment as it carried straight on. Any day now, Angus's Post Office van would bring her an envelope that promised her A-level results—her yellow brick road to a life that did not necessarily play itself out on the island.

Soon she would be eighteen. Surely a watershed moment for talks about prospects and opportunities? Instead, growing up felt like just another dirty secret she was hiding. Did her mother imagine that she would stay for ever on the island and work in the knitwear factory, listening to Donald John boo-booing away until she was as old and bowed? Oh, God help her . . .

She heard the noise of an engine. The mobile shop was idling outside the gate and she watched Jamie exchanging money for comics with a dark-skinned man in a boiler suit. How a Pakistani had ended up in the Outer Hebrides was one of the island's great mysteries. But, within a month of his arrival, he had set up the mobile shop, peddling everything from long-life milk to library books, and it was now a regular sight outside islanders' crofts.

Georgie slid to the floor. More than half a year had passed since her father's death but she looked no older. She felt like a dropped watch that had stopped ticking and she needed someone to pick her up, align their beating heart with hers, and kick-start her into living again. It was lonely keeping secrets. It was lonely being the oldest. On her sixteenth birthday, her father had released her from the daily news round, and she had considered it her best present ever. Now, though, those awkward moments were the ones she yearned for most. She would have given anything to put her arm round his neck as he turned the pages of *The Times*.

Leaving the bathroom and creeping into her mother's bedroom, she approached the chest of drawers and yanked open drawer after drawer, pulling out bits of clothing until, at last, there it was, on a handkerchief—a lingering trace of her father's scent. His very own piece of Stasi muslin . . .

'You have to understand that East Germany is a country run on suspicion,' he had told her on the drive to Berlin. 'The East Germans are incorrigible trainspotters when it comes to surveillance. Information is what makes their little hearts beat faster. It keeps thousands in work. They say that in another decade, the Stasi will have generated more surveillance documents since 1949 than documents of any other kind printed in Germany since the Middle Ages. Think about that for a minute. Think of the crates of pens, the oceans of ink and miles of typewriter ribbon. Imagine all those people poring over transcripts filled with the minutiae of other people's lives. "Monday, 3.04 p.m. Georgiana Fleming walked into her bedroom (untidy) picked up a black-handled hairbrush (dirty) and brushed her hair using fourteen long even strokes. Monday, 3.07 p.m. Georgiana put down her hairbrush and picked her nose." '

'I do not pick my nose.'

'Try denying that under interrogation,' he teased. 'And they don't just collect documents on people, you know. They collect their smells too.'

'That's disgusting,' Georgie said doubtfully. 'And you can't collect people's smells.'

'Indeed you can. If the Stasi suspect you of some infraction—let's say you've been associating with the wrong people or reading seditious literature—they'll pull you in for questioning. They make you sit on a seat with a muslin cloth underneath, then they interrogate you for hours on end until you've sweated out half your body weight in fear. After that, in the event they decide to let you go—your sweat-saturated muslin is whisked away and stored in a glass jar. Every jar is labelled, and should that person ever abscond in the future, the Stasi simply whip the appropriate cloth from their storage facility and have them followed by the dogs.'

'You deal in information,' she'd told him, 'so what's the difference?'

He had reached for her hand and squeezed it. 'The difference is that I'm one of the good guys.'

One of the good guys . . .

It had all been so different on the journey home from East Berlin. Half an hour after they'd passed through the border, Nicky had stopped the Peugeot, stumbled from the driver's seat and thrown up violently by the side of the road. He'd been ill at ease the whole day and she'd noticed his hand trembling as he twisted the key in the ignition.

'Are you all right, Dad?'

'I'm so sorry, George,' he'd said tersely. 'I'm so terribly sorry.'

'Don't be silly,' she protested. 'It must have been that horrid food.'

He lowered his head to the steering wheel and banged it once. Georgie sat very still. Lord knows, the minute the lights of West Germany had appeared she, too, had felt like throwing herself to the ground and kissing the soil. She had expected the uneasy atmosphere to fade with every mile, but instead she could still feel the raised hairs on the back of her neck. She wanted to ask her father about the church, whether the Stasi had followed them inside and recorded what they'd seen. She wanted to ask him why, at the checkpoint, the officer, disregarding her father's diplomatic card, had waved the Peugeot into an inspection pit and initiated a search, only to abandon it abruptly after receiving a phone call.

Even more than that she wanted to ask about the look on her father's face as he'd been ordered out of the car and towards the interrogation booth. It had been one of raw, unconstrained fear.

'Yes,' he agreed. 'The food.' He took her hand and held it to his cheek. 'Forgive me, my little George, forgive me. I should never have brought you.'

Now she buried her face in her father's handkerchief. She was not stupid. She was not a child. MI6 had reports to write and boxes to tick. What boxes could there possibly be? Accident. Suicide. Murder. There was another explanation. There had to be. For the trip to Berlin, for the meeting in the church and the whispered handover that had accompanied it.

'My father is not a traitor,' she whispered. 'My father is not a traitor.' For a second her spirits lifted, then she remembered—her father was dead.

JAMIE STARED AT the knife in Roddy's hand. The old man's income from wall building and antique dealing was supplemented by snaring rabbits. After they'd been cleaned and skinned, he would pack them up, five or six at a time in brown paper, and post them off to the mainland.

'D'ye want to take a turn, Jamie?' Roddy held out the knife towards him.

'Oh! Actually, no, thank you very much,' Jamie said. His relationship with rabbits was complicated enough without having to butcher them. He was not averse to them stewed in a casserole but preferred them alive and hopping about the sand dunes. He glanced at the pile of corpses on the table and shuddered. Sometimes it seemed that death was everywhere he looked.

Suddenly he had an idea. 'Roddy! You can see the future, can't you?'

'Aye, when the second sight grants it me.'

'If the bear was still alive, could you see where it might be tomorrow, or the next day?'

'I might. Who's to say?'

'What about my father? Could you try to see my father in the future?'

'The day will come soon enough.' Roddy looked dramatically towards the heavens. 'And when it does, I'll be sure to shake him by the hand and tell him you're doing all right, lad. Aye, your grandpa was well liked on the island. Your daddy too, and more's the pity your father's no' resting here as there's many a soul who'd like to pay their respects to him.'

'I don't think my father is resting anywhere, Roddy,' Jamie said reprovingly. 'He's lost.'

'Oh?' Roddy's eyebrows lifted in surprise. 'Jamie, your father's not lost. Why, he'll be up in heaven, keeping an eye on you.'

Georgie had talked about heaven just the other day. Now, Roddy's reintroduction of the subject came as a relief. It gave him something to think about, a trail of breadcrumbs to follow. He dared not provoke his mother by asking questions. Besides, she was so different these days. Her arms still went round him, she still lovingly pulled him onto her lap or dropped an absent-minded hand onto his head, but it wasn't the same. Her love used to feel so huge and all-consuming—as though he lived inside her very heart—but now there was an invisible barrier around her. He was too young to understand that she was not cross, but sunk in her own sadness. All he knew for certain was that his world had changed.

So, heaven was where fishermen turned into seagulls. It was where you went when you were dead, or a place you visited when you were sick. Jamie realised he'd been too quick to dismiss the notion that his father might be there. Clearly there was more than one kind of heaven.

'HOW COULD YOU, ALBA?' Letty stared at her daughter. 'How *dare* you?'

Alba sat on the sitting-room sofa, every muscle tense with defiance.

'Alba, look at me!' Letty ordered.

Alba raised her head. Her mother was white, her cheeks hollow. It was as though her anger had sucked all the oxygen out of the room and for a second Alba felt herself sag. Then she looked her mother straight in the eye. 'How dare I what?'

Letty kept an unsteady grip on herself. 'Don't you understand? Stealing is about the worst crime you could commit here. First, taking things from the mobile van and, then, I heard from Peggy this morning that you've been in the shop almost every day.'

'Peggy's a sneak and a gossip,' Alba said dismissively.

Letty grabbed her daughter's arm. 'Don't you dare speak like that about anyone. Peggy is an extremely nice woman. You're lucky she hasn't called the police. What's got into you, Alba?' she could not stop herself adding.

'Got into me?' Alba repeated coldly. 'Got. Into. Me?' She cocked her head to one side in mock thought. 'Golly gooseberries. I wonder? I don't suppose it might have something to do with having to live in this god-forsaken place, or'—her voice rose—'the fact that my father is dea—'

'Stop it.' Letty glanced at the door. 'Keep your voice down.'

'Oh, yes, because we don't want little Jamie upset now, do we?' Alba sneered. 'Can't you understand that he should be upset? That we should get him in here'—she glanced at the door—'and make him really cry!' she yelled.

Letty sank into a chair, mute with despair. She had a sudden flash of an eight-year-old Alba: the burning eyes, the passionate avowals of love. Alba, leaping off the bed like a ballet dancer, forcing her father to catch her whether he was ready or not.

'I don't understand you, Alba,' she said. 'You have no reason to be this unkind to your brother. Nobody was ever unkind to you in the way you are to him.' She rubbed at her face tiredly. 'Where does it come from, this . . . this . . . desire to hurt people?'

Alba worked her finger into the frayed hole of the loose cover.

'Talk to me, Alba,' Letty said, 'please.'

The questions ran through Alba's head like ticker tape. *Tell me why. Tell me how. Tell me what I don't know. Please, please, tell me what it is you're keeping from me.* She tried to speak but she couldn't force the words over the block of pride jamming her throat.

She closed her eyes and took herself back to her bedroom in Bonn—back to the safety of her bed, under the darkness of its covers, one evening after she'd been sent to her room in a tantrum. She'd felt the bed dip as her father leaned forward to smooth her hair behind her ears. 'Almost everything that goes wrong in the world is due to people not knowing how to talk to each other,' she could remember him saying. 'Humans are continually struggling to find ways of expressing themselves and, sometimes, with the best will in the world, we forget how to do it, or our problems become so severe that we can't bear to talk about them any more. This is where diplomacy comes in. In fact, this is the sole reason why I studied hard to become a diplomat—so that I could negotiate peace between you and your mother.'

Anger, he had gone on to argue, was the default emotion for the lazy. Reason, logic and patience, conversely, all required harder work than most people were prepared to commit to.

'But what happens when you can't agree on things?' Alba had sniffed.

'Well, humans fight and countries go to war. This is why diplomacy is important, because diplomacy is all about using words and not weapons.'

'But words are weapons,' Alba had told him, not because she particularly understood the meaning of the phrase but because she remembered her father saying it before and she knew he'd be impressed.

'Clever girl. Yes, they can be. But so is silence. So is anything you do to manipulate people. Bad moods, charm, sulking. So, you see, you have to be careful how you use these things.'

'Then your job is a weapon.'

'Very much so. But diplomacy is a good weapon. Countries talking to each other is a good thing. People talking to each other is a good thing—which is why, my little tree frog, you must apologise to your mother when she comes up to kiss you good night.'

'Alba . . .' Letty pleaded now. All she wanted was to take her daughter in her arms and hold her tight, keep her safe.

Alba's nose had blocked with mucus from the effort of not crying. She turned her head away and parted her mouth to breathe. Apologies had come so cheap when she was little, the price of a kiss or a hug—not any more. She no longer knew how to talk to her mother and her mother didn't know the person that she had become. She had no idea, for example, that Alba smoked cigarettes; she had not noticed that her daughter needed a bra or that she was currently in collision with her own puberty. She had no idea about anything.

Alba would not apologise, she would not. The silence between mother and daughter stretched long and shrill.

'JUST GET IT OVER.' Georgie rammed her hands deeper into her pockets and gazed up at the mottled sky. 'Why are you making such a fuss about it?'

Alba shrugged and stamped her gumboots on the wet tarmac.

'For God's sake. Bang on the door, say you're sorry, then run like hell.'

'Easy for you.'

'Well, he's not going to hear you shouting it from here . . . unless, of course, you go and shoplift yourself a megaphone or something.'

'You're hilarious.'

'Get on with it then. Besides, you got off lightly. He could have had you arrested.'

'Oh, right, as if there's a single policeman on this island.'

'There's nice Sergeant Anderson.'

'Who's probably still searching for that bloody dead bear. God, why is everyone making such a fuss about this?'

'Mum, you mean. You don't think she has enough to worry about without you being a thief?'

'It's none of her business. She didn't have to make me apologise.' Alba spat out the word like a bullet.

'Don't be so stupid. Of course she did.'

'If it's so easy, then you do it.'

'I would if it had been me stealing.'

'No, seriously, you ought to do it. It's embarrassing for me. Besides, aren't you even slightly curious to know what it feels like to be in trouble?'

Georgie sighed. This was Alba's magic trick. Making her own guilt disappear like a rabbit into a top hat. 'I'm not doing your penance for you. Forget it, Alba. It's not going to work.'

Alba yanked up her hood angrily. Rain was breaking like metal needles against her face. 'You think it's good for me to apologise. You think I need punishing. But I'm not sorry, so what's the point? A forced apology is just a lie dressed up in pretty clothes. So—pointless. If you do it, though, I'll give you something in return and then we'll both benefit.'

'What could you possibly give me?'

'Why, will you do it?'

'Depends.' An idea was occurring to Georgie. There *was* something she wanted from her sister.

'What about if I do your cooking rota for the next few weeks?' Alba offered. 'Shake on it.' She prised a hand from her pocket.

But Georgie had no intention of selling herself cheap. 'Yes, that,' she said coolly, 'plus you have to be nice to Jamie.'

Alba withdrew her hand. 'Define "nice".'

'It's not a word that normally needs defining.'

'Define "nice", and for how long exactly?'

'Alba . . .' Georgie held her ground. 'You have to be really properly nice to Jamie and do my cooking until the end of the month.'

Alba scowled. She glanced at the shopkeeper's house and tried to imagine forming the word 'sorry'. Most emotions were hateful, but humiliation had to be the most hateful of all. She was furious that Georgie had got the better of her, but then she remembered the neat pyramid of ash that was her sister's recently arrived offer of a university place, and felt better. 'The end of the month. But not one day, one hour, not one single minute longer.'

'Don't worry, Alba,' Georgie said resentfully. 'God forbid anyone should expect more of you than the bare minimum.' She trudged up the stony path, knocked on the door, then pressed her nose to the window. She wanted to leave, but, unless one of them apologised, the whole unpleasant episode would have to be repeated. She sighed heavily, then picked her way through wet thistles towards the mobile van parked to the side of the property. The back was rolled up and she peered in.

It was the second time Georgie had seen him, although he was now no longer a distant scarecrow figure but a flesh-and-blood boy, slumped against a packing crate, reading a book, his long legs stretched across the floor.

'Oh,' Georgie said. She took in the dark skin and the wild afro hair. Of course, it made sense. The shopkeeper's son. Had to be.

Equally startled, he scrambled to his feet, tipping his book onto the floor.

'I'm so sorry,' Georgie said. 'I didn't mean . . .'

'I wasn't expecting to see anyone.' He brushed down his trousers. 'We're not open.' He was staring at her almost rudely.

Georgie pushed a strand of wet hair off her face. Standing, the boy was a gangly, thinner version of his father. The trousers of his boiler suit stopped well short of his ankles and his feet were bare.

'Why are you in here if you're not open?'

'Reading.' He shrugged.

Only a year ago, Georgie's whole life had been about boys. How to meet them, when to meet them, in which café she and her girlfriends would congregate to get the best glimpse of them. But, after her father's death, she had avoided boys—and now it was as if she no longer remembered how to choreograph her body in their presence. She picked his book off the floor. '*Under Milk Wood*,' she muttered, feeling hopelessly self-conscious. 'I had to read that for A level. I even got to be Captain Cat in the school play.'

He scrutinised her as though she was some exotic object the tide had washed up on his doorstep. 'Were you any good?' he offered finally.

'Awful, I've never been able to act. I think they only asked me because they felt sorry for me. Mostly because I was new and . . . well, other stuff.'

The boy yawned and stretched one arm up to the roof of the van. There was something sleepy and fluid about him, Georgie thought; like a sloth that had woken up from a month-long nap.

'The school here never puts on plays,' he said. 'They just made us read, day in, day out. I used to hate it.' He felt around in his pockets and produced a packet of cigarettes. 'Now it's something to do when the weather's bad.' He glanced out at the clouded sky and grinned. 'I read a lot.'

'I like reading. You get to try out other people's worlds and see if they're any better than yours.'

'Are they?'

'Well . . .' she said carefully, 'not if you stick to the tragedies.'

The boy jammed a cigarette in his mouth and absently felt around with his foot for a boot. 'There's not much to learn about different worlds from *Under Milk Wood*. It might as well be set on the island.'

'I suppose so. I never really thought about it.' As it happened, she wasn't thinking about books at all, she was thinking about his subversive hair. She had seen hair like his in some newspapers. It was student-sit-in hair, anti-war-protester hair. If, one day soon, he drove the van through the township shouting communist slogans or preaching the evils of capitalism, no one could claim that they hadn't been warned. She wished she had hair that stood for something interesting.

The boy found his boot and jumped off the van. 'If you need anything, my father's doing the rounds tomorrow.' He rolled down the door and it occurred to Georgie that she'd missed her moment. The thing ought to have been done right at the beginning: a mumbled sorry and a lightning-fast exit. What a stupid idea, apologising for Alba. She suddenly felt tired. 'Are you saying that if I did want to buy something you wouldn't sell it to me because you're closed?'

'I've got no till.'

'What if I paid you the exact amount?'

'There's nowhere to put the money.'

'Couldn't you put it in your pocket?'

'I suppose if you really need something that badly . . .'

'I don't actually.' She couldn't work out why she was so cross. 'I was just making a point.'

'Look.' He glanced towards the house. 'It's not me. My father is fanatical about accounting. He would rather not make money than have it lying about in the wrong place or not know exactly what it was for. My father knows precisely how much money he's made every single day down to the last two-pence piece.'

'Oh.' Georgie's fingertips touched the edges of the coins in her pocket. 'I see.' No wonder Alba had been caught.

'It sounds crazy, but it's an obsession with him. When I was a boy, he would wait until he thought I was asleep, then he would whisper passages out of his accountancy manuals to me.'

'That *is* crazy,' she said unhappily.

'I don't care though.' He threw up the roller and jumped back in. 'You can get what you want. I won't tell him. Come on.'

Georgie looked hard at his hand before taking it. Unlike her light-fingered sister, she had never been inside the mobile van. The units to the right were tightly stacked with an assortment of sweets, tins and jams, while the other side housed a lending library of battered paperback books. There wasn't a lot of room for two people to manoeuvre in and Georgie could smell the peat and cigarette smoke on his clothes.

'Take anything you want.' Deftly he shuffled a few cans. 'We have beans, lentils, coconut milk, peppers, pine nuts—you can't get any of these things in the shop, you know.'

She was flustered by his closeness. 'It's OK, thanks.' Then, worried she sounded snobbish, added, 'I mean you obviously have really good things.'

'You can pay me tomorrow if you didn't bring enough money.'

'Honestly, it's not why I came.'

'I don't understand.' He was towering over her, blocking her escape.

'I came to apologise,' she mumbled. 'For stealing from you.' Her pink cheeks mutated to crimson.

'Oh.' A spiral of hair bounced across his eye. 'Well, that's interesting.'

Georgie felt as vulnerable as a tortoise tricked into parting with its shell.

Damn her sister. Damn her own pathetic lack of character for agreeing to take Alba's place. 'I brought money to pay you back.' She clanked her coins loudly and edged forwards in the hope he might follow suit.

He didn't. And now they were even closer. 'It was only a comic,' he said.

'And a mint Aero.' Georgie felt damp under her armpits. 'Plus a book.'

'Well, the book she'll have to return. There are people waiting for it.'

And still he didn't move. Georgie prayed for deliverance. It was only because Alba had nicked the island's most popular read that she'd been caught in the first place. Quite why she'd snatched Alex Haley's *Roots*, when there were already two copies at home, it was hard to say. Her sister was probably a kleptomaniac as well as a sociopath.

'I'll get you the book.' She raised her eyes to his with an effort.

He moved aside. The cool air felt like a poultice on her burning cheeks.

'Wait a minute.' Georgie found herself rewinding the conversation. 'You said "she". You said *she'll* have to return it.'

'My father said it was the younger sister. You're the older one, aren't you? I saw you at the meeting in the schoolhouse.'

'The bear meeting? I didn't see you.'

'The whole island was there.' He shrugged as if a crowd of elderly islanders were the perfect camouflage for a six-foot-three, smoky-brown boy with bedspring hair. He was Mowgli, Georgie thought. No idea that he was being raised among wolf cubs.

She took a deep breath. 'I'm Georgie.'

'Aliz.'

'Aliz,' she repeated unconsciously. 'So, did you look for him? The bear?'

'Nah, I reckon it drowned at sea.'

'That's what Alba thinks, but my little brother still goes out searching every day.' She remembered Alba was waiting. 'Look, I have to get back.' She scrabbled in her pocket. 'Here. I'm really sorry by the way.'

Aliz took the change from her. 'How did your sister get you to do her dirty work for her?'

'I don't know, she's cunning that way. She's like Typhoid Mary, she infects everyone around her.' Georgie then concentrated so hard on finding a way to end the conversation that accidentally she began a new one. 'So why do you keep that old school bus in your garden?'

'It's not a bus, it's a greenhouse. Want to see?'

Out of the corner of her eye, Georgie noticed Alba grimly enlarging the circumference of a pothole in the road with the toe of her gumboot. 'I really ought to get back.'

'Take these for your brother.' Aliz produced a packet of Fruit Pastilles.

'No, no, please.' She waved them away. 'I don't have any more money.'

'Good.' Aliz took her hand and closed it round the sweets. 'That means you have to bring it tomorrow.'

LETTY PICKED HER WAY over the rubbery grasses of the dunes. The sea was as flat as polished glass. She slipped out of her clothes, folding them and laying them on a dry patch of rock. The episode with Alba had shaken her badly. It wasn't the stealing, it was the impossibility of communication that floored her. Alba had stopped talking to her, and now they moved around the house like two repelling magnets. Why was it so hard to reach out to the very people closest to you? It had been the same with Nicky. They had stopped talking and everything had changed.

Rome had been the posting Nicky had been after for some time. So, after Gillian's little pep talk, and much as it went against her nature, Letty had made a conscious effort not to distract him with the mundane details of life. At first, the difference in their relationship was so subtle she barely noticed it. It was as though each sentence had one word less and each conversation was short of one sentence. Slowly but surely, though, whole paragraphs began to disappear from their lives until information was being exchanged on a need-to-know basis only. The less communication there is, the less is generated. Lack of it leads to misunderstanding, misunderstanding leads to resentment and the finger-pointing that inevitably follows leads to war. Nicky, busy negotiating with the rest of Europe, could not see that relations in his own tiny kingdom were in danger of imminent breakdown.

Letty waded into the sea. Happiness. Life. Family. Love. You only got one shot at them. She gasped involuntarily as the water closed round her. It was too cold to remain still and so she struck out purposefully, forcing her arms and legs into long, powerful strokes. For a while she was hypnotised by the view of the horizon. A tiny part of her thought how simple it would be to keep swimming . . . but already her mind was filling with an image of Jamie's face and she quickly turned round.

She stood naked by the rocks and waited for the wind to blow her dry. Afterwards, when she was dressed, she crawled into the shelter of the sand dunes and curled up, trying to find warmth. Why hadn't Nicky told her they weren't to be given Rome? It wouldn't have mattered. She could have been happy wherever they'd been posted. As long as it was away from Bonn and the Ambassadress. But after his and Georgie's trip to East Berlin, Nicky had been withdrawn. Overwhelmed with work, she'd diagnosed. And Gillian's warning had come back to her. She must not be too needy. Nicky must be allowed to get on with his job.

Below her, a group of ringed plovers pecked at their reflections on the mirrored sand. Suddenly, the memories crowded in. She and Nicky had made love in these sand dunes the summer after they'd been married. The weather had been freakishly warm. They might have been holidaying in the West Indies for the cloudless skies and emerald waters swaying in and out of the bays. She remembered the feel of his body close to hers, the taste of salt on his skin. 'What if someone sees us?' she had whispered. But nobody had been watching, only the nesting terns wheeling and screeching overhead.

Afterwards, walking a few steps ahead of her, Nicky had bent down to pick something off the sand. The stone had been pure white, perfectly round. When he was satisfied it had no flaws, he had hurried back and dropped it casually at her feet. 'Oh look!' he'd cried, pretending to spot it for the first time. 'A perfect stone! Fancy that.' He had plucked it off the ground again and pressed it into her hand. 'We must keep it and treasure it for ever. At least that's what penguins do, apparently.'

She'd looked quizzically at him. 'You are silly. What do penguins do?'

'They drop pebbles at each other's feet. It's more or less what they say when they want to have a nice egg together.' He drew her to him and laid his hand gently on her stomach. 'You're pregnant, aren't you?'

She'd been shocked at his perception. Hadn't yet worked out why she hadn't told him.

He'd laughed. 'Don't you understand? Everything you do, everything you are, everything that makes you happy or sad, it's all there for anyone to read in your face.'

'For *you* to read,' she'd said, mortified. 'Only you, not everyone else.'

'But I'm right, aren't I?'

'Oh, Nicky, I wanted to be sure.'

'Well, you're lousy at secrets, you know that, don't you?'

Who knew? she thought bitterly. Who knew that he would turn out to be so much better . . .

Something I've been keeping from you, the letter had said. *Something that's been preying terribly on my mind* . . . 'Oh, Nicky,' she said helplessly, 'what did you do? Tell me what you did, goddamnit! NICKY!' she shouted, but the wind tore his name from her mouth and flung it towards the sea. She closed her eyes, clenched her fists and roared until her throat burned. She didn't care what he'd done. Right then, she would have given everything she owned, she would have sold her soul, to have his arms round her. To know that he loved her.

A movement caught her eye. She scanned the top of the dunes. Had someone seen her? Heard her?

'Nicky?' she whispered.

She pushed shakily to her feet and stared out over the deserted sands, then pressed the pads of her fingers to her sore eyes before searching the dunes again. 'Nicky,' she breathed, half in fear, half in hope. 'Oh God. Nicky, are you here?'

Why was he shadowing them? Sometimes the girls, sometimes the mother, but most often the boy with his binoculars and little Bakelite lunchbox. Was he supposed to be keeping an eye on the family? He didn't know, but somebody should. Every day the tenuous threads that connected their lives frayed thinner. Did the children know that their mother cried in the dunes most afternoons? Did she, in turn, have any idea that her eldest daughter was dreaming of a boy, or that her son was riding on the trailer of an islander whose intake of alcohol doubled with every passing week?

And so he continued to watch them, guarding the house at night, observing the boy from the cave at the bottom of the Kettle, waiting for the girls to appear on the beach. And every day anxiety burned in his heart.

JAMIE DANGLED HIS LEGS over the edge of the Kettle and stared at the Penguin biscuit Alba had included in his lunchbox. As he carefully eased his finger under the metallic wrapper, his excitement at this act of kindness was tempered by wariness. As a general rule, 'nice' or 'helpful' were foreign concepts for Alba. Her cruelties only occasionally curtailed by flu or extreme exhaustion. To trust his sister was to place his head inside the mouth of a sleeping lion . . . But the chocolate biscuit was no one-off. When he'd knocked on the door of her room a couple of days earlier, instead of randomly selecting a reply from her usual store of put-downs, she'd cried, 'Enter my domain!' in an almost genial manner. Added to that had been two pats on the back, and the use of his name rather than 'moron'. And, most thrilling of all, special food allowances at mealtimes.

The previous evening, wandering into the kitchen to find her mashing potatoes, he'd enquired what was for supper.

'Mum and Georgie are having winkles but I've made you a sandwich.' Then, adding a dob of butter and a sprinkling of salt, she'd scooped the potato from the bowl, spread it between two pieces of white bread and slid it onto a plate in front of him.

'I love you, Alba,' Jamie declared before he could stop himself, but instead of snubbing him or hitting him, she had merely responded with a triumphant little smile directed at Georgie.

The rekindling of hope was so seductive. The thing was, if Alba could love him, then the impossible became possible. The bear would be found. His lost father would come home, the hole in his heart would mend. Greedily, Jamie took a nibble of his biscuit and then a bite. He almost moaned with pleasure as the rich sweetness filled his mouth.

ALBA, MEANWHILE, was cooking mussels. She wrenched the lid off the big saucepan and sniffed. Beneath the steam, the water glowed a synthetic blue. She had never made mussel soup before and it didn't look as she'd imagined, but she wasn't expecting complaints. Having exchanged her moral duties for Georgie's culinary ones, she'd as good as taken control of the kitchen in a bloodless coup. Her family would now eat what she wanted, when she wanted, and she had taken enthusiastically to food experimentation, rebuffing all questions about what was on the menu with an ominous, 'A little something I've thrown together.' At mealtimes she stood over the table, gimlet-eyed, wielding her spatula, determined that every last mouthful should be appreciated. Jamie had never been happier. Alba even excused him from her more ground-breaking recipes, such as razor-clam omelettes, on the grounds that he was too ignorant to appreciate the subtle flavours.

Still, as with the administration of most dictatorships, there were logistical matters to consider and Alba's initial problem had been one of supply. For obvious reasons she could no longer patronise the shop and, because she was punishing her mother by not speaking to her, there was no question of demanding that the necessary provisions be bought for her. Given the dwindling cupboard supplies, it was only a matter of time before she hit on the idea of living off the land.

The beauty of it grew on her. She became evangelical about the procurement of food for little or no money. Field mushrooms and seafood, disgusting though she found them, could be had virtually gratis. Alick had long ago taught them how to kill flounders by straddling the narrow channels on the incoming tide and stabbing them through with a pitchfork. Farther away, under the causeway, buckets of winkles and mussels could be harvested and, sometimes, when the fishing had been especially good, Alisdair would bring a sack of crab claws to the house.

The bovine Ambassadress, too, produced a bucket of warm rich milk a day, which, after a spell in a bowl on the top of the fridge, formed a thick layer of cream. Daily, Alba attempted to make yoghurt from the curdling milk and, soon, with a little more practice, even the creamy cheese, crowdie, would be within her repertoire. If all else failed, they could live on the island's potatoes—the best in the world, so soft and floury they fell apart underneath the fork.

'Indeed, we ate quite well before the shop came along,' Donald John confirmed when she quizzed him on the subject of self-sufficiency one day.

'Like what?'

'Well, I was very keen on the salted herring,' he offered. 'They sold it on the mainland in barrels and it came over on the boat.'

'Did you fry it?'

'No, no, we boiled it.'

'How revolting!'

'No indeed, it was very good, Alba,' he said, faintly insulted.

'What about crab? Lobster?'

'I ate a crab once but I didn't think much of him.'

'Mackerel?'

'Mackerel are villains! Oh, boo boo, I'd rather eat my sheepdog than a mackerel.'

'Is it worth shooting cormorants?'

'Well, they're very oily.' Donald John ironed his knees with his big flat hands. 'You have to take the skin off them because they're difficult to pluck.

After that you can boil them in a pan with an onion. When I was a boy we used to poach plenty of duck and many's the goose your father brought for us too. He was a fine shot, your father, a fine shot indeed.'

It was true, Alba thought wistfully. For as long as she could remember her father had been engaged in a highly personal war of wits with the island geese. When he saw that Alba had developed an interest, he began taking her along on the morning flight, and she would stumble behind him through the bogs while he tested the wind and planned the best place to hide to intercept the geese on their way to their feeding grounds.

'They're far more intelligent than people, of course,' he once told her. 'See that formation of dots in the distance? Greylags. They're a cunning bunch and they probably suspect I'm waiting for them. However, the wind is coming off the loch today, so you and I have decided to face north.' He winked at her. 'That'll fool them, you'll see.'

She checked the mussels again. She'd picked them that morning, hitching a lift to the causeway only to find a big yellow digger idling on the bank with a man perched on the driving seat, alternately gnawing at a boiled egg and pulling on his cigarette.

'What are you doing?' Alba had stared at the crater he'd gouged.

'It's a quarry, lass. We're digging up the whole of this bank. I haven't a clue what for. But the government is paying so we're doing it.'

'What are the government going to do with all this rubbish stone?' She'd kicked at the pile of rock.

'I don't suppose they'll do a thing with it, it's just that the money's there so they might as well spend it.' He'd winked. 'EEC grants and the like. There's nothing we won't dig up if we're paid to, so you'll soon be seeing a fine lot of progress on the island.'

'But what about my mussels?' she'd asked suspiciously. On either side of the causeway where the tide was seeping back into the channels, the water appeared to be tinted with rainbow colours. 'Can we still eat them?'

'To be sure,' he'd replied. 'A little oil in the water never hurt anyone.'

Alba now lifted the saucepan lid and stared down at the clunky gumbo of black shells. The *moules* were more 'Liquide de Fairy' than *marinières* and when she drained them, water frothed in the sink like the dregs of bubble bath. It was probably prudent to give them an extra rinse under the tap, but, really, who could be bothered?

'Supper!' she yelled.

ONE EVENING, Jamie trailed into the kitchen of the cottage behind his mother to find Alick pacing and sucking on his roll-up in short bursts like an expectant father in a hospital corridor.

'Ach, something terrible!' Alick exclaimed.

'What is it, Alick?' Letty asked, not even mildly alarmed. 'Terrible' was one of Alick's favourite words and he applied it equally to neighbours, slights, storms and joint pains. She saw at once that he was tipsy.

'There's a ghost up there.' Alick relit his cigarette end with trembling fingers.

'What do you mean?'

'Come with me, Let-ic-ia.' Alick grabbed her hand and pulled her out of the kitchen. At the top of the stairs he paused, then, with the exaggerated gait of a vaudevillian clown, crept along the corridor until he reached her bedroom door. 'Ready now?' he whispered.

'Yes, yes, we're ready.' Alick looked almost spectral himself, Letty thought. The lower rims of his eyelids shone red against the pallor of his skin.

'Right you are.' He threw open the door as though surprise was the only way to catch whatever menace was lurking within.

Letty and Jamie stepped briskly round him, then stopped. 'Alick, what—?'

Horrified, Letty surveyed the wreck of her bedroom. The bed had been moved away from the wall and positioned in the middle of the room. Balanced on top of it, in one vast, teetering pile, was every other piece of furniture along with whatever contents it had held.

'Alick, what happened?'

Alick explained that he'd been fixing the hinge of the door when he'd heard a moaning noise coming from the walls—and it had been a noise so dreadful, so chilling, that he had realised at once that it could not come from any mortal soul. Terrified, he'd run out of the house, across the garden and jumped over the yellow gate before even daring to look behind him—but when he did, he'd spotted something he'd never noticed before.

'There was a secret window there, Le-ti-cia,' he said. 'A secret window on the outside that canna' be seen on the inside.'

'Yes, it's a blind window, Alick.' Letty said with a trace of impatience. 'It's always been there.'

'Still and all, that's where the noise was coming from,' said Alick stoutly.

'Alick, it's just the wind.'

'It's no the wind. I've been living with the wind since the day I was born. I'm telling you, Le-ti-cia, there's something very queer in this room.

There's a secret place there between the walls.' Alick swayed backwards and forwards on his feet. 'Just like the one in that car.'

'What car? Alick you're talking nonsense.'

'It's not nonsense, it's proof of a mer-derr.' Alick rolled the word off his tongue. 'It's the ghost of poor Flora Macdonald, strangled by the captain and holed up behind that window.'

'Come on now,' Letty said. 'Everyone knows that Flora Macdonald ran away to Australia.'

'That's what they say.' Alick's eyes flashed. 'But who's to know what really happened. Neilly McClellan was a rascal, and he'd have had a job taking her all the way to Australia. In any case, ghosts canna just appear and start moaning for no reason. I'm telling you, she was mer-derred and now she's trapped.'

'But why does she have to live behind a window?' Jamie asked. 'Why can't she go to heaven?'

'Because when there's a *vi-olent* death'—he leaned his hand on Jamie's shoulder for support—'there's unfinished business.'

'Alick,' Letty said, uneasily. 'That's enough. Don't you think you're being a bit melodramatic?' There had never been so much as a handbag snatch on the island, let alone a cold-blooded act of filicide.

No amount of reasoning could deter Alick from his theory. 'Ach, poor Flora, poor soul,' he lamented. 'Lost for all this time. Not allowed to rest peacefully in heaven.'

This last statement started Jamie's brain whirring. *Lost for all this time*. Disappeared. Heaven. Resting. Here were the very same words struggling for order in his own confused lexicon. Wide-eyed, he turned to his mother, his mouth forming a question.

'Alick,' Letty said sharply. 'You're scaring Jamie with this talk of ghosts.'

'No, no,' Jamie protested. 'It's just that . . . I want to . . .'

Alick grinned wickedly, then lurched sideways. Letty put out a hand to steady him. 'All right, that's enough now.' She took stock of the precarious arrangement of furniture on the bed, and resolved to sleep downstairs.

Jamie had several searching questions for Alick on the nature of spirits, but Alick seemed suddenly too dizzy to answer. Neither did he appear well enough to explain why he had thought that the exorcism of Flora Macdonald's ghost might be achieved by pushing all the furniture away from the walls, and, after a while, once Alick had been seen safely home, Letty quietly but firmly suggested that Jamie put it all out of his head.

A NIGHT OF FREEFALL insomnia followed. To Letty it felt as though the room itself was conspiring to keep her from rest. The sofa cushions were lumpy and unyielding, a vicious west wind yowled through the chimney, and the blankets were scratchy. For the first hour, she lay supine, trying to clear her mind, but gradually every unfamiliar creak jolted her like an electric shock.

She turned and sighed and turned, all the while trying to identify a nagging pinprick in her consciousness. She couldn't shake the feeling that there was something important she'd overlooked. When, eventually, she slept, this unease followed her into a viper's nest of dreams, where she could only stand and watch, powerless to act, as disaster after disaster befell her family. First it was the Peugeot rolling backwards with Jamie at the wheel. Then they were going to miss the ferry, but Macleod wouldn't give her the car key. He stood in his garage, dangling it out of reach. *I can pull it out for you now if you like*, he was saying. *That plywood of yours . . .*

Except it wasn't Macleod any more, it was Alick's face leering at her. *There's a secret place there between the walls*, he had said. *Just like the one in that car*. She woke with a start, her heart beating fast.

LETTY'S WATCH READ a quarter past four. It was cold and damp and the wind blew her nightdress round her legs. She didn't need a torch—the moon was out and almost bright enough to read by—but she was scared and the torch in her hand felt reassuring. She walked swiftly to the Peugeot, fighting a sense of unreality. *A secret place*, Alick had said . . .

The day Georgie had crashed the Peugeot was the first time her father had allowed her to drive the car on the main road. Letty had been away, visiting her father's old cook. Barely a mile beyond the church loch, Georgie had whipped over a blind summit and swerved to avoid a duck. It was typical of Nicky's efficiency that he had arranged for the car to be mended and for parts to be ordered from the mainland before presenting the situation as a fait accompli on her return. There had been nothing for Letty to do but be thankful that no one had been hurt, and allow Alick to get on with the repairs.

Damn her naiveté. She turned the key in the boot lock. The 404 boasted a spacious luggage section, or so Nicky had always claimed when it came to packing the car. At the beginning of the summer, this job had fallen to the girls. The fact that the boot had taken fewer suitcases than usual Letty had put down to the girls' rookie status. Nicky would have taken everything out and begun again, rigorously matching size and shape to space available, but she hadn't cared. Grateful that the children had taken the initiative, she simply strapped the remaining suitcases on the roof rack.

Shivering, she worked her hands along the floor of the boot towards the rear of the back seat, feeling round the edges of the carpet. On the right-hand side the seam was intact, but the left side must have taken in the bulk of water when the car had gone into the river at a tilt, because here and there the carpet edge was disintegrating. Between the new tacks of Macleod's repairs, shreds of glue came away under her fingers. She ran and fetched a screwdriver from the outside room, then prised the staples out one by one until she was able to get some purchase on the corner of the carpet—enough to give it a yank. Underneath, was the yellowy chip of plywood.

That plywood of yours . . . That plywood of Nicky's.

Letty stared at it for a minute, then, putting the sole of her gumboots to it, kicked as hard as she could.

It had been done so cleverly you would never have known it was there. It was cut to exacting standards and fitted at a slight inward slant, creating a false divide between the boot and the void underneath the rear passenger seat. A void big enough for a person.

Afterwards she found she was shaking, cold to the bone. 'Damn you, Nicky.' She blotted her eyes on the sleeve of her nightdress. A percussion of rain started up on the metal roof, yet still she couldn't move. God knows, she understood the dangers of smuggling someone out of East Berlin, especially under the radar of the British government. Nicky would have had no official cover. No safety net.

Whatever you're doing, involve no one, Tom had warned. Except that Nicky hadn't involved no one. He'd involved his own daughter.

Now, finally, Letty had what she'd been fighting for—what she'd been demanding of the government. Proof.

Except now she knew that she hadn't wanted the truth at all. Only a truth she could live with.

'IT'S SO WARM IN HERE.' Georgie sketched a smiley face in the condensation on the bus window.

'I know. I'm sorry,' Aliz said.

'No, it's wonderful. Like being in some really exotic country.'

Aliz's father was a genius. He'd converted a van into a shop/library and an old school bus into a greenhouse. The bus had solar panels inserted into the roof and the rows of seats had been exchanged for trays of seed beds from which a jungle-like tangle of greenery was rising.

'Tomatoes, chillies, green beans . . .' The first time he'd shown her round, Aliz had pointed out every plant in turn. 'And these in here are herbs: coriander, parsley, fennel.'

'Why don't you sell all this stuff?' she'd asked.

'No one wants it. You can grow anything here but my father says the islanders don't like vegetables.'

'My mother loves them.'

'So take her some.'

'No, no,' Georgie said, having only just returned with the change for the Fruit Pastilles.

'Take something and come back with the money tomorrow.'

She cast a quick, curious look at him. Was this a game they were both supposed to be playing? 'I don't think I can come back tomorrow.'

He'd slipped some tomatoes into her hand. 'You have to, or my father's books won't balance.'

Georgie had come back every day since.

She sat down now on the slatted bench in the bus. The sun felt like honey on her back. 'What's that?' She touched a finger to a purple, bulbous-looking fruit.

'Aubergine. My father makes *kuku* with it but he complains it doesn't taste right. He says the aubergines don't get enough sun, even in here, so most of the time he strokes their skin and admires the colour. He likes to complain that the food on this island is all the same colour: white, grey or brown.'

'Last night my sister made spaghetti with Branston Pickle sauce.'

'And you ate it?'

'I had to. You have no idea what she's like.'

Georgie knew she should consider her manipulations a success but Jamie's rekindled hero worship of Alba made her uneasy. There was something about her sister's born-again sweetness that felt like the lull before the storm. Sooner or later, Alba would revoke Jamie's gift voucher of love once and for all. Then again, if she hadn't made the deal with her sister, she would not have met Aliz. Aliz who smelt of earth and minerals. Aliz who was sitting so close to her now that she could feel his breath on her cheek.

'Food is what my father misses most about home,' he was saying. 'He talks about it all the time. Ice creams made with pistachio nuts or scented with rose petals. Lamb seasoned with cinnamon and coriander or fried with apricots and figs. At night I hear him mumbling in his sleep about salted cheeses, bitter lemons or the minted lentil dishes my mother used to cook for him.'

It was the first time Georgie had heard Aliz mention his mother. She had presumed Aliz's father was a widower. Alba claimed that he'd come to Scotland to find a new wife, although somehow the idea of Morag or Peggy being whisked on his arm through customs in their beige mackintoshes and emerging onto the bustling streets of Karachi seemed a little far-fetched. Georgie had less trouble imagining herself there, standing in front of some ancient mosque, waiting for a bull cart to trundle by.

Accidentally, her knee touched his. 'What's it like in Pakistan?' she asked dreamily.

'No idea.' Aliz took out his tin of tobacco and began rolling a cigarette. 'I've never been.'

'Aren't you curious? Have you asked your father?'

'My father also has never been to Pakistan.'

'What do you mean?' She looked sharply at him.

'We are not from Pakistan.'

Georgie's city of sandcastles crumbled to the desert floor.

'My father came here from Syria after my mother and brother were killed during the Six Day War.'

'But I thought . . .' she said, mortified. 'I'm sorry, I don't know why I . . .'

'Everyone does. We're the Pakis who opened the Paki shop.'

Georgie hung her head.

'Don't worry, it doesn't bother me and my father likes the people here.' Aliz flicked a corkscrew of hair out of his eyes. 'He says many of the islanders haven't even been to the mainland, so how could they know the difference between Syria, Pakistan or the moon?'

'At my school in Germany, we had American, English, African, Korean, Indian, even Finnish kids. The first thing we had to learn was which country everybody was homesick for.'

'I've been here since I was seven years old. I don't know where I should be homesick for.'

'Maybe that means you belong here now.'

'Well, everyone has to belong somewhere.' He severed the stem of the aubergine between his nails. 'Take this home with you, and some more tomatoes for your mother.'

'I should pay you.' Georgie didn't even bother to check her pockets.

'Yes. You must. Tomorrow my father will be completing his tax returns for the year.'

'I thought tax returns were completed in April—that's seven . . . no, eight months from now.'

'My father hates to be late,' Aliz said gravely.

Georgie rubbed the burnished skin of the aubergine with her sleeve. 'I'll come back tomorrow, then.'

'Good.' His chipped front tooth gave him an uneven smile.

Georgie smiled back. She felt young. She felt old. She had no idea what she felt. She liked the way her body melted in the heat. At home she sometimes felt so brittle she feared her bones might snap, but here with Aliz, surrounded by plants and earth and the smell of fermenting fruit, her arms and legs felt supple and her heart simmered and burned.

She looked at his sharp cheekbones and the wild springs of his hair, but tried not to look at his mouth. Whenever Aliz opened it, Georgie thought about kissing him. Almost every physical part of Aliz was fascinating to her. More than anything she wanted to touch the pads of her fingers to his, to put her ear to his heart and hear the rhythm of its beat. She couldn't decide whether his lips were blue or purple or the inside of his mouth hot or cold. All she knew was that she had a strong desire to find out.

LETTY MADE ALICK show her exactly what Nicky's 'modifications' had entailed. She stood next to him, watching, feeling her world distort and spin further out of control as he enthused about the precision of the plywood template; how the switch he'd installed would cut the Peugeot's distributor and stop the car at any chosen moment. Alick had no curiosity about what his adaptations had been needed for—his only interest was whether he was mechanic enough to achieve them.

She had no such excuse. Had she chosen to look on the darker side of the facts, the signs had been there to see: Nicky's opting to take the car instead of flying, his resistance to taking Georgie with him. Then, on their return, hadn't there been some problem with the car? Hadn't the radio not been working or something? She thought back. Yes, it had definitely been the radio. Nicky had had it upgraded some weeks before the trip, relocating the speaker cones on the wooden plinth of the back shelf and covering them with a strip of smart blue perforated leather. Now, at her insistence,

Alick reluctantly cut through that leather and shone the torch downwards.

'Aye, they've been dislodged a wee bit.' He tapped the speakers with his screwdriver. 'See?'

'Yes,' she said shortly. 'I see.' Two of the four screws attaching the cones to the wooden plinth had been loosened and the speakers had been manually swung round and away from the perforated circles. No wonder the quality of sound had been poor. No wonder Alba had complained the whole journey up north. After all, Letty thought bitterly, a man had to breathe.

The week that followed her discovery was the worst week of Letty's life. She spent most of it in bed, away from the children, staring at the passport photo, passing her thumb over the stranger's face with increasing pressure as though some clue to his identity might reveal itself, like one of those novelty scratch cards. She couldn't bring herself to question Georgie. She dared not call Tom.

He has never been the man you thought he was. The accusation came back to her again and again, but if Nicky wasn't who he said he was, then who on earth was she? Her whole life, everything she stood for, unravelled until all she was left with were two hard knots of fury and grief.

One night, when it seemed as if her brain could no longer purge the poison from her thoughts, it was the memory of Tom's vice-like grip on her wrist that suddenly came to her. *Hold on to what you believe, Letty*, he'd said that day in Bonn.

She switched on the light, reached for her cigarettes and smoked three in a row, trying to imagine a Nicky committed to treason, involved in subterfuge—a secretive, bitter man exacting revenge on his government—but she knew then, with absolute certainty, that she could never square this picture with the man she loved. She thought instead of Nicky standing beneath her bedroom window. The Flora Macdonald story . . . Nicky had made it their story, too, and now this memory, on top of so many others, came back to haunt her.

'I'll make you a bet,' Nicky had said one day after he'd first been invited to lunch to meet her father. 'I bet you anything I can get you out of that window at Ballanish and down that tree without your father catching us.'

'This is assuming you'll be asked up to the island,' she'd teased.

'Whether I'm asked or not is irrelevant,' he had said. 'The question is, will you take the bet?'

'What are the stakes?'

'Oh, I'll think of something,' he had replied. 'Don't you worry.'

He'd been due to leave for Washington the following week and she'd been sure he meant to propose before he left, but he hadn't. And when the projected month in the US doubled and his letters started to arrive less and less regularly, she'd fled to the island to nurse her breaking heart. She hadn't seen him for three months—had almost forgotten the bet they'd made—when she was woken by the noise of stones hitting glass. She'd looked out of the window to find him grinning sheepishly up at her.

'Nicky,' she'd said faintly. 'Dear God, whatever are you doing?'

'I'm here to rescue you!' he'd cried in a not entirely successful attempt at a Hebridean accent. 'Come along now, Flora lass,' he'd added when she seemed too shocked to move. 'Down you pop. It's bloody freezing out here.'

When it came to it, Letty had been right. The old tree, more bowed than ever from the unrelenting wind, seemed just out of reach.

'Jump,' Nicky had said recklessly, 'and I'll catch you.'

'Nicky, no!'

'Climb over the ledge and then let go. I'll catch you, I promise.'

'It's too far.'

'Jump and we can elope.'

'Are you proposing to me from down there?'

'What does it look like, goddamnit?'

'Oh, Nicky.' She'd been half laughing, half crying. 'What if I say yes to the elopement thing, but come down the stairs?'

'No,' he'd said stubbornly. 'There are certain things that have to be done for love.' He'd stretched out his arms. 'Jump and I'll catch you. I promise.'

She'd looked down. The ground wasn't that far away, but it was the sort of uneven landing you could easily break a leg on. 'I'm scared.'

'No need to be scared, my love, trust me.'

'Nicky . . .' She'd faltered. She did trust him. Even the thought of him made her bones feel stronger, her blood thicker. Nicky Fleming knew who he was and what he believed in. It was the quality she most loved about him.

'Letty, trust me,' he'd ordered. 'And let go.'

THE PROBLEM WAS Jamie never put anything out of his head. All information received went straight to his 'brainbox' and from there was processed in a manner that made sense to him before any decision was taken on how to use it or where to store it.

His father had had an accident. His father had gone away for a long time. His father was lost. Jamie had tried to fit the clues together but the picture that had finally emerged made no sense to him. And all Jamie had ever wanted was a picture that made sense. Not good sense, not real sense or even common sense, but Jamie sense.

The idea of ghosts perplexed him. Ghosts were lost souls, ghosts had not yet made it to heaven. Neither had Dada. Ghosts could not get to heaven if they had unfinished business down below.

Jamie thought back to the papers scattered across his father's desk in Bonn. He remembered the telegrams that arrived twice a day, the contents of the mysterious 'diplomatic bag' . . . How could his father *not* have had unfinished business? And once again he found himself back on his unrelenting treadmill of sleuthing.

Eventually, tentatively, he turned his attention to the question he least wanted answered: What if his father was dead?

People died. It didn't matter how clever or strong you were. Death still happened. His grandfather had died. Even the bear, with all his strength, might have drowned. His father was a clever man, but wherever it was that he had gone might have been a place too far. He might have been too weak from the accident. The mission may have been too dangerous. His father would have tried his best to get back, but that didn't mean he hadn't failed.

To Jamie's intense surprise, the idea that his father was dead did not much increase the unhappiness he already felt. The emptiness inside him remained the same. Over the past months the memory of his father had continued to fade even as his belief grew stronger that his father would return.

It dawned on him why ghosts were so important: it was to do with this concept that a spirit could return as something else. Ghosts were a get-out clause in the contract with death.

LETTY DISLIKED CLEANING MUSSELS. Tugging at their beards and scraping off the barnacles made her feel like a nurse cleaning up grizzled old men on a geriatric ward. But now, as she dropped a gleaming shell into the saucepan of water, it struck her as a pleasantly mindless pastime. She was standing outside the back door, protected from the wind, and the sun was warm on her face.

The children had disappeared for the day with an assortment of picnic food. She had given up asking what they were doing. What did it matter, as long as they weren't lolling around on the sofa, tearing her heart in two with their listlessness.

She stole another look at Donald John, perched awkwardly on the far end of the bench, away from the mussels. It was unusual for him to pay her a visit, and after a lengthy preamble about the weather, he'd slipped into an even more uncharacteristic silence.

'So, you're keeping well, Donald John?' she ventured.

'Aye, well enough.' He slurped at a mug of coffee, then stretched his neck towards the sky like a stork conducting a survey of possible routes south. Letty could dimly make out the sound of a plane.

Donald John stared at the twin streaks of white cutting through the blue. 'These air-o-planes, where are they going? Forwards and backwards, backwards and forwards. Up in the sky . . . so high, so lonely.'

'They're transatlantic planes, Donald John. I expect they're on their way to America.'

'Aye.' He shook his oblong head in sympathy. 'Poor souls.'

'Yes,' she agreed. She too had no desire to be anywhere except on the beach, or trailing across the machair, blown by wind and rain. She understood why it was so hard for Donald John to leave. The island exerted a mesmeric pull. She had felt the magic of it all her life, but it was a magic that stayed on the island. You couldn't take it with you.

'Letitia,' Donald John began heavily, then broke off to gaze, seemingly with great interest, at an odd assortment of treasures stacked against the wall—glass lobster floats, whale vertebrae, sheep skulls, all bleached white by salt and sun.

'What is it, Donald John?' Letty pressed gently. 'What's bothering you?'

Donald John floated his big hands off his knees, then dropped them down again. 'It's about Alick.'

Letty laid down her knife. 'He's on the drink, isn't he?' she said quietly.

Within the community drinking was accepted as an everyday happening, like breathing or the baking of scones. But since the ghost incident, Alick's behaviour had become increasingly erratic. He had taken to pitching up at ungodly hours, sometimes painfully early or just as Letty was deciding to go to bed. Each time he'd take up position at the kitchen table to spin the most riveting tales from the most commonplace happening. He was a born storyteller and, to begin with, whisky enhanced his comic timing. As the bottle emptied, however, he'd descended into the repeated telling of shaggy-dog stories. There was no question that he was the kindest, most capable man. But she often had a terrible premonition of an Alick to come: embittered and paranoid, his fierce spirit and independence eroded by alcohol.

'He's been taking the oil from you,' Donald John suddenly blurted out.

Letty stared at him. Had Donald John told her that Alick was wanted for war crimes she would have been less shocked.

'He's been stealing oil to pay for the drink.'

'I see.' Letty picked miserably at a mussel beard, untangling it strand by strand. Alick's drinking always meant trouble, but she had not imagined this sucker punch of betrayal.

'Working at the croft all these years and nothing to show for it. Oh, boo boo, it's little wonder. And now with the cattle gone. Poor Alick never got a penny for all he did. Not a penny, no indeed.'

'No, quite,' she said hollowly. Then, more sharply, 'What do you mean the cattle gone, Donald John?'

Donald John raised troubled eyes to hers. 'I was sure he would have told you. Murdo Macdonald—Alick's brother—has sold his father's cattle.'

'He's done *what*?'

'Aye, every last one of them—at the cattle sales.'

'But the cattle are Alick's livelihood. I don't understand. Did Euan ask him to?'

'Indeed, Euan had no idea, Letitia. No idea at all. Why, when poor Euan found out he took a terrible shock. Murdo had no right to them.' Donald John began to rock backwards and forwards in agitation. 'Murdo has the croft in his name but not the cattle.'

Letty's understanding of Scottish inheritance was hazy, but she dimly remembered talk of Euan Macdonald turning the property over to his eldest son, Murdo.

'Aye, Euan left the croft to Murdo,' Donald John's voice rose, 'but that didn't mean he got the moveables along with it. Euan never meant for him to have the cattle, no indeed. Alick has taken it bad, right enough, working all these years, day and night, and getting nothing for his trouble.'

Letty bit her lip. 'He never said a word.'

'Well, it's put him on the drink and little wonder. Wee Alick was always the first to do a hands-turn for somebody. Oh my goodness, yes he was.'

'Oh, Donald John, I wish you'd told me earlier.'

'You have your own worries, Letitia.'

'But why would Murdo do such a wicked thing?'

'They say he needs the money for his contracts, yes indeed, that's it. His company is involved in building that new army base.'

Letty frowned. The army base was only a few years old. 'Why do they need a new one?'

'Well, I'm not sure if it's an army base exactly,' Donald John said thoughtfully. 'Angus Post Office says it might be some kind of nucular station.'

'Nuclear station! No, no. I don't think so. I mean, I think there must be a muddle of some sort,' she added tactfully.

'No one knows what it is supposed to be,' he conceded. 'Alisdair the fisherman had a letter from his cousin Duncan over in Lochbealach who said he'd heard it was a missile firing-range—like that one they built down on south island—but old Jackson up in Clairinish thinks it's an early warning system for Russian bombs.'

Letty was staring at him. 'Donald John, are you quite sure?'

'Well, that's what I hear anyways, and they'll be starting with the building of it pretty soon.'

'But it will be the ruin of Eileandorcha,' she whispered.

'Oh, tse tse, Let-ti-cia, it's not going to be in Eileandorcha, no indeed. It's going to be situated right here in the township.' He screened his eyes from the sun and pointed east. 'On the hill above the church loch. Just over there, at the very top of Clannach!'

'RODDY, DOES EVERYTHING get to be a ghost?'

'Well, I'm not sure I know what you mean.' Roddy wiped the blood from his knife onto a piece of paper. 'This rabbit, for instance. Will it get to be a ghost now it's dead?'

Jamie looked at the opaque, milky eyes of the dead animal. 'No, no, I don't think so. What about lobsters?'

'Lobsters . . .' Roddy appeared to give the matter of shellfish spirits some serious thought. 'Well, now, I can't say I've ever heard tell of a lobster ghost.'

'What about the bear, then? Would the bear get to be a ghost if it's dead?'

'Ghosts are for humans,' Roddy said firmly. 'Now, that's not to say that humans can't turn into rabbits or lobsters after they die, because they can and that's a fact.'

'Yes, I know,' Jamie said eagerly. 'Mrs Macdonald says that fishermen come back as seagulls and that they have the whole sea to fish in.'

'Folks can come back as all kinds of animals, why, seagulls, rats, cockroaches even.'

'But how does anyone know if they're going to come back as a ghost or an animal?'

'Now that depends entirely on the circumstances. If someone's been very brave, they might come back as an eagle, or a horse. But if they've been very bad and disliked by enough people, then they might come back as a fly or a mosquito.' Roddy tugged at a hair sprouting from his ear. 'Indeed, lad, there's many a wicked man I've ground under the heel of my boot.'

'But you've seen ghosts too, haven't you, Roddy?'

'Aye, plenty of them.'

'Alick thinks there's a ghost in mum's bedroom.'

'Well, then,' Roddy said lugubriously, 'I'm very sure there is.'

'Roddy, where do people go when they don't go to heaven?'

'To hell,' he said serenely. 'Down in the depths of the earth.'

'Where the earthquake people live?'

Roddy lifted his cap and scratched his head. 'I don't rightly know about that, Jamie, but there's plenty of room down there for all sorts. Hell is where the devil lives, right enough. Ach, the stories I could tell you about the devil.'

Jamie was well aware that Roddy seemed suspiciously privy to the devil's itinerary on any given day of the year, which he was happy to report to anyone who cared to ask, but Jamie had no intention of getting sidetracked. There was really no question of his father fraternising with the devil. He would take a very dim view of that sort of thing.

'What if you're not a wicked person, but you haven't made it to heaven yet?'

'Could be that a soul has unfinished business on earth. Folks can get trapped somewhere between the two until they see to whatever it is that's been bothering them.'

'Roddy,' Jamie took a deep breath, 'do you think it's possible my father's being a ghost or an animal somewhere?'

The hunchback eyed him thoughtfully. 'Well, that's hard to say, Jamie, indeed it is.'

'So who decides whether you get to come back as a person ghost or an eagle ghost?'

'It depends what you believe.'

'Yes, but what do *you* believe?'

'Well, now, I say if a man wants to come back as a ghost or an eagle, then that's his choice,' he pronounced philosophically. 'If it's a question of unfinished business, I would imagine it's whatever suits a man's purpose best, and if he's been a good enough fellow, why, who's to say he won't get what he wants?'

His body ached. Hunger had morphed into a fiend inside him, one that grew more demanding every day and, as it growled, raking its claws up and down the inside of his stomach, he was overcome with the doubt that freedom and choice brings. Why not end it? Lumber into the township and wait for the net to close round him.

As he began losing control over his body, the shape and pattern of his thinking began to change. His head filled with memories he didn't recognise, feelings he had never experienced. He didn't fully understand the journey he was on, but he sensed its magnitude and so he fought hunger and doubt as he'd never before fought any opponent.

From time to time, when energy returned to him, he left the cave, slaked his thirst in the small burn that trickled into the loch, then made his way to the house, staying as long as he dared. He leaned against the stone wall for support and reassured himself with the comings and goings of the family. But these forays tired him and were followed by extended periods of weakness spent in a trance-like state back in his cave.

Every night he dreamed of the boy—that serious little face, his puppet-and-string form, on top of the cliff, silhouetted against a thundery sky.

'Hello, bear,' the boy said.

'Come to me, boy,' he begged, and reached out . . . but the boy could not hear him, had yet to work out that he even existed.

LETTY SAT ON HER BED, trying to imagine herself walking downstairs, picking up the receiver and dialling the Foreign Office. It was months since she'd spoken to Tom, so how could she just say Nicky's name then stumble through small talk as if nothing had happened? Still, what choice did she have? The long arm of the government had snaked north and tightened its acquisitive fingers round this tiny space, this one-third of an acre that she'd carved out for her family, and she was damned if she was going to allow them to take it from her.

It had taken four telephone calls to secure the correct number for the Member of Parliament for the Highlands and Islands, and a further two to break through the protective guard of his staffers. Marriage to a diplomat had endowed her with a high tolerance for bureaucracy and she was prepared for further filibuster from the man himself, but Edward Burgh had been depressingly forthcoming. He had agreed with Letty that most people had little idea of the extent of Ministry of Defence activities in Scotland. In the Highlands and Islands alone, there was St Kilda, the army base on Shillaig, the missile firing-range at Gebraith. 'A number of other proposals are being considered,' he added. 'If there are no significant job gains or extensive upheaval is threatened, we argue there's a threat to the language, faith and culture of island people, but I have to advise you that the government is committed to the expansion of its military presence in Scotland.'

So Donald John had been right. After his visit that afternoon she'd gone straight to see Euan Macdonald.

'Oh, yes, Let-icia, there's been talk of it,' the old man had said.

'On Clannach.' Her throat had constricted.

'Aye, right up on the top.'

'But you'd be able to see it all over the island!'

'Aye, that's the truth.'

'But of all places, why here?' She'd paced the croft's smoky interior.

'They say it's a convenient place for tracking the enemy right enough.'

Euan looked ill, Letty thought. His eyes were watery and his whole physiology had changed, as though his iron spirit had been forcibly extracted leaving only a shell. He'd taken his son's treachery hard, Donald John had warned her and, God knows, she understood. Why was it that the people you loved were capable of betraying you with such apparent ease?

'Have you talked to the town council? Surely if there was enough opposition, they could stop it.'

'Why, there's plenty of opposition, Let-ic-ia. There's many a crofter who's been complaining. There was plenty of opposition to the military base on St Kilda and to that missile firing-range above Our Lady of the Isles, but they went ahead and built those anyways. Maybe it's no' so bad with the closure of the seaweed factory.' He'd stared into the fire, then raised his eyes pleadingly to hers. 'Murdo says the islanders would be involved in short-term building. He says the MoD might employ them there, as drivers or security.'

'And you believe that?' But Letty knew he needed little convincing about the fickleness of his own government. At the beginning of the First World War, the MoD had made lavish promises to all Hebrideans prepared to fight for their country, first and foremost being the ownership of their crofts should they return alive. They had reneged on the deal and most of the survivors who'd managed to make their way back to the island, demoralised by the horrors of war, had resignedly accepted the betrayal.

'Ach, the MoD has lied on more than one occasion,' Euan conceded unhappily.

Letty had been struck by the miserable irony. What if there should be a job for Alick on Clannach and what if her meddling threatened it? She was damned if she did and damned if she didn't. She didn't believe the MoD promises, not for a second. She realised, with a clarity that shocked her, how much she loathed her own government for conspiring against her husband and everything else she held dear. If, right now, someone were to demand of her a quid pro quo for preventing this newest monstrosity from being built, there was nothing she wouldn't agree to.

'There must be someone on the island who can help? Someone with influence.'

The old man had gripped her hand. 'There isn't a soul on the island with any influence with the Ministry, Letitia . . . except for you, *mo gràdh*.'

No one in the Fleming family took baths to get clean—only to keep warm. Hot water was limited and the family took their turn in strict pecking order, youngest being last. At least in the tepid soup of the family's collective dirt, Jamie could submerge himself completely for as long as he liked.

Under the water, his mind relaxed and his thoughts turned to his conversation with Roddy. Premonitions, ghosts, animals, insects. It seemed that people were able to return as just about anything. After some reflection, however, he decided he wasn't particularly keen on the idea of his father returning as a ghost. The practicalities of ghost life worried him. Ghosts, for example, could not drive cars or buy ferry tickets. To come back as a bird or an animal made so much more sense, and he could imagine his father appreciating the freedom and sheer fun of it.

He stretched his foot towards the tap. A thin trickle of hot ran over his toes. His father would have put considerable thought into the logistics of his return. His father was an important man, a good man. If he chose, he could be a unicorn or a golden eagle. Jamie closed his eyes and imagined his father swooping down and taking him on his back. He would hook his fingers through the soft vanes of the feathers, watch the wing tips twist in the wind, and together they would soar!

His eyes snapped open under the water—but surely his father, of all people, would realise that there was more than one eagle on the island. If he fancied returning as a gannet, well, there were 80,000 on St Kilda alone, so it would be the same problem, only worse. He would never choose a snipe or goose for fear of getting shot, and he would hate to be a black-backed gull or hooded crow because he referred to them as bloody vermin.

Jamie came up for air. He tried to visualise other birds he had noted down in his book—wagtails, starlings, curlews—but all struck him as too insignificant. It was possible, though, that Nicky might choose a deer . . .

Jamie's heart quickened. He scrambled out of the bath and grabbed a towel off the back of the chair. His father might appear to him at any moment, in any form. Whatever he decided to return as, whatever sign he chose to give, Jamie now made a promise of his own: he would be ready.

ALBA SQUINTED into the darkness. A bluebottle was hurtling around the room. The buzzing was intolerable and she fumbled for the switch on her bedside light. The noise stopped. The fly was squatting on the inside wall of the lampshade. She examined it sourly. What disgusting vampiric creatures flies were. Slowly, deliberately, she reached for her paperback but the fly evacuated with a furious buzz and began a retaliatory dive-bombing of each wall from the safety of the ceiling.

After several abortive attempts to kill it, Alba decided the more intelligent tactic would be to entice it from the room with a fresh electrical glow. She switched off her lamp and marched into the corridor. A cold draught was twisting up through the staircase. Christ, they might as well live in Siberia or the Ukraine. She walked on, then stopped abruptly outside her mother's room. A wedge of light was spilling onto the carpet. After a second's hesitation, Alba peered through the crack in the door.

Her mother was sitting up in bed, a letter in her hands. She appeared to be reading it fitfully, as though the contents were too painful to be absorbed more than a sentence at a time. As she put it down and picked it up again, her face contorted into expressions of sorrow, and Alba found the effect disturbing. Suddenly, her mother threw the letter away, then, balling up her fists, began to pummel her face. After that, the tears came in a seemingly unstoppable flow, bringing with them small, dulled-down animal noises.

Out in the corridor, Alba shivered in the cold night air, intrigued, deeply suspicious. What had made her mother cry? A note from the bank? A letter from the embassy? Could Georgie have confessed her sneaky rendezvous with the Paki's son? Well, serve her mother right for opting so comprehensively out of her children's lives.

She went back to her room, but couldn't forget the way her mother had cried, the desperate hold she'd kept on that letter. What was it all about? She would make it her business to find out.

IN LETTY'S DREAM, once she'd fallen asleep, she saw herself from the air, a dark speck silhouetted against the khaki fern of south Clannach. The wind toyed with the hood of her jacket while Alick pulled her by the hand up the hill's steep incline.

'Ach, there it is, Letitia!' he cried, as the twin funnels of a nuclear power station loomed into view. 'You'll not guess, but the fairies built this!'

And now she was being transported to the schoolhouse, where a meeting of the Ballanish township was in progress. The islanders were sitting in rows of chairs flanked by the military, who were standing to attention for the Ambassadress. Gillian, impeccably dressed in her family's clan-appropriate tweed, stood on stage, one hand resting on the burnished end of a warhead.

'It has come to our attention that a bear has been seen on this island,' she began. 'The bear is the symbol of Russia. Who knows how much information this enemy spy has already gleaned? Our existing defence plans have been compromised. The Outer Hebrides are now at the geopolitical axis of the Cold War and the facility we intend to build here will provide the integrated command and control system of Great Britain with early warning of approaching enemy aircraft and nuclear attack.'

'How much time?' One of the islanders raised a tentative hand.

'Two minutes,' the Ambassadress shot back her reply. 'Now, for those of you who may harbour doubts as to the validity of this project, let me remind you that any community hosting a military facility will provide an essential service to the nation. This should be considered an honour for a people whose sole purpose up until now has been the cultivation of potatoes and the export of rotting sea matter.'

Letty's eyes snapped open. For a moment she lay still, dismayed to find that the horror of her nightmare had not been alleviated by waking. Then she glanced at the clock and threw back her covers.

Tom's plane would be landing in just over two hours.

GEORGIE DIPPED HER FOOT into the cold green water of the swimming hole. A zigzag of baby eels panicked and changed direction. Beneath her toe, a bright red sea anemone was stuck to the rock like a wine gum.

'I had no idea this place even existed.' Aliz took a drag on his cigarette and passed it to her. 'It's grand.'

'I've always come here,' she said. 'Ever since I could first swim.'

Along the coast, a rising gale was whipping the sea into a foam, but within the protective curve of the cliff the rock pool was as calm as a millpond, the water clear twenty feet down to its white sandy bottom.

'Look at the sky,' Georgie said. 'It's such a weird colour. Like someone's placed tracing paper over the sun.'

'Ah, see the hand of God.' Aliz kicked at a limpet with the heel of his boot.

'What's that mean?'

'My father says it whenever he thinks something is beautiful, or when he cooks something tasty. "Ah, Aliz, my son," he cries, "see the hand of God," and then he rubs his chin in wonder.'

'I love days like this,' Georgie said, 'when the weather is suspended and you know a storm is coming.'

'Wouldn't you prefer it sunny?'

Georgie shrugged. She found it strange that of all planets, the sun was most revered. She connected with the earth. Soil. Mud. Rock. Sand. Somewhere, way below them, a magnificent geological pulse was sending electrical charges to every human being, keeping their hearts beating, keeping them alive. She pushed herself into the dip of the rock until she felt her chest constrict as the voltage passed though her. Maybe these were what growing pains felt like.

Aliz was leaning on his elbow, his bushy head propped up on one hand.

She laid her arm alongside his. 'Look at your skin against mine.'

'Yours is so white. Mine is made of peat. It looks like it's been stewing in the bog ever since the Vikings hacked it off and threw it there.'

Georgie laughed. 'Well, I still like yours better.'

'Take it, then.' He hooked it round hers.

She touched his skin. 'I don't like the hairs.'

'Pull them out.'

'No, it'll hurt.' Georgie sprinkled sand onto his arm then ground it in under the pad of her finger. 'Besides, I have my own ways of making you talk.'

They lapsed into silence.

'Doesn't it feel strange?' she said after a while. 'To be so different.'

'Because of my dirty peaty skin?' He looked at her and grinned. 'You don't know, do you?'

'Know what?' She reddened.

'It's not me. My family aren't the outsiders here. You're the ones the islanders talk about all the time. You, your sister, your father, grandfather.'

Georgie hugged her knees to her chest. 'What do they say?'

'I don't know.' He backtracked hastily. 'Lots of things.'

'What do they say about my father?'

Aliz hesitated, gouged a hole in the sand and dropped his cigarette inside. 'Everyone has their own idea of what happened to him.'

'Like what?'

'My father heard someone saying he'd been assassinated. Chrissie thinks it was a plane crash. Peggy said he got the cancer.' He looked at her for a reaction, but Georgie's face was turned away. 'You know what everyone's like round here,' he went on uncertainly. 'Angus Post Office is convinced that Russians have hold of him and are keeping him prisoner.'

'I wish that were true.' There was a hard edge to her voice. 'At least it would mean he was alive.'

'I'm sorry. You must hate people asking about it.'

'No one *ever* asks about it. At the beginning my mother didn't want to upset my brother, but now it's as if my father has become a taboo subject.'

'I shouldn't have brought it up.'

'No, I want you to bring it up.' Talking about her father felt as if someone had clamped an oxygen mask to her face. She was giddy for more. 'Ask me anything,' she blurted out. 'Ask me how he died.'

Aliz looked at her, shocked. He dropped his eyes, touched the veins in the rock with his finger. 'All right then, how did he die?'

'He fell. From the roof of the embassy.'

'He fell. How?'

It occurred to Georgie, in that moment, that 'how' was the one word which encompassed all her torment. People didn't spontaneously fall from roofs. People were pushed from behind or they leaned against railings that gave way . . . she took a deep breath. 'I think he jumped.'

'Jumped?' Aliz stared at her. 'Why?'

'No one knows,' Georgie said. Secrets you carried deep inside got heavier with each passing day. Aliz was still staring. Grains of sand glittered on the curve of his cheekbone. 'Except me,' she whispered. 'I know.'

'ALICK, WHY DON'T YOU come any more when we put the flag out for you?'

'Well, I've a good many things to do just now,' Alick said.

Jamie looked doubtful. It was early afternoon, but Alick had only just got up. His wire-brush hair was sticking up and his eyes were red-rimmed.

'Is it because you're scared of Flora Macdonald's ghost?'

'Not at all.'

'Because Mum said that Flora Macdonald went to Australia with Neilly McLellan and it's just the wind that makes that howling noise.'

'If Flora and that rascal got to Australia,' Alick said bitterly, 'then they're a lucky pair of devils and that's a fact.' He scrabbled some loose tobacco off the table and looked around for his papers.

Jamie watched him unhappily. The electric blower was on full and he could hardly breathe for the cloying heat. Usually, he liked the military tidiness of Alick's caravan, which served as both house and workshop. Today, though, the caravan wasn't orderly at all. Plus, the caravan smelt of something mildewy. Jamie wrinkled his nose and watched as Alick struggled with the buttons of his boiler suit. It was already clouding over and a storm was brewing. It would be no use looking for stags in bad weather.

'Were you scared of ghosts when you were my age?'

'The will-o'-the-wisp,' Alick said grimly. 'That's what I was scared of. I only saw it once, but it was made up of a whole lot of lights and seemed to move with the wind. It must have been phosphorous gases from the bog right enough, but still and all, we were terrified it would get us.'

Jamie looked out of the window. 'Alick, if you died and came back as an animal, what do you think you'd come back as?'

'Captain Alick is indestructible.' Alick flashed him a grin. 'So I'll not be dying any time soon.'

'But do you think people can come back as animals?'

'Of course. Why there's a sheep out on the machair, I swear is the very spitting image of Donald John's dead aunty.' Alick pushed open the door of the caravan and jumped down. 'Let's be off.'

'Can I drive?'

'Aye, if you don't put us in the ditch.'

Alick climbed up into the tractor seat and pulled Jamie up after him. Jamie sat on his lap, put the tractor in gear and turned the stiff key. There were few pleasures in life as great as operating heavy machinery but, to his frustration, they'd gone barely 100 yards before they were waved down by Peggy from the shop, a grim look on her face and a white plastic bag hanging from her wrist. Jamie's heart sank.

'If you're headin' to Horgabost, Alick, will you give me a ride?'

'We're away to the Committee Road, Peggy.'

'To the Committee Road! At a time like this? You've no' heard then?' Peggy was a determined competitor in the gossip race and nothing made her happier than being first over the line with the news.

'What is there to hear?'

'Why, word is all over the island,' she hedged. 'I'd be surprised if it's not on the wireless too.'

The skill of the game was to delay the actual information for as long as possible while systematically building up interest. Peggy had plenty more teasers up her sleeve, but hadn't allowed for the severity of Alick's hangover. 'Out with it, woman,' he commanded.

'Well, if you must know,' she said, 'they've spotted the bear.'

'The bear?' Jamie spluttered. 'My bear?'

'Aye, the wrestler's bear,' Peggy said.

'Are you sure?' Jamie sprang out of his seat.

'Quite sure, and what an excitement, with everyone thinking he was drowned all this time.'

'I knew it.' Jamie punched the air with his fist. 'I knew he was still alive.'

'Alive and well indeed,' Peggy said placidly. 'Old Archie down at Horgabost was getting ready to go out with the sheep when he saw a wee furry ear sticking up behind the rock. He reasoned at once that it must be the bear and he had that nice Sergeant Anderson down in a jiffy, bringing the wrestler with him. Why, the man was that keen to get here, they say he flew up in an army helicopter, all the way from Perthshire, with half the press on his heels.'

'So they've caught him?'

'Why, no.' Peggy, still working her way towards the actual essence of the news, shook her head in feigned disbelief. 'It's the strangest thing. Archie says the wrestler put down a bucket of fish not fifty yards in front of him and the bear didn'a move an inch towards him!'

'So he's still on the loose?' Alick squinted thoughtfully in the direction of Horgabost.

'Aye, took himself off at a run,' Peggy said triumphantly, 'and with the reward still on his head.'

Alick stabbed at the tractor's starting button and stuck out a hand for Jamie. 'Come on,' he said grimly. 'We'll get after him.'

'Well, you'd best be careful,' Peggy said, unwilling to relinquish her audience without an encore, 'for it's the greatest likelihood he's gone mad. Because if, after six weeks, that poor beast's not looking for his fish and he's not looking for his wrestler, then who on earth can he be looking for?'

Jamie almost heard the click in his head. He paused, his foot on the metal step of the tractor. 'What do you mean?' he asked slowly.

'Well, no doubt it was the commotion that scared him, but I heard Archie tell that the bear took off in such a hurry, why, anyone would think he had some kind of unfinished business to take care of.'

Now Jamie's brain was flashing like a circuit board. The bear . . . of course, the bear! Hadn't the bear been with him every step of the journey? From the *Zirkusplatz* in Bonn to the coach passing him on the Inverary road? If the Peugeot hadn't rolled into the river, wouldn't they have even crossed the Minch on the same ferry? Oh, he was stupid! It had been his father who'd made him love bears. The *Gummibär* sweets, the grizzly in the museum, the *Zirkusbär* balancing on his unicycle. His father had told him that bears were princely animals, highly intelligent, and this one had been well educated. Jamie felt his heart slam painfully against his ribs. If his father were to come back as an animal, then what else would he choose?

Alba was right. He was a retard! He was *nugatory*. He felt like smacking himself in the face. Of course the bear wouldn't allow himself to be caught. Of course he wouldn't be lured from his purpose by some smelly bucket of fish. His father had come back exactly as he'd promised. He had unfinished business, something to tell his family. And all this time he'd been waiting patiently for Jamie to find him, for Jamie to hear him.

For Jamie to understand.

GEORGIE TOLD ALIZ all that she could remember. How, when it had been Porter's turn to take notes, he had moved to the end of the table, while Norrell had repositioned himself next to her, the very personification of friendly informality. 'So, why don't you tell us what he looked like, this Torsten fellow. Where did your father meet him and what was discussed?'

Georgie had fixed her gaze on his jacket. It was virtually without creases. A pen was hooked by the lid onto his lapel. The door to the room had opened. The Ambassadress entered carrying a mug of hot chocolate, which she set on the table.

'How are we doing?' she enquired. When there was no reply, she stiffened her back. Protocol was not as clear as it might be on the interrogation of minors of deceased diplomats. She bore no particular fondness for the secret ferrets of the government, but Fleming had died on her watch and she would see to it that there was fair play. 'Mr Porter?'

'Very well, very well,' Porter responded with weary heartiness.

'Georgiana?' Again Gillian waited for an answer but Georgie was staring over her shoulder. Framed in the shadow of the doorway stood the familiar form of Tom Gordunson and she felt the tightness of fear loosen a notch. Tom would make it all right. Tom was family.

Or was he? As he stepped forward, she caught his brief nod to Porter and Norrell, before all three men turned once again to her. 'Are you all right, Georgie?' Tom asked. 'Would you like me to stay?'

Georgie's fraught brain whirled. *Trust no one*, her father had told her. *They're all watching you*. She pushed away the hot chocolate. She was no longer a child whose cooperation could be bought.

The Ambassadress absorbed the hostile atmosphere and recalibrated her tactics. 'Georgiana, these men are here to help. They understand how difficult this is for you and appreciate your desire to be loyal to your father, but you must realise that anything you tell them might help to put the record straight.'

'The record?' Georgie looked from the Ambassadress to the three men. It was a colossal gaffe and all of them recognised it. Georgie knew then she had been right to lie. That she would continue to lie.

'Just a turn of phrase, my dear.' The Ambassadress took barely a second to recover. 'I'm afraid that in the business we're in, even tragedy is subject to records and red tape. I'm so sorry.' She turned the handle of the mug towards Georgie and eased it gently in her direction. 'You'll tell them everything they want to know, won't you?'

Georgie nodded. The day she'd left East Berlin, she'd put it out of her mind—the echo of her feet on the stone flags in the church, the low whispers and the strained face of the man her father had met inside.

'Be careful, Georgie.'

She looked up. Tom was standing right over her. Suddenly, his eyes met hers and she felt weak with certainty. He knows, she thought. He knows.

'It's hot,' Tom warned. 'Take small sips.'

Georgie picked up the mug and gulped down as much as she could, wincing as the milk blistered her tongue. The pain was good. It made her less vulnerable.

'Don't keep her too much longer,' the Ambassadress instructed Norrell. 'After all,' she added with infinite compassion, 'she's only a child.'

After Tom and the Ambassadress had left, Georgie told Porter and Norrell everything. How the waiter in the hostel restaurant denied having a table for them. Then, in response to her father gesturing towards all the empty ones, had said coolly, 'Your eyes deceive you,' as he stared hard at the wallet in Nicky's hands. She told them that of the eight items listed on the menu, seven had been unavailable and that when her order of sausage and potatoes arrived, the meat gave off a lingering smell of lignite. She told how none of the streetlamps worked. And that Torsten had been wearing a knitted tie and orange shoes. She overwhelmed Norrell and Porter with information, drowned them in detail. And she could see the impatience in their eyes. Later, they would scour page after page in the hopes of identifying the one important lie.

'And what did they talk about, your father and this man?' Norrell, still deceptively relaxed, made a show of checking his own notes. 'Who did they talk about? Can you remember if they mentioned anyone in particular?'

'I was a bit bored, really.' Georgie matched her tone to his. 'I read my book most of the time. *The Mayor of Casterbridge*, we were studying it at school last term and there was a test coming up.'

It was true, Georgie *had* read her book. Still, echoes of the conversation kept returning to her. Schyndell. Torsten and her father's frustration with regard to the factory clean-up. The unanswered questions of who was at fault, whose head would roll. The determination of every tier of East German government to blame management, and for management to kick someone farther down the ladder. She clearly remembered her father saying quietly and furiously, 'It's nothing more than a witch hunt,' with

Torsten's reply coming in an equally low voice: 'Yes. Apparently this is the last we'll be seeing of our friend Bertolt Brecht—I'm afraid he's going to be scrubbing institutional toilets for the rest of his life.'

'Why would Bertolt Brecht be scrubbing toilets?' she'd asked later. 'I thought Bertolt Brecht was a playwright.'

Her father had been distracted. The Peugeot wouldn't start and they'd been waiting over an hour outside the hotel for the garage to pick it up.

'He is a playwright,' he answered after a second or two, 'but all the players in our little industrial accident have pet names. It makes the meetings a little more lively for us.'

He had been play-acting at jolly, she'd thought retrospectively; even at the time, he'd looked tense and worried.

'So, what happened in the church?' Porter asked again.

Georgie had sworn then and there—she would tell Norrell and Porter nothing. She would never tell her mother.

Now, sitting on the sand and looking towards the horizon, clouds were merging over the sea and there was a deep rumble of thunder.

'My father was a traitor,' Georgie whispered.

Aliz was sitting cross-legged. The bone of his ankle jutted out from underneath his trousers, hard and round as a pebble.

'My father was a traitor.' She said it louder and his face closed down in acknowledgment.

Georgie lay back against the cold rock. She took Aliz's hand then lifted her jumper and slid it onto her stomach. Above them, the storm hovered in the sky like a temper about to burst.

ALBA, SITTING ALONE at the table in the house, studied her father's letter—or should she call it his suicide note? For what, she had no idea, but hell, just add it to the list of everything else that had been kept from her.

Taken the only way out, her father had written. *Forgive me, my love*. And then he had given up on them all. Alba choked on a sob. Had he really loved them so little that death was preferable?

She wanted to shred the letter into a thousand pieces, but she knew it would make no difference. You couldn't rid yourself of knowledge once you were in possession of it. Hadn't she always known there was something more? Grown men did not tumble off roofs. They did not fall to their deaths. That her mother was somehow responsible, she had little doubt.

Why else had she been hiding the truth from her children? Alba reread the terrible lines, stoking the fires of her rage, adding up all the minutes and the hours and the days her mother had treated her like an idiot, making her guess and search for answers. As if it didn't make any difference how he'd died—as if she didn't have the right to know.

Of all the far-fetched scenarios she had concocted, this had been the one that had never occurred to her: her father had killed himself . . .

At that moment—at the very apex of her anger—Jamie careered through the door, literally flew into the kitchen like a runaway truck, with that ghostly white face of his so full of hope, so full of naked want that it both enraged and panicked her.

He opened his mouth and tipped a full load of his screwy thinking down on her like two tonnes of gravel until she could no longer breathe under the weight of it. She heard intermittent snatches—bears, mosquitoes, caves, Roddy, ghosts, heaven—but his voice kept passing in and out of audibility and there was no way it could compete with the roaring static in her head. Suddenly the noise stopped. She opened her eyes to find Jamie staring at her, a look of disbelief on his face.

'Alba, you're crying,' he stated flatly.

'Shut up.' She balled her hands into a fist.

'Alba, don't cry.' He took a step towards her. 'Don't be sad, it's OK.'

Jamie saw that she was shaking and his heart ballooned with sympathy. He remembered every day he'd spent grappling with his father's disappearance. 'Alba, don't be sad, we'll go to the Kettle. You were right all along, that's where he'll be.'

The absurdity of what Jamie was suggesting meant nothing—but his face, shining with conviction, was too much. How dare he have hope when she had none?

'I love you, Alba,' he announced simply. 'You were the first person I wanted to tell.' He plucked at her sleeve.

At his touch, her hand swung back and she struck him with the cumulated force of a year's misery. Jamie spun backwards, his foot caught on the mat's curling edge and he landed hard on the floor. For a second he lay stunned, then his hand floated to his face. 'Alba?' The disbelief in his voice was pitiful.

'Get away from me,' she shouted. 'Just leave me alone.'

'Alba, I don't understand.' A scarlet weal shone on his pale cheek like a burn from an iron. 'I thought . . .' Jamie felt as if everything meaningful was slowly draining out of him.

'You thought what?' she spat contemptuously. 'Oh, hell's teeth,' she said. 'Don't start crying. What have you got to cry about?'

He touched his raw cheek. 'You being nice to me. I thought it was real.'

'You're talking about people coming back as mosquitoes and bears and you're worried about whether me being nice to you was real?' Her face was hard as granite and, despite the distance between them, he shivered at her coldness. It quenched the flame of his hero worship, it froze his unconditional love and in that instant it was over. He felt curiously lightheaded.

'I'm going to the cliff.' He pushed to his feet. 'I'm going to find him.'

'Yes, well, off you pop, Jamie. It's a marvellous idea. Go to the cliff in a storm, why not? In fact, you know what's an even better idea? Why don't you just jump off the bloody cliff and have done with it.'

Even with his shortsightedness he had known who it was, from the way he was standing, the way he was holding that bucket. The big wrestler had come for him. Home was no more than a few hours away and all he had to do to get there was put one foot in front of the other. The sight of the bucket worked like a crank on his hunger and he moved towards the wrestler, drugged by the promise of salvation, the intoxicating smell of fish.

What happened next, no one would ever pretend to understand. All anyone could do was attribute it to the strangeness of the beast's half-human heart.

When the image first entered his brain, it was faint. Then it sharpened and his mouth filled with the sour anticipation of tragedy. The fear was so strong it felt as though it had the power to prise loose the very soul from his body. Because the image haunting him was a new picture, a terrible vision: the boy lying at the bottom of the cliff, still and lifeless. He faltered. For a moment he didn't know where he was. Then, out of the blackening sky, the wind picked up and breathed life back into his numbed soul and finally he understood.

Ignoring the shouts of the wrestler, he turned towards the cliffs and ran.

THE WAITING ROOM was fogged up with cigarette smoke, the meaty fumes of frying bacon and industrial shots of steam from a catering urn that was dispensing tea to a line of people. Letty had never seen the airport so busy. There were huddles of men, bulky canvas bags slung over their shoulders, some queuing for the single payphone, several with cameras dangling round their necks and almost all woefully equipped for the stormy welcome the island afforded them. Letty guessed they were journalists.

The knot in her chest tightened. Tom had become synonymous in her mind with the government and so her hatred for him and them was equal, but from the moment she'd raised the courage to call him, she'd been surprised to find that the details of her fury had become blurred. Had their fight been weeks or days after the accident? Had Tom's refusal to help Nicky really been a betrayal rather than a desperate attempt to prevent his friend from risking his career? Then she remembered Jamie's conspiratorial whisper—*Daddy's a spy, isn't he . . . Tom said*—and she felt a rekindling of all her frustration and anger. What Tom had said had been unforgivable. Christ, why had she even called him?

She'd spent the drive figuring out what to say, but now, faced with the sight of him, stooping a little as he levered his big frame out of the plane, she forgot her lines and felt a prickle of shame. She tried to reorganise her thoughts, but Tom was already walking across the runway, his tweed overcoat blowing about his legs, and nothing felt natural. Should she wave? Not wave? Should she smile or frown? What would he think? Did she look older? Defeated?

She swiped on fresh lipstick and, pulling herself together, went over to where he was already standing by the entrance door, his hair blown over his face. When he said her name and took hold of her shoulders, to her utter mortification, she burst into tears.

On the drive home, she tried to paper over the awkwardness with geographic reminders—look, there was the track down to Maleshare where Nicky had once taken him for a walk; on their right was the turning to the lobster factory, remember? But these dried up long before she reached the causeway and an unreasonably long silence formed around them.

'Letty . . .' Tom began judiciously, cleaning his glasses with his handkerchief. 'Letty, I'm glad you called. I tried to see you in London. I wrote to you.' He turned to look at her helplessly. 'I was never sure whether—'

Letty gripped the wheel and frowned at the road. 'I got your letters, Tom.'

'But you never wrote back.'

'No.'

'Letty.' He pressed on. 'Despite what you thought, despite what you may still think, I have always been Nicky's friend. I am still your friend.'

Letty stared straight ahead. The moment she had picked up the phone to him, she had decided she would tell him nothing of what she had discovered. She would betray Nicky to no one. Tom was here for Clannach, and Clannach alone.

'There's no point dredging it up again, Tom. God knows, nothing can be changed now.'

'Letty,' he said vehemently. 'We must talk about this.'

Letty swerved the car into a passing place and switched off the engine.

'You want to talk about it.' She turned on him. 'Fine, we'll talk about it. You were not a friend to Nicky. You didn't help him or believe in him. You were as quick to condemn him as everybody else.'

'No.'

'You even tried to turn me against him and then you told Jamie. Of all people, you told Jamie.'

'Jamie?' Tom looked baffled. 'Told Jamie what?'

She gave a bitter laugh. 'That his father was a spy.'

'Good God, Letty, how can you say such a thing?'

'Jamie told me. He knew his father was a spy because you told him.'

'I swear on my life I did no such thing. Whatever Jamie thinks I said to him, or whatever I did say to him, he must have misunderstood. Surely you know me better than that.'

'You were his best friend,' she said, and the words caught in her throat. 'Whatever he's done, you should have *fought* for him.'

'Of course I fought for him. MI6, the Foreign Office, the Ambassador; I fought all of them, but you can't disprove suspicion. It's as futile as trying to prove you never received a letter.'

Letty bit her lip miserably. She had no strength for this. '"Nicky has never been the man you thought he was." Isn't that what you said to me that day?'

Tom grimaced. 'It was a stupid thing to say. I've regretted it since.'

'But you meant it, didn't you?'

Tom sighed, pulled his overcoat round him. 'Letty, if Nicky had to choose between his family and his country, what would he have chosen?'

'I don't—' She felt wrong-footed. 'What—'

'You want to know if I trusted him? Yes, I trusted him.' Tom's eyes refused to leave hers and Letty felt the colour rise in her cheeks. 'When a man signs up to work for his country, he thinks he understands what that means. He walks into the job with an unshakable set of principles and the belief that he has the moral backbone to maintain them in some precise and unyielding order, but in the end it never works out that way. If you were to ask me whether I trusted Nicky to put his loyalty to his country over and above his wife and children? Then no. Most people are fortunate enough not to have to make that choice. Maybe Nicky wasn't.'

'Tom, what are you saying?'

'I think Nicky stuck to his own moral code, no matter what side of the line it put him on.'

Tears were rolling down her face. 'They never found anything. There was never anything to find.'

'Letty,' he said gently. He handed her his handkerchief and waited while she dabbed it over her eyes. 'Did I ever tell you why I recruited him?' he asked softly. 'First-rate mind and an apparent ability to gobble up languages notwithstanding?'

She shook her head.

'He was utterly protective of others, with a keen sense of right and wrong. He was idealistic, fair, passionate about Britain's democratic principles. Loathed the Communist regime for obvious reasons. Nicky was a born diplomat, except in one respect: he was a romantic. An impulsive and occasionally reckless one, and there is nothing quite so dangerous as that. It's why he didn't get Rome, Letty. He wasn't ready. He may never have been ready.'

'Oh, Tom.' Tears welled up again.

He waited till she had finished. 'When you called me last week, I did some snooping. It's not my department, as you know, but, well . . . Letty, did Nicky ever mention this proposed site on Clannach to you?'

'No.' She blew her nose. 'Never. Why, do you think he knew?'

'It's possible. He was privy to so much information. It just seems like too much of a coincidence.'

A little coincidental, Porter had said. *A little convenient, don't you think?*

'I had no idea until I looked at the map,' Tom went on. 'Clannach . . . the range . . . it would be right on top of you.'

'Yes.' She held his look. 'It would be.'

'What about Gebraith, the missile firing-range? Did he ever mention that?'

'No.' She looked down at her hands. Of all people, she should know better than to underestimate Tom.

'Letty,' he said quietly. 'Don't make me do this on my own.'

A sudden wave of loneliness overwhelmed her. Her world looked so much less distorted through his eyes. Maybe it was better for everything to come out—the painting, the car. It was the not knowing, the half-knowing. Secrets were corrosive and they made the living of any kind of truth impossible. 'All right,' she said, defeated. 'All right.'

Tom reached into his briefcase and handed her a thin blue leaflet.

'Naval Protection Services.' She opened the report to a subheading on the first page. 'Outer Hebrides. Radio Mist Distance Indicators.' She flicked through pages of tables, technical data and graphs. 'What is this?'

'It's a safety report for Gebraith—Our Lady of the Isles. "Where Religion Meets Radar", as I believe it's been rather wittily dubbed. When you called me,' Tom continued, 'I checked on the status of Clannach and I found the department's feathers were in a state of advanced ruffle about this report.'

Letty dug a nail into the palm of her hand. If Nicky had found out about the proposed plans for Clannach, he would have been in no doubt as to how she'd feel about them.

Nicky painted things he was interested in. He liked to find out how things worked. A study of a bird's beak, a missile firing-range. A nuclear power plant . . .

'The blueprint for Clannach is being lifted directly off the Gebraith model, but this report claims that Gebraith's surrounding areas, i.e. the hills, dunes and beaches, have all been contaminated by something called Cobalt-60.'

'Cobalt-60?' She frowned with recognition.

'Cobalt-60, or CO-60 as it's referred to in the report, is a radioisotope used to track missiles. The report claims that significant amounts of CO-60 have leaked onto the launch pad during the course of the last ten years.'

'And this CO-60. It's dangerous?'

'Highly toxic. If this report is correct, it could have caused a great deal of harm to the island.'

Letty stared at him, appalled. 'What sort of harm?'

'Radiological.'

'Dear God.' She covered her mouth with her hand.

'The report was commissioned following an accidental spillage that was brought to the MoD's attention two years ago.' Tom shrugged. 'Apparently, the missiles on the range were not stored safely. The magnesium in the cone head connected with sea water and that's how the original leak occurred.'

She closed her eyes. So Nicky had known and had said nothing. Magnesium. Cobalt. She saw the codings on his painting. CO-60, MG-137. They weren't colours. They were chemicals.

'Schyndell. Gebraith. One nuclear power, the other nuclear weaponry. Nevertheless much ties them together. Containment, waste treatment, risk of uncontrolled radiation—'

'This is exactly what I was worried about.' Letty stared unseeingly at the report in her lap. 'What about the islanders, have they been warned?'

'You're missing the point. If this report is true, it will have implications for the Clannach project.'

'Why do you keep saying *if* the report is true?'

'When this came in, everybody was so busy reacting to the content, they didn't initially look into where it had come from.'

'Stop being so bloody cryptic, Tom,' she said calmly, though her heart was thudding. 'Where did it come from?'

'That's just it. No one knows. This report was not commissioned by the MoD, or any other government body. Look.' He took the document from her and flicked to the last page. 'It's not even signed with a name, just initials: BB.' He looked at her keenly. 'I believe the report is fake.'

RAIN WAS SLUICING down the glass, wind howling through the pipes of the Raeburn. Alba clenched and unclenched her fists as she went from window to window scanning for any moving smudge that might turn into a boy. The storm should have forced Jamie's return long before now. He was obviously staying out on purpose to land her in trouble. If he was still out sulking in a storm when her mother returned, the crime would increase ten-fold in severity. Not that she cared about being punished. She had already decided on solitary confinement for the rest of her life, and her mother simply wasn't imaginative enough to top that, but it would be better if Jamie came back. None of them was allowed to go to the cliffs on their own. Especially Jamie. Especially in this weather.

He knew to be careful, but it was raining hard and it would be slippery, misty as well. And then there had been that look in his eyes, a glittering brilliance she'd never seen before. She felt the curdle of shame. She'd gone too far, but hadn't it been justified? If he was chasing about the island after some childish fantasy then why the hell should she get a soaking just to bring him down to earth? Let him take responsibility for once.

She sat down at the table but the rain continued to fall and the clock ticked. With each passing minute, she began to feel a sick uneasiness. What if he did something stupid, really stupid, as in attempt to climb down the Kettle to look for the bear? Suddenly, a horrifying image of his foot sliding on the wet grass passed through her head and she knocked back her chair abruptly.

'All right,' she said grudgingly. 'Bloody hell.' The sound of her own voice calmed her.

On the mantelpiece she caught sight of Jamie's collection of bird skulls. She identified a crow and a curlew, alongside something larger—a cormorant, perhaps. On a whim, she placed the skulls on three separate plates, arranging them on the table flanked by a knife and fork. She tore a strip of paper from Letty's writing pad and bent it into a placement card.

Enjoy, she wrote, then she propped the card in front of her mother's place setting and slammed out of the front door.

THE WEATHER WAS CLOSING in fast. Jamie was thankful for his coat as he stumbled across the bog, hardly bothering to aim for stepping stones. He was oblivious to both the wet and the cold. His body was on fire, his heart drumming as if a moth were trapped against his rib cage and, by the time he reached the cliffs, he was close to hyperventilating.

He threw himself down on the ragged side of the Kettle and attempted to untangle the strap of his binoculars from his pocket. 'Bear!' he shouted. 'Dada!'

No reply, only the pattering of rain on his anorak hood and the wind in his ears. He squirmed closer to the edge and peered over. The bottom of the Kettle was roiling with water. Out to sea, a long wave crested white, sending spray and specks of yellowing foam into the air.

'Dada!' he yelled again. The wind stole his voice and laughed in his face. A fulmar, hugging a ledge a few feet beneath him, looked up and squawked with distaste.

'Bugger off, fulmar,' Jamie said wildly. He tried wiping his jumper sleeve over the convex lens of the binoculars, but the wind was gathering strength and it was no longer possible to hold them steady. Besides, the

Kettle was too high and narrow for him to see into the tunnel. He stuffed the glasses back into his pocket and shuffled round the perimeter on his stomach. When he reached the ridged spine that funnelled down to the bottom, he stopped and appraised the descent with what he hoped was a professional eye. The day his father had climbed down had been the day he'd found the cave. Forbidden, dangerous, off-limits, yet . . . possible. And Jamie couldn't rid himself of the notion that he was meant to do it.

It began easily. The heather at the top was bunched and thick enough to take his weight. But as he progressed down, the clumps grew sparser. After thirteen or fourteen feet, the spine narrowed and steepened and Jamie spread-eagled himself across its width, hugging the sides with both arms and digging his fingers into the soil. He was wet through and didn't feel quite as confident as before, but scrambling back up seemed impossible.

He took a deep breath and continued down, itsy bitsy spider, synchronising his arms and legs, descending inch by precarious inch. After another few minutes he discovered his left foot waving ineffectively in space and was compelled to press his head into the mossy slope to stop himself falling. 'Dada!' he yelled, as the dread realisation hit him. He was stuck.

The shriek of the fulmar came a fraction of a second before its wings brushed against the back of Jamie's head. Instinctively, he took a swipe at it and his body came away from the cliff like a winkle kicked off a rock. Down he plummeted, another fifteen feet. There was an intense pain in an indefinable part of his body, and at the same time his head jerked backwards and smashed against something solid.

And then everything went dark.

GEORGIE STOLE a sideways look at Aliz. He was working the pedals with his boots undone and the laces dangled from the eyelets like spaghetti. When he turned and grinned at her, an electrical charge ran through her body. Under Aliz's touch, every awkward curve and angle of her body made sense for the first time. She could still feel the imprint of his fingers pressing against the arc of her ribs, a graze where sand had rubbed between their lips. She touched it with her tongue as the mobile van clattered over the watery potholes of the road.

Suddenly every tug of emotion she'd suppressed, every tiny bead of information in her abacus of knowledge felt relevant to her future, and, for the first time in a long time, the world glowed with possibility.

Through the window, Georgie watched a flock of geese take wing and assemble into a V formation, their long necks stretched out, their feathers glinting white under the thin seam of light in the dark sky.

Aliz stopped the mobile van at the yellow gate. When he blinked, his eyelashes closed down on his cheek like velvet claws. He took her hand and pressed the tips of her fingers one by one. 'Can you meet me tomorrow?'

Georgie nodded. She would meet him every tomorrow, she thought.

Happiness suffused her. She wafted into the house, floated through the kitchen door, his name whispering in her head, *Aliz, Aliz*. Every time she heard it, a tiny pair of bellows blew at her heart, making it glow red, making it spark, and when she heard a voice telling her that she looked chilled to the marrow, that her clothes and hair were soaked from the rain, she assumed her mother must be talking to someone else. How could she be referring to a person whose heart and soul were on fire? But then she heard another, strangely familiar voice and she plummeted down to earth with a jolt.

Tom Gordunson rose slowly from the kitchen table. 'So how's my favourite goddaughter?' He kissed her on the cheek and sized her up with a rueful laugh. 'Look at you, you look radiant . . . and, well, a little damp.'

'When did you . . . ? Why are you . . . ?' Georgie looked from Tom to her mother. 'I don't understand.'

'It was all somewhat last-minute,' Tom apologised.

'I wanted to surprise you all, darling,' Letty said. 'It's been such a long time since we saw Tom and—'

'Has something happened?' Georgie interrupted.

'Come and sit with us.' Nervously, Letty pushed out a chair.

'No.' Georgie stayed standing, thoroughly spooked. She had finally shouted her secret to the sea and her words had summoned up Tom Gordunson like the ghost of miseries past. 'What's going on? Why are you here?' She glanced at the canvas, partly covered by papers, which was lying between them. 'What are you doing with Dada's painting?'

Letty looked at the floor.

'Georgie, I want to talk to you about your father,' Tom said. 'About Berlin.'

'I don't want to.'

'Georgie, believe me, it's all right.'

'No!' *Aliz, Aliz, Aliz*, she chanted in her head.

'Tom, please.' Letty looked upset. 'If she doesn't want—'

'Something happened in East Berlin, didn't it?' Tom said urgently.

'No,' Georgie said again. She covered her face with her hands but she could remember the raw fear on her father's face as the Grenzer pulled them over. The jump and ring of the telephone in the interrogation room. She could smell the lignite in the air.

There was always the before and after, Georgie thought; something monumental happens and life divides sharply. What little peace of mind her mother had left, she was about to blow apart.

'There is a time,' Tom coaxed, 'when all secrets have to come out.'

'Mum?' she pleaded.

Letty touched the tips of her fingers to Georgie's hand. Her eyes were suddenly brilliant and clear. 'Whatever it is, Georgie, tell us.'

She began haltingly. Berlin was a long story hinging on a single moment, a swift handover. Tom asked a few questions, but listened attentively, drawing on a cigarette, his eyes never leaving her face.

The exchange had happened inside a church. After the car had been towed to the garage and their laborious paperwork had been signed, she and her father had walked through the empty streets, hand in hand.

Her father wanted to make an offering or light a candle. She couldn't remember which excuse he'd used. 'Stay here,' he ordered. 'I'll be back in less than a minute.'

And she had nodded, too cold to move and overcome with a powerful longing for home. Berlin was the saddest place she'd ever been. There was no spirit there, no hope or humanity.

A minute passed and then five. The afternoon was closing in. She began picking her way through the dilapidated headstones towards the church. She wandered through the big doors and towards the altar. When she reached the pulpit, she turned and headed down a side aisle but there was no sign of him, only the echo of her footsteps on the stone flagstones.

'Dada?' she called uncertainly. She started purposefully up the other side of the church, peering through arches and round balusters.

She spotted the shadow of his overcoat before she actually saw him. He was behind a pillar, speaking to someone in a low voice. She'd been so relieved to find him that she'd almost forgotten the conversation. It hadn't been until Norrell and Porter had posed the question about an illicit meeting that the scene had returned to her with all its damning implications.

'Instructions . . . map,' she heard her father emphasise as she crept closer. 'Take it,' he'd urged. Then, 'My friend, time is running out.'

Two more steps and she could see him clearly. He was holding out an envelope, thrusting it towards someone still hidden from Georgie's view. Suddenly, there was a fumble, the ring of something metal dropping onto the stone, and her father had started.

'Dada!' she called in a whisper, and only now as she moved closer did she catch sight of the second man behind the pillar, stooped, then rising quickly from the floor, the envelope already slipped into a pocket, whatever object her father had dropped enclosed by his hand.

'Dada!' she said again, and this time, as the stranger reacted to her voice and turned to look, there had been no hiding the guilt on his face.

Neither Tom nor her mother spoke for a long moment, then Tom reached for the papers on top of the canvas and handed them to her. 'Is it possible that this is the man you saw?'

Georgie frowned at the passport photograph of a stranger, his features flattened by over-exposure, his eyes dead-fish blank. 'Maybe,' she said, 'but I only saw him for a second. . . "Eugen Friedrich Schmidt".' She read the name printed on the ID document. There were small tugs of memory attached to the name, but they dissipated before she could get hold of them. 'Who is he?' She looked up at Tom, but he shook his head.

'I don't know. I was hoping you might. His picture and papers were hidden in your father's painting.'

'Eugen Friedrich Schmidt,' she repeated. She picked up the canvas and ran her hand over the thick paint. 'Why in Dada's painting?'

'Tell her,' Letty said to Tom.

JAMIE WAS FLOATING and the water felt as warm and protective as amniotic fluid. He crossed his arms on his chest. He heard the cry of a seagull, but after a while, nothing, just the persistent lapping of water round the edges of his consciousness.

'Jamie!'

And now his name was being called.

'JAMIE!'

His eyes flew open.

'Jamie,' the voice ordered. 'Don't move.'

Alba.

He stiffened and his knee exploded with pain. Nausea rolled through him. He turned his head to one side and, to his terror, saw that he was lying on a ledge barely wide enough for his body. All around, black rocks were speckled white from fulmars. He remembered the brush of wings against his head. Remembered letting go.

'JAMIE!' Alba's shout echoed around the walls of the Kettle. 'Can you hear me? Are you hurt?' Her voice sounded tinny and far away.

Threads of mist floated through the air. Time slowed while Jamie focused on this important question. Was he hurt? And if so, how badly? Above his head, two fulmars circled in a holding pattern.

'Alba,' he wailed.

'Stay still! Don't move.'

Jamie felt profoundly disorientated. It was as if someone had turned reality inside out as an unkind joke. The rain felt hot against his face. None of this was right. He lifted his head to protest.

'Don't look down!'

He looked down. Sixty feet below him, the bottom yawned. Above him the clifftop swayed. Rain, freefalling from the sky, slicked down the rocks, pooling in the crevices of his ledge, seeping between every stitch of his clothing. One of the fulmars swooped, its hostile yellow beak coming straight for his eyes. Jamie whimpered and turned his face to the cliff wall. 'Dear Lord,' he intoned numbly, 'help me in these troublous times.' He groped at the ledge but it crumbled under his fingers and now he began to cry in earnest.

Thirty feet above him, Alba stood, immobilised by panic. Jamie's sobbing sounded like the bleating of a lost sheep. Monotone, unstoppable, hopeless. She could barely see him through the mist. She needed to get help, but how could she leave him? Christ, if she could only trust him to stay still.

But Jamie could not stay still. He needed to move his leg away from the grinding ache of his pain. Another sliver of rock crumbled and fell. And now Jamie's thin body was wider than the ledge supporting it.

'Alba, help me!' he screamed.

There was a reciprocal yell but the desperation in it frightened him more than anything and this fear caused a seismic shift in his mind. His powers of logic began to shut down and a feral, more animal thinking took hold. Instinct told him it was only a matter of time before the ledge gave way. Instinct told him he was going to die. He was so tired of hoping, of not knowing. It was easier to accept—and accepting was easier than he had ever imagined.

He looked down again, this time with something approaching resignation, and suddenly—there he was. Oh dear God, there he was, waiting at the bottom. Jamie's vision cleared. A slow smile broke across his face. 'Hello, bear,' he whispered.

'Hello, Jamie,' the bear replied.

And at the sound of his father's voice, Jamie felt all the fear and tension, all the misery, doubt, confusion and longing, bleed slowly from his body.

GEORGIE TOUCHED HER HAND to the scratched paintwork of the Peugeot's boot. She was scarcely aware of Tom waiting next to her, shoulders hunched, his hands thrust deep into his pockets. It was raining but she felt so disconnected from the present that she was oblivious to the cold and the bitter wind. Overhead the clouds were darkening, and suddenly it was once again nightfall and she and her father were driving away from East Germany, the atmosphere in the car thick with unease. Still she couldn't shake the feeling they were being watched. Well, they *were* being watched. *I should never have brought you*, her father had said. Suddenly she gave a short laugh.

'Georgie?' Tom stepped forward and laid a hand on her shoulder.

She shook her head, unable to articulate her feelings, even to herself.

It had been complicated and confusing to piece together, but as Tom had worked through his theory, changing details, bending time lines, a story emerged that Georgie began to recognise as one that suited her father. It was the kind of story he would have liked. A fake report, an attempted defection, the very cloak-and-dagger, finger-to-lips drama of it all. And, had it not been for the ending, it was precisely the kind of story he might himself have told his children. She laughed again, except this time she couldn't quite control her voice and hot tears rolled down her face.

'Come on.' Tom wrapped his coat round her shoulders and Georgie let herself be guided back into the house.

'I BELIEVE YOUR FATHER found out that the MoD had plans to build a missile firing-range on Clannach and I think he wanted to stop it,' Tom had said earlier. And Georgie thought she could almost see his brain slotting it together, a mental crossword puzzle with cryptic clues. 'As you know, he was already shuttling backwards and forwards to East Germany as part of the Schyndell clean-up, and I suspect he came into contact with someone at Schyndell who could help him—someone who had a compelling reason to do so.'

Eugen Friedrich Schmidt. The name flitted through her head again and suddenly her brain locked onto it. A memory from the visit, the very smell of it opened up to her as chemically preserved and meticulously recorded as any Stasi cloth or file. 'Poor old Bertolt Brecht,' she said slowly.

Tom looked at her quizzically.

'Bertolt Brecht was going to be made to scrub toilets for the rest of his life. It was the nickname Dada and Torsten gave one of the environmental scientists at the plant. Torsten said the Schyndell investigation had turned into a witch hunt and that this trip was probably the last time they'd see him.' Georgie reached for the passport photo and ID documents. 'Yes.' She stabbed her finger at the name. 'Don't you see? Bertolt Brecht's real name—the playwright's full name—was Eugen Bertolt Friedrich Brecht.'

'Georgie!' Letty exclaimed.

'BB.' Tom nodded. For a while he sat silently, then he cleared his throat and leaned forward. 'Letty, if this Schmidt fellow was being blamed for the accident, he'd have been desperate to get out. The trouble is, unless he was important or senior enough, well, we, the British government, wouldn't have helped him. Nicky must have been a godsend for Schmidt: his defection facilitated in return for providing irrefutable scientific data of a toxic spill on Gebraith . . .'

'So Dada hid him in the car,' Georgie said. Her mind went back to when they were clattering over the potholes of the road. She remembered her father stopping the Peugeot, retching out his fear into the grass verge.

'Schyndell had already dragged on for so long. I imagine your father thought he had more time,' Tom said, his eyes trained on Letty. 'I'm sure he never intended the trip with Georgie to be anything but a dry run, but then Torsten tells him that Schmidt is about to disappear and, realising it's now or never, he decides to take action.' Tom looked at her shrewdly. 'My guess is it started out as a business arrangement, but then Nicky got to know this man and liked him. The idea that he would be persecuted—turned into a scapegoat—would have been unconscionable to him.'

'I still don't understand how he could even contemplate doing something so risky,' Letty said tightly.

'It was less risky than it sounds,' Tom said. 'As part of the delegation, Nicky would have had a degree of diplomatic immunity. Allied personnel are not supposed to be stopped in any zone. Nicky understood the thinking of the East German government better than anyone, though: as far as they were concerned, he was an interesting fish. He knew how closely they watched him, so he had to come up with an extra safety measure of sorts. He drives to Berlin in his conspicuous western model, and, with the aid of Alick's distributor switch, he breaks down in full view of his Stasi tails, knowing perfectly well the car would be towed to a garage and that, once it was, the Stasi would lose no time in bugging it. He hands over a key to Schmidt in the church—Georgie heard something metal drop—along with a map showing the location of the garage, and instructs the scientist to get himself into the car that night. "It's your only chance," your father must have told him. By the time the Peugeot is delivered back to the hotel the next morning, once again in full view of Stasi watchers, Schmidt is safely installed in the secret compartment.'

'But if the Stasi were bugging the car, then wouldn't they have heard him getting in?' Georgie asked.

'A Stasi listening device would most likely be fitted behind the dashboard or heater grill and powered by the battery. It would only be activated by the car being started. The point is, having bugged the car, the Stasi would never suspect that it would then become the means of exfiltration. As a rather ingenious example of hiding in plain sight, it was probably the least risky way to cross the border.'

'Except that we were stopped at the checkpoint.'

'And quickly released after a phone call. The last thing that the Stasi would want would be some oafish Grenzer dislodging their handiwork, but it must have been a terrible moment for your father.'

Georgie bowed her head. *Forgive me, my little George, please forgive me*, he'd said.

'Letty.' Tom took her hand. She had not spoken for some time. 'It's entirely supposition. It might never have happened.'

'Except for the compartment in the car. Except for the report.'

'The report, yes.' He sighed. 'For poor old Bertolt Brecht it was the perfect quid pro quo, but for Nicky . . .'

'He hated bullies,' Georgie said. 'He always backed the underdogs.'

'Yes.' Tom smiled faintly. 'Commendably British in that respect but still, I cannot over-exaggerate the phobia our people have about dealing with anyone from the GDR. I still don't understand, why take *any* risk? There are plenty of silent protestors, some in our own government even, who are virulently against the building of further military sites. Nicky could have convinced one of them to write the report.'

'No,' Letty said quietly. 'He would never have done that. That he would have considered a betrayal of his principles, a betrayal of his country. Nicky was motivated by personal not political gain.'

'So the land, the beaches . . . are they contaminated?' Georgie asked.

'That's the MoD's dilemma. They'd chosen not to investigate it before, but this report changes everything. They might not know by whose authority it was commissioned, but if the data that it is based upon is genuine, yes, the Gebraith site could very well be contaminated. Faced with this possibility, the MoD have no option but to commission their own safety report to check for certain. My guess is that this is what Nicky was banking on. He knew that any kind of civil protest would be pointless. Forcing the MoD's hand was his best option: if there were proven instances of toxic spillage in Gebraith, then, surely, not even the government would risk it happening again at Clannach.'

'So did it work?' Letty asked eagerly. 'Have they commissioned a report?'

Tom sighed. 'It seems that, once again, Nicky set too much store by the principles of our government,' he replied grimly. 'I'm afraid the MoD intend to suppress it.'

THE WORDS FLOATED UP, barely audible, jumbled by the wind. 'It's OK,' Jamie had shouted. 'He's here now. Dada's here.'

Alba forced herself to respond calmly. She had surely not heard him correctly. 'Jamie, listen to me. I'm going to get help. I need to find Alick and bring a rope.'

'Alba, I'm going to jump. Dada will catch me.'

'Jamie, no!' she shrieked.

She was sobbing now, running this way and that, trying for a better sight of him, but there was only the thinnest scrap of his anorak wedged between the dark rocks. Holy God, what was he thinking? She looked down through the dense mist and could just make out a near-solid brown mass at the bottom of the ravine . . . moving, gently swaying on top of the water.

'Oh, Jamie,' her voice rose, then broke with understanding. 'No, it's just seaweed. It's *seaweed.*'

'It's OK, Alba. The bear will catch me. Dada will catch me.' Jamie no longer felt the rain or the cold or the ache in his knee. A delicious warmth had enveloped him. He was dimly aware of the fade of Alba's voice, pleading, yelling, but it was no longer the voice he was listening to.

Jump, his father said. *Let go and I'll catch you. I promise.*

Jamie peered down. The sides of the cliff began moving in on him. 'I'm scared, Dada.'

Don't be scared, Jamie. Trust me and let go.

Jamie hesitated, then he rolled away from the cliff wall. From somewhere high above him he heard a scream, but he felt no fear. He felt nothing as he spiralled down—only a powerful and serene peace.

A SHORT WHILE LATER, Letty stood silent, her forehead pressed to the glass of her bedroom window. 'This island is where I belong,' she'd told Nicky. 'It's where I feel the possibility of hope and faith, and every morning when I look out of the window, I fall in love with it all over again.'

She remembered that day at Gebraith so well. Three-year-old Alba had been sticky with chocolate. 'Piggyback,' she'd demanded, and Nicky had wordlessly hoisted his daughter onto his back and started down the hill.

Had that been the moment, all those years ago, when the crank of fate began its slow turn?

He had put his faith in the government and, when it had failed to live up to its promise, those first lethal drops of disillusion had been released. If the MoD had taken the report on Gebraith's safety seriously, taken action to put it right, Nicky would have considered it fair play and that would have been the end of it.

She knew now why Nicky hadn't told her. He would never have shattered her peace of mind without first finding a way to put things right. Finding a way out. Tom couldn't have been more wrong—Nicky was exactly the man she thought he was.

'Mum.' Georgie was standing in the doorway.

As mother turned to daughter, her face softened. 'I've been such a fool,' Letty said. She held out her arms and Georgie went to her.

'I'm so sorry,' Georgie mumbled into her shoulder. 'If I hadn't lied to those men. If I'd told you earlier . . .'

'No.' Letty released her. 'You did the right thing and now . . . well, it makes sense of so much. It explains so much.' She gave Georgie the piece of paper she was holding. 'I want you to read this . . . It's from your father.'

Georgie held herself very still. 'Dada left a letter?'

Letty didn't flinch under her daughter's hostile gaze. 'Yes. They found it just after he died.'

'And you didn't tell me?' Georgie's voice rose. 'Why didn't you tell me?'

'Georgie,' Letty said quietly. 'You know why.'

Georgie sank down onto the bed. The surface of the paper was soft and creased into a hundred tiny triangles from repeated folding. *My darling love* . . . she scanned through the lines . . . *protect you and the children* . . . *the only way out* . . . She looked up wildly. 'So he did abandon us.' Her voice broke. 'He did jump.'

'No!' Letty took the crumpled paper from Georgie's hands. 'Look at this. It's not what you think. It's not even a letter, it's a collection of thoughts. They found it on his desk. Do you know what I think this is? A practice run for a conversation he dreaded having, nothing more. Trust me, if your father wanted to leave a suicide note, he would leave one—in an envelope, and properly addressed. He would never have left us like . . . well, like this.'

'But he'd smuggle someone out of East Berlin in the boot of our car,' Georgie said cruelly. 'Did you know he could do that?'

Letty sat down beside her. 'I think he felt desperately guilty about the danger he had put you in, his moment of madness, and for whatever reason—perhaps he was besieged by so many worries, perhaps because I didn't make it easy for him—he couldn't find a way of telling me about Gebraith.'

'But then how did he—'

'Georgie, I don't know what happened on that roof. I doubt we'll ever know, but I have to believe, I *do* believe, your father's death was an accident.'

Georgie sat silent for a minute. 'Do you think what he did was so very bad?'

'I think it's as he said—he was trying to protect us,' Letty said simply. 'To protect a place I love.' She stood up and moved to the window. Outside, clouds had merged to form a solid bank of grey. The wind had dropped.

'You have to tell the others,' Georgie said eventually. 'Jamie will work it out eventually and Alba will work it out sooner.'

Letty nodded. An imagined truth was always more frightening than the actual truth and she should have understood that long ago. She stared at the sky, her attention caught by a low humming noise. All of a sudden, an orange naval helicopter appeared from the east, flying low over the machair. She frowned. 'Where are the others, anyway?'

SHE HAD AS GOOD as killed him. Hunted him down and driven him off the cliff. Hoarsely, she kept calling out his name, until finally, recklessly, she grabbed at a bunch of heather growing round the top of the cliff's spine and lowered herself over the edge. She no longer cared if she lived or died, but she had to get to him before the sea water took him.

The rock was slick with rain water and she managed the first twenty feet in seconds. When the descent steepened, she spread her arms wide, as Jamie had done, and slid on her front. Almost immediately the corner of a ledge caught between her ribs and she had to fight for breath. As her speed increased, her arms felt as if they might snap out of their sockets. Something ripped across her cheek but even had she wanted to, there was no way of stopping.

Her legs hit the ground, jarring her spine. She stumbled and turned, only to be caught full in the face by an incoming wave. Choking, she rubbed desperately at her eyes, then blinked in disbelief.

Jamie was not there.

She yelled his name again. It was impossible. She could feel the undertow sucking at her calves, but the water was surely not deep enough to have taken him back out to sea. Another wave made her legs buckle. She struggled towards the tunnel and braced herself against the arch, scanning the water repeatedly. But as her eyes slowly adjusted to the light, realisation came to her that the shadows and contours of the rock face possessed an oddly three-dimensional quality, a gradation of black in the rock. She rubbed viciously at her stinging eyes but, yes, it was still there and all of a sudden she remembered. Her father's cave.

HE WAS LYING INSIDE, on the floor, curled in a foetal position, and the way his legs were hiked up, the way his arm was thrown over his face, made the air snag in her throat. 'Jamie,' she whispered. She fell to her knees. What if his head was crushed? What if he was disfigured? She forced herself to touch him, to lay a hand on his arm, but his eyes were closed and his skin clammy. 'Jamie,' she pleaded. 'For God's sake.'

A tremor shook him. His eyes jerked under their lids. 'Why do you hate me?' he mumbled, but his eyes remained closed.

Alba pushed back her tears. The air in the cave was arctic and he had to be badly hurt. People died of hypothermia, they died of shock or internal injuries. People died so easily. 'I don't hate you.' Quickly she stripped off her anorak and spread it on top of him. She could keep him warm. He wasn't dead and she could keep him warm. At least she could do that.

'Yes, you do.'

'I hate everyone.' She said it automatically, but her mind was clicking. She had to move him. Aside from the immediate entrance, the cave was dry and another foot above sea level. But water was surging along the channel and how much higher the tide would rise was anybody's guess.

'But you hate me the most.' Jamie blinked out into the dimness.

'Jamie, how are you even talking?' she whispered. 'How are you not dead? Can you move your fingers and toes? Can you walk?'

'Will you still hate me when I'm older and not so annoying?'

Alba shook her head. 'How did you get in here if you can't walk?'

'Dada carried me—in his mouth.'

'Jamie, please,' she beseeched.

'But it's true,' Jamie insisted. He had felt the jaws of the bear like a father's kiss on the back of his neck.

'I told you not to move. I told you I'd get help.' She knelt on her hands to stop her wringing them. 'Oh God, why did you have to jump?'

'Dada told me to.'

'Why, for God's sake? Why would Dada tell you to jump?'

'Because he knew he'd catch me.'

'I thought the bear caught you?'

'Yes, Alba,' Jamie said with infinite patience. 'I told you already.' He closed his eyes. He had put his arms round the bear's neck and held him close. He had felt the warmth of his father's body. He had felt the beat of his father's heart restart his own.

Alba took a deep breath. 'Jamie, there's no bear here.'

'He went back to get help. He ran away from the wrestler and now he's gone back to fetch him.'

Alba suddenly noticed blood seeping from under Jamie's head. 'Did you hit your head?' she asked, deliberately casual.

'A bit.'

Alba moved her fingers around the back of his skull until they connected with two seams of ragged flesh. Blood welled over her fingers and she felt dizzy with fear. He needed help, he needed a doctor. She thought back to the bird skulls she'd left on the table. Would her mother even notice she and Jamie were missing?

'Is my brainbox leaking?' Jamie asked.

'Your what?' Alba forced herself to concentrate. What were the basic rules of first aid? *Keep them calm, keep them warm, keep them alive*.

'My brainbox. It's where I keep all my information and words and intelligence and I don't want any of them to leak out.'

'God forbid.' Alba wrenched off her boot and dragged down her sock.

'What are you doing?'

'Jamie, why do you think the bear is Dada?'

'He just is, Alba. I know why you don't believe me. You don't believe in anything. You don't believe in the bear, you don't believe in God or Father Christmas and you don't believe in Dada.'

'Keep still.' Alba bit her lip and held the balled-up sock to the wound in his head. A spray of dirty foam blew in off the thundering channel and drifted across the threshold of the cave. The water was rising.

'Jamie, you understand that Dada is dead, don't you?'

Jamie turned his head carefully towards her. In the dark, his bright falcon's eyes gleamed. 'You worked that out too?'

'I didn't need to work it out.' She looked at him strangely. 'Dada fell off the roof of the embassy and the fall killed him. It was an accident. It was the day of the circus. Mum told you, don't you remember?'

'No! Mummy never said anything like that, Alba, never.'

'Well, that's what happened.'

'That's not what Mummy told me,' he said stubbornly. 'She said Dada had an accident and then after that he got lost. Everyone said he was lost. No one said he was dead. I only worked it out because he never came back.'

'Jamie, if you had jumped off that cliff and died, do you know what people would say? They'd all talk in soft voices to Mum and say, "I'm sorry you lost your son." Nobody ever says the word "dead". No one ever says it because . . . because it's just too awful.'

Jamie pushed her hand away. 'How could he fall? He's a grown-up. Why does everyone lie to me? Why? He was watching the circus being built from the roof,' Jamie went on. 'Every day, he told me.'

'Jamie, he could have tripped or felt dizzy, people have stupid accidents all the time.'

'Well, it doesn't matter anyway, Alba, because he's here now. He promised to come back and he did. This is his cave. This is where he's been waiting for me.'

There was an almost fanatical timbre to Jamie's voice, Alba thought as she looked distractedly around her. Collected against the walls of the cave were tangled lengths of seaweed and a few scattered bottles.

'He's coming back for us, Alba.' Jamie's eyes were closing. 'He promised me.'

Of course I promise, the bear had said. *Don't I always come back?*

'Jamie,' she whispered. 'Don't go to sleep.'

His lips were colourless. 'He promised, Alba. You believe me, don't you?'

She hesitated. 'OK, yes, Jamie, I believe you.'

Jamie stretched out his arm and touched the tips of his fingers to hers.

Alba looked down at the small white hand, so close, so hopeful. After a moment she took it in her own and squeezed.

She'd been staring into the darkness a long time before she noticed it—a pinprick of light, far back in the cave. Carefully, she extricated her hand from Jamie's and felt her way along the wall. The floor was on a steep incline and, as she moved deeper into the cave, the light mysteriously disappeared. The air smelled oily, earthy. The ceiling began closing in on her. She crawled on, eventually banging her head sharply as she came to a dead end. Disorientated, she tried to turn. There was the light again, now coming from a tiny hole right above her head. She worked at enlarging it with her fingers until she could get a fist through. Encouraged, she scrabbled at it with her hands, but her nails scraped against rock. She sank to her haunches, hope unspooling.

'Alba!' came the plaintive cry. 'Alba, where are you?'

'I'm here, it's OK.' In the murky light she could just make out the blue of her anorak covering Jamie and she frowned at an idea half forming.

'Jamie, it's OK. I know what to do.' She fetched a piece of seaweed, stripping off the ribbons until she was left with a bare, three-foot-long stick. Easing her anorak off Jamie, she wrapped it tightly along the whole length, winding the hood strings diagonally back over the brightly coloured nylon until the thing resembled a makeshift umbrella. She crawled back to the end of the cave and pushed the stick through the hole. Initially it resisted, the seaweed bending wilfully, but she forced it upwards, loosening the hood strings and poking them through after it. The wind took it immediately.

She hunched her knees and gripped the stick with both hands, holding it steady, keeping it upright as it jerked and quivered. After a while, the ache in her arms consumed her. She squeezed her eyes shut against the pain, unable to see that Jamie kept forcing his open, checking she was still there. Checking that she hadn't left him.

There was little strength in him, yet he ran. Behind him was a confusion of shouts, the rumble of Land Rovers and tractors, the thump-thump of a helicopter. For the second time that day, he ran towards the cliffs. The first time he'd left the wrestler behind. Now he would guide him to the cave.

The wind was sweeping the last of the storm away in quick, efficient gusts. His legs were weakening, but he was so nearly at the loch. It lay ahead of him, shining like a silver spill of mercury. From there it was a straight line to the sea and, if the end came after that, well, no matter. Life, death—neither ever worked out the way people imagined. Who can predict how the fate of one person will interlock with the destiny of another? As he struggled on, a phrase came to him out of the blue. 'Everything and every event is pervaded by the Grace of God.' Yes, he thought. Yes . . .

To have watched the boy jump; to have been able to count on that sweet trust one last time. The moment he'd felt that small heart beating against his, it had made sense to him: the hunger, the nostalgia, the unbearable yearning to be who he once was.

At last, memories came, each more poignant than the last; the way Jamie rubbed his feet together for comfort; the way his eyes turned owl-round when he listened to stories; the way he gnawed the skin off an apple and let the exposed fruit turn to pulp in his hand. How he wished these had come to him sooner, but now he had them they would belong to him for eternity.

And still he ran. He was right at the loch when it caught his eye—the bright daub of blue, fluttering in the colourless aftermath of the storm. He knew instantly what it was—Alba's anorak, bloated with wind. It was the children's signal, their SOS, and it should have been the flag of his own finishing line. Above him the helicopter hovered and to his dismay he realised that exhaustion had beaten him. His body had failed and he was no longer moving. He felt the sting of a dart and the world began to slow. 'No!' he tried to shout, 'not yet!' but the only sound to come out of his mouth was a croak, a hoarse animal growl, and he knew his time was running out.

At that moment, in his peripheral vision, he saw a lone tractor breaking away from the mass of vehicles, veering erratically towards the flag. There was no mistaking the wiry islander at the wheel, his side-rolls of hair blowing in the wind, his upper body craning sideways to see round the broken windscreen, and he understood then that it would be all right.

When the sting of the second dart pricked the bear's skin, what took him by surprise was how very familiar it felt. His heart skipped a beat. He felt the acute burn of longing in his chest, for home, for forgiveness and peace. As the drug took hold, there was no pain, only the sound of rain in his head and an incredible and welcome sensation of falling.

'Goodbye, boy,' he whispered and he knew he would be heard.

On the floor of the cave, the boy's eyes drifted open in his heart-shaped face and his answer came back on the last thread of the wind.

'Goodbye, my Dada,' he said, and smiled.

General Hospital, Stornoway, Isle of Lewis

'Your son has a fractured skull and a torn kneecap. I've put in a dozen or so stitches but he's going to be fine. What I'm trying to understand is that your daughter claims he jumped, though I'm assuming she meant he fell'—the doctor checked his notes—'sixty feet?' He arched an eyebrow in expectation of being corrected. 'You must be familiar with the geography of this place, Mrs Fleming—is that even possible?'

Letty spread her hands, unable to trust herself to speak. Had Jamie landed an inch to the right, had the bottom of the Kettle not been cushioned by seaweed, had the tide been higher, the water deeper . . . What if Alba had not gone after him—or Alick had not spotted her makeshift flag? And what if a helicopter hadn't been on hand. Right there! Less than 100 yards away, with the unconscious bear tangled in a net suspended underneath and half the island in pursuit with shovels and sticks, ready to dig out her children from under the ground. She gripped Tom's arm.

'Of course you get these cases from time to time,' the doctor was saying. 'There was one during my first-year internship. A toddler fell from the twelfth floor of a Sydney high-rise and walked away—so to speak—without a scratch.'

Alba had told Letty that Jamie had jumped. Might he have thought he could join his father in some way and, if so, then why hadn't she noticed? Why hadn't she been paying attention? But what *had* she paid attention to these last few months other than her own pain?

Earlier, when she had been taken into the curtained cubicle to see Alba, she had barely recognised the young woman lying on a narrow trolley bed, spindly as a monkey in her hospital gown. Alba looked so wan, so grown-up, her pointed little face positioned to the wall, hiding the wad of cotton wool taped to her cheek. Then she had turned and an expression of such child-like relief had passed across her face that Letty had sprung forward and gathered her up. 'Oh, Alba.' She cradled her. 'Alba, Alba.'

For a second, Alba had remained limp, then Letty felt thin arms slowly encircle her and tighten.

'I want to give you something,' Letty had said when she'd settled her daughter back against the pillow. She pressed a small square of folded paper into Alba's palm.

Without looking up, Alba turned the paper over, her eyes brimming as she saw the letters IOU written on the other side.

'Open it,' Letty said. 'Read it.'

Slowly Alba peeled the note apart. *Everything will be all right*. She read out her mother's promise in a whisper. *From now on, it will be all right*.

'HOW IS IT POSSIBLE, medically, I mean?' Tom was asking quietly. 'What do you think happened?'

The doctor made a frustrated gesture with his hand.

'If the child knows no fear. If the body is completely relaxed. If somebody up there is looking out for him . . . I have no logical answer for you. The fact is, however, it happened. A miracle is a miracle and all we can be is thankful.'

'Can I see him yet?' Letty asked. Her hold on Tom's arm loosened—not that she had any intention of letting go entirely. She'd taken possession of it when the phone had first rung bringing news of Jamie, and Tom had quietly assumed charge. She'd clutched it in the army plane he'd commandeered, and even tighter in the waiting room where she'd sat rigid on the edge of her seat, sending up entreaties to God, to Nicky, to the devil himself. She would renounce whatever future she was entitled to, she would offer up her very soul *if only* her children could be safe—*if only* she could be given another chance.

'We're still conducting tests,' the doctor said, 'but as soon as I have those results, I'll come and find you.'

'Tests for what?'

'Mrs Fleming, your son was hypothermic when they brought him in—both children were—and initially I put it down to that. Sometimes cold can account for these things.'

'I'm sorry, account for what?' she persisted.

'When I originally assessed him, apart from quite severe concussion, I noticed he had VPB, not enough to cause a—'

'VPB?' Tom interrupted.

'Yes. It stands for ventricular premature beats. When your heart skips a beat—I'm sure you've both experienced that? Well, that would be due to VPB, do you follow?'

Tom nodded.

'Anyway the point is that Jamie's was not enough to cause his blood pressure to drop dangerously low, but . . .' He shrugged. 'I've just completed a fellowship in cardiology, so I'm probably a little more neurotic about matters of the heart than most residents. Jamie's blood pressure was low enough to sound a few warning bells so I thought to myself—better get the boy an ECG and echo—'

'Echo?' Letty queried faintly.

'That's an electrical and sound wave test of the heart called an echo cardiogram.' He flashed her an apologetic smile. 'It will tell us a bit about the heart structure.'

'Are you saying there's something wrong with Jamie's heart?'

'Let's hope not, Mrs Fleming, but if there is, we will deal with it. In any event, I'm going to speak to your daughter again and I'll come back to you as soon as I know what's going on.'

'I'M PREPARED TO OFFER you a Fruit Salad.'

'Which is?' Alba inspected the doctor with narrow eyes.

'Fruit Salad is a collective phrase for a group of stroke patients, or if you like, there's Vegetable Garden which is a group of brain-damaged patients.'

'OK,' Alba conceded. 'One stitch for each.'

'Too kind.' He tilted her chin and threaded the needle through her cheek. 'Ten Fs is a good one, I promise, but I want three stitches for it otherwise we'll be here all day.'

'Go on, then. If you must.' Alba's posturing helped cover the fear. She'd had the shakes ever since arriving in hospital and, despite the blankets and hot sugary teas, could still feel a tremor in her hands and weakness in her legs.

'It stands for fat, fair, fecund, fortyish, flatulent female with foul, frothy, floating faeces.'

Alba giggled in spite of herself. 'Where did you learn these?'

'Med school, Sydney. Keep still.'

'You're from Australia?'

'The accent didn't give it away?'

'What are you doing here from Australia?'

'My great-grandparents originally came from the north of Scotland, so, you know, I thought I'd check the place out.'

'Sounds tedious.'

'It's actually a pretty romantic story.'

'I'm not a bit interested in romance but I'll take more medical slang.'

'Last one for four stitches and the knot then?'

Alba glanced hopefully towards the curtain, but she knew that her mother had finally been taken in to see Jamie and would not be out for while. She took a deep breath and offered her cheek. She felt for the note in the pocket of her hospital gown. More than anything she had wanted her mother to stay, hold her hand, but she'd forgotten how to ask.

'You're quite brave for a Sheila.' The doctor knotted and snipped the thread. 'I hope you're proud of your sister,' he said over his shoulder. 'Saving your little brother's life and everything.'

Georgie sat in a chair in the corner of the cubicle, watching.

'I didn't save his life,' Alba said.

'Oh, who did, then?' The doctor fiddled with his bleeper.

Alba touched a finger to the ridge of stitches. The thing was, she couldn't erase it from her head. The ragged edge of Jamie's wound, his plunge through the mist, the sound of the helicopter—and then that animal, the beast, so small and shrunken looking, balled up in the net. Dada will catch me, Jamie had shouted, and every time she closed her eyes she saw the mass of seaweed, moving, floating at the bottom of the Kettle.

'I don't know,' she said quietly. 'I honestly don't know.'

After the doctor took himself off, the two sisters eyed each other like battle-weary generals. Since they'd last come together, only twenty-four hours earlier, they'd discovered between them sex and spirituality—in other words, pretty much all the complexity the world had to offer—but the accumulation of prohibited subjects that had stacked up over the last six months prevented them sharing any of these revelations. They continued to stare at each other in uncompanionable silence until Alba finally blurted it out.

'I burnt your university offer letter.'

'You did what?' Georgie said, startled.

'I burnt your university offer letter,' Alba repeated hollowly. 'And your A-level results as well.'

Georgie gawped at her. 'You little bitch! Why?'

Alba pulled the thin sheet up to her chin. 'Because you're nearly grown-up.' She faltered. 'Because you get to leave home and start a new life. Because I'm stuck here for another three years, for an eternity.'

Georgie felt strangely disassociated from the endless drama of her sister's selfishness.

'You don't understand.' Alba's voice rose. 'You've escaped, but I'm doomed. "Oh, poor Alba,"' she mimicked, '"how could she not have turned out bad, I mean, those wretched Fleming children, they had the most awful childhood."'

'We haven't had a really awful childhood.'

'Well, losing Dada happened for me at a more damaging time than it happened for you. I think my formative years might have been ruined.'

'Rubbish, your formative years are something like two to six. These are your teenage years.'

'I know, I know,' Alba said piteously. 'I'm in the middle of puberty!'

Georgie sighed and closed her eyes. She saw Aliz's arm resting against hers. She heard the papery noise of waves against the sand. What Alba said was true. Her own clock was ticking again. She was growing up, moving on. 'Do you know something, Alba? You're not nearly as interesting as you think you are.' She pushed out of her chair.

Alba's head was turned into the pillow. 'Please don't leave me, Georgie,' she whispered. 'Please.'

'You're going to be fine.' Georgie pulled aside the curtain.

'I don't want to be fine. I want to be better than fine, I want . . .' Alba's voice caught then broke. 'I want Dada back.'

The minute that Georgie allowed to pass felt like a year. Then she turned and sat back down on the edge of Alba's bed. Her sister still existed in the before, while she had moved into the after. And the after was OK, it was better. In the way that most mattered to her, she had got her father back. 'Do you know what I think about sometimes?' she said softly.

'What?' Alba wiped her nose on the sleeve of her gown.

'That one day I will come across a door and through that door will be a room and in that room I will find all the precious things I have ever lost;

that beautiful necklace Grandpa gave me, my old teddy, the Biba cardigan with the striped sleeves, and . . . you know . . . Dada.'

A fat tear trailed down Alba's cheek.

'Look, I'll make you a deal.' Georgie pushed a damp length of her sister's hair away from her stitches. 'If I defer university for a while, if I stay with you a bit longer, will you tell me what I got in my A levels?'

ALL LETTY REMEMBERED afterwards was the absoluteness of her exhaustion. She and Tom had been fetched out of the children's ward by the doctor and had taken up position between the shiny cream walls of the second-floor corridor. The air had been warm and unpleasantly scented. Bad ventilation, Letty thought. No windows to open. Outside she could hear a siren, then the rolling slide of doors opening and shutting; voices, shouting. Somebody else's trauma beginning. A janitor moved through them, keys dangling from his leather belt. How late was it? Letty wondered vaguely. How long had they been there? Time in hospitals was not measured in hours and minutes but in shifts and rounds, the wait between painkillers.

'No history of heart disease in your family?' the doctor was asking.

'Not that I know of.' She didn't like the way that he was looking at her—concern mingled with a certain ghoulish curiosity adopted by the medical profession when they were diagnosing an interesting condition.

'On either your or your husband's side?'

'No.' Letty's teeth began to work at the inside of her lip.

'Any health issues affecting either of Jamie's two sisters?'

'None.'

'What about yourself and your husband?'

'Jamie's father was killed in an accident earlier this year,' Tom intervened quickly.

The doctor made a note. 'I'm so sorry. What about Jamie's grandparents, are they still living?'

'All died of old age—well, apart from my husband's real mother who died in childbirth. How is this relevant exactly?'

'As I mentioned earlier, I initially questioned whether Jamie's irregular heartbeat was due to the cold, or too much adrenaline, but the results of his ECG show that he does, in fact, have a slightly dilated heart.'

'What does that mean exactly?' Letty reached for Tom's hand again.

'I believe your son is suffering from cardiomyopathy.'

When this pronouncement elicited only a shocked, blank silence, he took a pen from his pocket and began sketching on his notes. 'Let me see if I can make this simple. The engine of a heart is driven by electrical waves. The sort of waves, say, a pebble would make if you dropped it into a still pond.' He squinted up at them. 'Those waves send out a signal to the muscles of the heart which, in turn, pump the blood through the body. Now, if there's an interruption in those electrical waves, it causes an abnormal heartbeat—your heart skips a beat.'

'And this is what Jamie has?' Tom asked. 'An abnormal heartbeat?'

'Well, yes and no. For most people, skipping the odd beat happens from time to time and, normally, when the electrical waves are interrupted the heart simply starts up again itself—but in those suffering from cardiomyopathy, the heart lacks the capability to restart. Instead it panics and this causes a sudden and potentially fatal drop in blood pressure.'

'Fatal?' Letty stumbled over the word. 'Wouldn't we know if Jamie had something wrong with his heart?' She tried to exorcise the shrillness from her voice. 'Wouldn't we have found out before now?'

'Well, patients are almost always asymptomatic. There are literally no clues whatsoever. Sudden Cardiac Death can happen at any time during a person's life. Too much exercise, one coffee too many, an over-strenuous walk, a shock to the system. It can happen in your sleep, or when you're quietly reading in a chair. A person might experience palpitations or feel faint but that would be all. One minute they're here, the next they're gone. And I have to say, given the enormous amount of physical and emotional stress your son has been subjected to, it's quite amazing that . . .'

'Yes, thank you so much, Doctor.' Tom stopped him with a warning look.

The doctor took in Letty's ashen face. 'Oh, no, Mrs Fleming, please don't worry. Jamie is in no immediate danger. Now we know what we're dealing with, we can treat it.' He put the pen back in his pocket, hesitated. 'Look, the miracle isn't just that your son survived a sixty-foot fall. The miracle is that if he hadn't been brought to hospital, his condition might have gone undetected.'

Letty felt like a weak imprint of herself, a cardboard cut-out. She leaned against the wall. 'Thank you.'

'Yes,' Tom said, 'thank you very much.'

The doctor grasped Tom's outstretched hand. 'We have a few more tests to run and then we'll have a talk about treatment.'

'Of course.' Letty stared through him unseeingly as he turned to go. The first light of dawn was seeping between the shutters on the window.

'By the way.' Tom put a hand on the doctor's arm. 'Why were you so interested in the family history? You never explained.'

'Yes, well, I'm afraid usually it's the family of the sufferer we get to treat. Cardiomyopathy is very often a hereditary disease, and in those cases where it is hereditary, it's almost always passed down from father to so—' He cut himself off. 'That's right. You told me earlier that Jamie's father had an accident.' He looked at Letty. 'Exactly what sort of accident was it?'

It had happened then. In the weightless gap between not knowing and understanding, Letty realised that she had stopped breathing . . . And just like that, she'd gone down.

LETTY WAS SLEEPING in her bedroom at Ballanish. Sleeping a dreamless sleep. She slept as if sleeping was a new hobby that she'd lately discovered and now couldn't get enough of.

When she woke, her thoughts veered off to the same place they had gone every morning since she'd returned from the hospital. To the embassy in Bonn, to Nicky's office and the desk where he'd sat writing, practising his confession, crumpling up his first draft, summoning up his courage. She imagined him stealing up to the roof, smoking a cigarette and smiling as he watched the ropes tighten on the Big Top of the circus below. Then, perhaps a frown as pain sliced across his shoulder to his chest. A moment of dizziness as his faulty heart skipped that beat . . . He'd have been dead before he hit the ground, dead before he even fell, and she could come to terms with that. It was a death she could live with. Nicky's arrhythmic, asymptomatic heart. It would not have shown up on an autopsy. It might have looked somewhat pallid, but no suspicions would have been aroused.

'I told you,' Jamie said in the hospital. 'I told you there was something wrong with my heart.' He hadn't remembered much about what had happened on the cliff, but Alba remembered. Alba remembered everything.

If the child knows no fear, the doctor had said. *If the body is completely relaxed. If someone up there is looking out for him.*

'He jumped,' Alba said simply. 'He just rolled away and let go.'

Jump. Letty saw Nicky under her bedroom window, his arms opened wide. *Let go and I'll catch you.*

Jamie had inherited his father's heart and his father had come back to warn him. At least that's what Jamie believed. Letty didn't know what she believed, but maybe she didn't have to. It was no longer a requirement of life that it should make good sense or even reasonable sense, only that it should make Jamie sense.

Recently, Letty had begun to understand that sense to Jamie was a complex and wonderful thing. Squirrelled away in his brainbox were soaring columns of words and phrases, fragments of song and the frayed edges of poems. There were tall stories and short stories, the vibrations of truth and lies and a thrumming of tiny fibs between; there were the spores of magic, the residue of dreams, a few sharp splinters of reality and then there were the shapes and patterns of wishful thinking all merging, intersecting with hope and optimism in an ever-changing kaleidoscope of possibility.

Life or death. Nobody understood the workings of either. There was only what you believed—what you managed to hold on to. Letty believed now that Jamie's logic had a cohesive quality that had glued their broken family together again. It had been the unfairness of tragedy, the agonising futility of 'if only' that had trapped her in the past, but now all the interlocking connections of fate and chance that had saved Jamie's life had rebalanced the scales of fortune and tipped her into the present.

Tom had taken the report back to London with him. It would have to be put into the right hands, he'd said. Someone outside the MoD. Someone powerful, who could and would have questions asked in Parliament. A minister senior enough to oblige the MoD to commission a new report. 'This is something I can do for Nicky,' Tom said before he'd left. 'Something I can do for you.' And he'd kissed her, briefly, on the cheek.

Downstairs, she could hear Georgie moving about in the kitchen, putting on water for the porridge. In just over two hours, they would go to the church by the loch for the memorial service. She had brought Nicky home, back from Bonn, to a place where he belonged.

She looked at Alba and Jamie, both hot with sleep and stretched across her bed, their bare feet inadvertently touching. There was a lot of growing up left to do.

Life was unfinished business. It was time to begin living it.

bella **pollen**

RD: Were your early years as privileged as they sound from your entry in Burke's Peerage?

BP: My grandmother was one of ten children of the Earl of Radnor. She left home at sixteen to marry a soldier, and they eloped to Rhodesia where they lived in a tent, and later a mud hut. She was fiercely independent, surviving on very sound principles and very little money for most of her life. My mother was raised in Africa and inherited my grandmother's rigid work ethic and strong sense of thrift. But my siblings and I grew up in New York in the Sixties—a very far cry from the starchiness of the British class system.

RD: When your parents moved back to England, you had problems settling into an English boarding school. What is your worst memory?

BP: Pretty much every day of the first two years. I had come from a very good school in New York and it felt like taking a backwards step. Then there were the gothic rules and punishments . . . It was in an old castle, too, so pretty scary for a thirteen-year-old.

RD: When you left, you started to design and make clothes for friends, teaching yourself how to sew. It was a great success, and soon, you had financial backing for a designer label, Arabella Pollen Ltd, which drew customers like Princess Diana. What was that like?

BP: I was hugely surprised by the success. Those initial years were hectic and very strange. The attention from the press came first, and then I had to learn about the business, very, very fast, to maintain the sales the press had generated.

RD: What triggered the writing career?

BP: I always wanted to write, but while I was keeping my company afloat there was no time for anything else. After I sold the company, writing was the first thing I turned to.

RD: Your family owns a house in the Hebrides, where you spent many summers as a child. Do you still feel you have roots there?

BP: A very large chunk of my heart resides in the Hebrides. It was idyllic in many ways, albeit a very different kind of idyllic from the perception of a good holiday now: rotten weather, no television or computer. We were largely left to make our own entertainment and enjoyed a freedom to roam wild, which, today, would be unthinkable.

RD: In an article for the *Daily Telegraph* in 2010, you wrote about the real-life grizzly and wrestler who inspired *The Summer of the Bear*. How did such a wild and strange story lead to the novel?

BP: The grizzly escaped on the island one summer when we were there and we spent most of the holiday looking for it. Even then, we humanised it. Why had he run away? What was he thinking? If only the bear could talk . . . The idea stayed with me, but it was only after I began writing *The Summer of the Bear* and climbed inside Jamie's head that I realised that the bear could somehow come to represent Jamie's missing father in his fevered imagination.

Back home. Wrestler Andy Robin and Hercules the bear after their Hebridean adventure.

RD: As mother to three sons (plus one daughter) you must have a good understanding of how the eight-year-old Jamie's mind would work?

BP: Jamie is a composite of many children, but my beloved nephew Hoagy, who is mildly dyslexic and dyspraxic, used to talk to me, as a small boy, about his 'brainbox' and the complicated systems he used for storing information. I was fascinated by this idea and it became the basis for Jamie's character.

RD: You've said that you find inspiration in 'situations with a degree of discomfort and uncertainty'—why is that?

BP: Because it's in such situations, where people are called upon to act or react in an exceptional and instinctive way, that you can explore their nature. I am fundamentally interested in what makes people tick.

RD: And what brings you most joy and fulfilment nowadays?

BP: I get an enormous amount of fulfilment from my work. I like exploring new places and situations; I like learning about things. I'm watching four children grow up and change on a daily basis. Not a lot beats that.

RD: Do you have any particular ambitions you'd one day like to fulfil—countries to be visited, mountains to be conquered perhaps?

BP: All of the above. Too many to name. I want to visit pretty much every country I've never been to, to achieve everything I haven't yet achieved. I am a great believer in the Groucho Marx quote: 'I don't care to belong to any club that will have me as a member.' Which I guess means that anything I manage to achieve never quite feels like a real achievement, so I end up going for more. I know a lot of people who feel this way, and actually it's a pretty irritating trait, but I have to accept it's what drives me.

Stagestruck

PETER LOVESEY

As singing star Clarion Calhoun takes the stage at Bath's Theatre Royal, the audience is expecting the performance of her career. No one could know that, within moments of curtain up, she will be rushed to hospital with third degree burns. No one could predict that her agony would be followed by a dramatic murder in the wings.

As Detective Superintendent Peter Diamond is called to investigate, he finds tensions mounting, rivalries aplenty, and all too many sound motives for murder behind the scenes. Clearly, the killer may, at any moment, strike again . . .

1

'People keep asking me if I'm nervous.'

'Really?'

Clarion Calhoun, that week's star attraction, gave a broad smile. 'Believe me, anyone who's played live to a million screaming fans on Copacabana Beach isn't going to lose sleep over a first night in an itsy-bitsy provincial theatre.'

But the face told a different story. The woman waiting to apply the make-up watched the confidence vanish with the smile and spotted the tell-tale flexing of the muscles at the edge of the mouth. Clarion was outside her comfort zone. Acting was a different skill from pop singing.

Because of her inexperience, she was getting special treatment from the Theatre Royal, Bath. Almost all professional actors do their own make-up. This one couldn't be trusted to create a simple 1930s look, even with nothing more technical than a Cupid's bow and kohl-lined eyes. She was getting the nursemaiding in spades.

'You'll be a knockout. They love you, anyway.'

'My fans, you mean?' Clarion looked better already. 'Every ticket sold, they tell me.'

The dresser, Denise, unscrewed a new jar of cold cream and picked up a sponge. 'Do you want to remove your day make-up yourself?'

'Go ahead. I'll think about my lines.'

Clarion meant the lines in the script, not her face. A few more of those were revealed as the cleanser did its work. She was past thirty and her days as a rock star were numbered. Time to revamp her career. She was playing Sally Bowles in a new production of *I Am a Camera*. With her name on the billing, it was almost guaranteed a transfer to London later in the year.

'Your skin is marvellous,' Denise said.

'It should be, all the money I spend on treatments. Is that the colour you're going to use? I don't want to look as orange as that.'

'Trust me. You won't.'

'What is it—greasepaint?'

'Glycerine-based cream. It's going to feel dry. That's why I used a base of moisturiser.'

'I may sound like a beginner, but I was drama trained before I got into the music scene. I always promised myself I'd get back on the stage.'

Denise passed no comment as she smoothed on the foundation. She did the shadowing and highlighting. Then she used a plump rouge mop to brush on some powder.

'May I see?' Clarion asked.

'Not yet. Eyes and lips make all the difference.'

In another ten minutes Clarion was handed the mirror.

'Hey! Transformation. Sally Bowles.' She switched to her stage voice. 'How do you do, Sally? I'm terribly glad to meet you.'

THERE WAS ALSO some nervousness in the audience. Towards the back of the stalls, Hedley Shearman was fingering his lips, trying not to bite his nails. He gloried in the title of theatre director, yet the casting of Clarion Calhoun had been made over his head by the board of trustees. Until now, he'd always had final approval of the casting, and it had more than once earned him certain favours. No chance with this megastar, who treated him no better than a call boy. Each time she looked at him he was conscious of his lack of height and his bald spot.

Clarion's name guaranteed bums on seats and a standing ovation from her fans, but Shearman dreaded the critics' verdict. He cared passionately about the Theatre Royal. In 200 years all the great actors, from Macready to Gielgud, had graced this stage. This woman was expected to get by on that dubious asset known as celebrity. True, she was a singer playing a singer, but this was entirely an acting role. She'd learned her lines, and that was the best you could say for her. Speaking them with conviction was a difficulty that had become obvious in rehearsal. He only hoped her glamour would dazzle the critics.

The lights dimmed and the buzz of excited voices was replaced by a scratchy phonograph tune evoking Berlin in the 1930s. The curtain rose on Fräulein Schneider's tawdry rooming house: tiled stove, bed partly concealed by a curtain, sofa and chairs. A single shaft of light on the writer Christopher Isherwood focused attention for a speech that set the tone for the entire play. Preston Barnes, playing Isherwood, had learned his craft at Stratford. Could he compensate for Clarion's wooden delivery?

The opening minutes couldn't have been bettered. Preston's soliloquy was exquisitely done. Yet Shearman couldn't ignore the fact that everything was just building up to the entrance of the real star.

And there she was. A burst of applause from her fans.

Give Clarion her due. She moved with poise. She had the figure, the strut, the sexuality of a nightclub singer, all the attributes of a Sally Bowles. Until she opened her mouth.

Shearman slid lower in his seat. It could be worse—couldn't it?

Others in the audience were shifting in their seats. The restlessness was infectious. Movement from an audience so early in a play was unusual.

On stage, Clarion pulled a face. Her mouth widened and brought creases to her cheeks. Her eyebrows popped up and ridges spread across her forehead.

Shearman sat up again. Nothing in the script called for her to grimace like that. Sally Bowles was supposed to be in command, a girl about town, out to impress. Instead she was staring towards the wings as if she needed help. Her eyes bulged and she was taking deep breaths.

Preston Barnes had spoken and Clarion needed to respond. She didn't. A voice from the wings tried to prompt her but she appeared dumbstruck. Gasps were heard from the audience.

She put her hands to her face and clawed at her cheeks, way out of character. Nothing the other actors could do would rescue the scene.

And now Clarion screamed.

This wasn't a theatrical scream. It was piercing, gut-wrenching, horrible, echoing through the theatre from backstage to the box office.

Someone had the good sense to lower the curtain.

BY THE TIME SHEARMAN got backstage, Clarion had been helped to her dressing room. She was crying out in pain, the sound muffled by a towel pressed to her face. The room was full of people.

A St John Ambulance man turned to Shearman. 'We need to get her to hospital.'

The theatre director asked if the understudy was ready and was told she could be on stage inside five minutes. An announcement would be made and the play would resume shortly.

Denise did her best to comfort the star in the back seat of the Jaguar as Shearman drove at speed to the hospital. There, still clutching the towel to her face, Clarion was rushed inside.

Not long after, a doctor invited Shearman and Denise into a side room.

'She appears to have come into contact with an irritant that inflamed her skin. Do you know if she used a cosmetic that was new to her?'

Denise reddened. 'She didn't do her own make-up. I looked after her.'

'You never know with skin,' Shearman said. 'What's all right for one person can produce a reaction in someone else.'

'We don't think it's allergic,' the doctor said. 'Our first assessment is that these are acid burns.'

'*Acid?*' Shearman said, horrified. 'There's no acid in stage make-up.'

'I'm telling you what we found,' the doctor said. 'She may have to be transferred to the burns unit at Frenchay.'

'I can't understand this. It makes no sense.'

'It's not our job to make sense of it,' the doctor said. 'All we want to find out is the source of the damage so that we give the right treatment.'

'AGONY ON STAGE' ran next morning's tabloid headline. The theatre was besieged by reporters, distressed fans and ticket-holders wanting refunds. Upstairs in his office, Hedley Shearman was urgently conferring with Francis Melmot, the silver-haired chairman of the theatre trust. At six foot eight, Melmot towered over the theatre director.

'The skin damage is severe,' Shearman said. 'I'm sorry to say it could be permanent.'

'Hedley, this is irredeemably dire,' Melmot said. 'How could it possibly have happened?'

'The obvious explanation is that her skin reacted adversely to the make-up. The burning is all on the areas that were made up. She rubbed some of the stuff off with a towel and they're having that analysed.'

'You've spoken to the make-up person, of course?'

'Denise Pearsall.'

'She's a dresser, isn't she?'

'Yes, but she was assigned to do the whole thing. She's in complete shock. She used her own make-up on Clarion, the same stuff they all use.'

'But was it new?'

'Well, yes. It's not good practice to use something that's been in contact with another actor.'

'So it's possible it was a bad batch—the fault of the manufacturer?' For Melmot, this was all about apportioning blame.

'I find that hard to believe. The hospital was talking of acid burns. Acid isn't used in cosmetics. Denise is devastated.'

'If this disaster is down to her, I'm not surprised,' Melmot said.

Shearman didn't like the way this was heading. 'I didn't say it was Denise's fault. She's a trusted member of the team.'

'Someone is responsible. This could bring us down, Hedley. We could find ourselves being sued for a small fortune. A large fortune if Clarion is permanently scarred. She's a mega earner and no doubt she had contracts lined up for months ahead.'

Sensing he was about to be unfairly blamed, Shearman surprised himself with the force of his anger. 'I'd like the board to know I was bulldozed into engaging the bloody woman. She's no actor.'

Melmot chose to ignore the outburst. 'Was Clarion in any discomfort before the show?'

'No—the first signs of anything going wrong were on stage. Twenty minutes after she was made up. If there was a reaction, why was it delayed? I'm mystified.'

'Have you impounded the make-up?'

Shearman clapped his hand to his head. 'God, you're right. We'll confiscate everything that was used last night and lock it in the safe.'

His phone beeped and he snatched it up. The switchboard girl said, 'The police are downstairs, sir.'

'The police? That's all we need.'

HEDLEY SHEARMAN told the police in a calm, considerate way that they weren't needed.

The senior of the two uniformed officers, a sergeant whose bearing suggested he was nothing less than a chief constable, said, 'It's not your call, sir. We don't work for you.'

'I'm aware of that, but this is my theatre. I'm the director here.'

The sergeant turned to his female colleague. 'He's the director here.

We're in the right place, then.' It sounded like sarcasm.

Shearman said with more force, 'But you're not needed, and I'm an extremely busy man.'

'Then permit me to introduce Constable Reed. Reed can write at speed, so Reed is needed. Oh yes, there is a need for Reed.'

The young policewoman looked at Shearman and winked, as if asking him to make allowance.

'And I'm Sergeant Dawkins,' the ponderous introduction continued. 'We're here about the occurrence in your theatre last night.'

'Occurrence?' To Shearman's ear the word carried dangerous overtones. 'I wouldn't call it an occurrence. One of the cast was taken ill, that's all, and we're dealing with it ourselves.'

'Dealing with it?'

'Of course. That's my job.'

'And we investigate. That's our job.'

Shearman felt as if he'd strayed into a play by Samuel Beckett. 'Who sent you?'

'Any unexplained injury of a serious nature that shows up in A & E gets referred to us. Did you see what happened last night?'

'I'm always in the audience on first nights.'

Constable Reed made notes, her hand moving at prodigious speed.

'You don't have to write all this down.'

'You're a witness,' she said. 'You just confirmed it, sir.'

'But nothing of a criminal nature took place. Look, everyone here is extremely concerned about what happened and I'm going to carry out a rigorous enquiry.'

'So are we,' Dawkins said. 'Rigorous and vigorous. And so are the press by the looks of it. Have you seen all the newshounds downstairs?'

'It's a matter of public interest when a celebrity of Miss Calhoun's stature is unable to go on. Nobody's broken the law.'

'We don't know that, do we—or do we?' the sergeant said, his eyebrows arching. 'She's in hospital with burns.'

'You don't have to tell me,' Shearman said. 'I drove her to A & E myself.'

'When were you first aware that Miss Calhoun was in trouble?'

'When she missed her line and started screaming.'

'Did you see her before the show?'

'Personally, no. Others who saw her said she was in good spirits.'

'Did she do her own make-up?'

'No. She's not experienced in the theatre, so we provided a dresser for her, and that's who looked after her make-up.'

'I know about dressers,' Dawkins said. 'Constable Reed thinks a dresser is an item of furniture, but this isn't my first time in a theatre and I know dressers don't do make-up.'

'This dresser was specially asked to assist Clarion with her make-up.'

'When was it applied?'

'Some time before curtain up. I wasn't there.'

'I expect this dresser has a name.'

'I'd rather not say. I don't attach blame to anyone.'

'Blame?' Dawkins picked up on the word.

'I said I'm not blaming anyone.'

'All the same, we need the name.'

'It escapes me.'

'You must know them.' Dawkins smiled. 'We may look like plodding policepersons, but we are not incapable of discovering the dresser's identity.'

Shearman sighed and gave in. 'Denise Pearsall.'

'And is Ms Denise Pearsall available for interview?'

'Now?' Shearman reached for the phone. He'd given up the struggle. Passing these two on to Denise would come as a massive relief.

Dawkins lifted a finger. 'Not until we've finished. Clarion Calhoun is not famous for being an actress. How did the rest of the cast feel about performing with a pop singer?'

'I'm not aware of any hurt feelings. She's pre-eminent in her field.'

'So you're telling me no one had any reason to dislike her?'

This was heading into dangerous territory. 'What are you suggesting—that she was injured deliberately? That would be outrageous. We're a theatre. We work as a team to produce a top-quality production, and we're too damned busy to go in for petty feuds. Whatever went wrong last night, it was not deliberate.'

'How do you know?' Dawkins asked.

'Because no one in this theatre would stoop to the sort of mindless attack you seem to be suggesting, and I must insist you say not another word about it. If the press get a sniff, there'll be hell to pay.'

'The press are not slow, Mr Shearman. They've got the scent and are in full cry. They'll be writing tomorrow's headlines as we speak.'

'They'll have it wrong, then.'

'Which is why we need to find out what really happened. I suggest you exit stage left and cue the dresser.'

THE TWO POLICE OFFICERS met Denise Pearsall in the café at the end of the theatre block. It should have been a relaxing setting, but Denise was too strung out to touch her coffee. In her forties, she was red-haired and pretty, with brown eyes dilated by fear. Or guilt. She stared in horror at PC Reed, waiting with pen poised, and then Dawkins.

The first thing she said was, 'Have we met before?'

'Not to my uncertain knowledge,' the sergeant said in his stilted style. 'Have you *seen* me before? Very likely. I'm often around the streets of Bath. Are you going to tell us about last night?'

'I've worked here for six years and never experienced anything so awful,' she said, plucking at her neck with anxiety, 'and I can't blame anyone else. I did Clarion's make-up myself. Most actors do their own, but she hasn't worked in the theatre for years. She was the female lead, she needed help and I was asked to give it.'

'Who by?'

'Mr Melmot, the chairman.'

'What did you use for make-up—greasepaint?'

'No, that's hardly ever used in the modern theatre. It's too heavy and oily. Basic foundation, rouge and blusher, the usual liners for eyes and lips. Professional brands. They shouldn't produce a reaction, certainly nothing like what happened last night.'

'Shouldn't, wouldn't or couldn't,' Dawkins said, and he seemed to be talking to himself.

Denise looked ready to burst into tears. 'Well, if an actor suffers from acne it can get inflamed, but Clarion had a healthy complexion.'

PC Reed looked up from her notes. 'Some people have sensitive skin.'

'Allergies, yes,' Denise said, 'but she'd have told me, wouldn't she?' Uncertainty clouded her face. 'Besides, we had the dress rehearsal on Sunday and she was perfectly all right.'

'With all the warpaint on?'

'That's what makes this so hard to understand. If there was going to be a reaction it should have happened then.'

'Except if you used something different last night.'

'I didn't. All the pots and sticks were freshly opened, but exactly the same brand.' She sank her face into her hands and sobbed. 'Oh dear, I feel dreadful about it.'

THE DAMAGE TO CLARION'S FACE was referred the same day to the head of Bath's CID, Detective Superintendent Peter Diamond, a man well used to dramas, but not of the theatrical sort. He wasn't by any stretch of the imagination a theatre-goer.

'We're in danger of getting ahead of ourselves, aren't we, ma'am?' he said to Georgina Dallymore, the assistant chief constable. 'How do we know it wasn't an accident?'

'There are grounds for suspicion,' she said. 'I'm not proposing a full-scale investigation yet, but we must be ready to spring into action. If this *is* a crime, it's a particularly nasty one. The poor woman may be scarred for life. The tabloid press are out in force. If there was foul play, we must get on to it before they do.'

Pressure as always, Diamond thought. One of these days she'll tell me to take my time over a case. And pigs might fly.

He hadn't yet fathomed Georgina's interest in the matter. She was talking as if she had a personal stake.

'What's Clarion saying?' he asked.

'She's refusing to be interviewed. The official line is that she's in no state to receive visitors. Her lawyers have brought in a private security firm to guard the hospital room.'

'Lawyers are involved already?'

'Anything like this and they home in like sharks. They'll sue the theatre for millions if it can be held responsible.'

'The theatre can't afford millions. Are they insured?'

'I hope so, or Bath may end up with no theatre at all.'

Even Diamond regarded that as not to be contemplated. The city would be a poorer place.

Georgina said, as if reading his thoughts. 'To me, it would be a personal loss. I joined the BLOGs this year.'

'Really?' he said, unimpressed. 'Rather you than me, putting your private life on the internet.'

'Not blogging,' she said. 'Singing. The Bath Light Operatic Group. You know I've been in various choirs. I'd like to get a part in *Sweeney Todd*, their annual musical. They take over the Theatre Royal for a week in September.'

That was the hidden agenda, then. The BLOGs could not be deprived of their week on the professional stage.

She continued, 'If the dear old theatre were to shut down, we'd all be devastated. I hope you can steer a way through this mess.'

'Me, ma'am?'

'It won't be easy.'

He could see that. A victim who was unwilling to speak. An injury of uncertain origin. And a potential lawsuit. 'Everyone's going to be on their guard.'

'Uniform managed to get some interviews this morning.'

'That's something. Who did we send?'

'Sergeant Dawkins.'

Diamond's face creased as if caught by a sudden Arctic gust. 'Him?'

'What's the matter with Dawkins?'

'How long have you got? Five minutes in his company would tell you. He keeps asking to join CID. He'd be a nightmare.'

'My contacts with him have always been agreeable. In my estimation he's a man of culture.' In Georgina's estimation most policemen were not cultured, and some were uncouth, Diamond more than most. 'But enough of Dawkins. It's your case from now on. Handle it with kid gloves, Peter.'

'I'd rather not. Theatre people aren't my cup of tea.' How feeble was that? he berated himself. There was no way he was getting lumbered. Working in a theatre was his worst nightmare. But he was too late.

'They're very friendly,' she said.

'That's half the problem. I'll delegate.'

'No.' A flat, unqualified negative. 'I want you for this, Peter.'

He changed tack. 'I'll call in forensics, then.'

She gave a gasp of disapproval. 'We're not being as obvious as that. The make-up is being analysed in the hospital lab. There was a towel Clarion pressed to her face after she left the stage. Quite a lot of the greasepaint, or whatever she was wearing, rubbed off. They need to know if it was contaminated, so that they can give the right treatment.'

'It's strange,' he said, getting drawn in, in spite of his misgivings. 'If the make-up was responsible, why didn't it hurt her when it was first put on? If it was acid, you'd expect her to have been screaming long before she made her entrance.'

'It is rather hard to understand,' Georgina said.

'To me, it sounds more like an allergic reaction that took time to develop.'

'If that's all it was, we can breathe again. I hope you're right, Peter. But can a skin allergy be as violent as that? Does it actually burn the flesh?'

THERE WERE LUNCHTIMES when Diamond escaped from Manvers Street Police Station. The city of Bath had enough pubs to suit all his moods but today he'd decided on the Garrick's Head, adjoining the Theatre Royal. A couple of beers with the backstage lads would be an agreeable way to check Georgina's story. He hadn't yet briefed his team.

Originally—in about 1720—the building had been the home of Beau Nash, the Master of Ceremonies who made the city fashionable. It became a drinking house in 1805 when the theatre was built next door.

Diamond ordered his pint of British Red and took it to the sofa under the window. The dark wood panelling, board floor and traditional fireplace fitted his expectation of what a public bar should be. Someone had left the *Daily Telegraph* on the sofa, so he read about the 'indisposition' of the star of *I Am a Camera.*

Illusion and special effects were the stock-in-trade of theatres, so he was wary of anything that happened on a stage in front of an audience, even when it was unscripted. His other concern was the possibility of fraud. By all accounts, Clarion the pop singer was looking for alternative employment. Did anyone expect she would go on to a second career in acting? She was expected to sue the theatre for a huge sum. Had she injured herself for the prospect of a multi-million-pound settlement? Of course, the scarring would need to be permanent to convince a court.

A nearby conversation was getting interesting. Diamond tried to listen to the man on a bar stool in dialogue with the barmaid.

'It's obvious she's deeply troubled.'

He heard the barmaid say, 'I wouldn't know.'

'I find the whole thing heartbreaking,' the man said. 'She's there on stage and this gorgeous man in one of the upper boxes seems to be giving her the come-on, then he cuts her dead, so in desperation . . . Do you know which door she used?'

'I haven't asked. It doesn't bother me.'

'Never smelt jasmine around the bar?'

The girl laughed. 'You get all sorts of smells in this place.'

Curiosity got the better of Diamond. 'I couldn't help overhearing what you're saying. This woman you're talking about. Who is she?'

'The grey lady,' the man said, treating Diamond to a dazzling smile. 'She's our theatre ghost.'

'Ah.' Spooks didn't interest Diamond. It must have been obvious.

'Don't look so disbelieving,' the man said. 'She's real enough. She strung a rope over a door right here in the Garrick's Head and hanged herself in 1812.'

'And came back as a ghost?'

'Are you old enough to remember Anna Neagle? Dame Anna was on stage in the 1970s and she saw the grey lady in the upper box, stage right, just as the curtain rose. Imagine that.'

'She probably did.'

The barmaid cackled with laughter.

'Be like that,' the man said, in an injured tone.

'I thought you were talking about Clarion Calhoun,' Diamond said.

'That poor creature? I shouldn't say this, but the accident is a blessing in disguise. She was dreadful in rehearsal.'

The barmaid said, 'Titus, that's unfair.'

Titus ignored her. His focus was on Diamond. 'Are you a fan, then?'

Diamond was well practised at giving nothing away about himself. 'I was just reading about it in the paper. They say she's receiving treatment for burns.'

'I shouldn't have been flippant. No one wishes that on her. I'm Titus O'Driscoll, dramaturge.'

'Peter Diamond. What's that—dramaturge?'

'Consultant on the theory and practice of writing drama.' Titus O'Driscoll paused for that to be savoured and for Diamond to volunteer more about himself, which he didn't. 'Do you have any theatrical connections, Peter?'

Everything up to now suggested that the man was gay and interested in finding out if Diamond was, too. He had himself to blame for getting on first-name terms. 'I just came in for a drink. Were you in the audience last night?'

There was a disdainful sniff. 'I took a squint at the dress rehearsal and decided to pass my time in here. You're not press, by any chance?'

'Lord, no.'

'It was panic stations this morning. The police were here. Hedley Shearman, our theatre director, was having kittens.'

'Why? Is he responsible?'

'Quite the opposite. He didn't want the Clarion woman on his stage, but the trust twisted his arm. The pressure was on for a commercial success, so they leaned on Hedley to give Clarion the star part.'

'They'll be regretting it now.'

'Too right they will. The box office is under siege with people returning their tickets.'

'The show's continuing, is it?'

'With the understudy, Gisella, yes. She's a far better actor than Clarion, but nobody cares.'

'Does anyone know the cause of the accident?'

'If you ask me,' Titus said, 'it's open to suspicion. She was hopeless in the part and she knew it, and now she's out of it and planning to sue.'

'How do you get skin damage on the stage? I suppose it's down to the make-up.'

Titus said in an interested tone, 'Do you know about make-up, Peter?'

'Not at all.' Diamond had walked into that. He wasn't homophobic but he didn't want to raise false hopes. 'I'm saying it's a possible cause, no more.'

'You could be right if something like chilli powder was mixed in with the foundation. Some irritant that would bring her face up in blotches and make it impossible for her to continue.'

'How could she get chilli powder in her make-up?' the barmaid said.

'Deliberately. She was looking for some reason to drop out of the play so she mixed it in herself. Unfortunately for her, the ingredients reacted badly and caused the burning.'

'If it was self-inflicted, she'll have no claim against the theatre,' Diamond pointed out.

The barmaid laughed. 'There you go, Titus. You've proved yourself wrong.'

Diamond didn't gloat. He'd decided Titus might be a useful ally. 'We were just exploring theories. What Titus was saying sounds possible.'

'You see?' Titus seized on that at once. 'Peter, how would you like to join me on a ghost hunt?'

'Inside the theatre, you mean?' Instinctively, he baulked at the prospect and it wasn't the ghost that troubled him. Old reactions were stirring, a profound resistance to stepping inside such places. Yet as a professional, he knew he ought to take up this chance. 'All right, Titus. You're on.'

Titus led the way outside to the theatre foyer. Inside, he made a beeline for the steps to the royal circle entrance. He had such an air of authority that no one gave Diamond a second look. If they had, they would have seen a face taut with stress.

Titus tapped out a code on the digital lock and pushed the door open. 'I'll begin by showing you the corridor where she's often been sighted.'

Diamond followed, deeply uncomfortable. The magic of theatre had always eluded him. His mother had never tired of telling friends how she'd taken the children to a theatre in Llandudno for a birthday treat only to have young Peter make a scene even before the curtain went up. He'd run out of the theatre and couldn't be persuaded to go back in. Years later, he'd been caned at grammar school for escaping from a trip to see *Julius Caesar*. He'd told himself there was drama enough in the real world, and that he didn't have to go to the theatre to experience it. But in his heart he knew there was something else behind his unease.

In a low-ceilinged corridor, Titus spoke in a hushed tone. 'The door to your right is the bar. Let's see if it's open.'

'Good suggestion,' Diamond said.

'The door, I mean. We won't get a drink at this time of day.'

They went in and Titus launched into a tour guide routine. 'I'm taking us back to June, 1981. A production of the Albee play *Who's Afraid of Virginia Woolf?* The audience are streaming in at the interval. Suddenly, a woman points at that wall behind you and demands to know what is wrong with the wallpaper. The wall is shimmering, as if in a heat haze.'

A summer evening, Diamond was thinking. All those people packed into this small bar.

'That is followed by a sudden icy draught. All the heads turn, sensing that something not of this world has rushed past them to the door. In its wake is a distinct smell of jasmine perfume.'

'The grey lady?' Diamond said, playing along. 'Were you present?'

Titus smoothed his hair. 'Too young. But there were numerous witnesses. Now allow me to show you the box where she was seen by Dame Anna.'

Leaving the bar, they crossed the corridor to the circle. The horseshoe-shaped auditorium was in darkness. Its crimson, cream and gold decorations were just discernible, the silk panels, gilded woodwork and crystal chandelier giving a sense of the antique theatre that was essentially no different from the interior known to the actors who had first played here in the reign of George III. Anyone but Diamond would have been thinking this was the prettiest theatre in the kingdom. His main thought was how quickly he could get out. To his embarrassment he was starting to get the shakes.

'The house curtains were a gift from Charlie Chaplin's widow, Oona,' Titus said. 'Chaplin loved this theatre. If you look in the corners, you'll see his initials in gold thread.'

Diamond muttered something in courtesy, but couldn't bring himself to look.

Titus beckoned to him to join him at the front of the circle. In this light, and without an audience, it was more claustrophobic than Diamond remembered from his only other visit, when he'd summoned the strength to take his friend Paloma Kean to see *An Inspector Calls.*

He forced himself to look at the upper box where the grey lady was alleged to appear.

'Some believe she wasn't an actress, but one of the audience who occupied the same box night after night to watch the actor she adored,' Titus said. 'Each of the boxes is endowed, you know. The grey lady box is named in memory of Arnold Haskell, the balletomane. The one opposite is the Agatha Christie. Her grandson sponsored it in her memory.'

'Have you actually seen the grey lady?'

'I've sensed her presence and smelt the jasmine more times than I care to remember.'

It was a huge relief to quit the auditorium. At the end of the dress circle corridor, Titus used the code system to open a door marked PRIVATE and started down some uncarpeted stairs. 'She's been known to terrify actors in dressing room 8.' His voice carried up the staircase. 'And that's before anyone has told them about her.'

'Incredible,' Diamond said. He felt more at ease now he was out of the auditorium. He needed to be alert for this part of the tour, a chance to see where Clarion had got ready for her performance.

They were backstage now and it became obvious that Titus wasn't just an armchair dramaturge. He knew his way around the place. 'We're fortunate in having eleven dressing rooms on three floors, and most of them are big enough for several actors,' he said.

'Which room was Clarion's?'

'The number 1, with shower and WC ensuite.' Titus opened a door.

Spacious, with a huge dressing table and ornate gilt mirror, the room would surely have satisfied the most exacting of actors. A chandelier, chaise longue, vases of flowers and a view of the lawn fronting Beauford Square.

Diamond crossed the room for a look at the dressing table and bent to look more closely at the surface.

'What are you doing?' Titus asked.

'Checking to see if there's any make-up residue.'

'I shouldn't think so.' Titus put out a hand to check for dust.

Diamond grabbed him by the wrist. 'Don't. Could be a crime scene. We don't want your prints over it.' He wished he'd sounded less like a policemen.

'I would never have thought of that,' Titus said, adding, 'That's a firm grip you've got, Peter. Strong hands.'

Diamond hadn't given any thought to security. 'I suppose the place ought to be locked.'

'Because it could be a crime scene?' Titus said with heavy irony. There wasn't much doubt he'd guessed the real incentive behind this tour.

At this point it didn't matter. Diamond got on his knees and looked under the dressing table. A tissue with some make-up left on it might have dropped out of sight. But it hadn't. Or had the cleaner been by?

'What are we looking for now—a hidden clue?' Titus asked.

Diamond hauled himself upright. 'You're thinking I'm here on false pretences, aren't you? You were kind enough to suggest a short tour and I took you up on it. I'm sorry if I gave you the wrong idea.'

'No offence taken,' Titus said.

Diamond moved across to the window. 'Here's a small tragedy.' He pointed to a dead butterfly on the sill. 'Looks to me like a tortoiseshell.'

Titus gave a gasp, rolled his eyes upwards and fainted.

HEDLEY SHEARMAN phoned Frenchay Hospital and was told all calls about Clarion Calhoun were being referred to her agent, Tilda Box.

'I'm not press,' Hedley said. 'I'm the director of the Theatre Royal.'

'We're not at liberty to say anything,' the hospital spokesman said. 'Ms Box is personally handling all enquiries.'

'Personally' turned out to be misleading. The agency had installed a recorded message: 'There is no change in Miss Clarion Calhoun's condition. We thank her many friends and fans for their good wishes for her recovery and will update this message when we have more news.'

'They've put up the shutters,' he told Francis Melmot.

'They don't want hordes of fans trying to see her.'

'But we're not fans. We have every right to know what's going on.'

'Look at it from Clarion's point of view. The first instinct of any woman whose looks are blemished is to hide herself away. You drove her to the hospital, Hedley. Just how badly is her face affected?'

'I couldn't see. She kept the towel pressed to her face. But it must be serious for them to transfer her to Frenchay. One of the cast tried visiting her this morning and was turned away by a security guard.'

'I wouldn't read too much into that. These celebs surround themselves with security. She's buying time while she considers her next move.'

This possibility plunged Shearman into greater panic. 'I think we've got to get our own house in order. A few words out of turn and we could find we're admitting to negligence.'

Even Melmot's self-possession took a knock at that. 'You're right. Make it clear that no one speaks to the press except the press officer, and she must get everything vetted by you.'

BACK IN MANVERS STREET, Diamond decided to update DCI Keith Halliwell and DC Ingeborg Smith.

'All this could come to nothing,' he summed up, 'but as Georgina put it to me, sitting behind her desk, we must be primed, ready to spring into action.'

Halliwell said, 'Just because Georgina doesn't want to miss her chance to sing in *Sweeney Todd*.'

'Be fair,' Ingeborg said. 'The story is all over the papers. If there is a crime involved, we'll be in the thick of it.'

Diamond said, 'Let's cut to the chase. Suppose it really is a crime. Who's in the frame?'

'The dresser,' Halliwell said at once.

'Too obvious,' Ingeborg said.

'Who do you suggest, then?'

'The understudy, Gisella Watling.' Ingeborg had that day's local paper open on her desk.

'Makes sense,' Diamond said. 'She gets the leading role for the rest of the week. But how would she get to damage Clarion's face?'

'By adding something to the make-up,' Ingeborg said. 'She'll be one of the cast, as like as not. Understudies usually have a small part in the play.'

'Done some acting, have you?' Halliwell said.

She gave him a sharp look. 'No, I was a critic. If you're a journalist, as I was, it's a good way to get complimentary tickets.'

Diamond steered them back on track. 'There are four parts for women in *I Am a Camera.* I can tell you that much.'

'So our understudy has a dressing room of her own. How about this?' Ingeborg said. 'Before the show, while Clarion is being made up, this Gisella calls to wish her luck and switches the foundation so that Clarion gets a faceful of acid. The damage was worse than Gisella intended. She didn't think it would disfigure Clarion for life.'

'Before we pin it on the understudy, let's think,' Diamond said. 'Do we know anything about Clarion's personal life?'

'She's one of those celebs with a paparazzi following. I'll do a profile.'

'Some rival singer could have got to her,' Halliwell said. 'Or a crazy fan.'

'The rival or the fan would have had to get backstage before the show. It's much more likely it was an inside job—someone who could get past the stage-door keeper without being challenged.'

'Plenty of people work backstage,' Ingeborg said.

'You're right, Inge. We need to find out who was around on the night.'

'I sense a job coming my way,' Halliwell said.

They knew Diamond's methods, these two. He shook his head. 'Not a job exactly. We don't have a case yet. More like a perk. If you happen to be free this evening I'll treat you to a theatre visit, the pair of you.'

'Me and him?' Ingeborg said, turning pale. Keith Halliwell was at least twenty years her senior, and married. She had an image to keep up.

'What's wrong with that?' Halliwell asked.

She didn't say. 'Can we get tickets as late as this?'

'They won't be hard to come by, with all the returns,' Diamond said. 'Aisle seats at the back if possible, leaving you free to move about. Before the show, test the security backstage. See if you can enter by the stage door. Failing that, there's a way down from the royal circle. I want to know which dressing rooms are in use and where everyone is.'

'And if we're challenged?' Halliwell asked. 'Do we own up to being cops?'

'They'll take us for press,' Ingeborg said. 'We can say we've been promised an interview.'

'Good suggestion,' Diamond said. 'Inge can be the reporter and, Keith, you'd better carry a camera.'

'Some treat, this.'

'A night at the theatre?' Diamond said. 'CID doesn't get better than that.'

2

The theatre seemed to be returning to normal as the day went on. Most of the press had given up and gone. The box-office manager reported that the night's house would be down in numbers, but not embarrassingly so.

Hedley Shearman went to see Basil, the stage-door keeper, on a mission he regarded as difficult, but necessary.

'Last night, were you here all evening, Basil?'

'Always am, Mr Shearman.'

'And do you remember admitting anyone you wouldn't have expected? No strangers? No one asking to go backstage on some pretext?'

Basil shook his head. 'Nobody gets past me unless I know them.'

'Is Denise in?'

'She was here all morning. She's entitled to time off. She won't be long.'

'The minute she arrives, tell her to report to me. And one other thing. Because of what happened, I'm making more use of security people. This is no criticism of you, but I've asked them to man all the entrances for the rest of the week. That includes the stage door.'

Basil's face creased into a frown. 'You're putting a security man on my stage door? As well as me?'

'Instead of you. I'm giving you the rest of the week off. On full pay.'

'Are you expecting more trouble, then?'

'It's not a case of that. I just want everyone to know that we're serious about security.'

'As you wish, Mr Shearman,' Basil said with dignity, as if he were Gielgud overlooked at an audition.

THE ECCENTRIC Sergeant Dawkins entered Diamond's office with a faint smile playing on his lips. 'You sent for me.'

'I did. Have a seat.' Diamond already felt blighted. Whichever way he started with Dawkins, awkwardness took over. 'You were at the theatre this morning checking on what happened last night. Would you give me a quick rundown?'

'That depends,' Dawkins said. 'How quick is quick?'

'A summary, then. You don't have to tell me every word.'

'Nor shall I,' Dawkins said, settling into a chair. 'First of all, may I be so bold as to ask the subtext?'

'You're losing me.'

'The hidden agenda.'

'I don't know what you're on about. All I want is a short report on what was said. You spoke to the theatre director. Did anything emerge?'

Dawkins gave a broader smile and said, 'Powers of observation, analysis, deduction.'

'I'm losing my patience, sergeant. You're wasting my time.' Diamond picked up the minutes of a Police Federation meeting and tried blocking out this pointless conversation.

But Dawkins had more to say. 'Put it this way: I can see where you're coming from.'

Diamond gripped his desk and made one more try. 'Listen, sergeant. There's no subtext, as you put it, no hidden agenda. I'm not coming from anywhere. I'm here, face to face with you.'

'Not coming, but come?'

'If that makes any difference, yes.'

'And if my report is satisfactory, may I look forward to going there?'

'Going where?'

'Where you're coming from.'

'And where is that?'

'CID.'

That was it. This pain in the arse thought he was being assessed for a plain-clothes job. Hell would freeze over first.

'No chance. You've got more front than the abbey,' Diamond told him. 'Get on with your report.'

Dawkins blinked in surprise. Finally he appeared to accept the inevitable. 'In plain words?'

'Plain, and to the point.'

Dawkins cleared his throat. 'First I questioned the theatre director, Mr Hedley Shearman. He was at pains to convey that the incident is being treated as an internal matter. He didn't see Miss Calhoun before the show, but he was in the audience. When the curtain came down he went backstage and drove her to hospital himself.'

'So he takes it to have been an accident?'

'Indeed, preferring accident to incident.'

'You also spoke to the dresser.'

'Ms Denise Pearsall, yes. She made up Ms Calhoun.'

'What's she like?'

'As a dresser? I wouldn't know.'

'In interview, I mean. What impression did she make?'

'Anxious, nervous, on her guard.'

Who wouldn't be, faced with you? Diamond thought. 'Suspiciously so?'

'Difficult to tell. In her position, anyone would be entitled to feel vulnerable. If there is blame, she is the prime candidate. However . . .' A finger went up.

Diamond had to wait. The man was like an actor playing to an audience.

'However, one other thing of interest emerged. On Sunday, they had a dress rehearsal in full make-up. Nothing untoward was reported.'

'Worth knowing,' Diamond said, nodding.

Dawkins almost purred at the praise. 'May I therefore look forward to a transfer to CID?'

'I didn't say that.'

'Pardon me, but you appeared to approve of my report.'

'You were simply doing your job, a uniformed officer's job,' Diamond said. 'It wasn't a secret test for CID.'

Dawkins's eyes bulged. 'I don't understand. You sent for me.'

'To get your report, yes.'

Dawkins shook his head. 'If you had wanted the facts, you needn't have asked me. You could have got them from PC Reed. She's the one who writes everything down.'

Diamond smouldered inside. How he wished he'd thought of that.

BACKSTAGE IN THE THEATRE, the male lead was the first to arrive for the next performance. Short for a leading actor and with a nose a pigeon could have perched on, he'd had to settle for character parts for most of his career. The role of Christopher Isherwood, a man of slight build and less than slight nose, presented a fine opportunity to get the name of Preston Barnes in lights.

'Has Basil been sacked? Some jobsworth is on the door.'

Hedley Shearman was in the dressing room area in case Denise Pearsall arrived. 'I've installed a security man. Basil will be back when the present emergency is over. Something went badly wrong last night, and we can't risk a repeat.'

'If you ask me, there was something dodgy with the make-up. The rest of us used our own and we were all right.'

'Did Clarion say anything about it before you went on?'

'I didn't see her. The first I knew there was anything wrong was when she missed her cue and started grimacing. I gave her the line again and she screamed in my face. How is she now?'

'Progressing, I understand, but we ought to assume she won't be back this week. Are you okay playing opposite Gisella?'

Barnes gave a shrug. 'She was better than Clarion. But the play won't transfer now. We'll all be looking for work after Saturday.'

'You'll be snapped up,' Shearman said.

'Do you think so?' Barnes enjoyed that. 'I must get to my dressing room and begin my preparation.'

He'd spoken before of his preparation. He arrived early and spent at least an hour in contemplation, 'connecting emotively with the role', as he put it. His door was closed to everyone.

'When you arrived last night, was anyone about?' Shearman asked. 'Denise, for example?'

'I've no idea. I went straight to my room to prepare.'

'That would have been early?'

'Five thirty or thereabouts.'

'Your dressing room is close to Clarion's.'

Barnes frowned. 'Does that make me a suspect?'

'Not at all. You've no reason to harm her. I was wondering if you heard anyone visiting her.'

'Certainly not. I was concentrating on my role and, if you don't mind me saying so, you should do the same. Don't play detective. It's a job for an expert. Let's hope we don't have need of one.'

LATELY, DIAMOND and Paloma had taken to going for walks. That evening found them on the towpath of the Kennet and Avon Canal, heading for the George Inn at Bathampton.

Diamond's friendship with Paloma was still just that. Neither of them wanted to co-habit. They slept together sometimes, finding joy, support and consolation in each other's company. You could have taken them for man and wife, but you would have been wrong. Diamond's marriage to Steph had been written in the stars and her sudden death had left a void in his life that no one could fill. Paloma had gone through a disastrous marriage to a man in the grip of a gambling compulsion. After the divorce, she had immersed herself in her career, amassing a unique archive of fashion illustrations used by film and television companies around the world. She couldn't imagine marrying another man.

As she had helped the Theatre Royal with research for costume dramas, it dawned on Diamond that his tour backstage might amuse Paloma, so he told her about the ghost hunt.

'What were you doing at the theatre?'

'Didn't you hear about Clarion Calhoun?'

She'd been working long hours and missed the whole story, so he updated her. 'It may come to nothing,' he said finally, 'but my boss Georgina has an interest in keeping the theatre going, so . . .'

'You chummed up with Titus?' Paloma said. 'He must have taken a shine to you.'

That nettled him. 'I didn't encourage him.'

'I'm teasing. Titus takes himself seriously, but then most of them do.'

'Is his health okay? He fainted in the number 1 dressing room.'

Her smile vanished. 'Poor Titus. What was it—his heart?'

'I hope not. I helped him back to the Garrick's Head and he seemed to be getting over it.'

'Did this happen suddenly?'

'We were talking normally. It was the room Clarion had used, so I was looking to see if any traces of the make-up were left. I went to the window and found a dead butterfly on the sill. I mentioned it to Titus and that was when he passed out.'

'You're kidding.' Paloma was wide-eyed. 'What sort of butterfly?'

'Tortoiseshell. Does it matter?'

'It explains why Titus fainted. Didn't he tell you the story of the butterfly and the Theatre Royal? It's more impressive than the grey lady.'

'Go on. Scare me.'

'Years ago, a family called Maddox ran the theatre and each year they put on a marvellous pantomime. Nellie Maddox made the costumes and Reg and his son, Frank, wrote the shows and produced them. In 1948, they put on

Little Red Riding Hood and there was a butterfly ballet, dancers in butterfly costumes moving around a big gauze butterfly that lit up and glittered.'

'It caught fire?'

'No. During rehearsals a real butterfly, a dead tortoiseshell, was found on the stage and, shortly afterwards, Reg Maddox suffered a heart attack and died. As a mark of respect they decided to cut the ballet from the pantomime. Just before they opened, a tortoiseshell was spotted backstage but this one was alive. Everyone got very excited and said it must be a sign from Reg. They reinstated the butterfly ballet and the show was a big hit.'

'Nice story.'

'There's more. The Maddox family decided to keep the gauze butterfly for good luck and it's been hanging in the theatre's fly tower ever since. You can see it to this day. And a butterfly has appeared for almost every panto they've put on.'

'In the depths of winter?'

'It's taken to be an omen of success. Sometimes they appear on stage. Most of the stars will tell you their butterfly story if you ask. Honor Blackman, June Whitfield, Peter O'Toole.'

'O'Toole? What was he doing in pantomime?'

'In his case it was *Jeffrey Bernard is Unwell*. On the opening night, he was on stage and the butterfly settled on the newspaper he was reading. He ad-libbed a chat with it. When it finally fluttered off, it got a round of applause.'

'Actors are superstitious, aren't they?'

'You're not convinced, then?'

'I'm an old sceptic. What matters is that people in the theatre believe it.'

'What about the butterfly? Is it still there?'

'It will be unless the cleaner has been by. Someone will have noticed, surely. From all you've told me, plenty of people have heard the story.'

'Everyone who works there gets to hear it.'

Diamond found himself thinking that among superstitious theatre people one dead butterfly could create quite a panic. 'I wonder if the understudy has moved into the number 1 dressing room.'

'They may not want the room disturbed,' Paloma said.

'But it isn't a crime scene. There's no official investigation. The management were playing it down this morning. The show must go on. That's why I'm thinking the understudy may have moved in.' He took his mobile from his pocket. 'Do you mind? I need to call Ingeborg urgently.'

Paloma sighed. Their walks were supposed to be a chance to get away from it all. 'Go on. It must be important.'

He got through and issued instructions.

After the call was over, Paloma said, 'You could have gone yourself instead of sending Ingeborg.'

'To tell you the truth,' he said, 'I don't like going into that theatre. It has an effect on me. Step in there and I can't wait to get out.'

'I noticed, the only time we've been there together,' she said. 'Is it just the Theatre Royal?'

'Any theatre. My parents gave up trying to take me to pantomimes.'

'You must have had a bad experience as a child.'

'If I did, I don't remember. No, it's more about my personality. I'm a logical guy. I prefer the real world.'

She shook her head. 'Forgive me for saying this, Peter, but that's bunk. You're giving in to this hang-up.'

Not many people could talk to him like that and get away with it.

'And you're missing so much,' Paloma continued. 'That moment when the house lights start to dim is magical.'

'It doesn't alter the feeling I get each time I go there.'

'How are you going to head this investigation, then?'

He laughed. 'With difficulty.'

She looked away, across the canal. 'Could the Clarion incident be a case of stage fright?'

He shook his head. 'The burns must be genuine, or she wouldn't have been moved to Frenchay.'

'I mean, if she was terrified of appearing, she could have induced the burns herself. How's this? She makes her entrance, does the screaming fit, gets off the stage and covers her face with the towel, giving her the chance to apply some chemical that burns. It would explain the delay in her reaction.'

'Until the make-up's analysed we won't know for sure,' he said. 'Shall we change the subject? What's the project that's taking up so much of your time?'

'Oh, it's a costume piece. *Sweeney Todd*.'

OUTSIDE THE THEATRE ROYAL, Keith Halliwell was waiting for Ingeborg. He had borrowed a camera from one of the police photographers and carried a professional-looking shoulder bag that was supposed to be filled with camera equipment. In reality, it contained his raincoat and the camera. He wouldn't know how to change a lens or what to do with a light meter.

'Yoo-hoo.' Ingeborg stood only a pace away from him, her hair pinned up and wearing a black velvet skirt and top. 'Did you get the tickets?'

'Royal circle, back row.'

'Shall we do the biz first? I've brought my old press card. You tag behind me with the camera in your hand.'

They turned right, past the Garrick's Head. The stage door stood open. Ingeborg tapped on the window and a heavy-jowled, unfriendly face appeared. 'Press,' she said in a matter-of-fact tone, allowing a glimpse of her card. 'May we go in?'

'Who are you?' the security man asked.

'Ingeborg, independent.' She made it sound as if Borg was her surname and the *Independent* was her employer. A national paper had to be treated with respect.

'The press night was yesterday.' Not a lot of respect there.

'Yesterday the story was all about Clarion,' Ingeborg said. 'Tonight it's Gisella, the understudy playing Sally Bowles. We're taking some pictures backstage for an exclusive. It's all been cleared.'

'No one cleared it with me.' The voice was deeply discouraging.

'Didn't she let you know? So much on her mind, poor lamb.'

Halliwell had to admire Inge's sales pitch. She must have learned how to blag in her days as a hack.

'Keith, why don't you get the picture of—what's your name, sir?'

'Charlie Binns.'

'Of Charlie Binns, while I go ahead and let Gisella know we're here,' Ingeborg said. 'I'll leave you guys to it.'

It was now up to Halliwell to work the camera. He touched each button on the camera and one produced a flash. He pointed the lens at Charlie Binns and pressed the same button again. 'Nice one.'

A relieved Halliwell was admitted to a passageway with several notice-boards. At the far end, Ingeborg was talking to a large-bosomed woman who was holding a dress on a hanger.

'This is my photographer,' Inge said as he approached. 'Keith, this is Kate, who runs the wardrobe. Gisella is still in number 8 upstairs. I thought we might get a picture of the number 1 room first.'

'That's on the prompt side—the left of the stage,' Kate told them, pointing. 'Are you sure you have permission to be here?'

'Yes, we have clearance from Mr Binns on the stage door.'

'Do we really want a picture?' Halliwell asked Ingeborg as they made their way up the corridor. People dressed in black were moving about with a sense of urgency as curtain up approached.

'We only need to get in there. Instructions from the guv'nor. He called me on the way here.' She looked at him suddenly. 'You wear specs sometimes, don't you?'

He patted his pocket. 'I thought I might need them for the play.'

'Are they in a metal case?'

He nodded, mystified.

'Ideal. Well done.'

He didn't ask why.

They were approaching the back of the stage itself. Above them was the cavernous fly tower with its complicated system of grids and catwalks. They turned right towards the wings. Stagehands hurried past.

A sign pointed to dressing rooms 1–7. Ingeborg was off like a shot, and Halliwell caught up with her only after she had opened the door of number 1 and gone in. No one was inside.

'We're looking for a dead butterfly.'

'You're kidding.'

'Them's the orders. It should be on the sill,' Ingeborg said. 'Voilà.' She pointed to the window. A small, speckled butterfly was lying there. 'This is where your specs case comes in useful.'

'Yes?' He took it from his pocket and removed the glasses.

'A perfect little coffin,' Ingeborg said, as she gently slid the tortoiseshell into the case and snapped it shut.

Suddenly, a voice shocked them both by saying, 'Beginners, please.' It came from a loudspeaker attached to the wall.

'Should we get to our seats?'

She crossed to the door and looked out. Dressing-room doors were opening and actors emerged. 'Let's hang back a moment. I'd like to meet Clarion's dresser. The one who did the make-up.'

'Is that a good idea? She's the main suspect and we're not acting officially.'

'The guv'nor asked us to check if she turns up.'

'That isn't the same as meeting her. We could blow the investigation.'

She saw sense. 'Let's find out from someone else, then.'

They waited in the dressing room with the door ajar. The play itself began to be broadcast, a man talking about Berlin.

'Time to move,' Ingeborg said.

Halliwell trailed behind her. He was alarmed to find himself in the wings, only a few yards from the actors on stage. Several people were standing in the shadows. He recognised one of the actors he'd seen leaving a dressing room. A young woman was facing the man, using a soft brush on his face. She looked too young to be the dresser.

The actor must have heard his cue, because he stepped behind a set of double doors. A doorbell was rung. The actors could be heard reacting.

As the dialogue on stage developed, Inge homed in on the young girl with the make-up brush. At heart, she was still a journalist eager for a story. She tapped the girl on the shoulder.

There was a whispered exchange that Halliwell couldn't hear. Then Inge returned. 'Let's go.'

Nothing was said until they were in the street, where she took her mobile from her bag.

'I'm calling the guv'nor,' she said. 'Denise didn't show up tonight. This has got serious.'

DIAMOND LEFT PALOMA ASLEEP in her bedroom in Lyncombe early next morning. There was much to do.

The drive in was quick and enjoyable, before the traffic became the morning crawl. At his first sight of Georgian elegance he reminded himself how privileged he was to be in one of the finest cities in Europe, a boost before moving on to the utilitarian block that was his workplace.

Looking forward to a quiet start, he did not expect to find anyone in the open-plan area that was CID's hub. So it surprised him to see a figure by the window looking out—no one he immediately recognised. None of the team wore a suit, except himself. And what a suit. This three-piece, patterned in squares too large to be called check, wouldn't have looked out of place in a circus ring.

'How can I help you?' Diamond asked.

'The boot is on the other foot,' the visitor said, turning round. 'How can I help you?'

Diamond's greet-the-day optimism evaporated. 'Sergeant Dawkins? Why aren't you in uniform?'

Dawkins chuckled. 'Have you not heard? I was assigned to your command late yesterday. A reinforcement, ACC Dallymore calls me.'

'We'll see about that.' Diamond marched straight through to his office, snatched up the phone and asked to be put through to the ACC, only to be told she wouldn't be in all day. Even before he replaced the receiver he saw the memo on his desk from Georgina: *Peter, I have assigned Sergeant Dawkins to CID for a probationary period. His individual qualities will, I am confident, strengthen the team. I may add that he comes with the recommendation of his senior officer.*

'I bet he does,' Diamond muttered with all the bitterness of a man who has been shafted. He opened the door. 'What's your first name?'

'Horatio.'

It was all of a piece. 'And is that suit your idea of plain clothes? You're going to stand out in a crowd wearing that. Haven't you noticed the others wear casual gear, like T-shirts and jeans?'

'T-shirts and jeans are not to be found in my wardrobe.'

'What do you wear then?'

'When not in uniform, I favour my dance things.'

'Say that again.'

'Singlets and leggings. I'm often barefoot around the house.'

'You're a *dancer*?'

'I do a certain amount, yes. Flamenco.'

Diamond couldn't see it going down well with the team. 'That's remarkable, but it doesn't solve the problem. We'll put up with this today and find some office work for you. Take off the jacket and sit behind a desk. Oh, and for your own salvation, we'll call you Fred.'

'Fred?'

'As in Astaire, but we needn't say so.'

'May I venture to ask why?'

'The dancing. And because other people can be cruel, that's why.'

A LITTLE LATER, Diamond addressed the troops. They'd taken stock of the new arrival and were keeping their distance.

'Some of you know Fred Dawkins already. He's on secondment from uniform. He comes at a critical moment, because we have a new line of enquiry. Keith and Inge went to the theatre last night.'

'We went backstage by passing ourselves off as press,' Ingeborg said.

'And you collected the little item I requested?' Diamond said.

Halliwell produced his specs case and opened it like a jeweller displaying a precious stone.

'This turned up in the dressing room used by Clarion Calhoun the other night,' Diamond said. 'A dead butterfly is a bad omen in the Theatre Royal. A live one would be good news. Don't ask me why. All you need to know is that theatre people are deeply superstitious.'

'Did Clarion see it?' Paul Gilbert, the youngest DC, asked.

'We don't know. And we're not even sure if she knows about the butterfly jinx.'

'Are you thinking someone placed it there to scare her?'

'Let's keep an open mind on that. This sad little critter may simply have been trapped in the room. I called Frenchay Hospital just now and Clarion's still in the burns unit. There can be no question that the skin damage is real.'

'Wounding with malicious intent?' DI John Leaman said.

'That's a possibility. Inge, tell the team.'

She nodded. 'After we found the butterfly, we went backstage and learned that Denise Pearsall had called in earlier to say she was too upset to carry out her duties properly.'

There was a sound like a liner being launched: Dawkins clearing his throat.

'You want to say something, Fred?' Diamond had a sense of dread.

'If you please, superintendent.'

'"Guv" will do if you want to call me anything at all.'

'This may or may not be significant . . . guv.'

'Spit it out, or we'll never know.'

'I interviewed Ms Pearsall yesterday. Conceivably, being questioned as a suspect caused her some alarm and she decided to stay away.'

'It can't be discounted,' Diamond said, adding, 'Fred was the officer who made the first contact with the theatre. This Denise isn't answering the phone or her doorbell this morning.'

'Can we get a warrant to search the house?' Leaman asked.

'We wouldn't get one. We don't have anything on her,' Ingeborg said.

'We treat her as any other missing person,' Diamond said. 'Find out her movements. See if she runs a car and if she does, we put out an all-units order to trace it. That's your job, Keith. We also step up the pressure on the hospital, insist on getting a statement from Clarion. Inge, you and I will go there together. And it's high time the hospital lab reported on the traces of make-up on the towel. I'll give them a rocket at Frenchay. We'll get our own analysis done by forensics.'

Another bout of throat-clearing from Dawkins.

'Fred,' Diamond said, 'you're going to ask me what I want from you. Can you use a computer?'

'One's keyboard performance is accurate, but not the quickest,' Dawkins began.

'The civilian staff will help you. Get Denise's statement on file, and Shearman's. When anything else comes in, every item relevant to the investigation, see that it gets into the system. You're acting as receiver. That's a key post, so don't let me down.'

Dawkins said no more.

THE BURNS UNIT at Frenchay Hospital was easy to locate and Clarion's private ward was obvious, thanks to a uniformed security man seated outside.

'She's with someone,' the man said. 'I'll have to clear it.'

Diamond was about to push past when Ingeborg touched his arm. 'She may be having treatment, guv.'

The upshot was that the 'someone' came out, a woman in her forties in a black suit with red tights and patent leather shoes, confident and businesslike. 'You'd better not be press,' she said.

Diamond held up his ID. 'And who are you?'

'Tilda Box, Clarion's agent. She's far too distressed to have visitors.'

'We're not visitors,' he said. 'It appears a criminal offence was committed on Monday evening and we have a duty to investigate.'

She folded her arms. 'Speak to me, then. I'm aware of all the facts.'

'No need,' Diamond said. 'We're going straight in. Inge, you go first.'

Tilda Box was incandescent, but stopped short of wrestling with them.

Diamond followed Inge into a large room. He was prepared to find a figure swathed in bandages. Not so. The patient was in an armchair looking at a television. Her face, neck and what was visible of her chest appeared to be coated in a yellowish ointment. The damage to her skin was evident, flakes of tissue hanging from raw burns. She tugged at her long, blonde hair to screen her face. 'Who are you?'

Diamond showed the ID and introduced Ingeborg.

'Now,' he said. 'I take it you didn't do this to yourself, so it's our job to find who is responsible.'

She appeared to think about playing dumb. There was a lengthy pause. Then she couldn't resist saying, 'The theatre is responsible and I intend to sue.'

'It may not be so simple,' he said. 'If someone wanted to harm you, they're mainly to blame.'

Startled, she turned, giving them a front view of her damaged face. Skin has a marvellous capacity for healing, but it was hard to imagine that the scarring would ever disappear. 'That's ridiculous. This is a clear case of negligence. They used some defective product that ruined my skin.'

'I doubt if any cosmetics firm would sell a product as harmful as that.'

'The doctors here are world experts and they're treating me for burns.'

'I'm not arguing with that. I'm saying we don't know how the make-up got to be so dangerous. Do you have any enemies, Clarion?'

'No.' The denial was total. Immediately she'd made it, uncertainty showed in her eyes.

Ingeborg said, 'Has anyone threatened you recently or in the past?'

'Of course they haven't.'

'Crazy fans? Someone else's fans?'

'My fans have grown up with me. I'm coming up to thirty. People of my age don't do crazy. They've grown out of all that hormonal silliness.'

'How did the theatre people treat you in rehearsal?' Diamond asked. 'You're an outsider, in a way, and you walked into a starring role.'

'They're professionals. My name sells tickets. That's how it is and they accept it.'

'Do you recall any hostility while you were rehearsing?' Diamond asked.

'If there was any bad feeling, I didn't pick it up.'

'Let's talk about Monday,' he said. 'What time did you arrive?'

'Before five. I went to my dressing room and sat going over my lines. Denise came with the clothes about forty-five minutes before curtain up.'

'She made you up for the dress rehearsal the previous day?'

'Yes.'

'And did your face react then? Any discomfort?'

'None whatsoever. And I didn't notice her doing anything different on the opening night. She brought her box of colours and brushes with her. She cleansed my face of day make-up and then put on a thin layer of moisturiser followed by the foundation and the highlights and the liners for the eyes and mouth and so on. I felt no discomfort.'

'What cleanser did she use?' Ingeborg asked.

'Cold cream and astringent, she told me. It all felt normal.'

'So there was this delay before you felt your face burning,' Diamond said. 'How long?'

'Between twenty minutes and half an hour.'

'This is the mystery,' he said. 'If we're right in assuming the make-up damaged your skin, why didn't it happen in the dressing room when it was being applied?'

'Slow-acting,' Clarion said.

'We'll get advice on that, but I've got my doubts.'

Her glare could have drilled a hole through his head. 'You can doubt all you want. I'm left with a face like a fire victim. And I'm suing for loss of earnings and disfigurement. You won't stop me.'

'BACK TO BATH NOW?' Inge said.

'Not yet. We'll find the hospital pathology lab first,' Diamond said.

'We'd better ask.' Inge stopped a porter, and they were soon heading in the right direction.

The scientist in charge, a bearded man called Pinch, jumped to attention when they showed their IDs. 'How can I help?'

They asked about Clarion's towel.

'There are traces of glycerine-based make-up and face powder, but also a corrosive I wouldn't recommend putting anywhere near your face. Sodium hydroxide.'

'Caustic soda,' Ingeborg said, with a sharp intake of breath.

Appalled, Diamond said, 'Isn't that what they use to unblock drains?'

'Right. We didn't believe it at first, so we repeated the tests. It's caustic soda for sure, available from your friendly, neighbourhood hardware shop. As you doubtless know, it comes in powder form as tiny flakes or granules. It's inert until added to water.'

'So it could be mixed with something dry, such as face powder, and it wouldn't react?'

'Correct.'

'And being white it would blend in with powder,' Ingeborg added.

'What would have activated it?' Diamond asked.

'Assuming it was applied to her skin?' Pinch said. 'The surface moisture may have been enough. If she was wearing a moisturiser, that would certainly have done it.'

'She had another layer over that, the glycerine-based cream you mentioned,' Ingeborg said. 'If it was mixed with that—'

'I'm not sure it was,' the scientist said. 'We recovered a number of dry particles from the towel. Actors powder their faces, don't they?'

'If they do, it's over some layers of make-up.'

'I understand it gets warm under the theatre lights. If she started sweating, the process would begin and she might not be aware at first. It would form a slime on the surface and the action can take out the nerve endings as well as the skin tissue. By the time she became aware, it would already have been well advanced.'

'This may explain the delay we've been puzzling over,' Diamond said. 'And it can't have been an accident. You don't add caustic soda to face powder through carelessness. This was deliberate.'

When they left, they took the towel with them in a sterile box. It would go to the forensics lab for them to run their own tests.

'What do we do?' Ingeborg said.

'We've got enough now for a search warrant to get into Denise's house and seize her make-up kit.'

Diamond called CID and got Dawkins.

'Is Keith in the office?'

'Would he be the gentleman with sideburns?'

Diamond gripped the phone harder. What could have possessed Georgina to dump such a nutcase in CID? 'That's Leaman. If he's there, hand the phone to him.'

'He is not. There is another officer with a more restrained haircut. I can only deduce he is DI Halliwell.'

'Put me on to him, for God's sake.'

Keith Halliwell said he'd organise the warrant directly.

'Any success tracing her car?'

'She owns a silver Vauxhall Corsa. The neighbours are pretty sure it wasn't there overnight. I've put out an all-units as agreed.'

Diamond updated Ingeborg.

She said, 'I can't think why Denise would do something as dumb as this.'

'You get people with a grudge and they lose all perspective. This could have been a personal spat with Clarion, or something different, like a grievance against the theatre.'

'So she scars Clarion for life?' she said on an angry, rising note.

'Stay cool, Inge. Up to now, nobody has said a word against Denise.'

'Because she's only known to us as a functionary. The dresser. We'll find out a whole lot more shortly.'

AS THEY STARTED the Bath Road stretch of the A4, Diamond said, 'I haven't heard what you dug up on Clarion.'

'She's not controversial, like some pop stars,' Ingeborg replied. 'There was a live-in boyfriend for a couple of years. An Australian who's gone back to Sydney. If there's anyone else she's kept them well hidden.'

'Does she do drugs?'

She laughed faintly. 'Don't they all at some point? Put it this way: she's not well known for it.'

'How does she spend her money?'

'Property. She has apartments in London and New York and a manor house near Tunbridge Wells.'

'A home-loving girl, then.'

'It doesn't stop her from eating out and clubbing.'

'Who with?'

'Lately with the agent we met, Tilda Box.'

'They go to nightclubs together?'

'There are plenty of magazine pictures to prove it.'

'Is Clarion bi, do you think?'

'I haven't seen it suggested.'

'If she's straight, she'd surely not want Tilda with her.'

'You could be wrong there, guv. A lot of women feel more comfortable with their own sex as company. If the break-up with the Australian guy hurt her, she may be pleased to coast along for a bit with Tilda.'

At Manvers Street, Diamond arranged for the towel to be driven to the Home Office forensic lab at Chepstow. He'd been impressed by Pinch, but he still needed official confirmation of the findings.

As promised, Halliwell had the search warrant ready. 'I was hoping for a few words in private,' he added.

'No problem. We'll talk on the way to Denise's. We can meet Inge there.'

In the car, it emerged that Sergeant Dawkins was the problem.

'He's an oddball,' Halliwell said. 'He means well—I think—but he says the strangest things. Our civilian women got the idea he was put in to spy on them. He was going on about time and motion to improve efficiency.'

This angered Diamond. 'He's got no right to talk to my staff like that. Time and motion is old hat, anyway.'

'I told him to shut up about it but he didn't seem to understand what the fuss was about.'

'I thought leaving him in the office was best. Now I'm not so sure.'

They crossed the River Avon to the Dolemeads housing estate. Ingeborg was waiting outside Denise Pearsall's narrow terraced house. She said she'd tried the doorbell and got no response. The neighbours hadn't seen her since the weekend.

Halliwell had brought a miniature battering ram used to open locked doors. 'Let's see if there's an easier way,' Diamond said. By sliding a loyalty card between door and jamb, he freed the latch.

In the hallway, the post showed Denise had not been there for a day or two. Ingeborg was sent to search upstairs while the men inspected the living room and kitchen. If her home was any guide, Denise was organised to the point of compulsion. Even the fridge magnets were in rows.

It didn't take long to discover that her professional make-up kit wasn't in the house. Ingeborg found some lipsticks and creams in the bedroom and there were a few sticks of greasepaint in a drawer that they put into evidence bags.

'She'll have her main stuff in the car,' Diamond said. 'We've got to find that. Is there a computer?'

'I checked it,' Inge said. 'She seems to delete emails she's read and there's little to see. I get the impression she doesn't use it much.'

'Did you search the bathroom?'

'Nothing much in there except toothpaste and shower gel,' Ingeborg said. 'She makes herself up in the bedroom.'

'I mean cleaning materials. I'm thinking of caustic soda.'

'There's a bottle of Sink Fresh. Not the same thing at all.'

Diamond checked all the cupboards downstairs, reflecting that the absence of caustic soda didn't mean Denise was in the clear. She would have taken the stuff to the theatre.

He decided they'd seen enough.

BACK IN MANVERS STREET, Diamond asked Dawkins to step into his office.

'What's this I hear about you upsetting the civilian staff? You were out of order talking about time and motion.'

'Time and motion?' Dawkins seemed genuinely at a loss. 'Ah, I have it. I was quoting Ford.'

'Henry Ford?' Diamond said, thinking of car production.

'John. '*Tis Pity She's a Whore*.'

'Sergeant, we don't go in for personal abuse in this department.'

'It's a Jacobean play.' Unexpectedly, Dawkins struck a theatrical pose and started speaking lines. ' "Why, I hold fate clasped in my fist, and could command the course of time's eternal motion, hadst thou been one thought more steady than an ebbing sea." '

One thing was clear. Manvers Street nick wasn't ready for Jacobean drama. 'Do you make a habit of quoting lines from plays?'

'I would characterise it as an occasional indulgence.'

'Well, knock it off. The only quoting we do in CID is the official caution.'

'I shall curb the habit,' Dawkins said, and added with an earnest look. 'I trust I haven't blighted my prospects . . . guv.'

They were blighted the moment you stepped in here in that clown suit, Diamond thought. 'So you are a theatre-goer?'

'One of my indulgences,' Dawkins said.

'I suppose it comes with the dancing. Do you know the play Clarion was in?'

'I haven't seen it, which is a pity. I was at some disadvantage questioning Mr Shearman, the director.'

'You also spoke to Denise Pearsall. Was there any aggro towards Clarion?'

'None that I noticed. I saw anxiety in plenty.'

'From guilt, would you say?'

'Difficult to divine. Conscience, possibly. She appeared to accept that her make-up was the likely cause of the occurrence.'

'Did you question her about it?'

'She told me she used new materials. The brand was the same she had used before, without ill effect.'

'She wasn't blaming anyone else, then?'

'The question of blame didn't arise. If you care to look at a transcript of the interview, it is now stored in the computer.'

'Good.' Somehow, Dawkins was coming out of this so-called roasting better than he came in. 'Watch what you say in future.'

Dawkins nodded and left the room. If there was a faint smile lingering, it may have been only in Diamond's imagination.

THE NOTICES WERE IN and Hedley Shearman was relieved. The critics praised Gisella Watling's performance and didn't make too much of Clarion's collapse. The sensational stuff had all been covered in news stories the previous day. 'UNDERSTUDY'S SUCCESS', went one headline. Another: 'GISELLA'S STARRY NIGHT'. Reviews like that would keep the show afloat until the end of the week.

He cut out the reviews to pin on the stage-door noticeboard. Before that, however, he would use them to boost his chances with Gisella.

'Have you seen these?' he said, when she arrived for the matinée.

She hadn't. She was over the moon, even if she tried to appear casual. She was taller than Clarion, with less of the showbiz glamour about her. For the play, her dark hair was styled with waves and cut short at the back, a style he could quickly get to like. She wasn't a starry-eyed beginner. She must have been on the stage some years. Even so, it had taken courage to go on.

'All sorts of people will read these, especially casting directors,' he told her, with a fatherly show of encouragement that often did the trick with young actresses. 'Clarion's misfortune is your opportunity. You never know where it will lead.'

'I don't think of it like that,' she said. 'I certainly wouldn't have wanted to get the part this way. I still feel bad about Clarion.' Her eyes confirmed it. To Shearman, she appeared utterly sincere.

'Why should you? You're not responsible.' After a pause he added, 'You could move into the number 1 dressing room if you wish.'

'I'm happy where I am, thanks.'

'Which room is that?'

'Number 8. I'd better get up there now.'

'Hope there's a good house in this afternoon, with at least one butterfly. You know about the Theatre Royal butterflies?' He was being over-friendly now. He'd got lucky like this a few times over the years.

'I've heard the stories.'

'I'll come with you and show you something. It's on the way.' She had to pass the fly tower to get to her dressing room.

He walked close behind her, enjoying the swing of her hips. 'Back in the 1940s, when the whole butterfly thing started,' he said, 'Reg Maddox designed a butterfly ballet for a pantomime. One of the big gauze butterflies made as the backdrop was kept hanging in the flies as a kind of talisman. You wouldn't know it was there unless someone told you where to look.'

They had reached the area immediately behind the stage. Above them, the steel-framed fly tower rose eight metres clear of the rest of the building.

'If you look straight up, you'll get a sight of the lucky butterfly right at the top.' He pointed upwards with his left hand and at the same time curled his right over her shoulder.

Gisella didn't flinch when Shearman touched her. He'd moved so close that he could feel her hair against his cheek. He wasn't looking up at the damn butterfly. He knew where it was.

Suddenly she tensed and her whole frame shuddered.

He jerked his hand away from her shoulder. 'It's okay,' he said.

'It isn't,' she said in a shocked voice. 'It's anything but okay.'

3

A police car and an ambulance were parked in front of the theatre and the whole area was congested with people arriving for the matinée.

'The stage door,' Diamond said to Keith Halliwell, heading up the steps into the dim interior. His negative feelings about entering the theatre had to be ignored. When you get the shout in CID you can't stop to think. They found their way backstage and emerged under the fly tower, where an assortment of actors and technicians were gazing upwards at two paramedics. They had made their way along a narrow catwalk close to where a body was jack-knifed over a pair of battens suspended from the grid under the roof. One arm hung down.

'Do we know who it is?' he asked a stagehand.

'It must be the dresser. She went missing earlier.'

Missing no longer. Diamond stood for a moment in silence. A fall onto steel battens, almost certainly fracturing the spine, was chilling to contemplate.

A man in a striped suit came over. 'I'm the theatre director, Hedley Shearman. I made the emergency call.'

'Are you certain who she is?'

'It's Denise, Clarion's dresser. You can see her red hair. She phoned yesterday and told me she couldn't face coming in for last night's performance. God forgive me, it didn't cross my mind that she was suicidal.'

'When did you spot her?' Diamond asked Shearman.

'Twenty minutes ago. Gisella—who is playing Sally Bowles now—had just arrived for the matinée and I wanted to point something out to her in the fly tower. She looked up and saw the arm. She's profoundly shocked, as I was. She wants to go on for the matinée, though.'

'No. Send the audience home.'

Shearman was appalled. 'What—cancel, at this late stage? Impossible. Denise wouldn't have wanted that.'

'Denise is out of the equation. It's my decision.'

'What can I possibly say to people?'

'Unforeseen circumstances. The truth will have leaked out anyway. They'll have seen the ambulance and the police cars as they came in. I suggest you make the announcement now if you want us out before the evening performance. Make sure the staff don't leave. I may need to question them.'

Red-faced and angry, Shearman used his phone to issue instructions.

'Did anyone see Denise arrive this morning?' Diamond asked him.

Shearman shook his head. 'Someone would have told me. I was trying to contact her.'

'So when do you think this happened?'

'I've no idea. You don't look up unless you have a reason.'

'What was your reason?'

'I told you, I was with Gisella. I wanted to show her the butterfly.'

Diamond's interest quickened. 'Butterfly?'

'A piece of scenery more than sixty years old, but we value it as an emblem of good fortune.' Shearman moved a few strides to the left and pointed upwards, at a higher level from where the corpse was lodged. Fortunately, the thing suspended among other strips of scenery was colourful enough to make out. 'It was for a pantomime.'

'Ah, I heard about this. So you're saying the body could have been there some hours without anyone noticing?'

'Quite possibly. It's dark up there and nobody would need to go up there between performances.'

'Denise wasn't at home overnight. We searched her house this morning.'

'Then it's not impossible she did this some time yesterday. She phoned in about two in the afternoon.'

'How did she sound?'

'Exhausted. She said she was sorry but she'd have to let us down because she couldn't face the evening performance. I told her to get some rest and we'd cope without her.'

'How would I get up there?' Diamond asked.

'The quickest way is up the iron ladder in the corner.'

Diamond eyed the ladder. A vertical climb with the rungs spaced a foot apart looked a stern test of an overweight detective's agility.

Shearman said, 'There's a little platform about every ten feet. Do you see?'

Diamond was having second thoughts.

The paramedics were coming down. 'She's well dead,' said one on reaching the ground. 'Her neck is broken.'

Diamond introduced himself. 'No indication how long she's been there, I suppose?'

'I wouldn't know. Are you going up to see?'

Duty demanded that he did. 'I'd better.'

He was canny enough to pause between levels and got to the catwalk breathing heavily, but without mishap.

Now it was a matter of edging out to view the body, making certain he clung onto the handrail. What he saw was Denise Pearsall's body lying face up along the battens, her head skewed into an unnatural angle, the hair red, the face deathly white. She'd dropped at least ten metres and hit the metal hard. It would have been instant death, he told himself. But to see where she'd fallen from, he'd need to climb a stage higher.

He hauled his overweight frame up the last set of rungs until, gasping for breath, he reached another catwalk. With only the briefest of glances downwards, he edged out to the position directly above the corpse. She'd have needed to step over the handrail. It couldn't have been accidental. Presumably she had intended to hit the floor, not the battens below.

Looking up, he noticed the piece of butterfly scenery: a psychedelic monster as tall as he, probably the last thing Denise saw before she died.

It hadn't brought her much luck.

With painstaking care he picked his way down. As he did so, an aroma of coffee wafted upwards. He saw Dr Bertram Sealy, the local pathologist, with his flask open. 'Should have guessed.'

'You should invest in one of these,' Sealy said, holding up the flask. 'You're sweating, Superintendent. Did you go up to the very top? You want to watch your blood pressure.'

'Coming from you, that's rich.'

'So what did you discover? I've heard of corpsing in the theatre, but this is excessive.' Sealy fancied himself a master of black humour.

'This wasn't a cry for help, that's for sure. If you take a jump like that, you mean to do the business.'

'Was she a headcase?'

'Not known to be. But it seems she may have blamed herself for an incident here two evenings ago.'

'The Clarion what's-her-name thing? Nasty. Is it a good play? My wife told me to ask for complimentary tickets.'

'I haven't seen it.' Diamond turned to Shearman. 'Does Denise have a room of her own somewhere?' he asked, thinking a suicide note might exist.

'The nearest thing to an office would be Wardrobe.'

'She worked out of a wardrobe?'

'It's where all the costumes and wigs are stored.'

'Beverages, too? I'm parched.'

'You won't get a drink in Wardrobe, but the bars were doing some trade until we sent the audience away.'

'Show me to the nearest, then.'

'IT'S A JEWEL OF A THEATRE,' Diamond said to soften up Shearman over a beer in the dress-circle bar. 'Are the finances in good nick?'

'Reasonably good. Mostly we play to full houses.'

'You need well-known actors to bring in the audiences. Clarion Calhoun was chosen for her box-office appeal. Is that right?'

Shearman glanced away momentarily. 'She wasn't my personal pick.'

'You'd have gone for someone else?'

'I had reservations about Clarion. She went to drama school, but hasn't done much since. It was a top-level decision.'

'How did Denise feel about the choice of Clarion?'

'No idea. I never discussed it with her. She was only a dresser.'

'But she was on the permanent staff. If there was a general feeling that Clarion wasn't up to the job, it would have fed through to Denise.'

'You're losing me.'

'There's a sense of unity in this theatre,' Diamond said, playing to Shearman's vanity. 'An outsider like Clarion—not known as an actor—is given the star part. There must have been some muttering in the ranks.'

'How does this affect Denise's suicide?' Shearman asked.

'I'm thinking aloud. She was well placed to get Clarion sidelined.'

'By making her up with something that damaged her face? No chance.'

'You may as well know. It was caustic soda.'

The man jerked back so suddenly that he spilt his beer. 'That isn't possible.'

'It is. It was analysed.'

Shearman said, 'I can't accept that Denise would have done such a thing.'

'Why else did she kill herself, then?'

Shearman released a long, audible breath. 'God almighty.'

'How well did you know Denise? Does she have any family?'

'I couldn't tell you. We weren't on close terms.'

'Who did she know best in this theatre?'

Shearman hesitated. 'She worked for Kate, the wardrobe mistress. You'd better speak to her. She objects to the official label, by the way. She likes to be known as Kate in Wardrobe.'

'Is she in the building now?'

'I'm sure she is.'

'I ought to be getting back.' Diamond drained his glass, but then paused. 'Just now, when we spoke about the choice of actress, you said it was a top-level decision. You're the boss, aren't you?'

Shearman gave a hollow laugh. 'Don't be deceived.'

'Who's the big cheese, if you aren't?'

'The chairman of the board. Francis Melmot.'

'He signed up Clarion?'

'I was asked what I thought, but the decision wasn't mine. He outranks me, and so do all the trustees, come to that.' The bitterness wasn't disguised.

'You're saying she was foisted on you?'

'I wouldn't put it like that. There was consultation.'

'But the decision wasn't yours. I'd better speak to Francis Melmot.'

Shearman's face flushed crimson. 'The casting has no bearing on what happened. Denise wasn't involved in theatre politics. She got on with her job like the rest of us. There must have been some dreadful error.'

'Caustic soda in the make-up?'

Shearman fingered his tie as if it was choking him.

HIGH IN THE FLY TOWER, photographs were being taken of the body, but Dr Sealy was back on ground level. 'We'll have her down presently, and I'll do the autopsy tomorrow morning.'

'Anything I should be told?' Diamond asked.

'Not really. The cervical spine appears to have snapped at the point where she hit the metalwork. Death would have been immediate.'

'Time?'

'I took a temperature reading, but it means very little. I can tell you it was some hours ago, but how many is another question.'

'Where would I be without your expert help?'

Sealy gave a shrug. 'Now, who do I see about those complimentary tickets?'

KATE IN WARDROBE sighed heavily. 'Denise was my senior dresser. I can't think what drove her to this.'

'She used this room as her base, I was told.' Diamond couldn't see how. He was wedged between an ironing board and a washing machine. Every surface was covered in layers of dress materials. Racks of costumes, hatboxes piled high, wigs on dummy heads and sewing machines filled all the other space.

'She did, but she always brought her own things with her and took them away at the end of the show.'

'What things?'

'Her bags, I mean, with all she needed. Dressers are expected to deal with all emergencies, anything from a missing button to a false moustache that won't stick.'

'Make-up?'

'In rare cases, yes. Like Clarion. She had a special bag for it.'

'Describe this bag, would you?'

'Black leather, rather like an old-fashioned doctor's bag, with all the pots and brushes inside. I expect you'll find it in her house.'

'We already searched. It isn't there.'

'In her car, then.'

'Do you know where she parked?'

'Anywhere she could. Finding a place is a lottery at this time of year.'

Diamond looked across the heaps of costumes and materials. 'I was wondering if she left a note somewhere.'

'A suicide note? I haven't found one. Things get covered over. If it's anywhere, it would be somewhere near the door where you're standing. She'd hang her coat there and chat, just like you are.'

After lifting everything within reach and finding no note he asked, 'Did she seem anxious about anything?'

'Anxious? Not Denise. She was as tough as old boots. At one time when she couldn't get theatre work she helped out at an undertaker's. She also toured with a theatre company in Bosnia when the war was going on. And when she was just a slip of a girl she was involved with a prison drama group in Manchester, with murderers and rapists. She was no wimp, bless her.' Kate produced a tissue and blew her nose, but Diamond had the impression it was more about self-pity than sympathy. The loss of the senior dresser would add to the workload.

'Did Denise have anything to say about the current production?'

'We consulted over the costumes and make-up.' A guarded answer.

'Yes, but did she say anything about the actors in particular?'

Kate shook her head. He had an instinct that this big-eyed, blousy woman would be a rich source of gossip if only he could tap into it.

'Come on, Kate,' he said. 'You just told me she liked a chat. Actors are fascinating to be around, aren't they?'

'Tell me about it,' she said, rolling her eyes, and then appeared willing to say more now that the focus had shifted from Denise. 'They're like kids, most of them. It's all "me, me". And if they're not full of themselves, they're sucking their thumbs in a corner, wanting to be mothered. It depends.'

'How was Clarion getting on with everyone?'

'All right. She was used to dealing with people, but it stood out a mile she was terrified of acting. She wasn't much good in rehearsal.'

'Forgetting her lines?'

'More the way she spoke them. It's not an easy part, Sally Bowles.'

'And how was Denise taking it? Was it personal for her?'

She was twitchy now that Denise's name had come up again. 'What do you mean—personal?'

'She worked here a long time. She was proud of the theatre, wasn't she?'

'She felt we'd been short-changed with Clarion getting the role, and quite a number of us shared her opinion.'

'But that didn't justify killing herself. Maybe there were other strains in her life. Was she romantically involved with anyone?'

'If she was, she never said a word about it.'

'On Monday when the play opened, did she call in here?'

'Always does, about six, in time to deliver the costumes to the actors. She was no different from usual.'

'Can you recall what was said?' he asked.

'Not much. I think we both said we hoped it would go better than the dress rehearsal. When the time came to sort Clarion out, she picked up her case and tootled off, as calm as you like.'

'You're speaking of the make-up case? Had she come straight here from her car?'

'I assume so. She was still wearing her coat.'

'So no one could have tampered with it before she got to Clarion's dressing room?'

'That's for certain.'

Useful information. Diamond had been toying with the possibility that some other person could have added caustic soda to the make-up before the show. This seemed to scotch the theory.

'You said just now when Denise left to see Clarion, she was calm.'

'She was her normal, placid self,' Kate said, 'well in control. What's wrong with that?'

'I'll tell you. She was on her way to smear caustic soda on Clarion's face and cause acute pain and third-degree burns, so how could she be so calm?'

'You'll have to work that out for yourself.'

One thing he had worked out. The wardrobe mistress and the dresser had not been on the best of terms.

DIAMOND HAD A STRONG dislike of being fobbed off. After seeing Kate, he asked to meet Francis Melmot and was told he had a prior engagement.

'Priority over the police? I don't think so.'

'All I can tell you,' said Shearman, 'is what he said to my secretary before he left the building.'

'So he was here today?'

'And yesterday. The chairman is taking a keen interest in what's happened.'

'So keen that he clears off as soon as the police arrive. Can you tell me where he lives?'

Shortly after, Diamond was driven by Keith Halliwell through the leafy lanes of Somerset about five miles south of the city. They were looking for Melmot Hall, where Melmots had lived since the Restoration.

For Diamond, getting out of that theatre was like being released from some hypnotist's instruction. Only now did he fully understand the paralysing effect the place had on him. If he didn't deal with it, he'd be forced to drop the case.

The sat-nav directed them through a quiet village to an imposing gateway: the entrance to Melmot Hall. A crowd of people were strolling round the edges of an immaculate lawn in front of a large gabled house with tall Tudor chimneys. They parked, and began walking up the drive. Halfway along, an elderly woman in a straw hat was seated behind a trestle table.

'Two?' she said when they reached her. 'That'll be six pounds, please.'

'We're visiting the owner, Mr Melmot. Is he home?'

She eyed them with suspicion. 'I'm Mrs Melmot. Everyone has to pay today. It's for charity.'

'We didn't come to see your garden, ma'am,' Diamond said.

'I guessed as much by the look of you,' Mrs Melmot said, 'and you're not the only ones. They come from miles around for a slice of my lemon drizzle cake, but the entrance fee is the same.'

'Is your husband on the premises?'

'I hope not. He's dead. He shot himself in 1999.' She announced it as if talking about a felled tree, in the matter-of-fact tone of the well-raised Englishwoman.

There wasn't anything adequate Diamond could say, so after a pause, he said, 'It must be your son we've come to interview. We're police officers.'

Leaving Halliwell to have a look around, Diamond marched up the drive towards the entrance porch and accosted a man in a blazer, who told him where to find Mr Melmot.

'He's in the orangery, around the building to your left.'

There, Diamond found a large octagonal Victorian structure. No oranges were visible, but there was a sizeable lemon tree and a sizeable man in a white linen jacket standing beside it, speaking to visitors.

'This isn't about the garden,' Diamond said when his turn came. He introduced himself. 'I'm following up on the fatality in the theatre. I was hoping to catch you at the theatre, but you'd left.'

'There was no more I could do. Extremely distressing, the whole thing. Shall we speak somewhere else? One's voice carries in here.' Melmot steered him through a walled garden to an open area with a sunken lawn. 'We use this as an open-air theatre for local groups.'

'You're heavily involved in the theatre,' Diamond said.

'Yes, I've always been drawn to the footlights.'

'So you became a trustee of the Theatre Royal?'

'When one is in a position to help out, one should, I feel.'

'I was told that the trustees had a hand in the casting of Clarion Calhoun.'

The first hint of ill humour surfaced on Melmot's face. 'Who told you that? Shearman, no doubt. He's touchy on this subject.'

'Is it usual for the board to make decisions like that?'

'This was a commercial decision. We need at least one sell-out production as well as the yearly pantomime to stay solvent.'

'I was told that Clarion can't act.'

Melmot's blue eyes bulged. 'That's hardly fair. She didn't get the chance to prove herself.'

'Everyone I've spoken to says she was rubbish in rehearsal.'

Melmot gave an impatient sigh. 'This isn't getting us anywhere. Why don't you concentrate on the suicide?'

'All right. It isn't entirely clear why Denise Pearsall, an apparently well-adjusted woman, decided to end it all.'

'That's plain enough, isn't it? She was responsible for the damage to Clarion's face. Apart from the personal tragedy, it has deeply worrying implications for the theatre.'

'The possibility of a lawsuit?'

'For obvious reasons, I'd rather not discuss that.'

'Clarion seemed ready to discuss it this morning.'

Melmot almost fell down the slope in his surprise. 'You've seen Clarion? I was told she was surrounded by security.'

'She is. She's instructing her lawyers, she told me. Suing for disfigurement and loss of earnings.'

Melmot groaned. 'I feared as much. Years of good housekeeping and fund-raising could be undone by this.'

'You heard about the caustic soda?'

'Yes. I can't think what drove the woman to it. Was it a dreadful error? How could it possibly have happened?'

Crucial questions, as yet unanswerable. 'Who first suggested Clarion for the part?'

'I did.' Melmot smiled. 'I'm a fan.' Difficult to credit, but the way his face had lit up seemed to make it believable. 'Followed her career almost since she started. I read somewhere that she'd been through drama college and also that she thought Bath was the loveliest city in England. I asked her out to lunch in London and sold the idea of Sally Bowles to her. She leapt at it. Tough negotiations followed with the agent, of course.'

'Tilda Box. I met her at the hospital.'

'Miss Box is a hard bargainer. Eventually we got the terms reduced to a realistic figure. God knows what we'll have to pay now.'

'Only if they can prove you were negligent,' Diamond said.

'Denise was in our employment, unfortunately. If the fault was hers I can't see us avoiding a substantial payout. Now, is there anything else you need to know? I really ought to be meeting my visitors.'

Diamond suggested walking back to the orangery. 'When Clarion came to Bath to start rehearsing, where did she stay?'

'Clarion put up here for a couple of days.'

'Here?' Diamond pointed a thumb at the stately home.

'One of the things I know about millionaire pop stars is that it pleases them to mingle with old money. It was all very proper. My mother lives here too, you know.'

'I met her when we arrived,' Diamond said. 'Famous for her cake.'

Melmot clicked his tongue. 'Is that what she tells people?'

'I was also told about your late father.'

'The whole family saga? Father had an accident while cleaning his shotgun. Mother was typically calm about the whole thing. They weren't close.'

They'd reached the orangery. Diamond thanked him and went looking for Halliwell. He found him at a table on the terrace. He had a cup of tea in front of him and an empty plate.

Diamond pointed. 'Was that the lemon drizzle?'

'I had the last piece. You can still get a cup of tea and a biscuit.'

Muttering, Diamond went over to where the tea was being served.

'I don't want you thinking this has anything to do with the cake I missed out on,' he said to Halliwell when he returned, 'but tomorrow morning you're standing in for me at the post-mortem.'

DIAMOND SHUT HIMSELF in his office and sank into the armchair there. On the face of it, the case could now be closed. Denise's suicide could only mean she held herself responsible for the damage to Clarion's face. What other interpretation could be put on it? By some freakish oversight she had used caustic soda with the regular make-up and her horror at what had happened must have driven her to take her own life.

But his self-respect as a detective wouldn't let him walk away. What would be the use of caustic soda in a theatre? The simple power to unblock drains seemed the best bet. But the mystery was how Denise could have made the mistake. Pure caustic soda came in sturdy containers with childproof lids and a printed warning. Could a professional like her have muddled one with a tin of talc?

He'd speculated whether someone else had tampered with Denise's make-up and this still seemed possible. People were unhappy that Clarion had the starring role, and she was the only cast member being made up by Denise. Doctor the make-up and it was obvious who would take the rap. But this line of thought presented two problems he hadn't resolved: opportunity and timing. First, Kate in Wardrobe had said Denise arrived with her make-up case and didn't open it or leave it lying around. She went straight from Wardrobe to Clarion's dressing room. And second, there had been that delay of at least twenty minutes before Clarion reacted.

He tapped the chair arm and stood up. He was no Sherlock Holmes. He needed a second opinion.

He put his head round the door. 'Is Ingeborg still about?'

The only response came from Sergeant Dawkins, still at his desk in the hideous check suit.

'Will anyone do? I'm ready for any assignment.'

'You're not, dressed like that,' Diamond told him. 'Do you know where Inge is?'

'She may have gone to powder her nose.'

Powder her nose? Which century was this stuffed shirt living in? At that moment Ingeborg came through the door.

'In here,' Diamond said.

Ingeborg followed Diamond into his office.

'If I have to put up with that pillock much longer, I'm taking early retirement,' he told her.

'He's not too bad if you make allowance.'

'Believe me, I've made all I can manage. I want to tap your brain. I asked you to collect the dead butterfly the other night to avoid hysteria. You know, the butterfly curse and all that garbage. The obvious explanation is that the thing flew in from outside. But there is another possibility, of course: somebody put it there.'

'What for, guv?'

'To distract us. When a dead butterfly is found, so the legend goes, something bad is about to happen.'

'Well, it had already. Clarion was in hospital.'

'This is what I'm getting at. This wasn't about Clarion. I don't think the butterfly was in the dressing room on Monday night. People crowded in there to see if they could help. One of them would have spotted it.'

'You're saying it was put there later?'

'Anyone could have gone in there on late Monday night or Tuesday morning. At the time I saw the butterfly, we were assuming Denise was alive.'

She took a sharp breath. 'The butterfly was supposed to be an omen predicting her death?'

He nodded.

She was staring at him. 'So everyone is meant to think the butterfly curse has struck again—that she was doomed to kill herself.'

'When in fact she didn't,' he said. 'The person who left the butterfly murdered her.'

'That's a whopping assumption. It opens up all kinds of questions.'

'Okay. Let's hear them.'

'Why would anyone want to kill Denise? From all I hear, she was difficult to dislike. And how would they do it? They'd have to persuade her to climb I don't know how many sections of a vertical ladder and jump off.' Ingeborg paused, thinking, and then said, 'Even so, there may be *something* in it.'

Diamond watched her face.

'If Denise was murdered, it would suit her killer to have everyone assuming she did it because of guilt over Clarion. Case closed. How convenient for this hypothetical killer of yours.'

'You're sounding like Fred Dawkins.'

'It's catching.'

'It's a peculiar thing,' he said, 'Dawkins talks a lot of rubbish but just now he made a remark that gave me an idea. He said you may have gone to powder your nose, and I had a mental picture of you in front of a mirror with an old-fashioned powder puff.'

'And did that inspire you?'

'I was trying to think of a way round one of the main puzzles in this case. How come Clarion wasn't in pain until she got on stage? But I think I know what happened, thanks to Fred Dawkins. Before the actors go on, isn't someone there to touch up the make-up to stop them shining under the lights?'

Ingeborg stared at him. 'I saw it last night when Keith and I were backstage. A girl was there with a make-up brush.'

'That's when Clarion got it.' One mystery solved. 'Got anything planned for tonight? Because I'd like to see this young woman at work and I need—'

'A sidekick?'

'A guardian angel.' And he meant it. A visit to the theatre was a test of nerve. Talk about stage fright. He had his own form of it.

AFTER INGEBORG had left, and Diamond had fortified himself with a coffee, he phoned his sister in Liverpool. He didn't spend long over the small talk.

'You remember how I hated being taken to the theatre as a child?'

'Do I just?' Jean said. 'It ruined a birthday treat for me, as Mum never stopped reminding us. You got over it eventually, I hope?'

'Actually, no. Just now I'm on a case involving theatre people, and the same old problem is getting to me.'

'But you're a tough old cop. You see all sorts of horrible things.'

'This is different. I get the shakes each time I enter the theatre. I've got to get over it. If I knew the cause, I could deal with it.'

'I don't think Mum and Dad ever worked out why you were like that,' Jean said. 'In those days nobody bothered with child psychology.'

'I was hoping you might throw some light.'

'One thing I can tell you is that you weren't born like it. When you were a little kid you really enjoyed strutting around on a stage. You did some acting in that one-act play at Surbiton.'

Another memory came back. His art teacher at junior school had recruited him for a costume piece about Richard III. He'd played one of the boy princes murdered in the Tower. 'Fancy you remembering that.'

'It got up my nose, that's why. Mum and Dad had booked a week on a farm to coincide with my birthday, and we were supposed to be leaving home on the Friday, but thanks to your play we lost two days and finally did the journey on the Sunday.'

'And it rained. I remember that.'

'The whole holiday was a washout. We didn't even get much sleep through that cow making pathetic sounds all night because the farmer had separated it from its calf.'

'That's coming back to me now.'

'And to cap it all, on the day of my birthday they took us to the theatre at Llandudno and that was when you came over all peculiar and absolutely refused to stay in there. The show hadn't even started. We had to leave.'

'I can only think something upsetting must have happened in the play the weekend before, but I can't work out what. There were two of us. I wish I could recall the other boy's name. What age would I have been at the time?'

'It was my eleventh birthday, so you were eight,' Jean said. 'I must admit it still irks me. Llandudno wasn't the only place it happened.'

'I know,' he said. '*Julius Caesar* at the Old Vic when I was fifteen. I was in real trouble for ducking out of that.'

'And some other shows we might have gone to as a family.'

'We did get to one Christmas show.'

'*Treasure Island* at the Mermaid Theatre,' Jean said at once. 'We all wondered if you'd make a dash for the exit, but you were fine.'

'I enjoyed it.'

'You see? It's all in the mind.'

He didn't need telling. 'You've been helpful.'

'Ring me if you ever get to the bottom of this,' she said. 'I'm rather curious.'

Rather curious? It's not a crossword clue, he thought.

4

The call to Jean had stirred some memories, but it made no difference to the mounting tension as he walked from his car to the theatre that evening. The only consolation was that he and Ingeborg were going backstage and not into the auditorium.

The security man, Charlie Binns, gave Ingeborg's warrant card a longer look than Diamond's, and passed no comment. The eyes registered much, however, not least that he wouldn't, after all, be gracing the *Independent*'s colour section in the foreseeable future.

Inge went first, moving confidently across the area behind the scenery. On the prompt side, they stood in the shadows. Above them, in a precarious cubbyhole reached only by ladder, the deputy stage manager was directing operations from a console. They heard him call the five minutes. Preston Barnes appeared from behind them and walked straight on stage, his eyes expressionless, as if all his thoughts were turned inwards.

'He has to be there when the curtain goes up,' Ingeborg told Diamond, in a low voice. Barnes had seated himself at the table. A young woman moved in to dust his face with a make-up brush. 'Belinda,' Inge said.

'We must question her,' Diamond whispered.

'Shortly.' Inge steered him round the back of the set to the opposite side. A large woman in a black dress wanted to pass.

'Fräulein Schneider,' Ingeborg muttered after they'd stepped aside.

The make-up girl came off the stage and checked Schneider with a mere two flicks of the brush. Diamond noticed that the powder came in a black, cylindrical box.

'And curtain up,' a low voice said through the tannoy.

The curtains parted and the stage came alight. Preston Barnes as Christopher Isherwood was in the spotlight at the desk, writing.

Diamond had been watching the young make-up artist. He didn't want her to vanish. Helpfully, two more actors, a man and a woman, were ready to go on. She was attending to one of them with more than the token flicks of the brush.

'Gisella,' Ingeborg murmured. 'Overnight star.'

His first sight of the understudy, the actress with a clear motive for ousting Clarion.

Barnes spoke his first lines, reading back the words his character was supposed to have written, about Nazis rioting in the streets of Berlin. He moved seamlessly into the 'I am a camera' line and was only interrupted by Fräulein Schneider's knocking on the double doors.

'Come in, Fräulein,' he said, and the big woman entered.

Diamond continued to watch Gisella. She was in a black silk dress with a small cape and patent leather high heels. He had to remind himself that he'd come to see the girl with the make-up brush but a problem was emerging. If each of the actors was given the last-minute touch-up from the same powder box, there was an obvious flaw in his theory.

From the wings, the flurry of action on the brilliantly lit stage was compelling. When he looked away, the make-up girl had gone.

'Where'd she go?' he asked Ingeborg.

'I'm not sure. Up the stairs, I think.'

'You go up. I'll try round the back.'

He thought he spotted the pale gleam of the young woman's face on the far side, turning right. A shout might have halted her. It might also have halted the play. He dodged past some waiting stagehands and away from the wings. No one was in the narrow passageway ahead.

A man wired up with a headset and mike appeared. Diamond asked if Belinda had come this way.

'Why don't you ask in Wardrobe?' The headset man pointed the way.

He recognised the door and opened it. Kate was at the far end, grappling with what he took to be one of her tailor's dummies until he spotted that her dress was pulled up to her waist and the dummy was the back view of Hedley Shearman, without trousers, humping her against a wall as if there was no tomorrow.

With his police training, Diamond first thought rape was being committed. Just in time, he registered that Kate was shouting, 'Yes!' with every thrust. He left them to it, too involved to have noticed him, and took the steps up to stage level. The phone in his pocket vibrated and Ingeborg's voice told him, 'First floor, dressing room 10.'

He found her standing beside the make-up girl, who looked about sixteen. She was still holding the brush and box.

'What's in the box?' he asked.

'Talc.'

'Hand it across.'

Tentatively he touched the powder with his little finger. There was no reaction. 'Where did you get this, Belinda?'

'The wardrobe department. It's a fresh box, opened this afternoon.'

'So you know why I'm asking?'

'Clarion Calhoun?' Alarm showed in her eyes. 'I had nothing to do with it.'

'Is it your job to touch up the actors' make-up before they go on?'

'One of my jobs. I help out in the box office and take phone calls.'

'And were you checking the actors' faces on Monday evening?'

'Not all of them. Clarion's dresser looked after her.'

'Denise was putting powder on Clarion's face while she was waiting in the wings?' This was dynamite if it was true.

'Yes.'

'Was she using the same stuff as you?'

She shook her head. 'She brought her own.'

This young girl came across as a convincing witness. More and more, suspicion was returning to Denise as the cause of Clarion's scarring. His hypothesis that Denise was innocent and also a murder victim was unravelling by the second.

'You'd better get back to your duties,' he said, handing back her talc. She took off fast.

'A useful witness,' he told Ingeborg. 'It's pretty obvious Denise was brushing caustic soda on Clarion's face while she was waiting to go on. If we can find the box she was using, we'll get the contents analysed.'

He passed a hand thoughtfully over his head and then told Ingeborg about the scene of passion he'd stumbled into.

'What an old goat,' Ingeborg said. 'I thought he fancied Gisella.'

'He fancies anyone willing to have him.'

AN ALERT POLICEMAN spotted Denise's Vauxhall Corsa when the huge Charlotte Street car park was just about empty. It was dark when Diamond arrived. Keith Halliwell was there with a torch, as was the young constable.

'Have you looked inside?' Diamond said.

Halliwell shone his torch over the interior. 'Nothing to see.'

'Let's have the boot open. Got the tools?'

Halliwell unfurled a cloth containing a set that had belonged to a housebreaker. He selected a jemmy.

Diamond told the constable they could manage without him now. 'Top result,' he added as an afterthought. 'What's your name?'

'Pidgeon, sir. PC George Pidgeon.'

Halliwell, meanwhile, was bending metal. The boot-lid sprang open to reveal a large, soft bag and a leather case.

'Huh,' Diamond said. 'This means she had no intention of reporting for work when she returned to the theatre. She'd have taken this lot with her.'

'She'd made up her mind to kill herself already?'

'Looks that way.'

Diamond was in the act of reaching for the make-up case when Halliwell said, 'You ought to be wearing gloves.'

'Raw caustic soda? You're right.'

'I was thinking about handling the evidence.'

Better protected, Diamond reached for the leather case and shone the torch over a neat arrangement of brushes, combs, lipsticks and eye-liners. Lower down were jars and tins, a roll of cotton-wool pads and a black, cylindrical box that he lifted out. 'Like the one Belinda was using.'

He handed Halliwell the torch and opened the box. A small amount of white powder lay inside. He moistened his gloved forefinger with spit and dipped it in the powder. 'It's supposed to form a viscous slime that burns through skin.' He rubbed thumb and finger together. 'Doesn't feel slimy.'

'We'd better get it tested properly,' Halliwell said.

'Can you get some of this to an analyst first thing tomorrow and stay with him till it's done?'

'Sorry, guv. I'm down for the post-mortem.'

A fixture not to be altered. 'So you are. Give it to Paul Gilbert.'

The interior of the car contained nothing of genuine interest.

'Where would she have left her handbag, I wonder?' Diamond said. 'I reckon it contains the parking ticket, her credit cards and her mobile phone, any of which could settle this.'

ON THURSDAY MORNING Diamond woke late. For much of the night he'd been unable to sleep, his brain in overdrive, trying to remember things from his childhood. The phone call to his sister had raised more questions than it had answered. The play about Richard III hadn't been a school play. The art teacher had belonged to some amateur dramatic society and they'd needed two boys. He'd been recruited along with another kid from his class whose name was somewhere in his brain. It began with G, he thought. Not Glass, but something roughly like it. Gladstone, Glaister, Glastonbury.

And then it came to him: Glazebrook. Mike Glazebrook.

At three in the morning, he was downstairs going through phone directories looking for Glazebrooks. Ridiculous. How would you trace a schoolboy more than forty years later? He'd heard of the Friends Reunited website and never looked at it until this night at 4.15 a.m. No joy. No Glazebrook. His contempt for websites was confirmed.

Before setting off for work he was phoning schools in the Kingston area. The second he tried came up trumps. 'We have a Mr M.G. Glazebrook on our board of governors,' the secretary said. 'I believe he attended the school as a child.'

'The M—does that stand for Michael?'

'I believe it does.'

'And does he live near the school?'

'I'm not at liberty to tell you where he lives.'

'If you're worried about data protection, I'm a police officer and a one-time friend of Mike's. He's not in any trouble, by the way.' He thought for a moment. 'What age would your gentleman be?'

'Fiftyish, I would say.'

'He was ten when I saw him last. Listen, would you do me a great favour and tell him his school friend Peter Diamond would like to hear from him today if possible? I'm at Bath Central police station.'

FIVE MINUTES AFTER he got in, Fred Dawkins walked in wearing a black leather jacket, white T-shirt and jeans.

'Strike a light!'

'Cool!' Ingeborg said.

Diamond couldn't bring himself to agree. 'How do you feel?' he asked Dawkins.

'Like the proverbial pox doctor's clerk,' the fashion victim answered. 'However, if it gets me out on active duties, I shall be more than compensated.'

'I'm promising nothing, Fred,' Diamond said. 'We'll see how the day develops. Is John Leaman in?'

'At the theatre with two from uniform searching for the handbag,' Ingeborg said.

'Okay,' Diamond said. 'The evidence is stacking up that Denise used the caustic soda on Clarion and killed herself when she realised the full extent of her action. Any ideas why?'

'Angry people lose all sense of proportion,' Ingeborg said. 'She may have been at her wits' end, wanting to stop Clarion.'

'But why?'

'God knows what went on between them. Denise had worked there for six years. She was under instructions to nursemaid Clarion. She may have felt her effort wasn't appreciated. Clarion is used to people idolising her.'

'A lot of actors are prima donnas,' Dawkins said. 'A dresser would be able to cope with that. Allow me to propose another motive. By sabotaging Clarion, Denise was saving her from a mauling from the critics.'

'Saving the theatre, too,' Diamond said. 'That's not bad, Fred.'

Ingeborg shook her head. 'No woman behaves like that, damaging someone's face as a good turn.'

'We're assuming she didn't expect the stuff to leave permanent scars,' Diamond said. 'When it happened, and she realised the theatre could be sued, she was devastated.'

'Driven beyond all,' Dawkins added in a sepulchral tone.

Ingeborg shook her head. 'You guys need to get out more.'

THE CALL FROM Mike Glazebrook came soon after eleven. It didn't take long for the two to convince each other that they were the former princes in the Tower.

'What's your line of work?' Diamond said.

'I look at old buildings and assess their safety. I'm often in Bath, as it happens. We have the contract for the abbey. If you'd care to meet, I could see you this afternoon, say in front of the abbey about three? It's on my way home.'

'How will I recognise you after all this time?'

'Look for the short, fat guy in a pork-pie hat.'

DI JOHN LEAMAN insisted on being admitted to every room in the entire theatre but he failed to find the missing handbag. Hedley Shearman offered to mention the missing bag at a meeting he'd called at noon to reassure everyone it was business as usual. 'Your poking around this morning had the opposite effect,' he told Leaman. 'People are behaving as if a crime has taken place.'

Leaman phoned to tell Diamond about the meeting but even before he'd arrived, it had been cancelled.

'What happened?' he asked.

'All I know is that the theatre director has been given a bloody nose,' Leaman said.

'Literally?'

'It's a right mess, I was told. He had it coming to him. Bumptious little sod. He's in the wardrobe department being patched up. The woman in charge won't let anyone near him.'

'We'll see about that.'

Diamond tried the door of Wardrobe and found it locked.

'Piss off, will you?' Kate in Wardrobe's voice yelled from within.

'It's the police. Superintendent Diamond. Open up, please.'

Diamond was presented with the bizarre spectacle of Shearman lying face upwards on an ironing board, holding a bloody tissue to his nose.

'It won't stop bleeding,' Kate said. 'I'm worried that it's broken.'

'Has he tried pinching it? It has to form a clot. Try gentle pressure.'

Shearman did so, and groaned.

'Who did it?' Diamond asked Kate.

'Preston. You'd think he'd learn to control himself. He was with the Royal Shakespeare.'

'What was this about?'

'About Preston's dressing room being searched,' Kate said.

'I'll hear it from Mr Shearman,' Diamond said and got closer.

Shearman responded on a low, nasal note. 'Preston said some of his personal things had been moved. He blamed me. He said I should have stood up to the police.'

'Where did this fight take place?'

'It wasn't a fight,' Kate broke in. 'It was a brutal, unprovoked assault.'

'In the auditorium,' Shearman said.

'In front of witnesses,' Kate said. 'Hedley was getting ready for a meeting.'

'If you don't button it, ma'am,' Diamond said, 'I'll ask you to wait outside. Now, Mr Shearman, what's behind this with Preston?'

'He was secretive from the first day of rehearsals, insisting he was given time to psych himself up. I'm not sure what he does, but he's there in the dressing room at least an hour and a half before curtain up and he turns off his phone and refuses to answer the door.'

'Was he okay about acting with Clarion?'

'That was never an issue. This is about Preston. He came with a reputation for awkwardness.'

If the man had been acting secretively, Diamond thought, he might be a suspect. 'I'd better speak to him.'

'Don't,' Shearman said, horrified. 'It will only make matters worse, and we have four more performances to go. As far as I'm concerned, the episode is closed.' He removed the tissue. 'Look, it's stopped bleeding.'

'Sorry, but my show has to go on as well as yours.'

Another locked door—to Preston Barnes's dressing room—frustrated Diamond, but not for long. He knew the layout. He went through the side door in Beauford Square. The principal dressing rooms, at ground level, looked out on to a quiet lawn. He picked the right window. As he'd anticipated, the casement was open at the top for ventilation. He slid the lower window up and climbed in. Leaman followed.

Barnes was on a chaise longue wearing only a pair of jockey shorts. He sprang up. 'What the—?' He was across the room and grabbing a bathrobe before they spoke a word. He wrapped it around himself as if playing the storm scene from *King Lear*.

Diamond made a point of introducing Leaman and himself, adding, 'We need to speak.'

'You've no right breaking in here.'

'Nothing is broken. What's your problem, Preston?'

Actually, Diamond had noticed one problem in the short interval before Barnes had wrapped himself up.

'I like to prepare before I go on.'

'What form does the preparing take?'

'I need to focus my energy, my emotions. Visualise the role. Become the character. I'm a method actor. In simple terms, I take a mental journey to Berlin in the 1930s and become Christopher Isherwood.'

'With all this preparation, you guard your privacy, obviously.'

'That's no crime,' Barnes said.

'It is, if it leads to an assault.'

'But—'

'As it happens, Mr Shearman wants to forget the incident.' Diamond glanced about him. 'Denise the dresser's handbag is missing. Did you know Denise?'

'We met. She was Clarion's dresser, not mine.'

'Were you worried about the play? I'm told Clarion wasn't much good in rehearsal.'

'She was crap. But I've been in the business long enough to know it *can* be all right on the night.'

'But it wasn't. What an experience you must have had.' Deliberately, Diamond was playing to Barnes's ego.

'It wasn't something I want to repeat,' Barnes said. 'One minute she seemed to have forgotten her lines and the next she was screaming in pain. I defy any actor to cope with that.'

'After the curtain came down, what did you do?'

'I waited to see what would happen next. They gave Gisella the part, as you know. She saved the night from total disaster. And she gets better with each performance.'

'Your own performance is worth seeing, I'm told.'

'Thanks.' Flattered, the actor was off-guard.

'What do you inject before the show?' Diamond asked in a matter-of-fact tone.

'What?' Barnes stared at Diamond.

'I noticed the needle marks.'

'I'm diabetic.'

'I don't think so. And I don't believe the horseshit you told us a moment ago about locking yourself in to visualise the role. You come here early to jack up.'

'You can't prove a damn thing.'

'I'm not investigating your habit. I know why you flew into such a rage over the search. You thought we'd find your syringes. And why you were so quick to cover your arms when we came in just now.'

Barnes had turned ashen. 'You people have no idea of the stress actors are under, night after night.'

'Heroin?'

'Methadone, on prescription.' His manner had switched from aggression to supplication. 'I'm fighting the addiction. I can give you my doctor's name if you keep this to yourself. I don't want the management finding out. Please.'

'Does anyone else in this theatre know?'

'Absolutely not. It would destroy my career.'

'We can count on your co-operation, then?'

In a voice otherwise purged of defiance, Barnes managed to say, 'Bastards.'

Diamond was about to respond when his mobile rang.

'She definitely broke her neck,' Keith Halliwell reported on his phone from the mortuary.

'I saw that for myself,' Diamond said, 'but was that the cause of death? She could have been dead already.'

This didn't persuade Halliwell. 'What—and somebody pushed her off the loading bridge? How would he have got her up there?'

Diamond's confidence was shrinking. His theory did sound far-fetched.

Halliwell continued, 'I was impressed by Dr Sealy. He said because of the position she was found in, she must have fallen backwards. Therefore she climbed over the rail and held on to it with both hands before letting go. Suicides often do it that way, not wanting to look down. That's why she didn't end up on the floor. She didn't see the battens that broke her fall.'

'No other marks or injuries?'

'None that he noticed. He said he'd wait for the lab test on the samples he'd sent. There was some suspicion she'd taken alcohol shortly before she died. Even I could smell it.'

'Dutch courage, I expect. What did he say about the time of death?'

'Probably between eight and twenty-four hours before she was found.'

'No use to us. But thanks, Keith.'

The theory he'd flirted with had withered away. Dr Sealy would surely have picked up some indications of murder. The case was moving to a conclusion. All it wanted was confirmation that Denise took responsibility for the Clarion incident. If her powder box contained traces of caustic soda, suicide would be hard to deny.

'Do I need a drink,' he said to Leaman.

THEY WERE GREETED in the Garrick's Head by the dramaturge, Titus O'Driscoll. 'My cup overfloweth. Well, it would have, if he hadn't arrived with someone else.'

Diamond raised a grin. 'John Leaman works with me. How are you, Titus? Fully recovered, I hope. Titus fainted and I caught him before he fell,' Diamond explained to Leaman.

'And the reason I fainted is one of the great, unsolved mysteries,' Titus said.

'You passed out,' Diamond said, 'because you saw a dead butterfly in Clarion's dressing room.'

For a moment Titus was speechless. 'Oh, my word! The curse strikes again.'

'But Clarion didn't die.'

'Denise did, the day we discovered it. Why didn't you tell me?'

'I know what theatre people are like. It could have caused a panic.'

'Really.' Titus rolled his eyes. 'As if we're the sort of people who panic.'

'It's summer,' Diamond said. 'Butterflies get trapped all the time. I dare say there are others lying around the theatre.' He turned to Leaman. 'Did you notice any on your search?'

Leaman shook his head. 'I wasn't looking for butterflies.' A simple statement and a reminder of how single-minded he was.

It occurred to Diamond that Leaman could have missed other items of importance. Tunnel vision, they called it in CID.

'Titus,' he said. 'Our tour backstage was cut short. Would you mind showing me the rest?'

'What about your colleague?'

'He'll wait here.'

'If you insist, then.' Titus drained his glass.

Inside the theatre, Diamond's nerve came under immediate test. The auditorium was visible through several entrances. He looked away. 'Shall we start with that haunted dressing room you mentioned?'

'We can't. Gisella is using it,' Titus said.

'She'll invite us in, won't she?'

They had reached the pass door to backstage. Titus quickly worked the digital lock.

'Is there one combination for all the doors?' Diamond asked.

'No, they're different. Newcomers are given a plastic card with the numbers. I long ago committed them to memory.' He pushed the door open and they went through. In the passageway close to the stage, he pointed ahead. 'Dressing room 8.'

'Let's see if she's in.' Diamond knocked on the door.

'It's open,' a voice came from inside.

He raised a thumb at Titus and turned the handle.

'Oh,' Gisella said from her chair in front of a theatrical mirror, fringed with light bulbs. 'I thought you were the boy bringing more flowers.' All they could see of her was the permed 1930s haircut above a slender, white neck. 'If you're press,' she said, 'it isn't convenient now.'

'Come on, Gisella,' Titus said. 'You know me. And this is my friend, Peter.'

She swivelled in her chair to look at Diamond. 'Are you an actor?'

Diamond realised she thought he was being shown the room because he'd be using it when the next production got under way.

'I'm a policeman,' he said. 'Do you mind if I look round the room?'

Gisella had the wit to press a hand to her brow. 'The police! I am undone.'

'Don't be like that,' Titus said. 'He's a nice policeman.'

She said in a more serious voice, 'If you think I had anything to do with Clarion's accident, you're mistaken. Just because I was understudying doesn't mean I wished her any harm.'

'Do you see the handbag?' Titus said.

'Where?' Diamond said, all attention.

'Behind you on the wall.'

He swung round, and was disappointed. Framed in a glass case were a bag and a pair of gloves.

'They belonged to one of the most exquisite beauties ever to grace the stage,' Titus said. 'Vivien Leigh. The room is named in her honour. But I don't think there's any suggestion that she is the visitor here.'

The room's spectral possibilities didn't impress Diamond at all. He was more interested in Gisella. 'Was Clarion a friend?'

'In the sense that we're all in the same company,' she said. 'We got along well. Most people here are friendly, some over-friendly.'

'A certain theatre director?' Titus said.

She gave a shrug that seemed to answer the question.

'He was with you when you spotted Denise's body,' Diamond said, wanting to hear her account.

'He was cosying up to me on the strength of some nice reviews I'd got. He offered to show me that butterfly in the wings and I could feel him pressing against me as I looked up. I watched him trying to hit on Clarion last week. She brushed him off like some ugly little insect. It creased me up.'

'Did you know Clarion before you were picked for this play?'

'I knew of her. Doesn't everyone? But we'd never met.'

'You must have met her in rehearsals.'

'Sure. She shared all the director's notes with me and showed me the moves, as you do with an understudy. And we practised lines together.'

'Was she nervous?'

'A bit. Well, a lot, actually, even though she wouldn't admit it. It's years since she'd done any acting.'

'You're the beneficiary of all this,' Diamond said. 'You stepped up and got rave reviews.'

'In this job, sweetie, you take whatever chance comes your way,' she said with a defiant stare.

There was a simmering resolve to this young woman. Four days had turned her from a bit-part actor into a leading lady—with attitude.

'Why don't you move to the number 1 dressing room? It's better than this.'

'It was offered, but I still think of that as hers. This is perfectly serviceable.'

The reason didn't ring true to Diamond. Here was a deeply ambitious actress turning down the star dressing room. Was there something about this less salubrious room she was reluctant to leave behind?

He crossed the room to inspect the hand basin. 'Does this sink ever get blocked?'

'Not while I've been here.'

He opened the cupboard underneath. No caustic soda. Not so much as a dead butterfly. 'We'll leave you in peace, then.'

In the corridor outside, Diamond said to Titus, 'Something is puzzling me. This is dressing room 8, while numbers 1, 2 and 3 are on the prompt side. What happened to dressing rooms 4, 5, 6 and 7?'

'Upstairs on the prompt side. And 10 and 11 are above us.'

'Who uses them?'

'In a small-cast play like *I Am a Camera*, scarcely anyone. There's no need.'

'I haven't been upstairs.'

They climbed the narrow staircase to dressing room 10, distinctly less glitzy than the ground-floor rooms. Diamond opened some cupboards and then asked if there were more rooms on this floor.

Titus shook his head. 'No—number 11 is up another flight of stairs.'

'Take me to it.'

Dressing room 11, when they got up there, turned out to be a barn of a place, with nine mirrors and dressing tables, bare of anything else except chairs and a clothes rail.

Diamond pointed across the passage. 'What's that room? Is it the cleaners' store cupboard?'

'I haven't the faintest idea.'

Diamond pushed the door open and got a shock. He was looking straight across the dark chasm that was the fly tower. This was the loading bridge, the same catwalk that he'd reached previously by climbing vertically hand over fist from floor level.

'Should have thought of this,' he complained more to himself than Titus. 'The scene shifters need to get access.' He leaned over the metal railing and reminded himself what a long way down the floor was. Already his mind was working on new scenarios. A major objection to his murder theory had been the difficulty of getting the body up to this level without assistance. Now he knew how it might have been done.

Equally, Denise could have used the back stairs herself to carry out her suicide plan.

They returned to dressing room 11. Diamond stood in the centre. 'Likely the cleaners wouldn't come in here when the room isn't in use.' He moved closer to the line of tables and crouched like a bowls referee judging a closely contested end.

'What are you doing?'

'Looking at the table tops. I was right. The place hasn't seen a duster for some time.'

Diamond completed his examination. Then he stood back. 'What we have here are nine dusty tables, and one over there'—he pointed to the one furthest from the door—'has a distinct curved shape in the dust at the front edge. You've heard of fingerprints? That looks to me like a bum print.'

5

'Pure talc and nothing else.'

'That's a pain. I thought we were getting somewhere.'

Diamond, Halliwell and Leaman had returned to find DC Paul Gilbert waiting in the CID room to report on the contents of Denise's box of powder. It wasn't the result anyone wanted to hear.

'If Denise's talc was harmless,' Diamond said, 'how did Clarion come into contact with the caustic soda? If Denise didn't do it, who did?'

From across the room, Ingeborg said, 'We've been over this, guv.'

'Yes, but since we spoke I've met some of these characters.'

'The understudy?' Ingeborg said without enthusiasm.

'Only four days into the run and already behaving like the prima donna. I also met the male lead, Preston Barnes, after he punched the theatre director on the nose for allowing John Leaman to search his room. Turns out Barnes had things to hide. He's a junkie.'

'What's he on?'

'Methadone, he says. He needs a fix before each performance.'

'But is he also a suspect? Why would he want to hurt Clarion?'

'Maybe, like me, she saw the state of his arms and worked out what he's doing. He's fearful of anyone in the theatre finding out.'

'But where's the logic in damaging her face?'

'To be shot of her. She's out of it now.'

'I suppose.' Ingeborg didn't seem wholly convinced.

Undaunted, Diamond moved on. 'Another one in the mix is Hedley Shearman. He claims he was railroaded into having Clarion in the cast.'

'Who railroaded him?'

'Francis Melmot, chairman of the board of trustees. Melmot is a Clarion fan. He came up with the idea of using her in a play and invited her to stay at Melmot Hall.'

'Get away,' Halliwell said, with relish. 'Did she go?'

'She did, for a couple of days, he said.'

'Couple of nights.' Halliwell got a laugh.

'I wouldn't count on that,' Diamond said. 'There's a domineering mother living there. Quite the duchess. I wouldn't care to cross her.'

'Then she wouldn't be troubled by bourgeois values,' Ingeborg said. 'Upper-crust mothers positively encourage their sons to get laid.'

'Is Melmot seriously in the frame?' Halliwell asked. 'What's his motive?'

'When it became obvious in rehearsal that Clarion was going to screw up. His own reputation was on the line. He had to find a way of stopping her.'

'Might I venture an opinion?' a voice said from close to Diamond. 'Regarding the fun and games.'

'Fred, if there's something you want to say, out with it.'

'There are ladies present.'

'Do you mean sex?' Ingeborg said.

'In a word, yes.'

'Say it, then.'

Dawkins tugged his leather jacket more tightly across his front. 'What if those nights in Melmot Hall didn't turn out as Mr Melmot hoped? If the sex was unsatisfactory, he may have panicked that Clarion would tell everyone and he'd be a laughing stock.'

'Good point,' Diamond said.

Leaman said, 'What about the gay guy? Titus. He knows his way around the theatre. He had the opportunity if he can come and go without anyone asking what he's up to.'

'Agreed, but I can't see why he'd want to damage Clarion's face.'

Ingeborg thought it was worth pursuing. 'As someone who cares about the theatre, he could have decided to stop her.'

'But not like that,' Diamond said. 'Don't get me wrong, but I have some respect for Titus.'

Dawkins cleared his throat. 'I've had a thought, guv. The box of talcum powder in Denise's bag was harmless. But what if there was a second box?'

Diamond frowned. 'There wasn't, not in her bag.'

'A box she used for last-minute powdering, one she kept in the wings? It could still be there.'

'Possible, I suppose,' Diamond said. 'Worth checking. Inge, you can take this on? And take Fred with you.'

The man was ecstatic. 'You're sending *me*?'

'Yes, but leave the talking to Ingeborg. Any problem with that, Inge?'

She said with an effort, 'No, guv.'

After they'd left, Halliwell said, 'He's keen.'

'Keen to get out of here, anyway,' Diamond said. 'Well, people. How has it been? Busy this morning?'

One of the civilian staff spoke up. 'A number of phone calls. Sergeant Dawkins handled them and emailed you about them. There was one message from the assistant chief constable.'

'Georgina? He didn't say.'

It was a good thing Dawkins had left the building.

GEORGINA WAS in a benign mood when Diamond entered her eyrie on the top floor and muttered an apology about not responding sooner.

'It isn't urgent, as I thought I made clear to Horatio.'

He had to dig deep to recall who Horatio was. How was it that Dawkins was on first-name terms with the assistant chief constable?

Georgina was thinking of other things. 'All the trouble at the theatre—did you get to the bottom of it?'

'Not yet, ma'am,' he said. 'It's more complex than I first thought.'

'The suicide?'

'I'm not a hundred per cent sure it was a suicide. She left no note.'

'I expect she was too distressed.'

'And we haven't proved a definite connection with the caustic soda incident. Denise Pearsall doesn't seem to have had any grudge against Clarion.'

'Are you suggesting she died by accident?'

'She may have been pushed. I had another look backstage. I'd assumed she climbed a ladder to get up to the loading bridge. Today I learned there's a way onto it from the second floor.'

'Is that significant?'

'It is if someone wanted to murder her.'

'*Murder?* Peter, are you serious?'

'There's a dressing room up there, not in use in the present play. I found clear evidence somebody was in there recently. It would make a useful base for anyone intending to ambush her.'

Georgina let him know she would need a lot more convincing. 'What would be the point of killing Denise? She was a nice woman, from all I heard, respected by people in the theatre. And she'd struggle with an attacker, surely. There would be marks on her body that would be obvious in the post-mortem. Was anything mentioned by the pathologist?'

'No, but there was alcohol in her system.'

'She may have taken a drink to get her courage up.'

'Or someone gave her a cocktail of drink and drugs.'

'Drugs were present as well?'

He cleared his throat. 'We won't know until the blood is tested.'

'And if, as I suspect, the results are negative?'

'I'll look at the possibility of more than one killer being involved.'

Georgina clicked her tongue. 'This is in danger of becoming an obsession, Peter.'

'If you remember, ma'am, you got me started on this.'

'Only because I could see the theatre being closed down. That seems less likely now, even if Clarion sues. The legal process would be slow to start.'

'Do I sense that you'd like to call off the hounds?'

She looked away. 'No, you can finish the job. I'm more confident than I was.' She turned to face him, eyes shining brightly. 'I was chosen last night for *Sweeney Todd*.'

'Nice work, ma'am. What part are you playing?'

'Not one of the principals. I have the voice but as a newcomer, I can't expect a major role this year. I'll be strengthening the company.'

In the chorus, in other words.

'Horatio doesn't do any singing,' Georgina added, 'but we couldn't stage a production like *Sweeney* without him.'

'Sergeant Dawkins is in the BLOGs?'

'Hasn't he told you? He's our movement director. All the action sequences are co-ordinated by him. Dances, fights, stunts, swordplay. He's a trained dancer, you know.'

'He told me that much. How long has he been doing this?'

'Before I joined.'

Now it was revealed why Fred Dawkins had been plucked from the uniformed ranks. He'd got to know Georgina through the BLOGs.

'I know exactly what's going through your head,' Georgina said, 'and I have to tell you I moved him into CID on merit. Don't mistake his speech for woolly thinking. You need to be sharp to choreograph an entire show like *Sweeney*. If anyone can get results for you, Horatio will.'

THEY WENT ABOUT the search systematically, each working at a different side of the stage, lifting props, discarded cloths and coils of cable.

'Putting myself in Denise's place,' Ingeborg called out across the stage after twenty minutes, 'if I had some powder laced with caustic soda I wouldn't leave it lying around. But then,' she added, 'if someone else doctored the stuff, Denise wouldn't have known.'

'Don't you think the someone else would also have got rid of it?' Dawkins said.

'In that case we're wasting our time.' Deadpan, as if she didn't remember, she asked, 'Whose idea was this?'

DIAMOND HAD an in-built resistance to computers and didn't make a habit of checking his email. If his own staff had anything to report, he expected to be told. Still, the thought nagged at him that there could be information waiting for him. He stepped into his office to check.

There wasn't much. Clarion Calhoun was moving out of the burns unit to a private hotel in Clifton called the Cedar of Lebanon. And there was a note that the crime scene investigation team had started work in dressing room 11.

With two separate searches now under way, he could keep the appointment with his old school friend.

On this fine afternoon, he chose to walk to Abbey Churchyard, zigzagging between crocodiles of French schoolkids waiting to tour the Roman Baths. He found the short, fat guy in a pork-pie hat standing below the bottom rung of the famous ladder to heaven carved into the abbey front. The years had been kind to Mike Glazebrook; he could have passed for forty-five. Diamond shook his hand and suggested they had tea at one of the outdoor tables on the sunny side.

'You've put on some weight since I saw you last,' Glazebrook said. 'Is it fattening, this police work?'

'I was going to ask the same about structural engineering.'

The banter was a useful way to roll back 40 years. They decided to order a cream tea.

Straight to business, Diamond thought. 'My recollection is that we got to know each other through that play we were in as the boy princes.'

'*Richard III*.'

'Wasn't it called *Wicked Richard,* so as not to confuse it with the Shakespeare version?'

'Shakespeare?' Glazebrook laughed. 'Who did they think they were kidding? But you're right about the title. Didn't one of the actors write it?'

'Maybe the art teacher who recruited you and me. What was he called?'

'Mr White—Flakey, to us kids.'

'Of course.' This was promising. The man had a reliable memory. 'I can't think why he picked you and me.'

'Can't you?' Glazebrook said, with a suggestive smile.

'We must have looked the part. Princely.'

Glazebrook laughed again. 'No chance. We were two miserable little perishers. I used to have a photo of us in costume and we didn't look overjoyed in breeches and tights. My mother tore it up when she read about Flakey in the *News of the World*.'

Diamond tensed. 'Read what?'

'Didn't you hear? He was sent down for five years for "interfering with schoolchildren"—as they called it then—at a private school in Hampshire. Dirty old perv.'

Pulsing spread through Diamond's arms and chest. 'I heard nothing of this.'

'It must have been five or six years after we'd left the school when he was found out. I was put through the Inquisition by my parents, wanting to know if he'd got up to anything with me. He hadn't, but then I wouldn't have told them if he had. You try and forget stuff like that.'

'Right,' Diamond said, his thoughts in ferment.

'He didn't try it on with you, did he? You'd have told me at the time, wouldn't you?' Glazebrook gave Diamond a speculative look.

'Sure.' But he wasn't. He was trying to remember.

'You can bet he didn't serve five years,' Glazebrook was saying. 'He'd have been out on probation, looking for more little kids to abuse.'

'They wouldn't have allowed him to teach again,' Diamond said.

'With his art, he could easily get other work. At one stage, he was illustrating books.'

They talked for another ten minutes, exchanging memories, but Diamond's heart wasn't in it. He was reeling from the shock. After he'd settled the bill, they shook hands and went their separate ways.

He stood with the crowd watching unicyclists performing in front of the Pump Room, but he saw nothing. All his perceptions were directed inwards. Everything connected with that play took on a new and sinister significance. Yet he was finding it difficult to pinpoint any one incident. The brain has ways of blocking traumatic experiences, particularly from childhood. He understood that. The one certainty was that he couldn't enter a theatre without fear. He could still only guess at what had happened, but the guessing was now more informed and more unpleasant.

A shout from the crowd brought him out of this purgatory. Time was going on and he was required to function as a detective.

FRANCIS MELMOT was outside the theatre stage door. He hailed Diamond. 'What a pleasure this is, Inspector.'

'Inspector' was a demotion, but the matter wasn't worth pointing out.

Diamond said he hadn't expected an official welcome from the chairman of the board.

'I just looked in to share some wonderful news with our staff. I was advised an hour ago that Clarion has withdrawn her threat to sue.'

'What happened? An out-of-court settlement?'

'No, we're not paying a penny. It's unconditional.'

'When I saw the lady yesterday, her mind was made up.'

'Yesterday, she was still in shock,' Melmot said. 'She's had time to reflect since then. There's even better news. She will be making a substantial private donation to the theatre.'

'Did you talk her round, then?'

'I haven't spoken to her.'

Mystified, Diamond refused to believe him. 'You're on close terms. I thought a word in her ear may have worked this magic.'

Melmot blinked. 'I'm not sure what you mean by close terms.'

'She stayed with you in Melmot Hall.'

'As a house guest. She didn't sleep with me, Inspector, if that's what you're suggesting.'

'Thanks for putting me right,' Diamond said, and trailed a warning. 'I was going to ask the lady herself. Now there's no need, but I'll visit her just the same. I'd still like to know why she's changed her mind about suing.'

'I daresay her lawyers talked some sense into her. I understand she's left the hospital.'

'It doesn't mean her face will ever be the same again.'

'Believe me, Inspector, she has the heartfelt sympathy of everyone in the Theatre Royal. Of course the saddest thing of all is that the dresser did what she did. I've no doubt she killed herself because she feared for our future, as we all did. She was deeply committed to this wonderful old theatre.'

'Yes, I've heard that,' Diamond said.

'Will you draw a line under the investigation?' Melmot asked, trying to sound casual. 'I believe some of your people are backstage at this minute.'

'The enquiry into Denise Pearsall's death continues until we find out exactly what happened. I'll be giving evidence to a coroner. I need all the facts.'

Diamond moved on into the building.

Clarion's decision baffled him. Her career was in ruins but she had a strong chance of winning a lawsuit. If Melmot hadn't persuaded her to drop the case, who had?

The back stairs to dressing room 11 were testing for a man of his bulk. He paused at the top to draw breath. He could hear voices ahead. Pleasing to know that the crime scene people were at work; less pleasing when he saw who was in charge, an old antagonist called Duckett.

'What's the story so far?' Diamond asked.

'Stop right there, squire,' Duckett called across the room through his mask. He looked risible in the white zip-suit and bonnet that was de rigueur for crime scene investigators. 'Don't take another step. You'll contaminate the evidence.'

Diamond waited for Duckett to come to the doorway. 'It was me who called you in.'

'I guessed as much,' Duckett said with a superior tone. 'A large room filled with trace evidence from I don't know how many people is about the most complicated scene any investigator can have to examine. So, thanks for that.'

'If you can tell me who was here most recently, that would help.'

'Apart from two lumbering detectives in size ten shoes, you mean?'

One detective and one dramaturge, Diamond was tempted to point out, but it wasn't worth saying.

'All I'm able to say at this stage is that within the last few days two people were in here and one at least had long, reddish hair.'

Two people, one of them Denise. This had huge potential importance.

'They weren't here long, going by what we found, but they seem to have done some drinking. The marks in the dust look like the bases of wine glasses and a bottle.'

'You haven't found the bottle?'

'Taken away, apparently. As were the glasses, the cork and the wrapping. The owner of the red hair sat in that chair at the end while the other individual perched on top of the dressing table opposite.'

'Didn't they leave any other traces?'

'We'll examine everything and let you know in due course.'

He heard the 'in due course' with a sinking heart. 'Signs of violence?'

'None that we've discovered. All the indications are that the people came in, enjoyed a drink and left. It's not what I call a crime scene.'

'A woman fell to her death from the loading bridge across the passage,' Diamond reminded him.

'I know, and we'll examine that, too.'

'Is there anything you can tell me about the second person, the one who sat on the dressing table?'

'Average-sized buttocks.'

'Average? What's that?'

'Slimmer than yours.'

'Nothing else?'

'We have a mass of trace evidence to examine in the lab. I can see this taking two to three weeks.'

'*What?* It's only dust.'

Duckett was equally outraged. 'I don't know if you appreciate how much work is involved. Each specimen has to be put through a battery of tests from simple magnification to infrared spectrophotometry.'

Science never intimidated Diamond. 'Three weeks, though. It's not as if you have a corpse in here. Just get on with it. I've got other fish to fry.'

The news that two people had definitely been in there fitted his theory, but the absence of violence did not. He couldn't reconcile the wine-drinking with the death leap. Had Denise become suicidal after a couple of glasses with a friend? Who was the friend? No one had come forward to say they were the last to see her alive.

For now, he turned his thoughts to the search downstairs.

DIAMOND FOUND his people on the stage, Ingeborg in Isherwood's chair and Dawkins horizontal on the sofa.

Ingeborg got up guiltily. 'Didn't know you were in the building, guv.'

'I can see. Are you comfortable, Fred?'

'We completed the search, your worship,' Dawkins said, 'and I proposed a pause for rest and recuperation.'

'We looked everywhere, guv,' Ingeborg said. 'We only stopped a few minutes ago.'

Diamond sank into the high-backed chair beside the tiled stove. He, too, had earned a break. 'I saw the chairman of the trust, Francis Melmot, and he told me Clarion has withdrawn her threat to sue. What's more, she's making a donation to the theatre.'

'Praise the Lord,' Dawkins said. 'Our ship is saved.'

'You emailed me this morning to say you took a message on the phone about Clarion's movements,' Diamond said to him. 'Did she say anything about this?'

'The message was from Bristol police, who were guarding her. They informed me she was leaving the hospital for a hotel in Clifton.'

'Good thing I checked my in-box. In future, Fred, speak to me.'

Ingeborg said, 'What changed Clarion's mind, I wonder? Do you think the damage to her face is not as bad as it first appeared? She'd look silly suing if she made a full recovery before the case came to court.'

'Which would make a mockery of Denise's suicide,' Dawkins said.

'Speaking of which,' Diamond said, 'I've just been up to dressing room 11.' He told them about two people drinking wine there, one a redhead like Denise.

'Then it wasn't suicide,' Ingeborg said, 'if there were two people, and one ended up dead.'

'Suppose the other person said something that so upset her she went straight over to the gallery and took her own life?'

'Her lover,' Dawkins said from the sofa.

Ingeborg said, 'Now you're talking, Fred. I reckon she was dumped. Hedley Shearman seems to have been everyone's lover.'

'Don't get carried away,' Diamond said. 'There's no evidence Denise or any other woman liked Shearman enough to kill herself for him.'

Dawkins had another theory. 'Here's a more down-to-earth scenario. She was told her services were no longer required.'

'Her job, you mean? By Shearman?' Ingeborg said.

'Or the chairman of the board.'

'Melmot?' Ingeborg seized on the possibility. 'Yes, he's the sort who'd pour you a glass of wine and sack you at the same time.'

Diamond was less enthusiastic. 'Why would Melmot invite her up to an empty dressing room?'

Nobody had an answer.

Diamond looked at his watch. 'Let's get out of here. You finished the search, you said?'

'We looked everywhere,' Ingeborg said. 'Shake a leg, Fred.'

Dawkins heaved himself off the sofa and performed a theatrical bow.

Ingeborg said, 'Why don't you show us a few steps? Go on. The boss doesn't believe you can do it.'

'Difficult on a carpet.' But the showman in Sergeant Dawkins couldn't resist. He performed a few stylish steps, a double turn and a slick finish. No question, he was a good mover.

Diamond gave a grudging nod. 'Where did you learn?'

'My parents sent me to dance school. At the time I didn't appreciate the opportunity, but later I saw some Fred Astaire films and took it up again.'

'*Top Hat*?' Diamond was more at ease now. '*Flying Down to Rio*?'

Surprised, Ingeborg said, 'You seem to know a lot about it.'

'Old films I know about. If you haven't seen Astaire dancing with Ginger Rogers, I'm sorry for you. He would have danced all over this set.' His eyes lighted on the stove. 'The only thing that might have defeated him is that ugly object.'

'The tiles are quite pretty.' Ingeborg said. 'Is it real?' She reached for the handle of the oven and was shocked by the door coming away in her hand and dropping to the floor. It was wood, painted to look like metal. 'Jesus, I've broken it.'

Diamond said, 'Pick it up and push it back in the slot.'

He could have saved his breath. Ingeborg had suddenly become more interested in the space she'd uncovered. She reached inside and took out an envelope. 'This looks like a letter. "To all at the Theatre Royal". Shall I see what's in it?'

'Let me,' Diamond said. He took it from her and withdrew a sheet of paper. 'This is a suicide note.'

My Dear Friends,

This theatre has been my life and you have been my family for six happy years. I can't thank you enough for all the wonderful moments we shared. I'm deeply sorry about what happened to Clarion and I hope by some miracle the theatre and all of you can survive this. But for me there can be no future.

Please don't mourn. If my ashes could be scattered in the theatre garden that would be more than I deserve.

Goodbye and blessings. Denise

Diamond handed the note to Ingeborg. Dawkins stood beside her and read the words at the same time.

'Poor soul,' Ingeborg said.

'It's been written on a computer,' Diamond said. 'Suicide notes are usually written by hand.'

'Guv, we're in the computer age now,' Ingeborg said. 'No one writes anything by hand apart from shopping lists. She's signed it by hand.'

'We'll get the signature checked.'

THE SAME EVENING when Diamond called for Paloma, she was in her office scanning pictures of frock-coated Victorians for the costume designer of *Sweeney Todd.*

'Did I tell you my boss has made it into the chorus?' Diamond said.

'Georgina? Good for her. She'll be one of the Fleet Street women, in a bright bodice and skirt.' Paloma picked up a book and opened it. 'I hope this damn show goes ahead. I've invested a lot of time in it.'

'It's on. The theatre has a future.' He told her about Clarion deciding not to proceed with the lawsuit. Then he told her about finding the suicide note.

'Not a bad day all round,' she said. 'The theatre is in the clear and the note proves what happened to Denise. Case closed.'

'If the note is genuine. It was hidden away inside a piece of scenery.'

'Come on, Peter. Where do you put something you want people to find? Centre stage isn't a bad idea. She was about to hurl herself off the gallery and hit the stage floor. That was clearly the intention. They'd find the body and see the note nearby.'

Put like that, it made sense.

'Denise killed herself. It's over, Peter. You can relax.'

How he wished he could. He'd been debating with himself whether to tell Paloma what he'd learned from Mike Glazebrook. Would he have confided in Steph, his wife? Certainly. Then why not Paloma?

'I met someone I was at school with today.'

Paloma listened in silence. 'You don't know for certain that the art teacher abused you.'

'White was a convicted paedophile and my theatre phobia kicked in immediately after that weekend.'

'Your school friend told you White didn't abuse him. Yet you feel sure you were taken advantage of?'

'If I was the kid he set out to entrap, he may have used Mike as a cover, to let me feel safe knowing there was another boy.'

'Is White still alive?'

The question unsettled him. 'No idea. He'd be over seventy.'

'You're in the police. They keep track of sex offenders, don't they? You could find out. You could meet him.'

He wished he hadn't started this. 'I don't know if I could trust myself. He'd deny it, anyway. I expect he changed his identity.'

'But the sex offenders register would list all the names he's used.'

'You have a touching faith in the system,' he said. 'He was convicted thirty years before the register was started.'

'There must be criminal records.'

'You're right. They're kept at Scotland Yard by the National Identification Service.' Keen to bring this conversation to an end, he added, 'I'll call them tomorrow and get them to run a check.'

'Why not do it now?'

She could have been Steph talking. He reached into his pocket for his phone.

Once he'd identified himself, the information was quick in coming. The civil servant at the Yard told him that Morgan Ogilby White, aged 31, had been convicted on three counts of indecency with minors at Winchester in 1965 and sentenced to five years, of which he had served three. He'd been released on probation in 1968.

'Is that it?' he asked. 'I was expecting more.'

'He hasn't re-offended—under that name, anyway. Paedophiles are crafty at changing their identities.'

'I was hoping to trace him.'

'Your best bet would be the police authority where he offended. Before the new legislation came in, they kept their own intelligence on sex offenders.'

THE THEATRE WAS three-quarters full that evening. Not bad, considering how bleak the prospects had been after Clarion had left the cast.

The mood backstage was upbeat. Melmot had made sure everyone knew of Clarion's decision not to sue. Gisella couldn't wait to go on stage. She'd heard that a casting director from the National had come to see her.

Hedley Shearman looked in with a bunch of roses when she was doing her make-up.

'These are from me, my dear, to spur you on.'

'Oh . . . thanks.' A guarded response. She hadn't enjoyed him pawing her the day before.

He continued, oblivious. 'You'll be marvellous. How about a spot of supper afterwards?'

'Thanks for the offer,' she said, 'and please don't take this personally, but I don't want company tonight or any night.'

As the beginners left the dressing rooms to take their positions, the buzz of expectant conversation out front was audible from the wings. The anticipation on both sides of the curtain was positive as Thursday's performance got under way.

Shortly before the interval curtain was lowered, Fräulein Schneider had an exit, followed soon after by Sally Bowles. In the wings, Schneider blocked Gisella's way.

'Did you see it?' Wide, startled eyes locked with Gisella's. 'The top box, stage right. The lady in grey.'

'The theatre ghost?'

'Staring at me. She was quite alone.'

'I expect it's just some member of the public.'

'That box is where the ghost is always seen,' Schneider said. 'I promise you, she was there, pale as death and all in grey. Is it bad luck?'

'I've no idea . . .' Gisella looked around for support. The curtain had just come down and Preston Barnes was walking off.

Schneider caught him by the arm. 'Did you see the grey lady?'

He wasn't as polite as Gisella. 'For Christ's sake, I don't have time to piss around.' With that, he marched on.

Gisella wished she'd been as firm. 'I'd forget about it if I were you,' she said.

'I'm scared,' Schneider said in a little-girl voice.

Soon, the news of the sighting circulated backstage. Scene-shifters tried peeping through the slots in the curtain. The grey lady was no longer on view. 'She must have gone for her interval drink,' was the quip. The word got through to the Garrick's Head, where Titus O'Driscoll was holding court. He left his half-finished wine and hurried round to the theatre. The royal circle bar was the obvious place to check first but the talk was all about the play, not the grey lady.

A clear view of the box could be had from the royal circle. Disappointing:

no grey lady. Frustrated, Titus went backstage, hopeful of a firsthand account from Schneider.

The place was charged with nervous energy. The five-minute bell had gone and the audience were coming back to their seats. Preston was on stage ready for the second half and Gisella stood in the wings ready to make her entrance.

The deputy stage manager's voice was coming over the tannoy system. 'Will someone please put a bomb under Schneider? She has to be out here and ready.'

Two stagehands were trying to coax Schneider out of her dressing room and back to the stage, but she was implacable. 'I won't be treated as a half-wit. Mr Shearman was downright rude to me. He seemed to think I imagined it. I know what I saw.'

Titus took over. 'I'm Titus O'Driscoll, dramaturge. I understand you had a sighting of the lady in grey. What was her appearance?'

One stagehand said, 'Sir, we don't have time. She's needed for her first entrance.'

'Grey. She was all in grey, with cold, glittering eyes I shall never forget so long as I live,' Schneider said.

'Was she wearing the costume of a nineteenth-century lady?'

She became more animated. 'Yes! It looked like a cloak.'

Titus gasped. 'This is truly momentous. Why don't you go on stage now and meet me afterwards to talk about this amazing occurrence?'

Mollified, Schneider swept out of the room and beetled towards the wings, elbowing Hedley Shearman aside as he arrived.

'Is she going on?' Shearman asked.

'Under protest,' Titus said. 'I doubt if you've heard the last of it.'

'Whatever you said appears to have worked.'

'The lady has my sympathy,' Titus said. 'I've no doubt in my own mind that the theatre ghost was among us tonight. I propose to go into the box and check for proof positive: the scent of jasmine.'

'Not now. The box is locked on my instructions. As soon as this daft rumour started I knew some idiot would want to get in there.'

'You can unlock it for me,' Titus said. 'I'm not "some idiot".'

'There is no ghost and there never has been,' Shearman said, practically stamping his foot. 'It's a myth put about by people who ought to know better. This has been one hell of a night, and my job is to restore sanity to this theatre. I suggest you return to the Garrick's Head, or wherever it is you came from.'

'There's gratitude,' Titus said, knowing he'd lost this skirmish.

The play resumed. Schneider may have appeared subdued but she didn't miss a cue. Gisella was in fine form and this seemed to inspire Preston. The second half sparkled.

From the back of the royal circle, Titus kept a vigil on the box opposite and was disappointed. The grey lady failed to appear.

In the understage area, Kate found Shearman alone in the company office, hunched over his desk, his hands covering his face.

'Someone obviously needs some therapy,' she said, putting an arm round his shoulders and nudging his face with her breast. 'As a matter of fact, I feel the need myself.'

He tensed. 'Leave me alone.'

'Not in the mood?' she snapped. 'That's got to be a first.'

'We're in deep trouble,' he said. 'There's been another death.'

6

Diamond and Paloma were debating whether to finish a vintage Rioja or have it corked and take it with them. They had eaten well in the Olive Tree at the Queensberry Hotel and his thoughts were turning to a taxi ride to Paloma's house and a romantic end to the day.

'So what are you going to do about Flakey White?' she asked.

'I can try Hampshire, where he was convicted, and some of the adjacent police forces. He may have died. He'd be an old man now.'

'You need to know. This goes deep. I see it in your eyes each time it's mentioned.'

'I'm on the case.' He released a long breath. 'But it's really not an after-dinner topic.'

They were interrupted by an old-fashioned phone bell.

'Sorry,' he said, fishing in his pocket.

Paloma watched in amusement, half expecting him to produce a phone set with receiver and cord. In the event, he took out the mobile she herself had given him over a year ago. Some playful member of his team had programmed a ring tone from the 1960s.

A few minutes later, two taxis left the Olive Tree. One took Paloma home, the other took Diamond to the Theatre Royal.

THIS TIME DIAMOND didn't pander to his anxieties by using one of the side doors. Taking a grip on his nerves, he marched straight into the foyer and was directed down some stairs and along the red-carpeted passageway leading to the front stalls. Through open doors to his right he couldn't avoid glimpsing the stage itself, yet he was relieved to see that the house lights were on, the safety curtain down and the cleaning staff at work. Access to the boxes was up the curved stairs at the end of the passage. This little theatre was an obstacle course of different levels.

A uniformed female constable guarded the door of the upper box.

'Who are you?' he asked.

'PC Reed, sir.'

'I expect you have a first name.'

She blinked in surprise. 'It's Dawn.'

'Who's inside, Dawn?'

'DI Halliwell and the manager, Mr Shearman. Oh, also the deceased.'

'Bit of a squeeze, then. Don't let anyone else in.'

He pushed open the door. The single wall light didn't give much illumination. Halliwell was bending over the body of a woman, shining a torch on the face. Shearman was in shadow on the far side.

Halliwell looked up. 'She's been confirmed dead by the paramedics.'

'Any idea who she is?'

Halliwell sidestepped the question. 'Mr Shearman identified her.'

'It's a nightmare,' Shearman said, 'and just when I thought we were getting over our difficulties.'

Diamond moved in for a closer look. He wasn't often thrown by surprises. This ranked high and he took several seconds to absorb it. The dead woman was Clarion Calhoun.

'For the love of God. She's only just out of hospital. What's she doing here?' he asked Shearman.

'She called Mr Melmot with a request to see the play, but not from the public seats where people would recognise her. She was brought in wearing one of those hoodie things and given this box.'

'Did you know about this?'

'I was in on it, yes. Mr Melmot told me.'

'Who else knew?'

A shrug. 'Now you're asking. Word gets round.'

'Who brought her up here?'

'One of the security people, name of Binns. I was waiting in here to welcome her.'

'How was she looking?'

'I couldn't see much. She was holding a scarf across her face and seemed calm. I offered to send up a drink, but she didn't want one. It was obvious she wanted to be left alone.' He shook his head. 'What the press will make of all this, I dread to think.'

'I can't disagree with that,' Diamond said. 'Look, it's ridiculous, using a torch. It's a theatre, for God's sake. They can point a spotlight straight in here.'

'I'll see to it at once,' Shearman said, eager to be out of there. He left, looking relieved.

'Give me that torch,' Diamond said to Halliwell.

No question: this was definitely the woman he'd visited at Frenchay Hospital. The scarring was still apparent, even if most of the redness had faded. As to a cause of death, he could see no bleeding at the mouth or nostrils. Although a grey chiffon scarf was around her neck, it wasn't tight and there were no obvious ligature marks. She appeared to have fallen sideways from her chair.

'Has anyone else been by?' he asked Halliwell.

'The two paramedics. A pathologist is on his way.'

'Who discovered her?'

'Shearman, when the show ended. I suppose he came up here with the idea of escorting her to a taxi.'

'It's very odd, Keith. If she was murdered—and we'd better assume she was—it throws new light on the previous incidents.'

'The dresser's fall?'

'And Clarion's scarring. Is someone responsible for all three?'

The spotlight suddenly came on, dazzling them and depriving the box of its previously lush look. There were cracks in the paintwork, stains on the carpet and a dead butterfly tangled in a cobweb on the ceiling.

Diamond gave it a glance and passed no comment.

Halliwell spotted Clarion's black leather handbag on the floor.

'Leave it,' Diamond said. Proper forensic procedure debarred them from handling anything. 'We're doing everything by the book. She's so famous that every action we take is going to be picked over by the media. And what is more, from now on, anyone backstage from the manager down has the chance of making big money by selling exclusives.'

'Christ, they'll be round here with their mobiles, taking pictures. Do you want to seal the building?'

'That would be a start. This theatre has more entrances than Victoria Station. Get our team in and a scene-of-crime unit. Tell them to bring arc lamps and some kind of screen for the open side. And where does this other door lead to?'

He opened it: the dress circle.

He told PC Reed she now had two doors to guard, so she'd better come inside the box with the body. 'Does that bother you?'

'No, sir.'

'Good answer. You're the speed-writer, I believe. Do you get every word?'

'I try to.'

'May I see?'

She took her notebook from her pocket and opened it at an example.

'What's this, then?' he asked.

'The interview with Denise Pearsall.'

'On Tuesday morning? You and Sergeant Dawkins?'

'Yes.'

He frowned at the first few letters—*Hv w mt b4*—and then smiled. 'Neat. May I tear these pages out? I'd like to read the rest.'

'Take the notebook, sir.'

'No, you're going to need it.'

He spotted a movement in the royal circle, one level down. He shouted through his hands. 'Mr Shearman, make an announcement over the public address. Nobody leaves the building. Everyone here is to assemble in the stall seats: actors, crew, cleaners, front-of-house people, the lot. That's an order.'

Halliwell, phone in hand, told him CID and uniform were alerted. More officers were already downstairs and security had been told to seal the building. 'But if she was murdered, whoever did it is likely away.'

'Which is one good reason to find out who's still here,' Diamond said. 'Get them listed when they're together. I'll speak to them as a group.'

Dr Sealy, the pathologist, arrived, grumbling that he'd been watching an old *Inspector Morse* and now he wouldn't find out who did it.

'Give me strength! This is the real bloody thing,' Diamond said.

Over the public address, Shearman made his announcement telling everyone to assemble in the stalls. From the dress circle, Diamond watched the actors and staff take seats. There must have been forty to fifty people.

Diamond took the stairs down to the ground floor and was pleased to find his CID team already there, listing the names of all present.

'So where's Melmot?' Diamond asked Shearman. 'Was he in tonight?'

'Yes. He was doing the hospitality bit with our special guests. It was Francis who told me Clarion wanted to come. We decided between us that a seat in the box was the best way to keep her hidden.'

Titus gave a gasp. 'I knew it: we've been duped.'

Diamond glared. 'What do you mean?'

'There was a sighting of the theatre ghost this evening. A reliable witness saw her in the box, the one with the spotlight on it.'

All the conversations around them had stopped.

'This evening?' Diamond said.

'During the play. She was all in grey. Where's Fräulein Schneider?'

'Here.' The big woman turned a stricken look on Titus.

'Tell them what you saw,' he urged her.

Her words soared melodramatically. 'She was here tonight, staring at me from the upper box where she is known to materialise.'

'Dressed in grey?'

'Totally. In a hooded gown. Most of her face was veiled in some shroud-like material.'

'What time was this?' Diamond asked.

'I don't know. Before the interval.'

'Was she there after?'

'I can't say. I was too petrified to look.'

'She was not,' Titus broke in. 'I observed the box for the second half.'

'Are you doubting me as well?' Fräulein Schneider asked Titus.

'Not at all, but I fear Mr Diamond can account for what you saw.'

'The dead woman everyone is talking about?'

Diamond spoke. 'What you've told us, ma'am, could be important, and I want to hear more from you in a moment.' While he had everyone's attention, he announced what he could about Clarion, stressing that she'd been wearing a grey scarf and dressed in a grey hooded jacket.

Fräulein Schneider gave vent to a theatrical sigh.

Diamond said he expected a number of witnesses had seen Clarion and he would need statements from all of them.

'Did someone murder her?' Preston Barnes asked.

'It's an unexplained death. We have a duty to investigate.'

'We'll be here all bloody night, then.'

This prompted a hubbub of alarm over personal arrangements.

Diamond briefed his team. The key points to discover, he told them, were whether anyone had seen or heard anything about Clarion's visit. He named his interviewers and sent them to various parts of the auditorium. He was left with Fred Dawkins.

'Marshal this lot in an orderly way, Fred. Send them one by one to whoever is ready to see them. Can you handle that?'

'Only if I get a badge and a gun.'

The man had a glimmer of humour. Given time, he might fit in.

A gap in the sequence of events needed explaining. Diamond took Shearman on one side. 'You told me you went to the box at the end of the play and found the body.'

The man had turned pale. 'That is correct and I called 999.'

'I'm more interested in what you didn't tell me. At which point of the evening did you know she was dead?'

Shearman's mouth moved without any words being spoken.

'No one was visible in the box during the second half. She was already dead, wasn't she?'

Still he didn't answer.

'There she was, your VIP guest. It would be extraordinary if you didn't look in during the interval to see if she was comfortable.'

Shearman finally found some words. 'I had a theatre full of people and a performance in progress. To interrupt it would have created mayhem.'

'You haven't answered my question. When did you find out?'

'Shortly before the second half started. I took her a glass of champagne. I looked inside and had the shock of my life.'

'Are you certain she was dead?'

'Definitely. I spoke her name several times, and felt for a pulse. Absolutely nothing. I was petrified.'

'The show must go on. That's the mantra, isn't it? You had a dead woman lying in the box—'

'No one could see her. She'd fallen on the floor.'

'How long is the second half?'

'About an hour and a quarter.'

Diamond was appalled. 'You left her lying dead for all that time?'

'It seemed the best thing to do. It was all down to me. Francis wasn't around to ask.'

'He'd already left, had he?'

'I've no idea.'

'Did you tell anyone?'

'I kept it to myself, I swear.'

'If Clarion was murdered—and it's quite possible she was—we'll need to know where everyone was during the interval.'

'I was trying to speak sense into Schneider.'

'Schneider?'

'It's the part she plays. Everyone calls her that. She was ranting on about the grey lady. She'd obviously noticed Clarion in the box but I couldn't tell her who it was. She's a blabbermouth.'

'Wasn't Clarion visible from the audience?'

'No. She was sitting well back in the box. Only someone on stage would catch a glimpse.'

'Any one of the actors could have spotted her, then?'

'They may have seen a figure there. Hard to recognise who it was.'

It was clear to Diamond that anyone who went to investigate could have attacked Clarion. Anyone in the cast or crew might have learned that Clarion had been in the theatre. Melmot and Shearman knew for certain, and so would the security man, Charlie Binns. For a would-be murderer, the opportunity had been there: Clarion alone in the box during the twenty-minute interval.

Binns was next up.

'How did you learn about Clarion's secret visit?' Diamond asked.

'Mr Melmot came to the stage door and told me.'

'Tell anyone else, did you?'

He didn't like that. 'What do you take me for?'

'So what happened?'

'I carried out his instructions to the letter. Waited out front for her to come in her black limo. Escorted her round to the side door and up the back stairs to the top box.'

'Was anything said when she got out?'

'Not by her. She had a scarf across her face and the hood of her jacket was over her head. I told her to come with me and she did.'

'Did she appear nervous?'

'How would I know when all I could see was her eyes?'

'Was anyone lurking around the stairs to the box?'

'No. After I took her upstairs I went back down to the stage door. I was there for the rest of the evening.'

Just a functionary. That was his defence, anyway.

Diamond returned upstairs, fixed on dragging some definite information out of Dr Sealy.

'What killed her, then?' he said. 'I've got fifty people down there wanting to get home. Is there anything I should be told?'

'About her death? I reserve judgement. I'll do the PM tomorrow.'

'Not even a suspicion?'

'I'm a scientist, my dear fellow. Suspicion is speculative.'

'Put it this way, is it possible she was killed and no mark was left?'

'Entirely possible, but don't ask me to list the possible causes or we'll be here all night.' He stood up. 'It gets to your knees, all this stooping.'

'Look, if you're not going to tell me anything, I might as well be off.'

'There *is* something I can tell you about the victim,' Sealy said. 'Take a look at her arms.' He rolled back one of the sleeves of the grey jacket as far as the elbow.

Diamond leaned over for a better look. There were scars on the inner side of the forearm. 'She was a druggie?'

'No. These old injuries are not the same as you get from shooting up. She's cut her wrists more than once. Clarion Calhoun was a self-harmer.'

AN EVENT AS SENSATIONAL as the death of a major pop star is international news. Well before midnight on Thursday, the police switchboard was jammed with media enquiries. Diamond issued a statement confirming that a woman had been found dead at the Theatre Royal and a press conference would be held next morning.

Early on Friday, he phoned Ingeborg. 'When I asked you to bone up on Clarion you didn't tell me anything about self-inflicted injuries.'

'She must have kept it well hidden. Thinking about it, all the pictures I've ever seen show her with her arms covered up.'

'Sealy says he can use ultra-violet light to enhance old scars and give us an idea how long she was doing this.'

Ingeborg moved on to the key question. 'Are you thinking she may have damaged her own face with the caustic soda?'

He'd debated this for much of the night. 'Tilda Box must know what her client got up to. Where is she? London, I suppose.'

'We have her mobile number.'

'You'll get more out of her if you meet.'

'We need someone to identify the body.'

Not for the first time, he valued Ingeborg's quick brain. 'Wake her up and tell her we want her here before they start the PM. Call me back as soon as you've fixed it. I'm at home.'

In his kitchen, his cat Raffles started pressing against his leg, reminding him of his duty. He'd barely opened a pouch of tuna before the phone rang.

'She's catching an early train,' Ingeborg told him. 'I'm meeting her at the station and driving her to the mortuary.'

'You can you handle this, can't you, Inge?'

'Getting her to open up? No problem, guv.' Cracking a difficult witness was a skill Ingeborg had learned in her days as a journalist.

'You hear quite a lot about self-inflicted injuries among young women. Why do you think they do it?'

'It's often a teenage thing,' she said. 'I did see a theory that they're suffering such pain from within that they take to cutting themselves to transfer the pain to the outside. The cutting brings temporary relief.'

'By pain from within, you mean anxieties?'

'You know how tough it can be when you're growing up.'

'Clarion was no teenager.'

'Right, but she was into the world of pop from an early age. Her growing up must have been distorted.'

'Arrested development?'

'If you want to put a label on it. Her great days as a singer were over. She may have started cutting herself when she was younger, but all the recent disappointment must have been hell to endure.'

'Damaging her own face would be a step on from cutting her arms,' Diamond said.

'Self-harmers use anything that comes to hand. And she had the extra incentive that scarring her face would save her from being savaged by the critics, something that she must have been dreading.'

'I thought self-harming was done in secret and covered up.'

'She did cover it up by blaming the theatre. She could have secretly brushed caustic soda on her face just before going on. She had the credit of making an entrance and the agony that followed saved her from having to remain on stage.'

'Why did she threaten to sue? Wouldn't a self-harmer stay silent?'

'To make her story stand up, she would have had to point the finger at someone else. She waited a few days and then withdrew the action.'

He was being persuaded. 'I wonder if she ever did instruct her lawyers. That's something else you should ask the agent.' He drummed his fingers on the worktop. 'And so we come to the even bigger question: does self-harming lead to suicide?'

'You mean did she kill herself? I don't think it follows. Most are content to damage their bodies without wanting to destroy them. But you'd have to ask an expert.'

He'd done enough theorising. 'We should find out what killed her from the post-mortem, but we'll have the usual wait for test results.'

IT WAS STILL EARLY. After shaving, Diamond put in several calls to police authorities in the home counties, seeking information on Flakey White. Everyone he spoke to said they would 'look into it'.

His next move of the day was south, into Somerset, with Paul Gilbert as chauffeur for an early call on Francis Melmot.

'Do you like lemon drizzle cake?' Diamond asked as they approached the pedimented entrance of Melmot Hall.

'I don't even know what it is, guv.'

'You've led a sheltered life. They're famous for it here.'

After a long delay their knock was answered by Melmot, wearing an ancient brown dressing gown. 'Do you know what time this is?'

'Time for some questions about last night,' Diamond said. 'You know what happened in the theatre?'

'Of course. I was there.'

'Not when I needed to question you. May we come in?'

Melmot showed them into a large, high-ceilinged room almost empty of furniture, with patches on the wallpaper where pictures had hung.

'Find yourselves a pew.'

The only possibilities were dining chairs heaped with cardboard boxes containing crockery.

'These things are waiting for a valuation,' Melmot said.

'Selling up?' Diamond asked, gesturing to DC Gilbert to clear some space. The prospect of lemon drizzle cake had vanished.

'Not the house. Just some of the contents. You wouldn't believe the upkeep of a place this size. It's death by a thousand cuts. And each time I sell something I have to justify it to my mother who, by the way, won't interrupt us if you're brief.'

'Let's go for it, then. You were phoned some time yesterday by Clarion, who wanted to see the evening performance?'

'That's correct.'

'You knew she'd dropped the lawsuit. You told me. So you were well disposed to the lady?'

'I told you I was a fan.'

'But your admiration must have been very much tested by the lawsuit hanging over you.'

'Others took it more seriously than I.'

'Denise, for one.'

'That's a matter of conjecture, isn't it?'

'Not since we found the suicide note.' Diamond watched the reaction. The discovery had been known only to Ingeborg, Dawkins and himself. No point now in keeping back the news.

'How desperately sad,' Melmot said after he'd been told, but anyone could tell he was neither desperate nor sad.

'Yes, if Clarion had withdrawn her threat earlier, Denise might not have taken the action she did. But, getting back to Clarion, can you recall her exact words when she phoned you yesterday?'

'She'd asked if I'd heard she was out of hospital and wondered if she could get to see the play. She said she wanted to come in secret. She wasn't ready yet to meet the cast or any of her fans.'

'Because of the scarring?'

'We didn't go into that. I had the idea of letting her see the show from a private box. If you sit back, you're invisible to the audience.'

'So you made plans?'

'She told me to look out for a black Mercedes limo. I laid on my end of things, getting Binns to escort her upstairs.'

'Did you tell anyone else?'

'Only Hedley Shearman. I asked him to look in at the interval and make sure she was comfortable.'

'Didn't you see her yourself?'

'Only when she arrived. I had other duties in the interval, so I had to rely on Hedley to take care of her.' He rolled his eyes. '*Take care of her*. God only knows what happened.'

'Where were you?'

'In the interval? In the 1805 Rooms—our VIP suite. Named after the year the theatre was built. We had a casting director from the National and several of our sponsors.'

'You were there for the whole twenty minutes?'

'It went on for longer, in fact. Some minor alarm backstage.'

'This would have been Fräulein Schneider reacting to the grey lady. Were you in the 1805 Rooms for the whole of the interval?'

'I slipped out towards the end to find out what the delay was about.'

'So there was a period when you were between the 1805 Rooms and backstage?'

'Is that significant?' Melmot managed a look of innocence.

'And at what point did you learn that Clarion was dead?'

'After the final curtain. One of the front-of-house staff told me someone had collapsed and died in the Arnold Haskell box. I knew who it was, of course. They told me Hedley was dealing with it. I couldn't face anyone. I returned here in turmoil and spent a sleepless night trying to work out what to tell people.'

'People like us?'

'Not you. I've told you the honest truth. It's all those reporters I dread. They'll twist it into a filthy scandal. They always do.'

'Have you been on the receiving end before?'

'Not in a serious way. This is something else.'

'Yes, it's huge,' Diamond said. 'I'll be holding a press conference about it this afternoon.'

On the drive back to Bath, he asked Gilbert what he'd made of Melmot.

'Didn't like him, guv. He's all front. There wasn't much real sympathy for either of the women who died in his theatre. All he thinks about is what the press will make of it. He said he was a Clarion fan, but he isn't grieving.'

'He had great hopes.' Diamond said. 'He was getting credit from the theatre people for finding a star performer and she was supposed to be grateful for getting the part. But it all turned sour.'

'His reputation was under threat.'

'You've got it. People of his sort, heirs to a big estate, don't like to be thought of as living off their capital. The theatre is a perfect vehicle for someone like him to earn extra status. But he let slip an intriguing remark.'

'About being treated unfairly by the press?'

'There's some skeleton in Melmot's cupboard. When we get back, do some digging.'

TILDA BOX was dressed in purple and black, an outfit straight out of *Vogue* but appropriate for the occasion. She spotted Ingeborg in the station forecourt and came over. She'd obviously just refreshed her make-up.

'I hope you weren't trying to phone me on the train. I had to switch off. It's been non-stop.'

'It's like that at the nick,' Ingeborg said. 'My boss is giving a press conference some time soon.'

'What will he say?' She was eager for information.

'Not a lot. He'll want to confirm Clarion's identity. That's up to you, of course.'

Tilda frowned. 'There's no question that it's her?'

'Not so far as I know.' Ingeborg started the car and headed west towards the hospital. She had a miniature tape-recorder running under the armrest between them.

Tilda was uneasy. 'I thought this was just a formality.'

'Absolutely,' Ingeborg said, noting how panicky her passenger was starting to sound. This would be as good a time as any to pounce. 'How long has she been cutting herself?'

'Cutting herself?' Tilda made a show of sounding baffled.

'You must have seen her arms,' Ingeborg said. 'You of all people will know about the self-inflicted injuries—as her professional adviser.'

Briefly, there seemed to be a danger of Tilda leaping out of the car. Then she gave up any pretence of not knowing. 'For some years, in fact. Top performers like Clarion are under enormous pressure.'

'Did she talk openly about the self-harming?'

'I wouldn't say openly. To me in confidence, yes.'

'It must have been a huge worry for you.'

'That goes without saying.'

'But she told you everything. A sympathetic ear.' A touch of flattery, opening the way for the key question. 'We could see you were very close when we met after her face was damaged. Did she tell you she did that to herself?'

Tilda hesitated. Then the words tumbled out. 'It was so sad, really. She was worried sick about the first night and she needed a get-out. She'd used corrosives on her skin before. There was caustic soda under the sink in one of the dressing rooms. She collected some in a tissue and dabbed it on her face before she went on. I don't think she knew how excruciating it would be. She almost passed out with the pain.'

'And then she blamed the theatre?'

'Poor darling. The doctors told her she was scarred for life. Having to admit to the world that she'd done it to herself was more than she could cope with, so she started this talk of legal action. She even convinced me—and I know her history. That morning when you came to the hospital I was sure she had grounds for damages. I called her lawyers.'

'When did she tell you the truth?'

'Later, over the phone. The lawyers advised the theatre she'd decided not to sue. Without disclosing the reason, of course.'

Ingeborg breathed a quiet sigh of relief. One part, at least, of the mystery was solved.

'Did you see her after she came out of hospital?'

'I'd already returned to London. We spoke on the phone and she told me of her plan to see the play. I couldn't see any harm in it, so I didn't try to dissuade her.' She reached for a tissue. 'If only I had.'

'Would you say she sounded suicidal?'

'Oh my God—do you know something?' Tilda's voice piped in horror.

'I'm just asking.'

'Oh.' Deflated, she said, 'No, the thought hadn't crossed my mind.'

OUTSIDE BATH CENTRAL police station, impatient pressmen were taking pictures of everyone, regardless of who they were. 'Can't you let them in?' Georgina said, not pleased at being called love and asked if she was Clarion's mother.

'I know what they're like, ma'am,' Diamond said. 'Stuck in the conference room, they'll get even more bolshy.'

It was eleven thirty. The post-mortem should have started at ten. He phoned the mortuary and asked for Halliwell. They said he was still observing.

'It could take another hour or more,' the mortuary keeper said.

'For crying out loud. You'd think it was brain surgery.'

'Well, it is.'

Diamond was forced to admit that this was true.

At least Ingeborg had delivered. He'd listened to the tape. Tilda's confirmation was a breakthrough. He hadn't yet worked out the full implications. If Clarion had damaged her own face, why had Denise killed herself and left that suicide note?

'Is this a good moment, guv?' Paul Gilbert asked. 'You asked me to check on Francis Melmot.'

'Well? Do we have anything on him?'

'Nothing on record. But there was a complaint of assault that was later withdrawn in connection with his father's death in 1999.'

'The old man shot himself, supposedly while cleaning his gun.'

'Well, not long after that, a reporter turned up at Melmot Hall and made some remarks Francis didn't appreciate about his father's private life. The old boy had been screwing a barmaid and Mrs Melmot had got to hear of it. The reporter suggested the old lady told her husband to do the decent thing and shoot himself and wanted to see if he could get a quote from Francis. Instead he got his nose broken.'

'He's a big guy to tangle with. This tells us he's capable of violence but I have some sympathy, especially as it was a poxy pressman. Nice work, Paul. Get a note of it on the case file.'

Around noon, Ingeborg came in. 'Is your phone dead, guv? Keith was trying to reach you from the mortuary.'

He sat forward. 'He was? Is it over?'

'Depends what you mean. You could say it's just beginning. They're saying Clarion was suffocated.'

'CONVINCE ME,' Diamond said.

Halliwell, back from the mortuary, gave his humour-the-boss grin. 'Dr Sealy wasn't in any doubt.'

'I'm no pathologist,' Diamond said, 'but even I know they turn purple if they suffocate. I saw the body. She was as pale as your shirt. What is more, they get those little blood marks in the eyes and the skin. Petechial haemorrhages. There weren't any.'

'He said the so-called classic signs were absent.'

'So how does he know she was suffocated?'

'He found marks at the base of her neck.' Halliwell tapped his own shoulders where the collar of his T-shirt met his neck. 'Here, on each side, where the killer pressed into the flesh with thumbs and knuckles.'

'To obstruct the arteries?'

Halliwell shook his head. 'Dr Sealy said she was suffocated with a plastic bag pulled down over her head and held there until she stopped struggling, which happened rapidly. The killer would have entered the box from behind and slipped the bag over her head.'

'Simple as that?'

'Not quite. You and I might think she died from lack of oxygen, but sometimes a neurochemical reaction kicks in and the death is from cardiac arrest. Sealy said in cases like that, the skin turns pale and there aren't any of the signs you'd normally expect in asphyxia.'

'As I noted,' Diamond said, with a hint of self-congratulation.

'It was a quick death, apparently, and the panic in the victim very likely contributed to the speed of it.'

Diamond exhaled sharply. 'Nasty. Surely she'd have grabbed at the bag and tried to pull it off.'

'Very likely, but the force downwards is stronger than her trying to get a grip and push it up.'

Halliwell had sketched the scene vividly enough for Diamond to visualise how it may have worked. 'We didn't find a bag at the scene.'

'The killer wouldn't have left it there.'

He had to agree. 'You're right. This wasn't the work of someone careless.'

'Will you tell the press?'

A difficult question. Sometimes details known only to the killer are held back for tactical reasons. To reveal that Clarion had been murdered in this manner would put the media machine into overdrive and make his task that much harder. Yet if the press weren't told, they'd ferret out the truth in a matter of hours. 'I'll lay out all the main facts.'

HE KEPT THE PRESS CONFERENCE down to twenty minutes. His stark opening statement made the strong impact he intended and gave the hacks their juicy quotes. He came out feeling less battered than some other times.

In the CID room he braced himself for a more searching examination.

Everyone was there. Even Georgina had come downstairs to listen.

'It's the most public murder enquiry we've ever had in this city,' Diamond told them. 'Put your private lives on hold. It's overtime for everyone. Now, where's John Leaman?'

A hand went up at the back of the room.

'You're in charge of the search of the theatre. Comb the place for the murder weapon, the plastic bag. The killer may have dumped it in some bin thinking it wouldn't be noticed. Take as many coppers with you as uniform can spare. Inge, you go through all the statements we took in the theatre last night. Look at everyone's movements, especially during the interval. We have three obvious suspects: Shearman, Melmot and Binns. Each of them knew ahead of time that she was coming to the play. See if what they said checks out.'

'Right, guv.'

'Then there's the actors. Find out how they spent the interval. Did they go to their dressing rooms and stay there? Were they alone?'

'Fräulein Schneider wasn't,' Halliwell said. 'She had stagehands with her trying to calm her down.'

'We can't ignore any of the crew,' Ingeborg said. 'They could have heard Schneider panicking about the grey lady.'

'And there's the wardrobe woman,' Halliwell said.

'Not to forget the dramaturge,' Dawkins added. 'He was with Schneider towards the end of the interval.'

Diamond said, 'I'm assigning Keith, Inge and Fred to getting the fullest possible profiles of our three main suspects—everything about them, their past, present and, above all, any link, however remote, to Clarion.'

Dawkins smiled broadly. 'Which one is mine?'

'That's up to Keith.'

'You can take Binns,' Halliwell said at once.

'I shall take him and dismantle him. I'm a fully fledged member of the team now.'

'I wouldn't say that,' Diamond said. 'Let's see how you cope.'

Then Georgina spoke. 'Please bear in mind, Peter, that Sergeant Dawkins has a rehearsal tonight.'

He jerked back in disbelief. 'Rehearsal?'

'For *Sweeney Todd*. We're doing a walk-through of the moves. As our choreographer, he's indispensable.'

Diamond felt his blood pressure rocket. He hadn't asked for Dawkins in the first place. The man was a pain, anyway. Let him do his bloody walk-through—walk through the door and out of CID for good.

With a huge effort, he controlled himself. 'Let's not lose sight of the other unexplained death at the theatre. There's compelling evidence that Denise was not alone in the minutes before she fell from the fly tower. I can't see a definite link but Denise's death is still high priority. The so-called suicide note has gone for analysis and we should find out if it was genuine. From what we now know, it appears Denise wasn't responsible for scarring Clarion, so she had no reason to blame herself.'

'A double murder looks likely,' Halliwell said.

'One more thing,' Diamond said. 'With all the media interest, we're liable to be approached by every kind of snoop. Keep it buttoned, okay?'

The briefing over, he followed Georgina from the room. 'About Sergeant Dawkins, either he's on the squad or he isn't . . .'

'You're right,' she conceded. 'I spoke out of turn. But if you can release him for a couple of hours tonight, I'll make it up to you in human resources. We have some bright young bobbies in uniform keen to get CID experience.'

'I'll take Dawn Reed and George Pidgeon,' he said at once.

Georgina looked surprised that he knew any names outside his own little empire. 'Agreed.' She moved at speed towards the stairs to her eyrie. She hated being outmanoeuvred.

7

I Am a Camera was forced to end its run prematurely. Even Hedley Shearman admitted that to have carried on would have been insensitive. The actors and crew were asked not to leave Bath and to be available for more questioning if required.

Alone in his office, Diamond studied printouts of the statements made by Shearman and Denise on the morning after Clarion's face was damaged. Thanks to PC Reed's speed-writing and Dawkins's faultless typing, they were lucid accounts, but they didn't yield anything new. No doubt Dawkins had done most of the talking. A proper check was a high priority, and best left to Halliwell and his team. More would definitely emerge.

In the calm at the eye of the storm, Diamond's thoughts turned to his early life. He'd not heard back from any of the police authorities he'd contacted about Flakey White.

Still uncomfortable using the computer, he Googled the man's full name. It gave several hundred so-called 'hits' that he could tell straight away were nothing to do with Flakey. Disappointed, he sat back and tried thinking of another way of tracing an ex-teacher with a prison record. Then he remembered something Mike Glazebrook had said. He reached for the phone.

'Mike? Peter, your old schoolmate here. When we talked about Flakey White, you said something about him surfacing as a book illustrator.'

There was a pause. 'Couple of years ago I saw something in a magazine in my barber's, a feature about illustrators. There were photos of these guys and one of them was called Mo White. It was definitely Flakey. He was white-haired and wore glasses, but the face hadn't changed much.'

'What was he illustrating?'

'It looked like comics to me.'

'For kids, you mean?'

'Who else reads comics?'

'There are books for adults called graphic novels,' Diamond said. 'Can you recall the magazine?'

'No chance. A couple of years could mean five or six. Oh, and one other thing, Peter—when you put the boot in, give him one for me.'

Even Diamond was shaken by that. 'He must be seventy-five, at least.'

'So what? He didn't care about the age of the kids he abused.'

The internet finally came in useful. He found a website devoted to graphic novels. An artist called Mo White was credited with rendering Dickens novels into illustrated books for adults. The publisher was Stylus of New Oxford Street, London.

A woman at Stylus confirmed that White had produced two books for them in 2003. She was guarded when Diamond asked for a contact address.

Silently Diamond cursed the Data Protection Act. 'What a disappointment after all the research I've done,' he said. 'He was my art teacher forty years ago. It's a school reunion. I was so looking forward to seeing the look on his face.'

She melted. White was living in Forest Close, Wilton.

Only about an hour's drive from Bath.

A CALL CAME IN from an unexpected quarter. It was Duckett, the crime scene investigator.

'We found something of interest in dressing room 11. We analysed the dust and found some particles of a chemical called flunitrazepam. Better known as the date rape drug, Rohypnol.'

Diamond was fully alert. 'Go on.'

'It's a prescription drug ten times more potent than Valium. In its original form it was colourless, odourless and tasteless, but since 1998 the manufacturers have added a blue dye that will appear when it dissolves. There are still supplies in circulation of the pure version. This tested neutral, so it must be pre-1998. Have you had the blood-test results from the post-mortem on Denise Pearsall?'

'Not yet.'

'I would expect them to confirm that she was drugged.'

'For sex?' Diamond said. 'Nothing about recent intercourse was mentioned by the pathologist.'

'I wouldn't place too much emphasis on the date rape connection. The purpose would have been to induce passivity. Within ten minutes, the subject feels euphoric and relaxed. She could then have allowed herself to be taken across to the gallery from which she fell or was pushed. In other words, Mr Diamond, I have just provided you with potential evidence of malice aforethought.'

'I'm obliged to you.'

Shortly after, Diamond stepped into the CID room to tell the team.

'How do people get hold of this drug?' Paul Gilbert asked.

'I expect you can get it on the internet,' Halliwell said.

'This was old stock.'

'Plenty of it is still in circulation,' replied Halliwell. 'We've got it off blokes going into nightclubs. There are evidence bags downstairs with the stuff.'

'Of more importance to us,' Diamond said, 'who in the Theatre Royal would be likely to have a supply?'

Dawkins said, 'Hedley Shearman. The little man with the large libido.'

'Fred's right,' Halliwell said. 'Shearman is just the kind of shagbag who would use the date rape drug. He has plenty of form as a seducer. Before coming to Bath, he was front-of-house manager at a theatre in Worthing and got one of the box-office ladies pregnant. His second wife divorced him on the strength of it.'

Diamond was less convinced. 'There's no evidence that he or anyone else had sex with Denise.'

'Maybe she gave him the brush-off and threatened to report him to the board. He got scared and set this trap for her.'

'Is that enough to justify murder?'

'He's still paying for the divorce. Losing his job would be a disaster. That's the motive and we know the opportunity was there.'

'But would he risk the theatre closing?'

'It didn't, guv. Everything carried on as usual after Denise's death. He was one of the keenest to let the show go on.'

'He looks the strongest suspect we have,' Paul Gilbert said.

'Are you also suggesting he murdered Clarion?'

'He was the man on the spot, wasn't he?' Halliwell said. 'He arranged for her to be seated in the box. He admits she was dead at the interval and he delayed reporting it. If that isn't guilty behaviour, what is?'

'But why murder Clarion?'

Halliwell shrugged. 'He fancied his chances with her and she told him to get lost.'

'And he happened to have brought along a plastic bag? I don't think so, Keith.'

Halliwell wasn't giving up. 'Well, he tried it on earlier and she laughed in his face. Humiliated, he went back with the bag and suffocated her.'

'I'll bear it in mind,' Diamond said in a tone suggesting the opposite. 'Has anything else been uncovered?' Everything went quiet.

Just then, one of the civilian staff called him to the phone. 'DI Leaman would like a word, sir. He's at the theatre.'

He picked up. 'John?'

'Guv, I'm in Wardrobe. You asked us to look for carrier bags. The thing is, Kate in Wardrobe has a stack of bags. So far I've counted forty-seven.'

EXPERIENCE HAD TAUGHT Diamond that you can't rush the people who work in forensic labs. The blood-test results from Denise Pearsall would be revealed only when the scientists were ready. The men in white coats were well used to dealing with impatient policemen. However, the same constraints didn't apply to document examiners. They were used less often, so fair game for some badgering, in Diamond's opinion. The suicide note supposedly written by Denise had been sent to an expert called Lincroft.

‘I can’t help you much,’ Lincroft said when Diamond phoned. ‘There isn’t much to go on.’

‘A signature.’

‘Half actually. She signed with her first name only. If it’s a forgery, it’s a good one. Often you can tell under the microscope, for example, when there’s some shakiness to the writing from the effort to make an exact copy. There is slight evidence of a tremor here, but one has to make allowance for the writer’s state of mind.’

‘I don’t know how you ever reach a conclusion,’ Diamond said.

‘Sometimes the deception is obvious, when, say, they trace over a signature in pencil and ink it in after. This certainly didn’t happen to the note in question.’

‘But I can’t look to you for a firm opinion?’

‘I’ve spent considerable time examining this document. Even if I work on it for another week I’m unlikely to say what you want to hear.’

‘Oh, brilliant.’

‘If I were you, I’d come at this from another direction. The letter was computer-generated. Did this lady possess her own printer?’

‘Yes, but you can’t tell anything from printed stuff. The days are long gone when we all used typewriters with chipped keys.’

‘Some modern printers still give information. I noticed some specks down the right edge, very small, deposited by the toner.’

Diamond picked up the photocopy of the note. He’d already seen some tiny dots and hadn’t thought anything of them.

‘Cleaning the drum removes them,’ Lincroft went on, ‘but people tend to wait until the marks get worse and become obvious. There must be enough here to identify the printer that was used. I suggest you run some paper through the lady’s printer and then compare it.’

Diamond was impressed. ‘Sounds like good advice.’

He checked with the store downstairs where evidence was kept. They had what they called Denise’s motherboard, but not her printer. They said they would send someone to fetch it.

‘What I really want is for someone to run a dozen sheets of blank paper through the thing and have them on my desk within the hour.’

Noticing the time, he went down to the canteen, where he’d arranged to meet his new recruits, George Pidgeon and Dawn Reed.

When they were settled with tea and Bath buns, he said, ‘You’re asking yourselves why you've been plucked from the ranks. It's because I've seen you in action, both of you, and I liked what I saw. I want two reliable officers for a job I wouldn't care to do myself. It's secret. Do you know the difference between secret and need to know?'

'If it's secret, no one needs to know,' Reed said.

'Correct. Not your family, brother officers, the chief constable, not even the theatre ghost. Afraid of ghosts, are you, either of you?'

They shook their heads.

'That's good, because you'll be spending the next two nights on duty inside the Theatre Royal, supposedly one of the most haunted buildings in Bath. It will be dark when you go in and I want it to remain in darkness. You'll be alone in that spooky old building, apart perhaps from the grey lady. How does that strike you?'

'Not a problem for me, guv,' Pidgeon said.

'Me neither,' Reed said.

'Here's the deal. We've had two murders in the theatre in two days. One thing we know for certain about the killer is that he or she is familiar with the place. The digital security system is no bar to this individual. I believe the killer may return to the scene of the crime for some giveaway clue they left behind. If this happens you'll be lying in wait and you'll arrest them.' He took out one of the cards issued to theatre staff, which he had requested that morning. 'These are the security codes. Get there by ten. Your shift ends at first light. I suggest you get some sleep in the next few hours.'

He watched them leave. He hoped his faith in them would be justified.

THE PAPER that had been run through Denise's printer had some marks that didn't remotely match the suicide note. Diamond showed them to Paul Gilbert and explained their significance.

'Is this good news, or bad?' Gilbert asked.

'Good and bad. It's more evidence that we're working on the right assumption, that she was murdered, so that much is good. If she'd printed the note at home, suicide would have been a safe bet.'

'So what's bad?'

'We don't know which machine it was printed on.'

'I expect the murderer has a printer,' Gilbert said.

'It's quite possible our crafty killer didn't use his own computer at all,' Diamond said. 'But you can start by getting specimen sheets from the printers at the theatre. When you've eliminated them, start going into people's homes. Don't let anyone offer to do the printing for you.'

'Guv, if I was the killer, I'd already have cleaned my printer so it wouldn't leave marks at all.'

'Let's hope he hasn't thought of that. Run these tests discreetly.'

Gilbert looked as if he'd rather stack shelves in Sainsbury's.

MOTIVE WOULD BE the key to the murder of Clarion Calhoun.

Alone in his office, Diamond turned to the classic trinity for all crimes: opportunity, means and motive. In a theatre where so much was going on, the opportunity had been there for the taking. The means, a plastic bag, was so commonplace that there was doubt if it was worth searching for. Leaman had found fifty-six at the latest count.

Only the motive was worth pursuing. Why would anyone want to kill Clarion when she had withdrawn her threat to sue? Who stood to gain financially from Clarion's death? She had property and money. She had intended to make a substantial donation to the theatre. Was that the trigger that had killed her? Did someone foresee their inheritance being frittered away on wigs and make-up and weird experimental plays?

He made a note to find out the terms of Clarion's will and who the main legatees were. There had been a live-in boyfriend but they'd split up. There was a manager called Declan Dean, but she'd dumped him, too. Anyone else? Tilda Box would probably know. Indeed, Tilda might be the beneficiary. She seemed to have been more than just an agent. But then Tilda had been in London at the time of the murder, apparently.

The more he thought about it, the more he was convinced that nothing would be gained by treating the two murders in isolation. The theatre had brought them together as actress and dresser, and Clarion's extravagant act of self-harm had thrown blame on Denise. The unfortunate dresser's death must have been cunningly arranged by the killer, who evidently knew the theatre intimately—the butterfly superstition, the empty second-floor dressing room, the door to the fly tower and the compartment in the stove where the note was discovered.

Equally, Clarion's killing required the knowledge that the injured star was secretly visiting the theatre. Only three people knew in advance. Others may have worked it out for themselves after the "ghost" was sighted, but the killing didn't have the feel of a last-minute decision. The murderer had come prepared with the airtight killing bag and chosen the interval when most of the audience were outside. He or she had left unseen. It was hard to imagine one of the actors having committed the murder on the spur of the moment and then going back on stage for the second half.

Realistically, Shearman, Melmot and Binns were the prime suspects.

DIAMOND LOOKED into the CID room. 'Anything I should be told?'

'Keith just called from the theatre,' Ingeborg said. 'He said to tell you about a fourth suspect.'

'Who's that?'

'Kate the wardrobe lady. Turns out she knew Clarion was in the theatre the evening she was killed.'

'I'd better get down there.'

He took his car, left it on the double yellow line outside, took a deep breath and . . . felt the first wave of nausea. Nothing had altered. If anything, it was worse. Ridiculous.

Another gulp of air and he forced himself to go in.

The foyer was empty, the box office closed. He gritted his teeth, took a security card from his pocket and pressed the keys that admitted him to the royal circle. Inside it was darker than usual. He heard voices from the bar; one was Halliwell's.

Keith was seated across a table from Shearman.

Diamond pulled up a chair. 'You left a message about Kate.'

'That's right,' Halliwell said. 'Talking to Mr Shearman, I discovered that she knew Clarion was in the theatre last evening.'

'How is that?' Diamond said, turning to Shearman. 'You told her?'

'I'm sorry. It was stupid of me.'

'When? When did you tell her?'

'During the first half.'

Halliwell said, 'Kate and Mr Shearman were at it in the wardrobe room.'

'Shagging? Does this happen every night and twice on matinée days?'

'It's not like that,' Shearman said, blushing. 'She's been through a hugely difficult time and so have I. There's no law against it.'

'What exactly was said?'

'I said I couldn't stay long because I'd need to go up to the box during the interval to take care of a VIP. Of course she wanted to know who, and in the end I told her.' He paused. 'She had nothing to do with Clarion's death.'

'Where is she now?'

He shook his head. 'She left earlier, after your man finished his search of Wardrobe. She has nothing to keep her here.'

'Tidying up would be good. Wardrobe was a mess when I saw it.'

'Her heart isn't in it any more.'

Diamond leaned closer to him. 'So why did you lie?'

'I didn't want her put through the mill. She's no murderer.'

'Do you know where she's gone?'

'Home, I expect. She lives in Warminster.'

Diamond cast his thoughts back to the interview he'd had with Kate shortly after Denise had been found dead. He said to Shearman, 'I picked up some tension between Kate and Denise.'

'I wouldn't make too much of that if I were you. Denise came under Kate's supervision but she'd worked here more than Kate had. There was bound to be some professional awkwardness.'

'Kate didn't seem too cut up about Denise's death.'

'I expect she was putting a brave face on it.'

'Just now you said her heart wasn't in it. What did you mean by that?'

Shearman hesitated. 'Oh, I was talking about the dreadful things that have happened. It's enough to sap anyone's morale.'

Smart answer, but not convincing, Diamond thought. Kate was definitely in the frame now. Her dislike of Denise had been obvious all along. It wasn't beyond her to have lured Denise upstairs, slipped her the drug and pushed her to her death to fake the suicide. Working so closely with Denise, she would be familiar with her signature and able to forge the note. Up to that point everything seemed to be going to plan. Then she'd found out that Clarion was making this secret visit to the theatre. Did alarm bells go off in her head—that Clarion had worked out the truth and was coming to expose her as the killer? How simple to have picked up one of the many plastic bags in Wardrobe and gone to the box and suffocated Clarion.

He turned to Halliwell. 'This stinks. I'm going to see her.'

Shearman was shaking his head. 'She'll think she's under suspicion.'

'She is and I don't want you tipping her off.' He told Halliwell to stay with Shearman for the next hour.

'Don't you understand that I have a job to do?' Shearman demanded. 'I've got to organise a team to strike the set.'

'To *what*?'

Halliwell said, 'He means moving the scenery, guv. They want to clear the stage for the next production.'

Diamond pointed a finger at Shearman. 'Leave everything in place, exactly as it is. That's an order.'

SOUTH-EAST OF BATH in the thick of the Friday afternoon commute along the A36, Diamond drove at his usual steady forty miles per hour. At his side was a detective sergeant who had transferred from Chipping Sodbury a couple of months back. Lew Rogers had merged into the CID room almost unnoticed. This was a chance to get to know him better. All Diamond had discovered was that he cycled to work.

'Does Kate live alone?' Rogers asked Diamond.

'As far as I know, yes.'

'Are you going to nick her?'

'If necessary.'

Two minutes later, all the brake lights started going on. The carriageway was blocked as far ahead as Diamond could see.

'Could be road works,' Rogers said.

'I don't think so.' Diamond had heard the two-tone wail of an emergency vehicle, and an ambulance snaked a route through the stationary traffic. He took out his phone. After speaking to the traffic division, he informed Rogers that the problem was half a mile ahead. 'Some idiot managed to turn his car over.'

He dialled CID for an update and was pleased when Ingeborg answered. He knew she was just back from a visit to Melmot Hall.

'Learn anything new?' he asked.

'Yes. Melmot told me he sacked Kate a week ago. He said there'd been problems with her before, not doing the job properly. She'd clung on because of her relationship with Shearman, who always backs her. But when Melmot was approached about the state of the wardrobe room he went to see and was so appalled he fired her.'

'Shearman did say at one point that her heart isn't in it any more. That should have alerted me. He doesn't give much away.'

'Do you want to know who the whistle-blower was? Denise Pearsall. She showed Melmot photographs of the wardrobe room on her phone.'

Diamond gave a whistle. 'She was asking for trouble, shopping her boss. Kate must have known who dropped her in it.' The facts were slotting in like the last pieces of a jigsaw. 'This is dynamite, Inge. It means she had a red-hot motive for revenge on Denise. And if she thought Denise had mentioned any of this to Clarion, she had a reason to kill Clarion as well.'

Ingeborg sounded a note of caution. 'Let's not forget Shearman, guv. He's Kate's lover. He could have killed Denise. In his case, there was a personal element because Denise went over his head and complained to Melmot.'

'Point taken. And he was the best placed of everyone to murder Clarion. When I get to see Kate, I'll know. The one small problem is that I'm stuck in a bloody traffic jam.'

A further ten minutes went by. 'When we find the house,' he said to Rogers, 'I'll park some distance up the street and you can make the first approach. She knows me. I don't think she's met you.'

Ahead, progress was still slow, but there was movement. A police car with its blues flashing and a uniformed cop were guiding the traffic past the scene of the accident.

'Nasty,' Diamond said as they came alongside a mangled blue saloon being lifted onto a breakdown truck. 'Must have hit that tree.'

Away from the town centre, Warminster was a maze of side streets and dead ends, but Rogers was good with the map. He directed them to the estate where Kate lived. Some boys were kicking a football in the road.

Diamond parked at the kerbside. 'Did you spot the house?'

'The one with the yellow door. Shall I see if she's in, guv?'

'Why not? Give me a wave if she is.'

Rogers walked back, watched by the young footballers, and rang the bell. Diamond watched and waited. The footballers had suspended play.

No one came to the door.

Presently Rogers returned. 'Nothing doing. The kids say they know when she's home because she parks her car outside, a blue Vauxhall Astra.'

A disquieting thought popped into Diamond's mind, but he dismissed it. Instead, he took another look at the house. 'Was that ground-floor window open when you went to the door?'

'I'm sure it was.'

'Careless of her. We shouldn't leave it unsecured. In fact, we have a civic duty to investigate.'

The two of them approached the house. A small top window was open.

Diamond said. 'See if you can reach in and unfasten the catch.'

The footballers came closer while Diamond was helping Rogers get a foot on the outer ledge. The smallest of them said, 'What are you doing, mister? Are you breaking in?'

'We're the police,' Diamond called back, 'making sure it's safe.'

Rogers lifted the catch and they both climbed in. The place was appreciably tidier than Kate's workplace. A black sofa covered with a purple throw. Afghan rug. Flat-screen TV.

'See if you can find her computer and run a sheet of blank paper through the printer.'

'It's right here against the wall.' Rogers checked that the paper in the feed was clean, then passed a couple of sheets through and handed them to Diamond. 'I don't know what you're expecting to find, guv.'

'It isn't this,' Diamond said. The sheets were pristine. 'Mind, she could have used another machine.'

A swift tour of the small house revealed no second printer and nothing else in the way of evidence. Up in the bedroom he started in surprise when his phone emitted its archaic ring-tone.

It was Ingeborg. 'Kate was in a car accident on her way home. She turned her car right over, only a short way from the town.'

That disquieting thought chided him, gloating: *I told you so*.

'Is she alive?'

'So they're saying. She was taken to A and E at Salisbury Hospital. I don't know what condition she's in.'

'We're halfway there. We'll find out.'

AT THE A&E enquiry desk of Salisbury hospital, Diamond learned that Kate was not critically injured. She was being assessed for concussion.

'This could take a long time,' Diamond said to Rogers.

'Shall I fetch some coffee?'

'Good thinking. And a beef sandwich would go down well.'

He called Ingeborg again. The mobile was getting more use in one day than it had in months. 'How did the accident happen?' she asked.

'We don't know yet.'

'Is it possible more than one vehicle was involved?'

He sensed at once what she was thinking, that Kate may have been forced off the road in an attempt to kill her. Kate as victim would mean a reversal of the way he was thinking.

'Hard to tell until we get a chance to speak to her. What's going on at your end?'

'Not much,' Ingeborg said. 'Paul is back from checking the printers at the theatre. There wasn't a single match with the suicide note.'

'He'll just have to visit each of the suspects. Tell him Kate's machine has been cleared. Who else is around?'

'John Leaman found I don't know how many carrier bags in the theatre. And Fred has left for that *Sweeney Todd* rehearsal. He's done a solid job on Binns, checking with previous employers. He doesn't seem to have had any previous connection with Clarion or Denise or the Theatre Royal.'

'So what's your take on Francis Melmot?'

Her sigh could be heard down the phone. 'I'm in two minds, guv. He's far from silent, but he gives nothing away. I'm sure he's an excellent chairman of the trustees because he's so discreet. Personally I find him charming and I think he truly cares about the theatre. But his decision to employ Clarion was a disaster and I suspect there's more he hasn't told us.'

'Like sacking Kate? How did you wheedle that out of him?'

'I made some suggestive remark about Shearman and Kate and he obviously didn't know what they get up to in Wardrobe. He was shocked into telling me she'd already been dismissed.'

'Shearman didn't tell us anything about the sacking, either.'

'Well, he's been exploiting it, hasn't he? Encouraging Kate to think that by cosying up to him she'll get a reprieve. Small chance. Shearman has hardly any influence with Melmot.'

This was a new angle on the goings-on in Wardrobe. 'So you think Kate is pulling him to save her job?'

'I'd put it another way. Shearman is taking advantage.'

'I thought it was straightforward sex.'

'A typically male assumption, if I may say so.'

He wouldn't get into a debate with Ingeborg about that.

Ingeborg rang off and he stepped up to the desk again, and asked if he could see Kate. He was told firmly to wait with everyone else. More marking time. He wasn't good at it. But an idea was coming to him.

When Rogers returned with the coffee, Diamond said, 'There's someone I wouldn't mind seeing while I'm over here. Lives at Wilton. It's not police business, and I'd be leaving you in charge for an hour or so. Would you mind?'

'I'll still be here,' replied Rogers, equably. 'I don't have my bike with me.'

'NO VIOLENCE,' Diamond kept repeating aloud while skirting Salisbury on the road to Wilton. The next hour would test him. The anger simmering for days was already threatening to boil over. No, he must keep reminding himself of the purpose of meeting Flakey White: to find out for certain what had happened when he was a child. Only by getting to the truth of it could he hope to remove the block his brain had put up and give himself the possibility of closure.

He'd thought about phoning White to let him know he was coming. But surprise was essential. As it was, there was no guarantee he'd be at home.

The house was a squat, stone structure with the look of a converted farm building. Crucially, the lights were on inside.

He rang the bell and was relieved to hear movements inside. The door opened on a chain. He couldn't see much of the person inside.

'Mr White?'

'Yes.' The voice was tentative, unwelcoming.

'My name is Peter Diamond and you were once my art teacher. It's late to be calling, I know.'

Without any more being said, White released the door chain. He was shorter than Diamond remembered, dressed in a thin cardigan, corduroys and carpet slippers. 'Do come in,' he said.

Then he held out his hand.

The handshake was a pitfall Diamond hadn't foreseen. Visiting the old paedophile was one thing. Touching his flesh was another. He told himself it was only a formality. How many hands had he shaken in his lifetime—hands that had thieved, assaulted or even committed murder? He felt White's palm against his own; limp, bony, lukewarm. He couldn't stop himself rubbing his hand against his hip afterwards to cleanse it.

White didn't appear to notice. 'I'll make some tea.'

'Please don't,' Diamond told him. 'I had some not long ago. I was visiting the hospital. That's how I was in the area.'

The old man matched him for courtesy. 'Whatever the reason, it's an unexpected pleasure to meet a former pupil. Come through to the kitchen. I use the living room as my studio. Still doing art, you see.'

To reach the kitchen they took a few steps through the studio. An ink drawing of a city street was in progress on a drawing board. Beyond question, it was the work of a skilful artist.

'What did you say your name is?'

Diamond repeated it. 'I was at Long Lane Primary School.'

'I remember the school. I don't remember the names of any of the scholars, I'm sorry to admit. Were you any good at art?'

'Useless. Sport was my main interest. I wonder if you can recall a school friend of mine called Michael Glazebrook?'

A shake of the head. 'I'm afraid I can't.'

'Well, he remembers you, alright. He saw your picture in a magazine some while back.'

White frowned. He was very uneasy.

Diamond said, 'It was a piece about book illustrators.'

The frown gave way to a look of relief. 'Oh, yes. I can recall being photographed for that.'

'At school you had some connection with a local drama group. Mike Glazebrook and I took part in one of the shows, about Richard III.'

White raised both hands. 'Ah, you were the princes in the Tower.' This was said with the pleasure of recognition. 'That's forty years ago, if not more. I'm pleased you mentioned it, because I can place you now.'

I bet you can, you pervert, Diamond thought. 'It isn't a pleasing memory for me. I was put off theatres for ever.'

'Oh, dear,' White said, with what sounded like genuine concern. 'On reflection it was a gruesome story to be in.'

'It wasn't the play that affected me.'

'Stage fright, was it? You seemed very confident.'

'Come on, we both know it wasn't stage fright.'

'You'd better enlighten me.'

'No, Mr White. I want you to enlighten me. I want to know what happened between you and me.'

The old man blinked. 'I'm sorry. I'm at a loss. To the best of my recollection nothing "happened", as you put it.'

'Why did you choose me for the play?'

'I expect because you were a confident child. If you don't mind me saying so, you have quite a forceful presence as an adult.'

'I'm a police officer.'

The effect was dramatic. White's face drained of colour.

'I know about your prison term,' Diamond said.

Almost in a whisper, White said, 'That was a long time ago. And I served my sentence.'

'Early release after three years.'

'It was no picnic. They make sure everyone knows what you're in for and you get it tougher than anyone else.'

'You won't get sympathy from me.'

'I'm not asking for any. I deserved all I got. I did my time and I haven't offended since. You can check the records.'

'All it means is you weren't caught again. The perversion is permanent.'

White nodded. 'I'm a child molester and that's how the world will always see me. Is this about the sex offenders register?'

'No. It's about you and me.'

As if he hadn't heard, White continued, 'I never worked in a school again. I was unemployed for a long time. It was my facility at drawing that was my salvation. I could have illustrated books for children but I deliberately stayed out of that. Eventually I found a niche in graphic novels for adults.' There was a pause and then, 'Why are you here, Mr Diamond?'

The anger was hard to hold down. 'You say you changed your job and your style of life. It's not so easy for your victims, is it?'

White lowered his head. 'I'm aware of that. As a child I was abused myself. Please believe me, after I came out of prison I stopped.'

Diamond still despised him. 'Mr White, I'm here because of what went on when I was a kid with a teacher I trusted.'

White looked up, wide-eyed. 'I didn't abuse you.'

Now he was denying it, the filthy creep. Red mist descended. Diamond grasped him by the shoulders. 'Are you saying that it wasn't abuse?'

'I swear to God I didn't do anything to you.'

'Don't give me that.' Diamond held him up. They were eye to eye. 'Each time I step inside a theatre something so foul is triggered in my brain that I want to throw up. I don't know exactly what it is. A shutter comes down. But I know precisely when all this started—during that weekend when I was in the play.'

White's face was contorted with terror.

Diamond shoved him away and White screamed. Blood oozed from the corner of his mouth. When he opened his mouth it was obvious that he'd bitten his tongue.

The blood was White's salvation. The sight of it acted as a check on Diamond. It wouldn't take more than a few blows to kill this old perv, and what would that achieve?

'Admit it,' he said, panting for breath. 'You know what you did to me. I need to hear you say it.'

White simply shook his head.

Diamond made a fist and then unclenched it. He was making huge efforts to stay in control. He took a step back. 'The least you can do is tell me the truth.'

White wiped some blood from his chin and succeeded in saying, spacing the words, 'I have never assaulted you in any way. I wasn't ever attracted to small boys. My offences were all at Manningham Academy, a private school for girls. I took advantage of under-age girls of fourteen and fifteen.'

Diamond did a rapid rethink. Mike had said his mother had read that White had been convicted of sex offences against minors at a private school in Hampshire. Mrs Glazebrook had evidently assumed that the victims were young boys.

Yet the truth solved nothing. He could trace his theatre episodes back to immediately after the Richard III play.

'I'm certain something deeply upsetting happened to me over the weekend of the play,' he told White. 'Was there anyone else who could have targeted an eight-year-old boy?'

'I think not,' White said. 'Anyway, there wouldn't have been the opportunity. It was a church-hall production and always crowded.'

This chimed with Diamond's memory. He was forced to conclude that he wasn't being duped.

'What will you do about me?' White asked. 'If it gets known locally, people are going to feel threatened. It's happened before. I've had to move out each time.'

'Why didn't you change your name?'

'Because when you get found out, as you will in time, you become an even more sinister figure, a pervert trying to pretend he's someone else, somebody normal.'

Diamond saw sense in that. 'This was a personal visit, nothing to do with my job. I know of no reason why someone in the police should ask me if I know your whereabouts. Glazebrook won't come near you.'

During the drive back to the hospital, Diamond reflected on his failure. He'd messed up, big time. He could have killed that old man, and all through a mistaken assumption. He felt shamed. And he still didn't know how to deal with his private nightmare.

8

Lew Rogers was still waiting in Accident and Emergency.

'What's the latest?' Diamond asked.

'They're keeping Kate overnight but there's nothing seriously wrong. She's being moved to another ward and we can talk to her there. Two local traffic guys are waiting to interview her as well—they're getting a coffee.'

'Let's beat them to it.'

They found Kate in a room of her own, seated in an armchair beside the bed. Her forehead was bruised and she had a bandaged arm. She produced a smile fit to fill the royal circle.'Hi, darlings.'

'You're lucky,' Diamond told her. 'We saw the state of your car. Do you know what caused the accident?'

'I got into one almighty skid coming round a bend and hit a tree.'

'Were you trying to avoid another vehicle?'

She giggled. She was in a strangely playful mood. 'Are you offering me an alibi? I appreciate that. But the crash was down to me entirely, driving too fast with my little mind on other things.'

'Like being sacked from the Theatre Royal?'

'God, no, that's water under the bridge. I was daydreaming about all the gorgeous fellows I'd like to sleep with.'

Diamond muttered to Rogers, 'Was she breathalysed?'

Rogers nodded. 'At the scene. Negative.'

Kate's light-minded talk had to be put down to shock, or a side-effect of medication.

She said to Diamond, 'I don't drink and drive. But they rescued my handbag and I keep a small pick-me-up for stressful situations. No need to look so disapproving, ducky. It's brandy. It's medicinal.'

The good thing was that the drink hadn't taken over entirely. She was speaking coherently. Maybe a few extra truths would come out. 'So were you on your way home?'

'Yes. Today was my last in the Theatre Royal. I collected my few possessions and walked.'

'Feeling depressed?'

'Positively murderous. There are sod-all Wardrobe jobs in these parts.'

'Why did you let it happen? You can't deny that Wardrobe is in a mess.'

'It wasn't until lately. I ran it like Buckingham Palace for two years. No complaints and oceans of praise, and I dressed some spectacular productions in that time, I can tell you, gents. Imagine all the costume changes in a musical: not just a handful of actors, but twenty or more dancers with about nine changes. Wardrobe has to run like mission control to stay on top.'

'What went wrong, then?'

'Sabotage by a certain member of my team.'

'Denise?'

She rolled her eyes upwards. 'I shouldn't speak ill of the dead, but that bitch was out to get me. She'd worked in this theatre longer than anybody and wanted to queen it over us all backstage. She saw I was running my wardrobe superbly and she hated it.'

'Jealous?'

'And some. Things started going wrong. Clothes went missing, the washing machine kept flooding. One morning I came in and found my button collection, thousands of them, all over the floor. Actors would come complaining and I'd find the labels in their costumes had been switched or seams had been loosely tacked. I was forever trying to catch up. In the end, I thought what the hell and just did the minimum. I can't tell you the snide remarks I endured from that woman. She could have run Wardrobe so much better, in her opinion.'

'Had she put in for the job when you applied?'

'No. She was one of those people who won't take responsibility but are the first to slag off anyone who does.'

'I thought she had some high-powered jobs before coming to Bath.'

'I wouldn't call putting cosmetics on corpses high-powered.'

'Didn't you say she ran a drama group in Manchester?'

'The prison. It must have been voluntary work, not professional. I'm sure the screws were there to make sure no one stepped out of line.' Kate wasn't giving an inch in her demolition of Denise's CV.

'She also toured Bosnia with some theatre group. Presumably they were professional?'

'It was only a road show, darling. They all fitted into a minibus. That's not theatre. That's busking.'

'Did you ever accuse her of undermining you?'

'Frequently, but she had a line into the boardroom. Every time I had a crisis in Wardrobe, Melmot would hear about it. Bloody Denise was running a campaign to get me fired and eventually she succeeded.'

'Was she sleeping with him?'

'I doubt it. She may have dangled the bait, but he's an odd fish.' She smiled. 'I expect she told Melmot about Hedley and me.'

'How long have you and Hedley Shearman been . . .?'

'Having it away? Not long. He's a serial flirt, I know, but he's sweet and does his best to fight my cause.' She sighed. 'I don't think he has much influence. He told them Clarion would be a disaster and they ignored him.'

'On the evening Clarion was killed, you and Hedley were together in the wardrobe department.'

'Having a five-star shag. You don't have to be coy. Hed was over the moon because the theatre was saved. I was in a great mood, too, thinking I might get my job back.'

'This was when he told you Clarion was actually in the theatre?'

'Bless her little cotton socks, yes.'

'Did anyone else backstage know that she was in the box?'

'Melmot, of course. And the security man, Binns.'

'Binns has the freedom to move around the theatre, doesn't he?'

'Part of his job. He makes sure it's safe to close up at night.'

'Can the staff get in after hours?'

'No problem if you know the security codes. I could go back tonight if I wanted and burn the whole place down.'

'But you won't, because you'll be here.'

Her mouth curved upwards. 'Unless I discharge myself. I could bum a lift back to Bath with you.'

'No chance,' Diamond said at once. 'You've got an interview coming up with the accident investigation team.'

On the way back to the car, Rogers said, 'Is she innocent?'

'That isn't the word I'd choose but I doubt if she killed anyone.'

'She had motive, means *and* opportunity.'

'In spades, Lew. But there's a clear brain behind these killings, someone confident enough to think ahead and pass off the murder as something it wasn't. Kate is capable of managing a wardrobe department if everything goes well, but under pressure she lost it. We're not looking for someone who runs her car into a tree and gets half-pissed in hospital.'

CID WASN'T EXACTLY buzzing when Diamond walked in about 9.30 p.m. Leaman had his feet up. Paul Gilbert had found a football match on the internet. Halliwell was eating a pasty. Ingeborg was texting.

'Okay, people,' Diamond said.

Order was restored. Gilbert replaced the football with a screen saver. 'Hi, guv.'

'I thought you were out testing printers.'

'I've checked more than twenty. No joy.'

'What about the actors—Barnes and the rest of them?'

'They're in digs. They don't have printers.'

'Their landladies do.'

Gilbert blushed.

'Tomorrow morning,' Diamond said.

Ingeborg said, 'The lab has detected significant levels of Rohypnol in Denise's blood.'

'That ties in nicely. Are we any further on with our major suspects? Keith, you were marking Shearman's card.'

'He's a bundle of nerves,' Halliwell said. 'He's worked in any number of provincial theatres. Wants desperately to hang on to this job, so he kowtows to Melmot. If he planned these murders, I can't work out why.'

'And Melmot?'

'He likes everyone to think he's the money behind the theatre,' Leaman said, 'but in reality his only asset seems to be the house. I checked with the land registry and it's owned by his mother.'

'So what would he have gained from killing Denise and Clarion?'

'He'd be better off killing his mother,' Ingeborg said.

There were some smiles. Not from Diamond. 'Is that where we are—reduced to making tasteless jokes about old ladies?'

Ingeborg turned scarlet.

'How about Binns?' Halliwell said. 'Fred made some notes before he left for the *Sweeney Todd* walk-through.'

'Fancy going to all that trouble,' Diamond said with such sarcasm that even he regretted after speaking it. His mood was bleak.

Ingeborg handed him Dawkins's notes. 'Fred worked hard on this before he had to leave.'

Diamond put up a hand in conciliation. 'I'm sorry, team. It's been a bloody long day. Let's draw a line under it. See you in the morning.'

They didn't need any persuading. After they'd left, he called Paloma.

'Are you still there?' she said.

'Winding down. It wasn't one of my better days.' He told her about his visit to Flakey White. 'I came away feeling a bully and an idiot. He appears to have led a blameless life since he got caught.'

'But something still happened to you. Something deeply upsetting,' Paloma said. 'Let's get this clear. After the play finished you went directly on holiday to the farm in North Wales.'

Her desire to help was well meant. He suppressed the sigh that was coming and repeated the salient facts. 'Where my sister had her eleventh birthday and for a treat we were taken to the Arcadia Theatre at Llandudno. I kicked up a fuss even before the show started.'

'So you hadn't objected to going into the theatre? Do you see what I'm saying, Peter? It wasn't the idea of going inside.'

'It is now. I damn near throw up when I approach the entrance.'

'But the first time it happened, you didn't. And you said it didn't affect you some time later when you were taken to the Mermaid Theatre.'

'For *Treasure Island*. I was fine. Loved it.'

'Yet *Julius Caesar* at the Old Vic made you ill.'

'I walked out before it started. Are you going to tell me the play makes the difference?'

'No, I'm not. It's obvious that the theatre does.'

He stared unseeing across the empty CID room. 'But why?'

'Can you remember any other theatre where you just enjoyed the show?'

His theatre-going didn't amount to much. 'Once when I was in Chichester with Steph we saw a comedy. It was very funny. There were no alarms for me.'

'That's interesting,' Paloma said. 'Chichester has a thrust stage. It projects out into the audience, with the seating around it. And the Mermaid was open stage as well. There's no curtain in an open-stage theatre. No curtain, Peter, and no problems for you. Do you follow me?'

'Are you saying I have a fear of curtains?'

'Theatre curtains. Bath has curtains. So does the Old Vic. And no doubt the Arcadia at Llandudno. Did something unpleasant happen with the curtain in that play you were in as a child?'

'Nothing I can remember.'

'Give it some thought. It may come back to you.'

After putting down the phone he picked up the notes Dawkins had made on Charlie Binns. Fred was a pain in many ways, but give him a job like this and he was as reliable as anyone on the team. Binns, aged thirty-six, was a Londoner, a poor scholar who joined the army as an apprentice and served until 1996. He'd had a series of jobs including two years as an assistant undertaker. He had then started in the security business as a part-time bouncer. Over the last three years he'd held down a regular job with a security firm and lived alone in a rented flat in Twerton. He belonged to a martial arts club and was a black belt in judo. Below, Dawkins had written:

FOR FURTHER INVESTIGATION
<u>Possible links to Denise:</u> 1. Army experience. Bosnian War? Check if his regiment was there when she was touring. 2. Employment in undertaker's. Where did she work?
<u>Possible links to Clarion:</u> Bouncer at clubs. Pop concerts? Protection?

Even if none of these potential links matched up, the analysis was intelligent and thorough. Dawkins was thinking outside the box.

The motive wasn't clear, but there was enough to keep Binns in the frame. If he and Denise had crossed paths in Bosnia or even some funeral parlour, and chance brought them together again at the theatre, maybe there was a motive. Old enmities could have triggered the violence.

Diamond decided to take another look at Denise's original statement. Dawkins had put it on the computer, but Diamond had a printed version along with the pages from Dawn Reed's notebook.

A sound outside disturbed him. Dawkins had walked in.

'You gave me a shock, guv,' he said. 'I was starting to think CID had closed down for tonight. Do you mind if I check my voicemail? I'm hoping for an answer to an enquiry I made about Mr Binns.'

'Go ahead.' He returned to his desk but hadn't been there long when Dawkins reappeared.

'A development, guv. I asked Binns's employers how he came to be assigned to the Theatre Royal and they said he volunteered.'

Diamond nodded. 'Interesting.'

'There is more. I asked about Binns's other duties in recent months and was informed that he is often on nightclub duty.'

'As a bouncer?'

'Indeed. And on occasions they seize drugs.'

'I think I see where this is going.'

'That was the voicemail I just got. They confirm that on two occasions in the past six months Binns confiscated a quantity of Rohypnol.'

'Now you're talking. Mr Charlie Binns has some questions to answer. Right, you'd better get a good night's sleep, but one thing before you go: have you mentioned the suicide note to anyone in the theatre?'

'No, guv. You asked us not to.'

'Good. The killer will be getting nervous about that note, not knowing it was found. He or she will think it's still tucked away in the play's stove. In fact, now that we're saying openly that Denise was murdered, it's a liability. The killer needs to remove it before the set is broken up tomorrow. I've laid a trap in case this happens tonight.'

'May I help?'

Diamond smiled. 'No, two officers are there already. Dawn Reed and George Pidgeon. Anyone gets inside the theatre, he's nicked.'

'If I may put it succinctly, guv, that's neat.'

'I wish you'd put it succinctly more often.'

After Dawkins left, Diamond remained in his office until after midnight. This was a useful time to be at work, when the phones were silent and he could deal with the information in his own way, on paper, rather than a screen. Methodically he went through the process of sorting fact from mere suspicion.

Until recently, the killing of Denise had seemed like a direct consequence of Clarion's scarring. Now he was considering it in isolation. He returned to the statement made by Denise about the scarring incident. Thanks to Dawn and Dawkins, it was a virtual transcript of the words Denise had used. Not all the asides in the speed-written version were in the printed statement, but her testimony about the Clarion incident was entirely accurate.

'Bloody hell.'

He held the witness statement closer and stared at it. He had the answer in his hand. He reached for the fake suicide note.

He was stunned, but there was only one conclusion. Both documents had been printed on the same machine.

He knew what he must do. He went back to the computer and accessed the personal files of his CID team. Then he turned to the notes he had on Denise's early career. Manchester Prison interested him most. He phoned and asked for the duty governor. The man on the end of the line had obviously been asleep. He sounded peeved to get a call at this late hour, but he soon understood the urgency and promised to check.

Diamond was getting close to a result and the indications couldn't have been worse. His reasoning was taking him into territory he hadn't visited until tonight, moving from disbelief to inescapable fact to near horror.

A mass of information was faxed from Manchester. He leafed through it rapidly and with a heavy heart.

Then his mobile rang. 'Yes?'

'Guv, this is Dawn Reed. Someone has got into the theatre. George and I separated but arranged to stay in contact on our personal radios. Now I can't raise him.'

'Where are you now?'

'The front stalls, crouching down between the seats.'

'Don't move from there, whatever happens, do you hear me? I'm coming at once.'

THE TIMING HAD BROUGHT its own problems. The key members of Diamond's team were all off duty, settling into deep sleep by now. He could rouse them, tell them he needed them at the theatre in the shortest possible time, but for what? He didn't know yet, so there was no way of briefing them. They would come ready for action, expecting an emergency. Experience told him it was a huge error to go in with all guns blazing. Lives could be at stake here. Better, surely, for him to assess the dangers. But he would still need back-up.

He paused at the front desk to tell the duty sergeant a major incident was taking place. Armed police were needed immediately at the Theatre Royal, enough to cover every exit. They were to stand guard outside the building pending instructions. Then he dashed to his car.

When he'd asked PCs Pidgeon and Reed to patrol the theatre at night it had seemed a smart idea. The killer would surely want to retrieve that so-called suicide note. Huge mistake. What he'd done was set up the young officers as targets.

They could be dead already.

THE SQUARE, three-storey façade loomed over Saw Close, a sinister grey-black monolith deprived of any of the magic of theatre. No response cars had arrived. This was it, then. Diamond was going in alone.

A side entrance would be best. He chose the door for the pit and fished in his pocket for the card with the door codes. He could just read the combination in the faint illumination from the street-lamps. He stabbed in the code, pushed the door inwards and closed it behind him without a sound.

Total darkness. Good thing he knew he was in the corridor to the left of the auditorium. He'd be acting on memory from this point on. By a series of shuffling steps he progressed down the slope as far as the door leading to the stall seating area. It was already ajar. Either the young officers or the killer must have come this way.

Dawn Reed had said she was crouching between rows of seats in the front stalls, but where? He groped his way forward until he felt the padded arm of a seat and listened for some sign of life.

Absolute silence.

He made a throat-clearing sound that wouldn't carry. If she was close and heard him she might respond.

Nothing. His eyes were adapting to the dark and he could make out the nearest row of seats, the vertical pillar of the proscenium structure and the curve of the royal circle. He could see enough to move along the gangway to check whether Dawn was still hiding. She wasn't there.

Then he heard a small sound. Something hit the floor not far away. In an old building like this it could have been boards contracting, or a fragment of plaster dropping, or a mouse. The sound had come from up on the stage. Up to now he'd avoided looking there. He turned.

His nightmare. The huge velvet curtains hung across the proscenium, thirty feet in length, crimson and gold when the lights were up, black as sin right now, and he knew for certain that Paloma had been right. He was terrorised by curtains, drawn curtains hiding something bad.

Pull them aside, Peter Diamond, and see what you get.

The shakes began. They started in his hands and spread rapidly through his entire body. Get a grip, Diamond. This is your trauma. Engage with it. Analyse. Understand.

His heart thumped. An image was forming in his brain.

As an eight year old, he was back in the Welsh farmhouse his family had rented. Night-time: his sleep disturbed by a strange sound. He'd crept downstairs. The sound was close by, outside the house. In the living room, a floor-to-ceiling window looked out towards Snowdonia. A stunning view by day. By night, long curtains drawn across. He had pulled the curtains aside.

He pictured what he'd suppressed all these years: the massive head of a beast with gaping, blood-red jaws and hairy lips drooling saliva in long threads. A huge, pink, lolling tongue. Manic, staring, white-edged eyes. And devilish horns.

Stay with it, Diamond. Part of his brain resisted, wanting to cut the scene. He refused. He had to know the truth. By force of will he succeeded. Out of the horror came an explanation. After all the years, he recognised the monster for what it was: a cow. His sister had told him about the distressed cow parted from its calf and keeping the family awake with its heart-rending sounds of distress. The poor beast had come close to the house, right up to the window, to make its protest.

To a young boy unused to the country, the sudden close-up of the cow's head at a level with his own had been enough to traumatise him. From that night on, drawn curtains would induce this petrified reaction while the censor in his brain would dumb down the real cause.

Was the fear conquered? To understand is to overcome, he told himself. Dawn Reed was in danger of being murdered. It was essential to look behind those curtains.

He reached up to the stage. He was no athlete, but the strength had returned to his limbs. He hauled himself up, thrust his arms between the heavy drapes and parted them.

SOME LIGHTS WERE ON, not powerful, but dazzling to Diamond's eyes. The set was still in place, the three walls lined with the solid-looking furniture dominated by the stove. On the sofa at centre stage lay PC George Pidgeon, bound hand and foot with duct tape. A strip of it was across his mouth. His eyes were open, but not moving.

Dead?

Diamond pushed the curtain aside and crossed the stage.

The eyes slid to the right and fixed on him. The young man was alive. Diamond started easing the gag from his cheek, but Pidgeon jerked his face away, ripping the tape off quickly and yelling, 'Behind you!'

Diamond flung himself across the constable's body and the blow caught his shoulder. It felt as if it had splintered his shoulder blade. All he could do for protection from another blow was make a piston movement with his arm. His elbow struck something solid.

Pidgeon yelled, 'Guv!'

He rolled left. The weapon whizzed past his ear, struck the upholstery and ripped a gash in the fabric. It was a claw hammer. Diamond's reflex action brought him crashing to the stage floor and he made a grab for his attacker's legs. He got a hand on one leg, but the other kicked his arm away. He watched the legs turn and run off the stage.

Go in pursuit, or release Pidgeon? His right arm felt numb. He was going to need assistance. He worked at the tape around Pidgeon's wrists.

'Guv, you won't believe who did this,' Pidgeon started to say.

'I don't need telling,' Diamond said. 'Where's Dawn?'

'I don't know.'

'When did you last see her?'

'I've no idea. He grabbed me from behind and put something over my face. I think it was chloroform. When I came to, I was lying here.'

'Dawn phoned me,' Diamond told him. 'Said she was hiding between the seats, but she's not there any more. He could mean to kill her. He must have got her backstage.'

'He could have left the building.'

'No chance. All the exits are covered. We need the house lights on.'

Pidgeon finished freeing his legs. 'I'll see what I can do.'

'Right. I'll check behind the scenes.'

Diamond crossed to the prompt side and moved along the passage towards the three main dressing rooms. He found them locked. What next? He moved on to the fly floor. Faint beams of light leaking from the other side of the scenery allowed him to see his way. He edged forward with caution, primed for another attack.

He'd just crossed to stage right when he was stopped in his tracks by a voice speaking his name immediately above his head.

He heard the hiss of static. He squinted and found himself looking at a loudspeaker. 'You can stop charging around like a demented elephant. She's been dead twenty minutes.'

'You bloody maniac. Where is she?' he shouted back, and got no reply except the click of a disconnection.

Dead twenty minutes: callous words spoken with the disregard he expected of this killer. If true, this was the worst outcome imaginable. He should never have sent Dawn Reed in.

He urged himself to concentrate. The building was too large for two men to search. Soon there would be reinforcements he could call on.

The arrest would follow. The real urgency had been to save Dawn's life. But how much reliance could he place on the words of a murderer?

Enough for huge concern.

The tannoy crackled again. The voice was Pidgeon's. 'House lights are on, guv.'

Diamond moved fast around the set. The curtain held no fears now. He parted the heavy lengths of velvet and the auditorium was before him in all its magnificence, every light glowing. The great actors of seven generations had stood on this spot. But the significance was lost on Diamond. There was no one in sight.

The sound of a handclap began, a slow, ironic slapping of palms. He couldn't tell where it came from, except it seemed close. Presently, it died away but he knew that the killer was out front and could see him.

A voice called out, 'What are you up to, standing centre stage? Is this an audition? You'll never make a Hamlet, but you might get by as one of the gravediggers.'

He knew who it was. He glanced right and left.

'That's a clue for you, the *Hamlet* reference. They always use the trap for the graveyard scene. Her body is in the understage.'

Now he could see the speaker in the lower of the two boxes to his right: the Agatha Christie, a fitting place for a murderer's last stand. Fred Dawkins.

'I was streets ahead of you before tonight, Superintendent. What changed your mind? You weren't planning to come here when we last spoke.'

The sensible response was to engage with Dawkins for as long as possible in the hope that Pidgeon would come to his aid.

'I got your number, literally,' he told Dawkins. 'Convict 5189, on a seven-year rap in Manchester for fraud. I spoke to the deputy governor. You're a con man, known at that time as Hector Dacreman.'

'Quite a leap from Strangeways to sergeant of police,' Dawkins said, unimpressed, as if there was room for doubt.

'Yes, but you're good at what you do. I asked for the names of prisoners active in the drama group that Denise Pearsall supervised and I was told Dacreman, 5189, was one of the leads in the 1988 production of *Waiting for Godot.* There is even a photo, emailed to me. The likeness satisfies me. They're sending your fingerprints, too.'

'You seem to think you have snared me.'

'You snared yourself, the first day you worked in CID. I asked you to type up the witness statements. When I compared the printout with the notes Dawn Reed made, I noticed you left off the first words Denise spoke when she saw you: "Have we met before?"'

'You don't put small talk in a witness statement.'

'Not small in this case. It came as a huge shock for you that Denise recognised you. You quickly glossed over that by saying she must have seen you patrolling the streets of Bath and she seems to have accepted that. She wouldn't have expected one of her former convict actors to reinvent himself as a police officer.'

Dawkins smirked in self-congratulation. 'Do go on. I'm learning volumes.'

'So the moment you met again at the theatre and she thought she knew you, she was at risk of being murdered. You're a vastly ambitious man. Conning your way into the police after serving a prison term was a triumph. I've seen your record: the lies, the forged references that got you into Hendon as a recruit. Eighteen weeks of training and within four years a sergeant's stripes and you'd set your sights on CID. And what an opportunity arrived when the assistant chief constable joined the BLOGs group you were choreographing.'

Dawkins smirked. 'There is a saying, "He dances well to whom fortune pipes."' His ego couldn't resist these asides, regardless that they were confirming Diamond's case.

'Yet Denise had the knowledge to destroy all you'd achieved. She had to be eliminated. You thought of a way of killing her that would be passed off as suicide. You set an elaborate trap. First you armed yourself with Rohypnol. You'd had ample opportunities to acquire the drug, confiscating it from nightclubbers.'

'Speculation.'

'We found traces in dressing room 11.'

'You can't link it with me.'

'Forensics will. Let's stay with the trap you set for Denise. You sent Denise some kind of message to lure her into the theatre on Tuesday night after everyone had left. My guess is that you offered to tell her the true explanation for Clarion's accident. Poor woman, she was distraught about it, fearing she'd made some terrible mistake with the make-up, so the chance of redemption was sure to reel her in. She was to meet you in dressing room 11. You're familiar with the layout of the theatre, having choreographed several BLOGs productions. Knowing the door codes, you could come and go at will. You met Denise, slipped Rohypnol into her drink, took her onto the riggers' platform in the fly tower and pushed her off. It was meant to be interpreted as suicide.'

'And does that complete the case for the prosecution?' Dawkins asked.

'There's more. It became clear to me that someone on our side was bent. The murderer was getting inside information.'

'Such as?'

'The call from Bristol Police about Clarion discharging herself from hospital. You put it on computer instead of telling me directly.'

'I acted properly, filing the call.'

'That wasn't the reason. You were alarmed. Clarion was a loose cannon. None of us knew what she'd been thinking while she was stuck in hospital or what she intended to do next. You could see the suicide theory being blown out of the water.'

'Immaterial,' Dawkins said. 'You insisted on keeping an open mind about Denise's suicide.'

'Which was precisely why you decided the time had come to remove all doubt. You came up with the suggestion that an extra powder box spiked with caustic soda was hidden backstage. I sent you and Ingeborg to search for it. You had the fake suicide note in your pocket and planted it in the stove. Neat. But there was a flaw.'

'The famous specks of ink?' Dawkins said.

'Yes. Tonight I examined the statements you typed and saw the tell-tale specks in exactly the formation we found on the suicide note. It was obvious it had been printed in our own office.'

'Admirable,' Dawkins said in a flat voice. It may have been meant as sarcastic, but it sounded like defeat.

'Getting back to Clarion,' Diamond said, 'Bristol Police told you the hotel she was staying in. You called on her there, didn't you?'

'What makes you think I did?'

'It's logical. Clarion had a bad conscience about the caustic soda she'd smeared on her face without fully realising how damaging it was. Denise was dead and the theatre faced disaster. She wanted to make amends. You learned that she was about to confess everything to the theatre management, destroying the theory of Denise's suicide.'

'What am I supposed to have done about it?'

'You must have thought about murdering her in the hotel but I guess something went wrong. Maybe you were seen on a security camera. Whatever it was, you got back in your car and followed her to the theatre. You waited for the interval, entered the box and suffocated her with a plastic bag. You were out of there and away without anyone seeing you.'

'Leaving no traces.'

'I wouldn't count on that. The scene-of-crime people have been thorough. DNA is a marvellous aid to detection.' Diamond paused. 'Where are you?'

Dawkins had vanished.

Simple, of course, to do a disappearing act when all it needs is a step backwards into the box. And Diamond had no way of stopping him. But with all exits sealed, Dawkins wouldn't escape.

Diamond's mind was on a more disturbing duty. He let himself down to the orchestra pit. There were steps down into the band room. He discovered Dawn Reed lying on the floor towards the back, bound and gagged as Pidgeon had been.

She was still alive. Dawkins had conned and lied to the last.

THE FINAL-NIGHT PARTY for *Sweeney Todd* was held in the Garrick's Head. The show had been a resounding success. The reviews were better than anyone could remember for a BLOG production. If some of the choreography had looked a little under-rehearsed, not one of the critics mentioned it. Allowance was made for the loss of the movement director before the rehearsals got serious.

Paloma was there as costume consultant and she insisted that Diamond was present.

'A good show?' Paloma asked him after he'd downed a large beer.

'Very good. Pretty graphic, some of the throat-cutting.'

'Don't throw a wobbly. You're over all that, I thought.'

'Happily, yes.'

'And the case? Is that all wrapped up now?'

'It is.'

'Georgina was telling everyone about PC Pidgeon making the arrest on the staircase behind the boxes. He and Dawn Reed are both being recommended for promotion.'

'So I heard.'

'And the armed police weren't needed after all.'

'Right,' he said. 'Georgina is pissed off about the cost of the operation.

It was all double-time, being at night. I told her if she hadn't insisted on Dawkins joining CID, none of this would have happened.'

'Are you certain of that?'

'I guess he would still have done the murders, but it would have been more difficult covering them up as a uniformed sergeant.'

Titus O'Driscoll joined them. 'Do you mind if I butt in? There's something I'm anxious to know. When you and I went backstage, we found a dead tortoiseshell butterfly and to my embarrassment I passed out. Furthermore, I was informed that when you searched the box where Clarion was murdered, you found a second butterfly.'

'That's right.'

'My question is: did the murderer have anything to do with the butterflies?'

'You mean did he place them there himself?' Diamond paused for thought. 'If you want my opinion, Titus, they found their own way. It was a natural occurrence, or supernatural, depending on your point of view. And I think I know what yours is.'

Titus smiled.

peter **lovesey**

RD: What is your most vivid childhood memory?

PL: Being collected from our school air-raid shelter in suburban Whitton in 1944, when I was seven, and taken along the street to the heap of rubble that had been my home, destroyed by a V1 flying bomb. Miraculously, my two brothers were dug out alive and neither of my parents was in the house. That night we slept on the living-room floor of the vicar's house and in a few days we were transported to a farm in Cornwall. As a family we learned a valuable lesson about starting over.

RD: Looking back over your seventy-four years—national service in the RAF, teaching English, athletics, acting, writing and overseeing TV dramatisations of your books—which of these experiences do you think most influenced or moulded you?

PL: My wife Jax takes the major credit. Without her encouragement and gentle prodding I wouldn't have taken a commission in the RAF, or written a novel or completed TV scripts or gone freelance—all of which required more self-confidence than I had at the time. I like to think that I have influenced and moulded her too, but we've never discussed this and it's a lady's privilege not to admit it.

RD: You started writing professionally after winning a prize in *The Times* for a debut crime novel in 1969. Did Jax help you onward from that point?

PL: Her support was critical. I had little knowledge of crime-writing, but she devoured whodunits from the library at the rate of three or four a week. The £1,000 prize was more than my annual salary as a teacher and I was willing to try for it, but I needed her experience of the genre to understand how to begin. She suggested an original approach would be to use my interest in athletics history, so I did that and wove a mystery into it.

RD: What was hardest part of learning the craft?

PL: Plot. The background was always easy. For the early books I used aspects of Victorian entertainment such as the music hall, boating, the seaside and the waxworks. I had a wonderful time collecting all the vivid detail and thinking of characters, but then I had the hard task of creating a convincing plot with surprises. The mechanics, the sleight of hand, had to be learned. With experience, it has become a more organic

COPYRIGHT AND ACKNOWLEDGMENTS

WORTH DYING FOR: Copyright © Lee Child 2010.
Published at £18.99 by Bantam Press, an imprint of Transworld Publishers.
Condensed version © The Reader's Digest Association, Inc., 2011.

DAMBUSTER: Copyright © 2011 Standing Bear Ltd.
Published at £16.99 by Little, Brown, an imprint of Little, Brown Book Group.
Condensed version © The Reader's Digest Association, Inc., 2011.

THE SUMMER OF THE BEAR: Copyright © Bella Pollen 2010.
Published at £12.99 by Mantle, an imprint of Pan Macmillan, a division of Macmillan Publishers Ltd.
Condensed version © The Reader's Digest Association, Inc., 2011.

STAGESTRUCK: Copyright © Peter Lovesey 2011.
Published at £19.99 by Sphere, an imprint of Little, Brown Book Group.
Condensed version © The Reader's Digest Association, Inc., 2011.

The right to be identified as authors has been asserted by the following in accordance with sections 77 and 78 of the Copyright, Designs and Patents Act, 1988: Lee Child, Robert Radcliffe, Bella Pollen, Peter Lovesey.

Spine: Shutterstock. Front cover (from left) and page 4 (from top): Andy Kerry/Alamy; *Operation Chastise* by Robert Taylor © The Military Gallery, England; John Spencer; © Richard Nixon/Arcangel Images. Page 5 (top) © Mike Lawn/Rex Features. 6–8: photograph: Tom McGhee/Photis; illustration: Kate Baxter@velvet tamarind; 152 © Johnny Ring. 154–6 illustration: Alec MacDonald; 290 © courtesy of Robert Radcliffe. 292–4 illustration: Simon Mendez; 295–428 bear woodcut © Benjamin Cox; 438 © Jane Hilton; 439 Andy Robin and Hercules © Trinity Mirror/Mirropix/Alamy. 440–2 images: Shutterstock; illustration: Rick Lecoat@Shark Attack. 574 © Kate Shermilt; 575 © David Sellman/www.photolibrary.com.

Reader's Digest is a trademark owned and under licence from The Reader's Digest Association, Inc. and is registered with the United States Patent and Trademark Office and in other countries throughout the world.

All rights reserved. Unauthorised reproduction, in any manner, is prohibited.

Printed and bound by GGP Media GmbH, Pössneck, Germany

020-271 UP0000-1

process and now, sometimes, mysterious things happen without me shaping them.

RD: Peter Diamond, the detective hero of *Stagestruck*, first appeared in *The Last Detective* in 1991. Has he changed at all over the course of the eleven books in which he has now appeared?

PL: I'm sure he has. He remains stubbornly resistant to change in the police, yet he can see with hindsight that the rough justice in which he was reared won't do in the present century. I gave him a life-changing tragedy midway through the series and after that he can't possibly be the same. He is accident-prone and vulnerable, yet presents a personality that appears pugnacious and confident. In *Stagestruck*, he is compelled to face demons from the past.

RD: Was there a particular performance, or aspect of Bath's Theatre Royal that inspired this latest novel?

PL: It's one of the most gorgeous small theatres in the world, 250 years old, all gilded and red plush velvet. The moment when the Chaplin curtains part is magic. I lived near Bath for twenty years and saw numerous productions there. The ones I remember best were Alan Ayckbourn comedies, but I wouldn't say they inspired the novel. Samuel Beckett's *Waiting for Godot* influenced *Stagestruck*. I leave it for the reader to work out why.

RD: The theatre's history sounds fascinating. Did any of it surprise you when you were researching?

PL: I knew a little of the superstition about butterflies being a good or bad omen depending whether they were alive or dead. I discovered many actors and audiences had been visited by them on stage. Peter O'Toole, for example, did some inspired ad-libbing when the tortoiseshell settled on a newspaper he was supposed to be reading. There is also a surprisingly impressive list of actors claiming to have seen the theatre ghost, the Grey Lady . . .

RD: Is it true that you're a good cook? And, if so, do you have a *pièce de résistance*, recipe-wise?

PL: Let's say a keen cook rather than a good one. But I have to say my slow-cooked beef casserole is worth committing a crime for.

RD: And, finally, would you go back and change anything, if you could live our life over again?

No. I've been remarkably lucky. I wouldn't insult whoever is pulling the strings by ing it any different.